STOP

This is the back of the book!
Start from the other side.

NATIVE MANGA
readers read manga
from right to left.

If you run into our **Native Manga** logo on any of our books... you'll know that this manga is published in it's true original native Japanese right to left reading format, as it was intended. Turn to the other side of the book and start reading from right to left, top to bottom.

Follow the diagram to see how its done. **Surf's Up!**

READ RIGHT TO LEFT

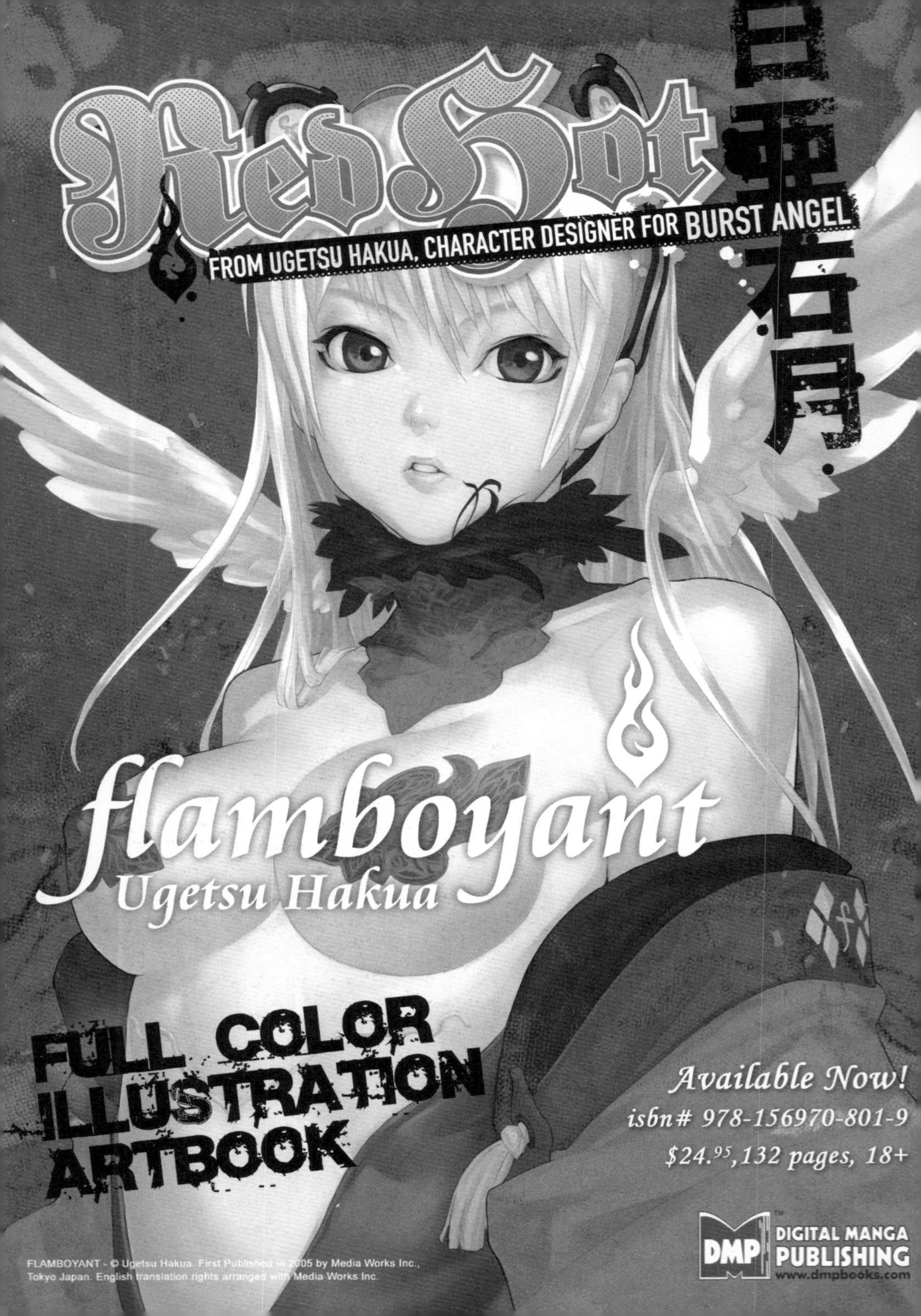
Red Hot
白亜右月
FROM UGETSU HAKUA, CHARACTER DESIGNER FOR BURST ANGEL
flamboyant
Ugetsu Hakua
FULL COLOR ILLUSTRATION ARTBOOK
Available Now!
isbn# 978-156970-801-9
$24.95, 132 pages, 18+
DMP DIGITAL MANGA PUBLISHING
www.dmpbooks.com
FLAMBOYANT - © Ugetsu Hakua. First Published in 2005 by Media Works Inc., Tokyo Japan. English translation rights arranged with Media Works Inc.

join the party!

register now at www.anime-expo.org

 L.A. CONVENTION CENTER
ANIMEEXPO® **AX** 2008
JULY 3-6

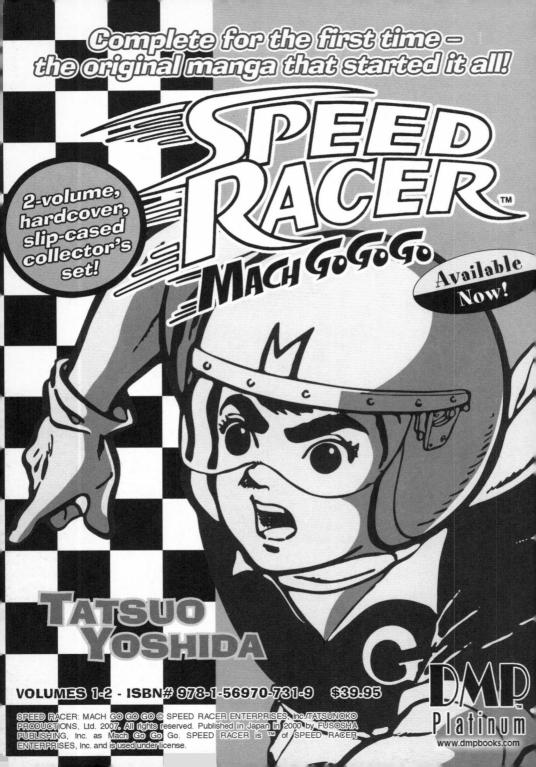

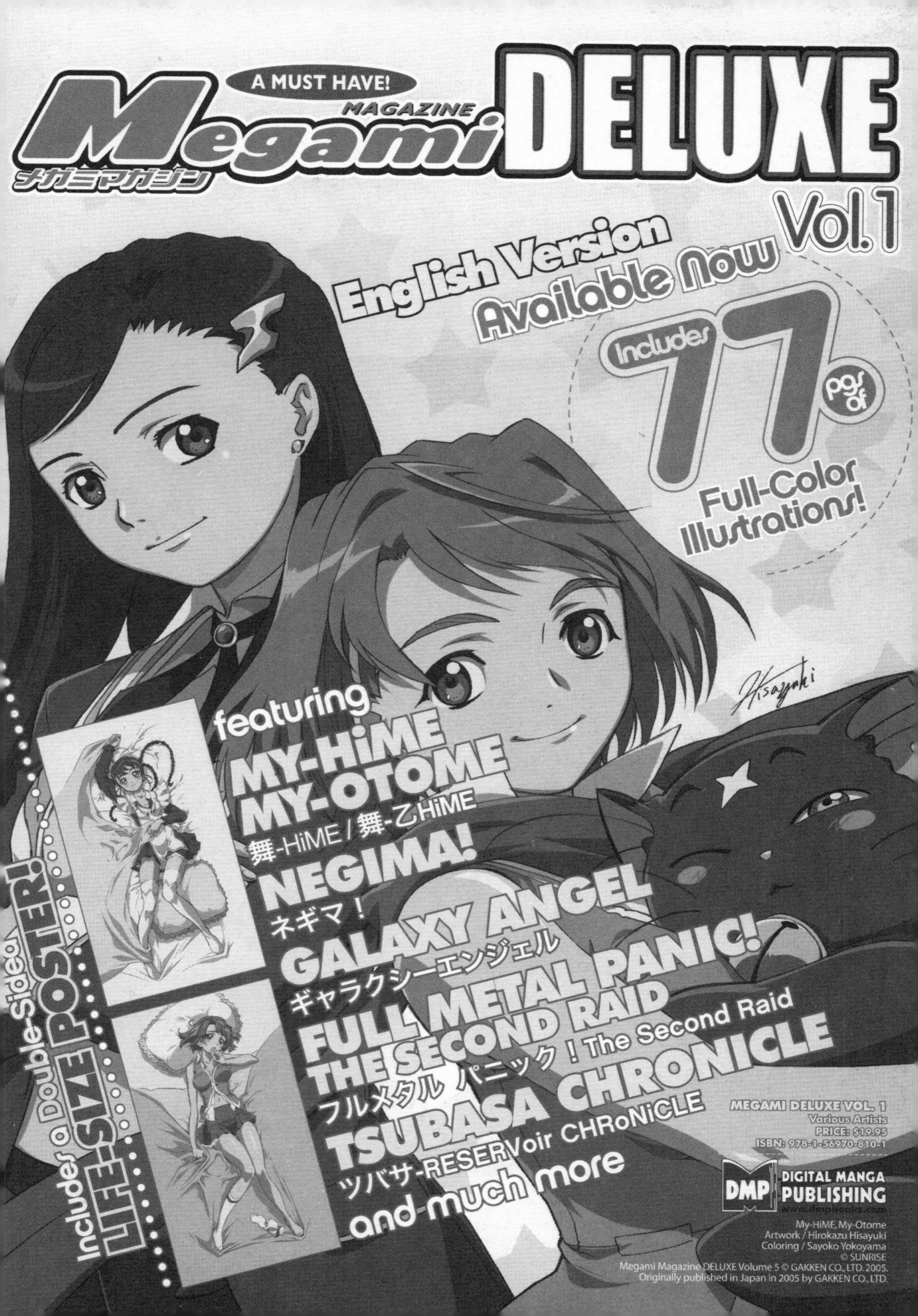

A MUST HAVE!
Megami MAGAZINE DELUXE
メガミマガジン
Vol.1
English Version
Available Now
Includes 77 pgs of Full-Color Illustrations!
featuring
MY-HiME
MY-OTOME
舞-HiME / 舞-乙HiME
NEGIMA!
ネギマ！
GALAXY ANGEL
ギャラクシーエンジェル
FULL METAL PANIC!
THE SECOND RAID
フルメタル パニック！The Second Raid
TSUBASA CHRONICLE
ツバサ-RESERVoir CHRoNiCLE
and much more
Includes a Double-sided LIFE-SIZE POSTER!
MEGAMI DELUXE VOL. 1
Various Artists
PRICE: $19.95
ISBN: 978-1-56970-810-1
DMP DIGITAL MANGA PUBLISHING
www.dmpbooks.com
My-HiME, My-Otome
Artwork / Hirokazu Hisayuki
Coloring / Sayoko Yokoyama
© SUNRISE
Megami Magazine DELUXE Volume 5 © GAKKEN CO., LTD. 2005.
Originally published in Japan in 2005 by GAKKEN CO., LTD.

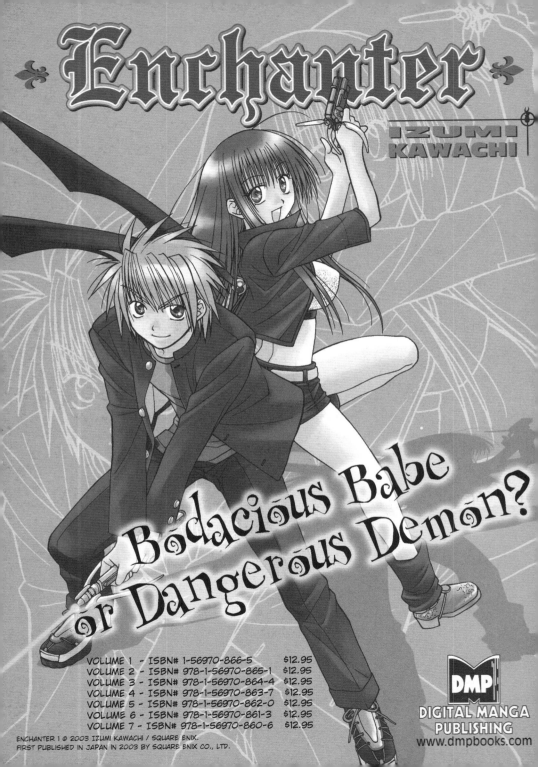

Enchanter

IZUMI KAWACHI

Bodacious Babe or Dangerous Demon?

VOLUME 1 - ISBN# 1-56970-866-5 $12.95
VOLUME 2 - ISBN# 978-1-56970-865-1 $12.95
VOLUME 3 - ISBN# 978-1-56970-864-4 $12.95
VOLUME 4 - ISBN# 978-1-56970-863-7 $12.95
VOLUME 5 - ISBN# 978-1-56970-862-0 $12.95
VOLUME 6 - ISBN# 978-1-56970-861-3 $12.95
VOLUME 7 - ISBN# 978-1-56970-860-6 $12.95

DMP
DIGITAL MANGA
PUBLISHING
www.dmpbooks.com

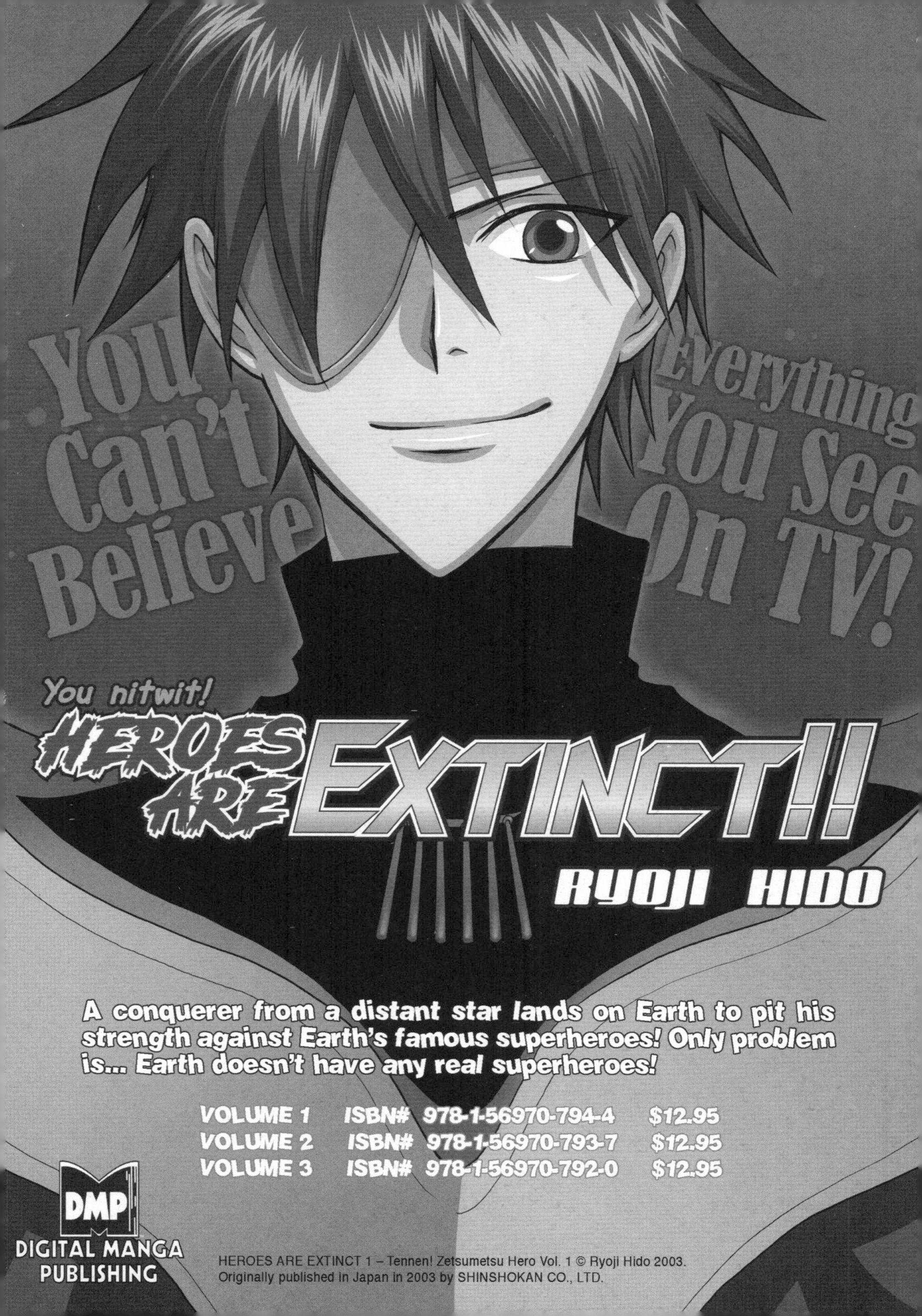
You Can't Believe Everything You See On TV!
You nitwit!
HEROES ARE EXTINCT!!
RYOJI HIDO
A conquerer from a distant star lands on Earth to pit his strength against Earth's famous superheroes! Only problem is... Earth doesn't have any real superheroes!
VOLUME 1 ISBN# 978-1-56970-794-4 $12.95
VOLUME 2 ISBN# 978-1-56970-793-7 $12.95
VOLUME 3 ISBN# 978-1-56970-792-0 $12.95
DMP
DIGITAL MANGA PUBLISHING
HEROES ARE EXTINCT 1 – Tennen! Zetsumetsu Hero Vol. 1 © Ryoji Hido 2003.
Originally published in Japan in 2003 by SHINSHOKAN CO., LTD.

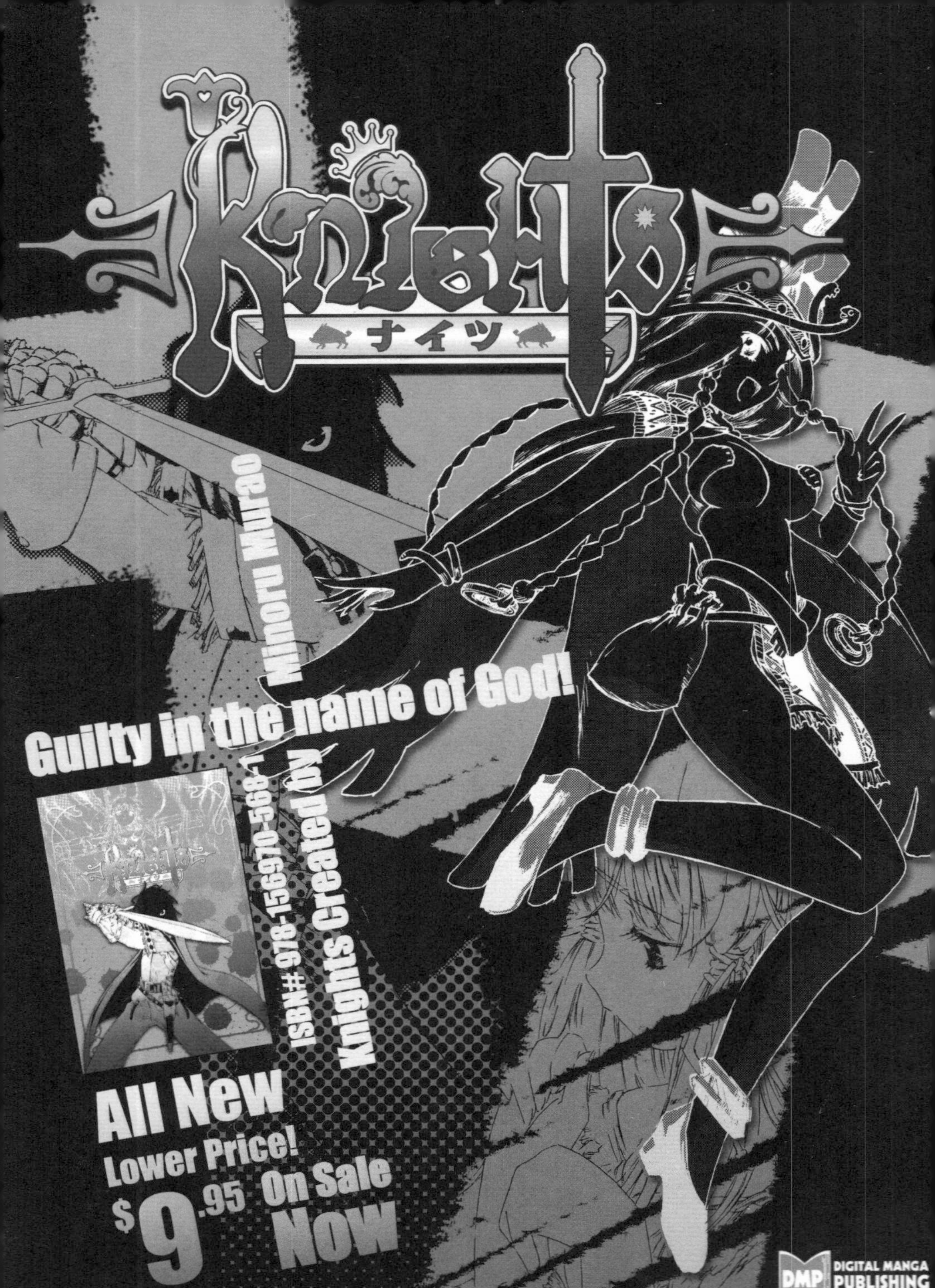
Knights
ナイツ
Guilty in the name of God!
Knights Created by
Minoru Murao
ISBN# 978-156970-568-1
All New
Lower Price!
$9.95 On Sale Now
DMP DIGITAL MANGA PUBLISHING
www.dmpbooks.com

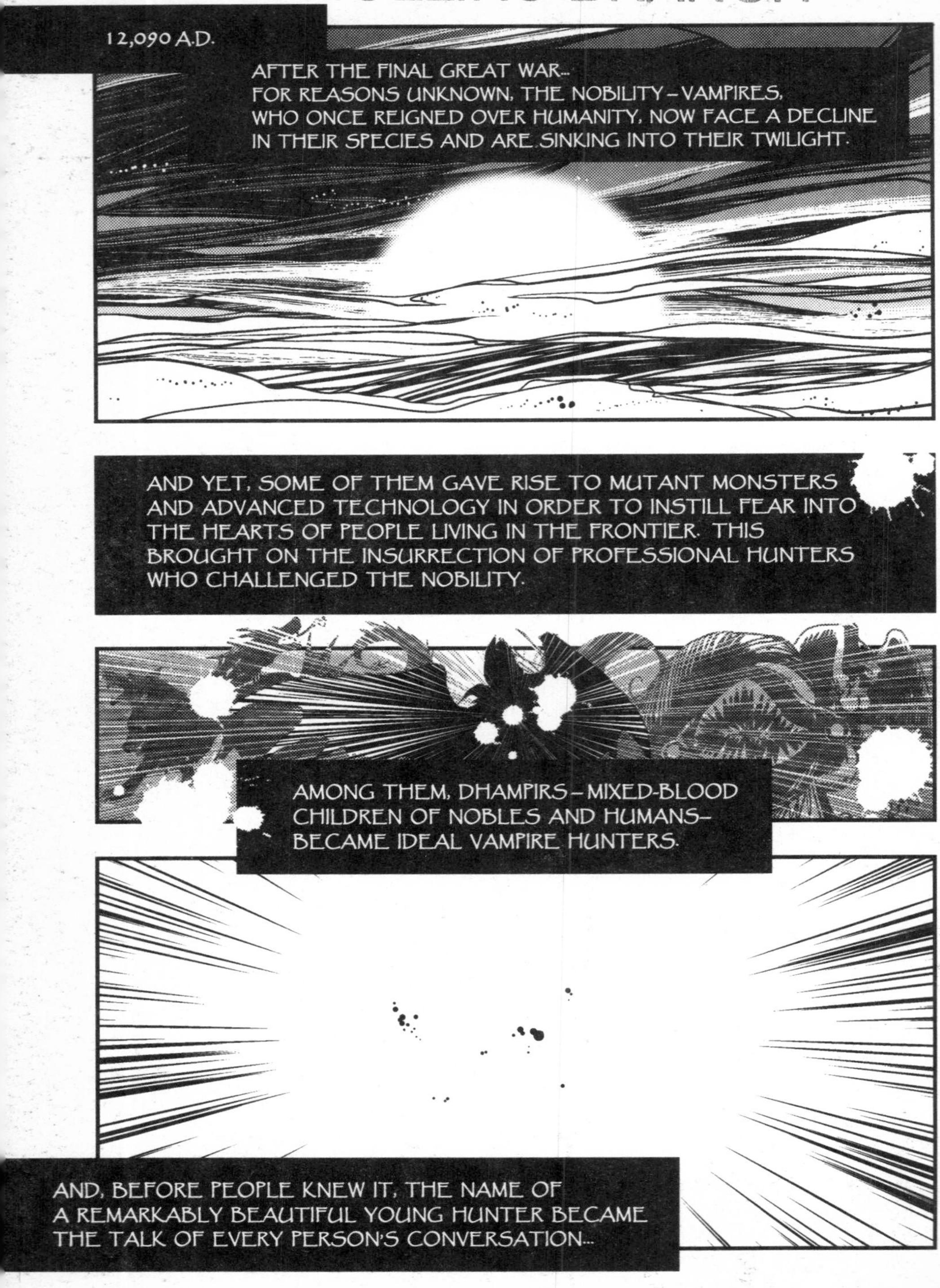
12,090 A.D.
AFTER THE FINAL GREAT WAR... FOR REASONS UNKNOWN, THE NOBILITY—VAMPIRES, WHO ONCE REIGNED OVER HUMANITY, NOW FACE A DECLINE IN THEIR SPECIES AND ARE SINKING INTO THEIR TWILIGHT.
AND YET, SOME OF THEM GAVE RISE TO MUTANT MONSTERS AND ADVANCED TECHNOLOGY IN ORDER TO INSTILL FEAR INTO THE HEARTS OF PEOPLE LIVING IN THE FRONTIER. THIS BROUGHT ON THE INSURRECTION OF PROFESSIONAL HUNTERS WHO CHALLENGED THE NOBILITY.
AMONG THEM, DHAMPIRS—MIXED-BLOOD CHILDREN OF NOBLES AND HUMANS—BECAME IDEAL VAMPIRE HUNTERS.
AND, BEFORE PEOPLE KNEW IT, THE NAME OF A REMARKABLY BEAUTIFUL YOUNG HUNTER BECAME THE TALK OF EVERY PERSON'S CONVERSATION...

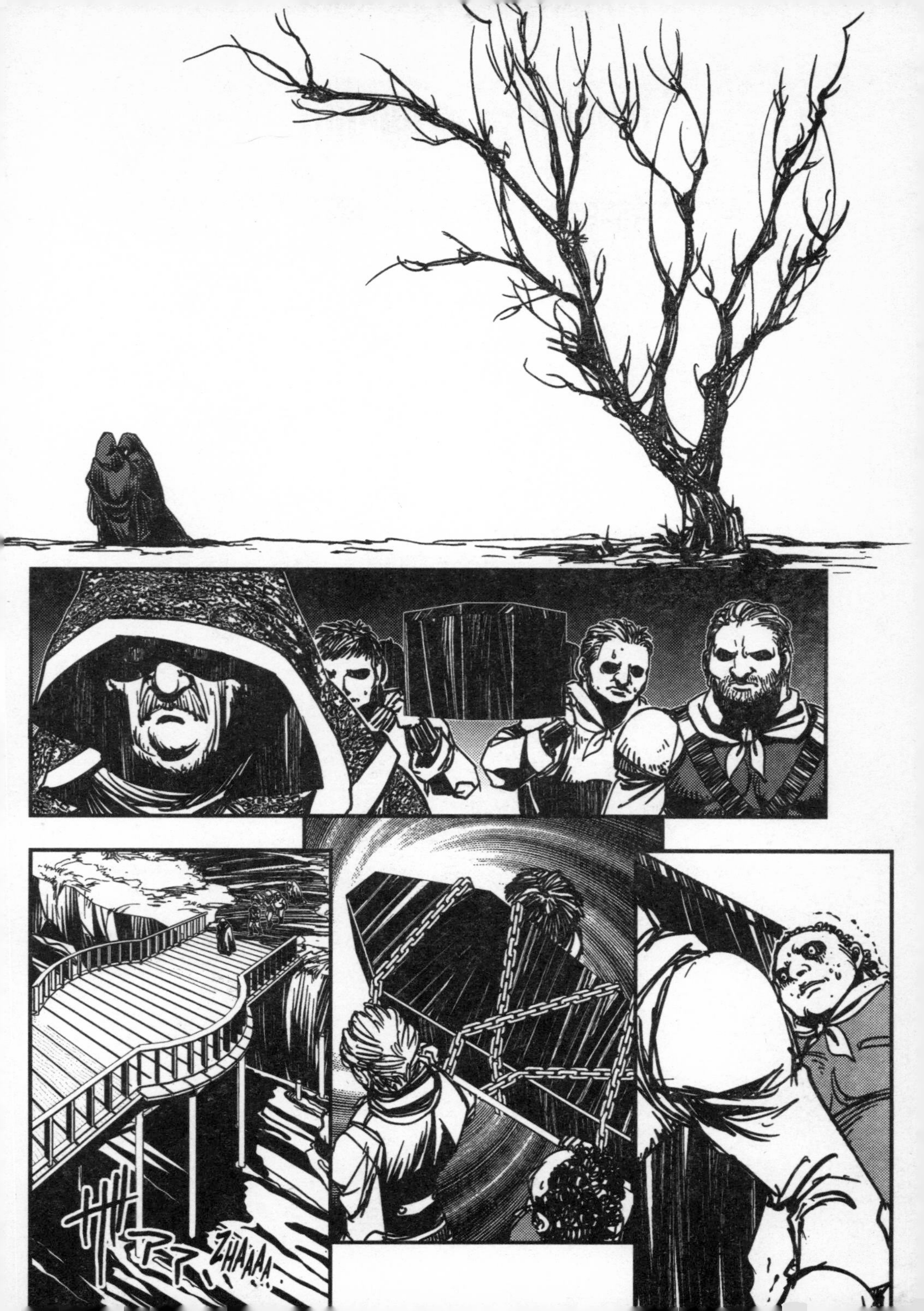
ZHAAAA

Hideyuki Kikuchi's Vampire Hunter D

Adapted and Illustrated By
Saiko Takaki

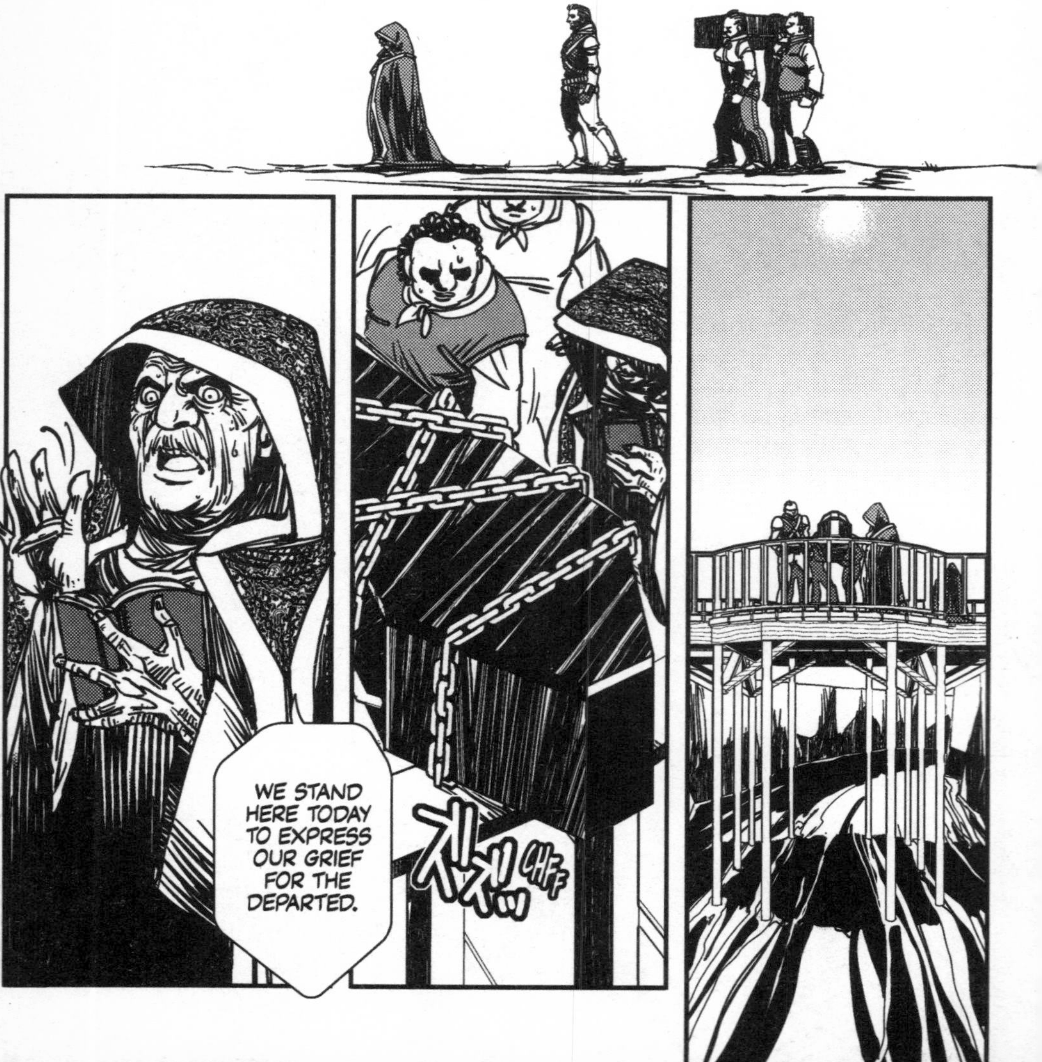
CHFF
WE STAND HERE TODAY TO EXPRESS OUR GRIEF FOR THE DEPARTED.

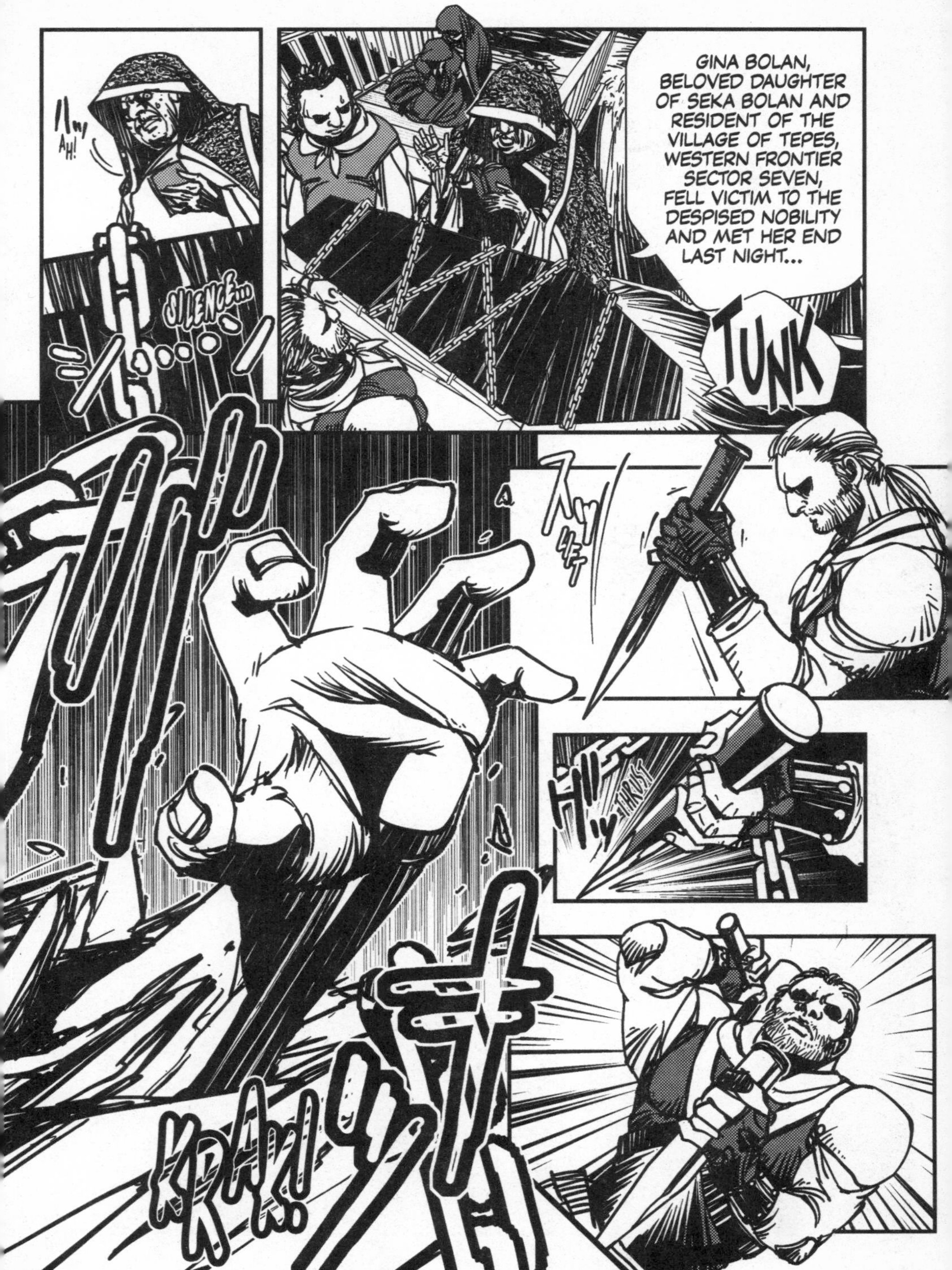
GINA BOLAN, BELOVED DAUGHTER OF SEKA BOLAN AND RESIDENT OF THE VILLAGE OF TEPES, WESTERN FRONTIER SECTOR SEVEN, FELL VICTIM TO THE DESPISED NOBILITY AND MET HER END LAST NIGHT...
TUNK
AH!
SILENCE...
LIFT
THRUST
KRAK!

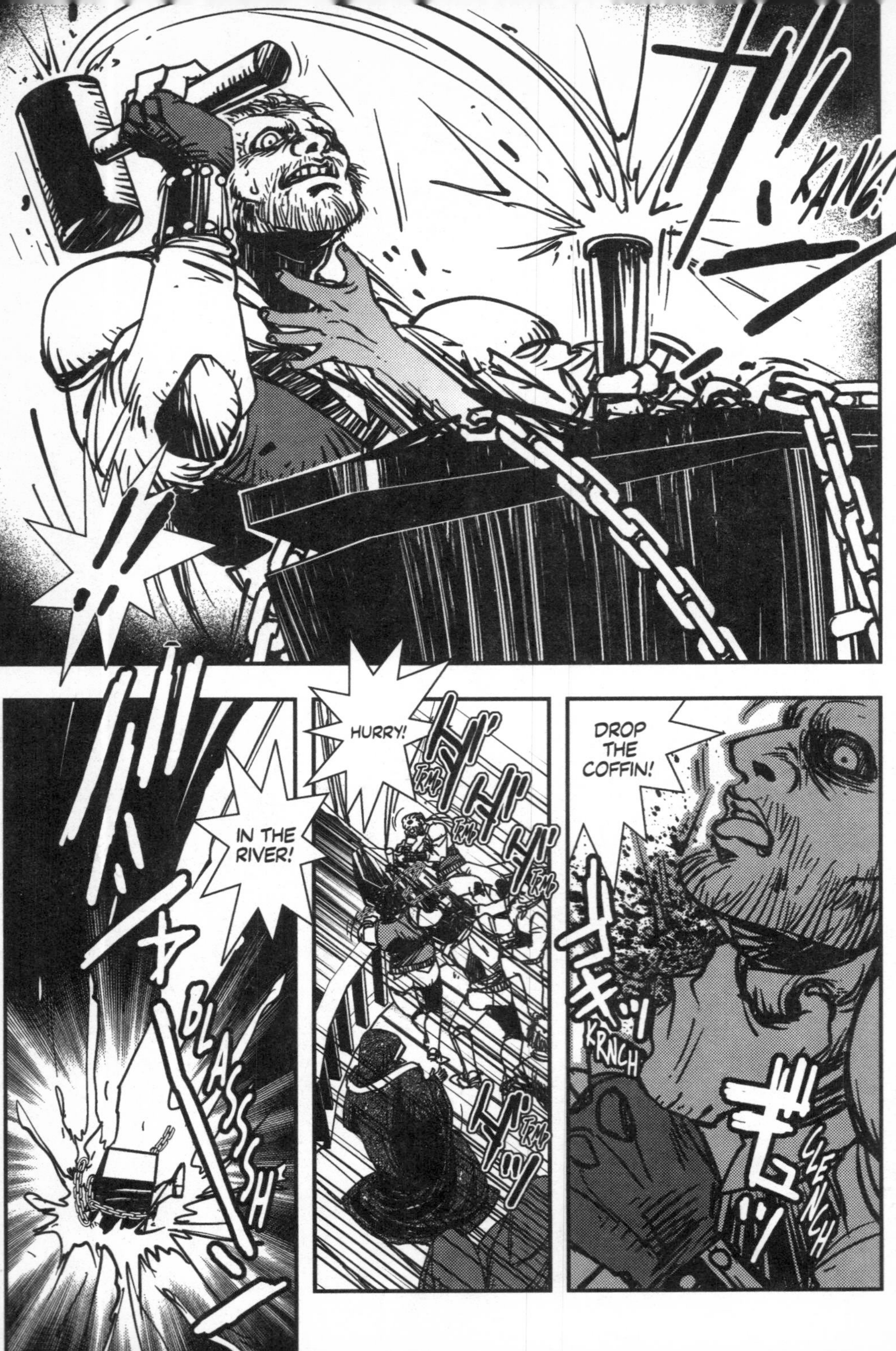
KANG!
DROP THE COFFIN!
KRNCH
CLENCH
HURRY!
TRMP
TRMP
TRMP
TRMP
IN THE RIVER!
BLASSSH

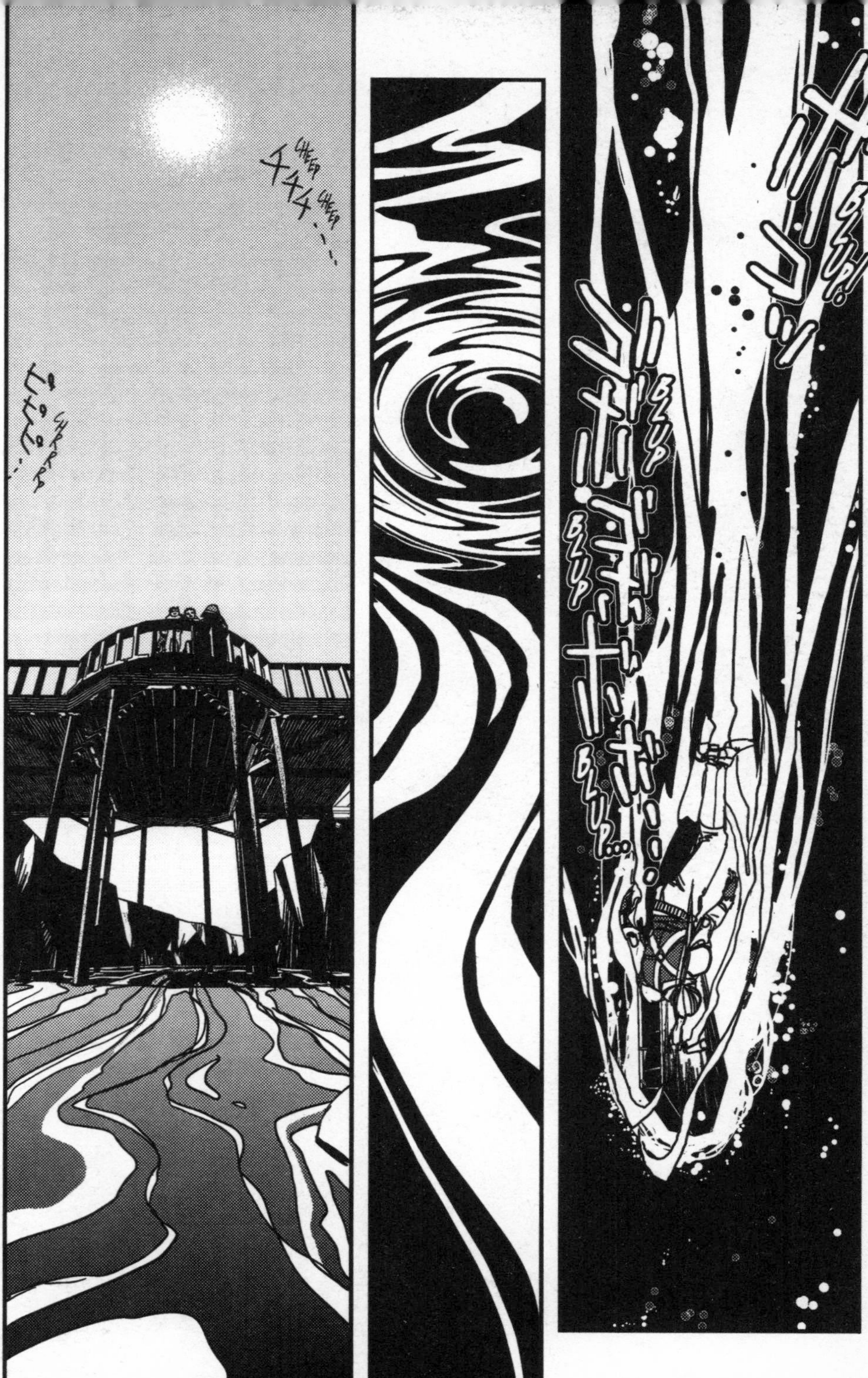
BLUP!
BLUP
BLUP
BLUP...
CHEEP
CHEEP
CHRRRR

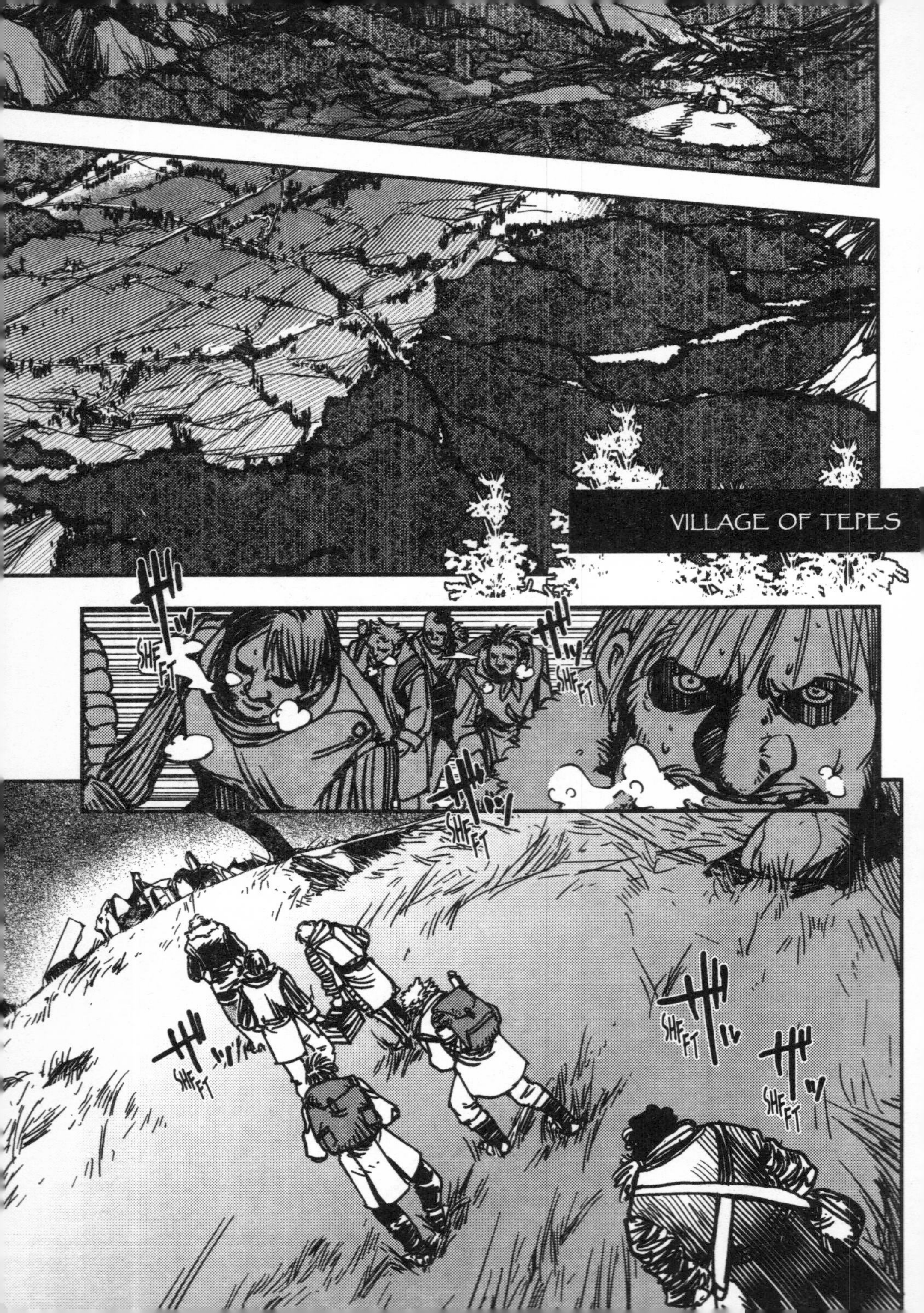
VILLAGE OF TEPES
SHFFT
SHFFT
SHFFT
SHFFT
SHFFT
SHFFT

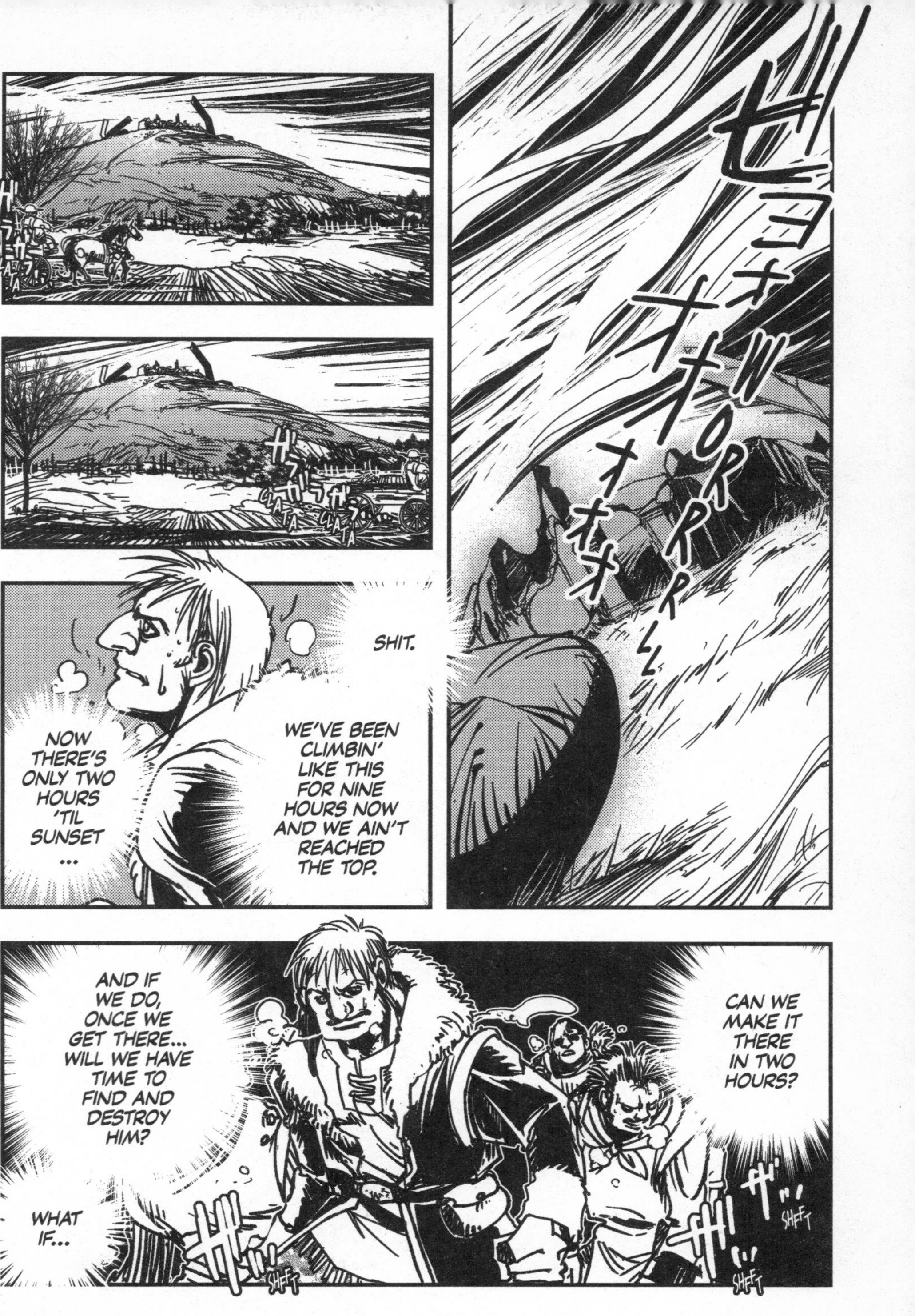
WORRRRLL
CLATA CLATA
CLATA CLATA
SHIT.
WE'VE BEEN CLIMBIN' LIKE THIS FOR NINE HOURS NOW AND WE AIN'T REACHED THE TOP.
NOW THERE'S ONLY TWO HOURS 'TIL SUNSET ...
CAN WE MAKE IT THERE IN TWO HOURS?
SHFFT
SHFFT
AND IF WE DO, ONCE WE GET THERE... WILL WE HAVE TIME TO FIND AND DESTROY HIM?
WHAT IF...
SHFFT

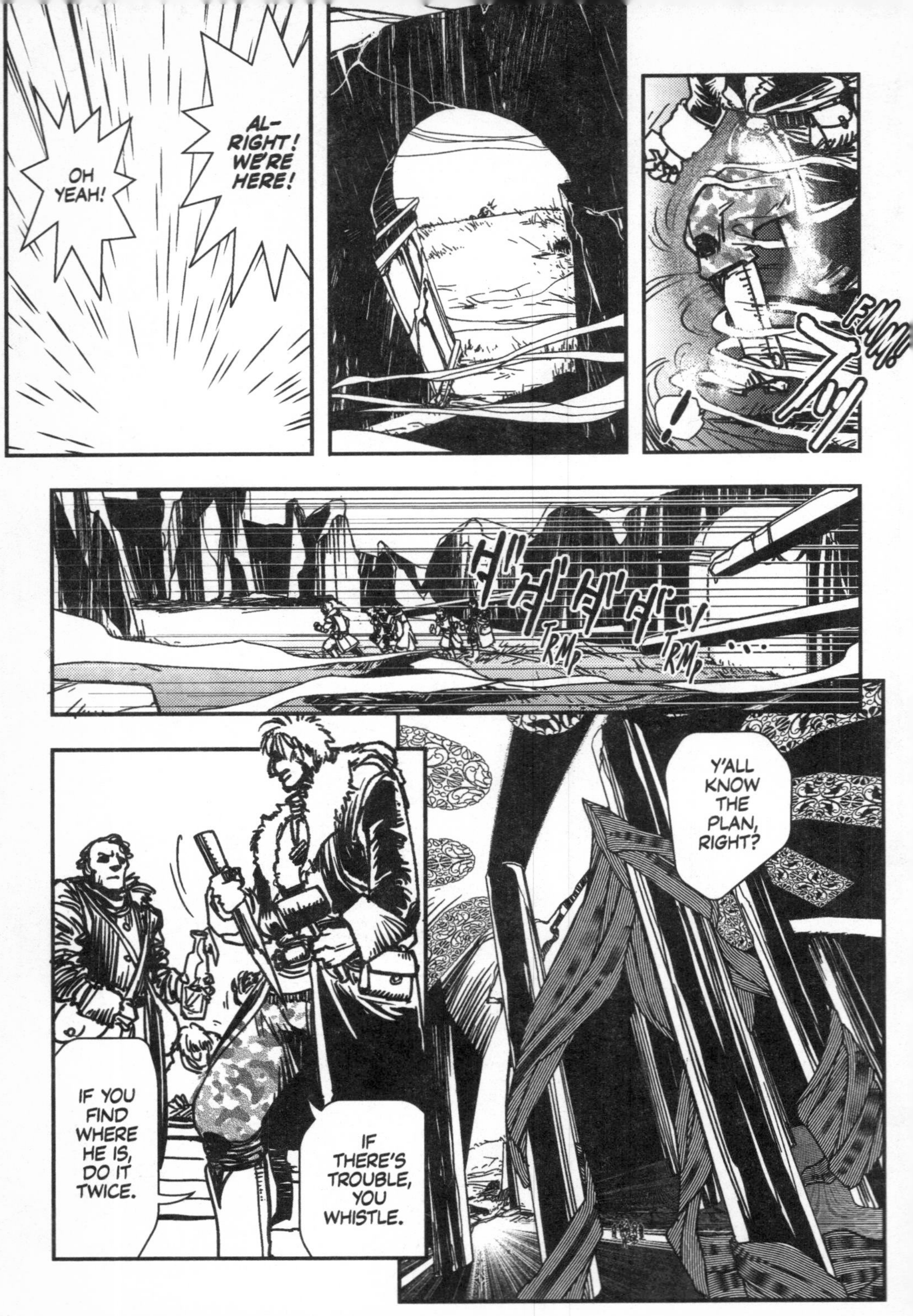

FMM!
AL-RIGHT! WE'RE HERE!
OH YEAH!
TRMP
TRMP
...
Y'ALL KNOW THE PLAN, RIGHT?
IF THERE'S TROUBLE, YOU WHISTLE.
IF YOU FIND WHERE HE IS, DO IT TWICE.

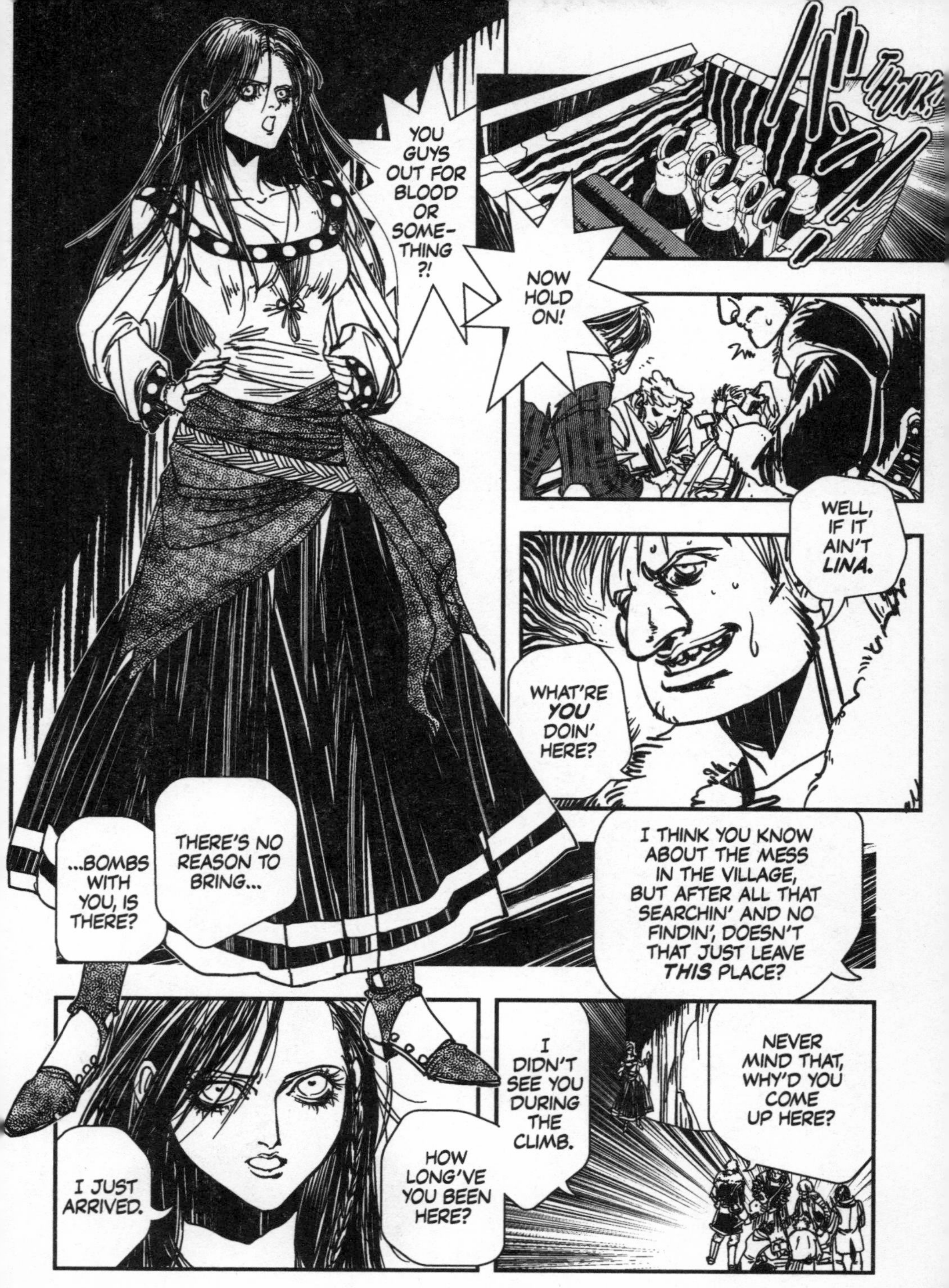

THUNK!
NOW HOLD ON!
WELL, IF IT AIN'T ***LINA.***
WHAT'RE ***YOU*** DOIN' HERE?
I THINK YOU KNOW ABOUT THE MESS IN THE VILLAGE, BUT AFTER ALL THAT SEARCHIN' AND NO FINDIN', DOESN'T THAT JUST LEAVE ***THIS*** PLACE?
YOU GUYS OUT FOR BLOOD OR SOME-THING?!
THERE'S NO REASON TO BRING...
...BOMBS WITH YOU, IS THERE?
NEVER MIND THAT, WHY'D YOU COME UP HERE?
I DIDN'T SEE YOU DURING THE CLIMB.
HOW LONG'VE YOU BEEN HERE?
I JUST ARRIVED.

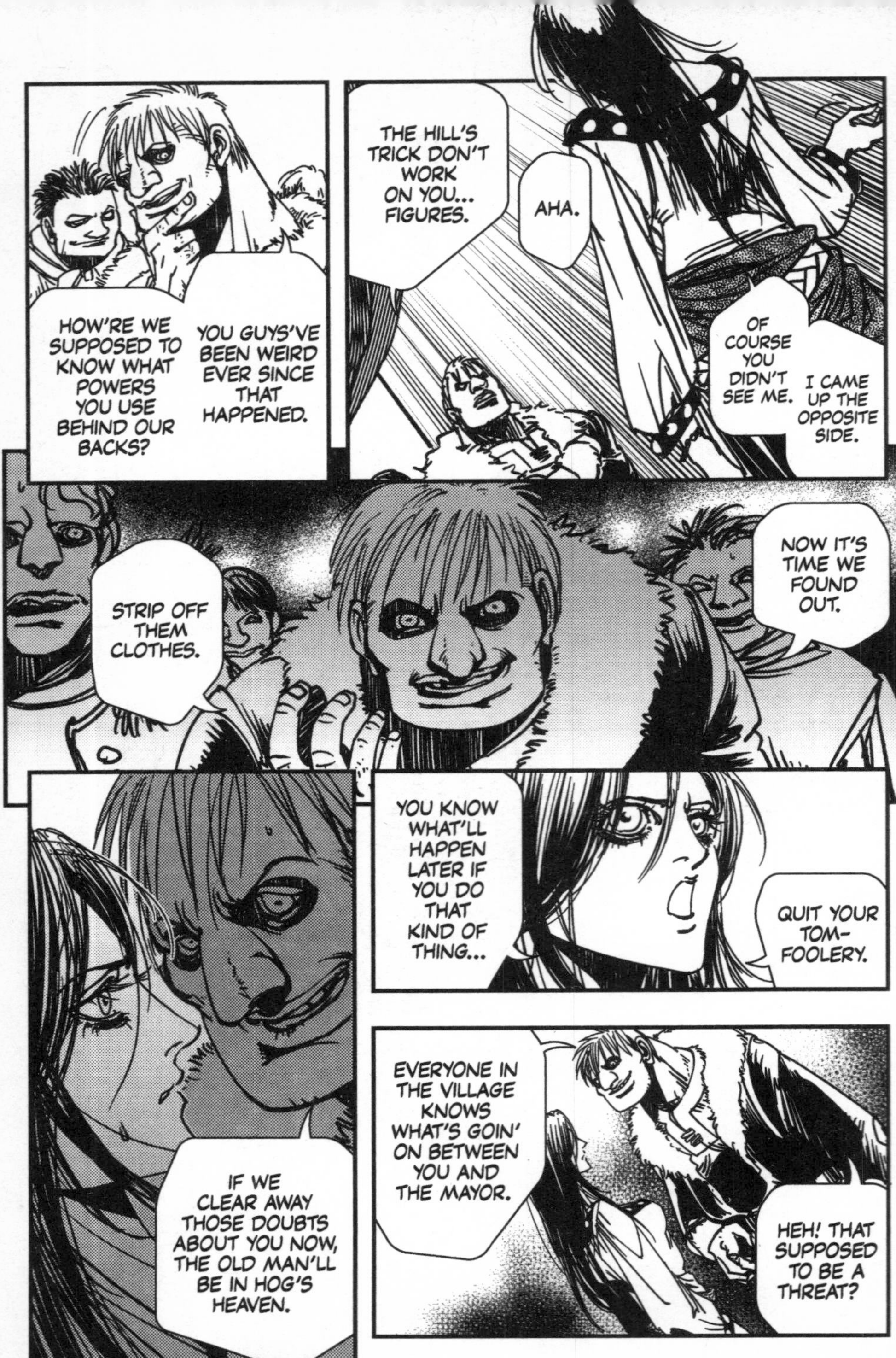
AHA.
THE HILL'S TRICK DON'T WORK ON YOU... FIGURES.
OF COURSE YOU DIDN'T SEE ME.
I CAME UP THE OPPOSITE SIDE.
YOU GUYS'VE BEEN WEIRD EVER SINCE THAT HAPPENED.
HOW'RE WE SUPPOSED TO KNOW WHAT POWERS YOU USE BEHIND OUR BACKS?
NOW IT'S TIME WE FOUND OUT.
STRIP OFF THEM CLOTHES.
QUIT YOUR TOM-FOOLERY.
YOU KNOW WHAT'LL HAPPEN LATER IF YOU DO THAT KIND OF THING...
HEH! THAT SUPPOSED TO BE A THREAT?
EVERYONE IN THE VILLAGE KNOWS WHAT'S GOIN' ON BETWEEN YOU AND THE MAYOR.
IF WE CLEAR AWAY THOSE DOUBTS ABOUT YOU NOW, THE OLD MAN'LL BE IN HOG'S HEAVEN.

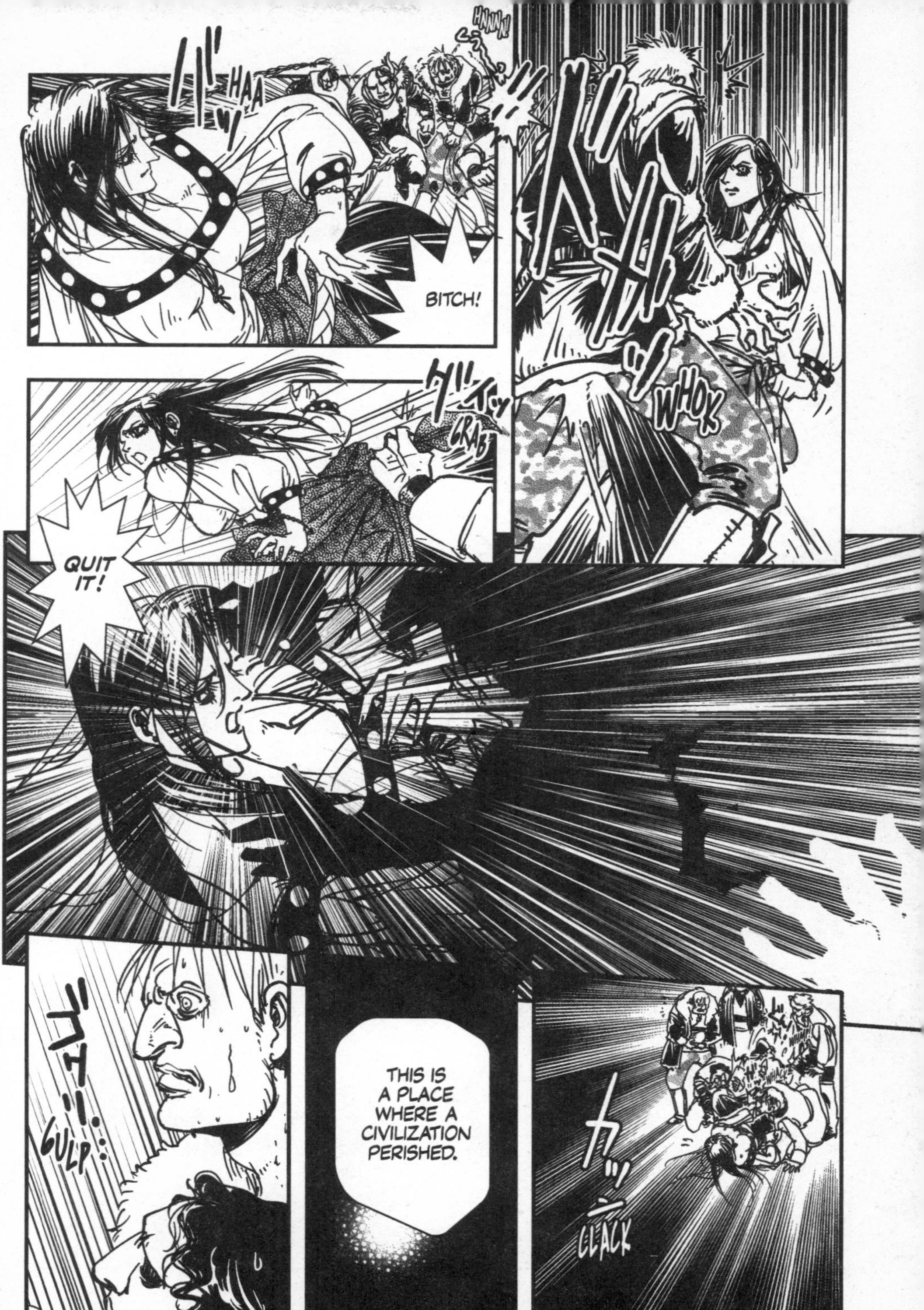
HNNN!
WHOK
HAA
BITCH!
GRAB
QUIT IT!
CLACK
THIS IS A PLACE WHERE A CIVILIZATION PERISHED.
GULP

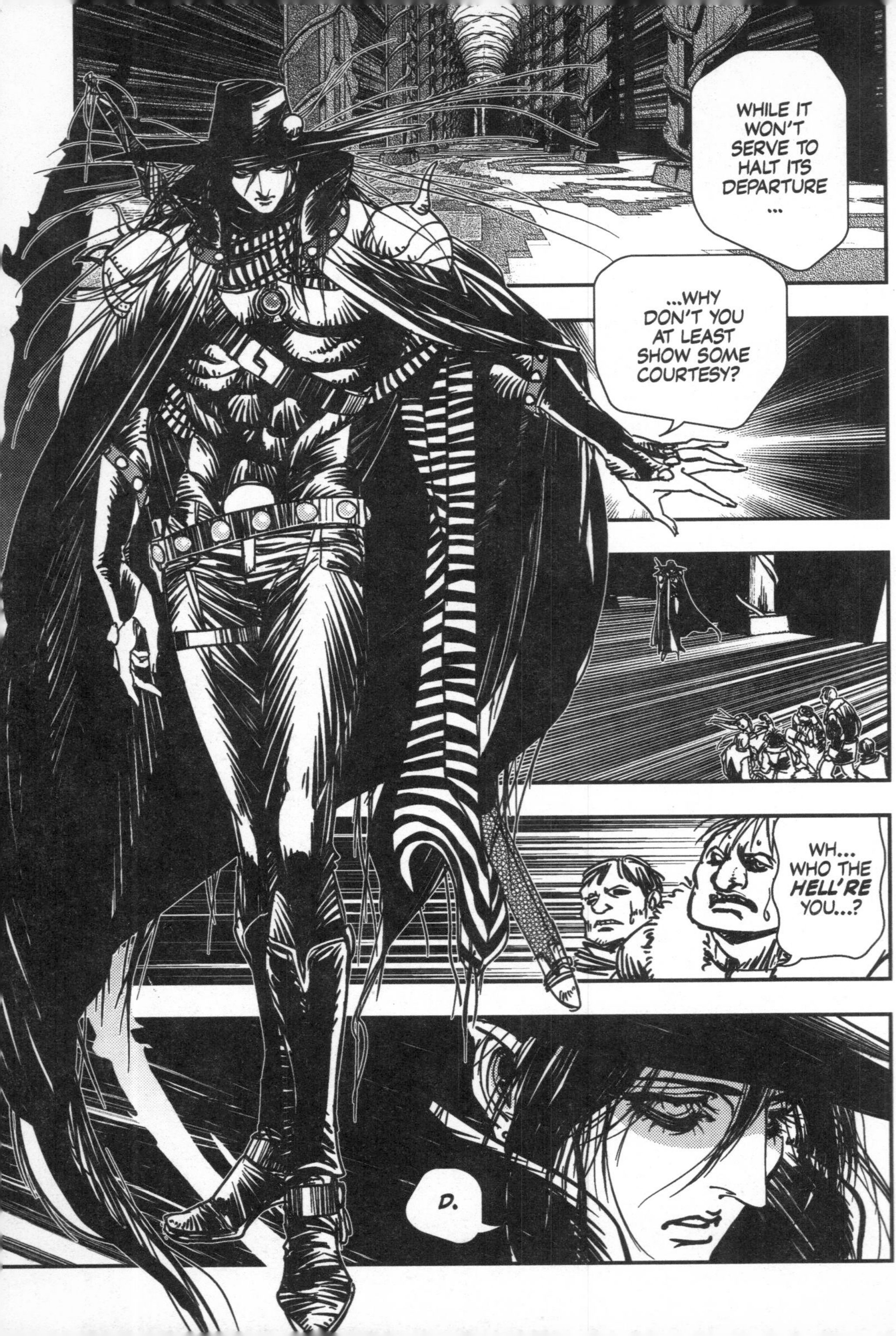
WHILE IT WON'T SERVE TO HALT ITS DEPARTURE ...
...WHY DON'T YOU AT LEAST SHOW SOME COURTESY?
WH... WHO THE *HELL'RE* YOU...?
D.

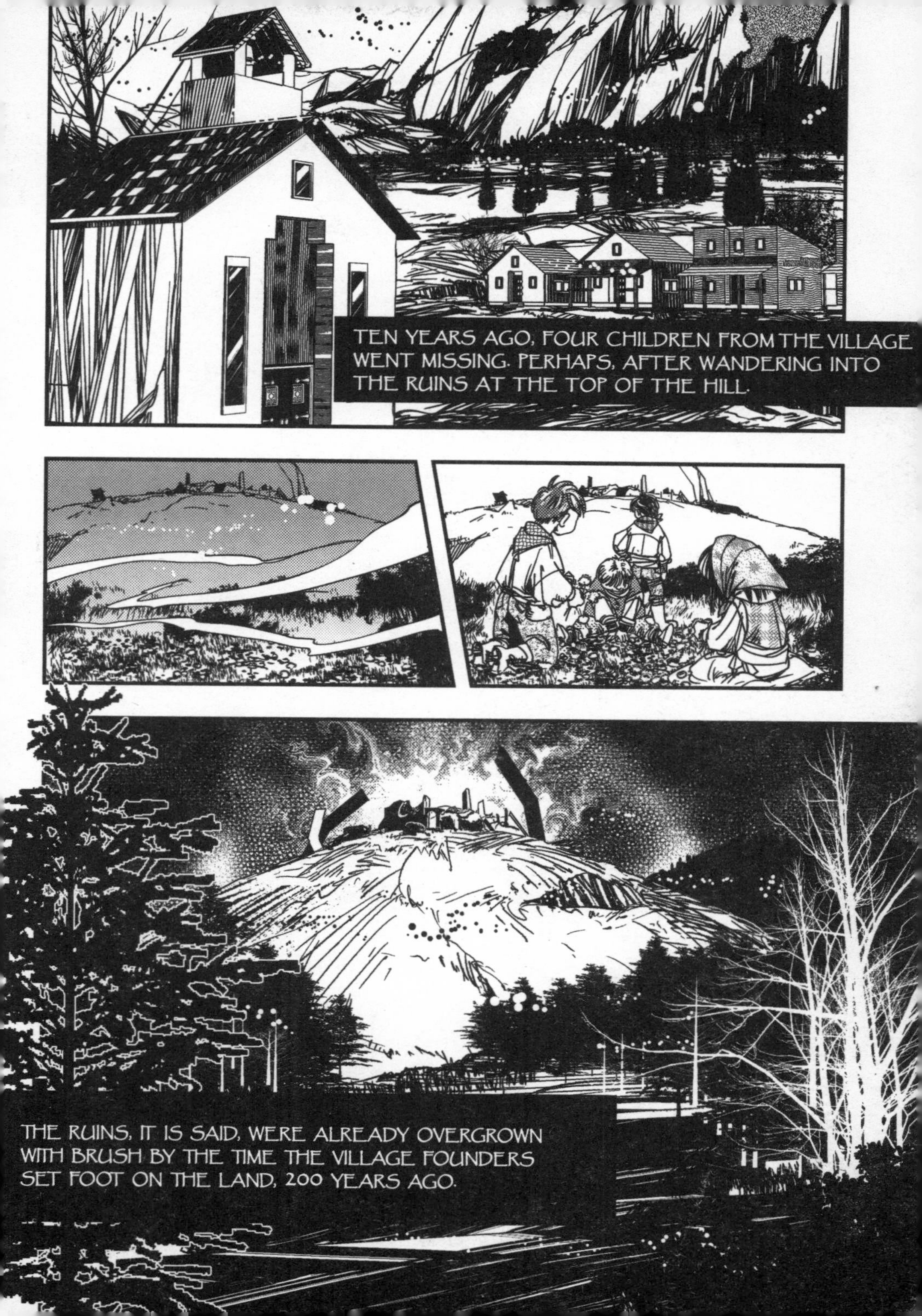
TEN YEARS AGO, FOUR CHILDREN FROM THE VILLAGE WENT MISSING. PERHAPS, AFTER WANDERING INTO THE RUINS AT THE TOP OF THE HILL.
THE RUINS, IT IS SAID, WERE ALREADY OVERGROWN WITH BRUSH BY THE TIME THE VILLAGE FOUNDERS SET FOOT ON THE LAND, 200 YEARS AGO.

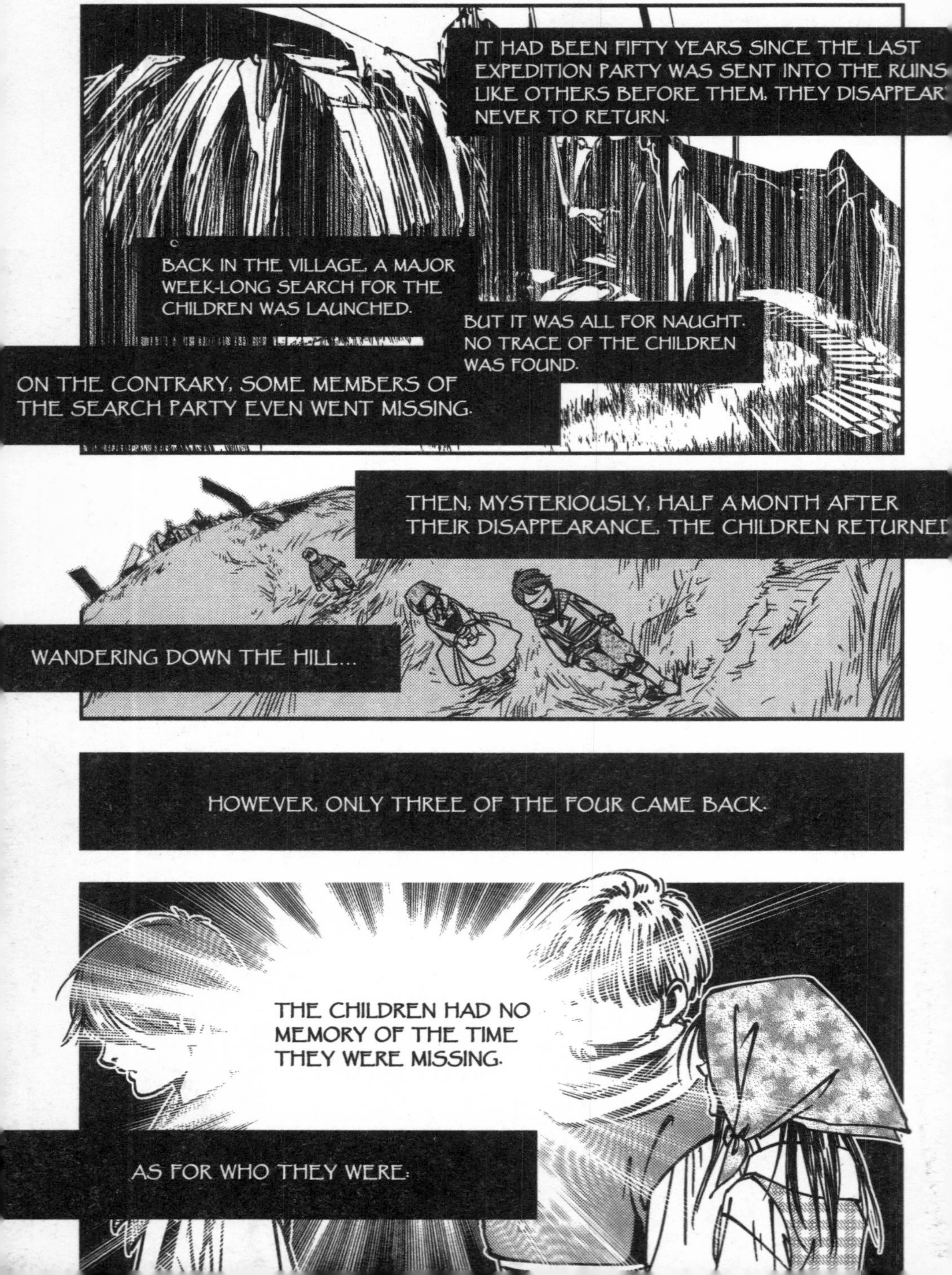
IT HAD BEEN FIFTY YEARS SINCE THE LAST EXPEDITION PARTY WAS SENT INTO THE RUINS. LIKE OTHERS BEFORE THEM, THEY DISAPPEAR NEVER TO RETURN.
BACK IN THE VILLAGE, A MAJOR WEEK-LONG SEARCH FOR THE CHILDREN WAS LAUNCHED.
BUT IT WAS ALL FOR NAUGHT. NO TRACE OF THE CHILDREN WAS FOUND.
ON THE CONTRARY, SOME MEMBERS OF THE SEARCH PARTY EVEN WENT MISSING.
THEN, MYSTERIOUSLY, HALF A MONTH AFTER THEIR DISAPPEARANCE, THE CHILDREN RETURNED
WANDERING DOWN THE HILL...
HOWEVER, ONLY THREE OF THE FOUR CAME BACK.
THE CHILDREN HAD NO MEMORY OF THE TIME THEY WERE MISSING.
AS FOR WHO THEY WERE:

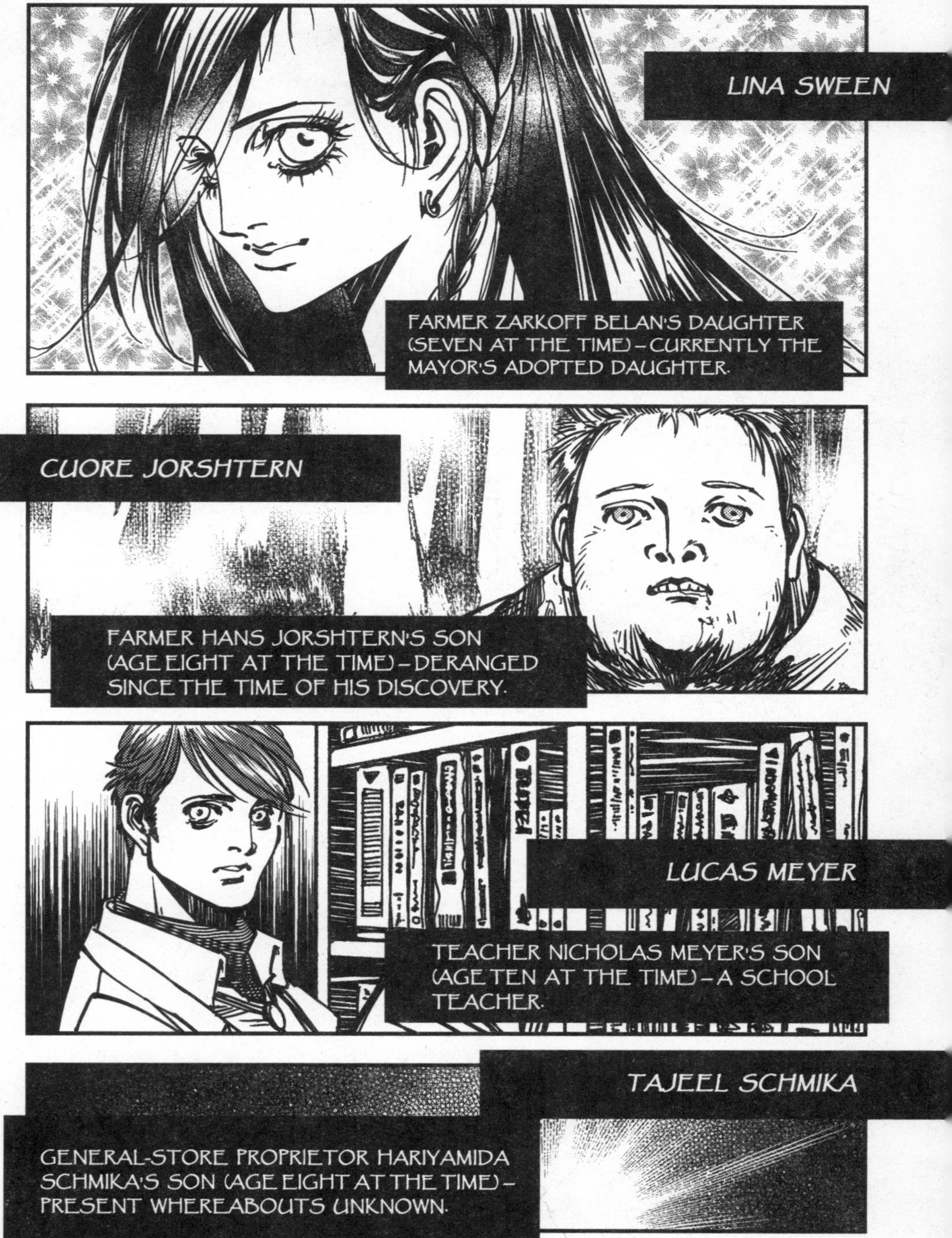
LINA SWEEN
FARMER ZARKOFF BELAN'S DAUGHTER (SEVEN AT THE TIME) – CURRENTLY THE MAYOR'S ADOPTED DAUGHTER.
CUORE JORSHTERN
FARMER HANS JORSHTERN'S SON (AGE EIGHT AT THE TIME) – DERANGED SINCE THE TIME OF HIS DISCOVERY.
LUCAS MEYER
TEACHER NICHOLAS MEYER'S SON (AGE TEN AT THE TIME) – A SCHOOL TEACHER.
TAJEEL SCHMIKA
GENERAL-STORE PROPRIETOR HARIYAMIDA SCHMIKA'S SON (AGE EIGHT AT THE TIME) – PRESENT WHEREABOUTS UNKNOWN.

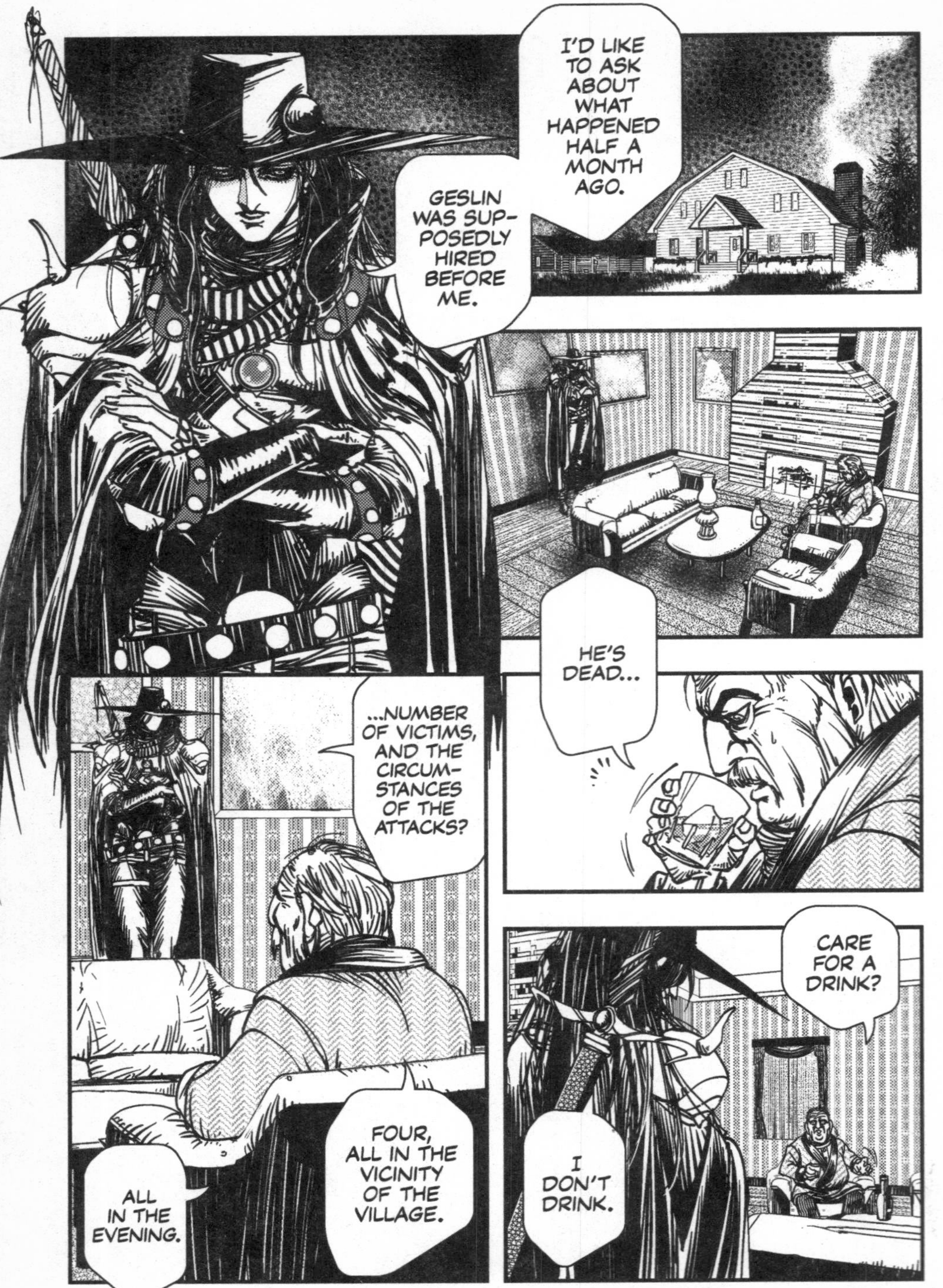

I'D LIKE TO ASK ABOUT WHAT HAPPENED HALF A MONTH AGO.
GESLIN WAS SUP-POSEDLY HIRED BEFORE ME.
HE'S DEAD...
...NUMBER OF VICTIMS, AND THE CIRCUM-STANCES OF THE ATTACKS?
FOUR, ALL IN THE VICINITY OF THE VILLAGE.
ALL IN THE EVENING.
CARE FOR A DRINK?
I DON'T DRINK.

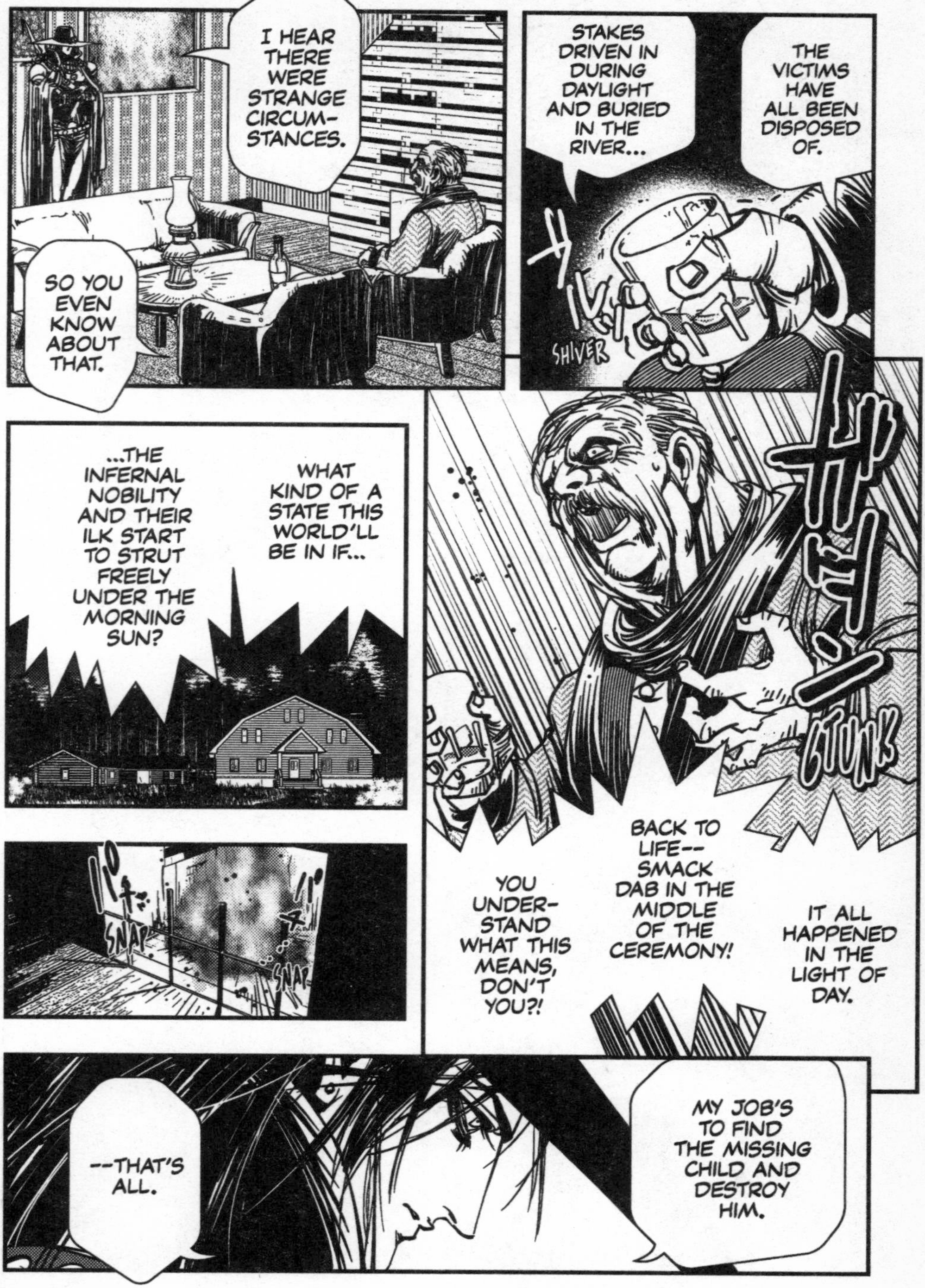
THE VICTIMS HAVE ALL BEEN DISPOSED OF.
STAKES DRIVEN IN DURING DAYLIGHT AND BURIED IN THE RIVER...
SHIVER
I HEAR THERE WERE STRANGE CIRCUM-STANCES.
SO YOU EVEN KNOW ABOUT THAT.
GTUNK
IT ALL HAPPENED IN THE LIGHT OF DAY.
BACK TO LIFE-- SMACK DAB IN THE MIDDLE OF THE CEREMONY!
YOU UNDER-STAND WHAT THIS MEANS, DON'T YOU?!
WHAT KIND OF A STATE THIS WORLD'LL BE IN IF...
...THE INFERNAL NOBILITY AND THEIR ILK START TO STRUT FREELY UNDER THE MORNING SUN?
SNAP
SNAP
MY JOB'S TO FIND THE MISSING CHILD AND DESTROY HIM.
--THAT'S ALL.

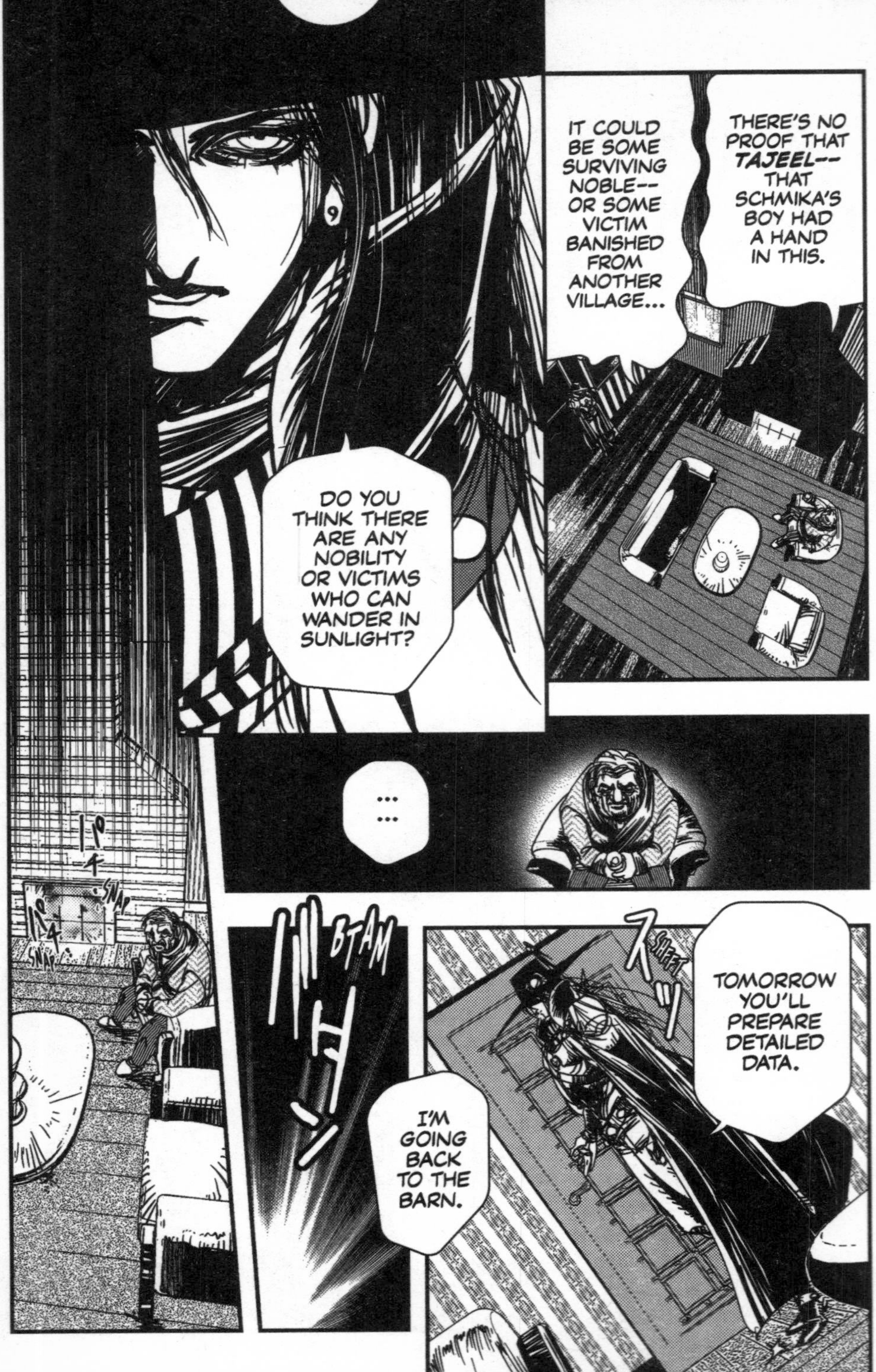
THERE'S NO PROOF THAT *TAJEEL*-- THAT SCHMIKA'S BOY HAD A HAND IN THIS.
IT COULD BE SOME SURVIVING NOBLE-- OR SOME VICTIM BANISHED FROM ANOTHER VILLAGE...
DO YOU THINK THERE ARE ANY NOBILITY OR VICTIMS WHO CAN WANDER IN SUNLIGHT?
...
...
SHFFT
TOMORROW YOU'LL PREPARE DETAILED DATA.
BTAM
I'M GOING BACK TO THE BARN.
SNAP
SNAP

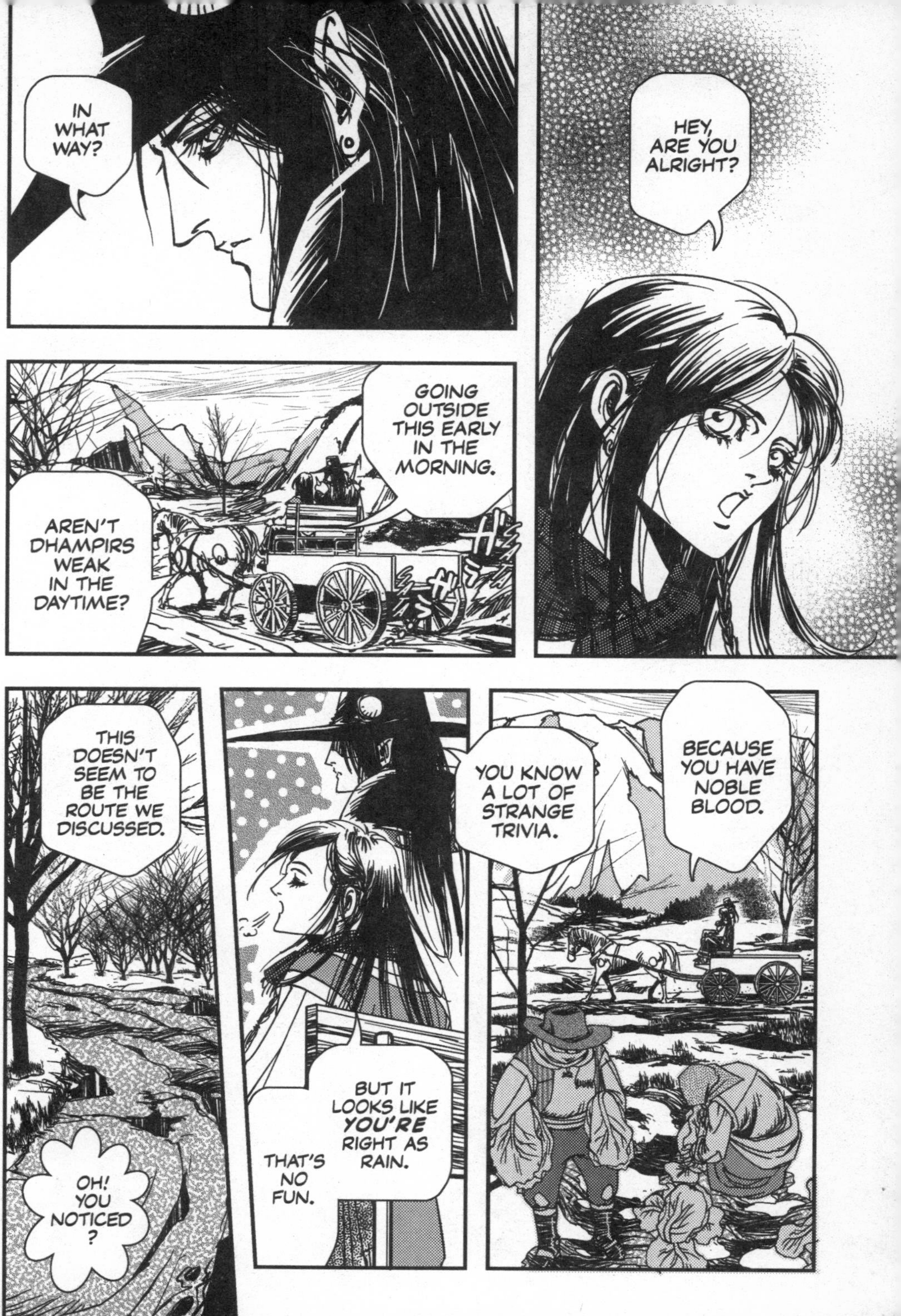
HEY, ARE YOU ALRIGHT?
IN WHAT WAY?
GOING OUTSIDE THIS EARLY IN THE MORNING.
AREN'T DHAMPIRS WEAK IN THE DAYTIME?
BECAUSE YOU HAVE NOBLE BLOOD.
YOU KNOW A LOT OF STRANGE TRIVIA.
BUT IT LOOKS LIKE *YOU'RE* RIGHT AS RAIN.
THAT'S NO FUN.
THIS DOESN'T SEEM TO BE THE ROUTE WE DISCUSSED.
OH! YOU NOTICED?

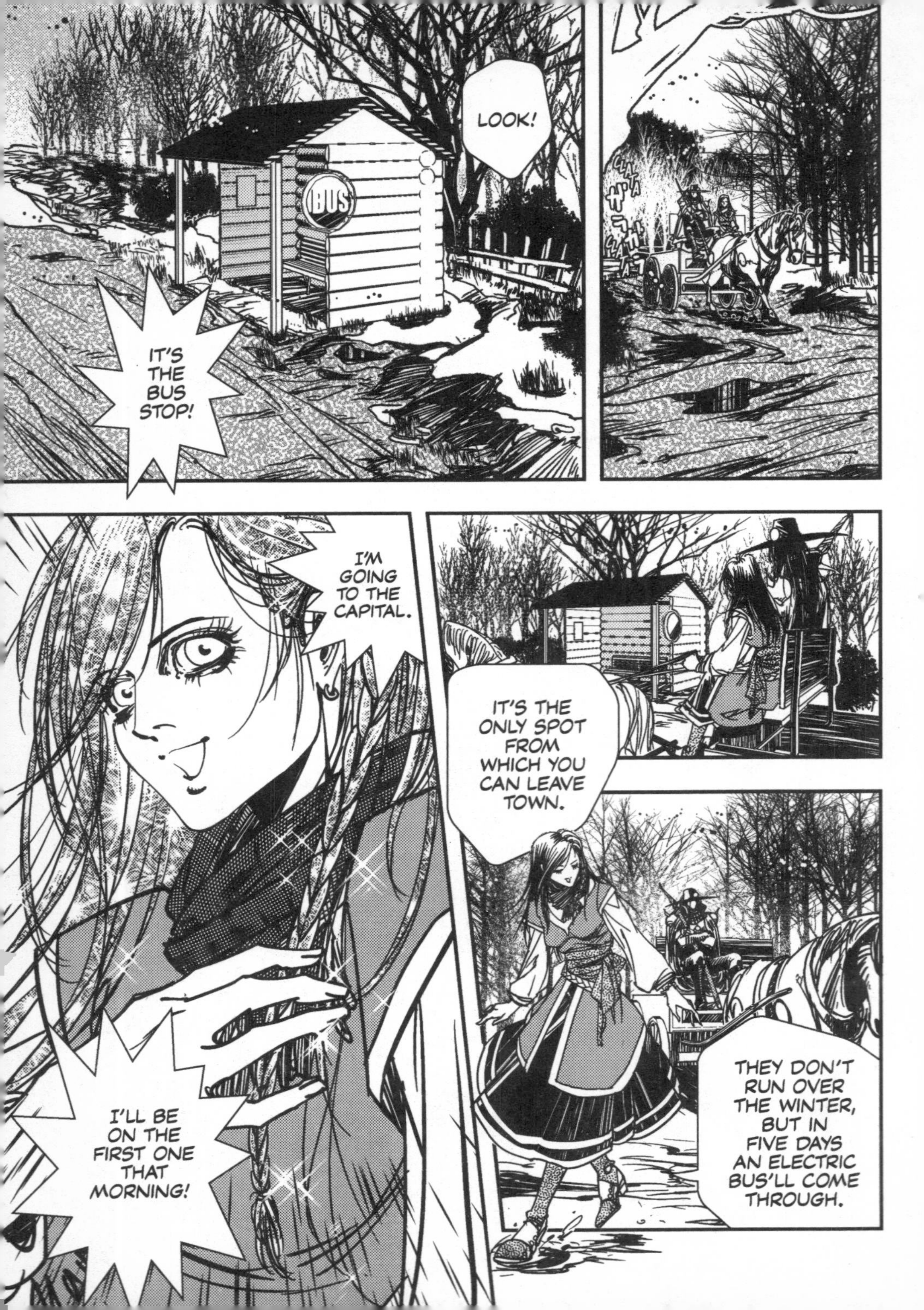
LOOK!
BUS
IT'S THE BUS STOP!
IT'S THE ONLY SPOT FROM WHICH YOU CAN LEAVE TOWN.
THEY DON'T RUN OVER THE WINTER, BUT IN FIVE DAYS AN ELECTRIC BUS'LL COME THROUGH.
I'M GOING TO THE CAPITAL.
I'LL BE ON THE FIRST ONE THAT MORNING!

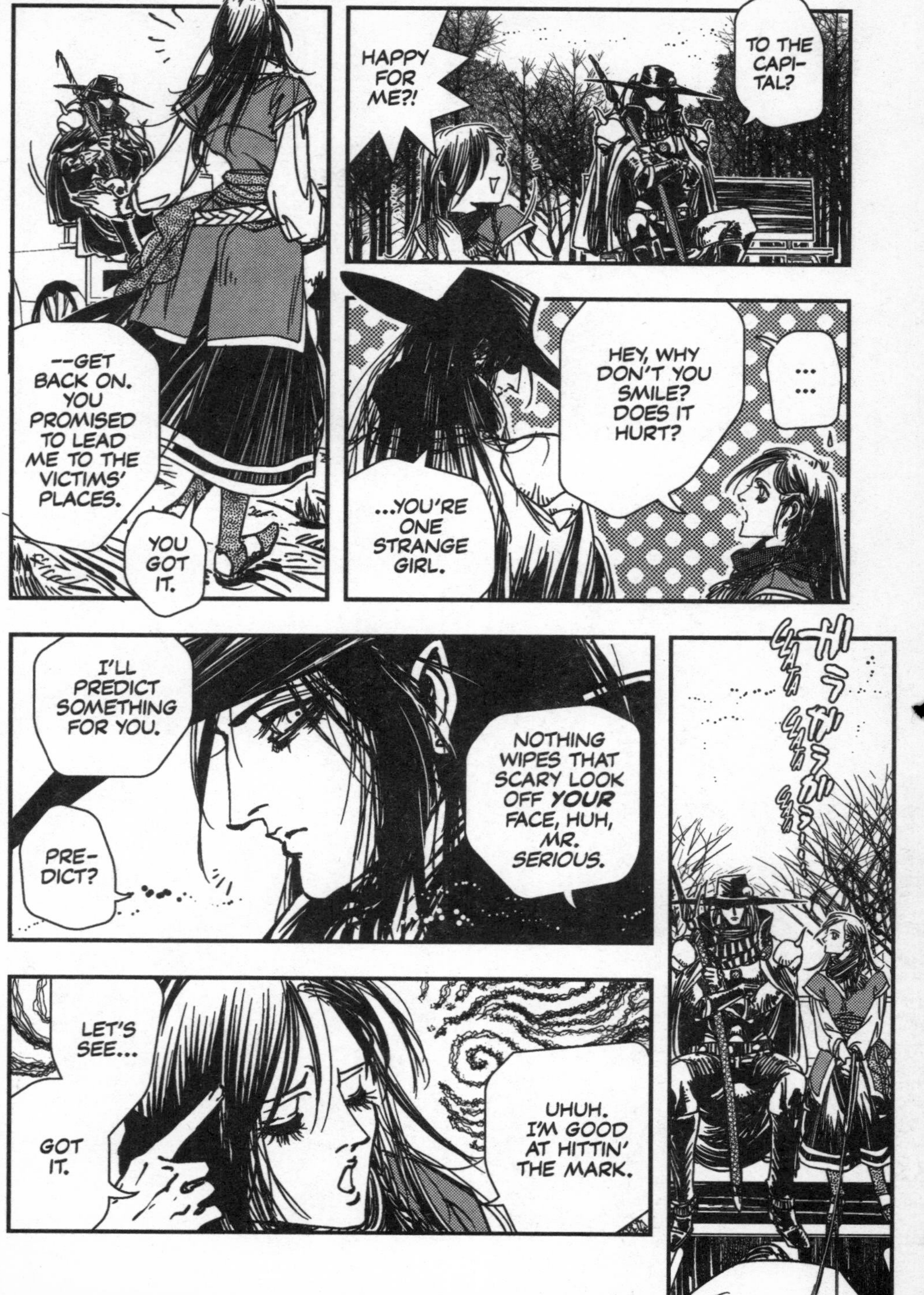
TO THE CAPI-TAL?
HAPPY FOR ME?!
...
...
HEY, WHY DON'T YOU SMILE? DOES IT HURT?
...YOU'RE ONE STRANGE GIRL.
--GET BACK ON. YOU PROMISED TO LEAD ME TO THE VICTIMS' PLACES.
YOU GOT IT.
ガラガラガラ…
CLATA CLATA CLATA
NOTHING WIPES THAT SCARY LOOK OFF *YOUR* FACE, HUH, MR. SERIOUS.
I'LL PREDICT SOMETHING FOR YOU.
PRE-DICT?
UHUH. I'M GOOD AT HITTIN' THE MARK.
LET'S SEE...
GOT IT.

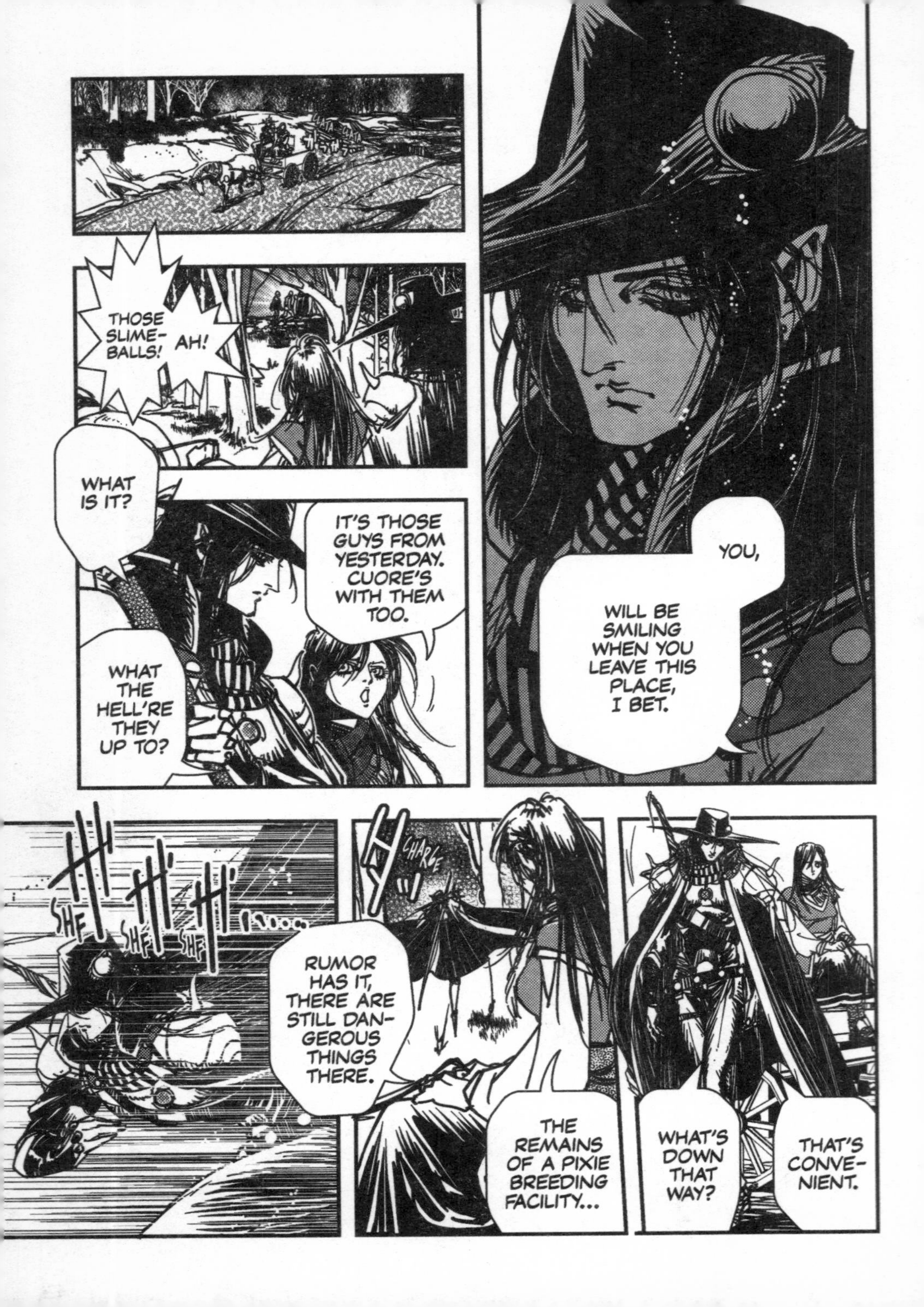

YOU,
WILL BE SMILING WHEN YOU LEAVE THIS PLACE, I BET.
AH!
THOSE SLIME-BALLS!
WHAT IS IT?
IT'S THOSE GUYS FROM YESTERDAY. CUORE'S WITH THEM TOO.
WHAT THE HELL'RE THEY UP TO?
WHAT'S DOWN THAT WAY?
CHARGE
THE REMAINS OF A PIXIE BREEDING FACILITY...
RUMOR HAS IT, THERE ARE STILL DAN-GEROUS THINGS THERE.
THAT'S CONVE-NIENT.
SHF
SHF
SHF

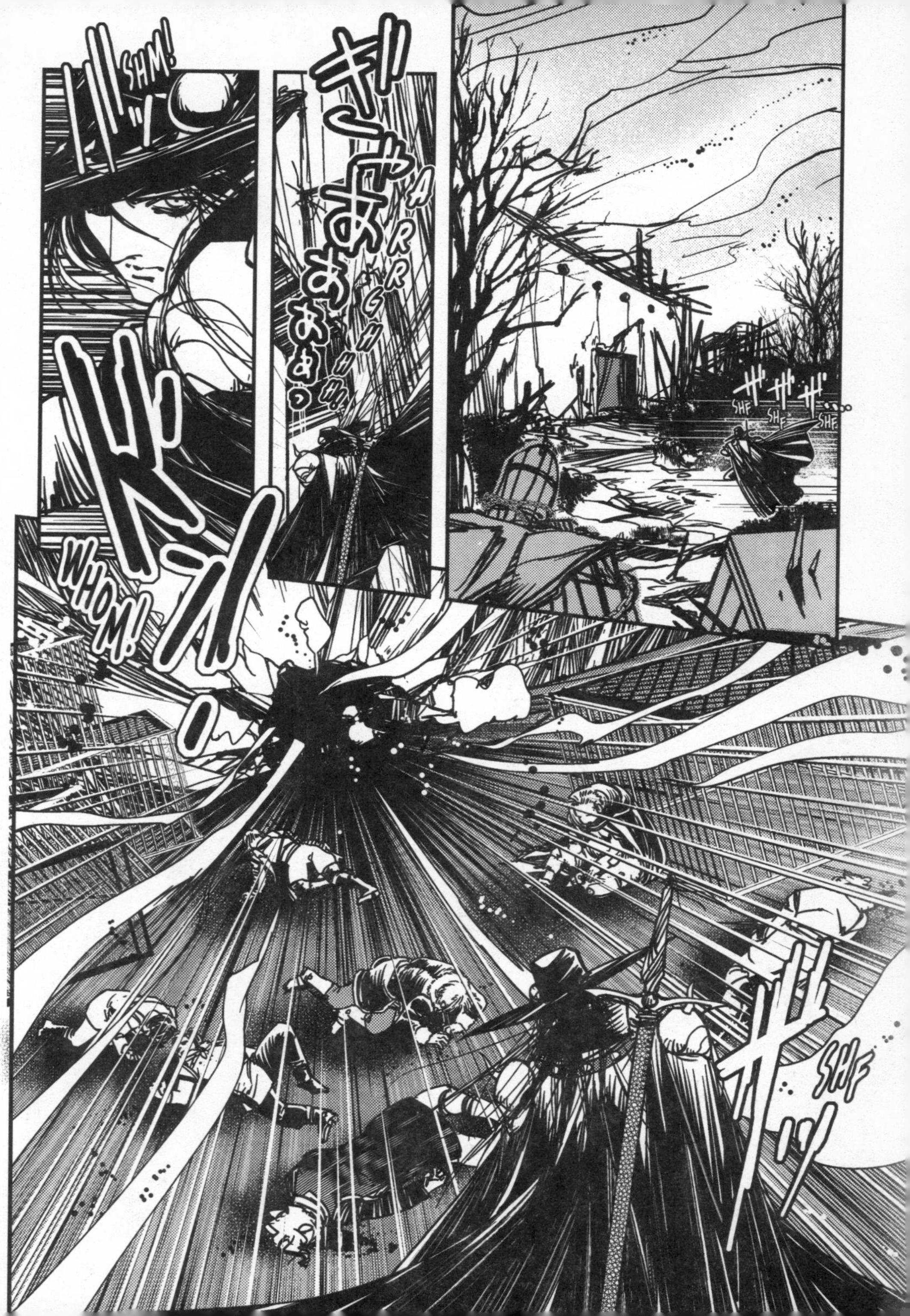

SHF
SHF
SHF
ARRGHHH!!
SHM!
WHOM!
SHF

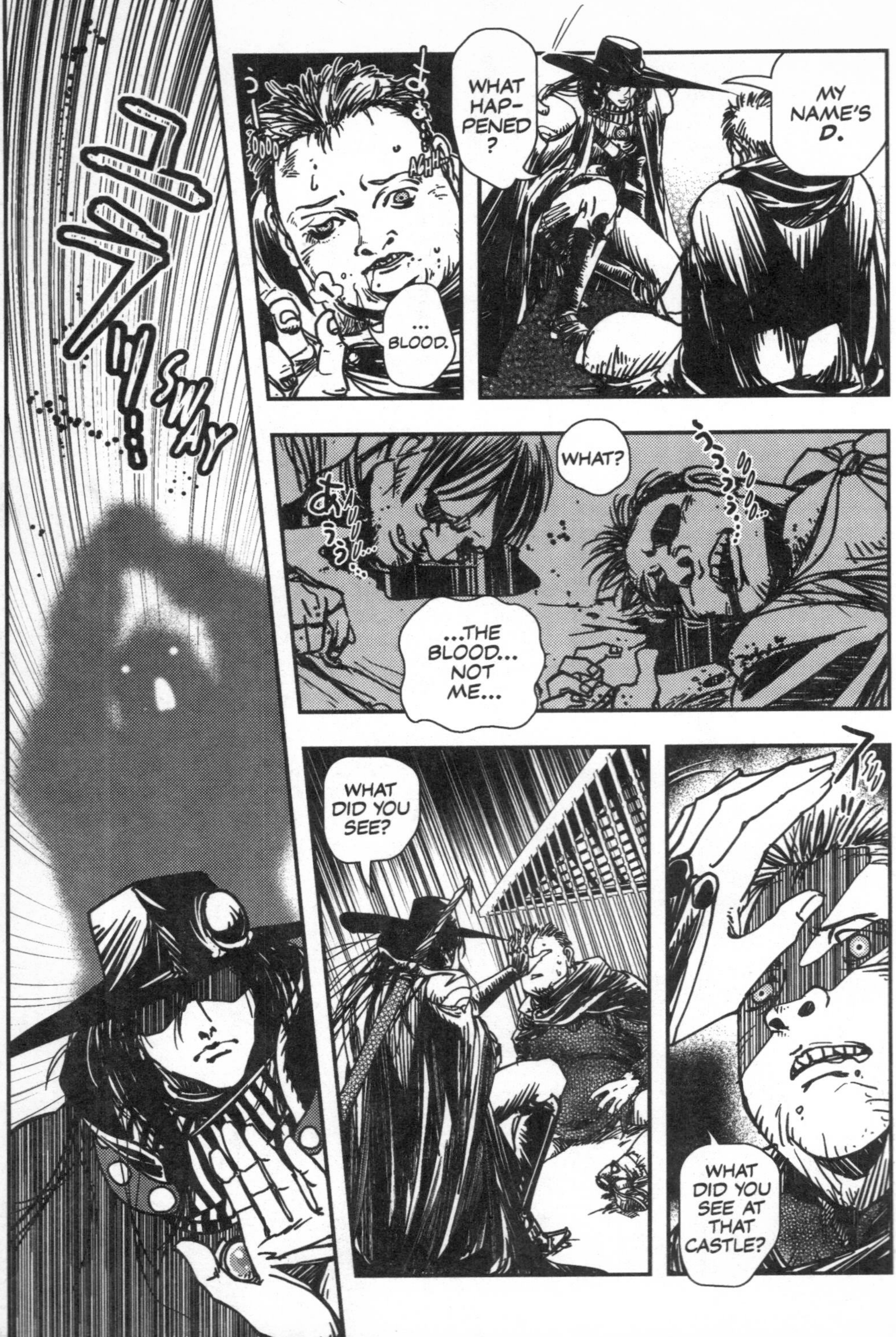

MY NAME'S D.
WHAT HAP-PENED?
ACHH...
...BLOOD.
WHAT?
...THE BLOOD... NOT ME...
WHAT DID YOU SEE AT THAT CASTLE?
WHAT DID YOU SEE?
SWAY

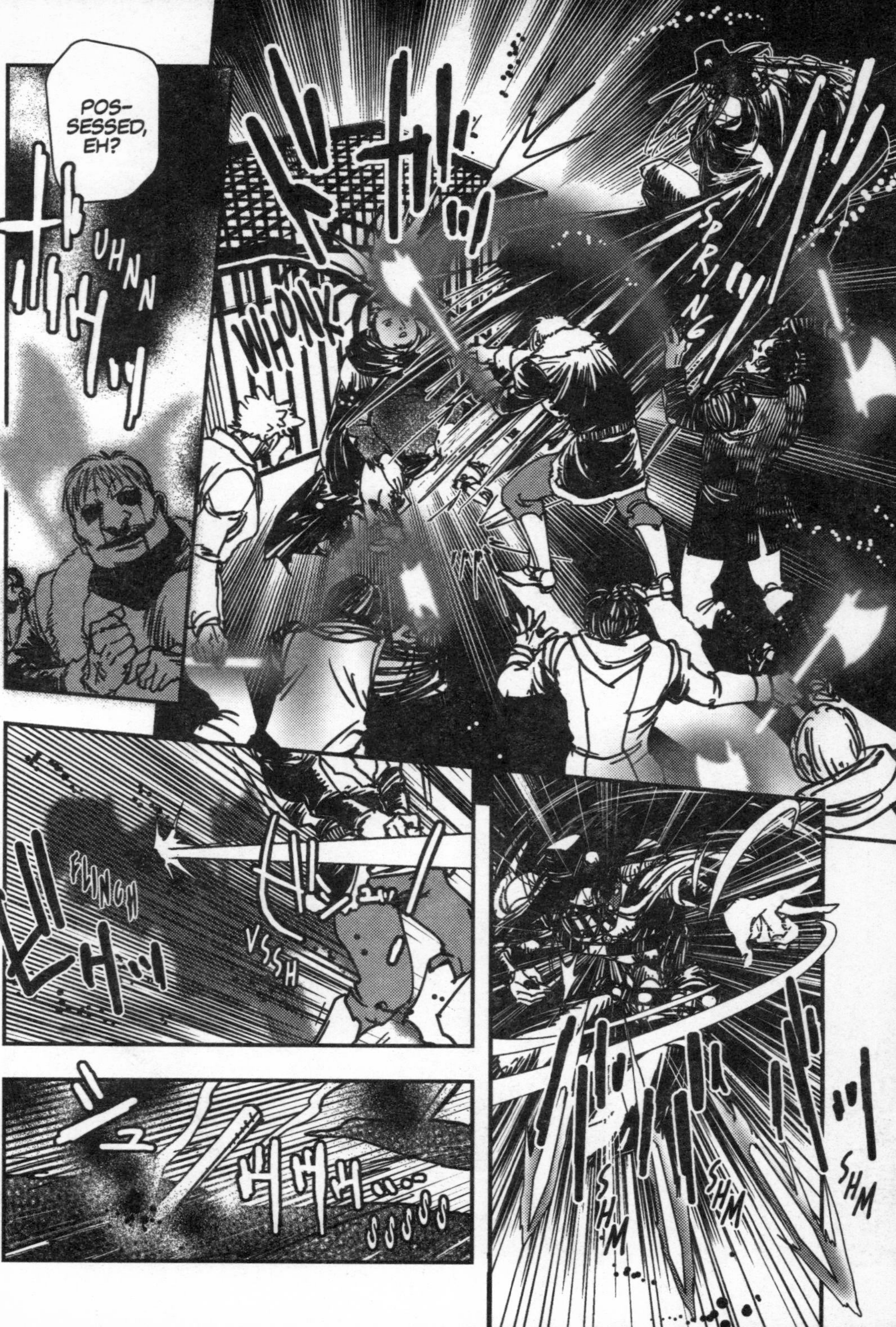
SPRING
WHONK
POS-SESSED, EH?
UHNNN
SHM
SHM
SHM
FLINCH
VSSH
SSSSS

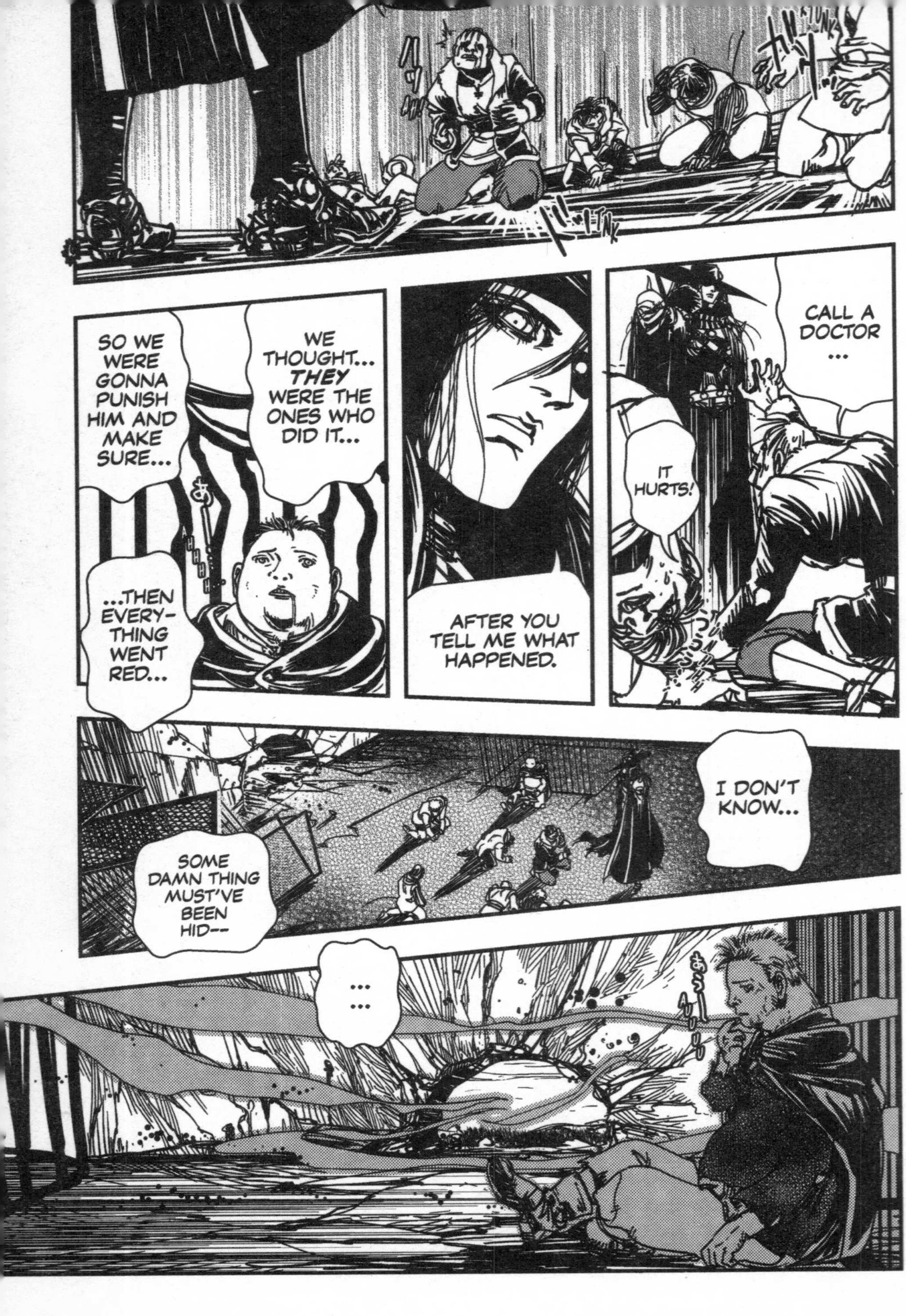
CALL A DOCTOR ...
IT HURTS!
AFTER YOU TELL ME WHAT HAPPENED.
WE THOUGHT... *THEY* WERE THE ONES WHO DID IT...
SO WE WERE GONNA PUNISH HIM AND MAKE SURE...
...THEN EVERY-THING WENT RED...
I DON'T KNOW...
SOME DAMN THING MUST'VE BEEN HID--
... ...

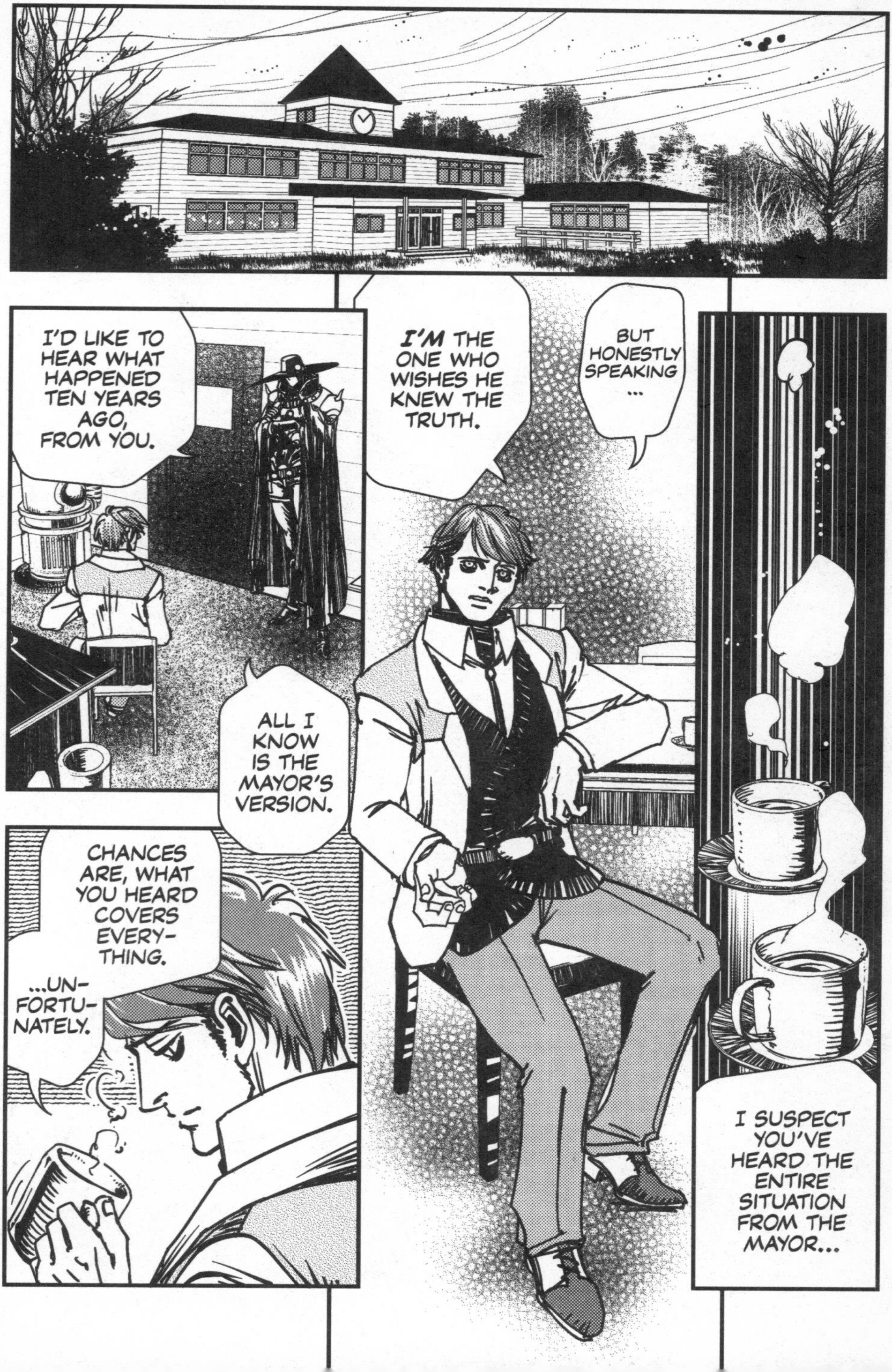
I SUSPECT YOU'VE HEARD THE ENTIRE SITUATION FROM THE MAYOR...
BUT HONESTLY SPEAKING...
I'M THE ONE WHO WISHES HE KNEW THE TRUTH.
ALL I KNOW IS THE MAYOR'S VERSION.
I'D LIKE TO HEAR WHAT HAPPENED TEN YEARS AGO, FROM YOU.
CHANCES ARE, WHAT YOU HEARD COVERS EVERY-THING.
...UN-FORTU-NATELY.

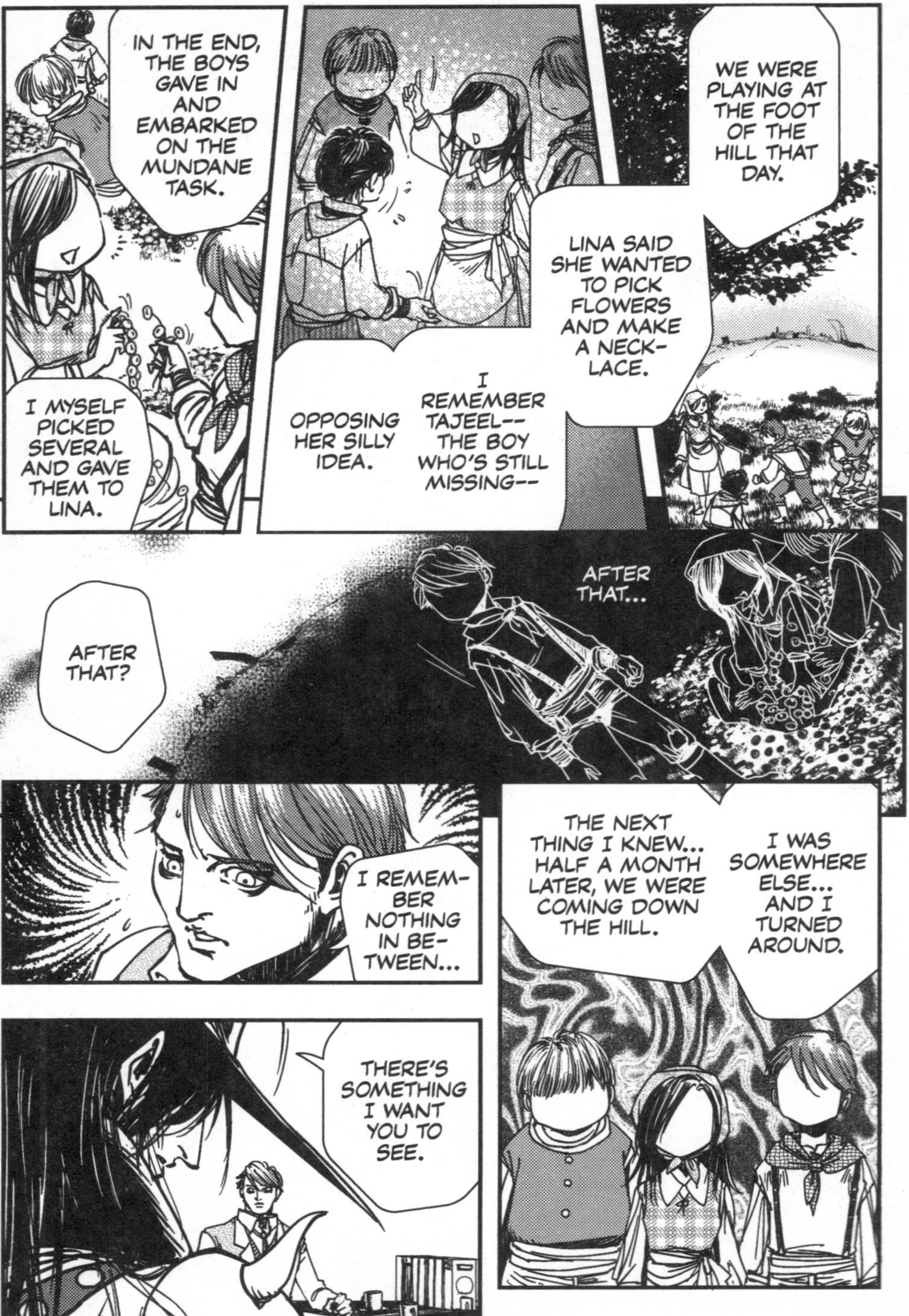
WE WERE PLAYING AT THE FOOT OF THE HILL THAT DAY.
LINA SAID SHE WANTED TO PICK FLOWERS AND MAKE A NECK-LACE.
I REMEMBER TAJEEL-- THE BOY WHO'S STILL MISSING--
OPPOSING HER SILLY IDEA.
IN THE END, THE BOYS GAVE IN AND EMBARKED ON THE MUNDANE TASK.
I MYSELF PICKED SEVERAL AND GAVE THEM TO LINA.
AFTER THAT...
AFTER THAT?
I WAS SOMEWHERE ELSE... AND I TURNED AROUND.
THE NEXT THING I KNEW... HALF A MONTH LATER, WE WERE COMING DOWN THE HILL.
I REMEM-BER NOTHING IN BE-TWEEN...
THERE'S SOMETHING I WANT YOU TO SEE.

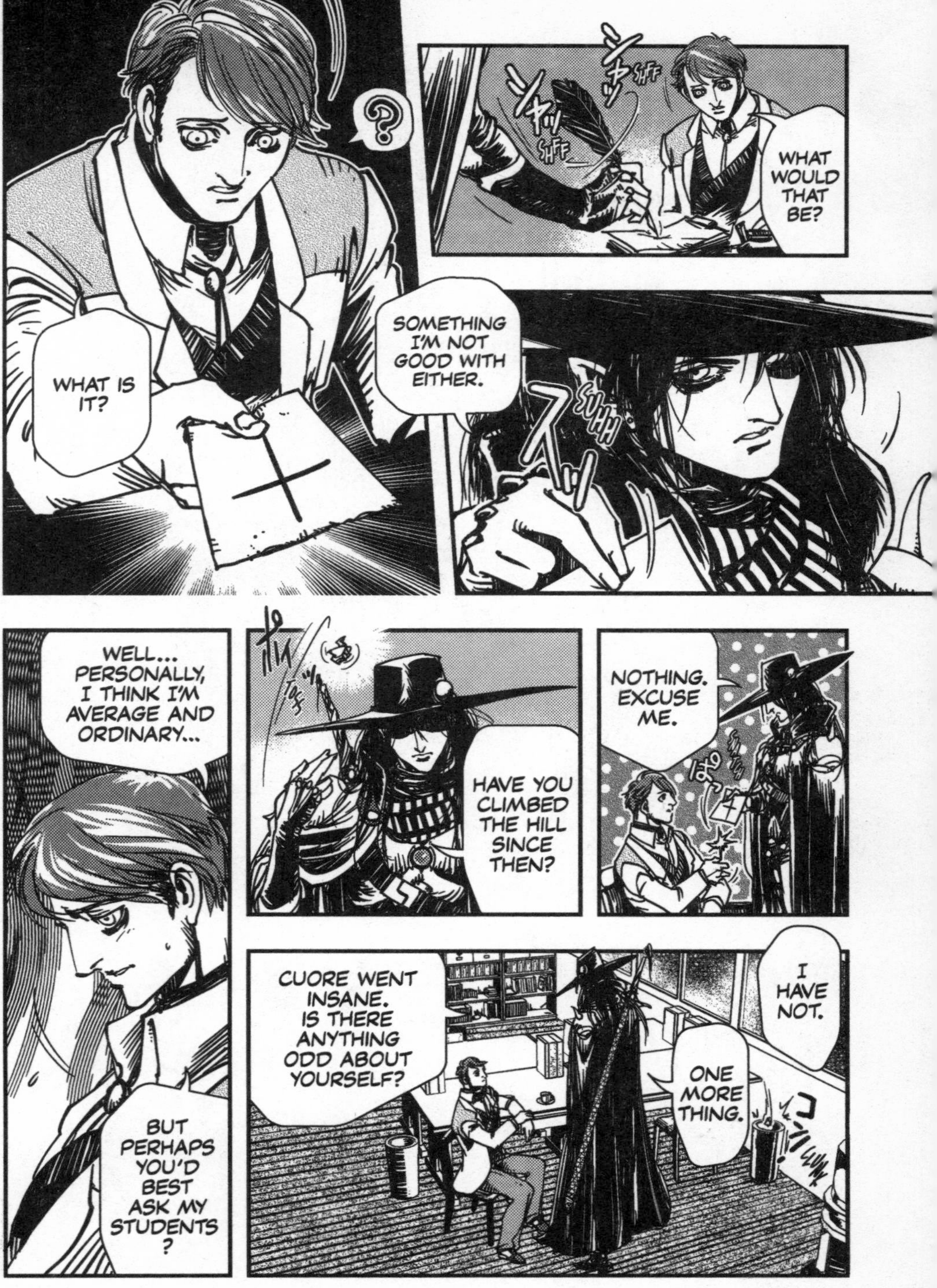
SHFF
SHFF
WHAT WOULD THAT BE?
SOMETHING I'M NOT GOOD WITH EITHER.
?
WHAT IS IT?
NOTHING. EXCUSE ME.
HAVE YOU CLIMBED THE HILL SINCE THEN?
I HAVE NOT.
ONE MORE THING.
CUORE WENT INSANE. IS THERE ANYTHING ODD ABOUT YOURSELF?
WELL... PERSONALLY, I THINK I'M AVERAGE AND ORDINARY...
BUT PERHAPS YOU'D BEST ASK MY STUDENTS?

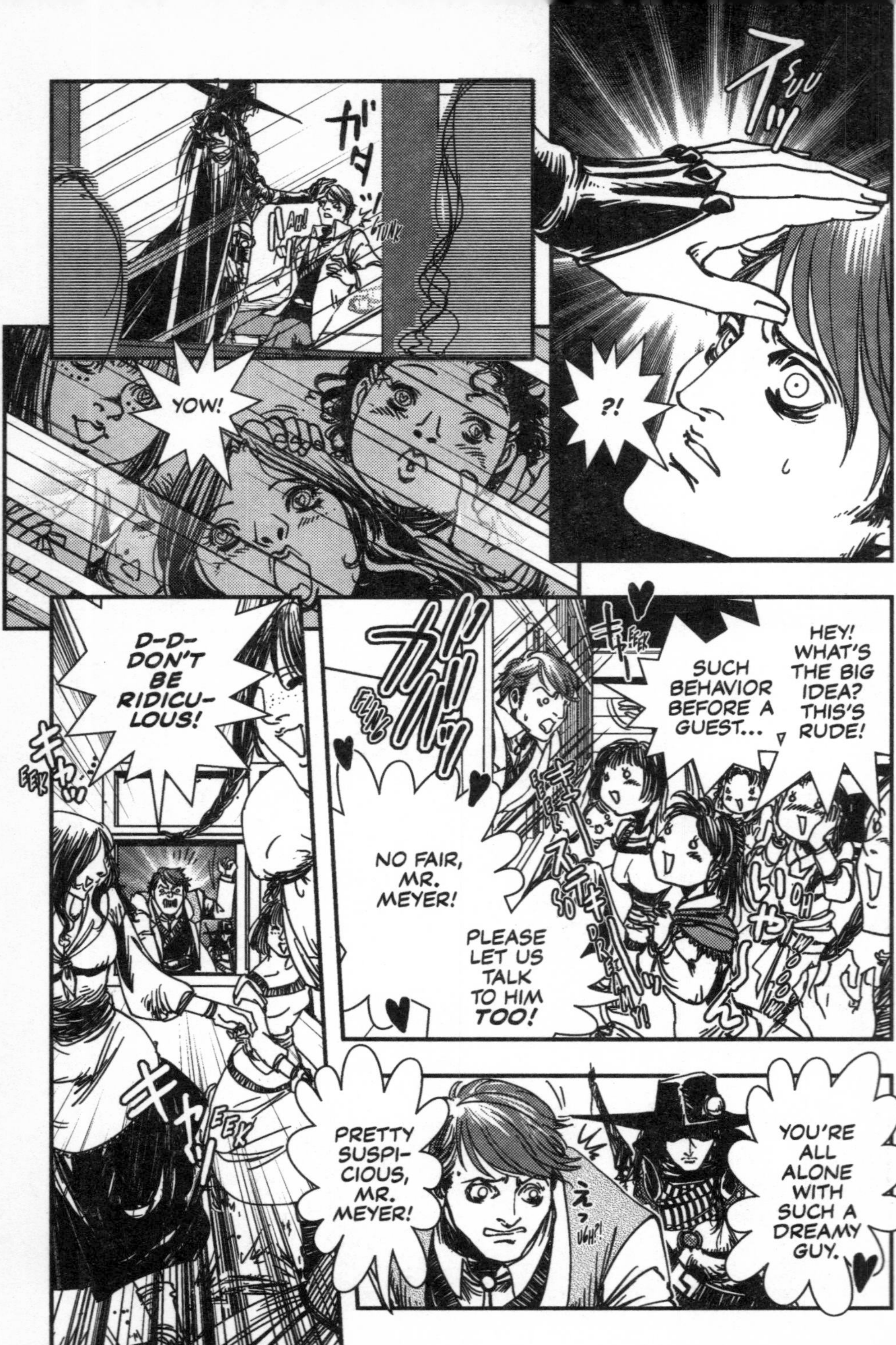
SUU
?!
NAH!
GLINK
YOW!
EEEK
HEY! WHAT'S THE BIG IDEA? THIS'S RUDE!
SUCH BEHAVIOR BEFORE A GUEST...
FLING
NO FAIR, MR. MEYER!
PLEASE LET US TALK TO HIM TOO!
D-D-DON'T BE RIDICULOUS!
EEEK
YOU'RE ALL ALONE WITH SUCH A DREAMY GUY.
UGH?!
PRETTY SUSPICIOUS, MR. MEYER!
EEEK

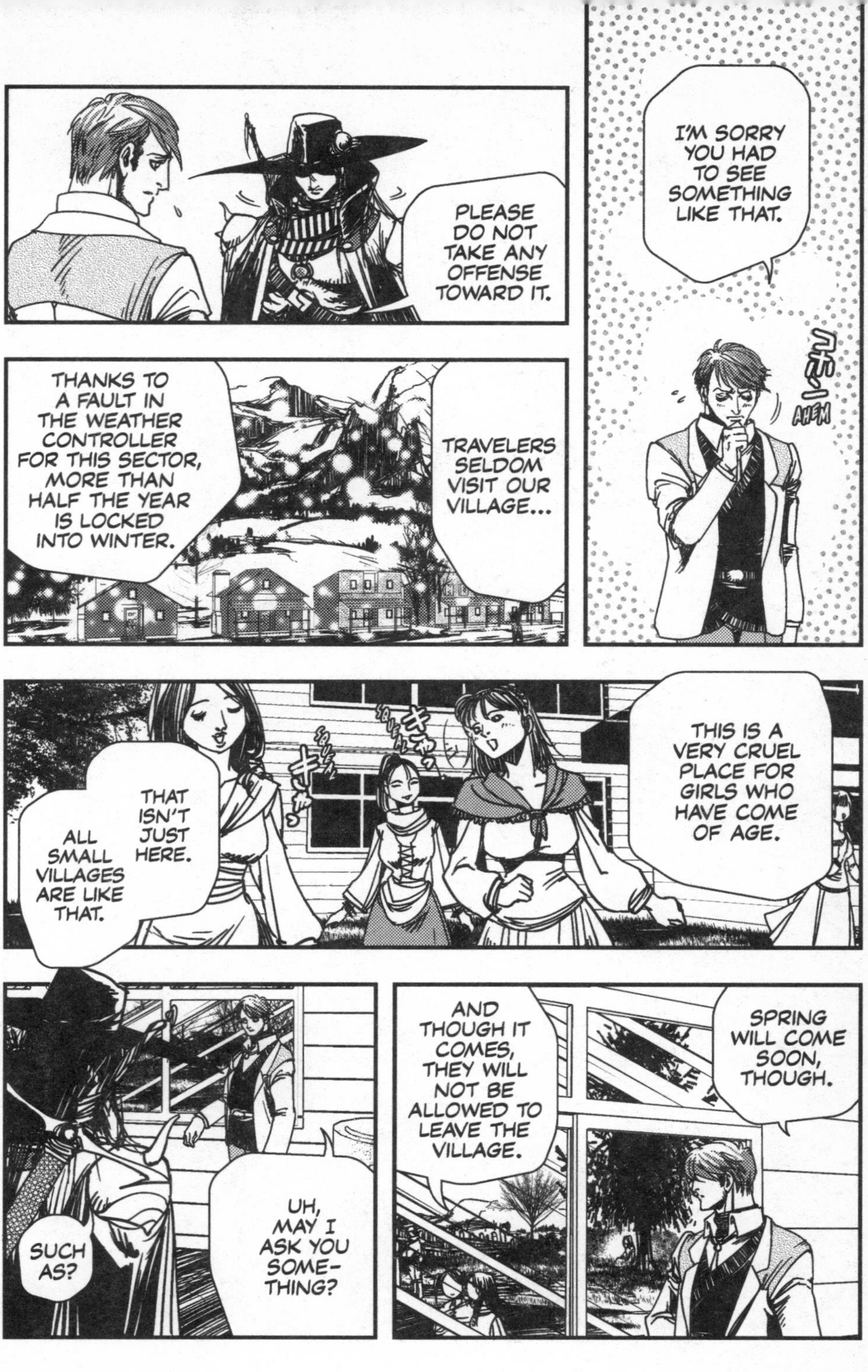
I'M SORRY YOU HAD TO SEE SOMETHING LIKE THAT.
AHEM
PLEASE DO NOT TAKE ANY OFFENSE TOWARD IT.
TRAVELERS SELDOM VISIT OUR VILLAGE...
THANKS TO A FAULT IN THE WEATHER CONTROLLER FOR THIS SECTOR, MORE THAN HALF THE YEAR IS LOCKED INTO WINTER.
THIS IS A VERY CRUEL PLACE FOR GIRLS WHO HAVE COME OF AGE.
SQUEAL
SQUEAL
THAT ISN'T JUST HERE.
ALL SMALL VILLAGES ARE LIKE THAT.
SPRING WILL COME SOON, THOUGH.
AND THOUGH IT COMES, THEY WILL NOT BE ALLOWED TO LEAVE THE VILLAGE.
UH, MAY I ASK YOU SOMETHING?
SUCH AS?

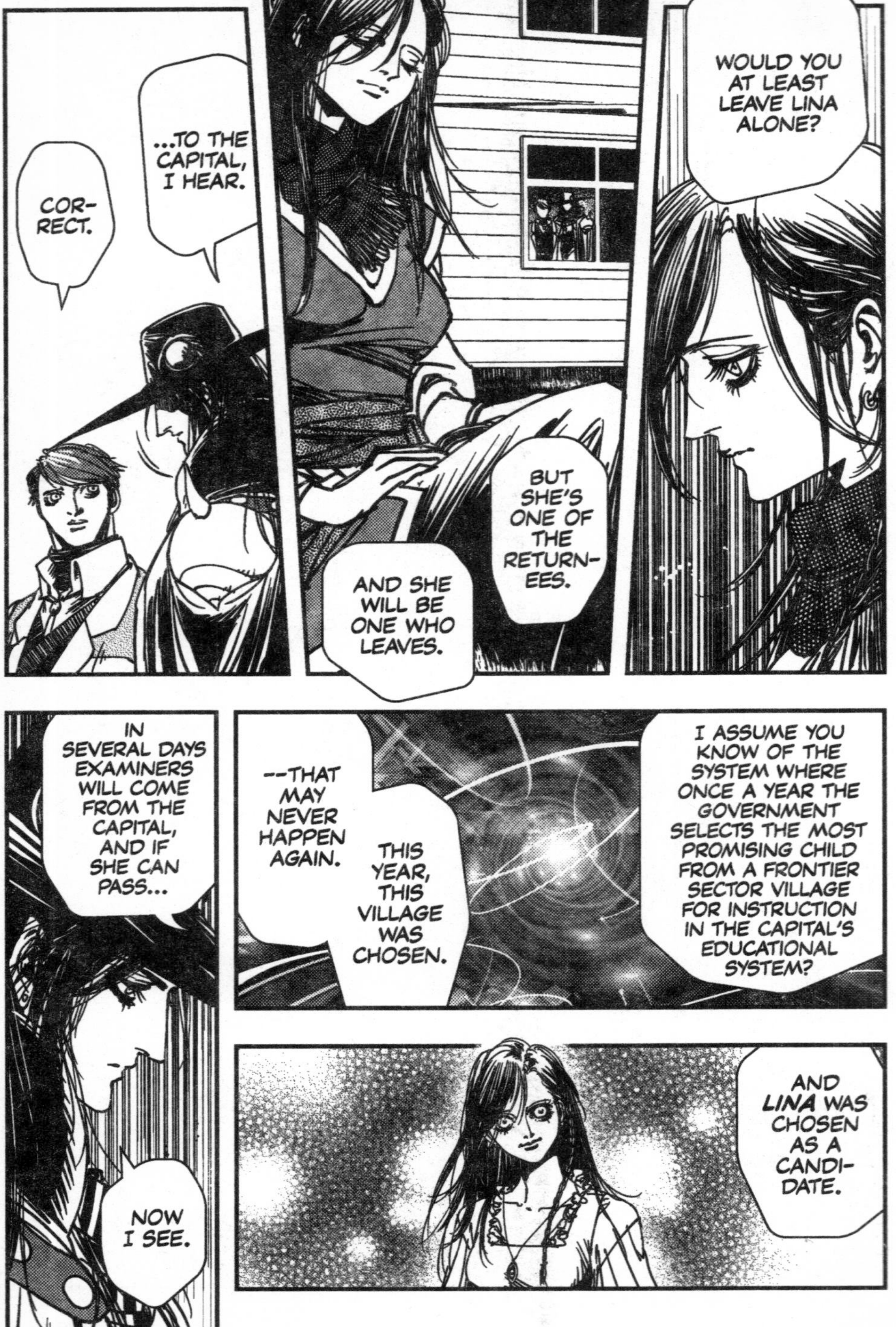
WOULD YOU AT LEAST LEAVE LINA ALONE?
BUT SHE'S ONE OF THE RETURN-EES.
AND SHE WILL BE ONE WHO LEAVES.
...TO THE CAPITAL, I HEAR.
COR-RECT.
I ASSUME YOU KNOW OF THE SYSTEM WHERE ONCE A YEAR THE GOVERNMENT SELECTS THE MOST PROMISING CHILD FROM A FRONTIER SECTOR VILLAGE FOR INSTRUCTION IN THE CAPITAL'S EDUCATIONAL SYSTEM?
THIS YEAR, THIS VILLAGE WAS CHOSEN.
--THAT MAY NEVER HAPPEN AGAIN.
AND LINA WAS CHOSEN AS A CANDI-DATE.
IN SEVERAL DAYS EXAMINERS WILL COME FROM THE CAPITAL, AND IF SHE CAN PASS...
NOW I SEE.

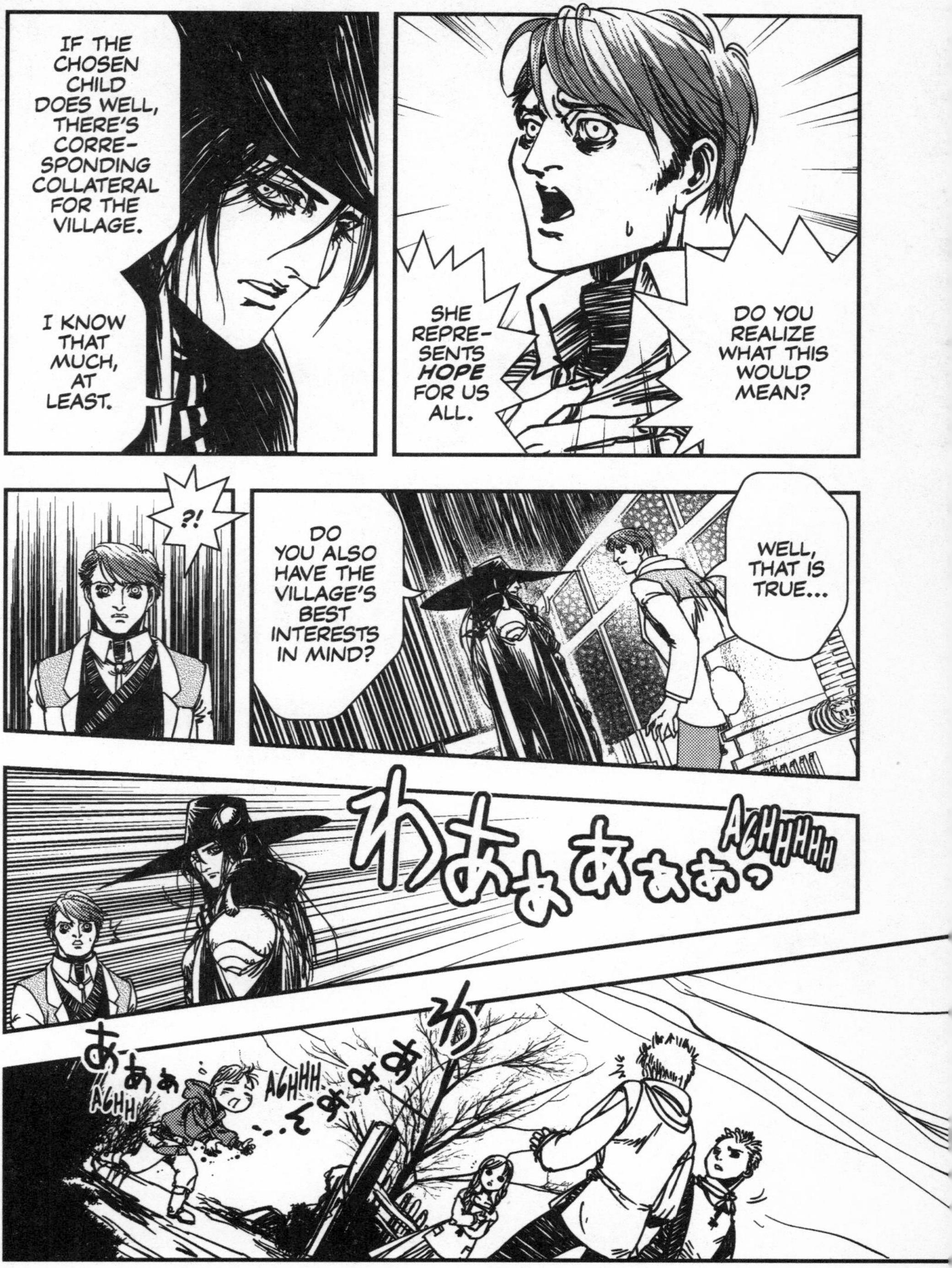
DO YOU REALIZE WHAT THIS WOULD MEAN?
SHE REPRESENTS *HOPE* FOR US ALL.
IF THE CHOSEN CHILD DOES WELL, THERE'S CORRESPONDING COLLATERAL FOR THE VILLAGE.
I KNOW THAT MUCH, AT LEAST.
WELL, THAT IS TRUE...
DO YOU ALSO HAVE THE VILLAGE'S BEST INTERESTS IN MIND?
?!
わあぁあぁあっ
AGHHHHHH
わあああ
AGHHH
ああぁ
AGHH

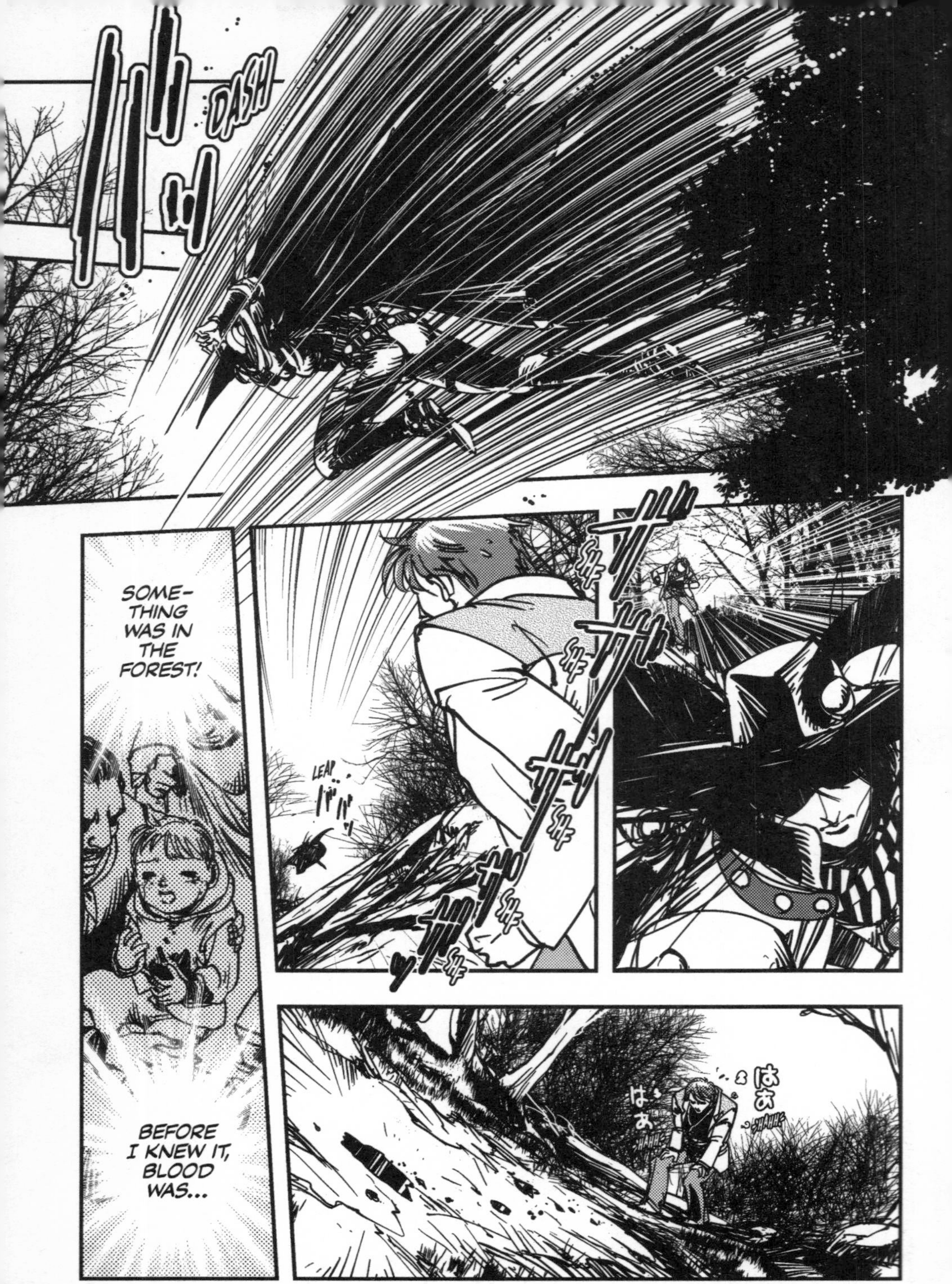
DASH
SH
SH
SH
SH
SH
SH
LEAP
はあ
はあ
SOME-THING WAS IN THE FOREST!
BEFORE I KNEW IT, BLOOD WAS...

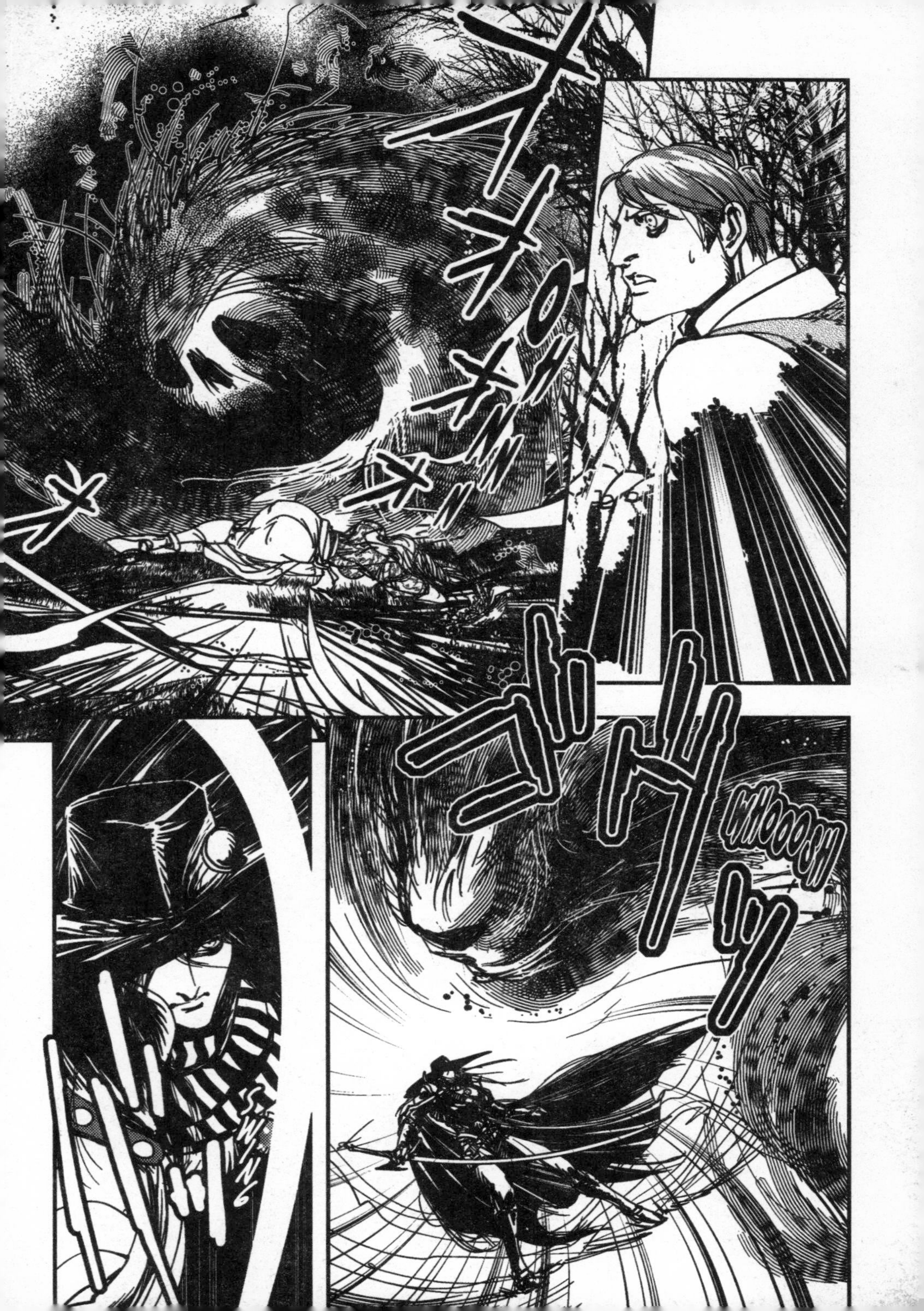

WHOOOSH
SWING

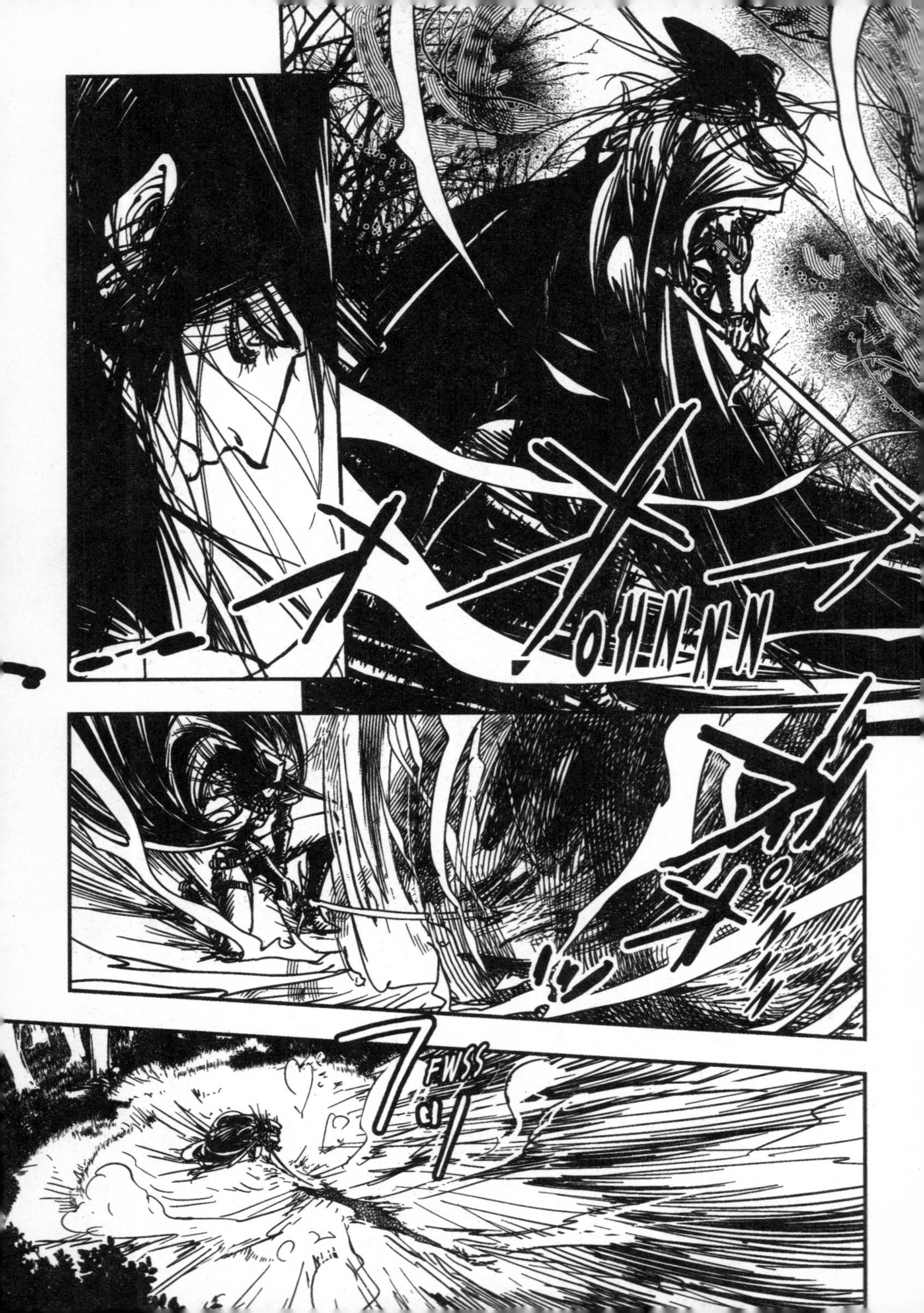
OHNNN
OHNNNN
FWSS

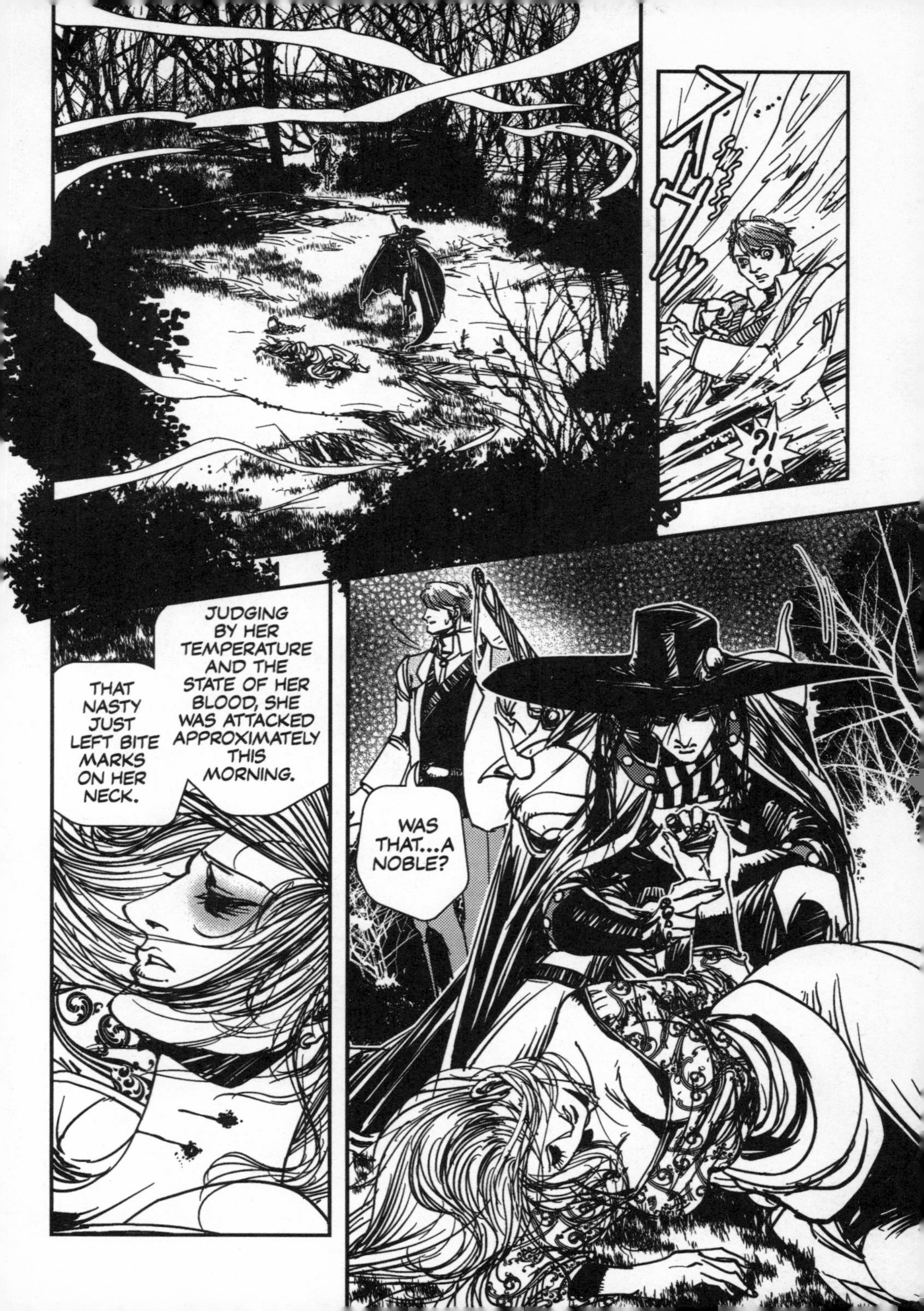
?!
WAS THAT...A NOBLE?
JUDGING BY HER TEMPERATURE AND THE STATE OF HER BLOOD, SHE WAS ATTACKED APPROXIMATELY THIS MORNING.
THAT NASTY JUST LEFT BITE MARKS ON HER NECK.

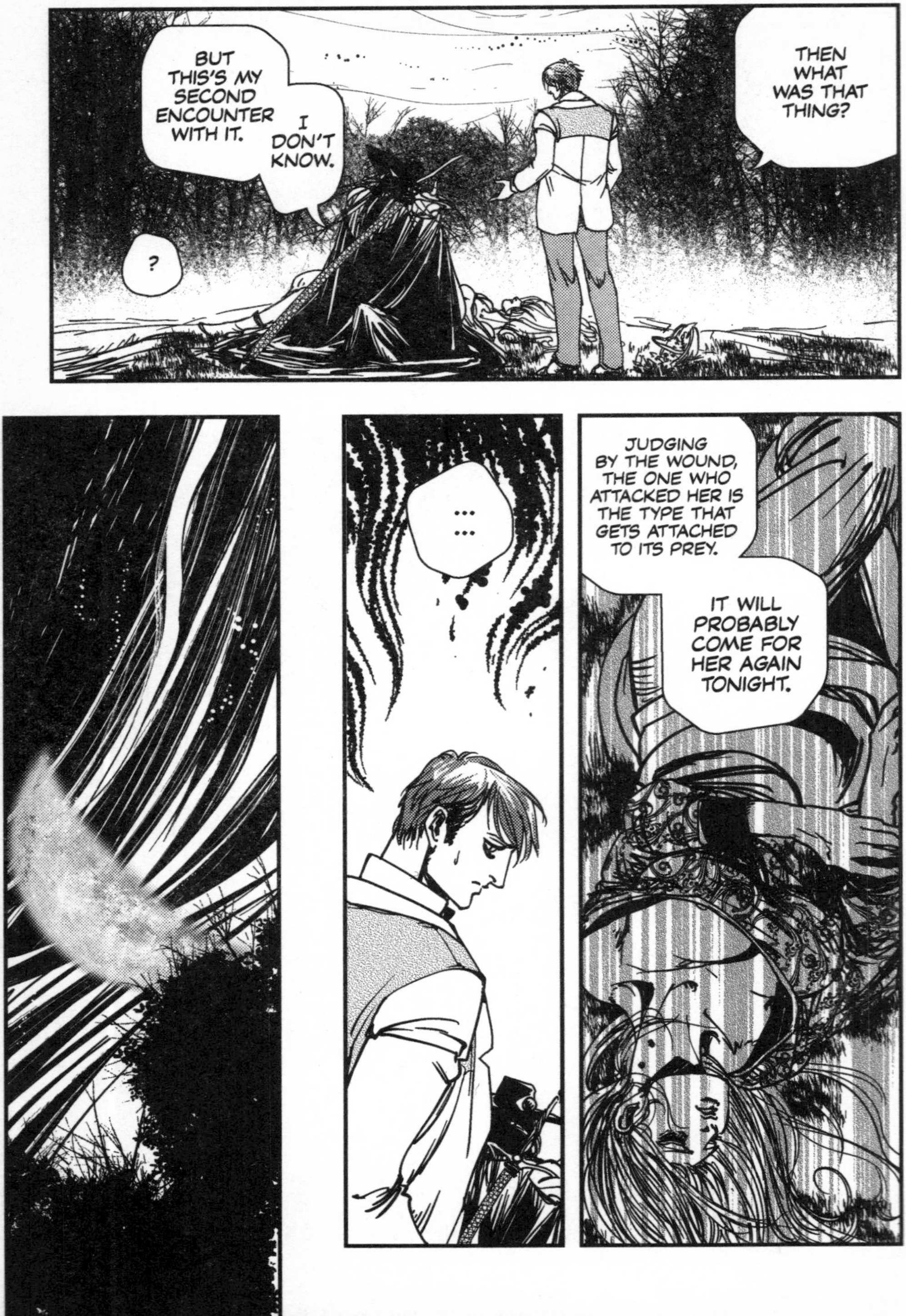
THEN WHAT WAS THAT THING?
I DON'T KNOW.
BUT THIS'S MY SECOND ENCOUNTER WITH IT.
?
JUDGING BY THE WOUND, THE ONE WHO ATTACKED HER IS THE TYPE THAT GETS ATTACHED TO ITS PREY.
IT WILL PROBABLY COME FOR HER AGAIN TONIGHT.
... ...

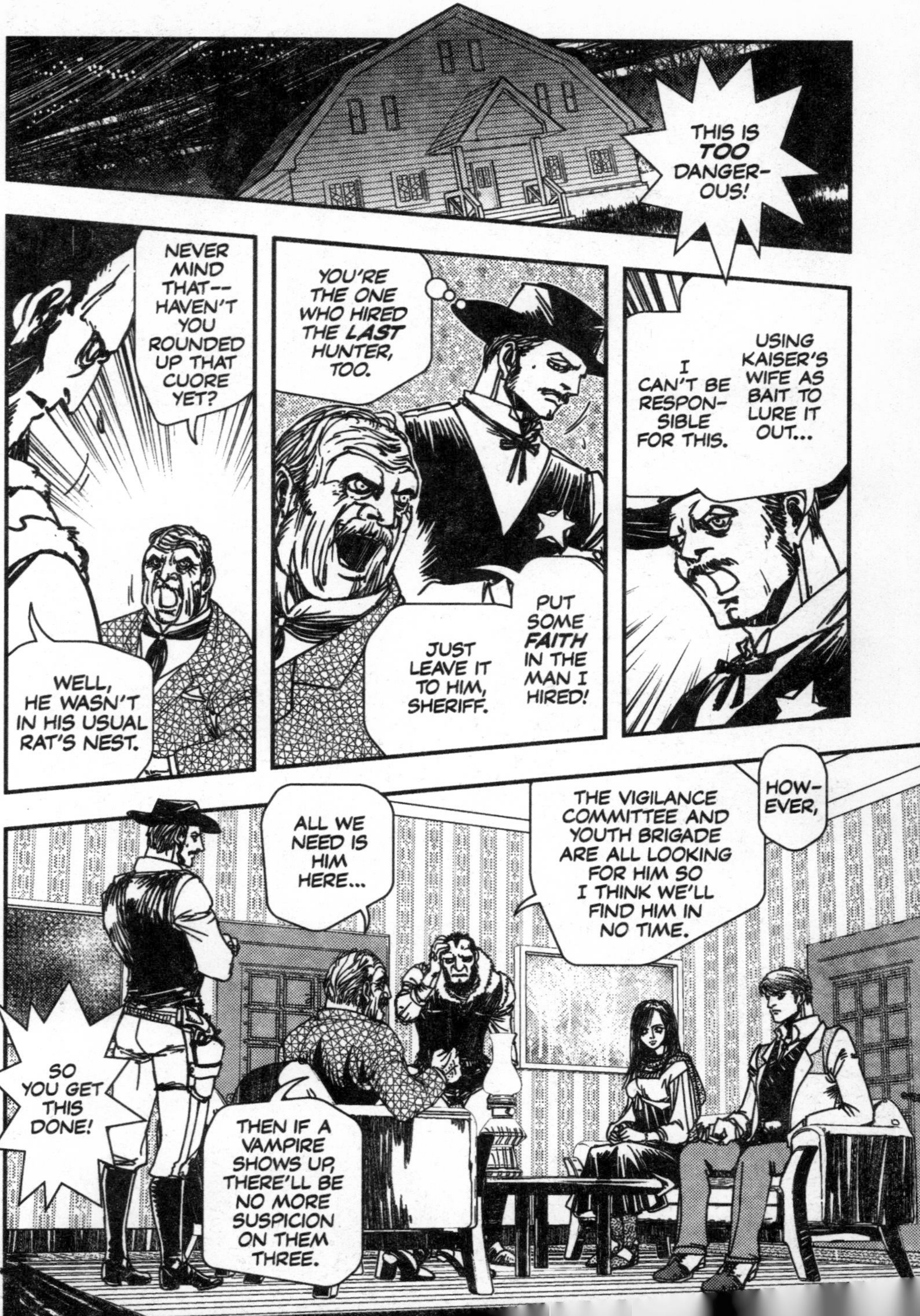
THIS IS TOO DANGER-OUS!
USING KAISER'S WIFE AS BAIT TO LURE IT OUT...
I CAN'T BE RESPON-SIBLE FOR THIS.
YOU'RE THE ONE WHO HIRED THE LAST HUNTER, TOO.
PUT SOME FAITH IN THE MAN I HIRED!
JUST LEAVE IT TO HIM, SHERIFF.
NEVER MIND THAT-- HAVEN'T YOU ROUNDED UP THAT CUORE YET?
WELL, HE WASN'T IN HIS USUAL RAT'S NEST.
HOW-EVER,
THE VIGILANCE COMMITTEE AND YOUTH BRIGADE ARE ALL LOOKING FOR HIM SO I THINK WE'LL FIND HIM IN NO TIME.
ALL WE NEED IS HIM HERE...
THEN IF A VAMPIRE SHOWS UP, THERE'LL BE NO MORE SUSPICION ON THEM THREE.
SO YOU GET THIS DONE!

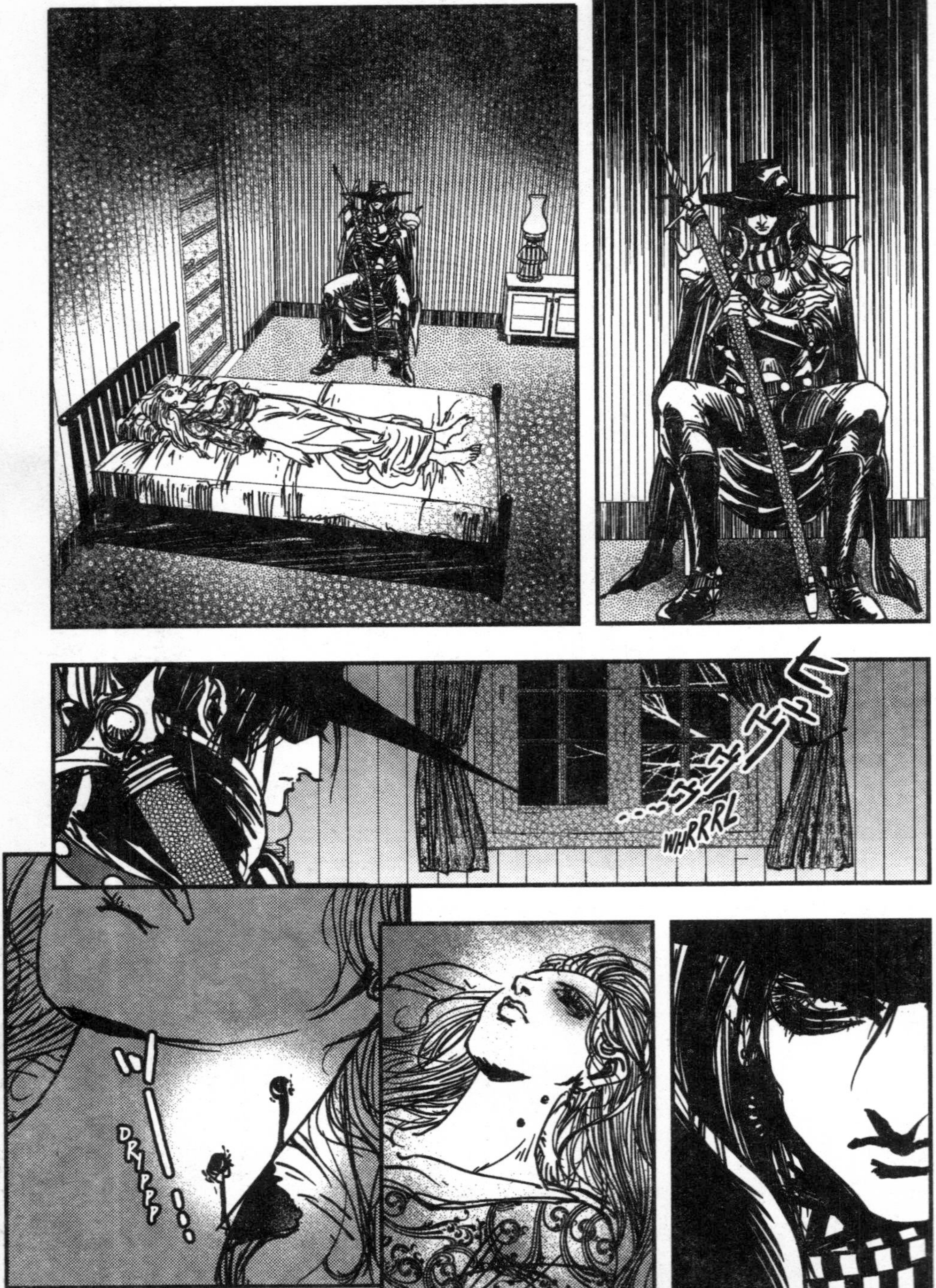
WHRRRL
DRYPPP

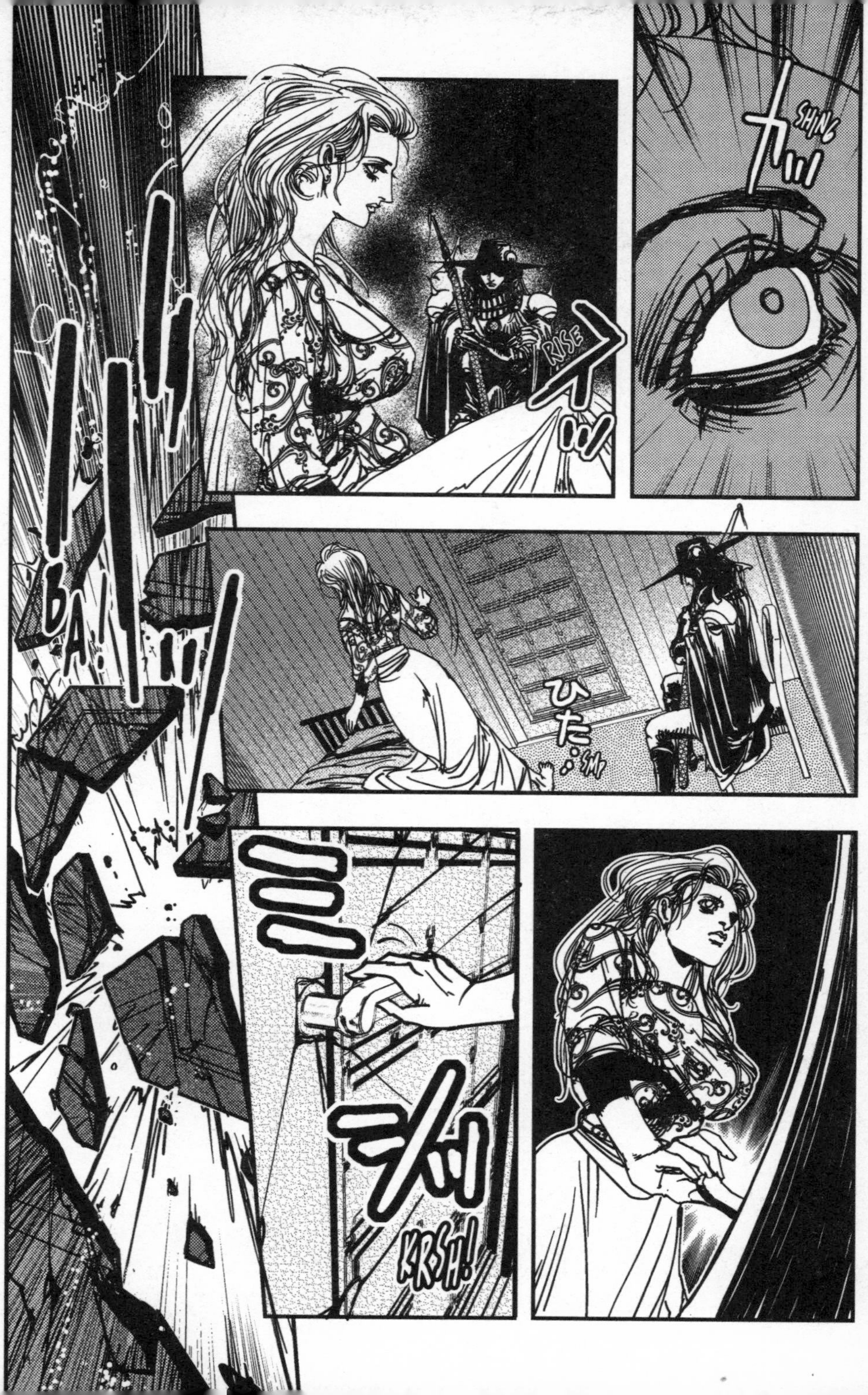
SHING
RISE
ひた
KRSH!
BA!!

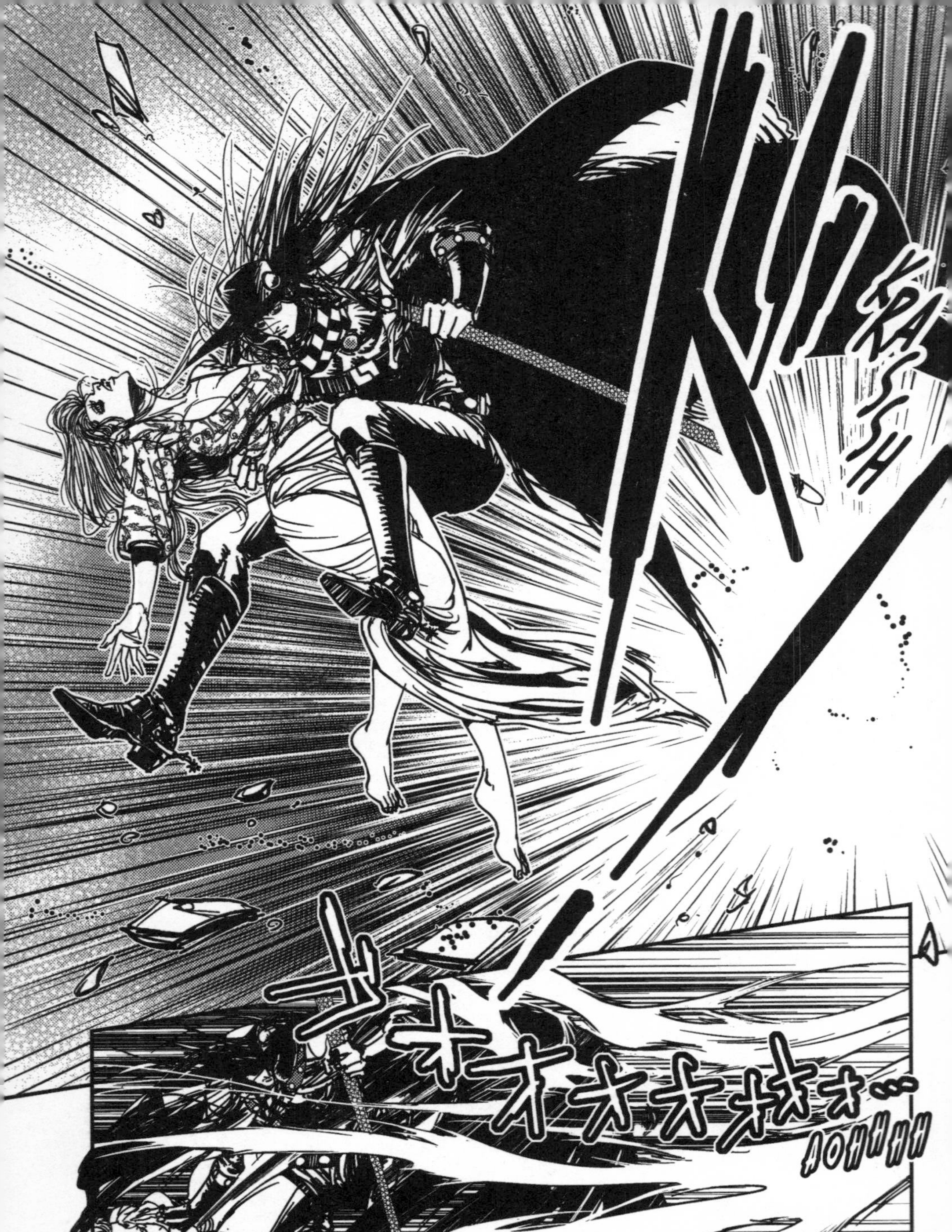
KRASSH
ゴオオオオォォ…

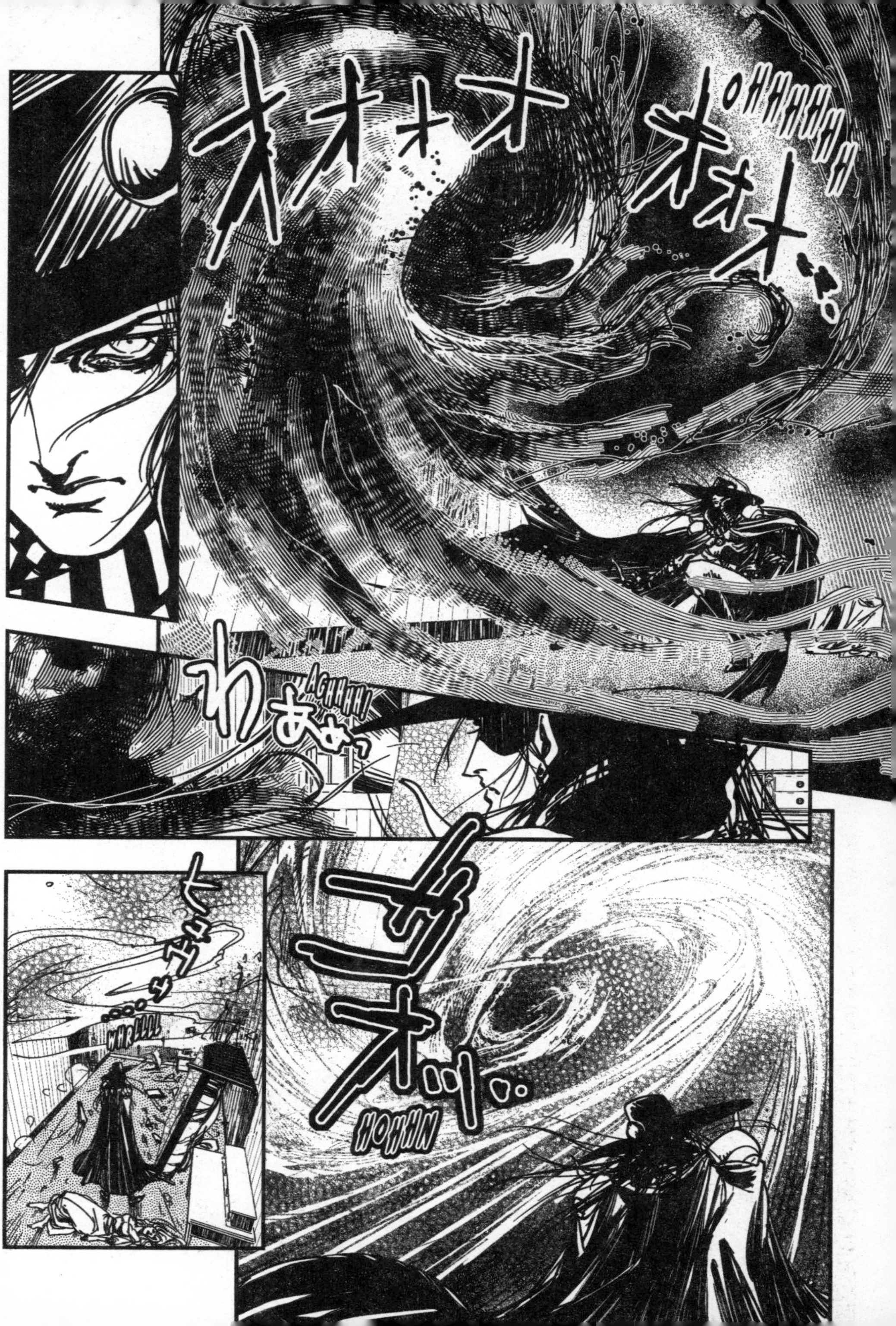
オォォオ
オォオ…
OHHHHHHHH
わぁぁっ
AGHHHH!
ゴゴオッ..
HOHHN
ヒュウゥゥ…
WHRLLLL

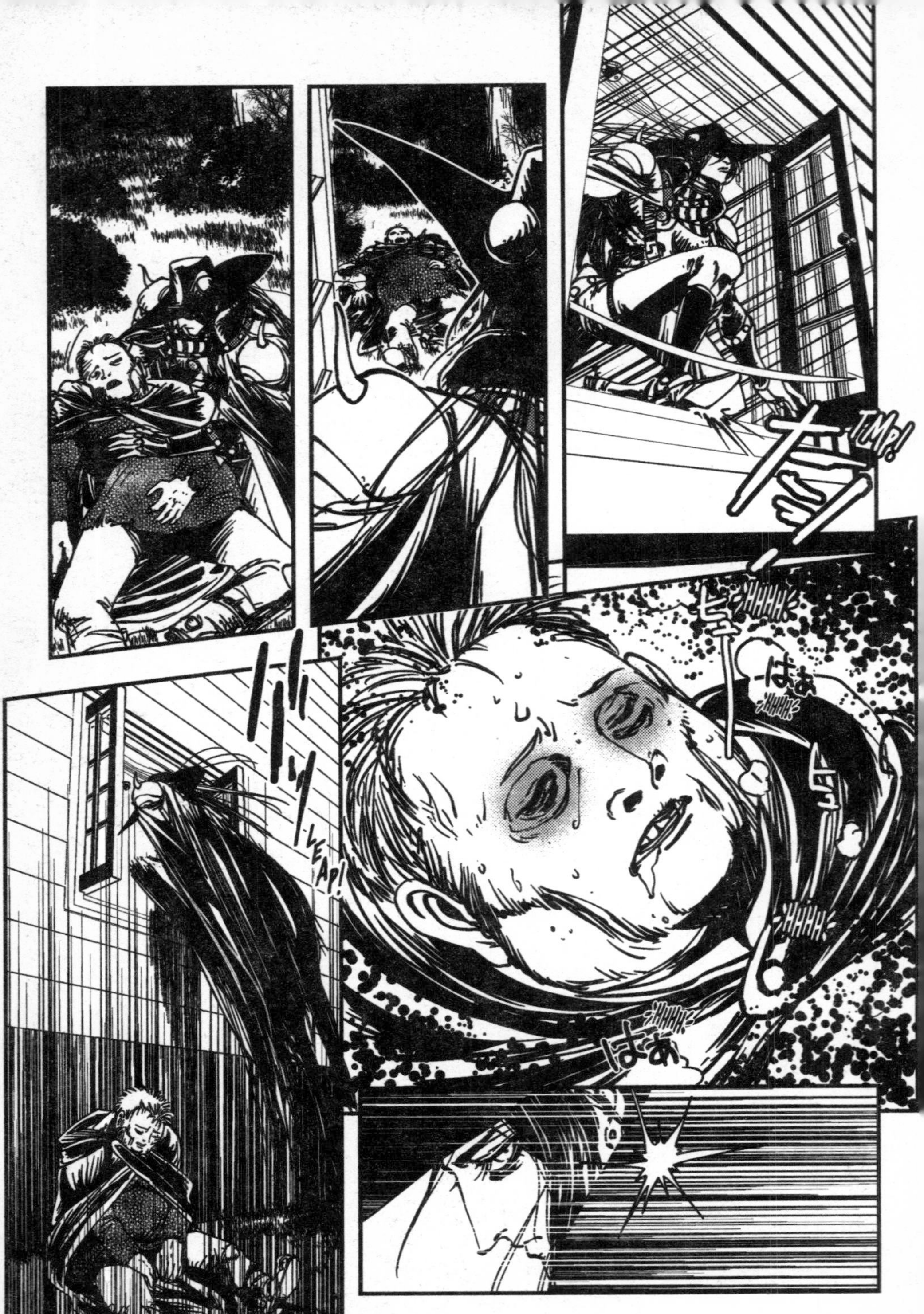
TMP!
HHHHH
はぁ
HHHH
HHHH
はぁ
HHHH
LEAP!

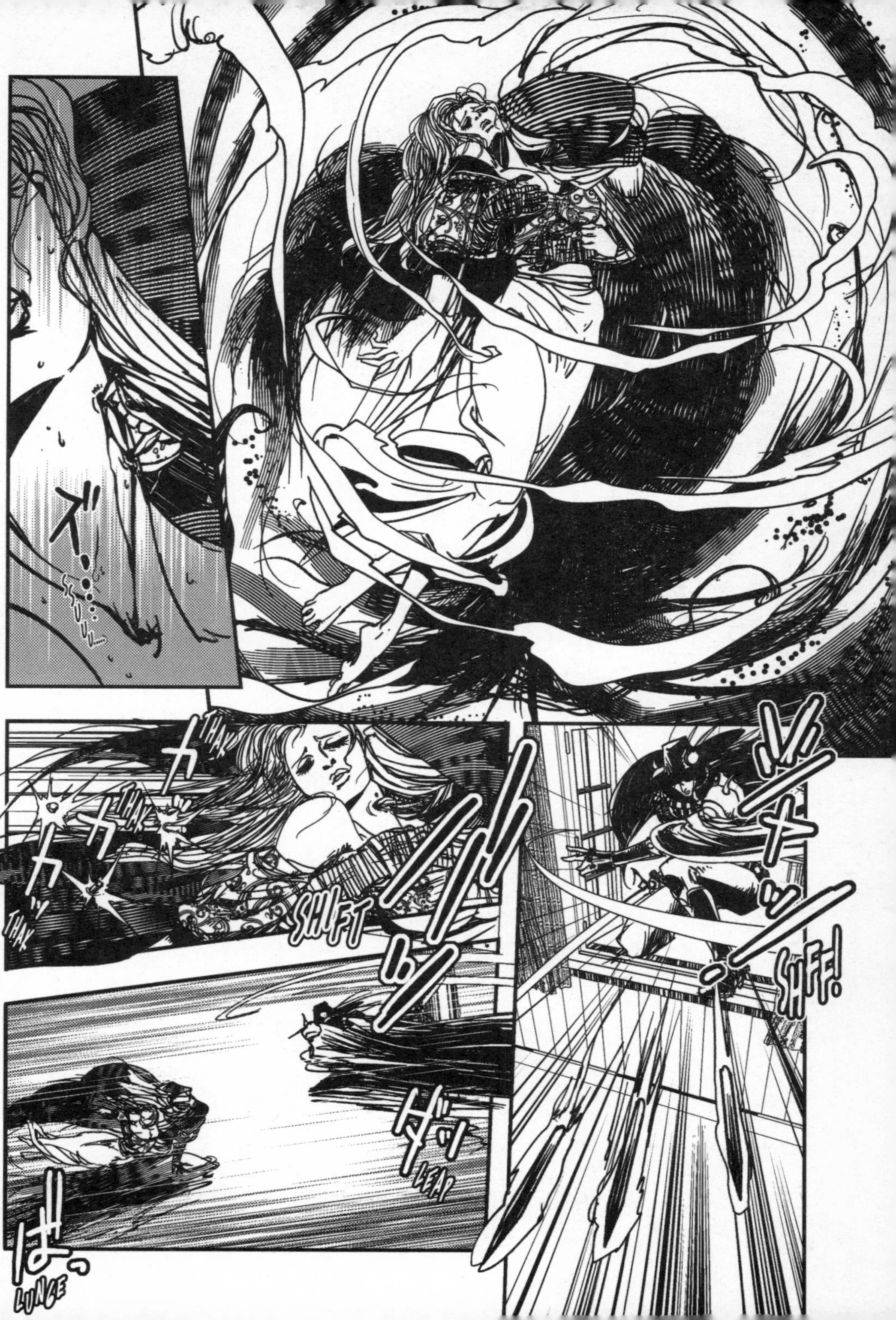
ズ…
SHFF!
カ THAK
カ THAK
カッ THAK
SHIFT
ザッ LEAP
ばっ LUNGE

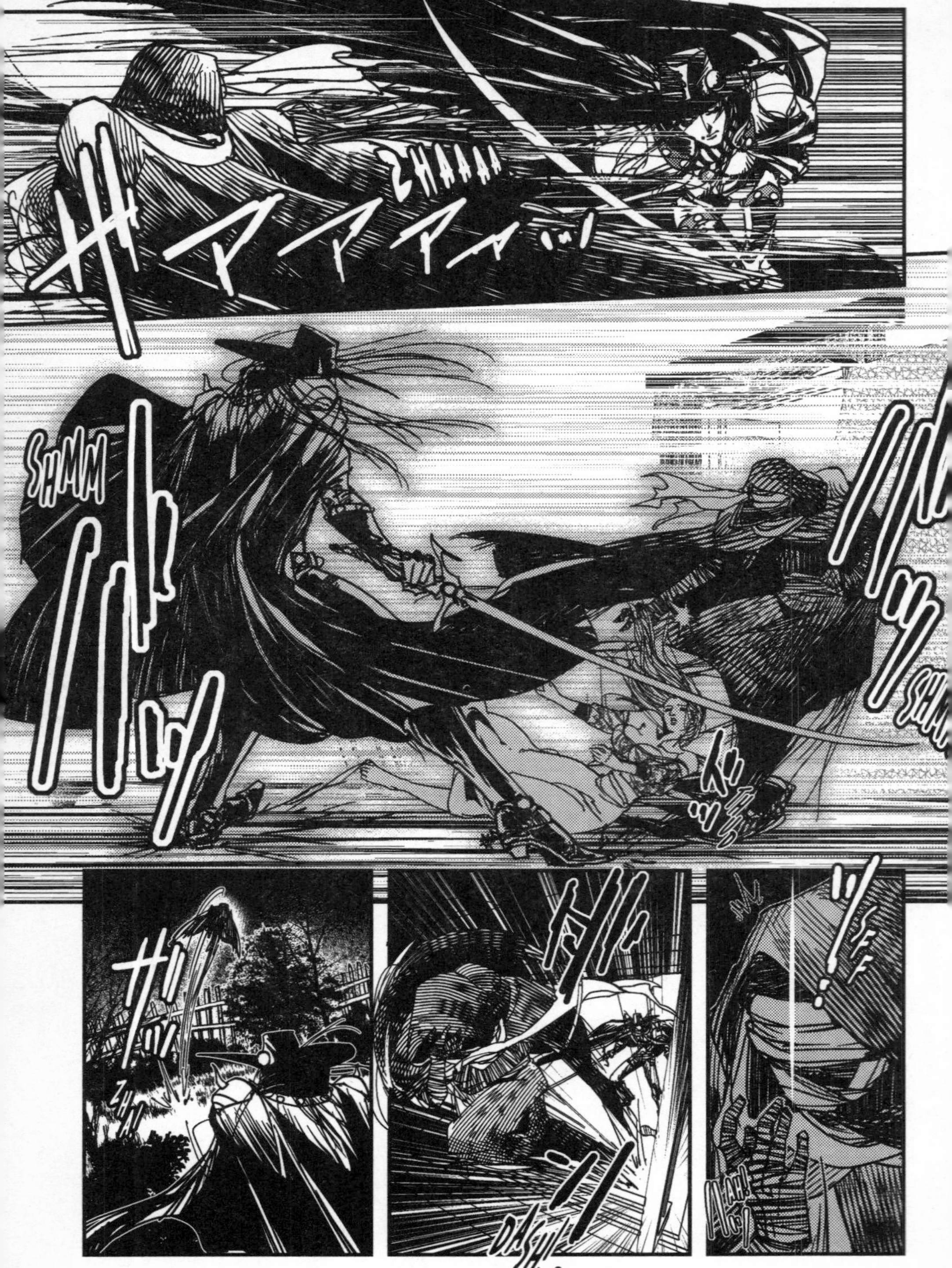
ZHAAAA
SHMM
SHMM
DASH!
ZH!

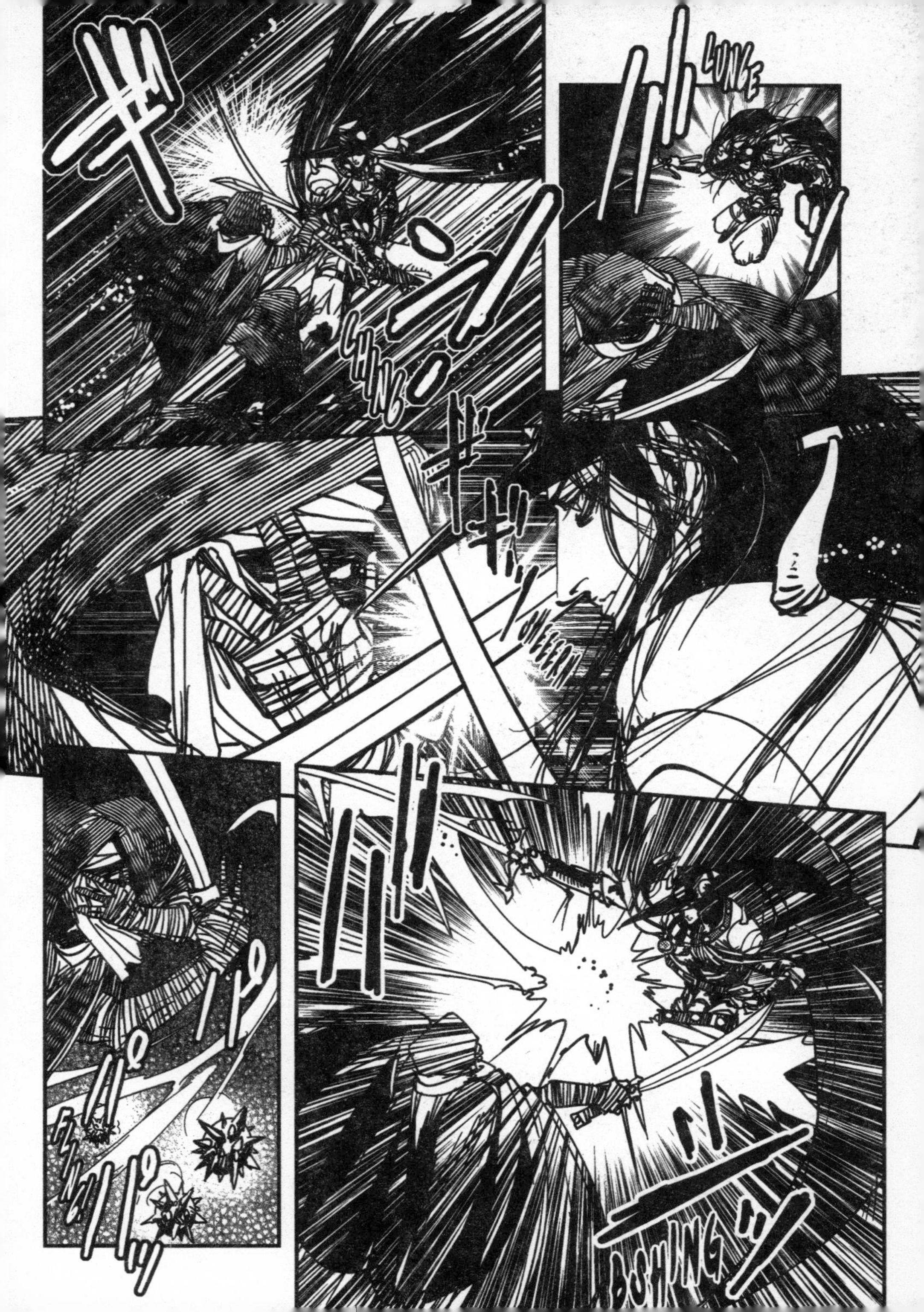
LUNGE
CHING
SWEEEN
DSHING
FZING

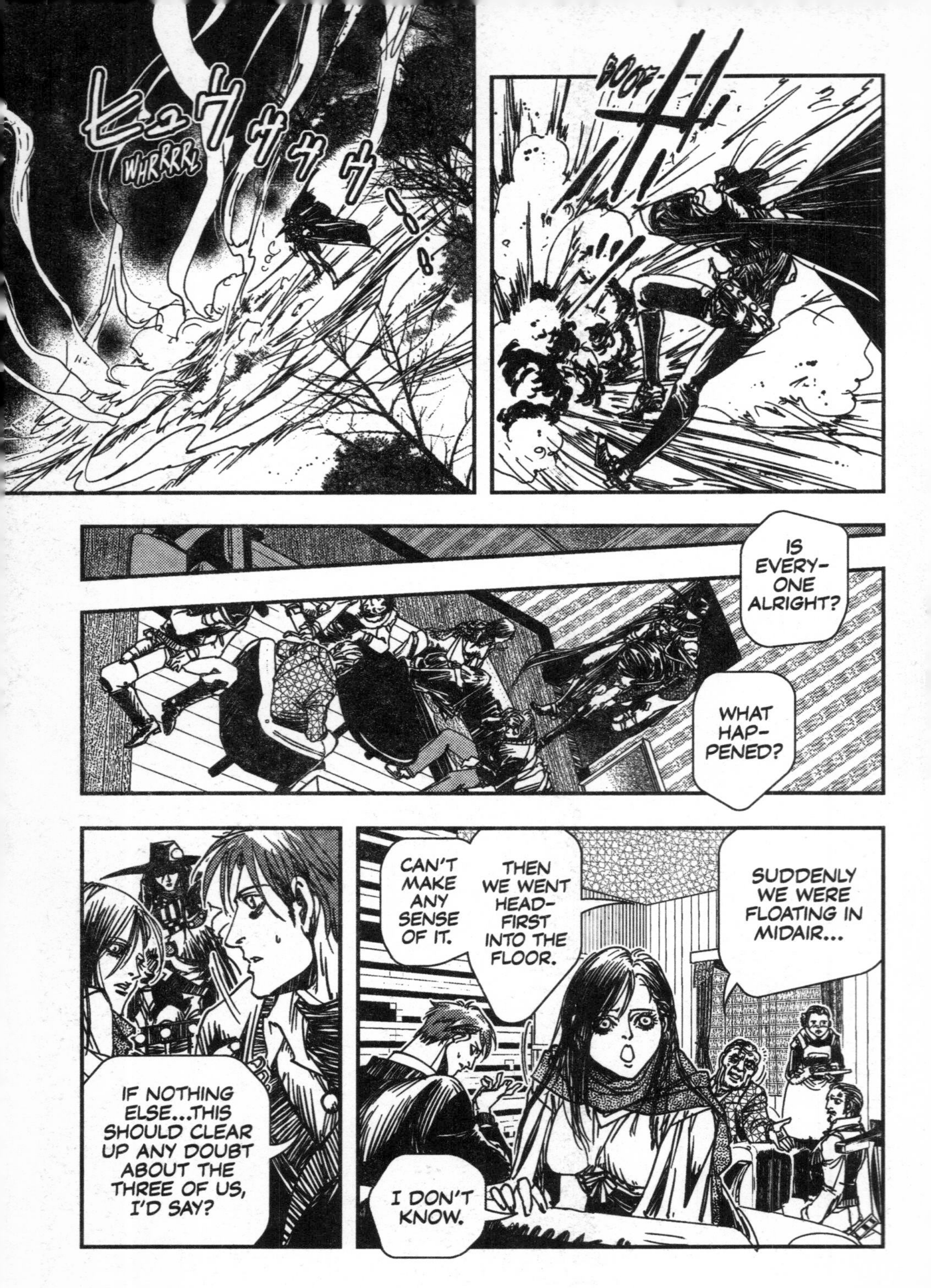
BOOF-
WHRRRRL
IS EVERY-ONE ALRIGHT?
WHAT HAP-PENED?
SUDDENLY WE WERE FLOATING IN MIDAIR...
THEN WE WENT HEAD-FIRST INTO THE FLOOR.
CAN'T MAKE ANY SENSE OF IT.
I DON'T KNOW.
IF NOTHING ELSE...THIS SHOULD CLEAR UP ANY DOUBT ABOUT THE THREE OF US, I'D SAY?

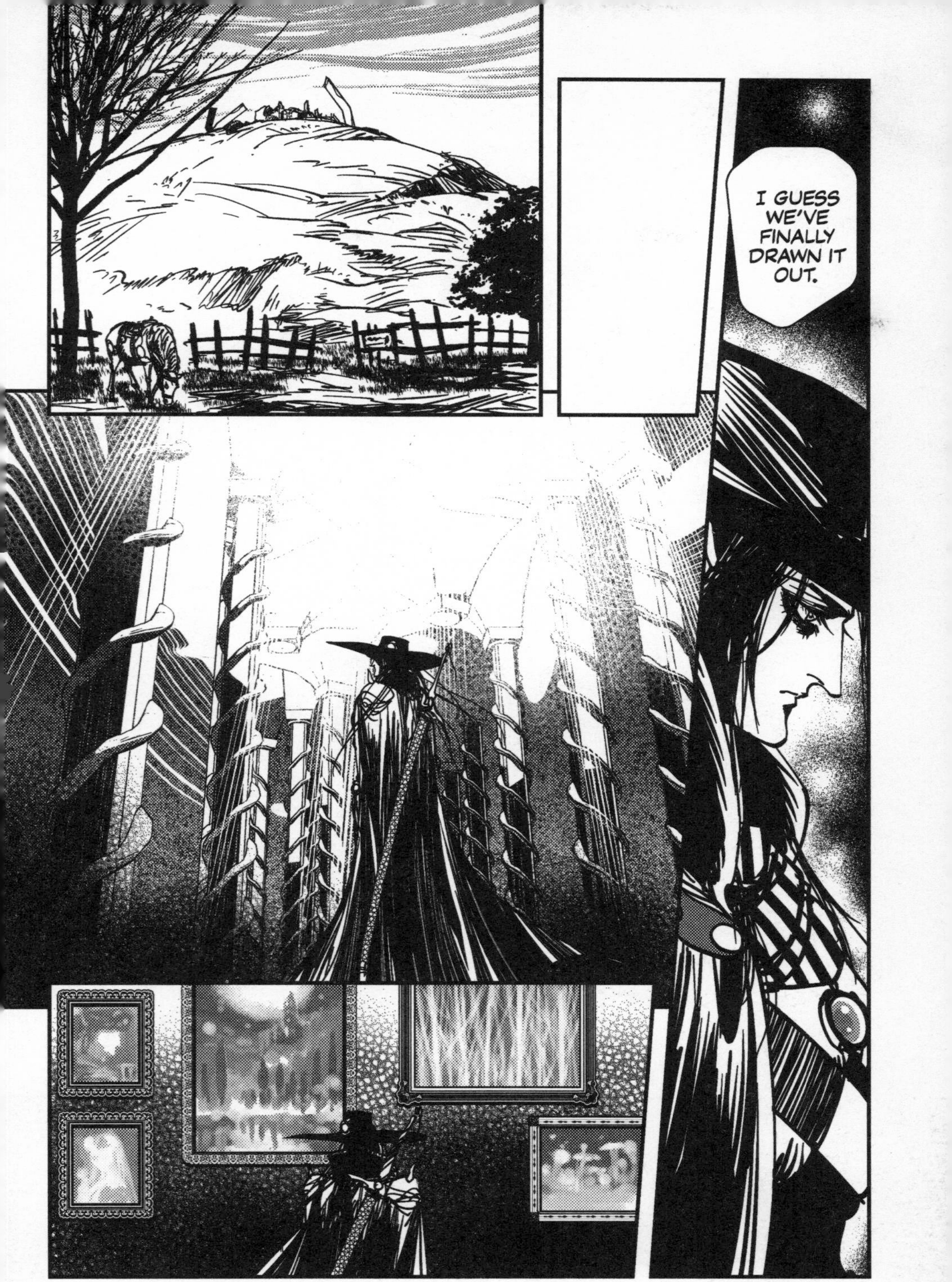
I GUESS WE'VE FINALLY DRAWN IT OUT.

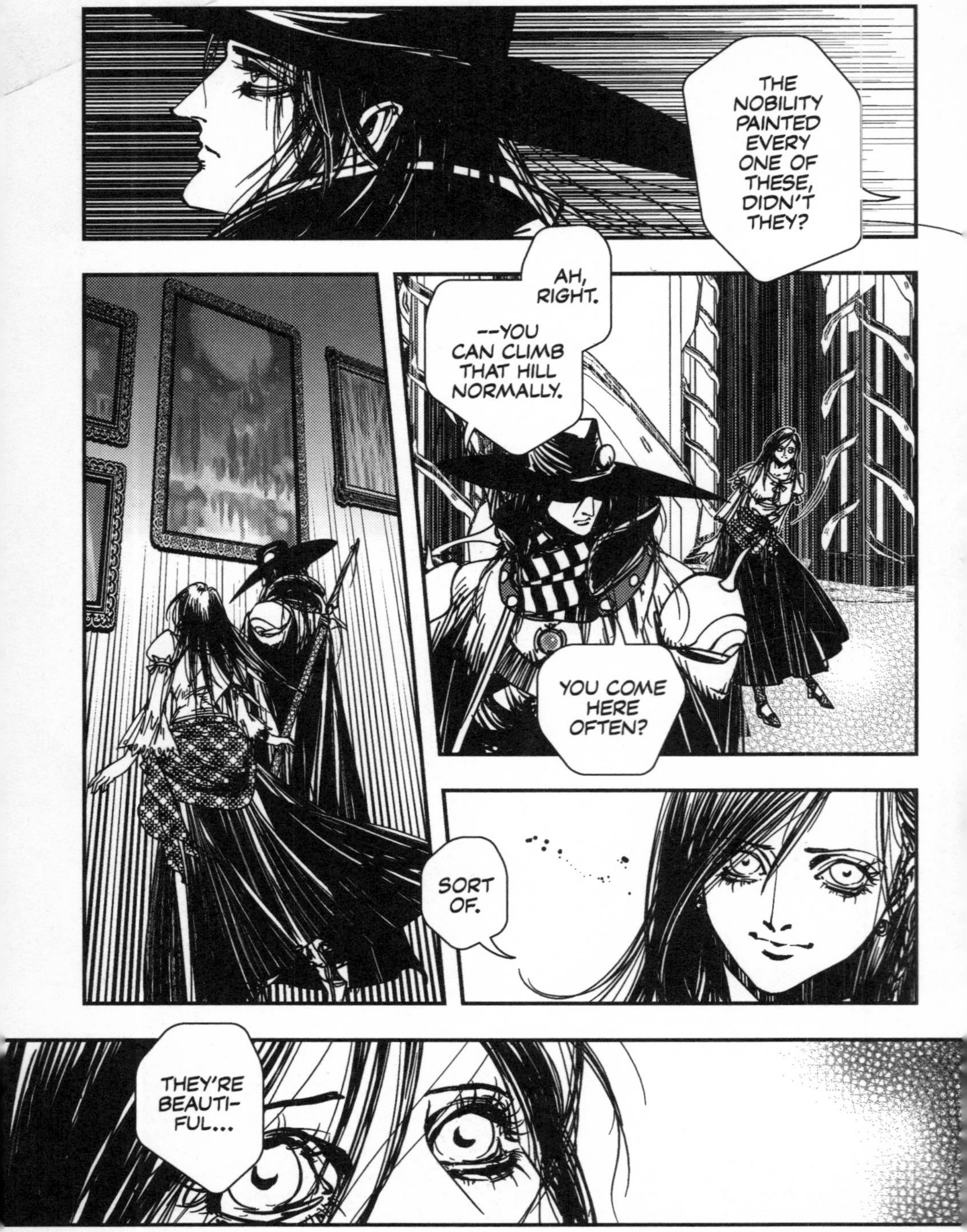
THE NOBILITY PAINTED EVERY ONE OF THESE, DIDN'T THEY?
AH, RIGHT.
--YOU CAN CLIMB THAT HILL NORMALLY.
YOU COME HERE OFTEN?
SORT OF.
THEY'RE BEAUTI-FUL...

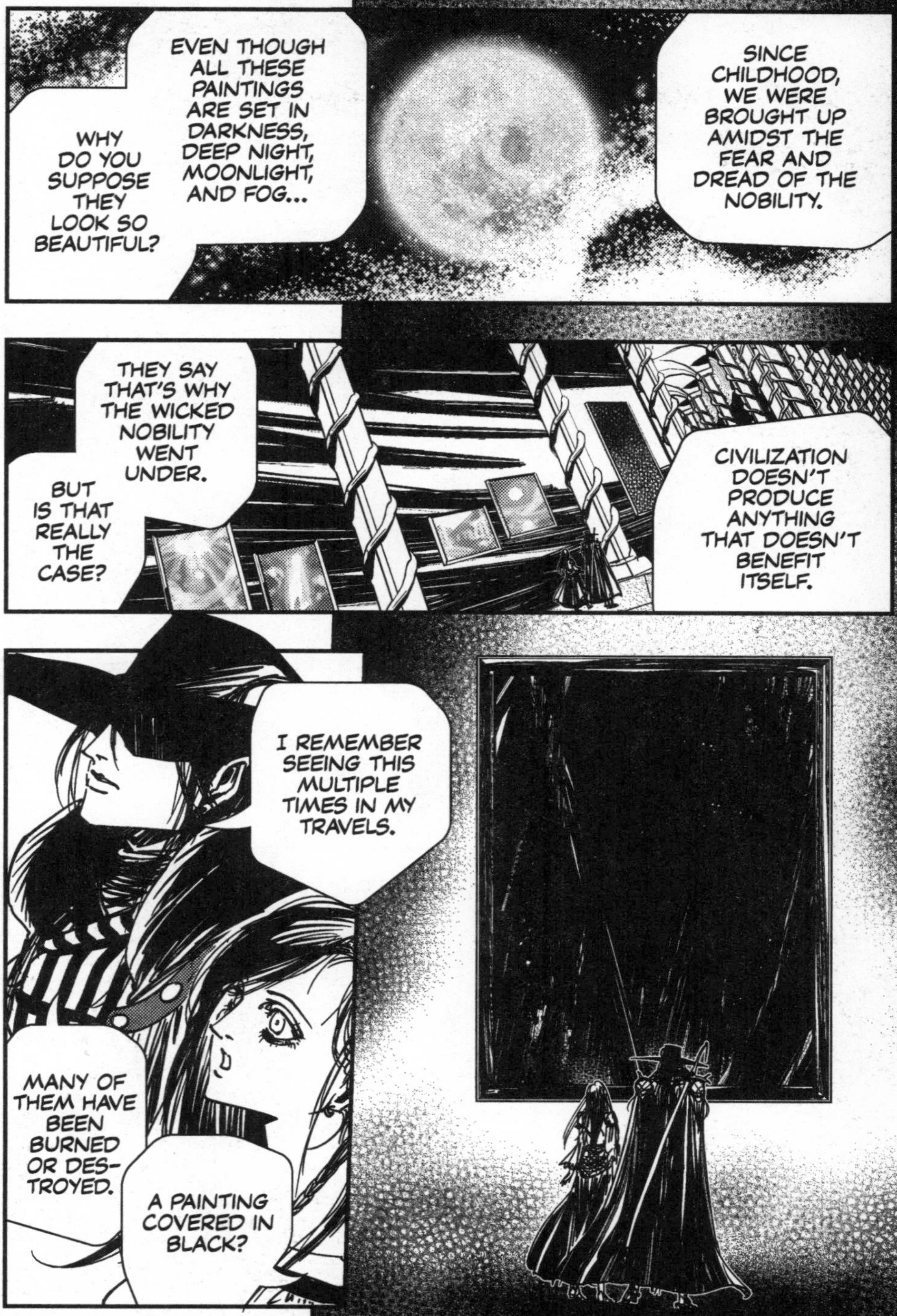
SINCE CHILDHOOD, WE WERE BROUGHT UP AMIDST THE FEAR AND DREAD OF THE NOBILITY.
EVEN THOUGH ALL THESE PAINTINGS ARE SET IN DARKNESS, DEEP NIGHT, MOONLIGHT, AND FOG...
WHY DO YOU SUPPOSE THEY LOOK SO BEAUTIFUL?
CIVILIZATION DOESN'T PRODUCE ANYTHING THAT DOESN'T BENEFIT ITSELF.
THEY SAY THAT'S WHY THE WICKED NOBILITY WENT UNDER.
BUT IS THAT REALLY THE CASE?
I REMEMBER SEEING THIS MULTIPLE TIMES IN MY TRAVELS.
MANY OF THEM HAVE BEEN BURNED OR DES-TROYED.
A PAINTING COVERED IN BLACK?

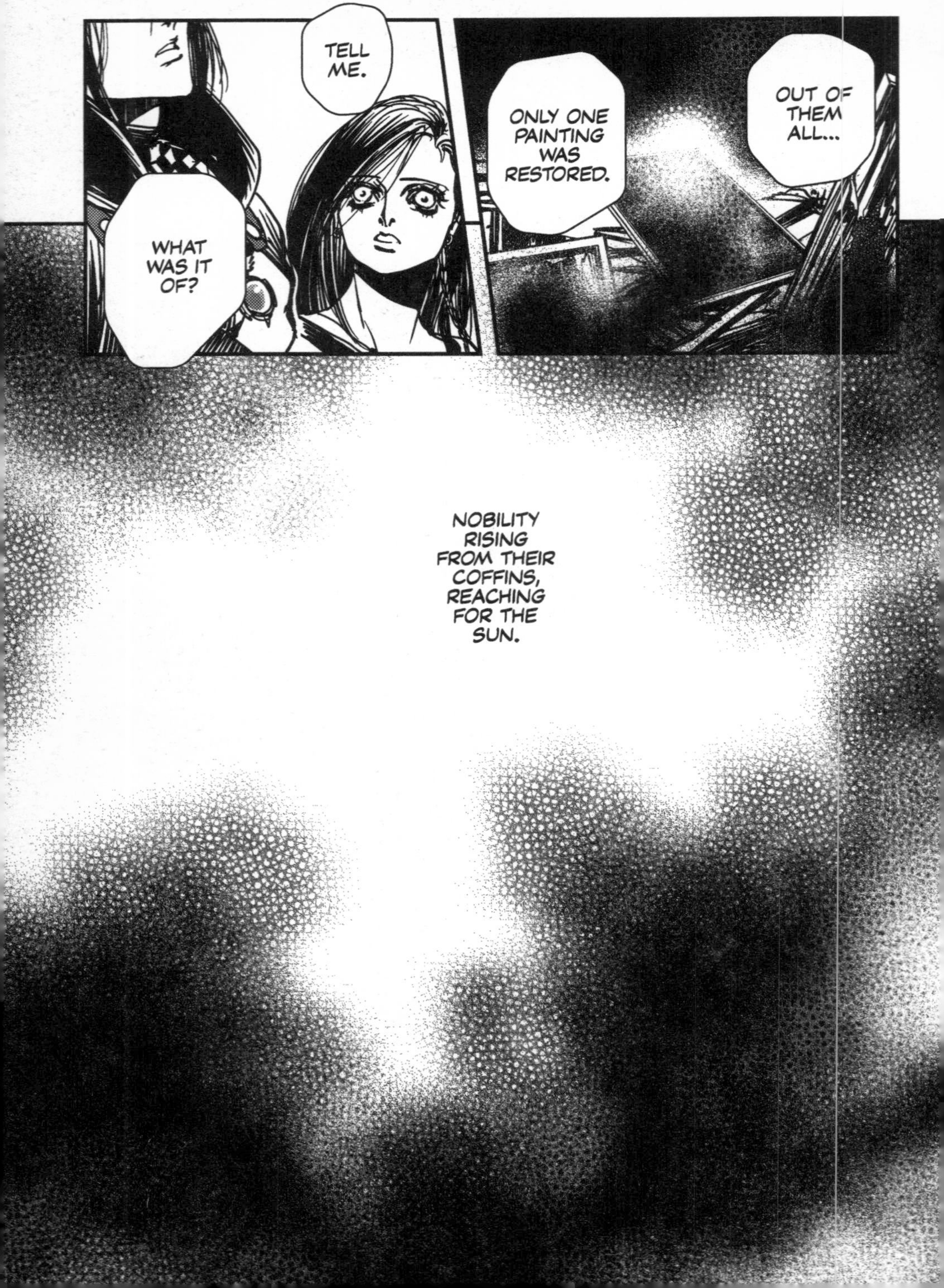
OUT OF THEM ALL...
ONLY ONE PAINTING WAS RESTORED.
TELL ME.
WHAT WAS IT OF?
NOBILITY RISING FROM THEIR COFFINS, REACHING FOR THE SUN.

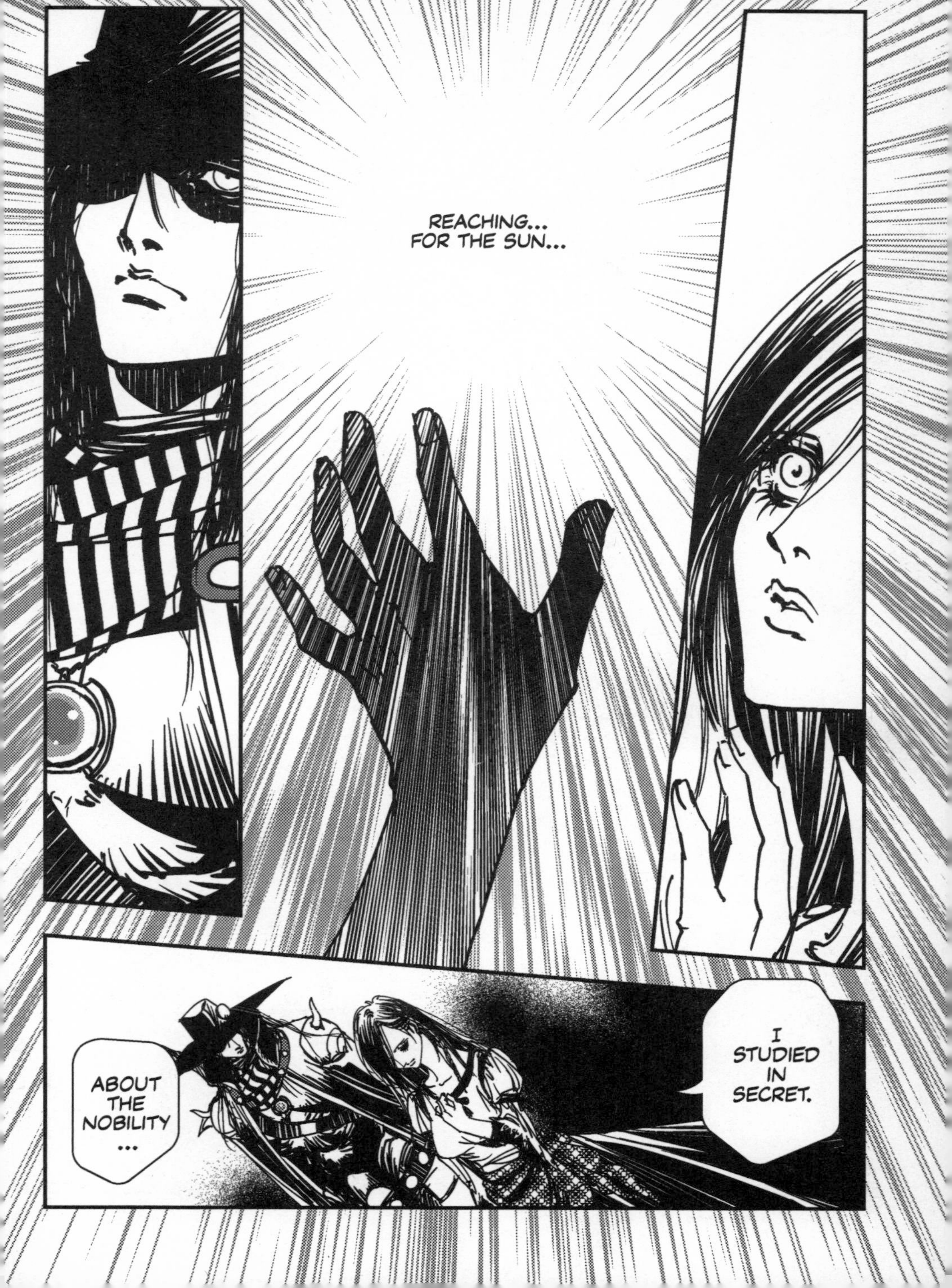
REACHING... FOR THE SUN...
I STUDIED IN SECRET.
ABOUT THE NOBILITY ...

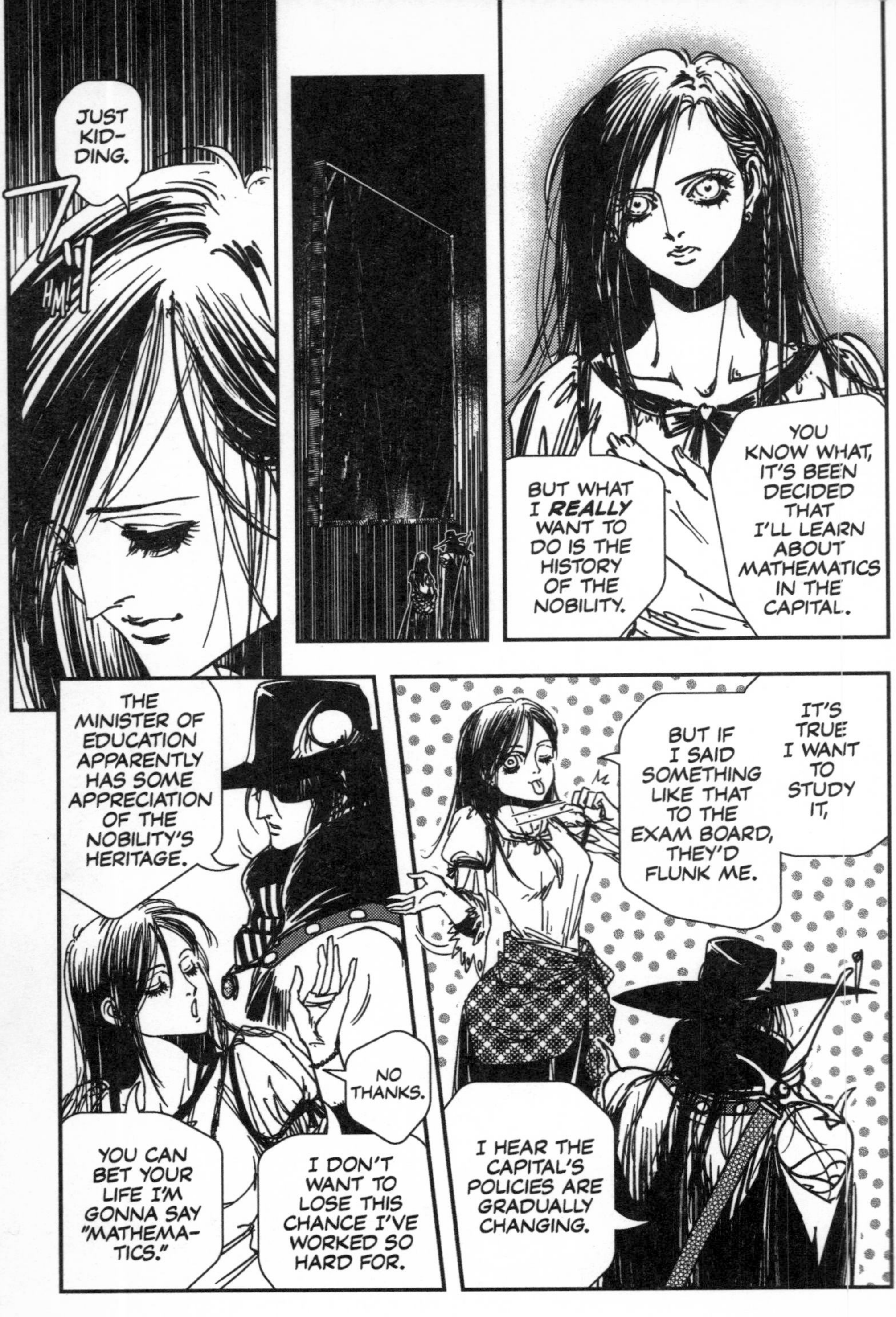
YOU KNOW WHAT, IT'S BEEN DECIDED THAT I'LL LEARN ABOUT MATHEMATICS IN THE CAPITAL.
BUT WHAT I ***REALLY*** WANT TO DO IS THE HISTORY OF THE NOBILITY.
JUST KID-DING.
HM!
IT'S TRUE: I WANT TO STUDY IT,
BUT IF I SAID SOMETHING LIKE THAT TO THE EXAM BOARD, THEY'D FLUNK ME.
I HEAR THE CAPITAL'S POLICIES ARE GRADUALLY CHANGING.
THE MINISTER OF EDUCATION APPARENTLY HAS SOME APPRECIATION OF THE NOBILITY'S HERITAGE.
NO THANKS.
I DON'T WANT TO LOSE THIS CHANCE I'VE WORKED SO HARD FOR.
YOU CAN BET YOUR LIFE I'M GONNA SAY "MATHEMA-TICS."

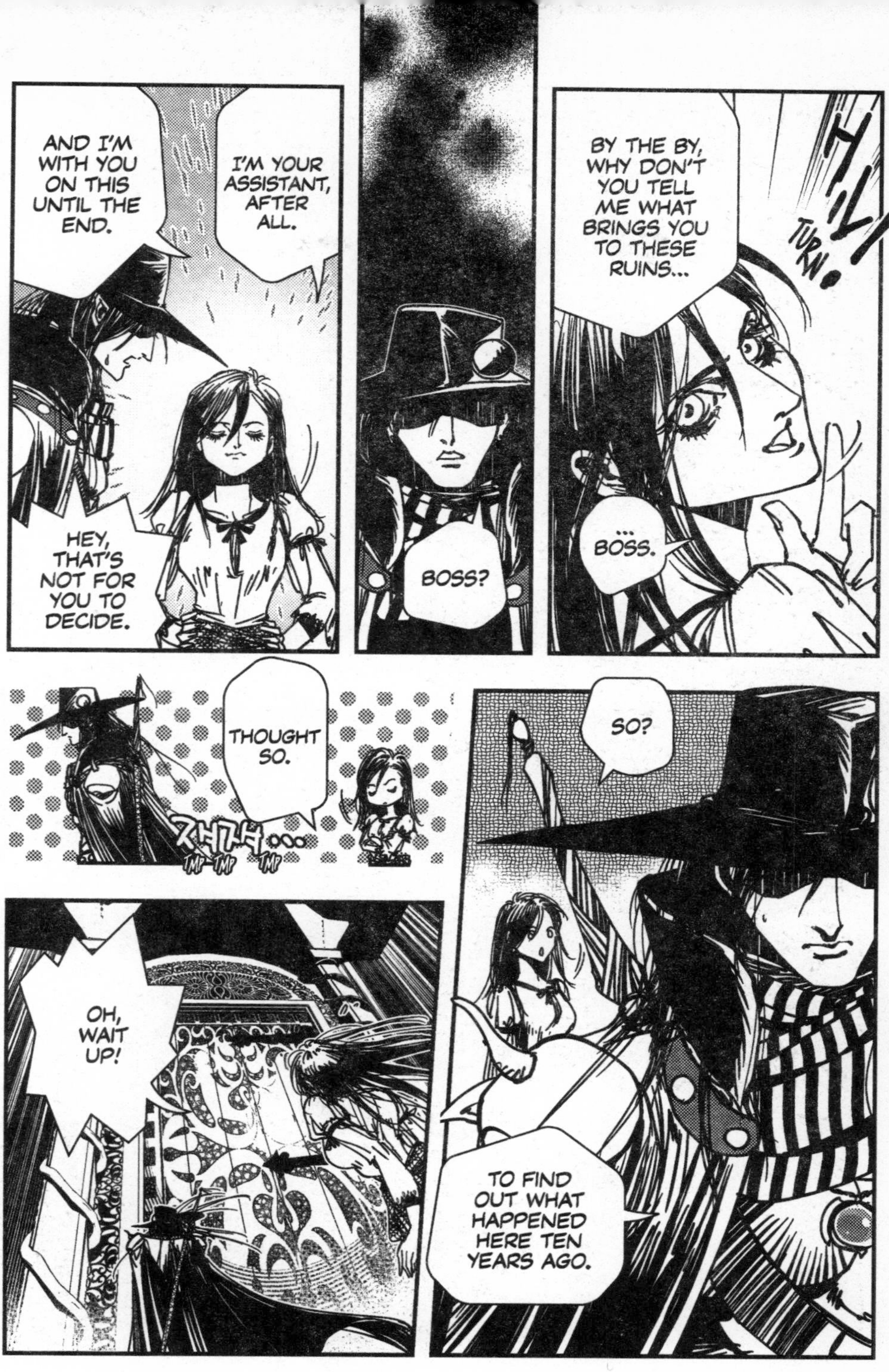
BY THE BY, WHY DON'T YOU TELL ME WHAT BRINGS YOU TO THESE RUINS...
TURN!
...BOSS.
BOSS?
I'M YOUR ASSISTANT, AFTER ALL.
AND I'M WITH YOU ON THIS UNTIL THE END.
HEY, THAT'S NOT FOR YOU TO DECIDE.
SO?
TO FIND OUT WHAT HAPPENED HERE TEN YEARS AGO.
THOUGHT SO.
TMP TMP TMP
OH, WAIT UP!

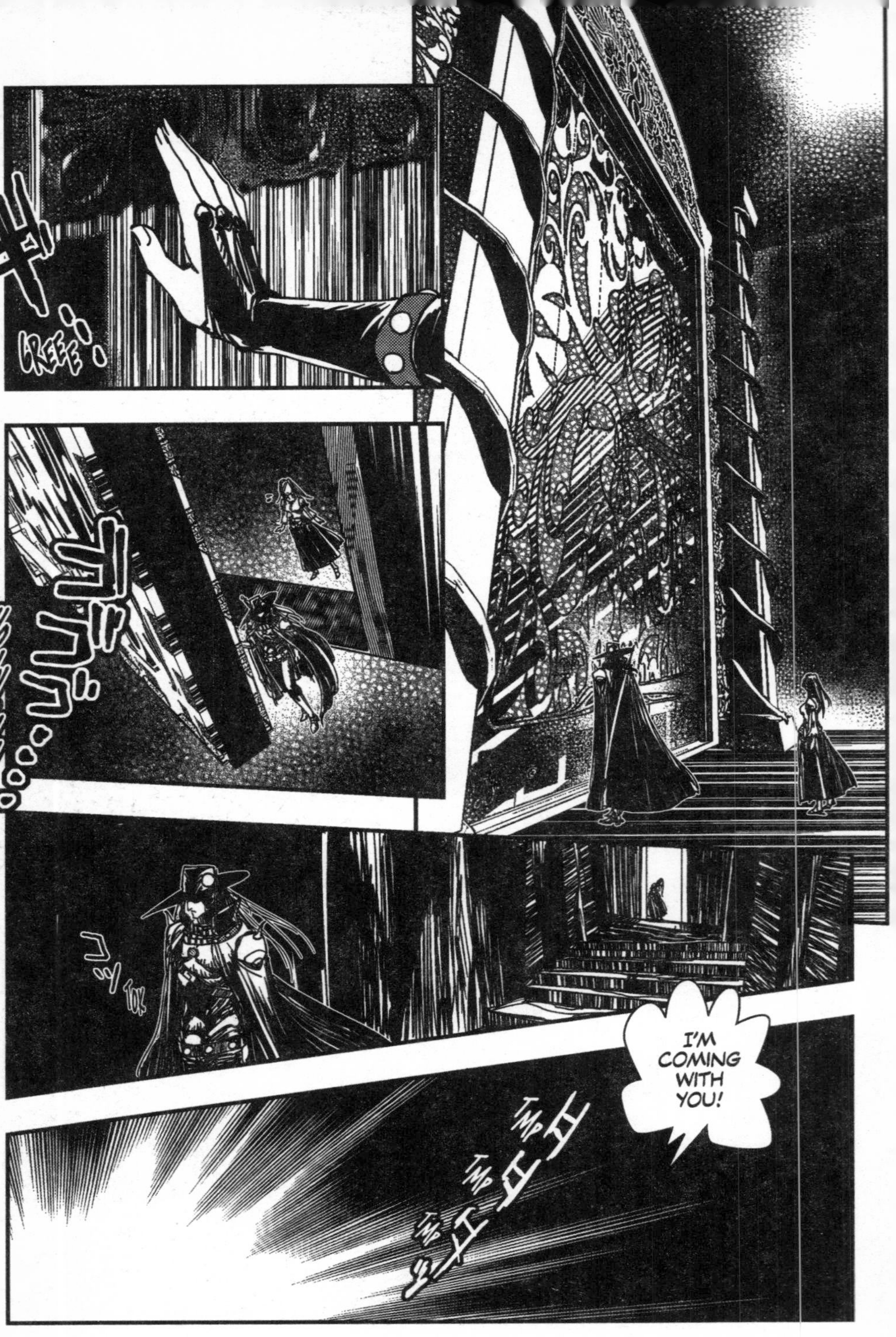
CREEE...
GONNNNNN...
TOK
TMP TMP TMP
I'M COMING WITH YOU!

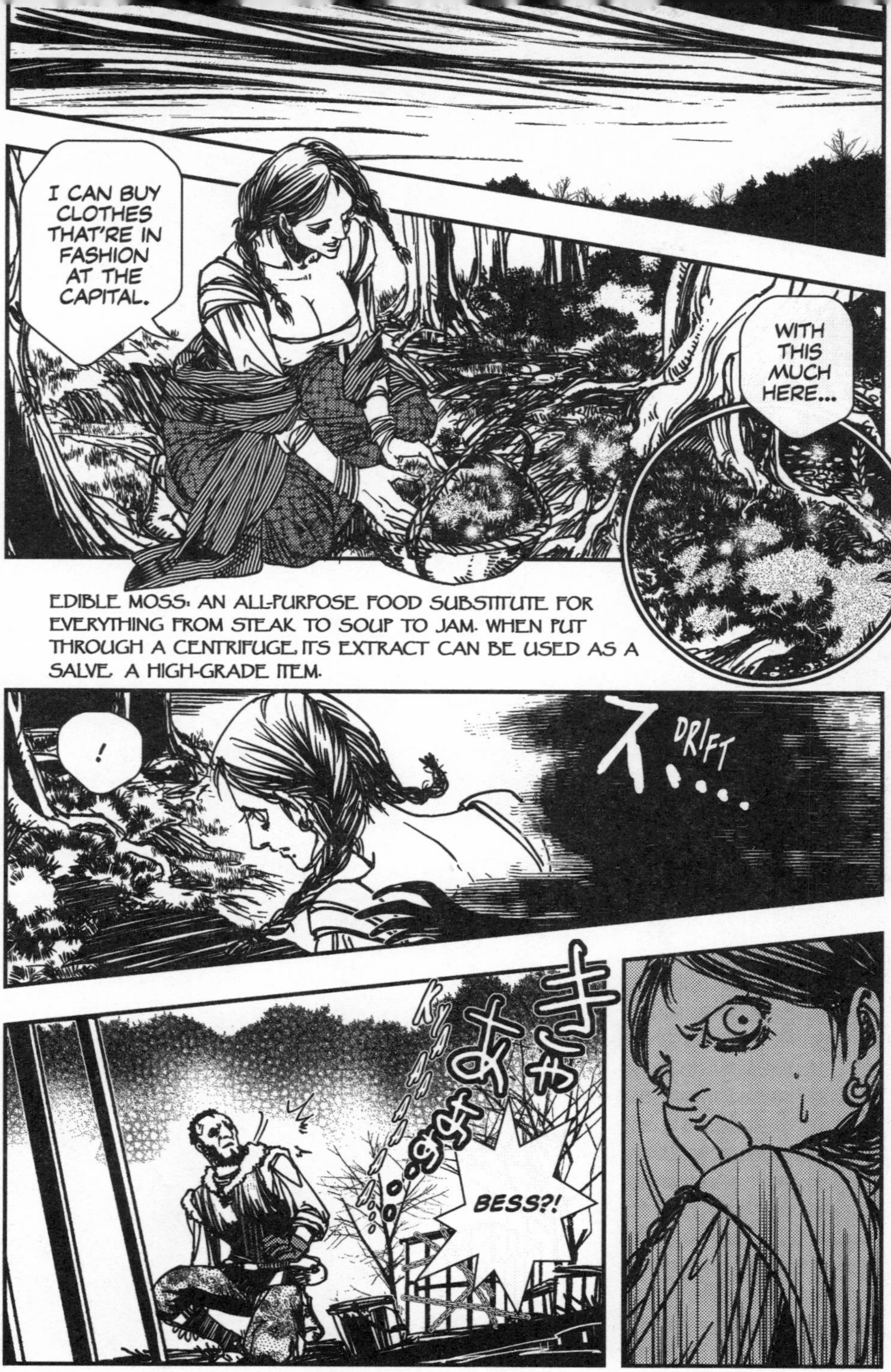
WITH THIS MUCH HERE...
I CAN BUY CLOTHES THAT'RE IN FASHION AT THE CAPITAL.
EDIBLE MOSS: AN ALL-PURPOSE FOOD SUBSTITUTE FOR EVERYTHING FROM STEAK TO SOUP TO JAM. WHEN PUT THROUGH A CENTRIFUGE, ITS EXTRACT CAN BE USED AS A SALVE. A HIGH-GRADE ITEM.
ス DRIFT...
!
BESS?!

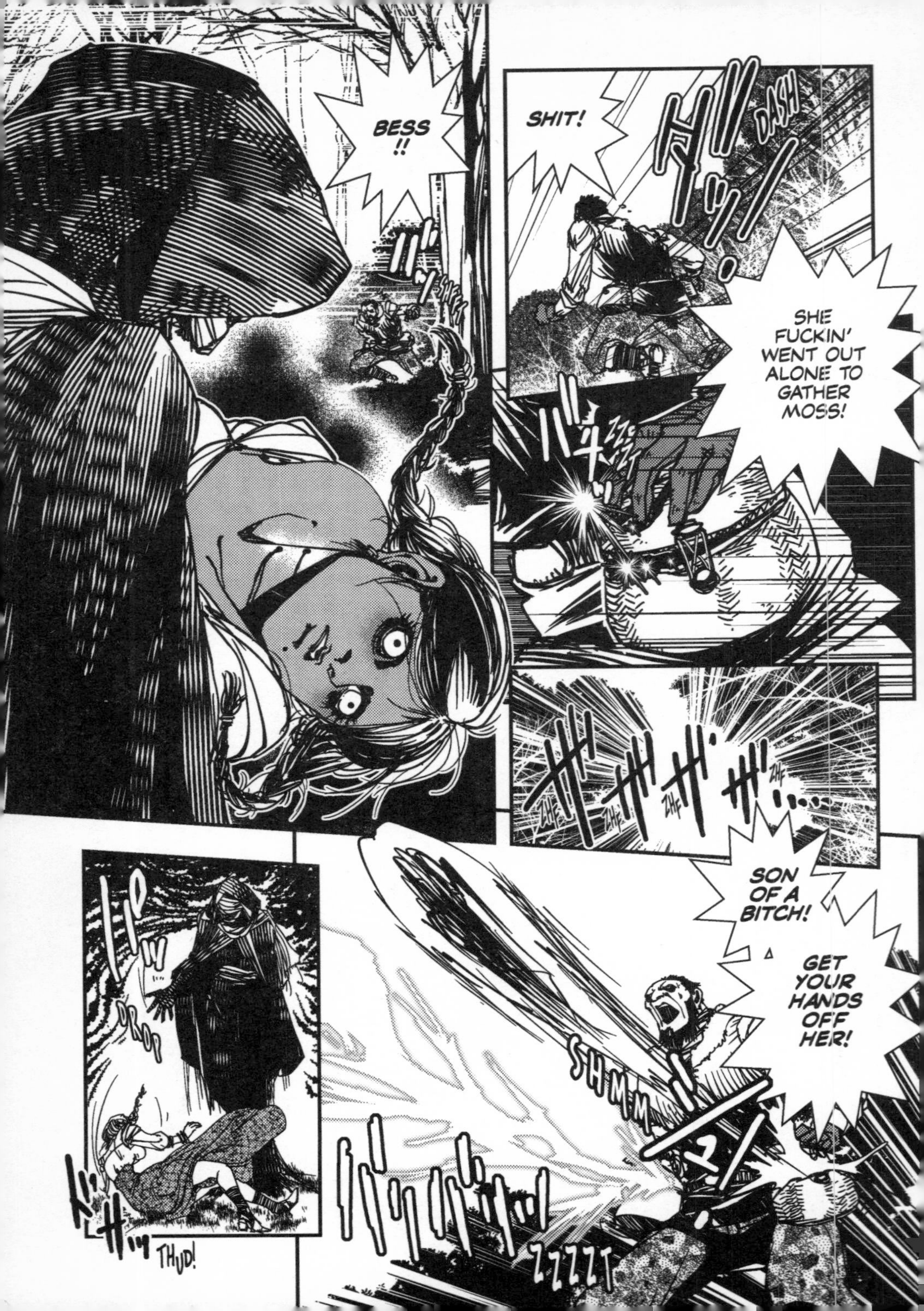
SHIT!
DASH
SHE FUCKIN' WENT OUT ALONE TO GATHER MOSS!
ZHF
ZHF
ZHF
BESS !!
SON OF A BITCH!
GET YOUR HANDS OFF HER!
SHMM
ZZZZT
DROP
THUD!

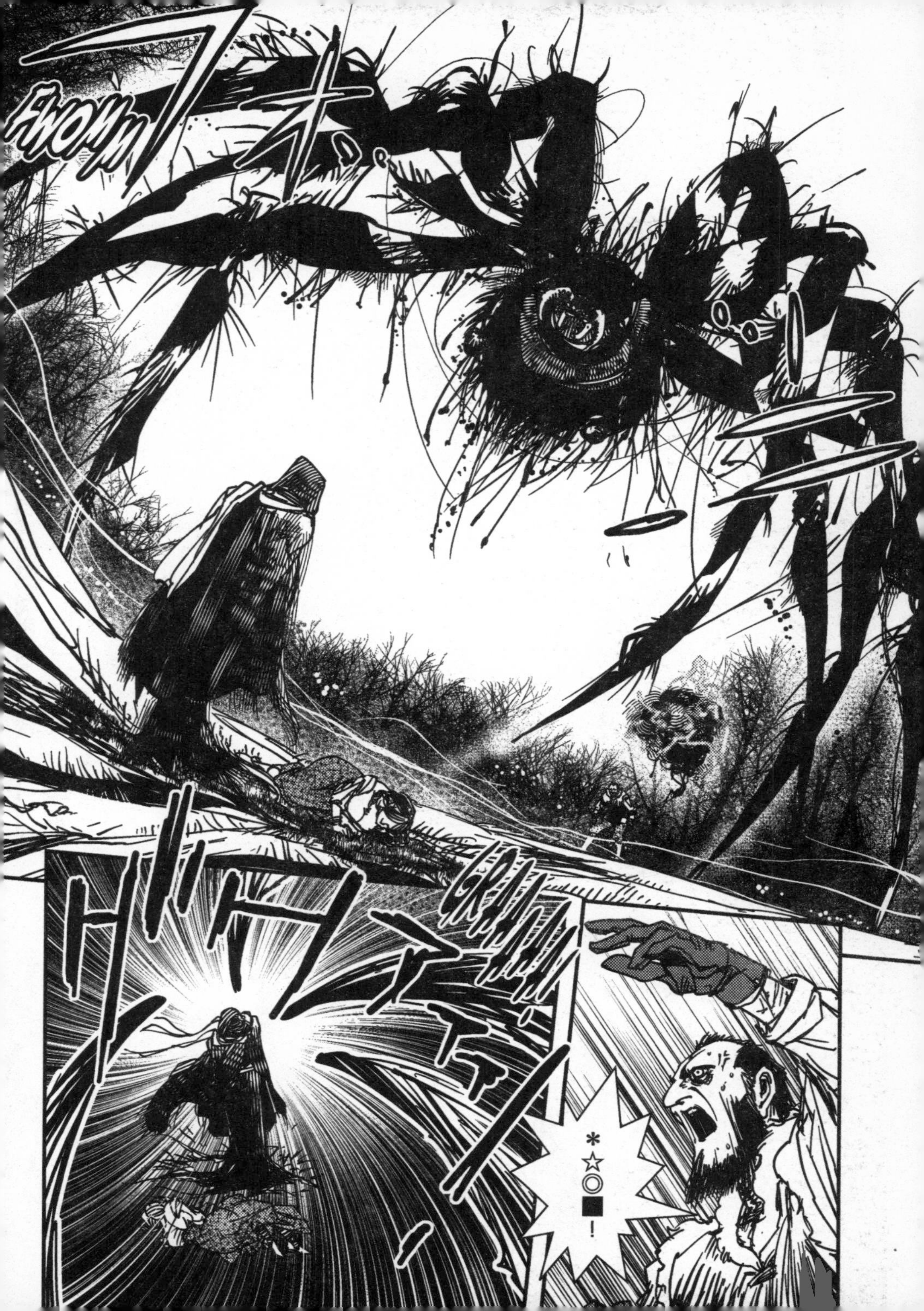
FWOMM
フォッ
*☆◎■!

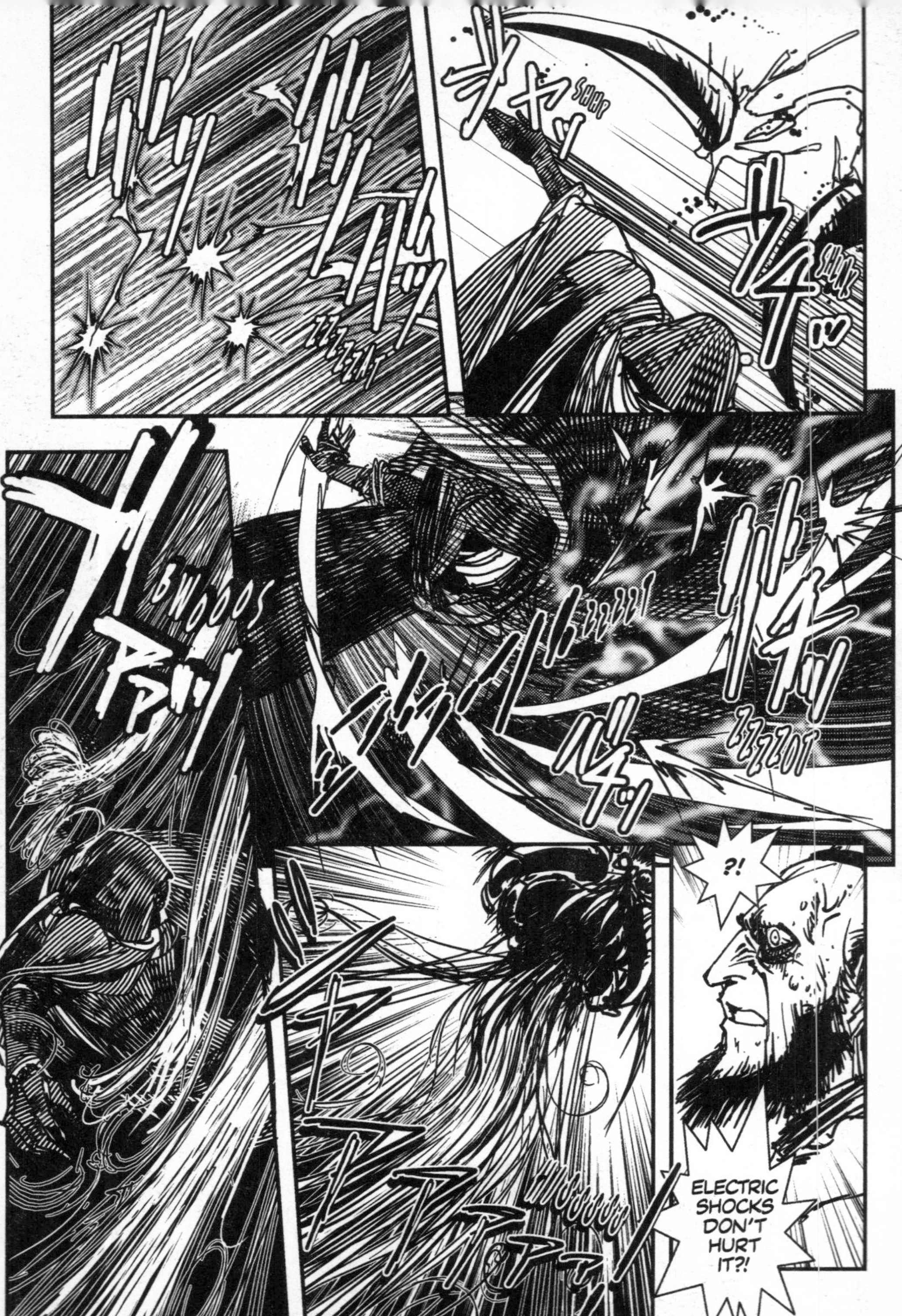
SHHP
BWOOOS
?!
ELECTRIC SHOCKS DON'T HURT IT?!

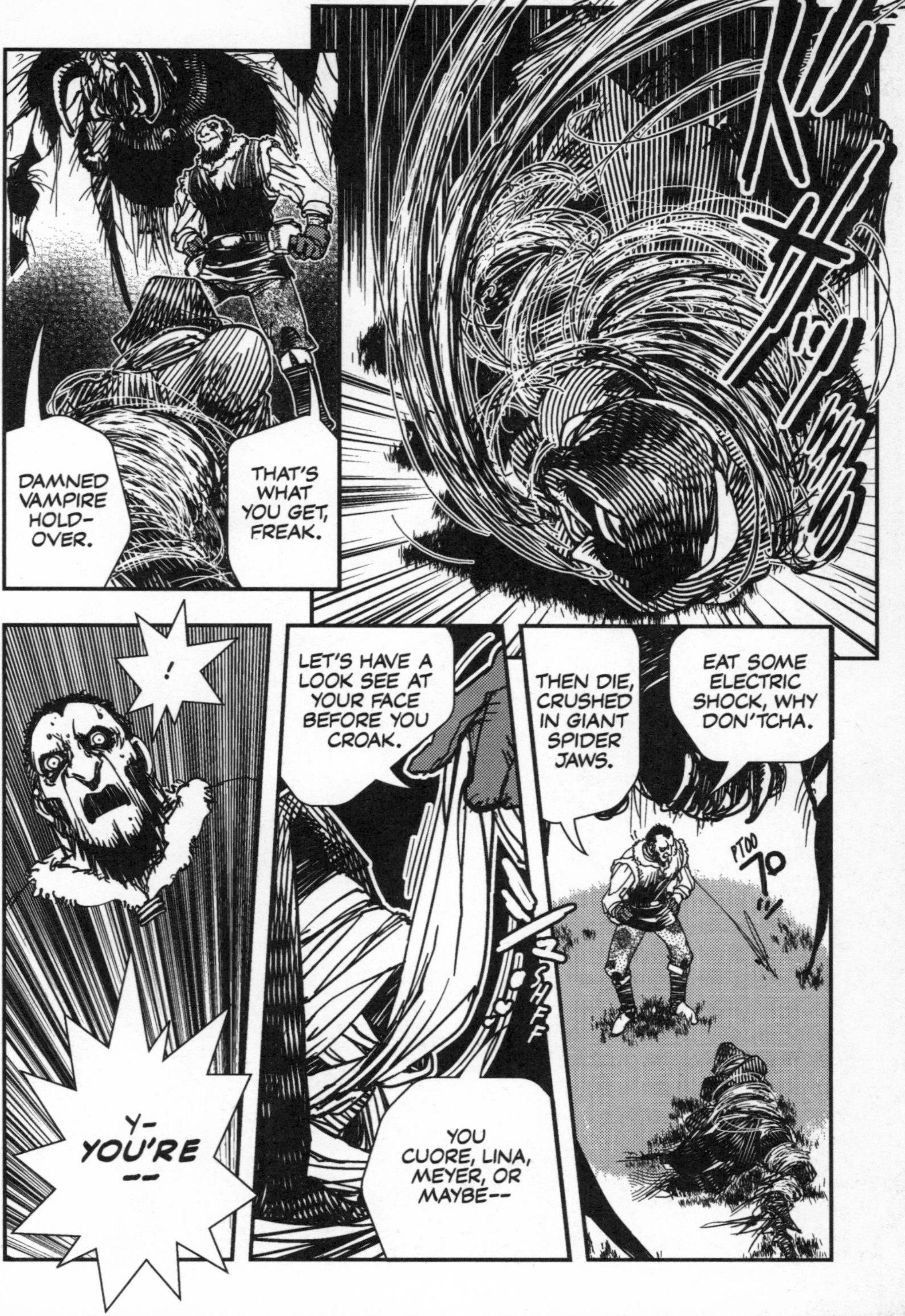
THAT'S WHAT YOU GET, FREAK.
DAMNED VAMPIRE HOLD-OVER.
EAT SOME ELECTRIC SHOCK, WHY DON'TCHA.
THEN DIE, CRUSHED IN GIANT SPIDER JAWS.
PTOO
LET'S HAVE A LOOK SEE AT YOUR FACE BEFORE YOU CROAK.
YOU CUORE, LINA, MEYER, OR MAYBE--
!
Y- *YOU'RE* --

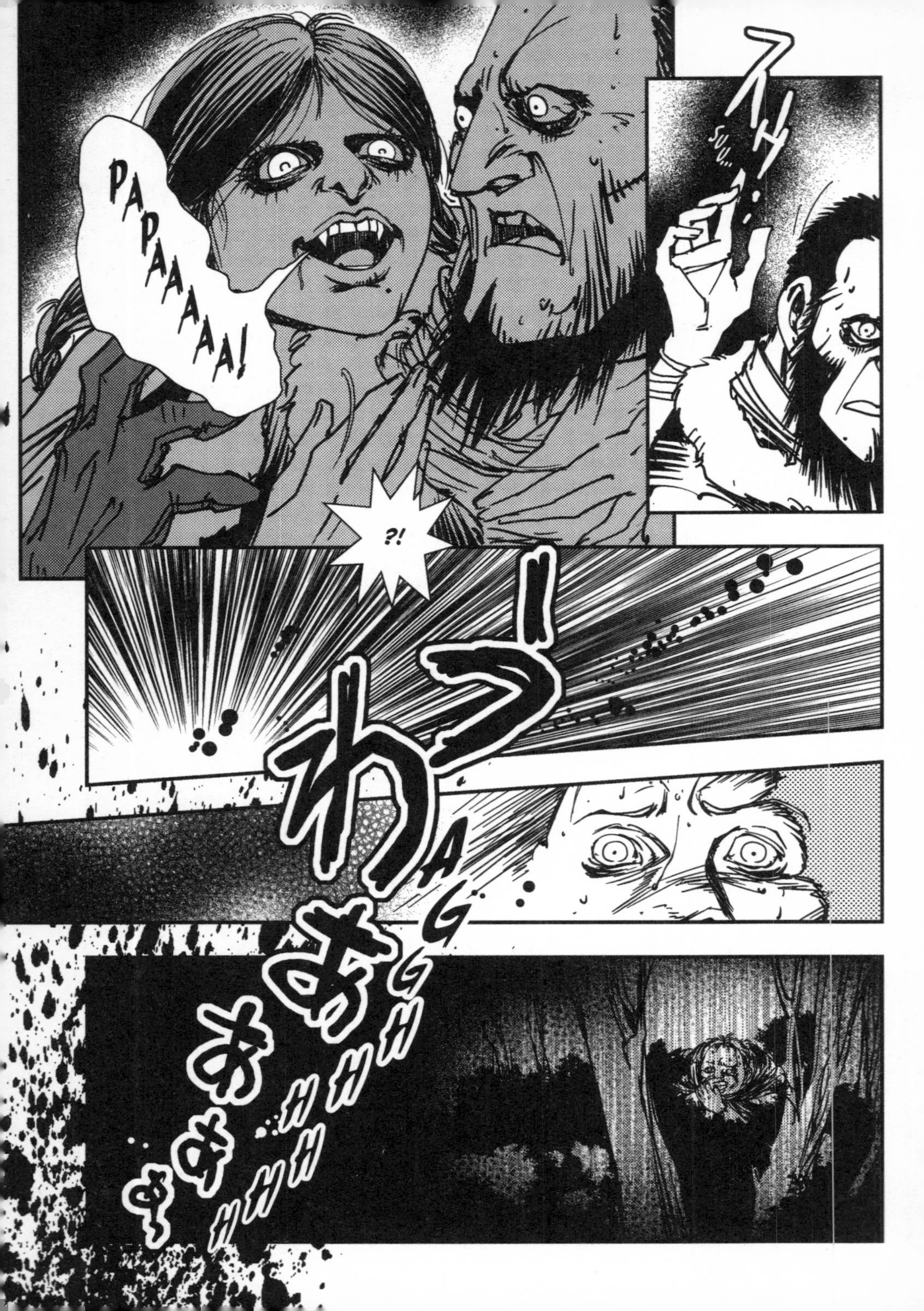
スッ…!
SUU...
PAPAAAAAAA!
?!
AGGGHHHHHHHHHH...

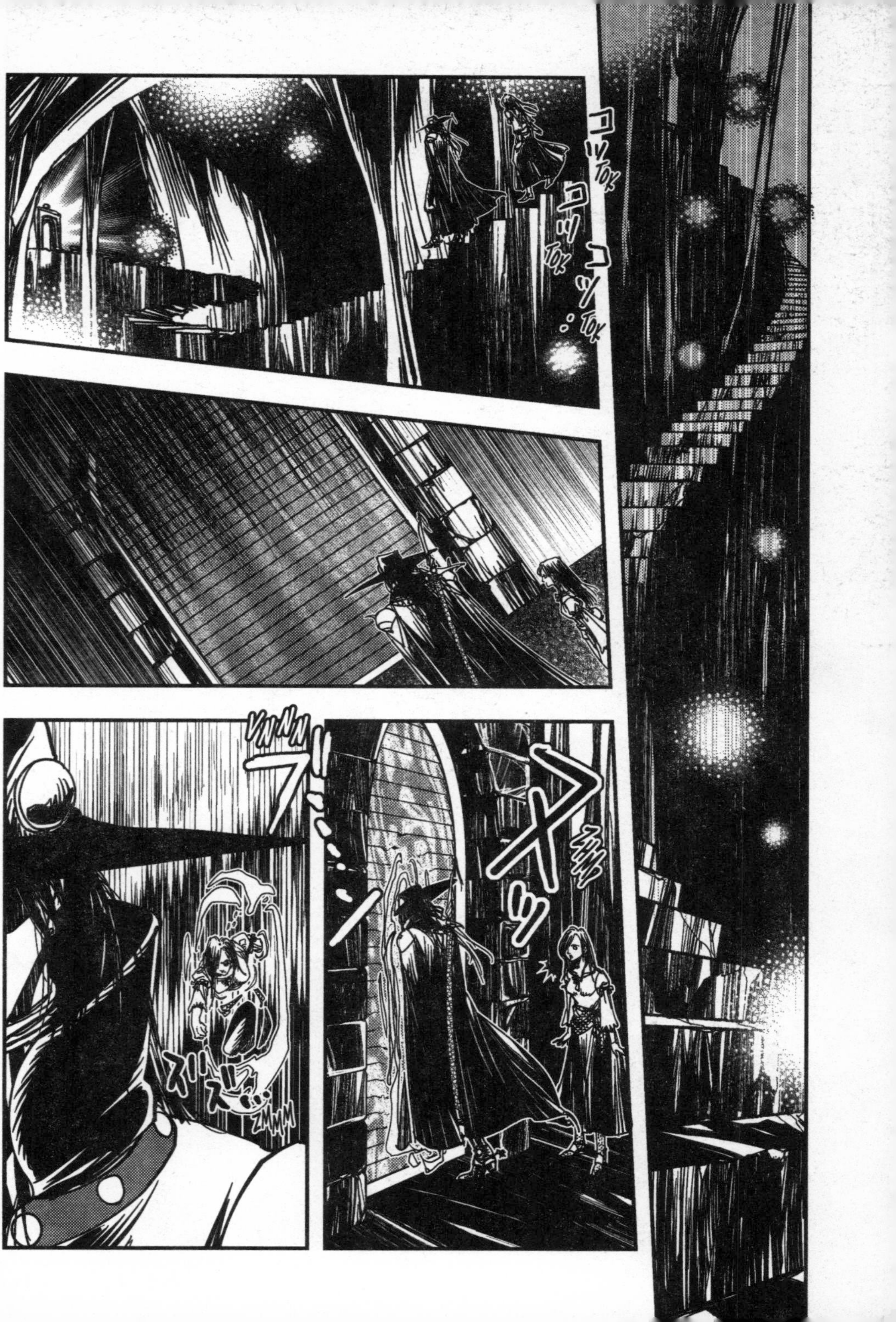
コッ
TOK
コッ
TOK
コッ…
TOK
ヌッ
ZMM
ブ……ン
VNNN
ズズ…
ZMMM

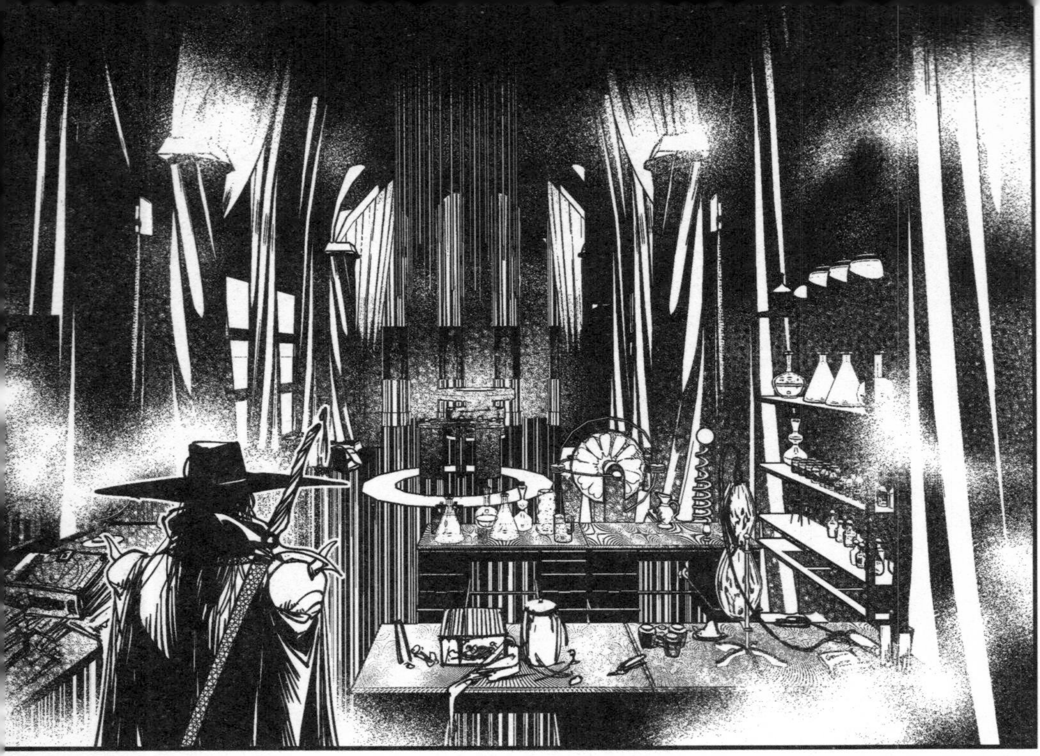

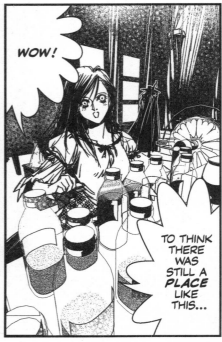

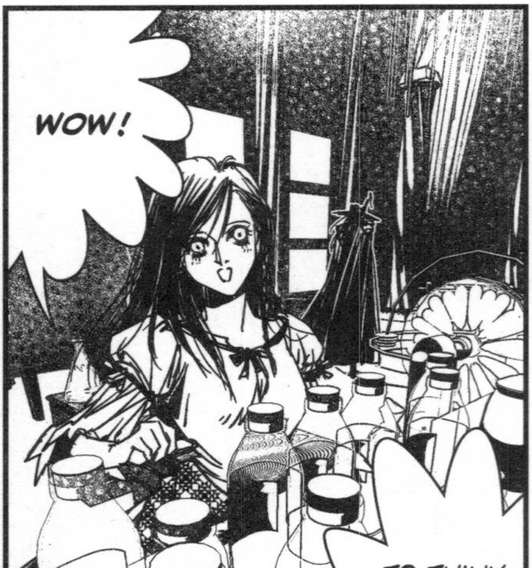
WOW!
TO THINK THERE WAS STILL A PLACE LIKE THIS...

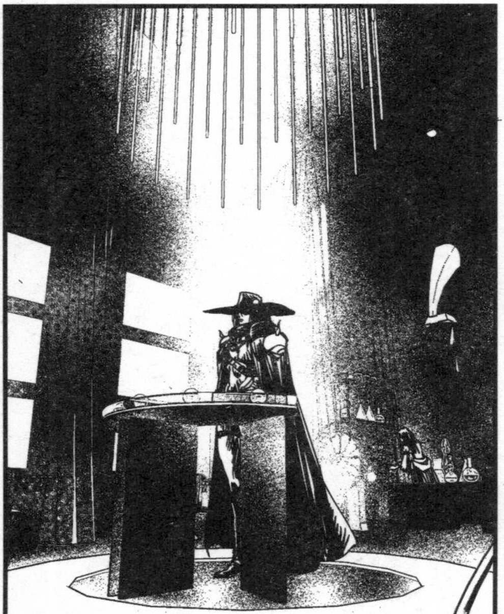

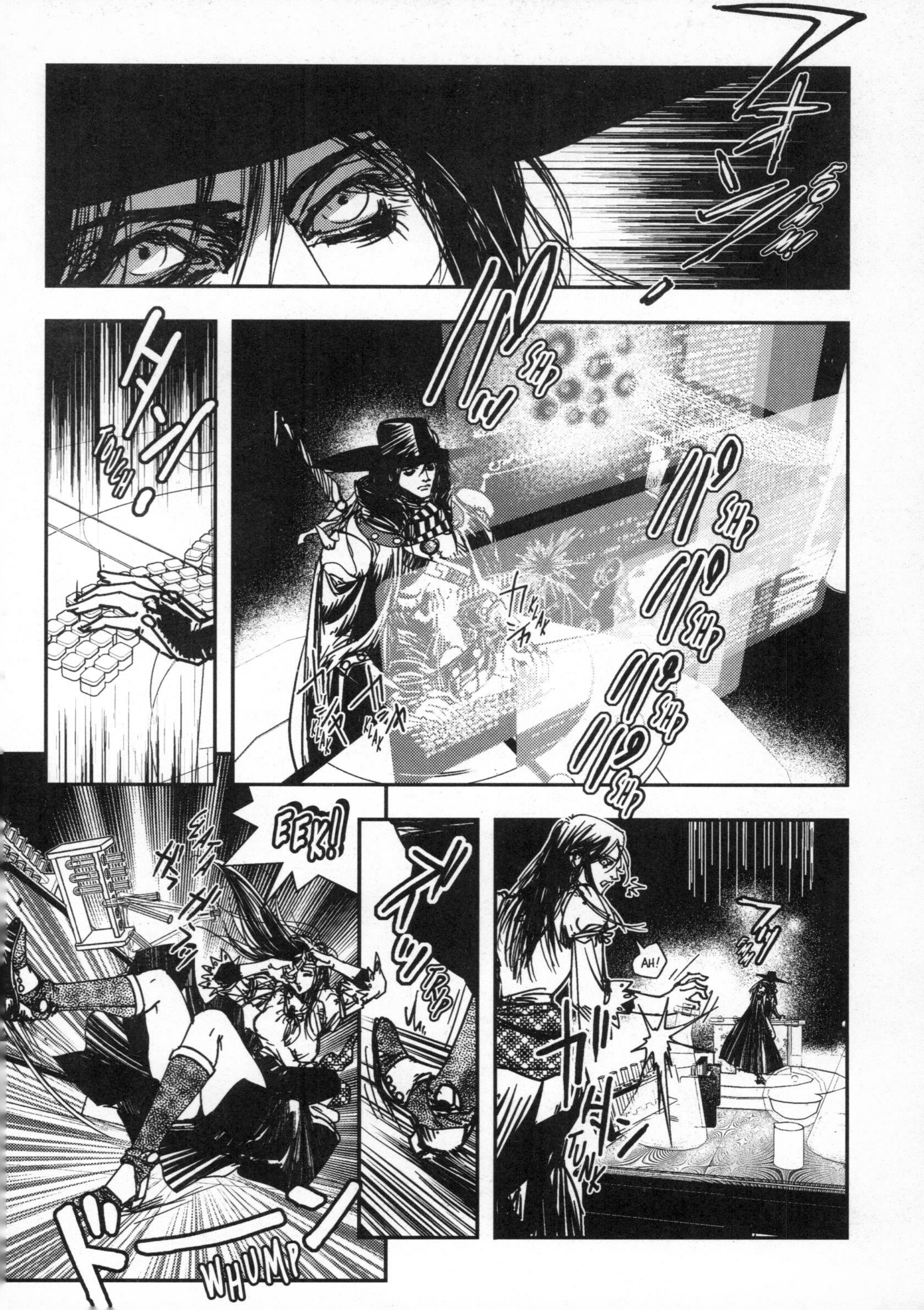
FOMMM
SHK
SHK
SHK
SHK
SHK
SHK
KLAK
KLAK
KLAK
TOUCH!
AH!
TUNK
TRIP
EEK!!
WHUMP

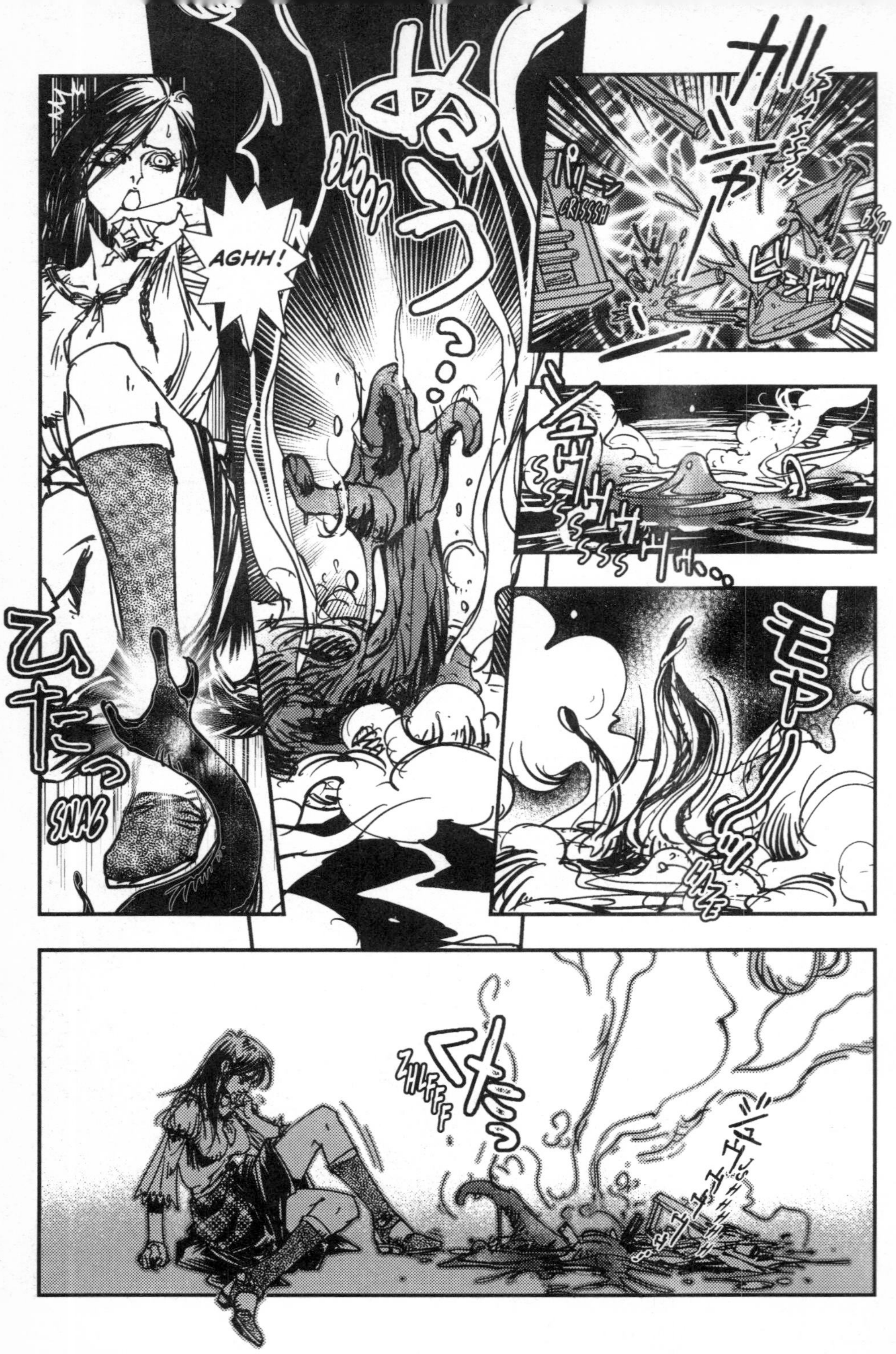

ガシャーン
SRASSSH
パリーン
CRISSSSH
ビシッ
BSSH
シュウウウ
SSSSSSS
モヤーン
HAZE
ぬうっ
BLOOP
AGHH!
ひたっ
SNAG
くたっ
ZHLFFF

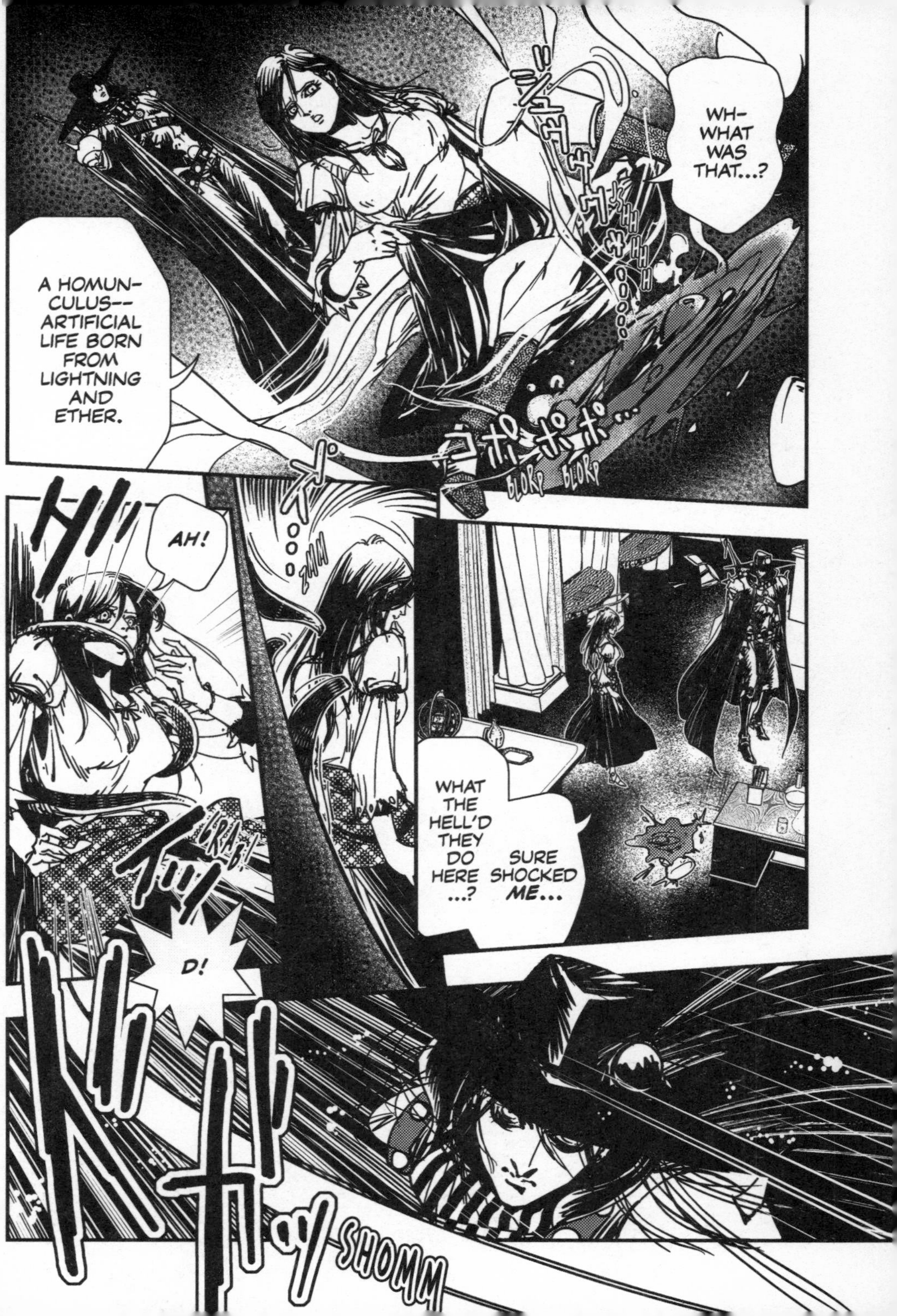
WH-WHAT WAS THAT...?
A HOMUN-CULUS--ARTIFICIAL LIFE BORN FROM LIGHTNING AND ETHER.
BLORP BLORP
WHAT THE HELL'D THEY DO HERE ...?
SURE SHOCKED ME...
AH!
GRAB!
D!
SHOMM

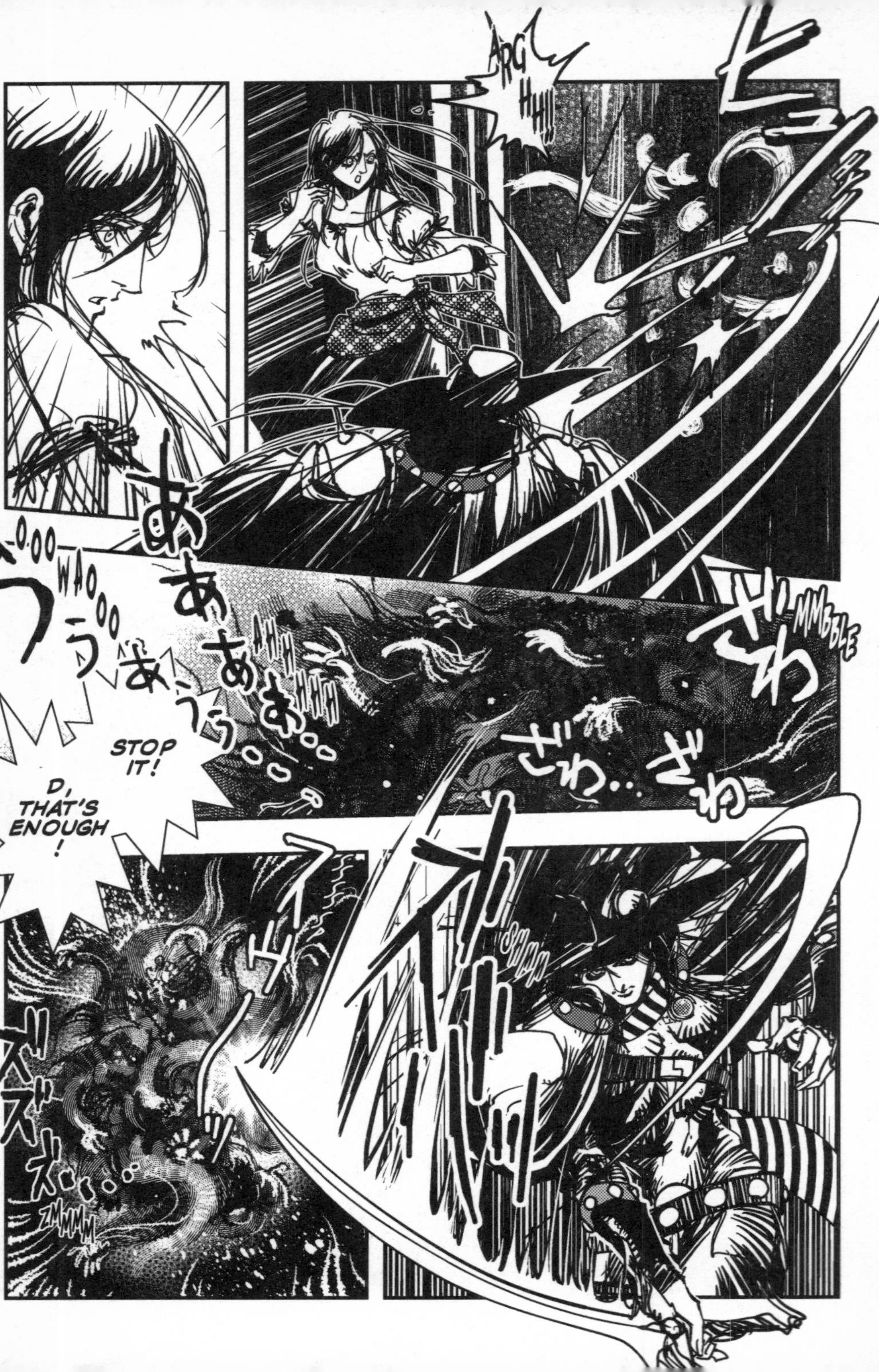
ARGHH!!
MMBBLE
ざわ
ざわ… ざわ
ざわ
AHHHHHHH
WAOOOOOOO…
STOP IT!
D, THAT'S ENOUGH!
SHNNN
ZMMMM

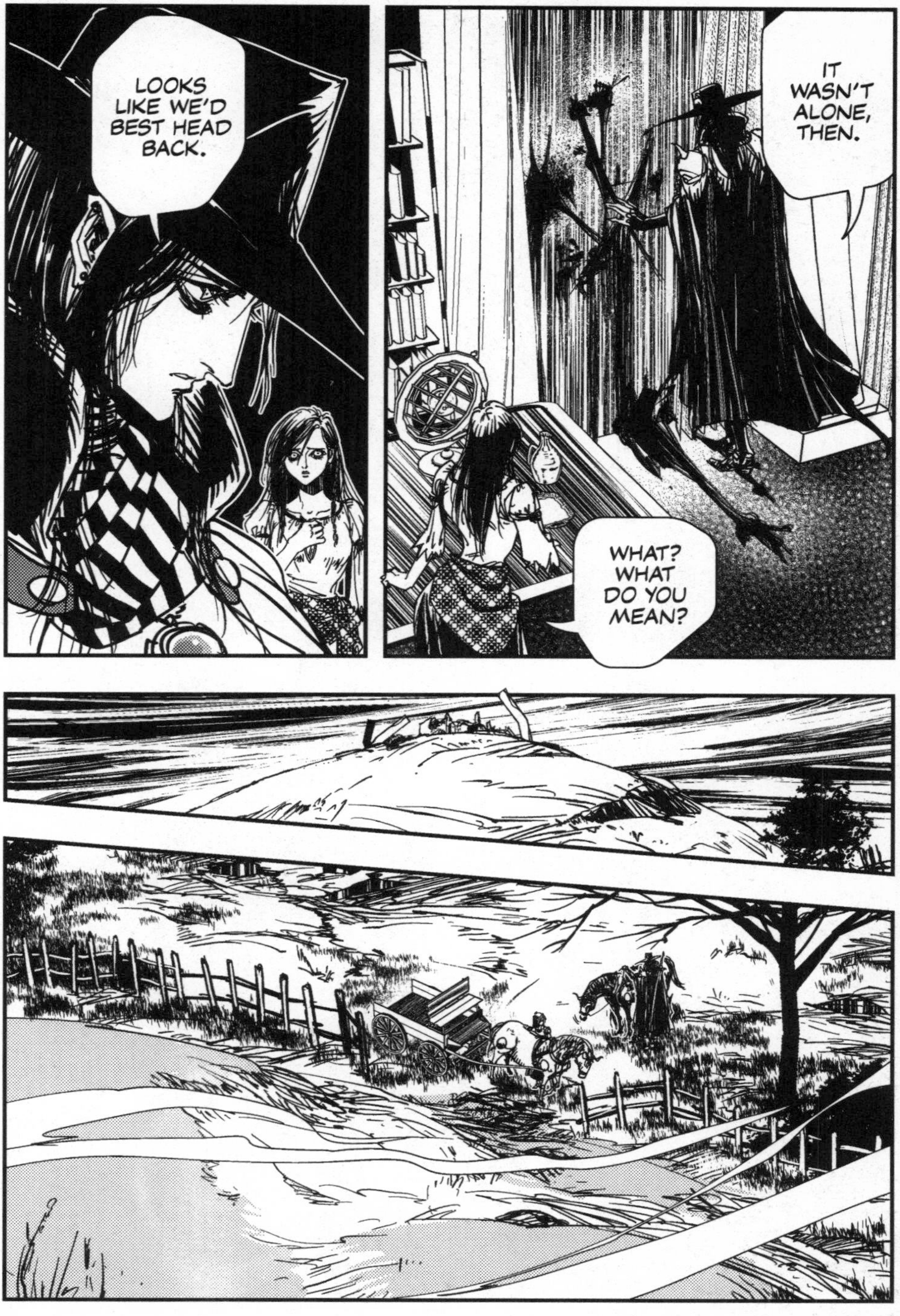
IT WASN'T ALONE, THEN.
WHAT? WHAT DO YOU MEAN?
LOOKS LIKE WE'D BEST HEAD BACK.

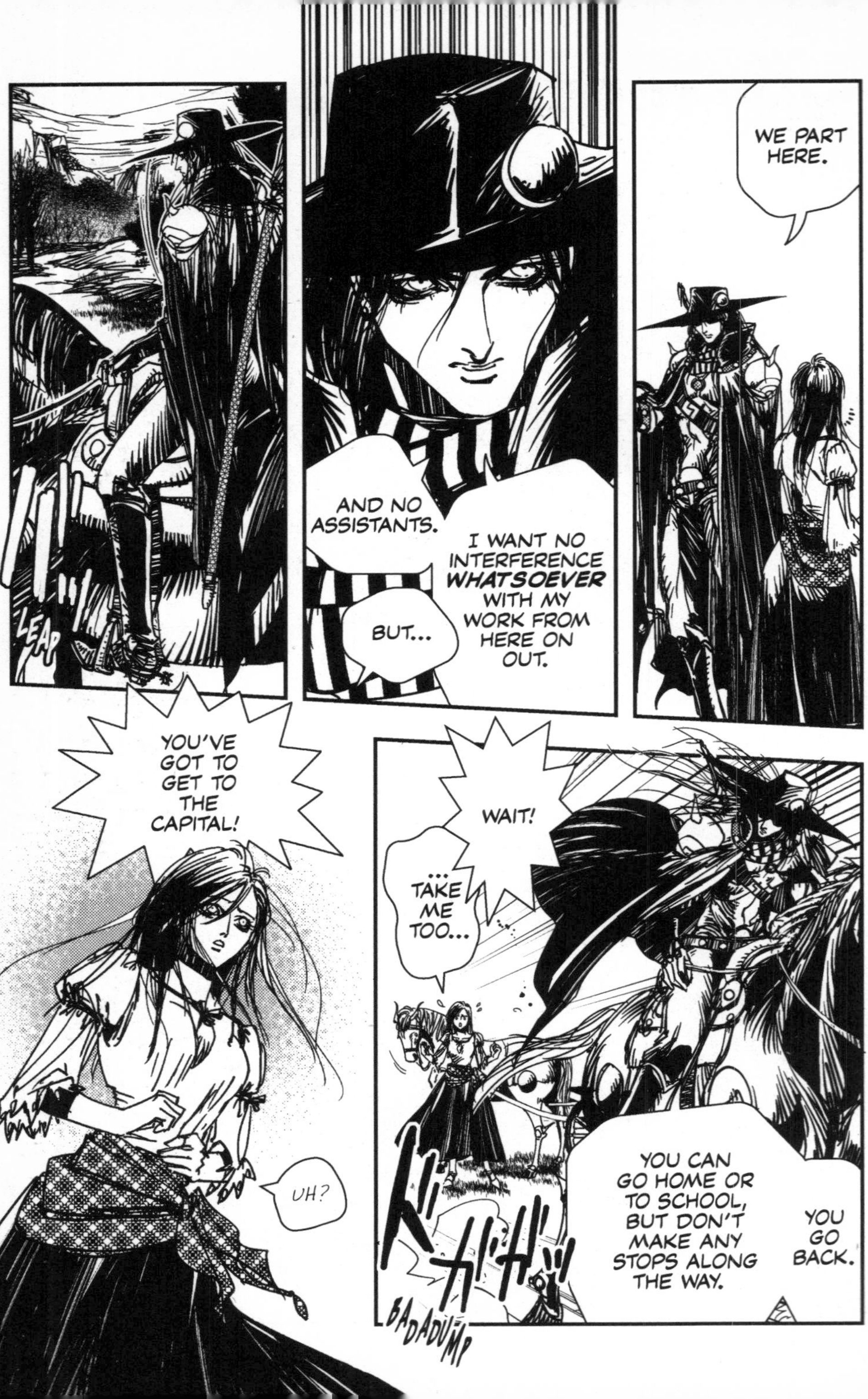
WE PART HERE.
I WANT NO INTERFERENCE ***WHATSOEVER*** WITH MY WORK FROM HERE ON OUT.
AND NO ASSISTANTS.
BUT...
LEAP
YOU GO BACK.
YOU CAN GO HOME OR TO SCHOOL, BUT DON'T MAKE ANY STOPS ALONG THE WAY.
WAIT!
...TAKE ME TOO...
BADADUMP
YOU'VE GOT TO GET TO THE CAPITAL!
UH?

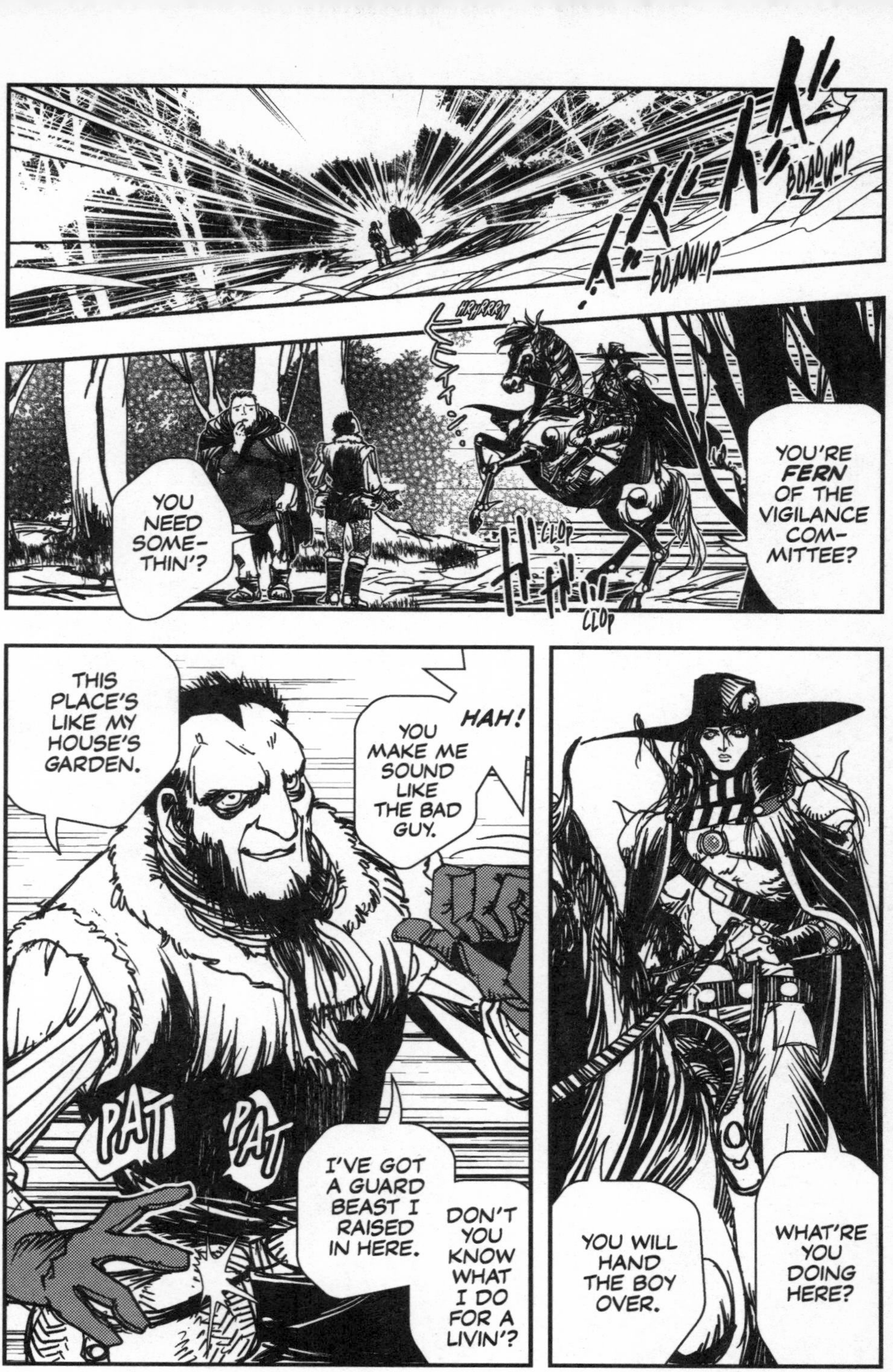
BOADUMP
BOADUMP
HRHRRRN
YOU'RE **FERN** OF THE VIGILANCE COM-MITTEE?
CLOP
CLOP
YOU NEED SOME-THIN'?
WHAT'RE YOU DOING HERE?
YOU WILL HAND THE BOY OVER.
HAH!
YOU MAKE ME SOUND LIKE THE BAD GUY.
THIS PLACE'S LIKE MY HOUSE'S GARDEN.
DON'T YOU KNOW WHAT I DO FOR A LIVIN'?
I'VE GOT A GUARD BEAST I RAISED IN HERE.
PAT
PAT

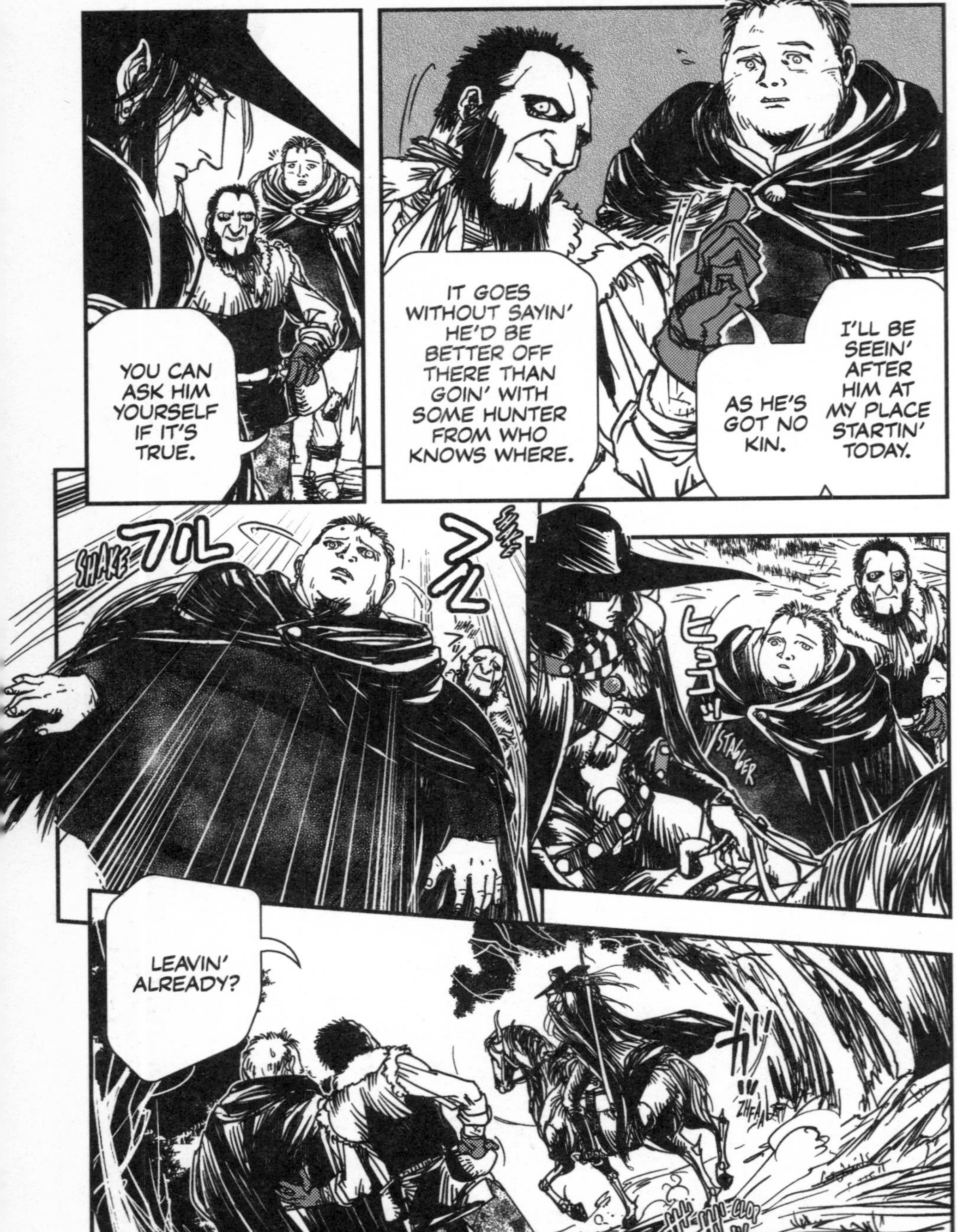
I'LL BE SEEIN' AFTER HIM AT MY PLACE STARTIN' TODAY.
AS HE'S GOT NO KIN.
IT GOES WITHOUT SAYIN' HE'D BE BETTER OFF THERE THAN GOIN' WITH SOME HUNTER FROM WHO KNOWS WHERE.
YOU CAN ASK HIM YOURSELF IF IT'S TRUE.
STAGGER
SHAKE
HMPH
SHAKE
LEAVIN' ALREADY?
ZHFAA
CLOP

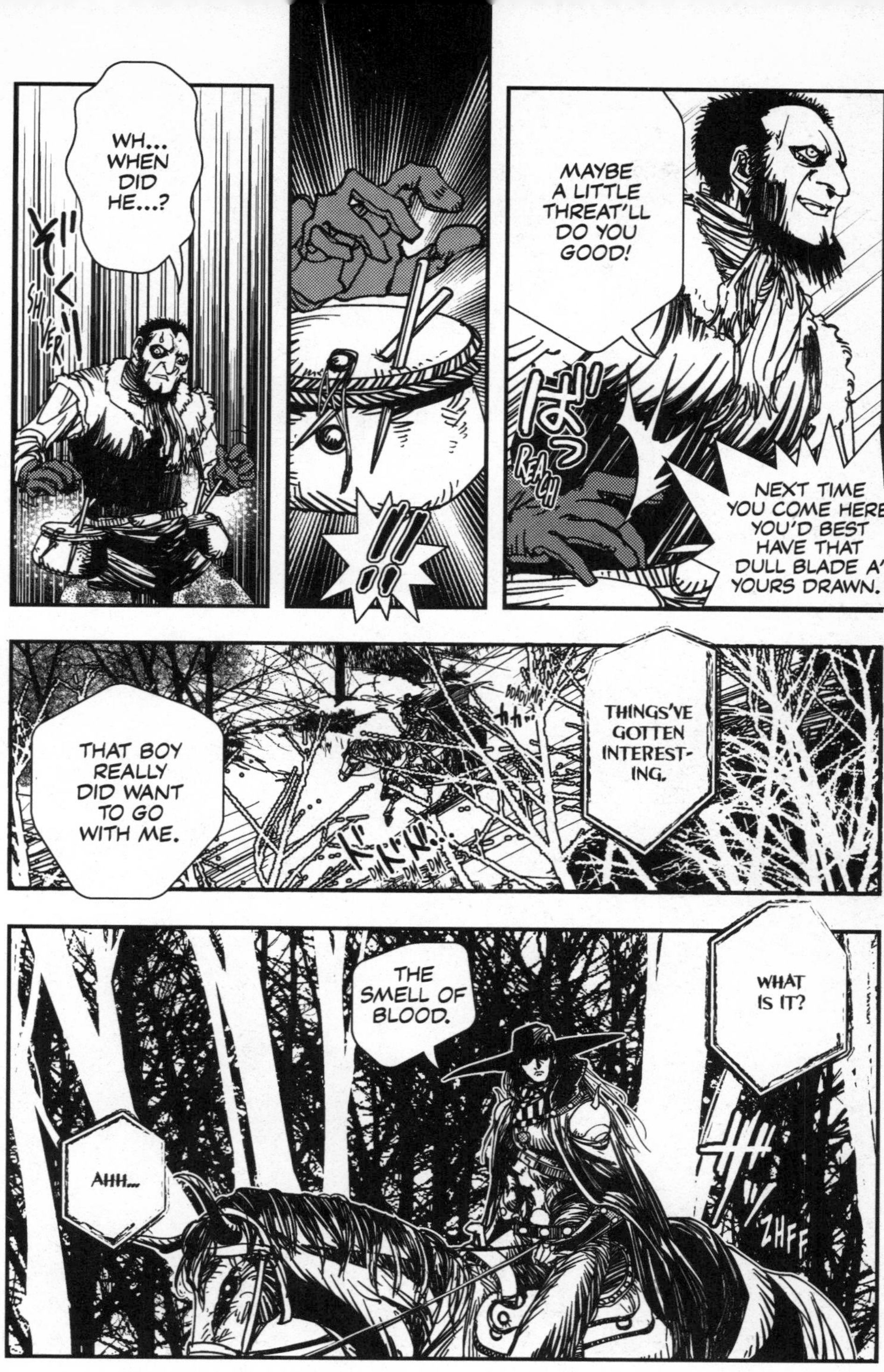
MAYBE A LITTLE THREAT'LL DO YOU GOOD!
REACH
NEXT TIME YOU COME HERE, YOU'D BEST HAVE THAT DULL BLADE A' YOURS DRAWN.
!!
WH... WHEN DID HE...?
SHIVER
THINGS'VE GOTTEN INTEREST-ING.
DM DM DM
THAT BOY REALLY DID WANT TO GO WITH ME.
WHAT IS IT?
ZHFF
THE SMELL OF BLOOD.
AHH...

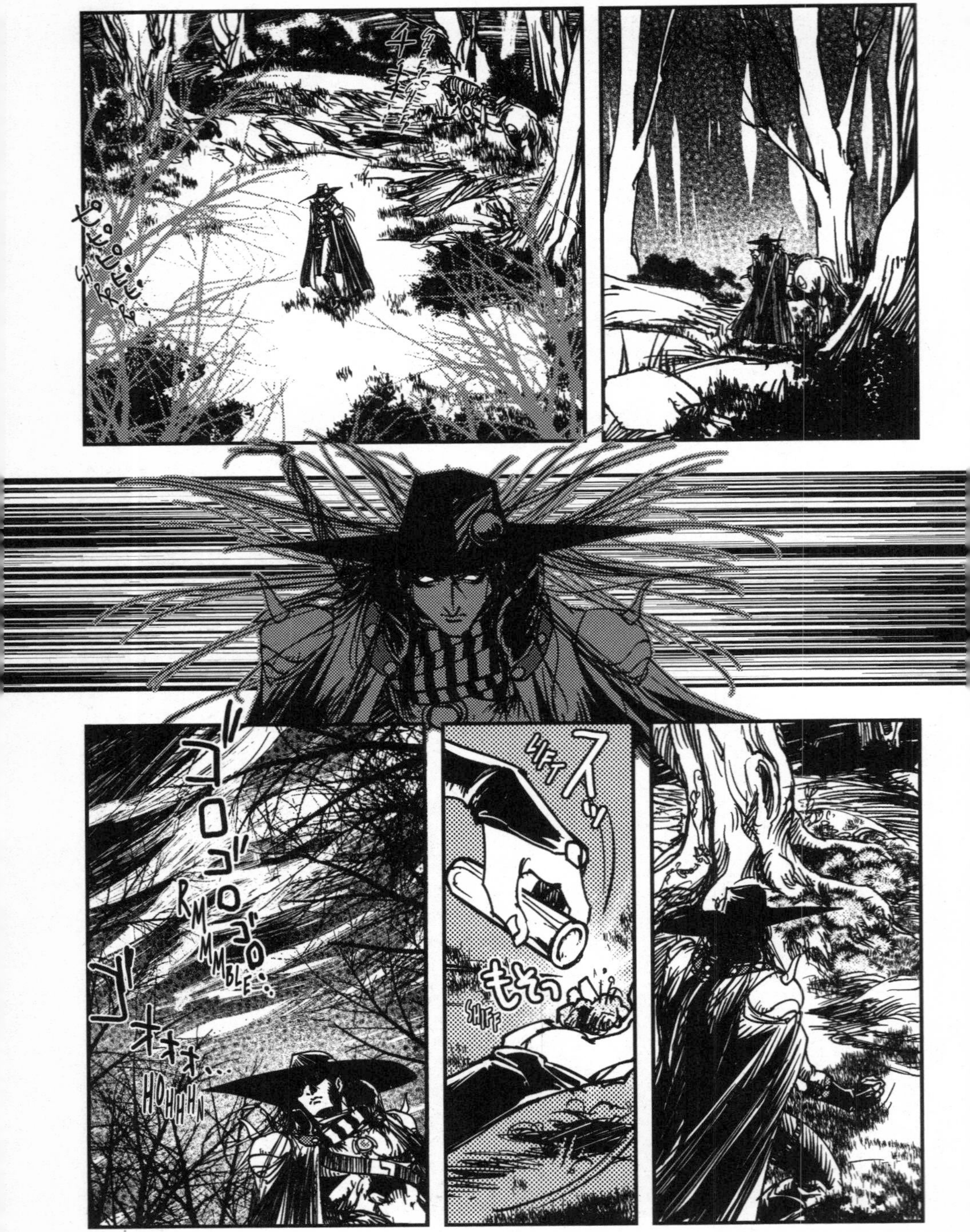
チチチ…
ピピピピピ…
スッ
LIFT
もそっ
SHIFF
ゴロゴロゴロ…
RMMMMBLE…
ゴオオオ…
HOHHHN

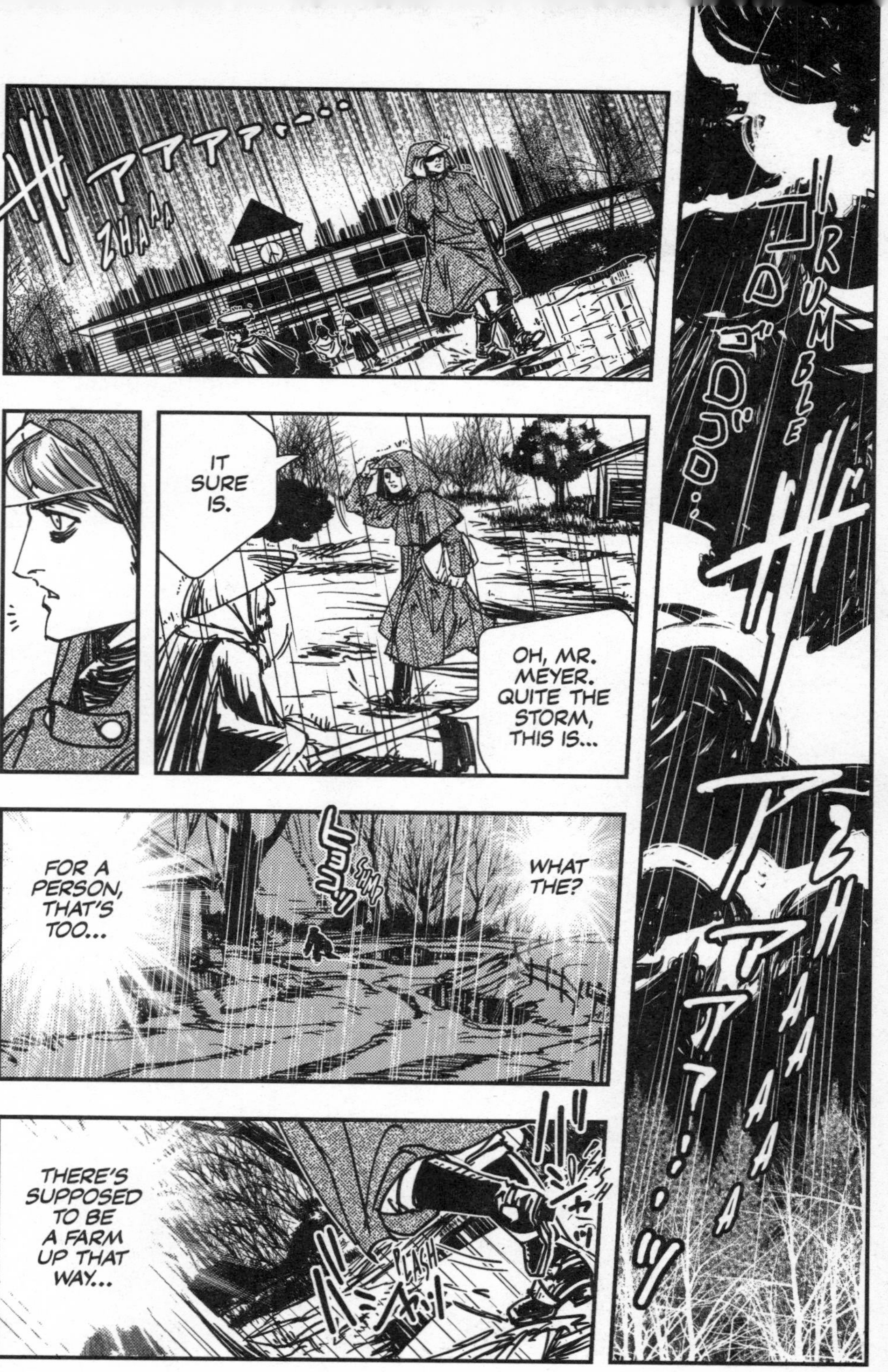
RUMBLE
WHAAAAAA
ZHAAA
OH, MR. MEYER. QUITE THE STORM, THIS IS...
IT SURE IS.
WHAT THE?
FOR A PERSON, THAT'S TOO...
CLASH
FLASH
THERE'S SUPPOSED TO BE A FARM UP THAT WAY...

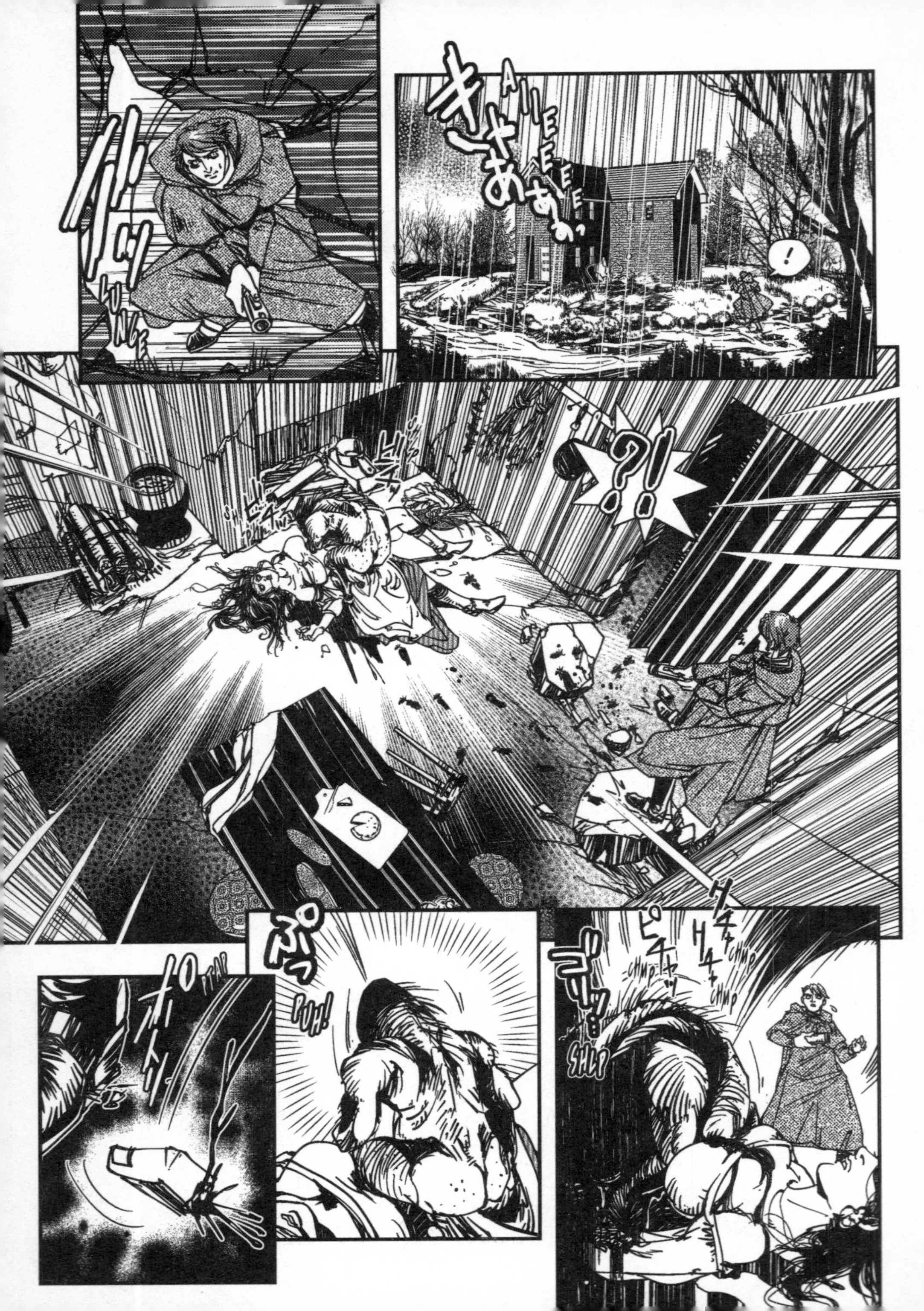

きゃあああっ
AIIEEEEE
!
LUNGE
?!
PUH!
ぷっ
PTAK

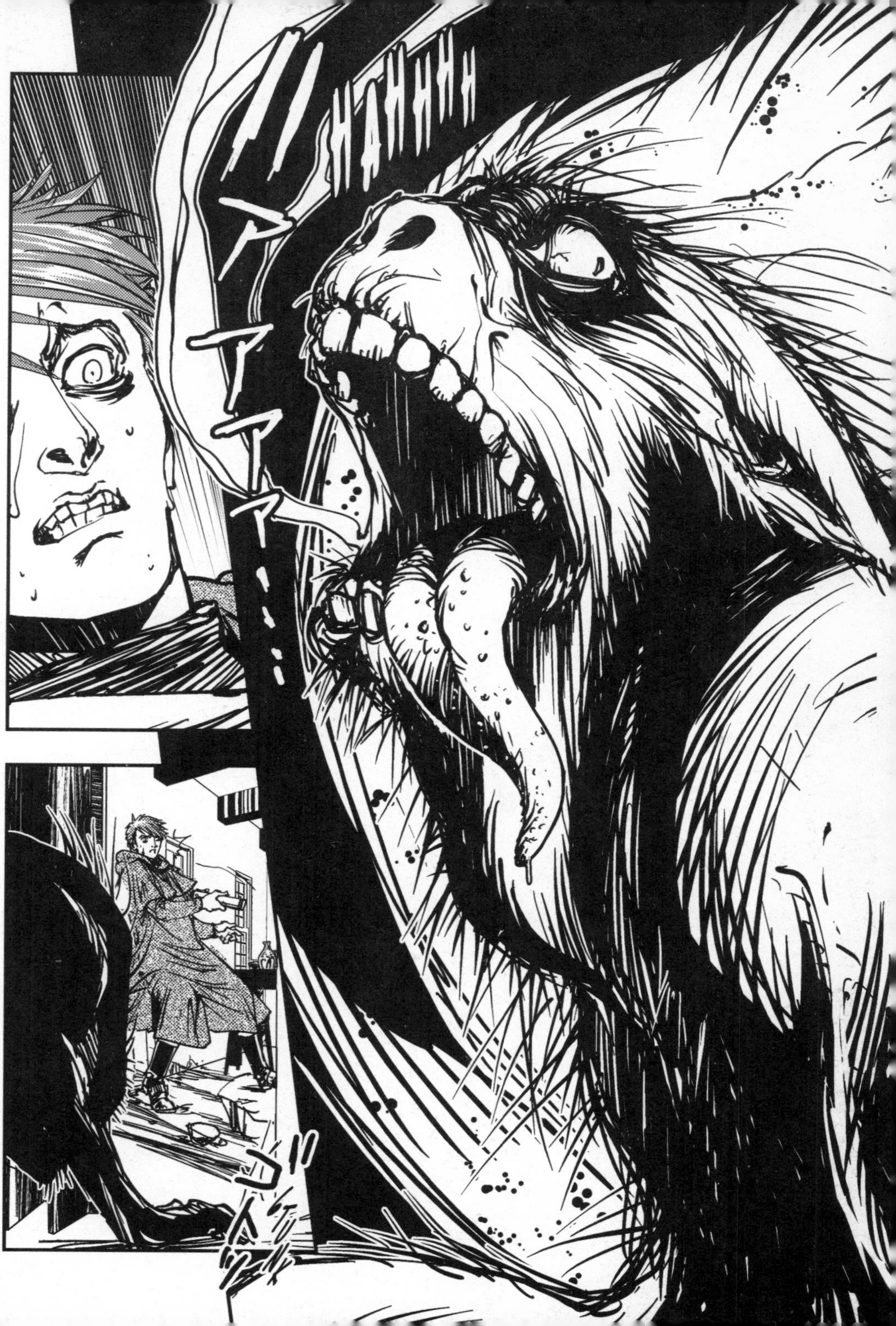
HAHHHH
アァァァァ…

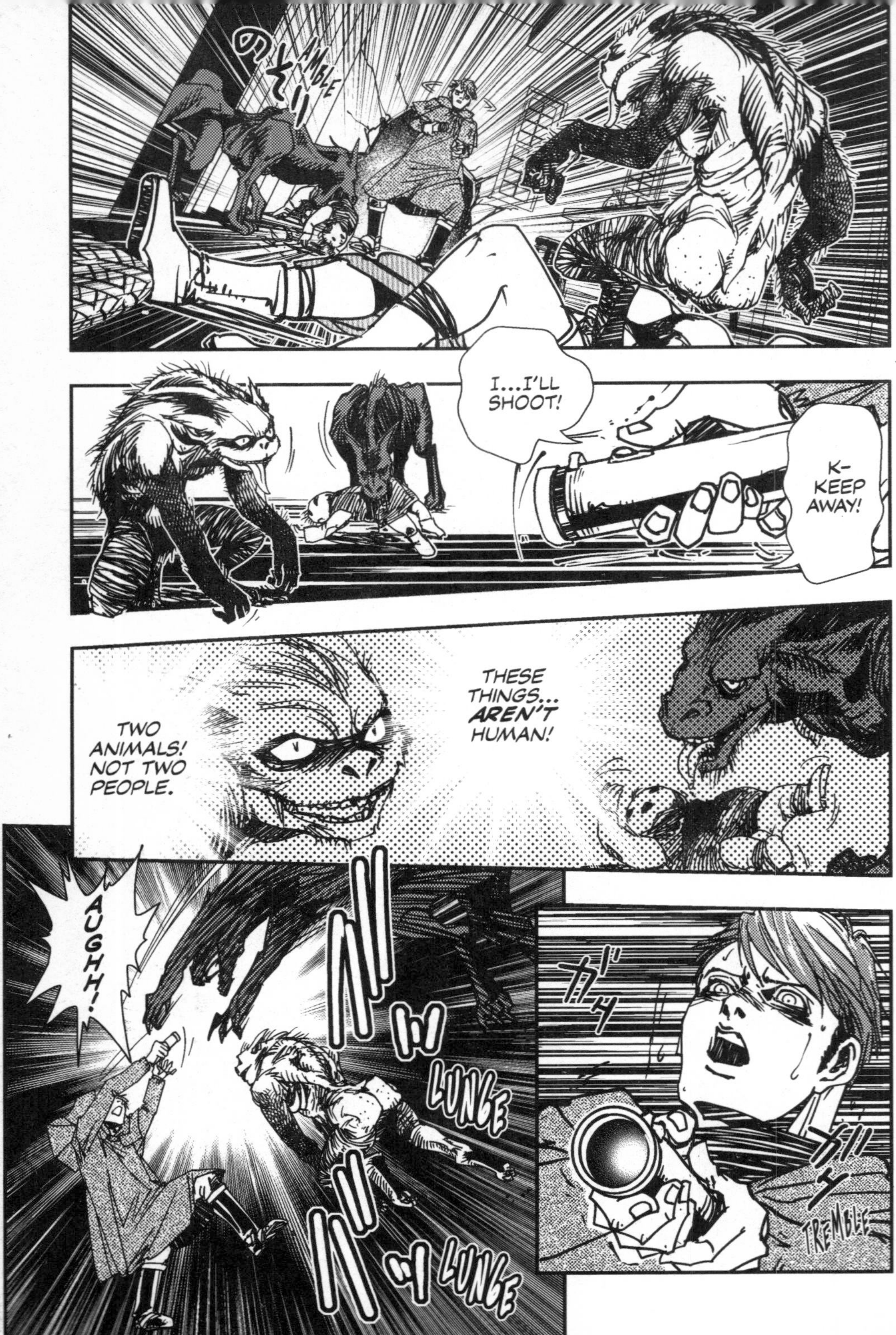
のそ
AMBLE
I...I'LL SHOOT!
K-KEEP AWAY!
THESE THINGS... AREN'T HUMAN!
TWO ANIMALS! NOT TWO PEOPLE.
ガタ
ガクッ
TREMBLE
AUGHH!
LUNGE
LUNGE

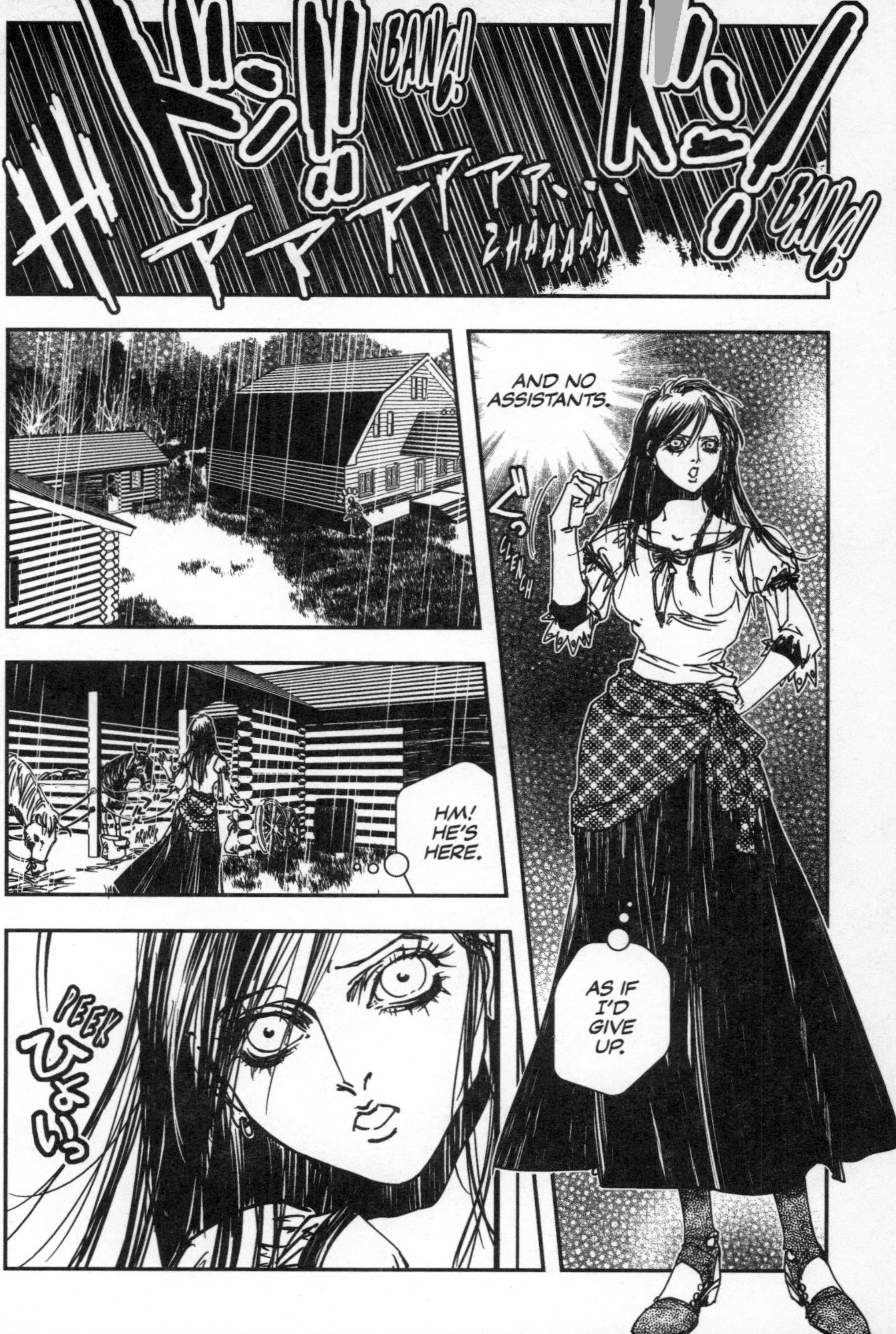
BANG!
ZHAAAAA
BANG!
AND NO ASSISTANTS.
CLENCH
AS IF I'D GIVE UP.
HM! HE'S HERE.
PEEK

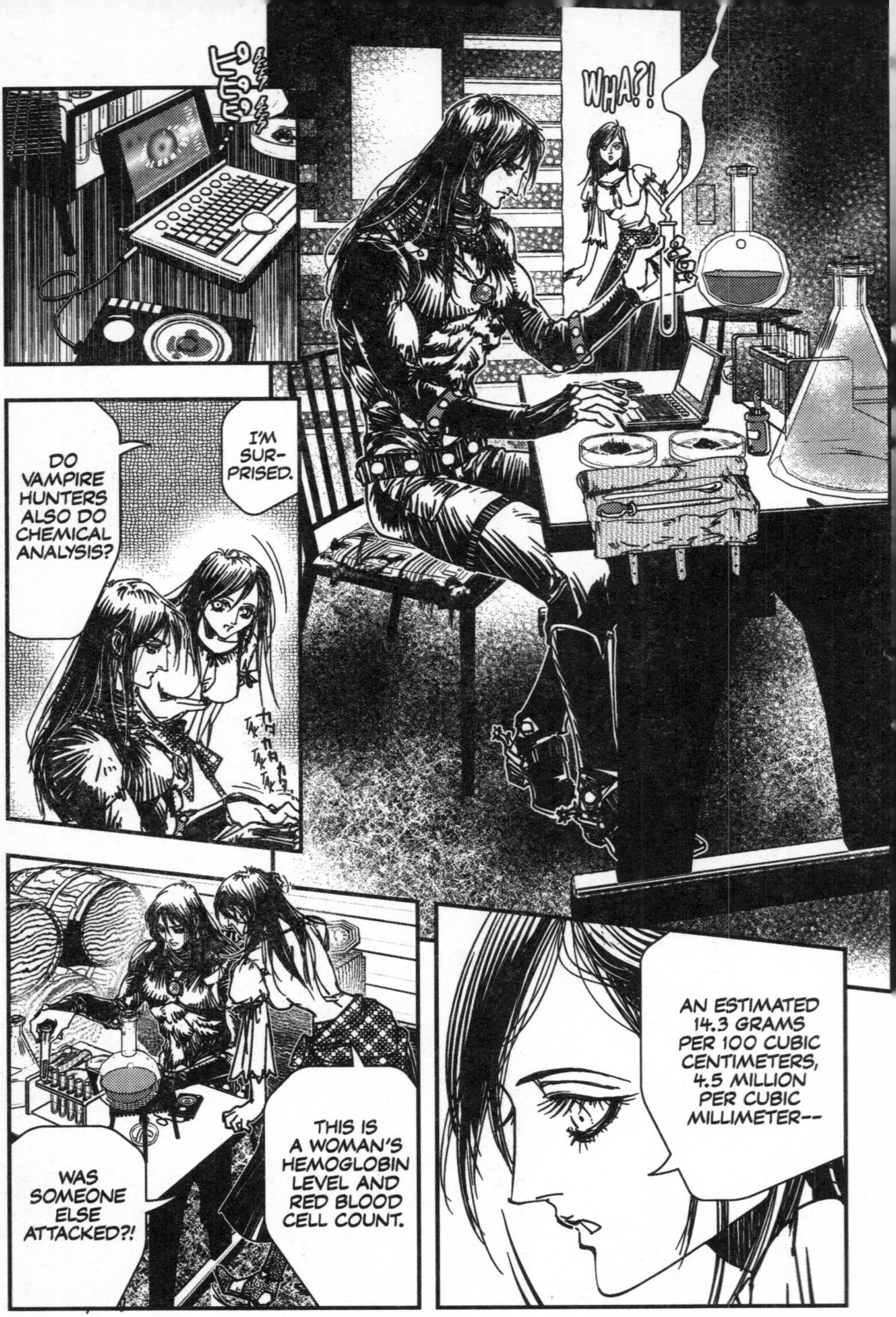
WHA?!
I'M SUR-PRISED.
DO VAMPIRE HUNTERS ALSO DO CHEMICAL ANALYSIS?
AN ESTIMATED 14.3 GRAMS PER 100 CUBIC CENTIMETERS, 4.5 MILLION PER CUBIC MILLIMETER--
THIS IS A WOMAN'S HEMOGLOBIN LEVEL AND RED BLOOD CELL COUNT.
WAS SOMEONE ELSE ATTACKED?!

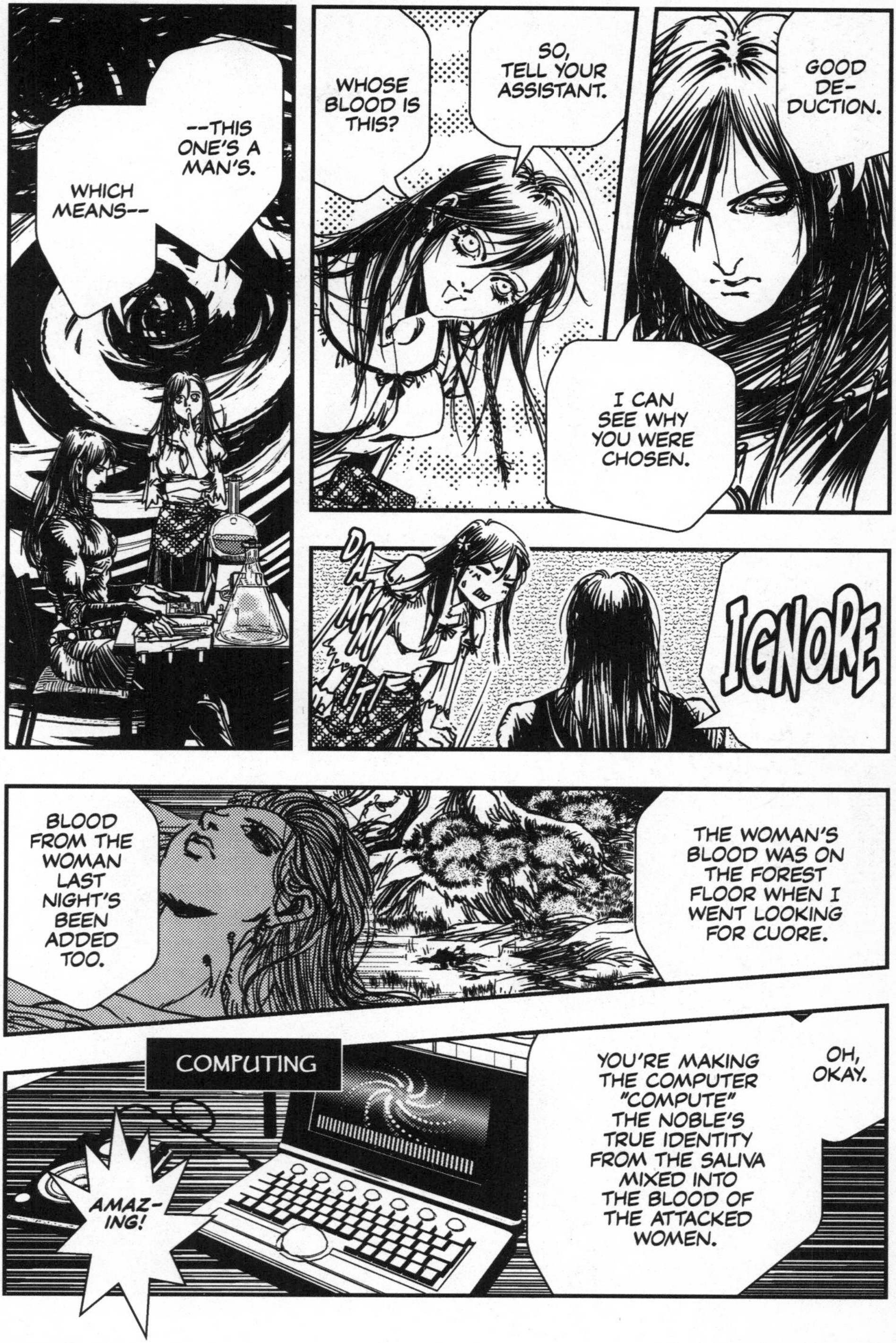
GOOD DE-DUCTION.
I CAN SEE WHY YOU WERE CHOSEN.
SO, TELL YOUR ASSISTANT.
WHOSE BLOOD IS THIS?
IGNORE
DAMMIT!
--THIS ONE'S A MAN'S.
WHICH MEANS--
THE WOMAN'S BLOOD WAS ON THE FOREST FLOOR WHEN I WENT LOOKING FOR CUORE.
BLOOD FROM THE WOMAN LAST NIGHT'S BEEN ADDED TOO.
OH, OKAY.
YOU'RE MAKING THE COMPUTER "COMPUTE" THE NOBLE'S TRUE IDENTITY FROM THE SALIVA MIXED INTO THE BLOOD OF THE ATTACKED WOMEN.
COMPUTING
AMAZ-ING!

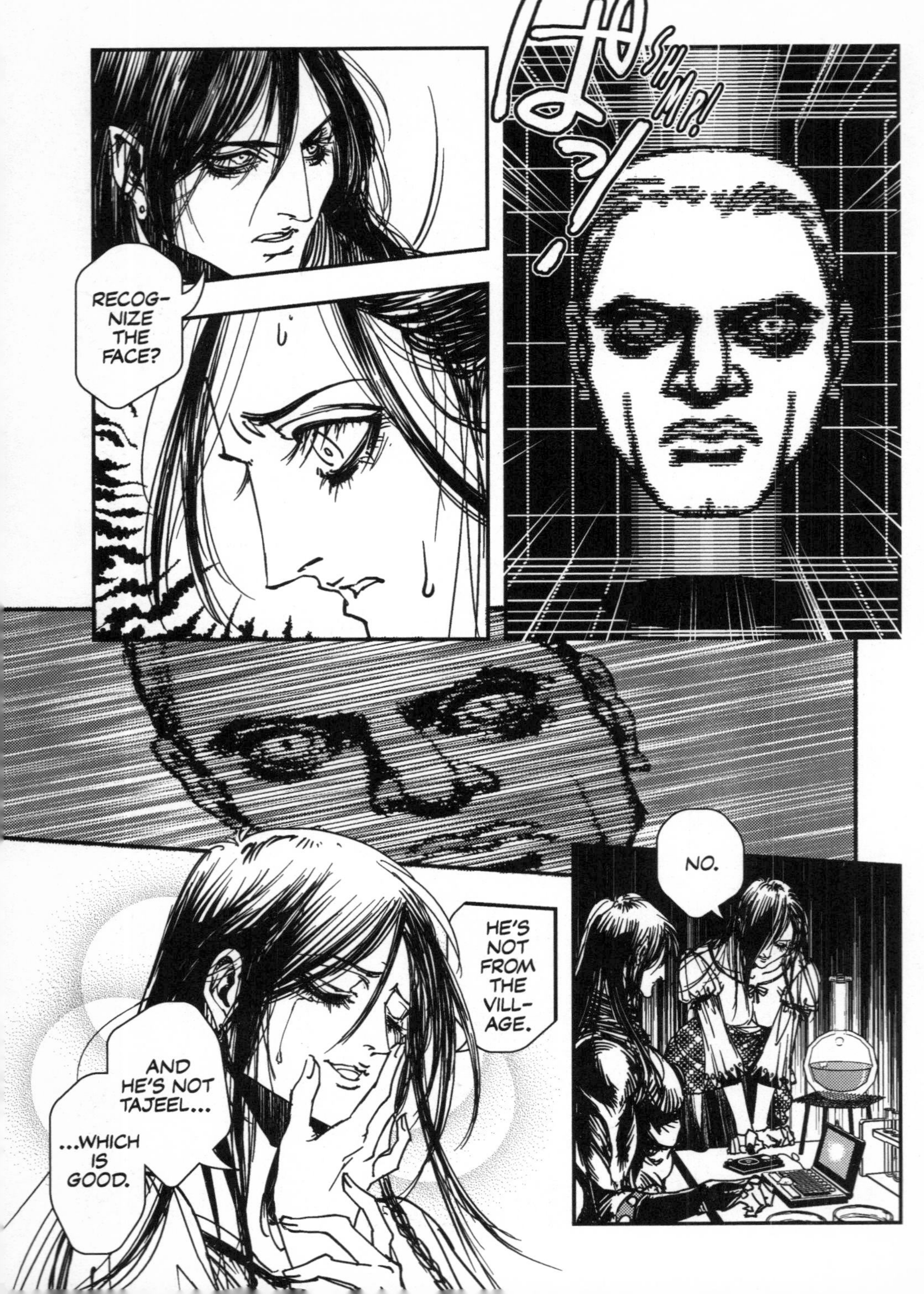
はっ!
SHMP!
RECOG-NIZE THE FACE?
NO.
HE'S NOT FROM THE VILL-AGE.
AND HE'S NOT TAJEEL...
...WHICH IS GOOD.

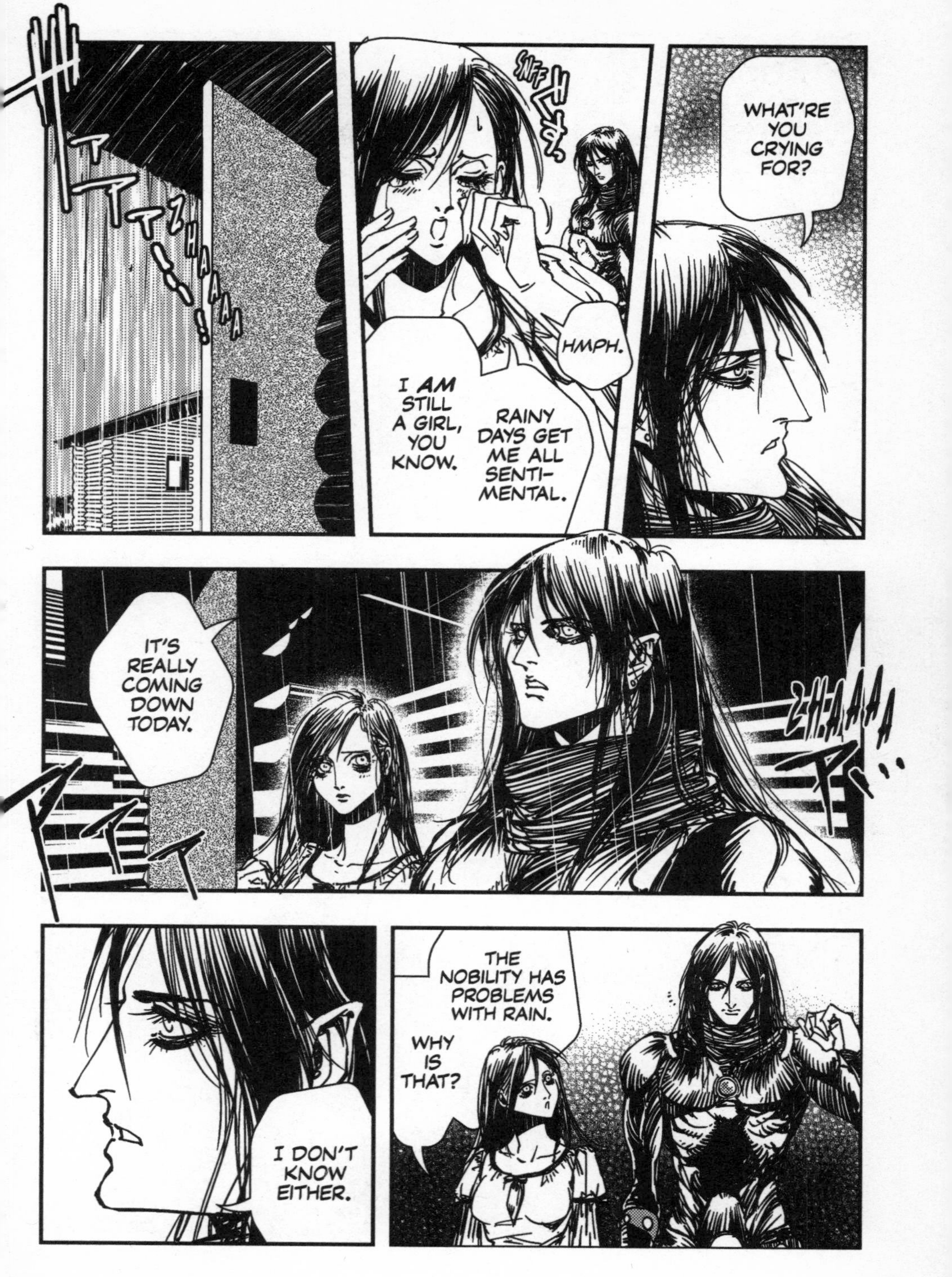
WHAT'RE YOU CRYING FOR?
HMPH.
RAINY DAYS GET ME ALL SENTI-MENTAL.
I **AM** STILL A GIRL, YOU KNOW.
ZHAAAAA
IT'S REALLY COMING DOWN TODAY.
THE NOBILITY HAS PROBLEMS WITH RAIN.
WHY IS THAT?
I DON'T KNOW EITHER.

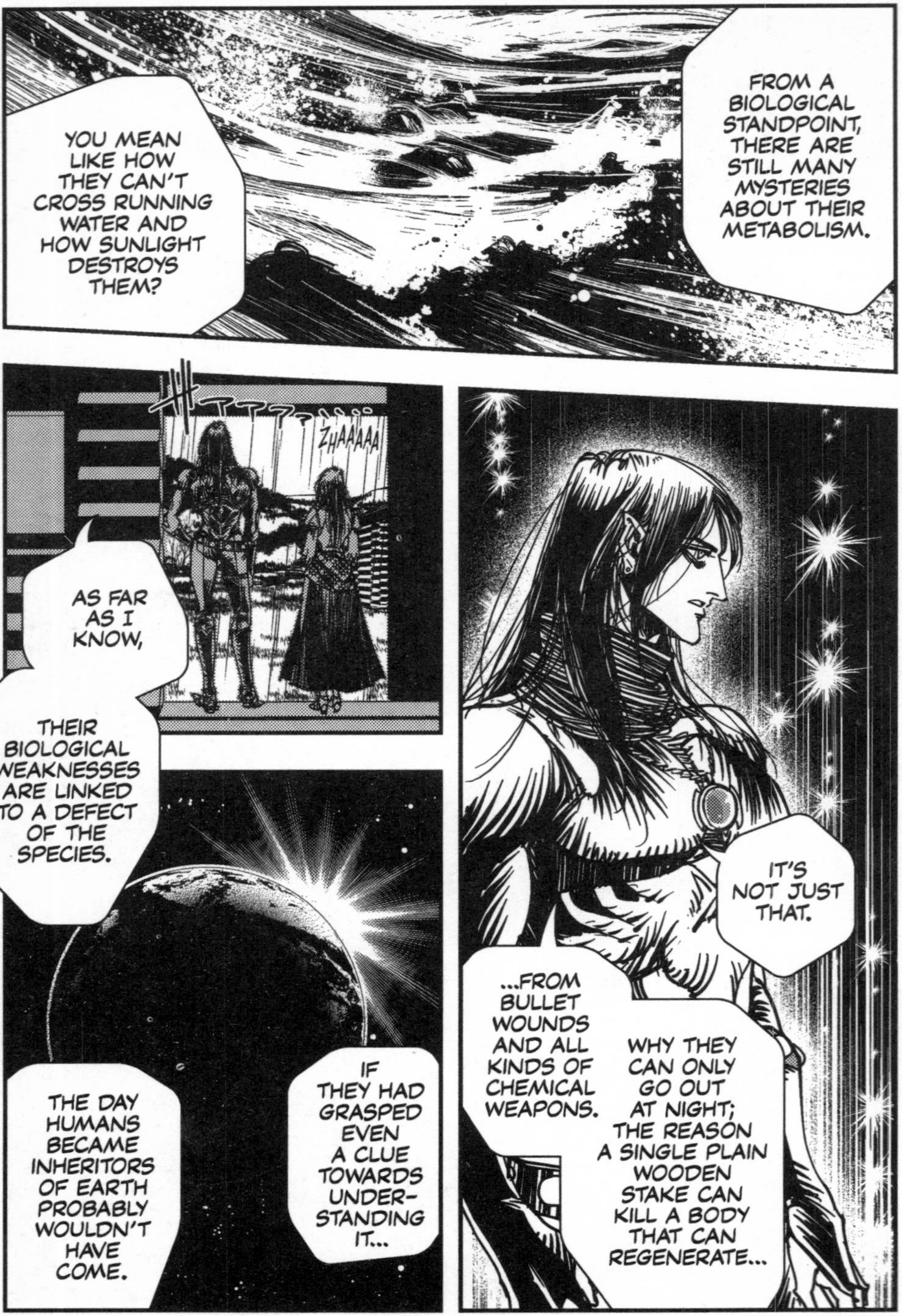
FROM A BIOLOGICAL STANDPOINT, THERE ARE STILL MANY MYSTERIES ABOUT THEIR METABOLISM.
YOU MEAN LIKE HOW THEY CAN'T CROSS RUNNING WATER AND HOW SUNLIGHT DESTROYS THEM?
IT'S NOT JUST THAT.
WHY THEY CAN ONLY GO OUT AT NIGHT; THE REASON A SINGLE PLAIN WOODEN STAKE CAN KILL A BODY THAT CAN REGENERATE...
...FROM BULLET WOUNDS AND ALL KINDS OF CHEMICAL WEAPONS.
ZHAAAAA
AS FAR AS I KNOW,
THEIR BIOLOGICAL WEAKNESSES ARE LINKED TO A DEFECT OF THE SPECIES.
IF THEY HAD GRASPED EVEN A CLUE TOWARDS UNDER-STANDING IT...
THE DAY HUMANS BECAME INHERITORS OF EARTH PROBABLY WOULDN'T HAVE COME.

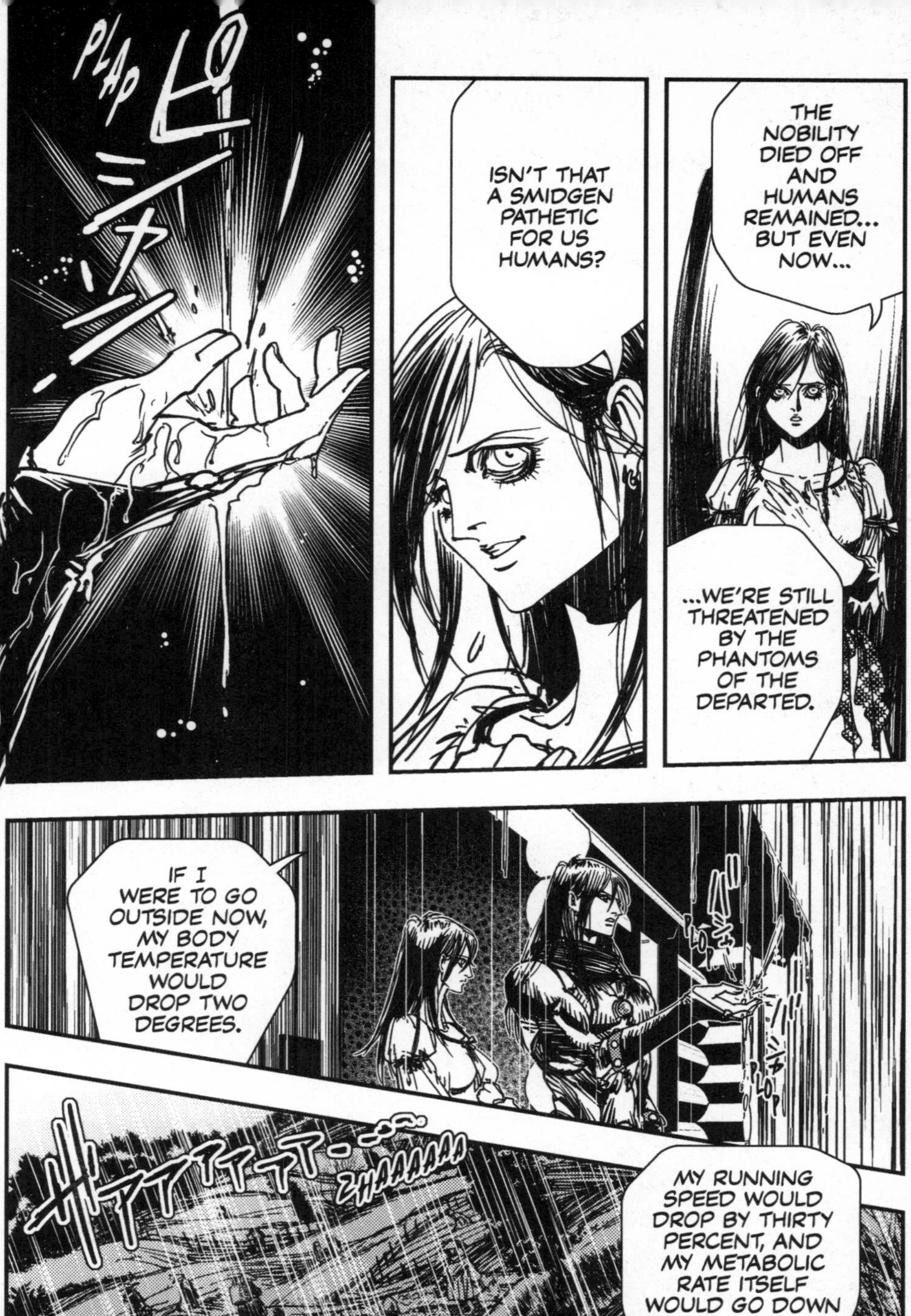

THE NOBILITY DIED OFF AND HUMANS REMAINED... BUT EVEN NOW...
...WE'RE STILL THREATENED BY THE PHANTOMS OF THE DEPARTED.
ISN'T THAT A SMIDGEN PATHETIC FOR US HUMANS?
PLAP
IF I WERE TO GO OUTSIDE NOW, MY BODY TEMPERATURE WOULD DROP TWO DEGREES.
PLOP
PLOP
ZHAAAAAA
MY RUNNING SPEED WOULD DROP BY THIRTY PERCENT, AND MY METABOLIC RATE ITSELF WOULD GO DOWN A LEVEL.

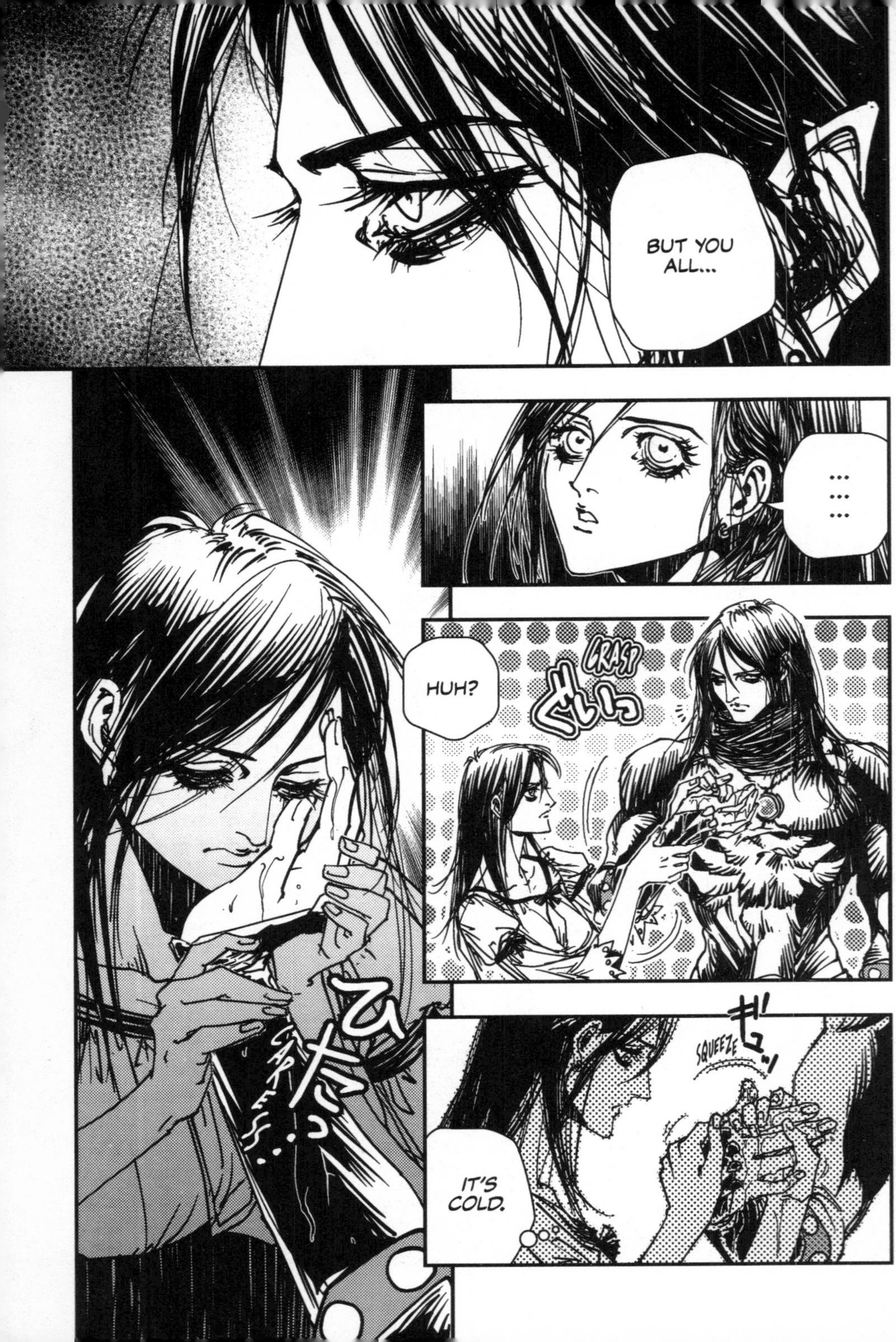
BUT YOU ALL...
...
...
...
CRASH
ぐいっ
HUH?
SQUEEZE
ギュッ
IT'S COLD.
ひたっ
CARESS...

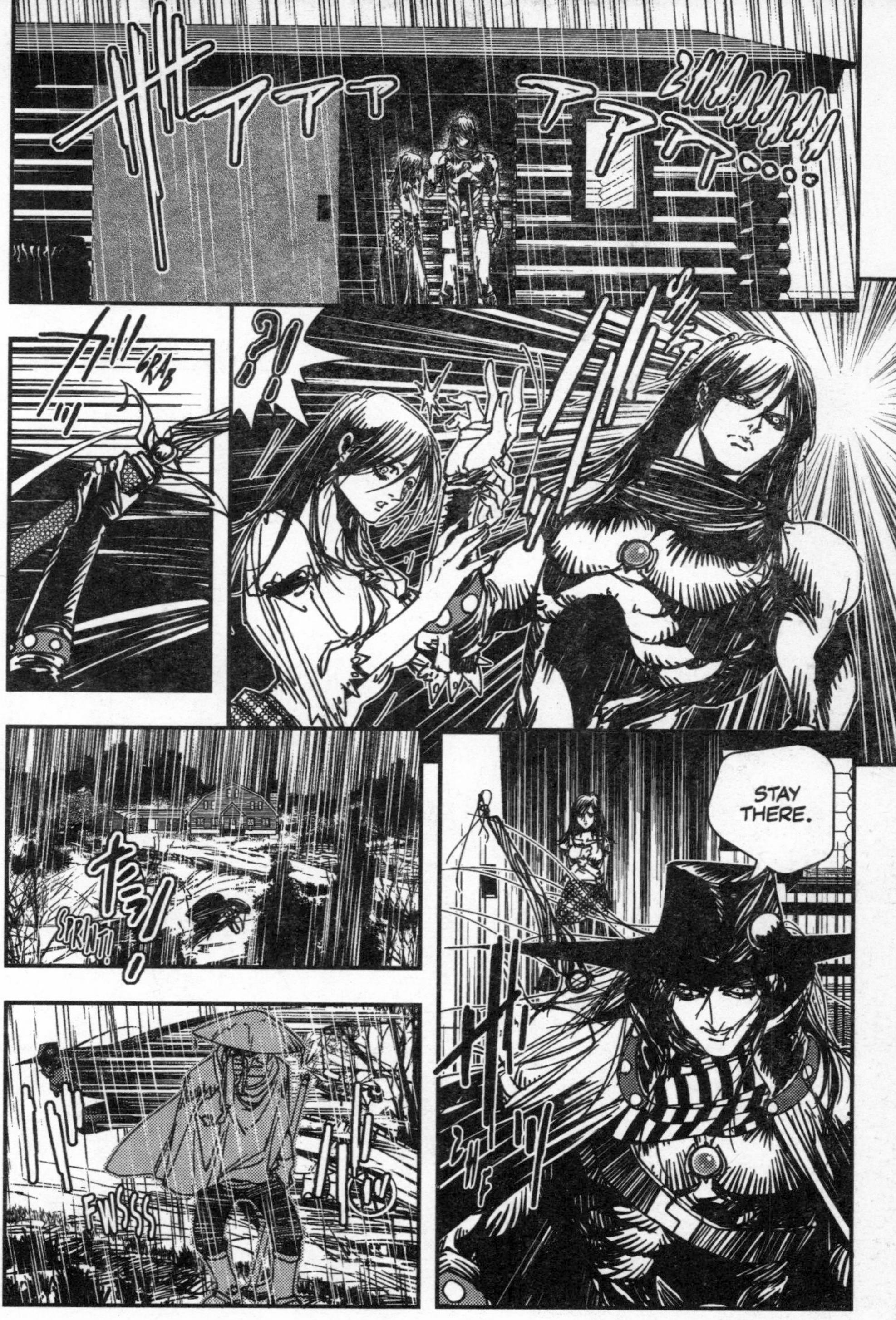

ハァァァ アァァ…
EHAAAAAA!!
?!
GRAB
STAY THERE.
SPRINT!
FWSSS

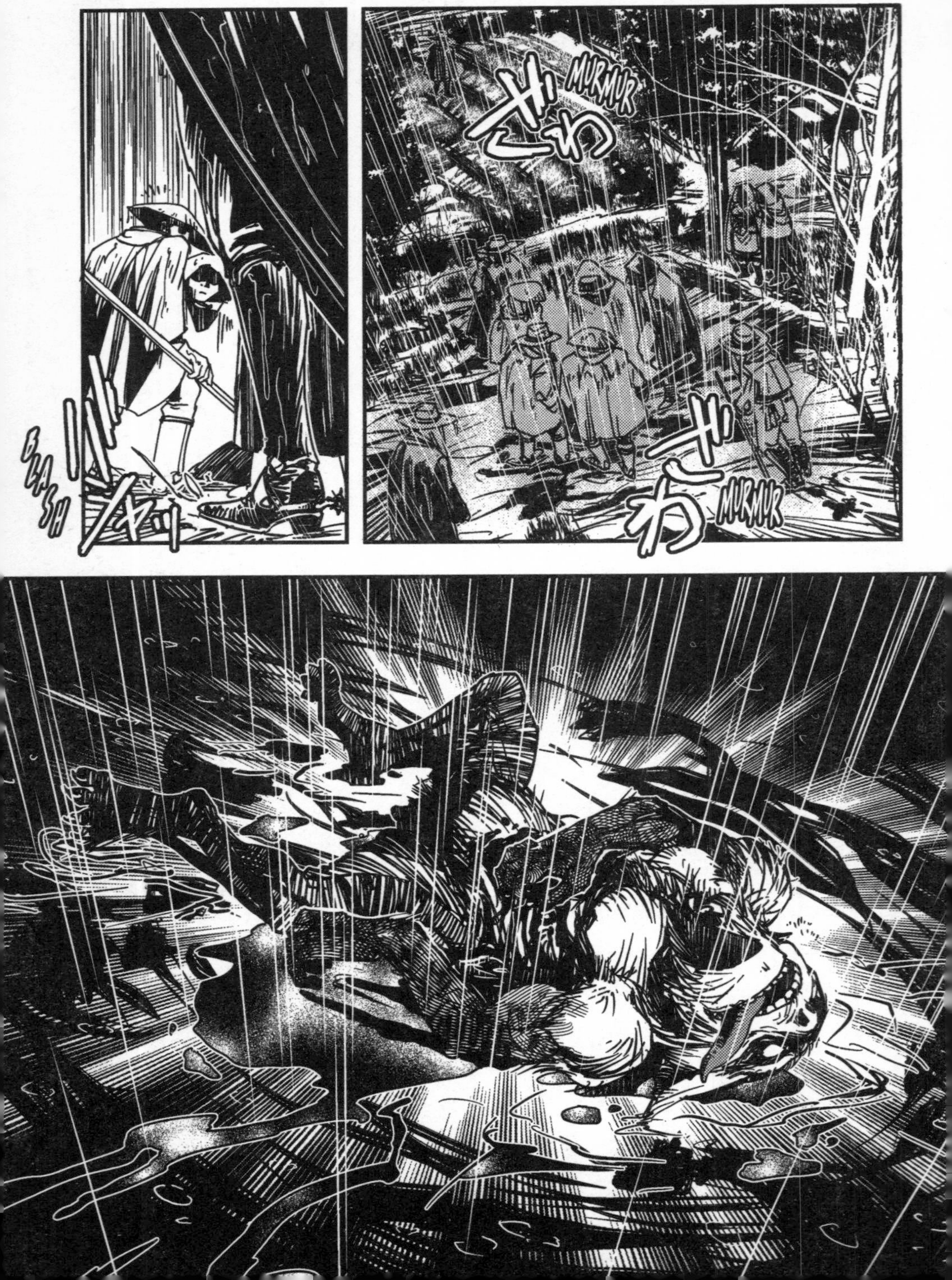
ざわ
MURMUR
ざわ
MURMUR
BLASH

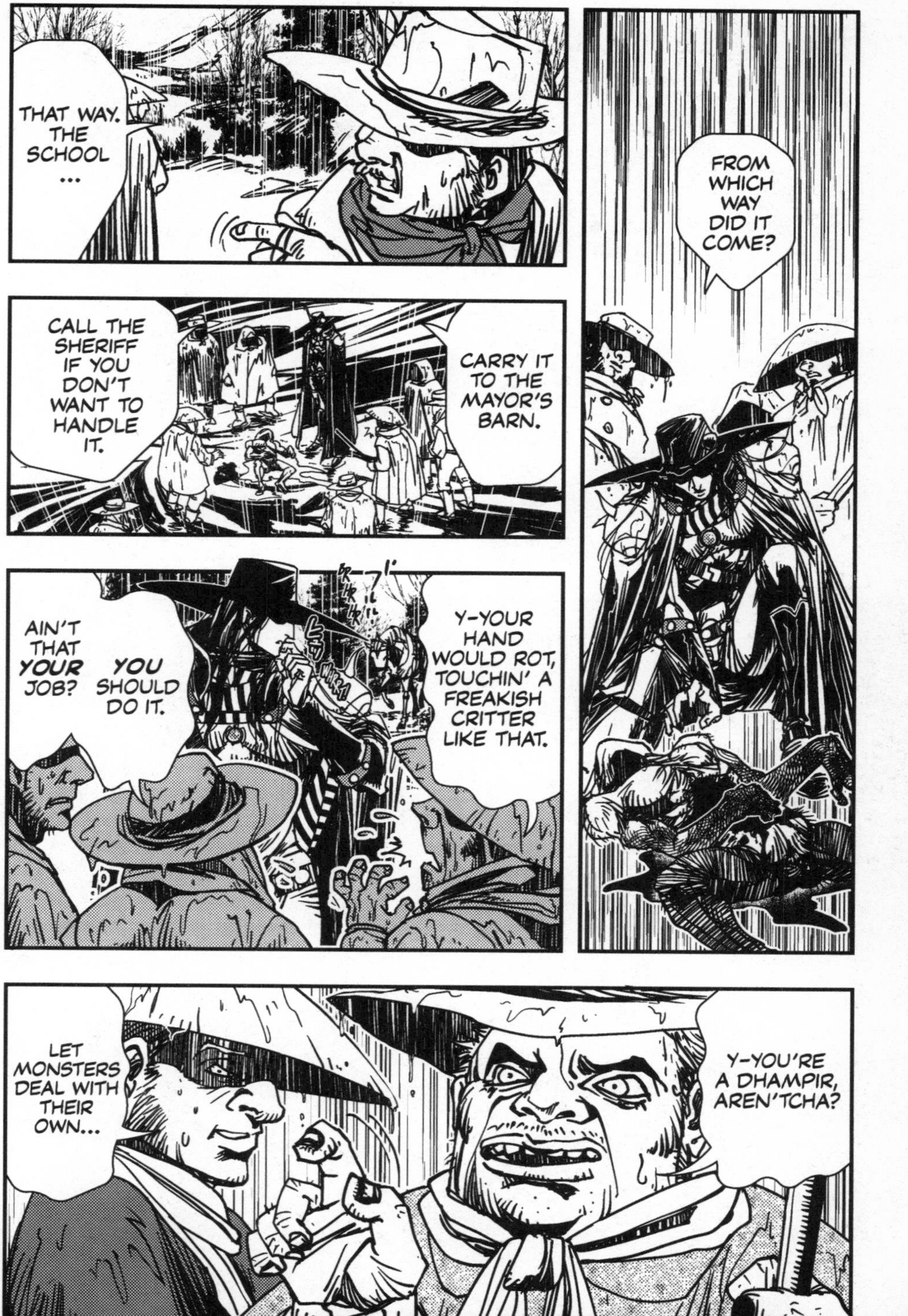
FROM WHICH WAY DID IT COME?
THAT WAY. THE SCHOOL ...
CARRY IT TO THE MAYOR'S BARN.
CALL THE SHERIFF IF YOU DON'T WANT TO HANDLE IT.
Y-YOUR HAND WOULD ROT, TOUCHIN' A FREAKISH CRITTER LIKE THAT.
YOU SHOULD DO IT.
AIN'T THAT *YOUR* JOB?
Y-YOU'RE A DHAMPIR, AREN'TCHA?
LET MONSTERS DEAL WITH THEIR OWN...

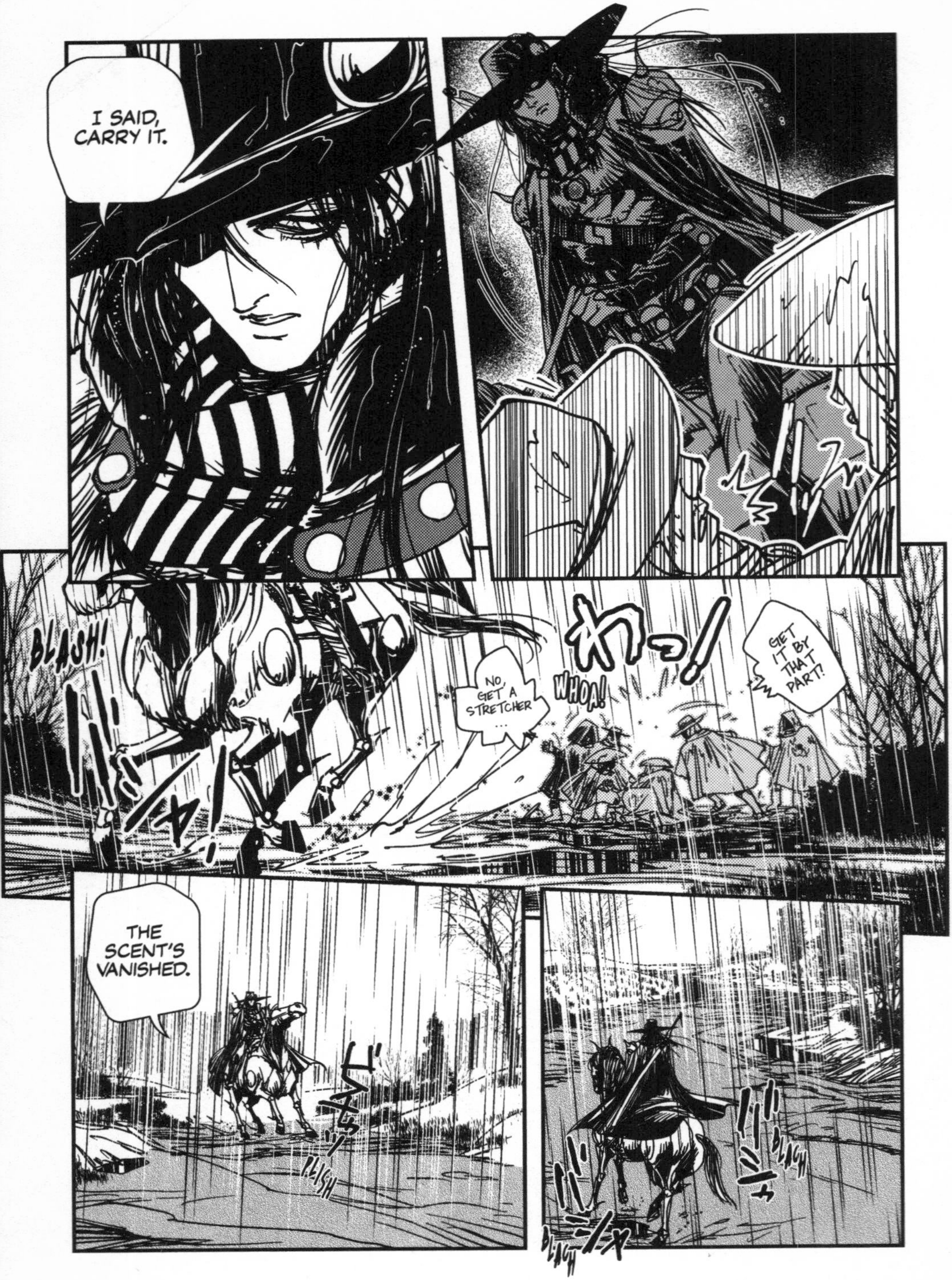
I SAID, CARRY IT.
GET IT BY THAT PART?
わっ!
WHOA!
NO, GET A STRETCHER …
BLASH!
BLACH
BLACH
THE SCENT'S VANISHED.
PLISH

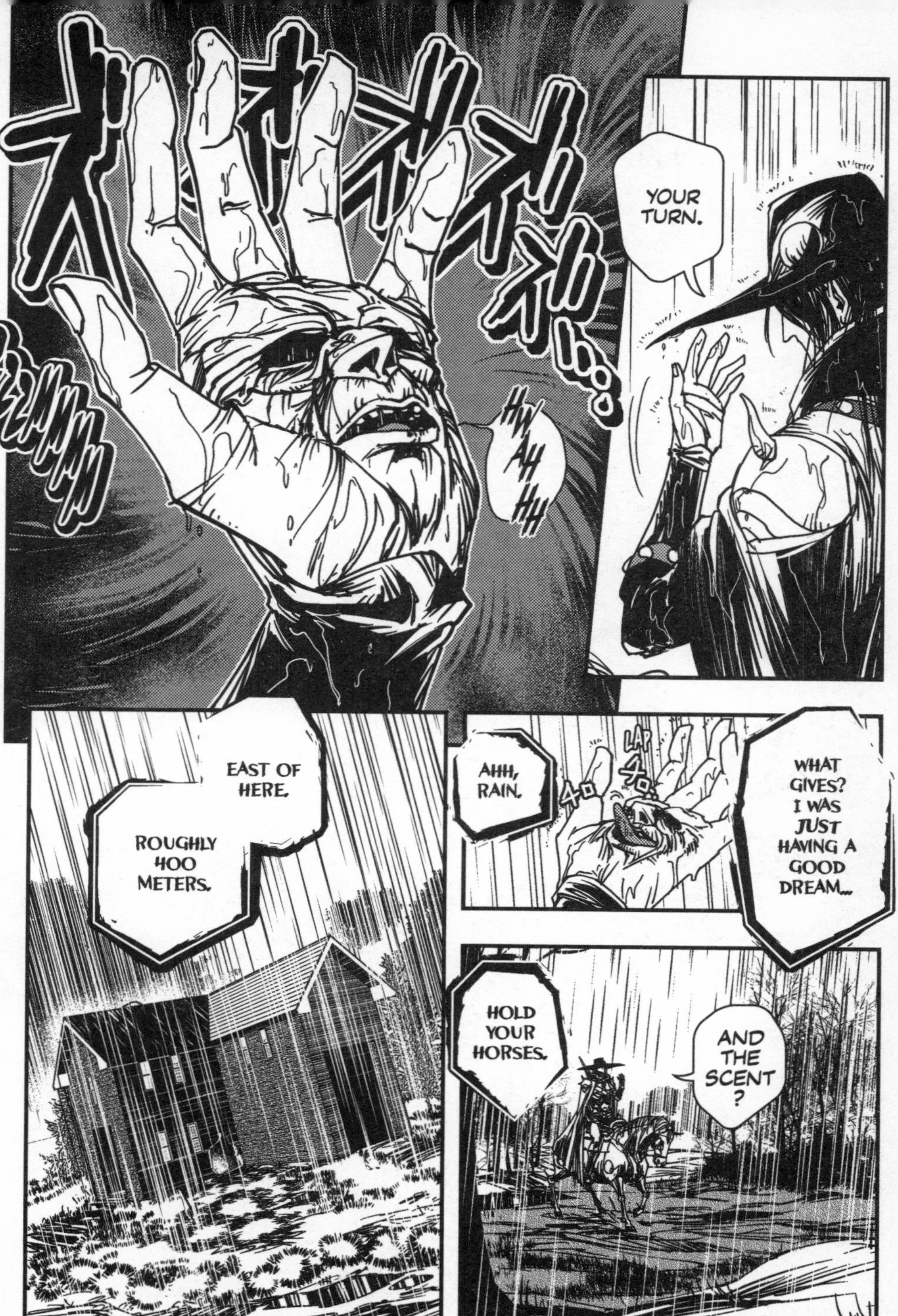
YOUR TURN.
HWAHHH
WHAT GIVES? I WAS JUST HAVING A GOOD DREAM...
LAP
AHH, RAIN.
AND THE SCENT?
HOLD YOUR HORSES.
EAST OF HERE.
ROUGHLY 400 METERS.

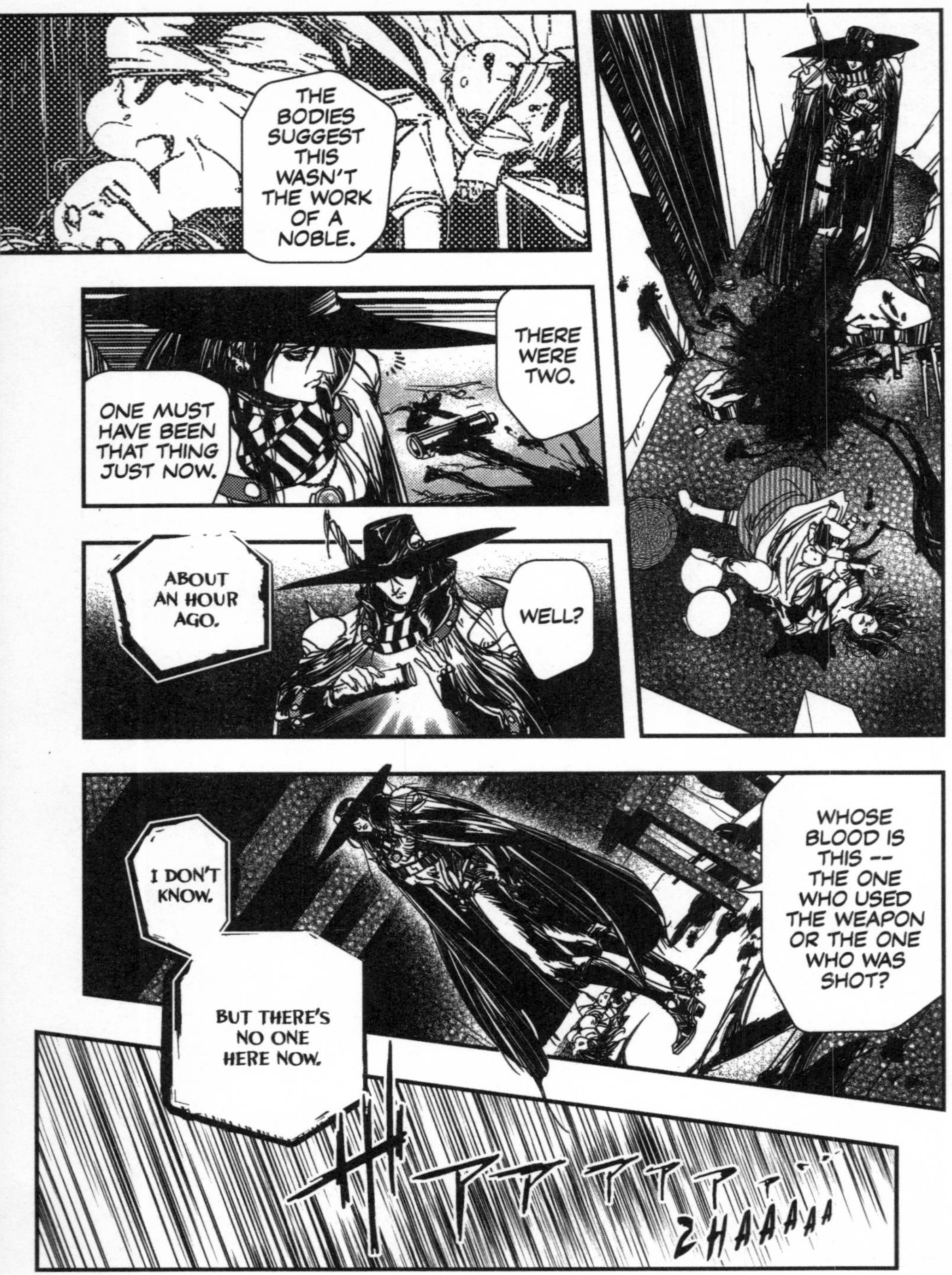
THE BODIES SUGGEST THIS WASN'T THE WORK OF A NOBLE.
THERE WERE TWO.
ONE MUST HAVE BEEN THAT THING JUST NOW.
WELL?
ABOUT AN HOUR AGO.
WHOSE BLOOD IS THIS -- THE ONE WHO USED THE WEAPON OR THE ONE WHO WAS SHOT?
I DON'T KNOW.
BUT THERE'S NO ONE HERE NOW.
ZHAAAAA

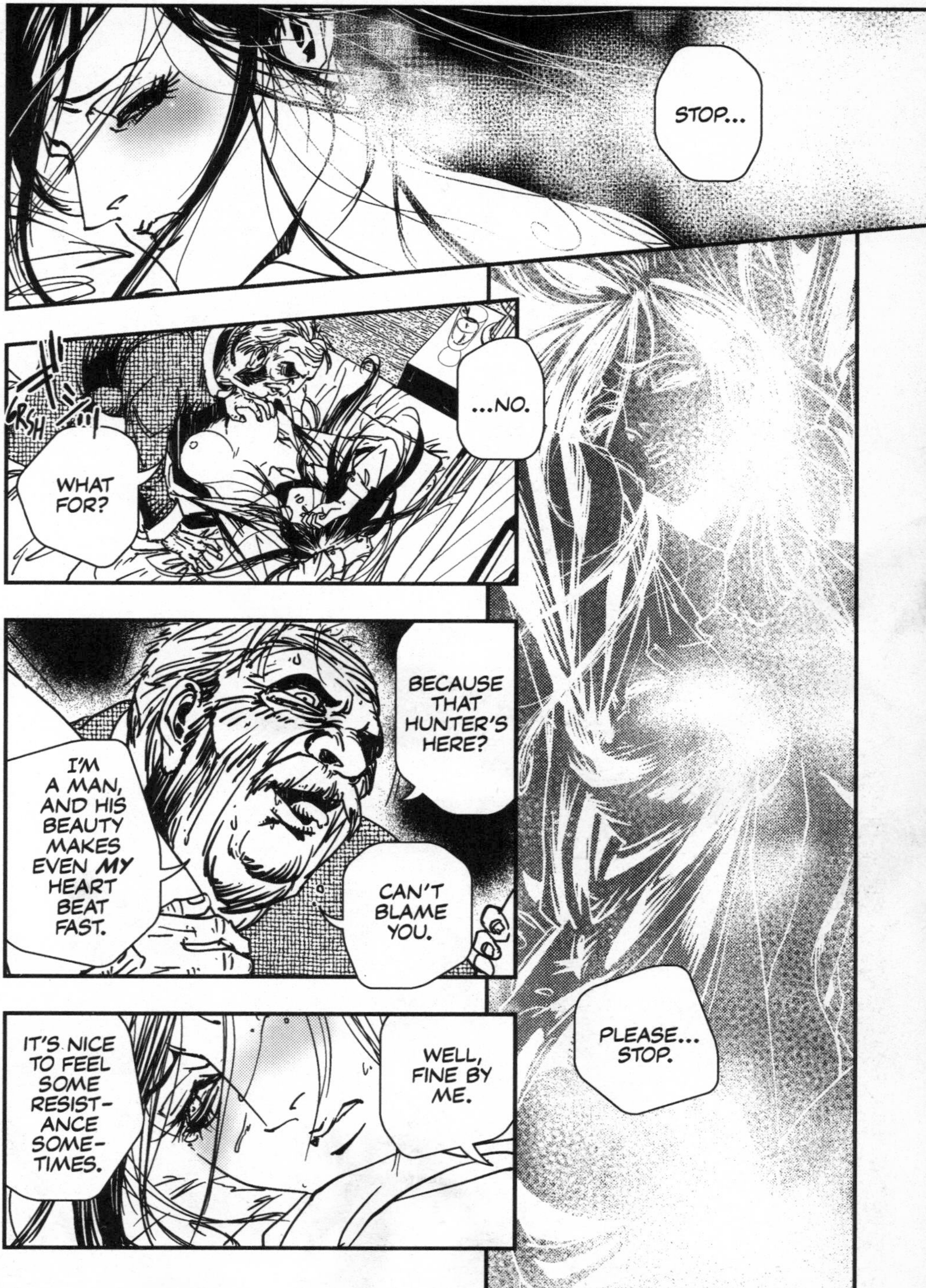
STOP...
PLEASE... STOP.
...NO.
GRSH
WHAT FOR?
BECAUSE THAT HUNTER'S HERE?
CAN'T BLAME YOU.
I'M A MAN, AND HIS BEAUTY MAKES EVEN MY HEART BEAT FAST.
WELL, FINE BY ME.
IT'S NICE TO FEEL SOME RESISTANCE SOMETIMES.

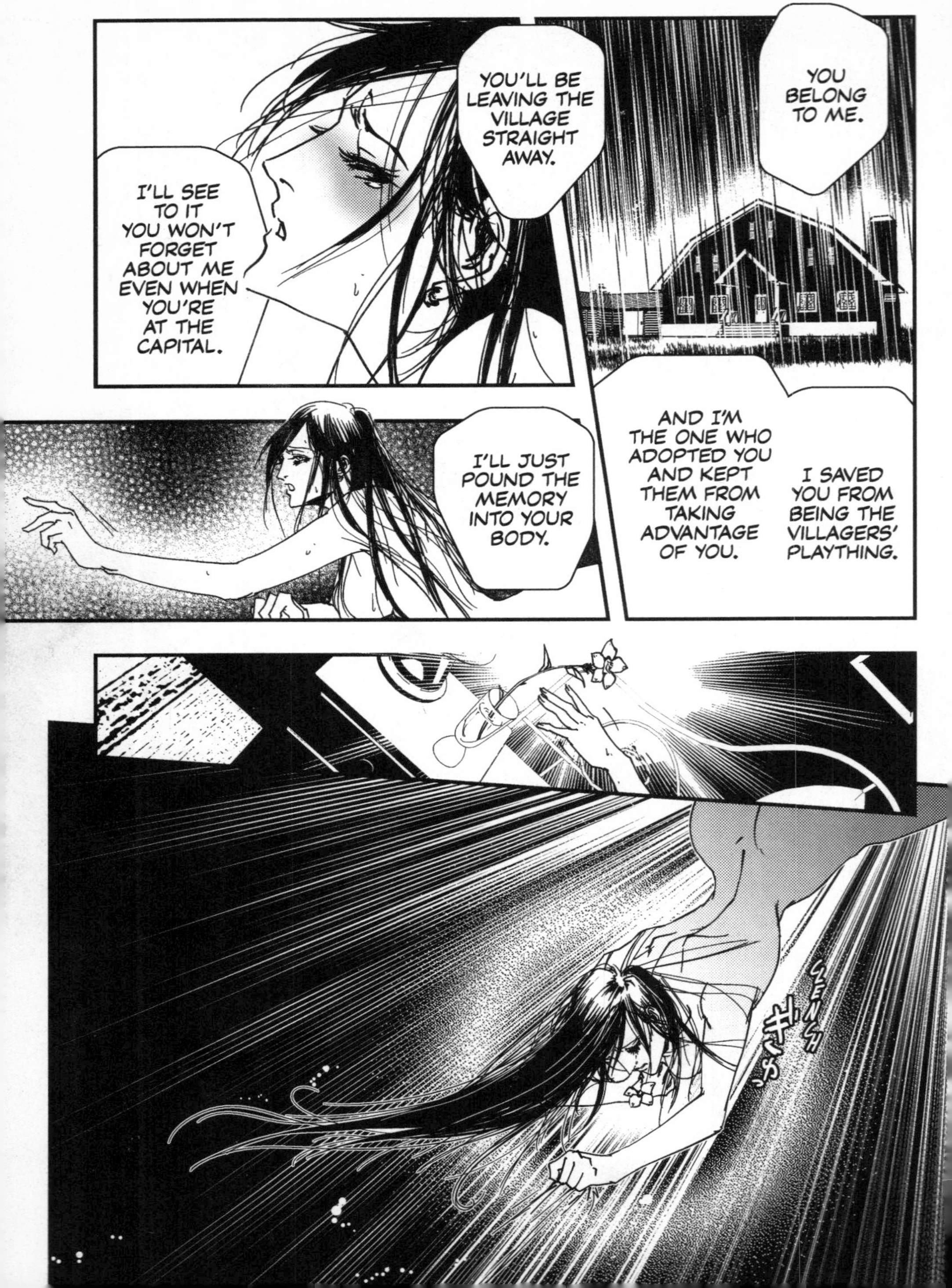
YOU BELONG TO ME.
YOU'LL BE LEAVING THE VILLAGE STRAIGHT AWAY.
I'LL SEE TO IT YOU WON'T FORGET ABOUT ME EVEN WHEN YOU'RE AT THE CAPITAL.
I SAVED YOU FROM BEING THE VILLAGERS' PLAYTHING.
AND I'M THE ONE WHO ADOPTED YOU AND KEPT THEM FROM TAKING ADVANTAGE OF YOU.
I'LL JUST POUND THE MEMORY INTO YOUR BODY.
CLENCH
ギュッ

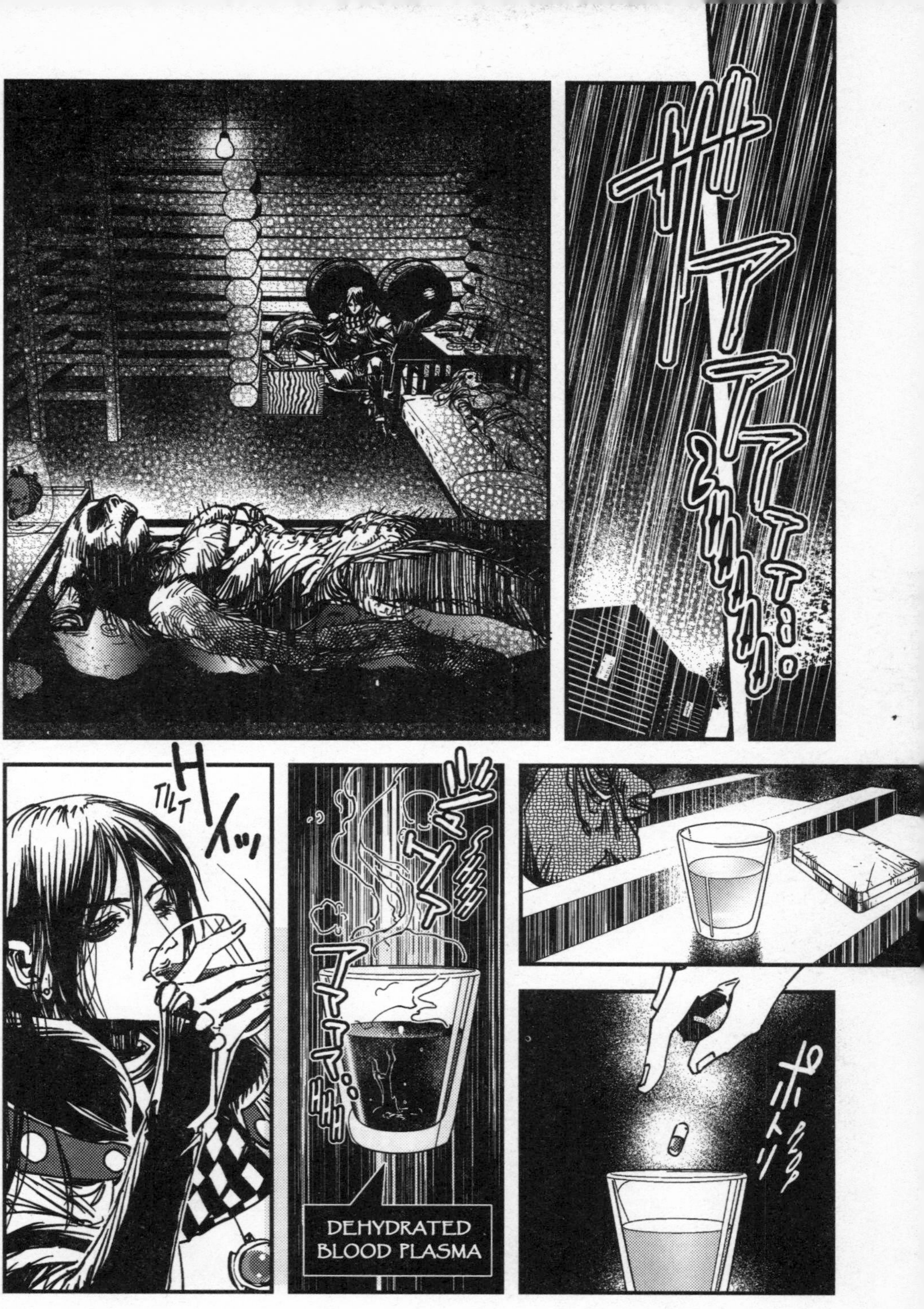
ハァァァ…
ポトリ
plop
ジュワァァァ…
DEHYDRATED BLOOD PLASMA
クイッ
TILT

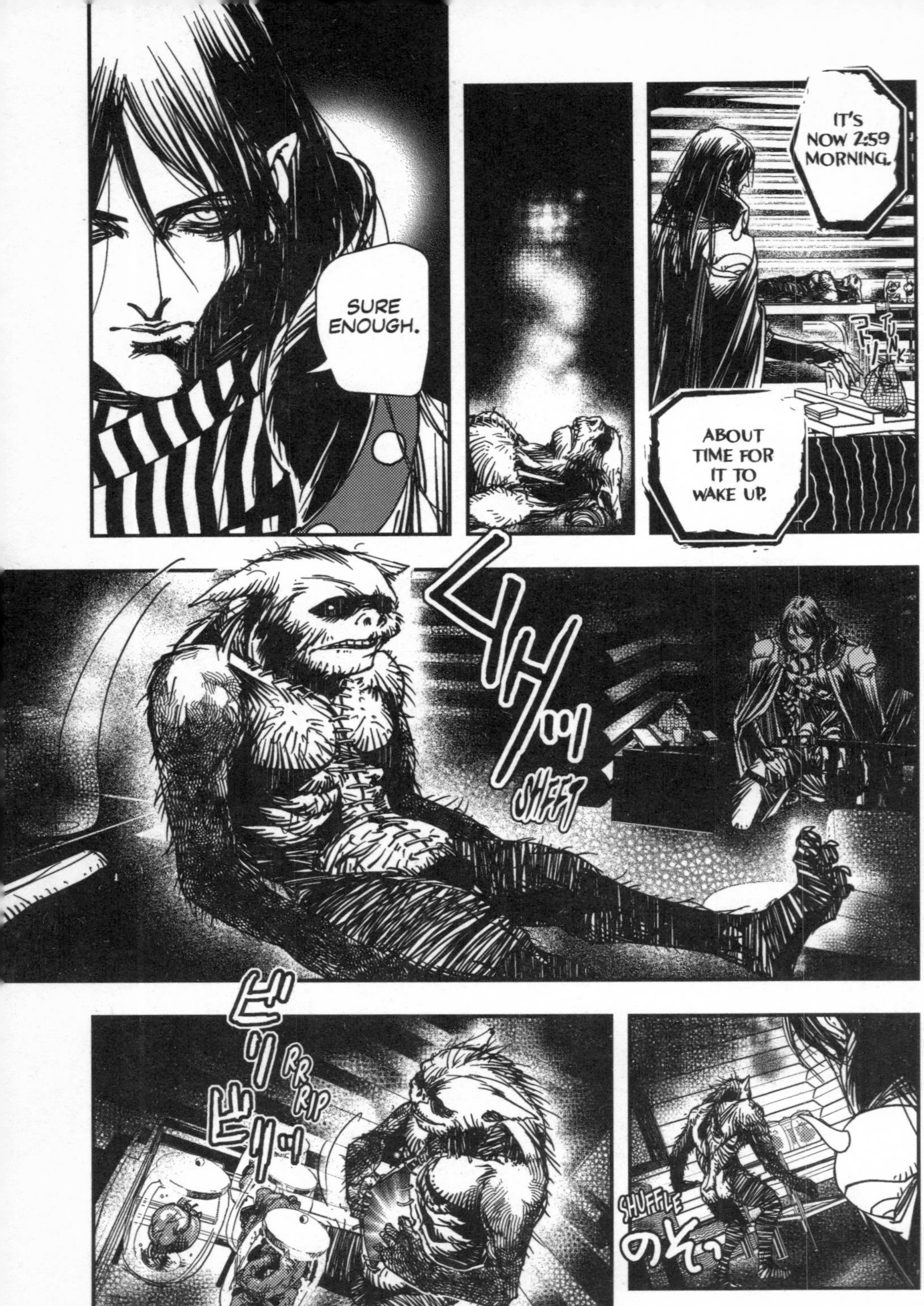
IT'S NOW 2:59 MORNING.
TUNK
ABOUT TIME FOR IT TO WAKE UP.
SURE ENOUGH.
SHIFT
RRRIP
SHUFFLE
のそっ

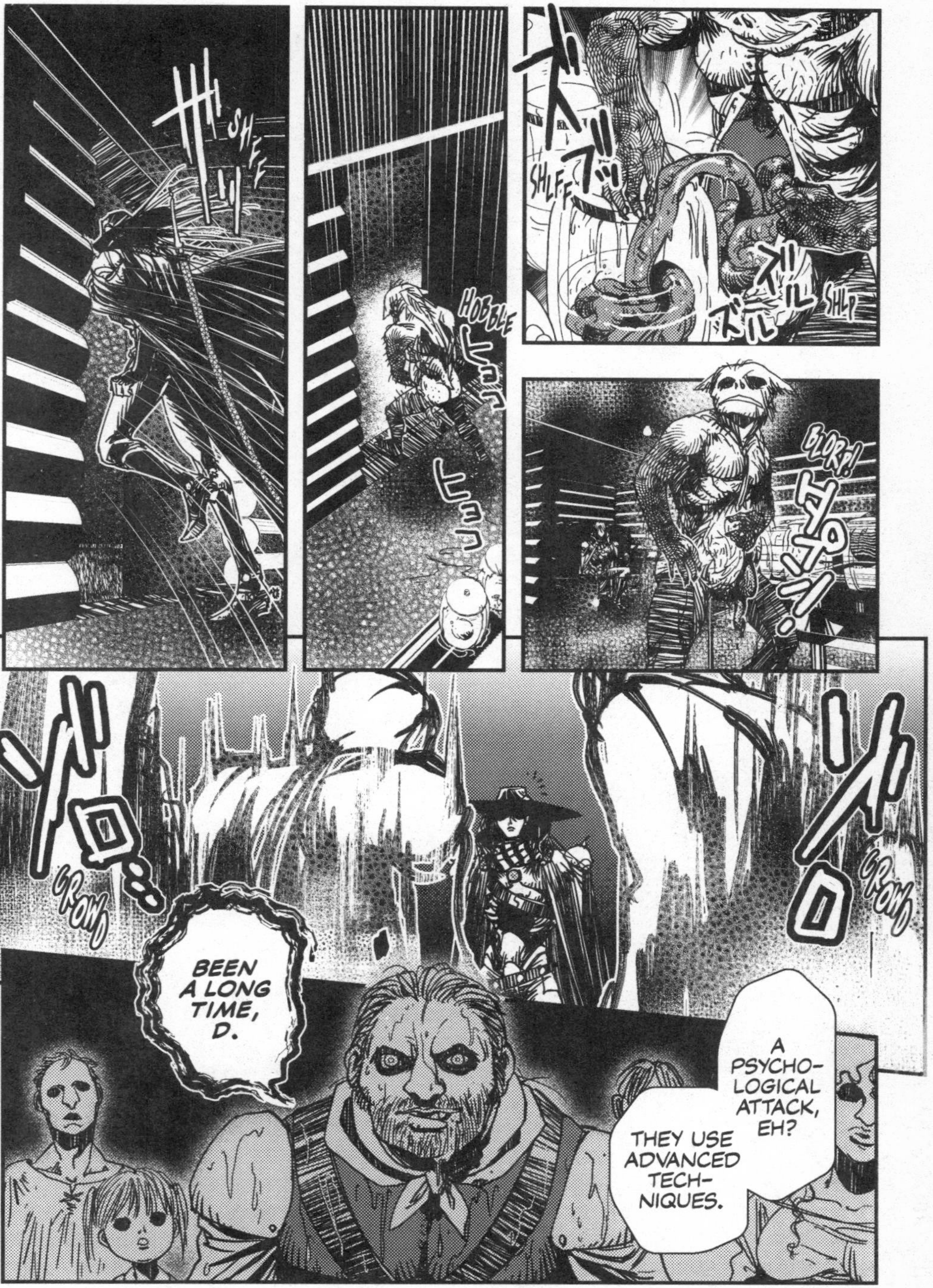

SHLFFF
SHLP
HOBBLE
ヒョコ
ヒョコ
SHFFF
BLORP!
GROWD
GROWD
BEEN A LONG TIME, D.
A PSYCHO-LOGICAL ATTACK, EH?
THEY USE ADVANCED TECH-NIQUES.

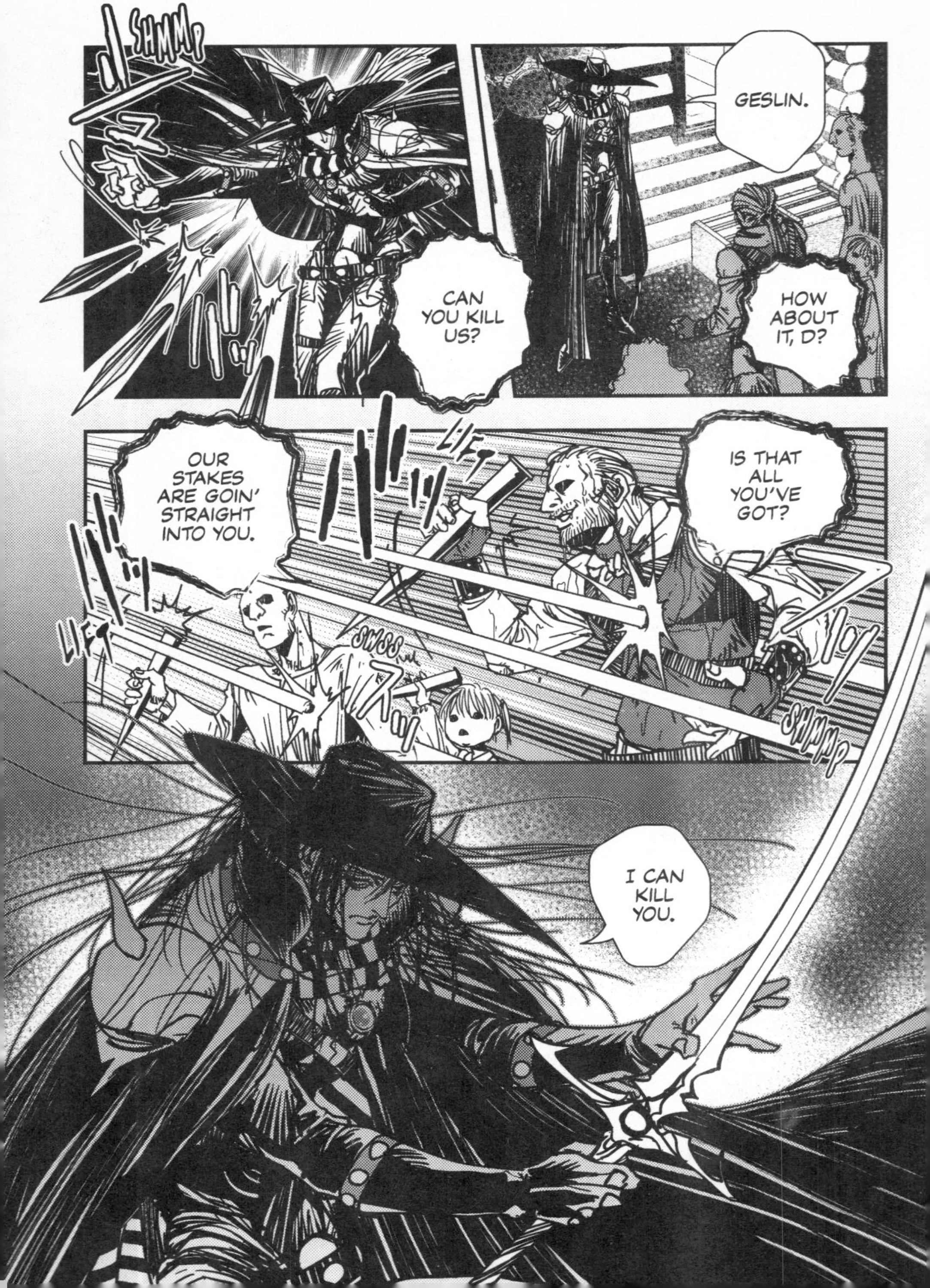
GESLIN.
HOW ABOUT IT, D?
SHMMP
CAN YOU KILL US?
IS THAT ALL YOU'VE GOT?
LIFT
OUR STAKES ARE GOIN' STRAIGHT INTO YOU.
LIFT
SWSS
SHMMP
I CAN KILL YOU.

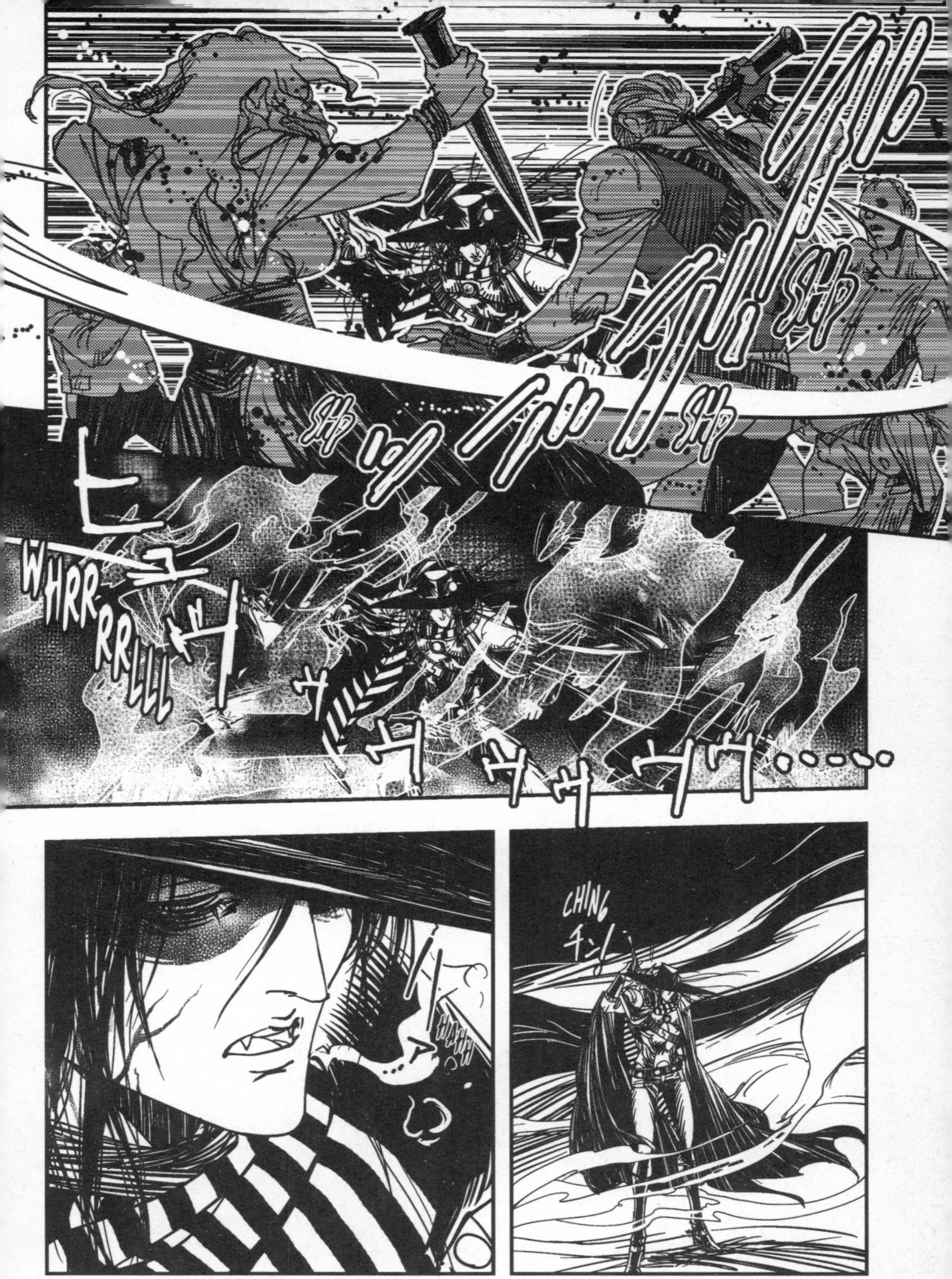
SHP
SHP
SHP
SHP
WHRRRRLLL
CHING
チン!

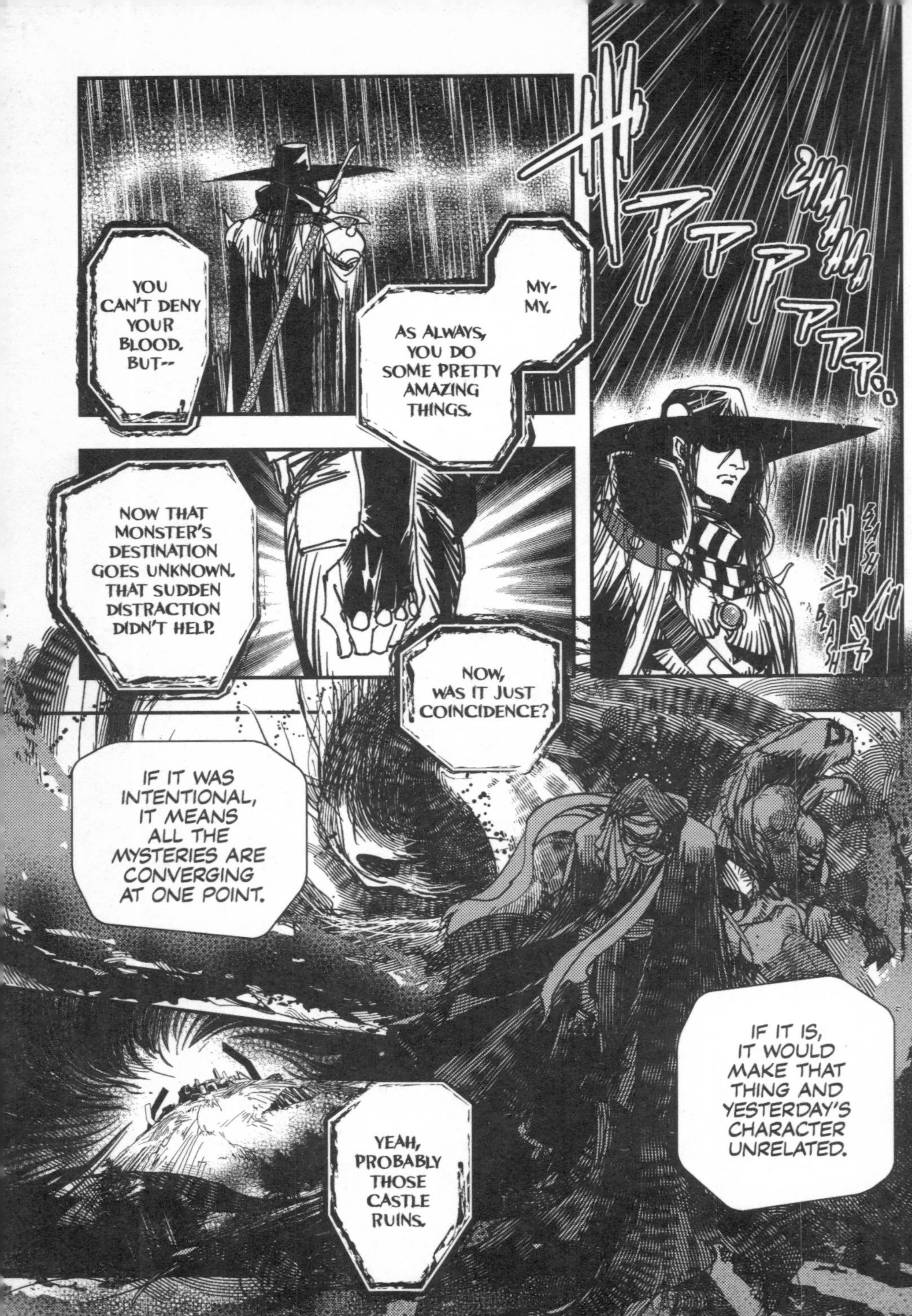
MY-MY.
AS ALWAYS, YOU DO SOME PRETTY AMAZING THINGS.
YOU CAN'T DENY YOUR BLOOD. BUT--
NOW THAT MONSTER'S DESTINATION GOES UNKNOWN. THAT SUDDEN DISTRACTION DIDN'T HELP.
NOW, WAS IT JUST COINCIDENCE?
IF IT IS, IT WOULD MAKE THAT THING AND YESTERDAY'S CHARACTER UNRELATED.
IF IT WAS INTENTIONAL, IT MEANS ALL THE MYSTERIES ARE CONVERGING AT ONE POINT.
YEAH, PROBABLY THOSE CASTLE RUINS.

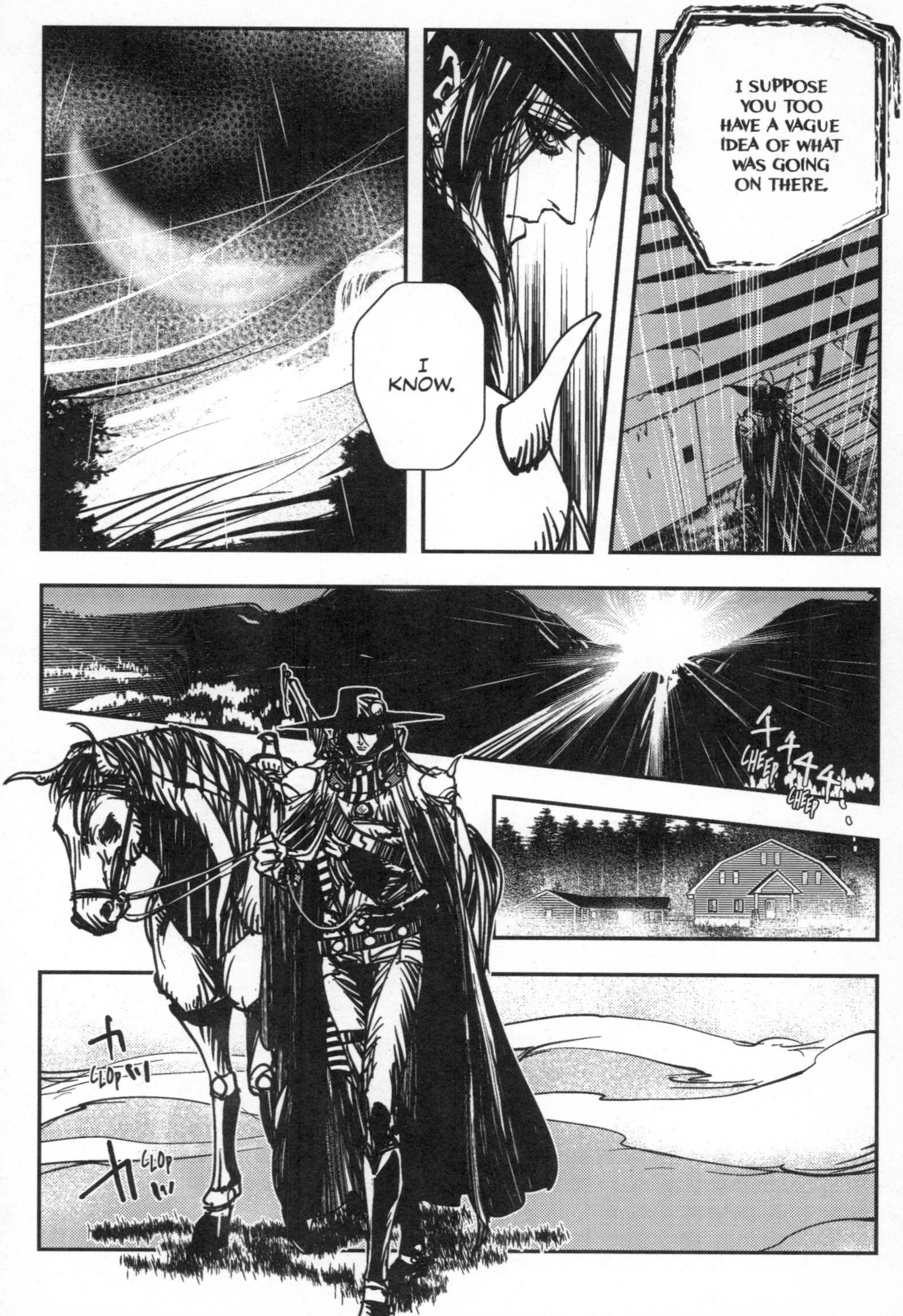
I SUPPOSE YOU TOO HAVE A VAGUE IDEA OF WHAT WAS GOING ON THERE.
I KNOW.
CHEEP
CHEEP
CLOP
CLOP

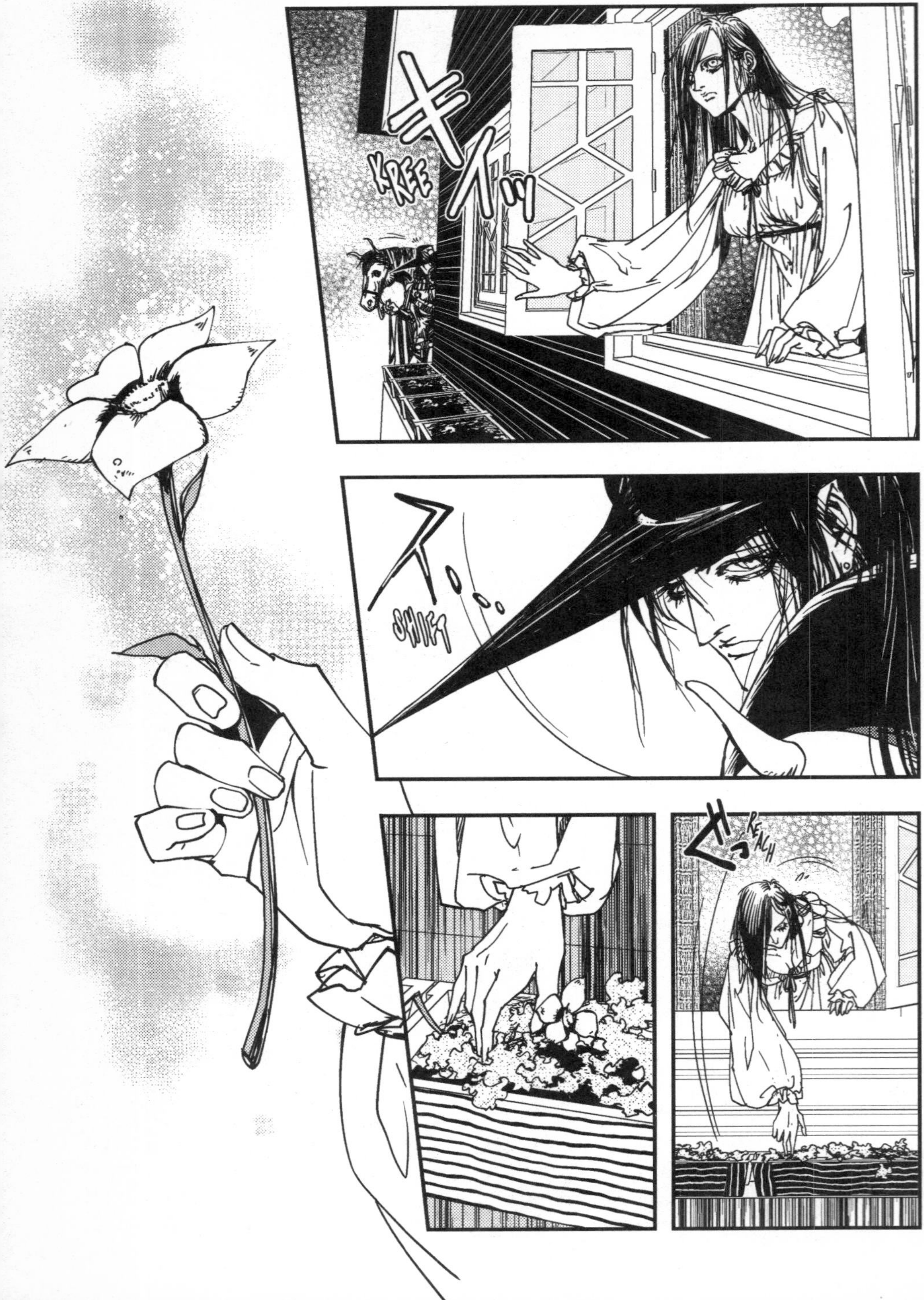
キイィッ
KREE
ス…
SHIFT
ぐっ
REACH

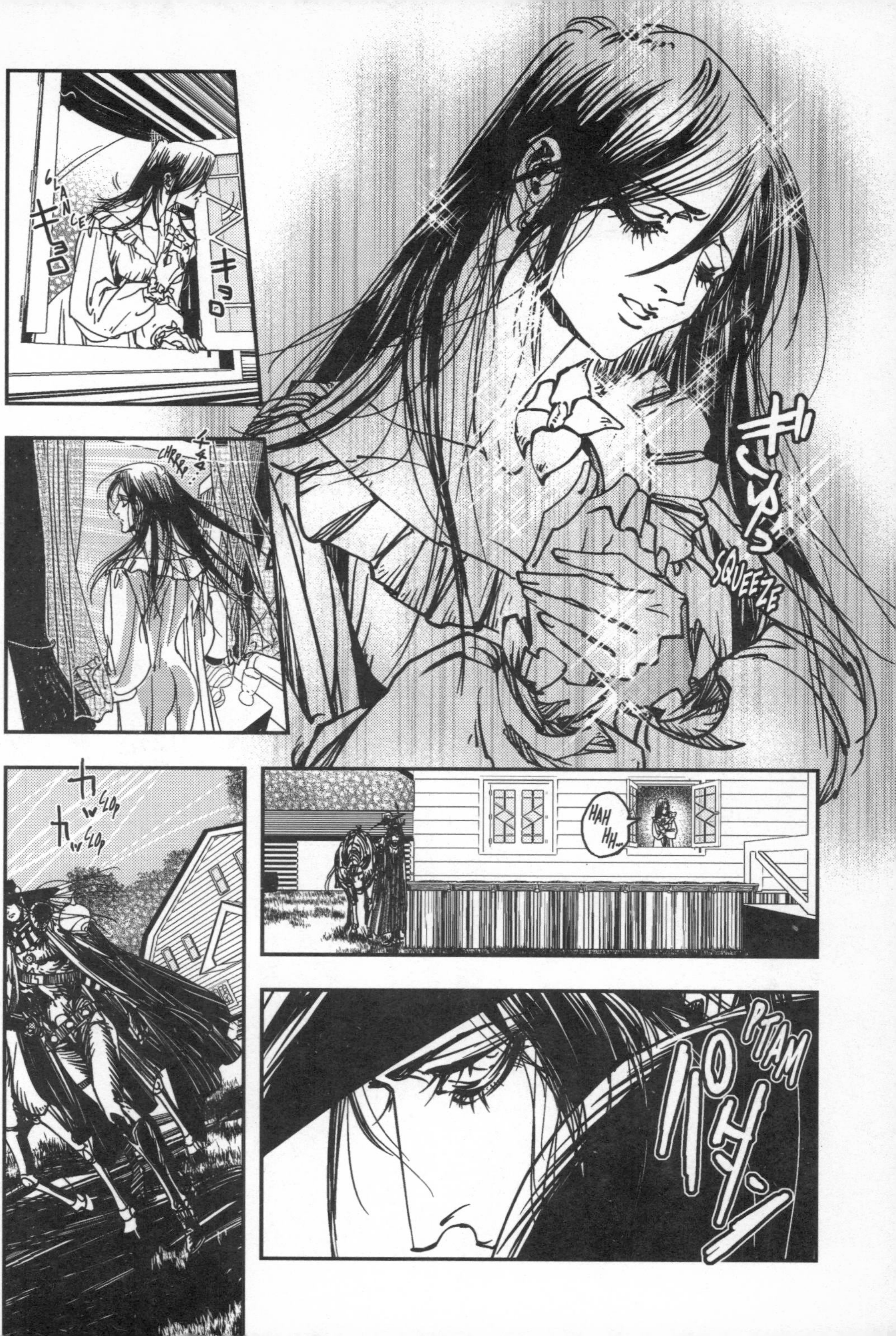
ぎゅう
SQUEEZE
キョロ
キョロ
GLANCE
CHRRRR
HAH HH...
パタ-ン
PTAM
カッ
CLOP
カッ
CLOP

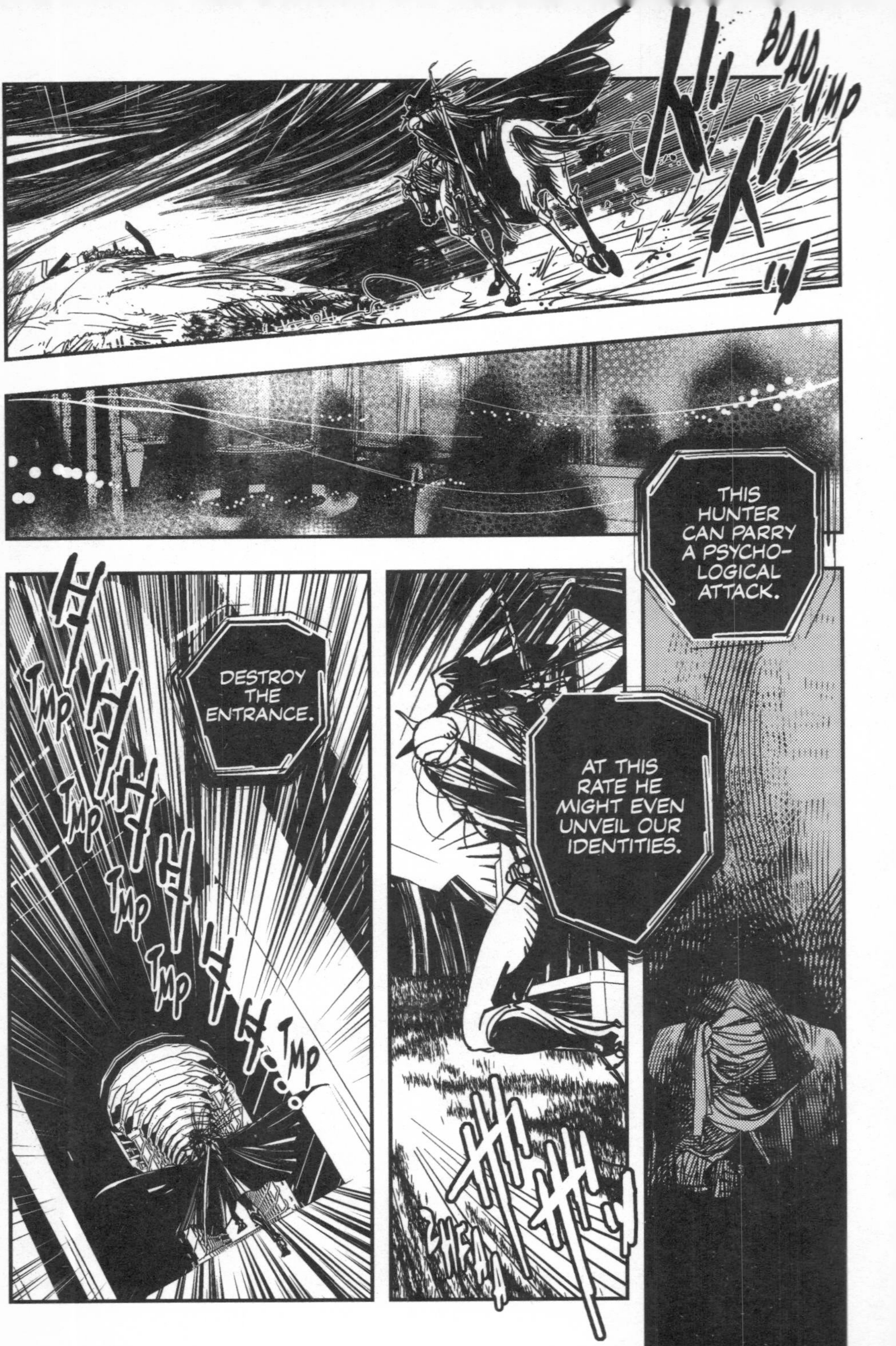
BOADUMP
THIS HUNTER CAN PARRY A PSYCHO-LOGICAL ATTACK.
AT THIS RATE HE MIGHT EVEN UNVEIL OUR IDENTITIES.
DESTROY THE ENTRANCE.
TMP TMP TMP TMP TMP TMP

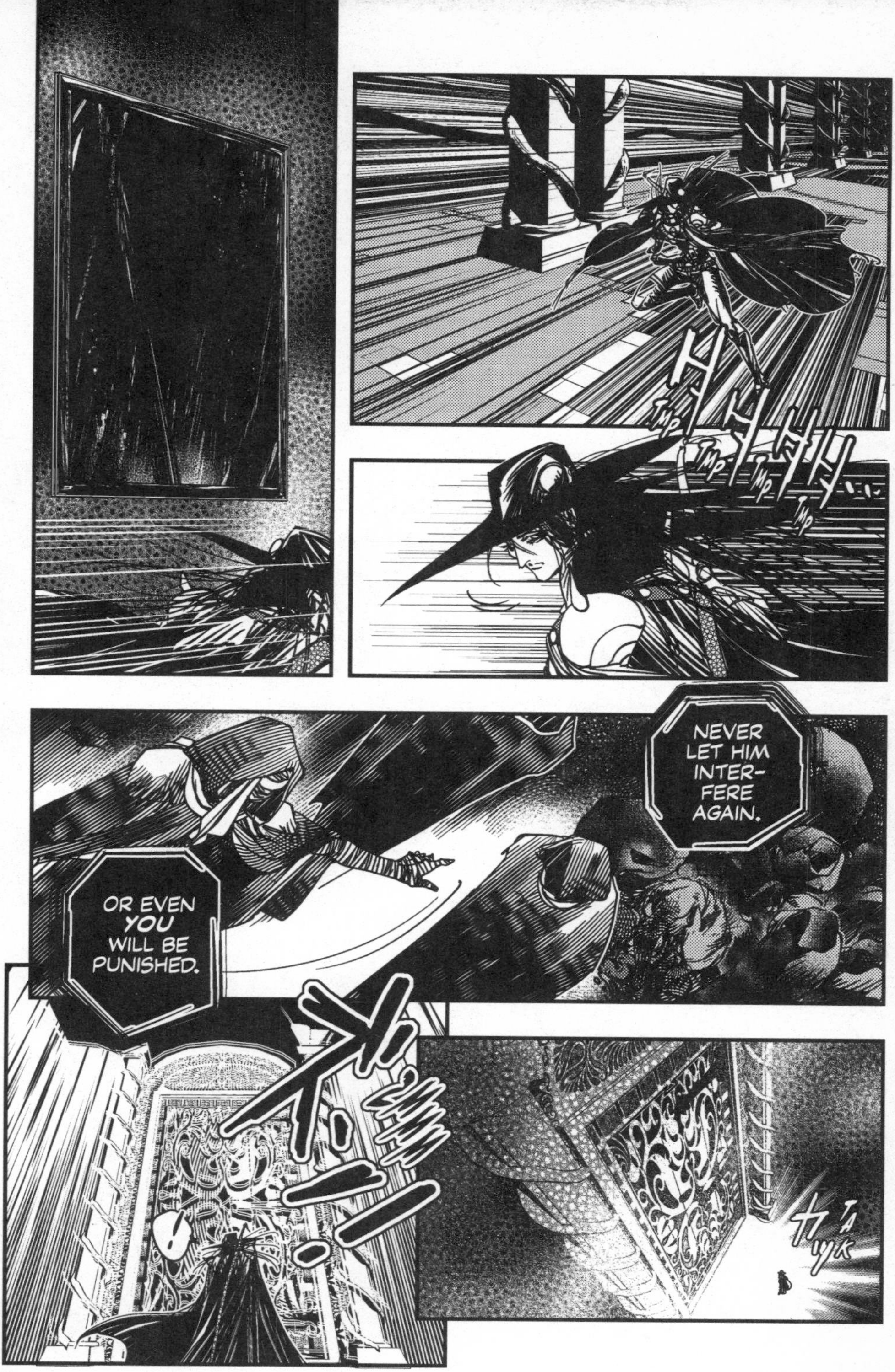
TMP TMP TMP TMP
NEVER LET HIM INTER-FERE AGAIN.
OR EVEN *YOU* WILL BE PUNISHED.

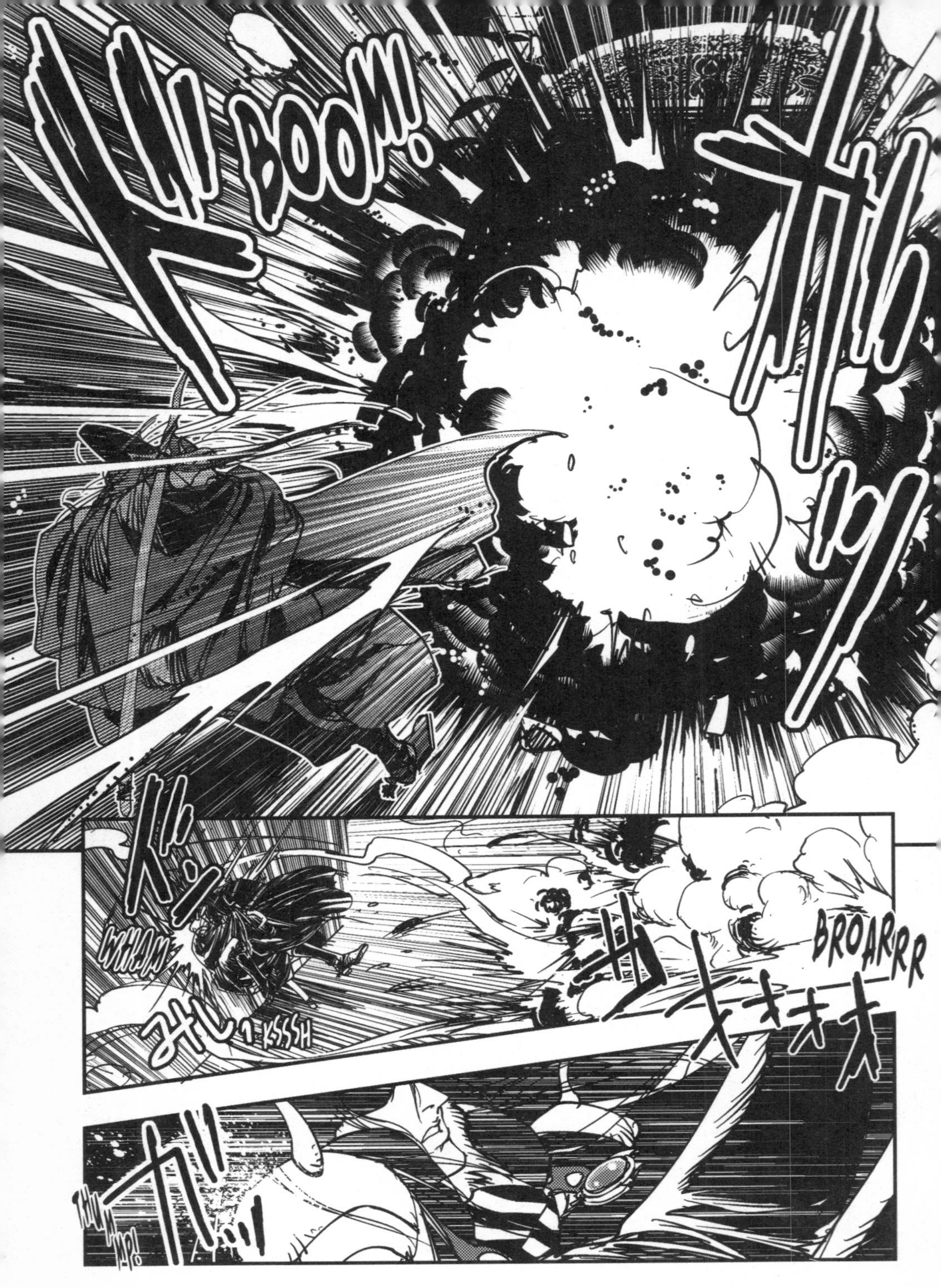
BOOM!
BROARRR
WHAM
みしっ
KSSSH
THUMMMP!

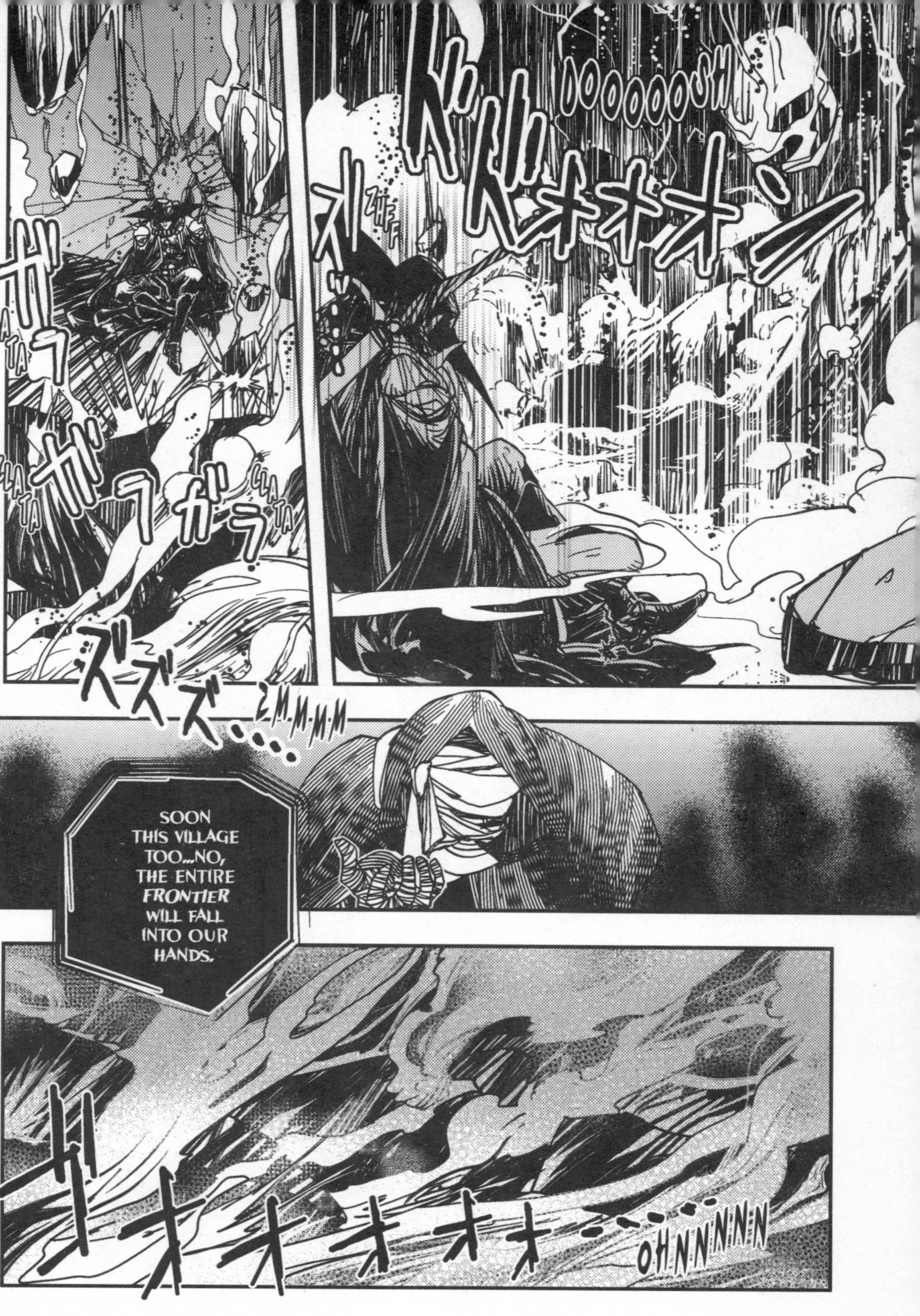

DOOOOOOSH
ZHFF
CLATA
CLATA
CLATA
ZMMMMM
SOON THIS VILLAGE TOO...NO, THE ENTIRE *FRONTIER* WILL FALL INTO OUR HANDS.
OHNNNNN

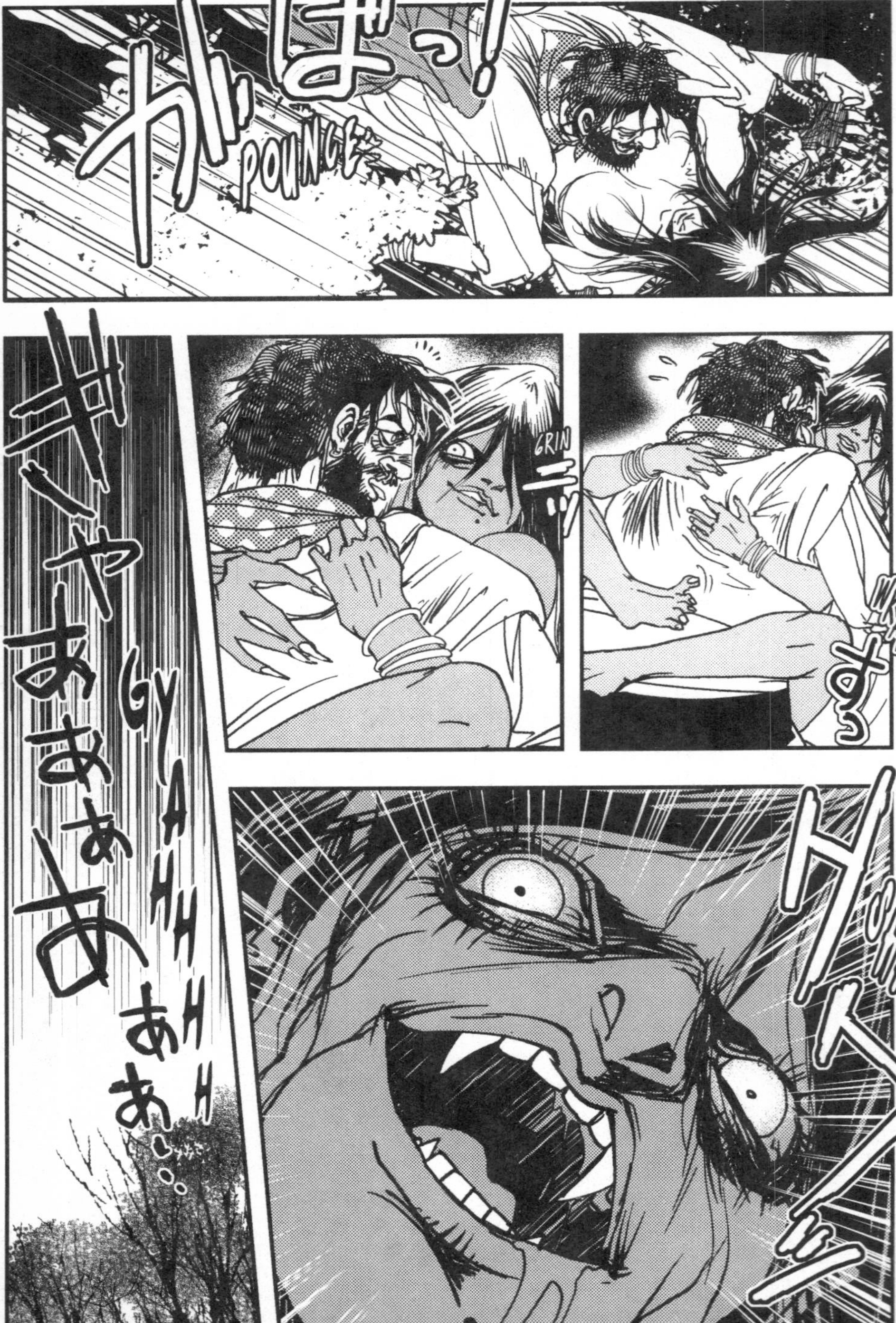
がばっ!
POUNCE
すっ
WRAP
GRIN
ぎゃあぁぁあぁあぁ…
GYAAHHHHHH

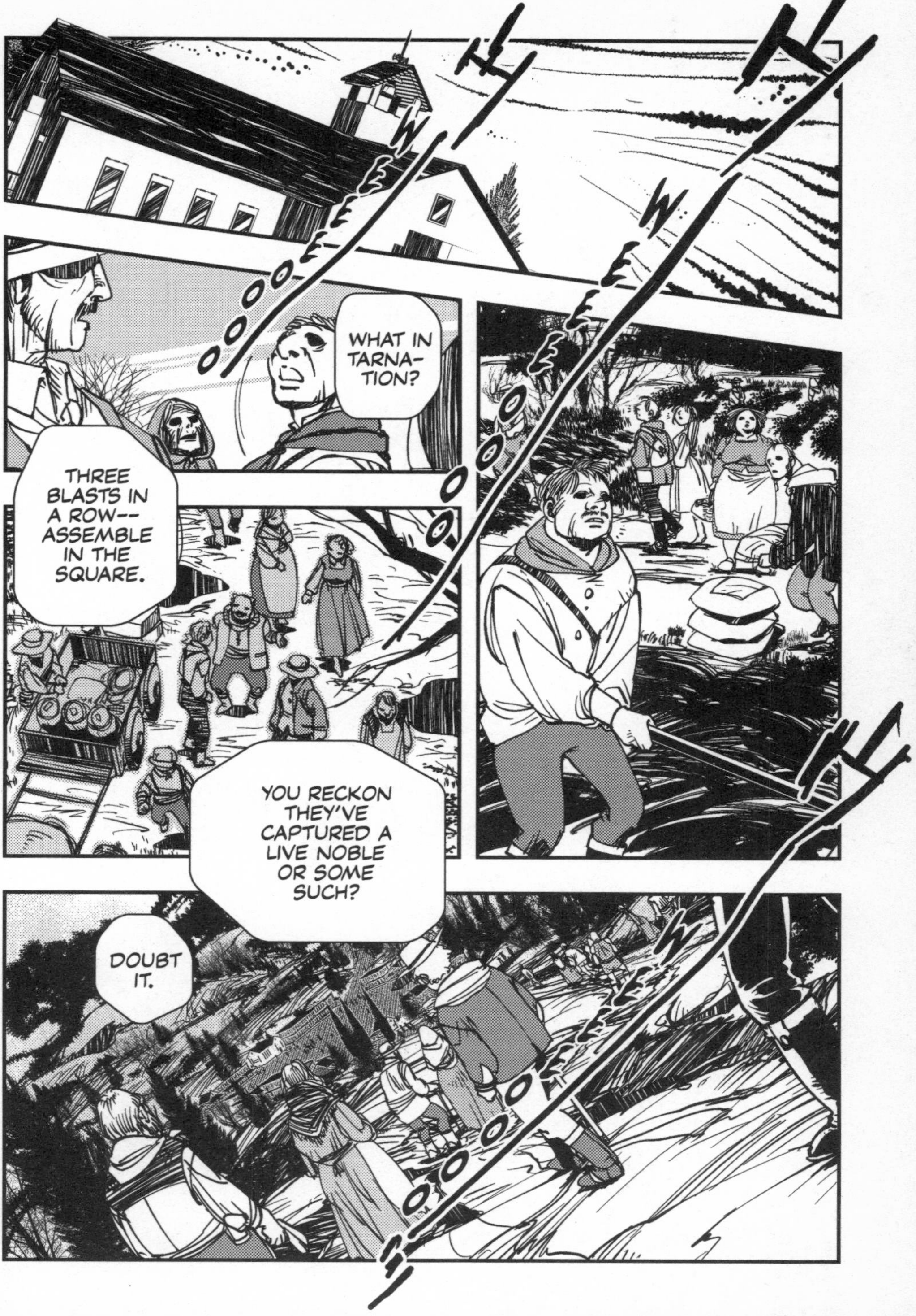
HWEEEEOOOOO
HWEEEOOOOOO
WHAT IN TARNATION?
THREE BLASTS IN A ROW--ASSEMBLE IN THE SQUARE.
YOU RECKON THEY'VE CAPTURED A LIVE NOBLE OR SOME SUCH?
HWEEEEOOOOOO
DOUBT IT.

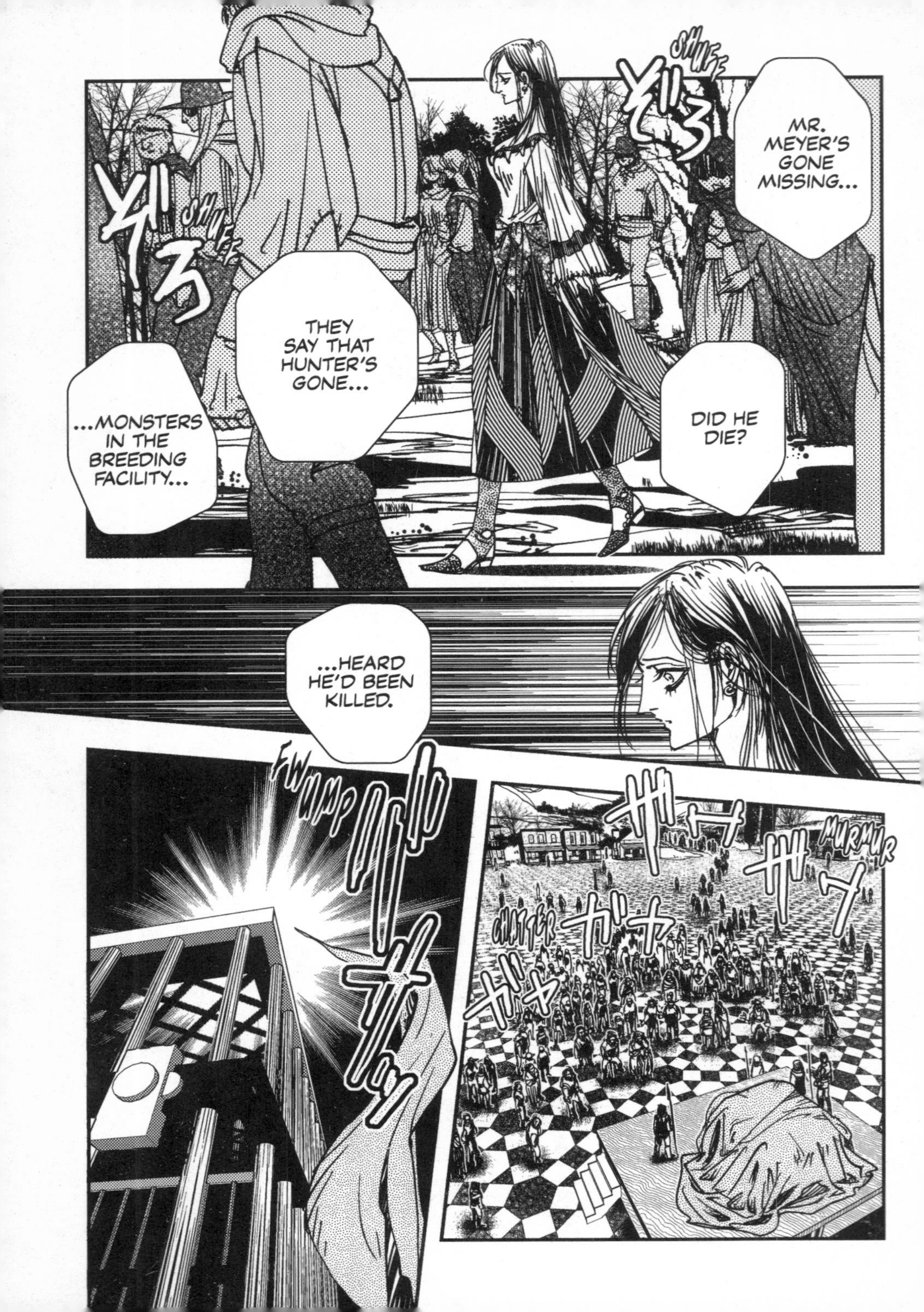
SHUFF
MR. MEYER'S GONE MISSING...
DID HE DIE?
THEY SAY THAT HUNTER'S GONE...
SHUFF
...MONSTERS IN THE BREEDING FACILITY...
...HEARD HE'D BEEN KILLED.
MURMUR
CHITTER
FWUMP

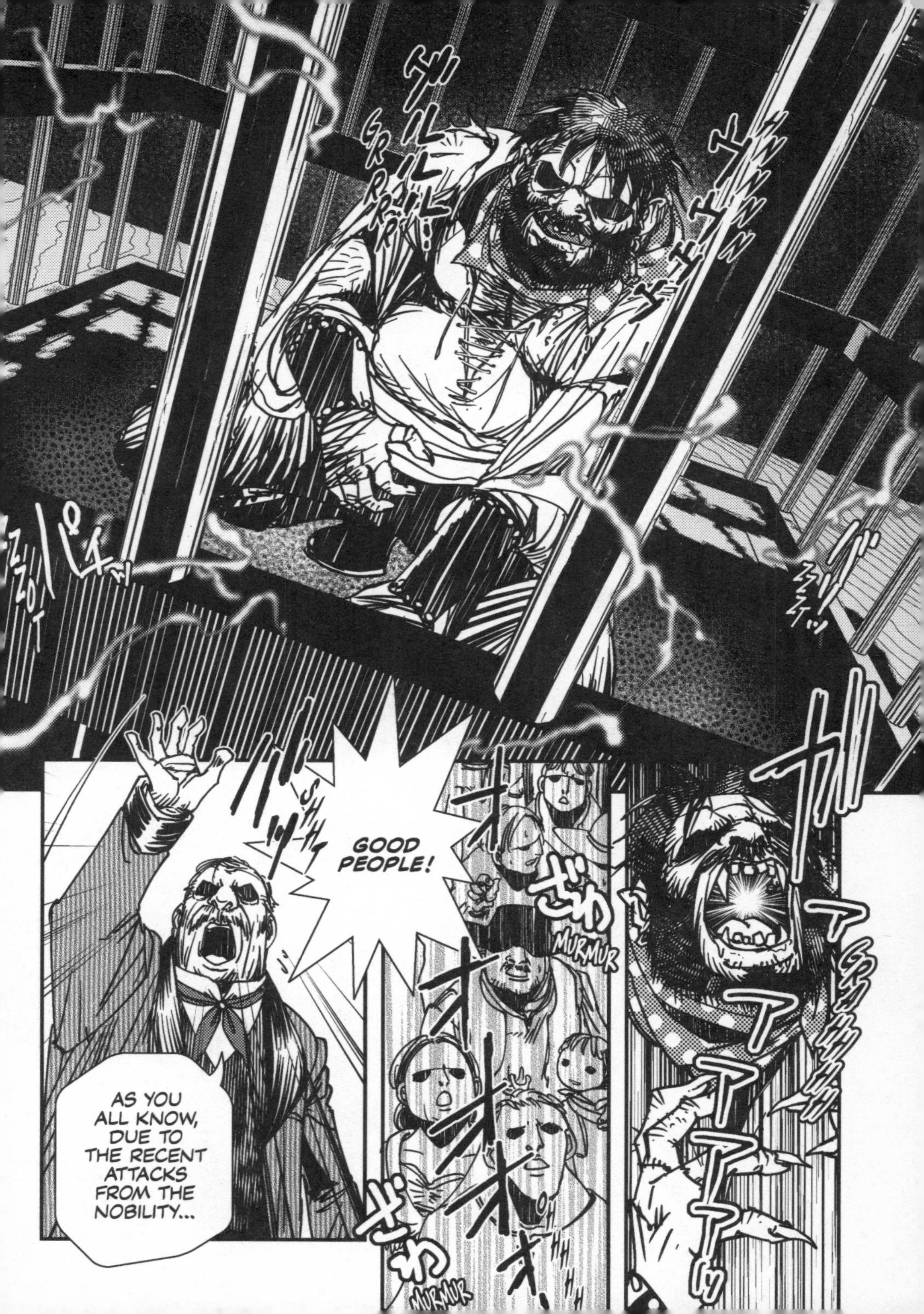
GRRRR!
ZZZOT
MURMUR
MURMUR
GOOD PEOPLE!
AS YOU ALL KNOW, DUE TO THE RECENT ATTACKS FROM THE NOBILITY...

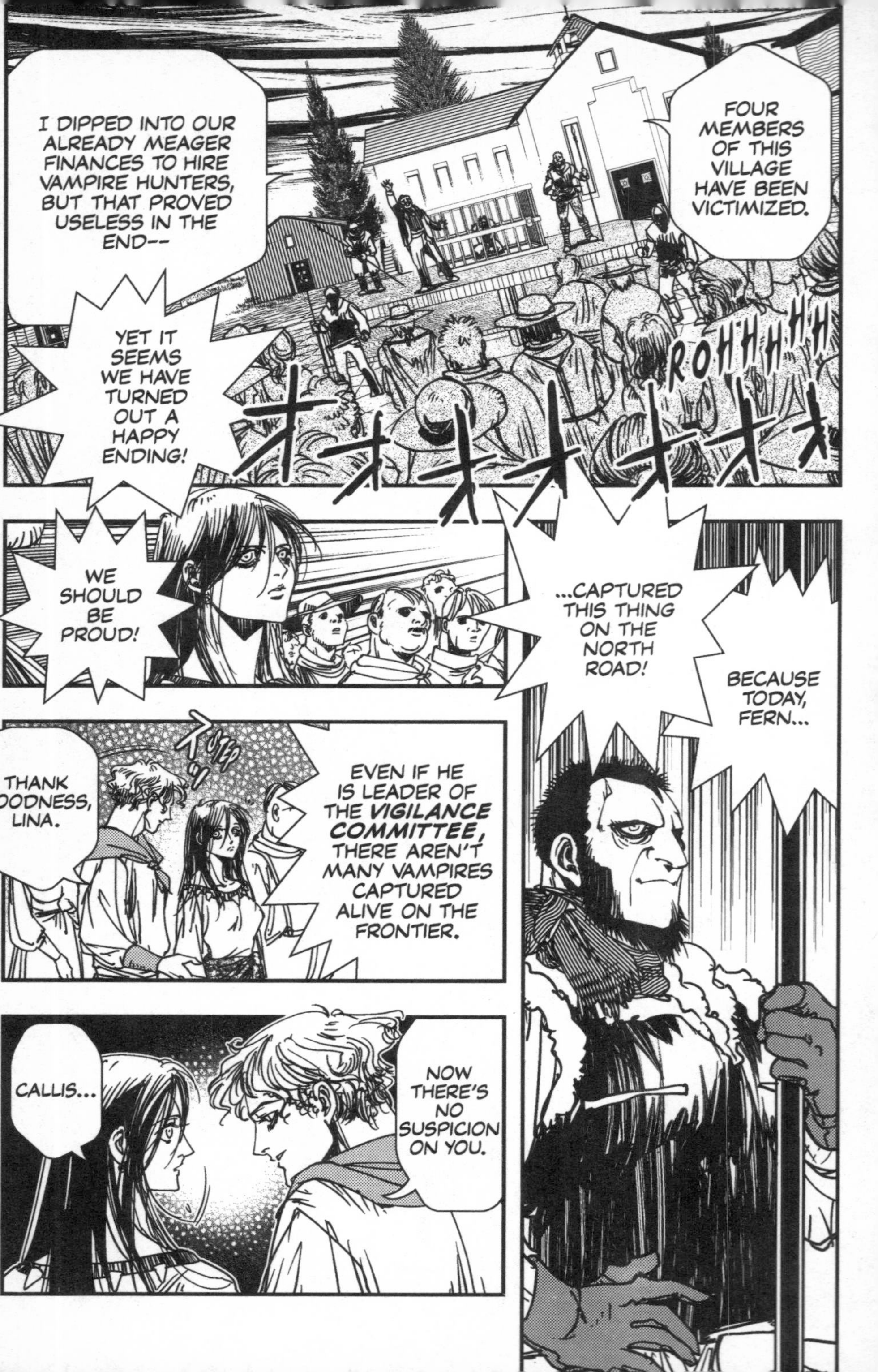
FOUR MEMBERS OF THIS VILLAGE HAVE BEEN VICTIMIZED.
I DIPPED INTO OUR ALREADY MEAGER FINANCES TO HIRE VAMPIRE HUNTERS, BUT THAT PROVED USELESS IN THE END--
ROHHHHHH
YET IT SEEMS WE HAVE TURNED OUT A HAPPY ENDING!
BECAUSE TODAY, FERN...
...CAPTURED THIS THING ON THE NORTH ROAD!
WE SHOULD BE PROUD!
EVEN IF HE IS LEADER OF THE ***VIGILANCE COMMITTEE***, THERE AREN'T MANY VAMPIRES CAPTURED ALIVE ON THE FRONTIER.
STEP
THANK GOODNESS, LINA.
NOW THERE'S NO SUSPICION ON YOU.
CALLIS...

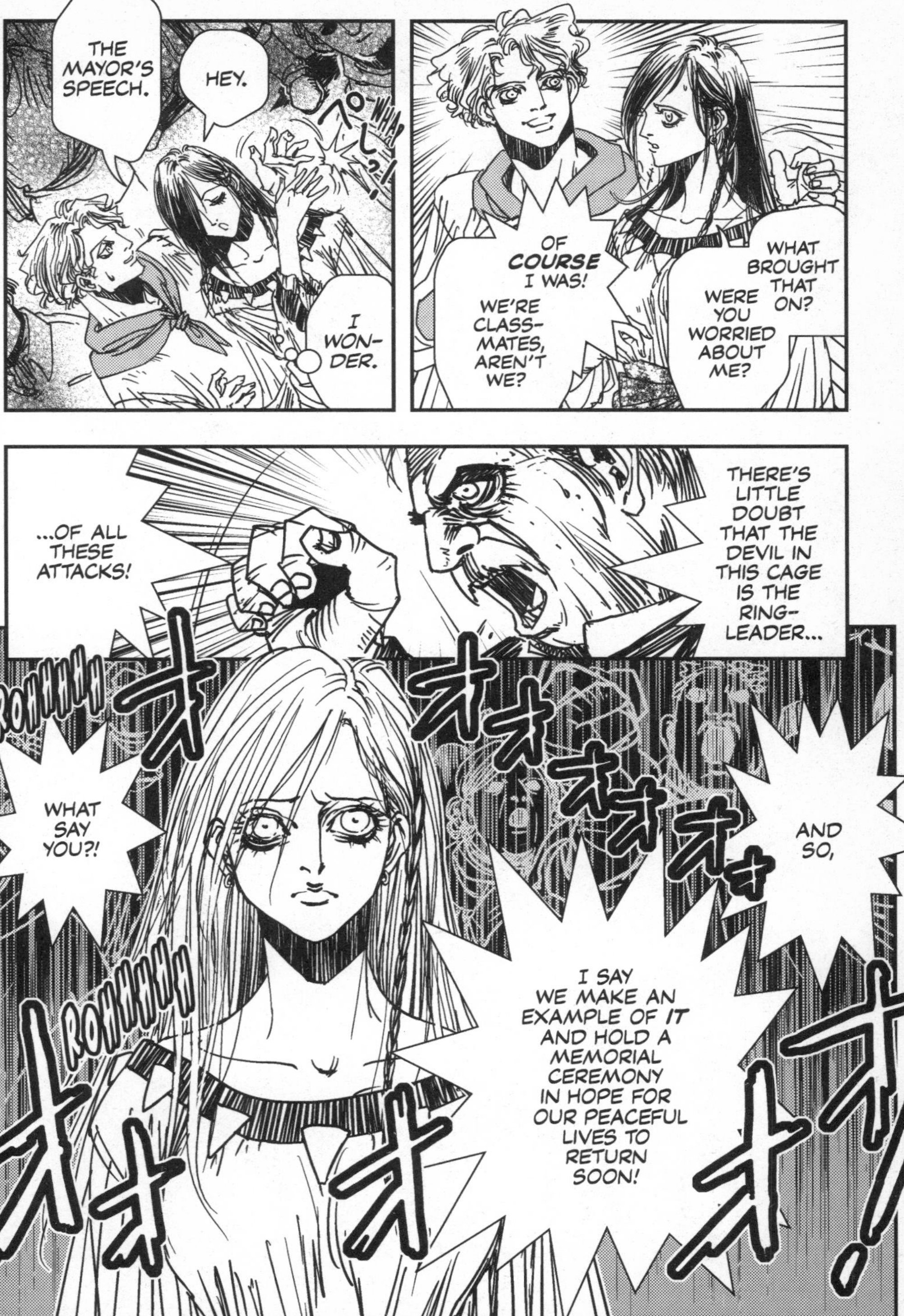
WHAT BROUGHT THAT ON?
WERE YOU WORRIED ABOUT ME?
OF COURSE I WAS!
WE'RE CLASSMATES, AREN'T WE?
HEY.
THE MAYOR'S SPEECH.
ぺしっ WHAP!
?!
I WONDER.
THERE'S LITTLE DOUBT THAT THE DEVIL IN THIS CAGE IS THE RING-LEADER...
...OF ALL THESE ATTACKS!
AND SO,
I SAY WE MAKE AN EXAMPLE OF IT AND HOLD A MEMORIAL CEREMONY IN HOPE FOR OUR PEACEFUL LIVES TO RETURN SOON!
WHAT SAY YOU?!
オオオオオオ ROHHHHHH
オオオオ! ROHHHHHHH

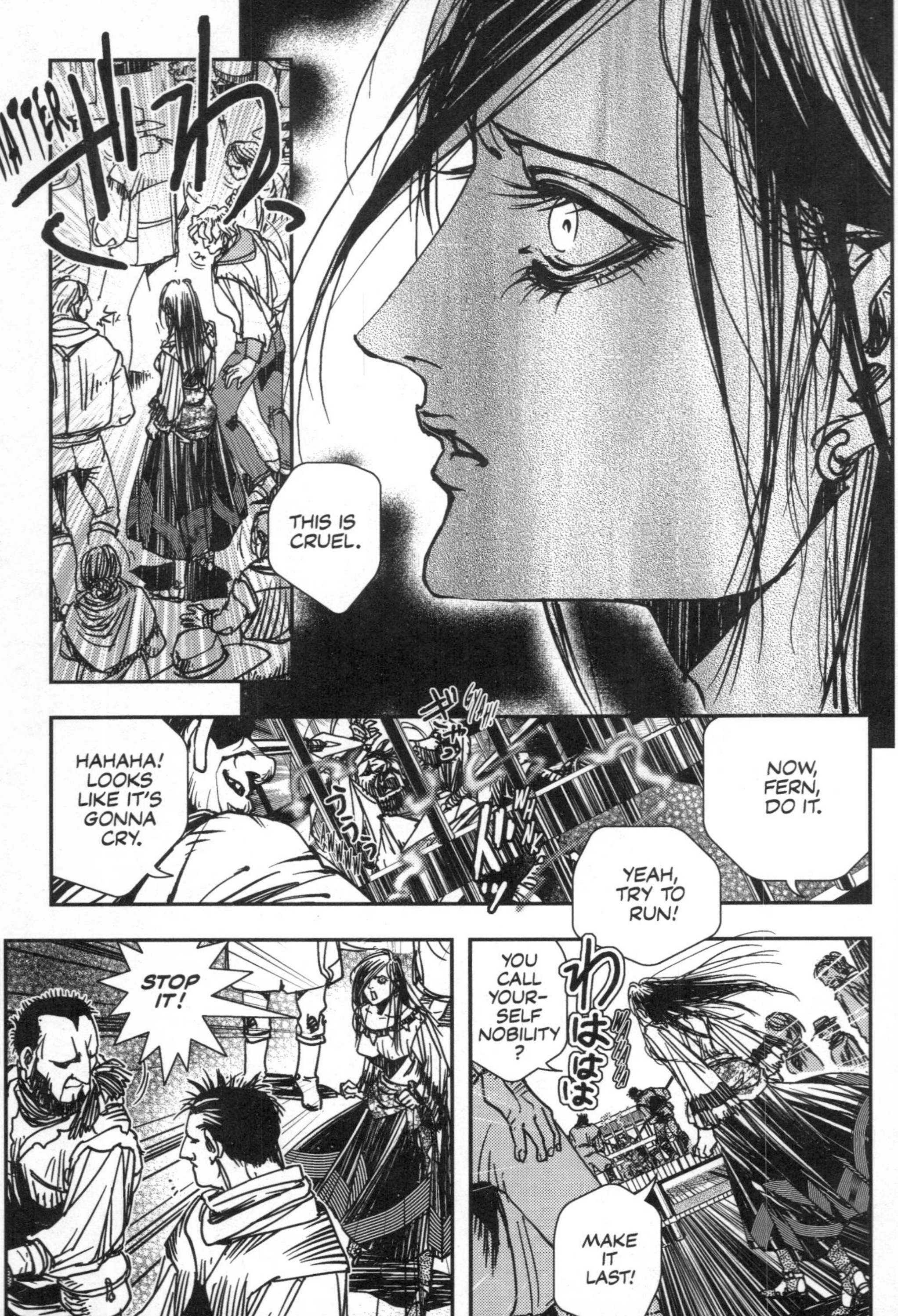
THIS IS CRUEL.
CHATTER
NOW, FERN, DO IT.
YEAH, TRY TO RUN!
HAHAHA! LOOKS LIKE IT'S GONNA CRY.
YOU CALL YOUR-SELF NOBILITY?
MAKE IT LAST!
STOP IT!

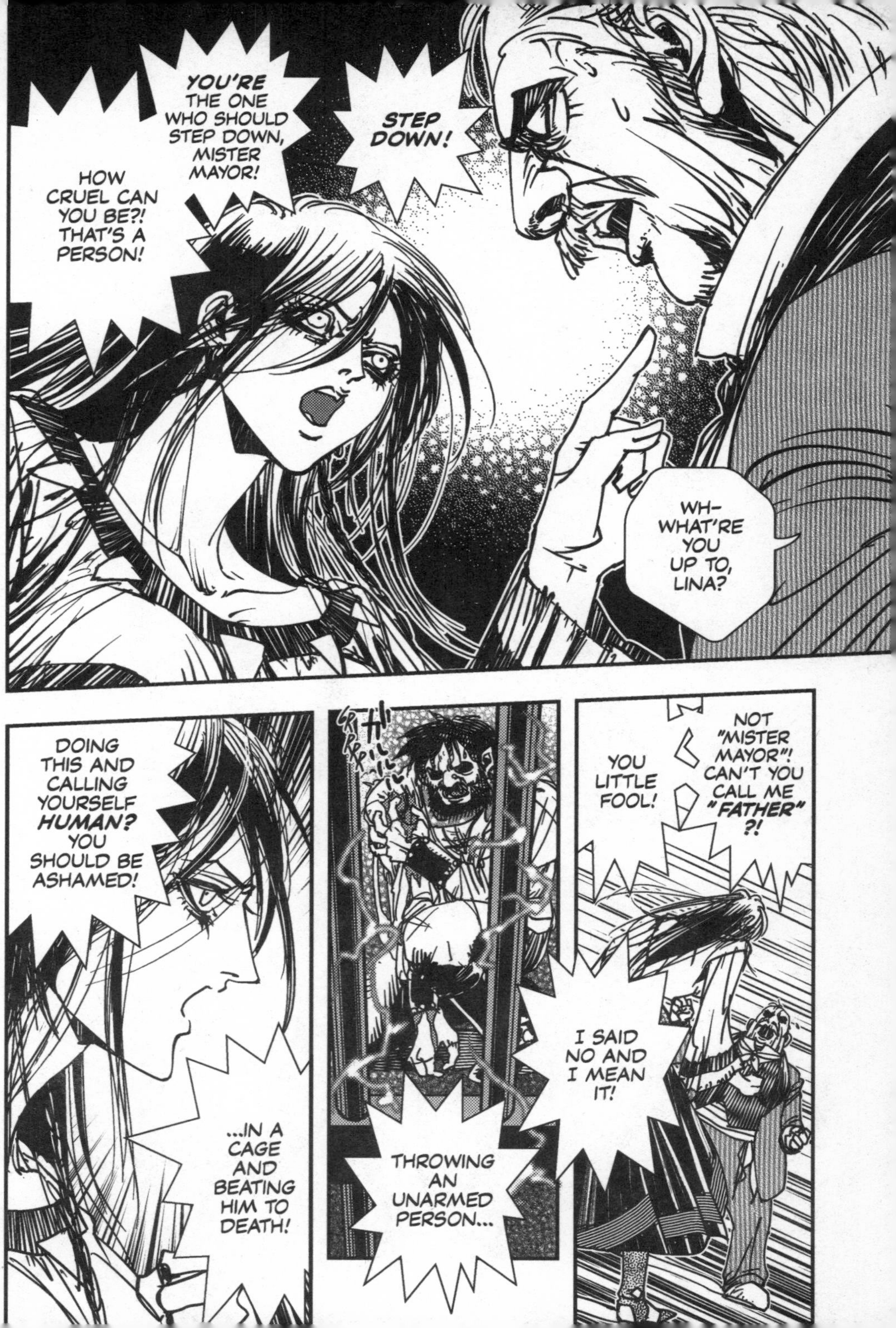
STEP DOWN!
YOU'RE THE ONE WHO SHOULD STEP DOWN, MISTER MAYOR!
HOW CRUEL CAN YOU BE?! THAT'S A PERSON!
WH- WHAT'RE YOU UP TO, LINA?
NOT "MISTER MAYOR"! CAN'T YOU CALL ME "FATHER"?!
YOU LITTLE FOOL!
I SAID NO AND I MEAN IT!
THROWING AN UNARMED PERSON...
...IN A CAGE AND BEATING HIM TO DEATH!
DOING THIS AND CALLING YOURSELF HUMAN? YOU SHOULD BE ASHAMED!

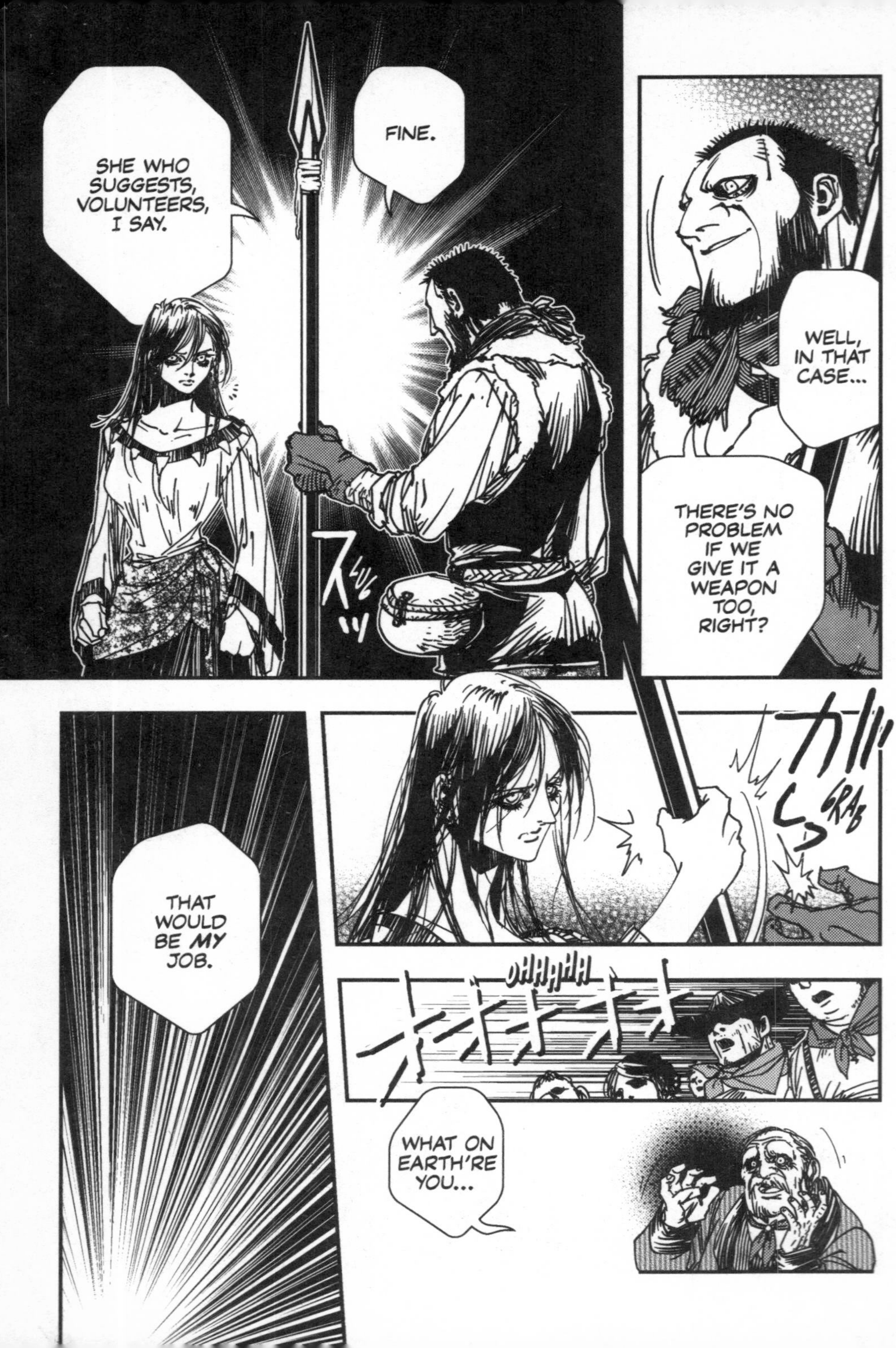
WELL, IN THAT CASE...
THERE'S NO PROBLEM IF WE GIVE IT A WEAPON TOO, RIGHT?
FINE.
SHE WHO SUGGESTS, VOLUNTEERS, I SAY.
GRAB
WHAT ON EARTH'RE YOU...
THAT WOULD BE *MY* JOB.

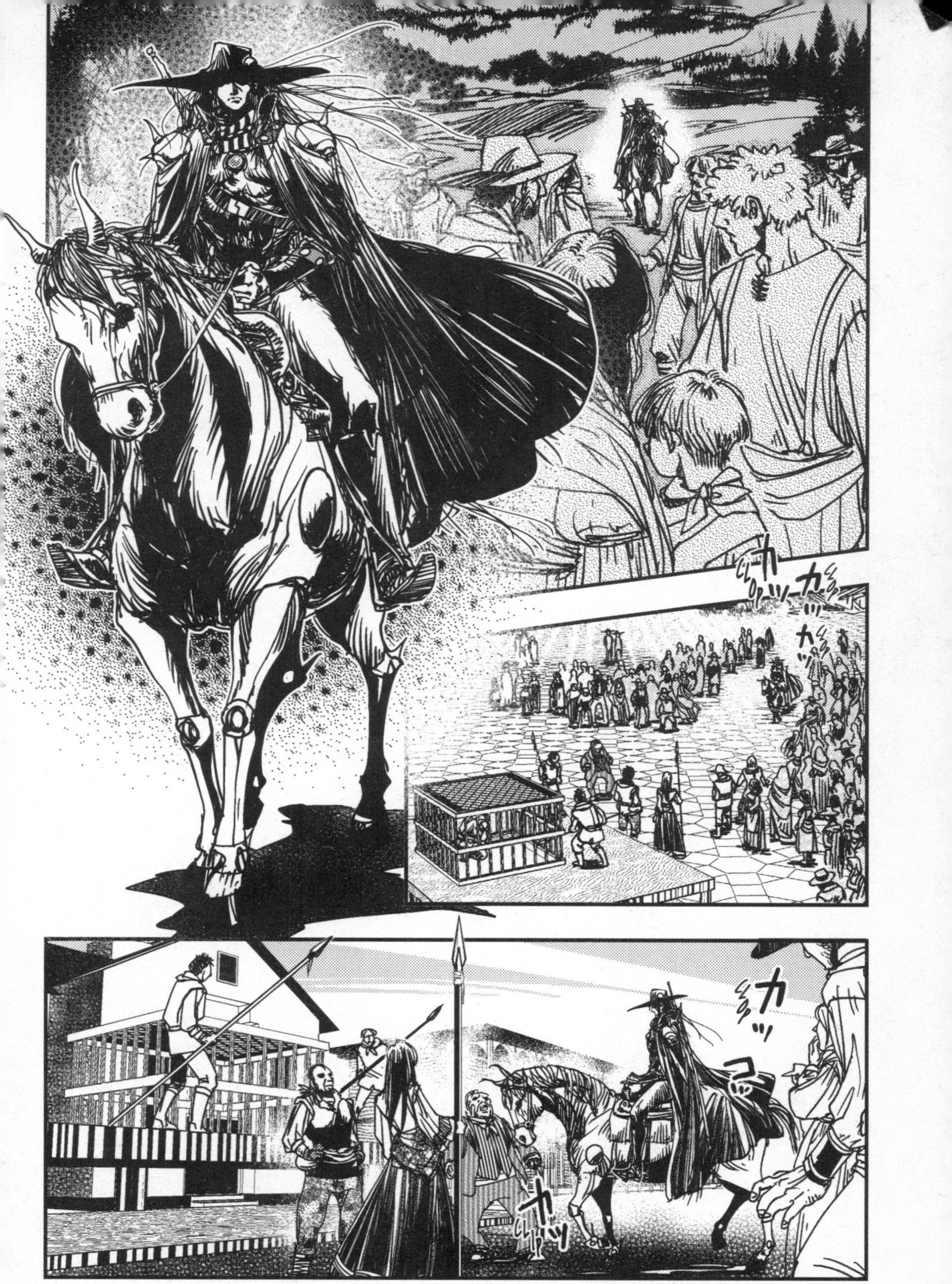
CLOP カッ
カッ CLOP
カッ CLOP
カッ CLOP
コッ
カッ CLOP

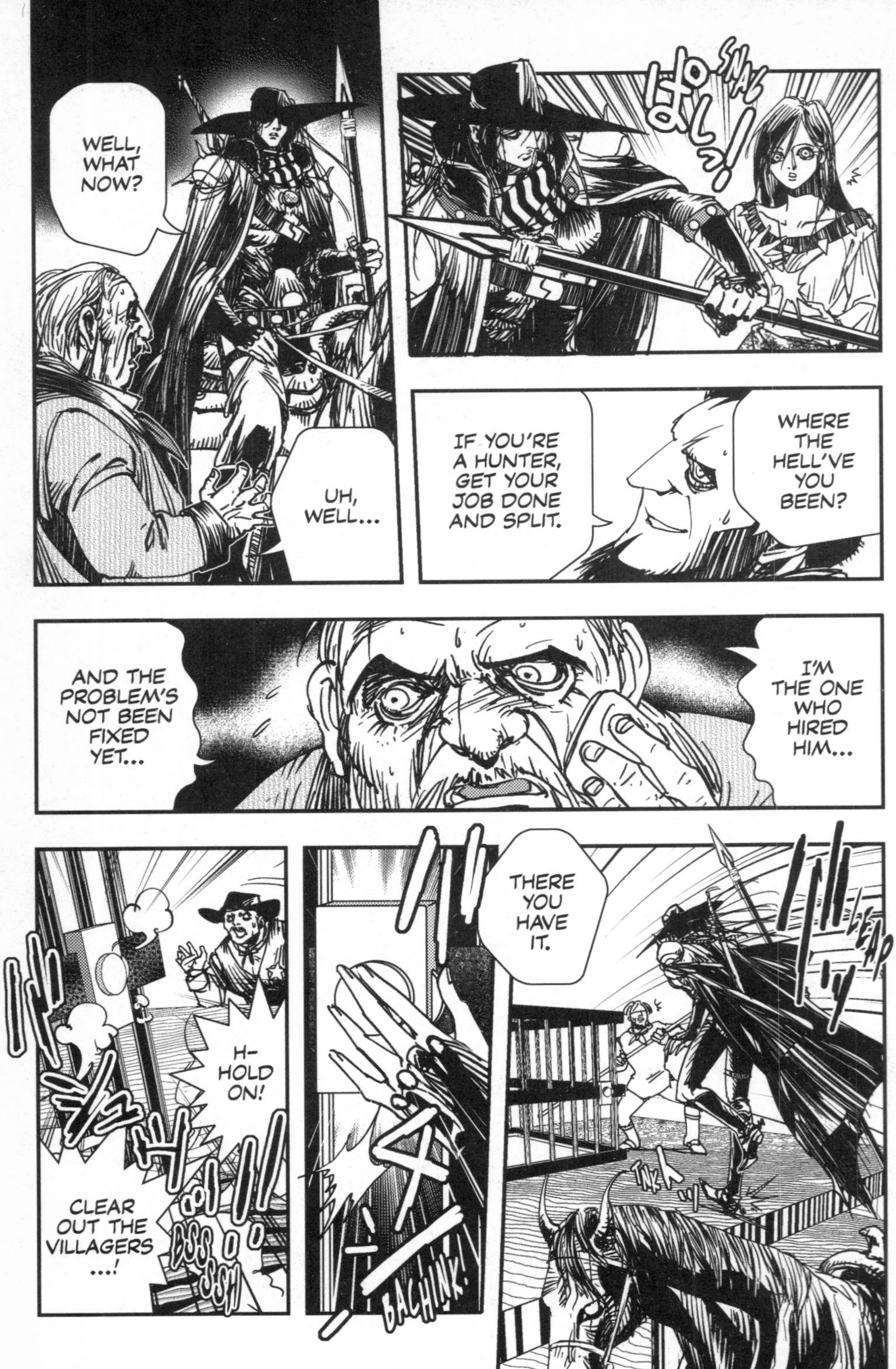
SNAG
ぱしっ!
WHERE THE HELL'VE YOU BEEN?
IF YOU'RE A HUNTER, GET YOUR JOB DONE AND SPLIT.
WELL, WHAT NOW?
UH, WELL...
I'M THE ONE WHO HIRED HIM...
AND THE PROBLEM'S NOT BEEN FIXED YET...
LEAP
THERE YOU HAVE IT.
TNK
BACHINK!
H-HOLD ON!
CLEAR OUT THE VILLAGERS ...!
BSSSSH

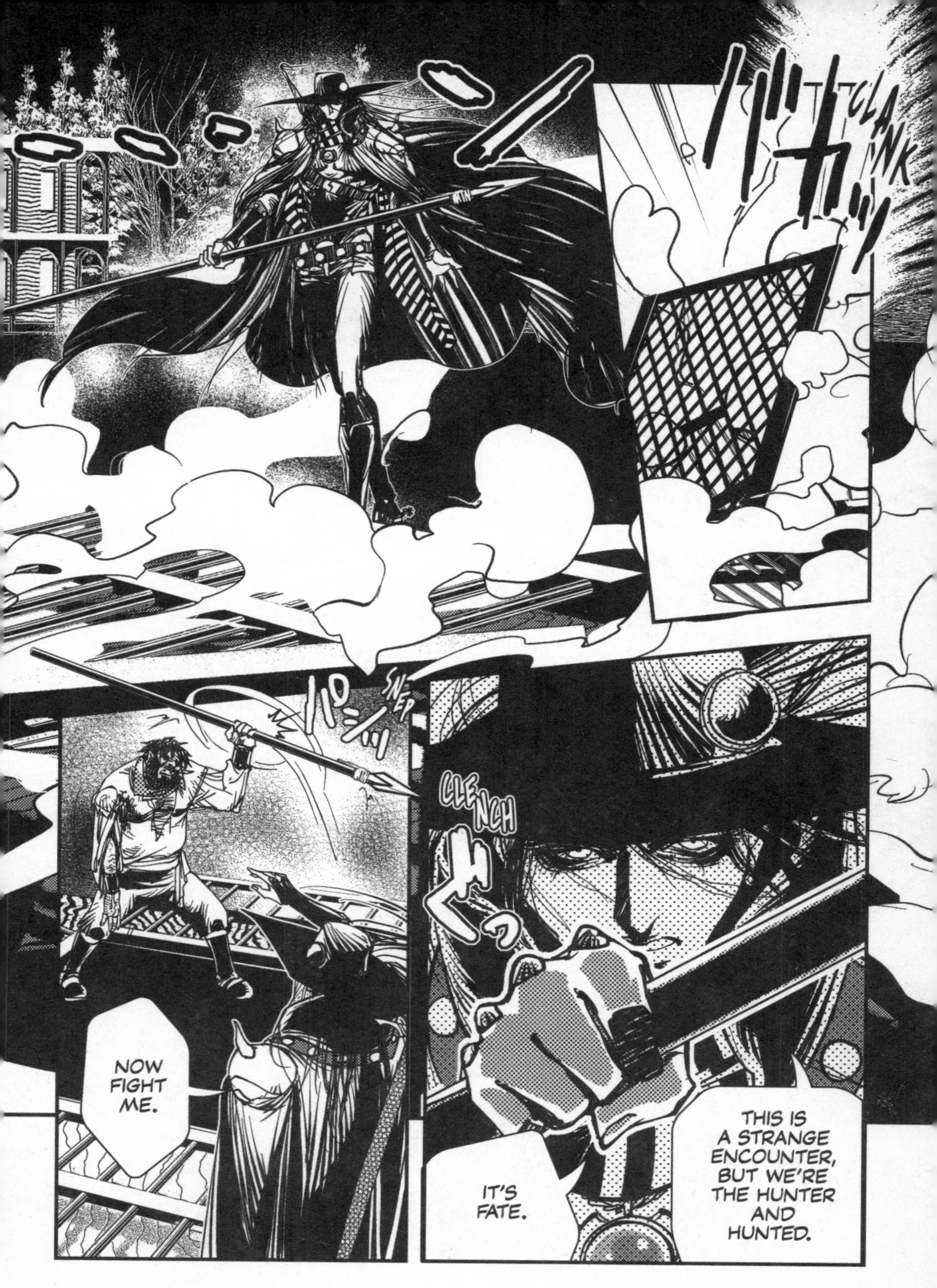
CLANK
CLENCH
THIS IS A STRANGE ENCOUNTER, BUT WE'RE THE HUNTER AND HUNTED.
IT'S FATE.
SNEP
NOW FIGHT ME.

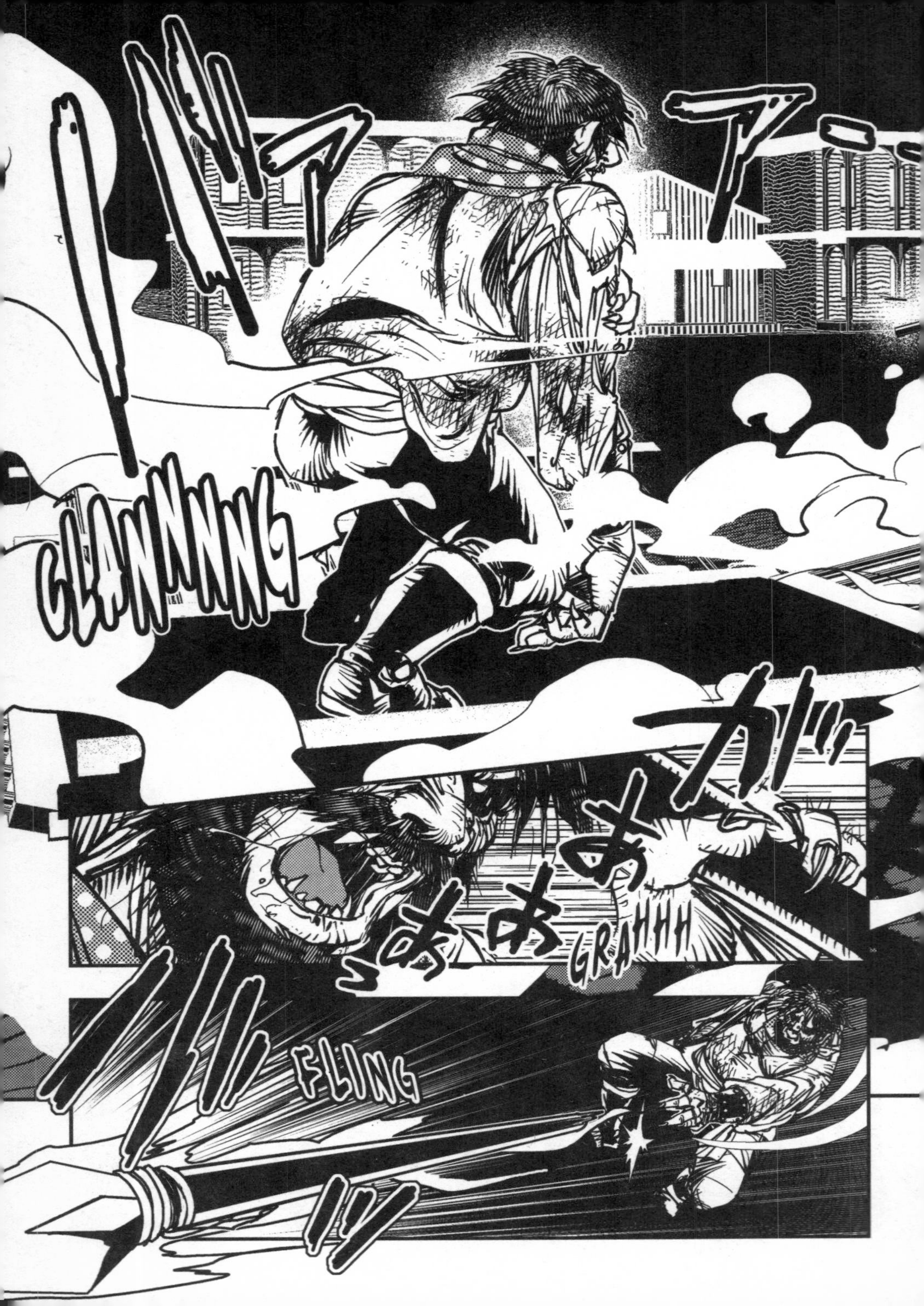
CLANNNNG
GRAHHH
FLING

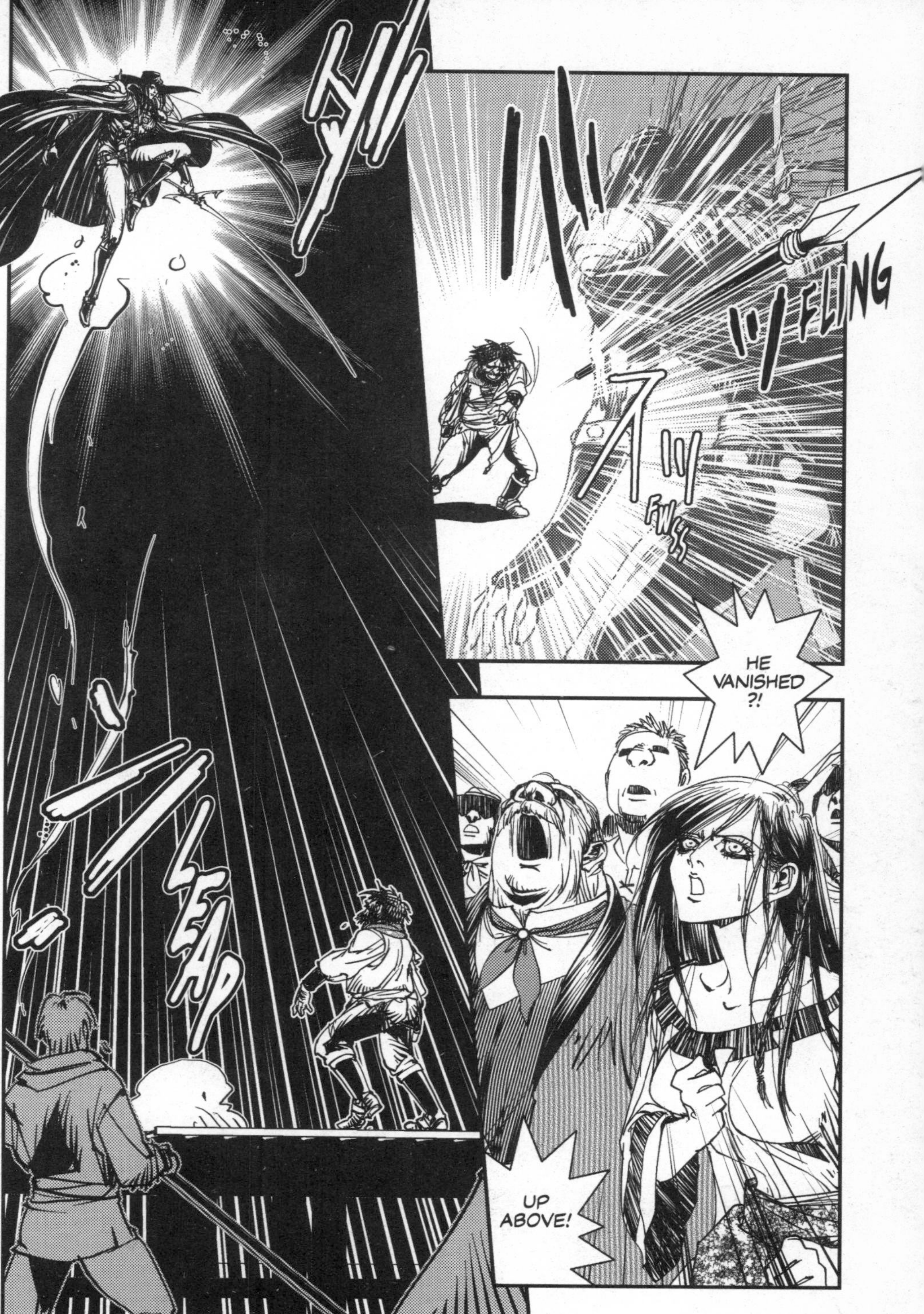
FLING
FWSS
HE VANISHED?!
UP ABOVE!
LEAP

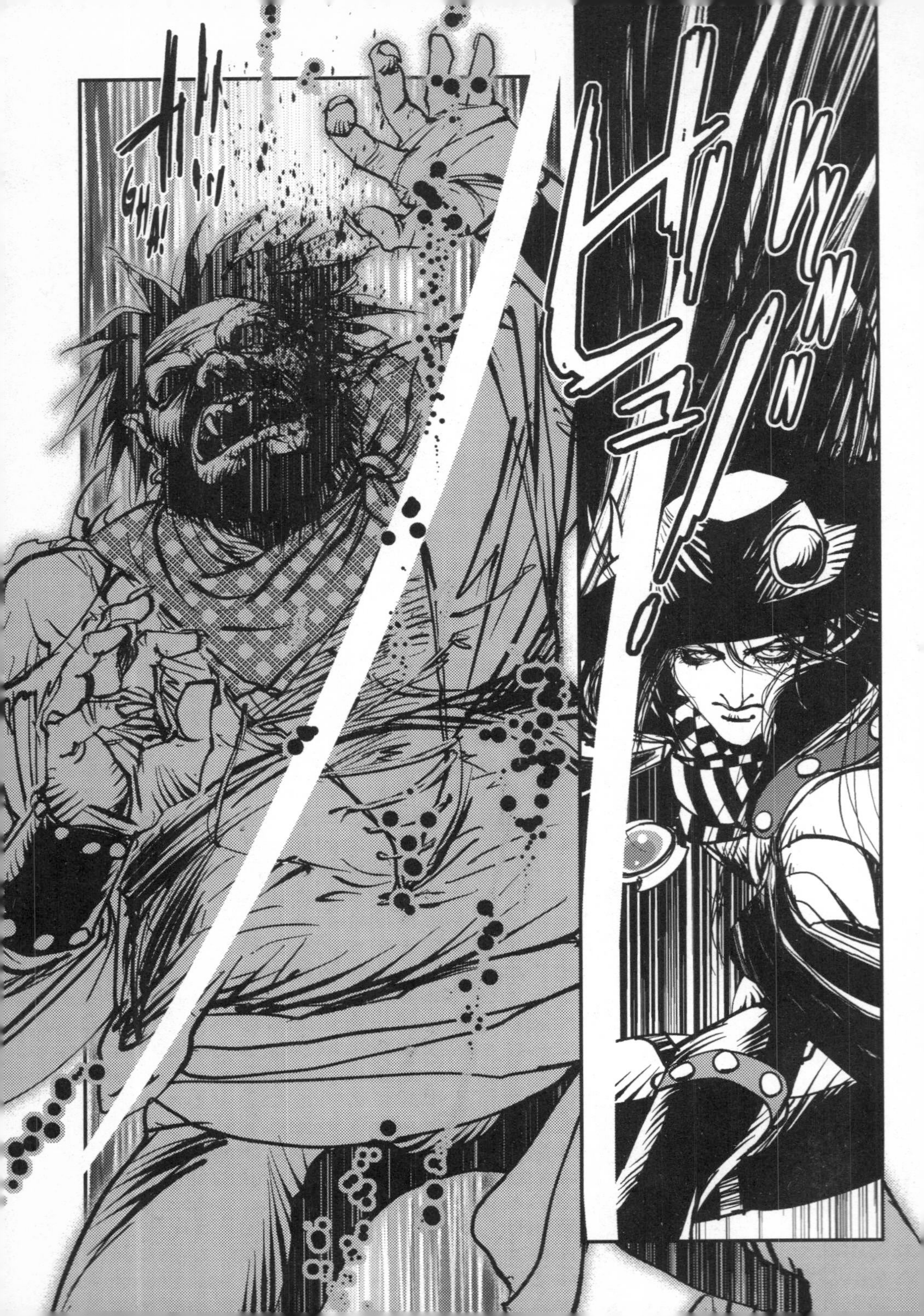
ヒュン
ガッ
GHA!

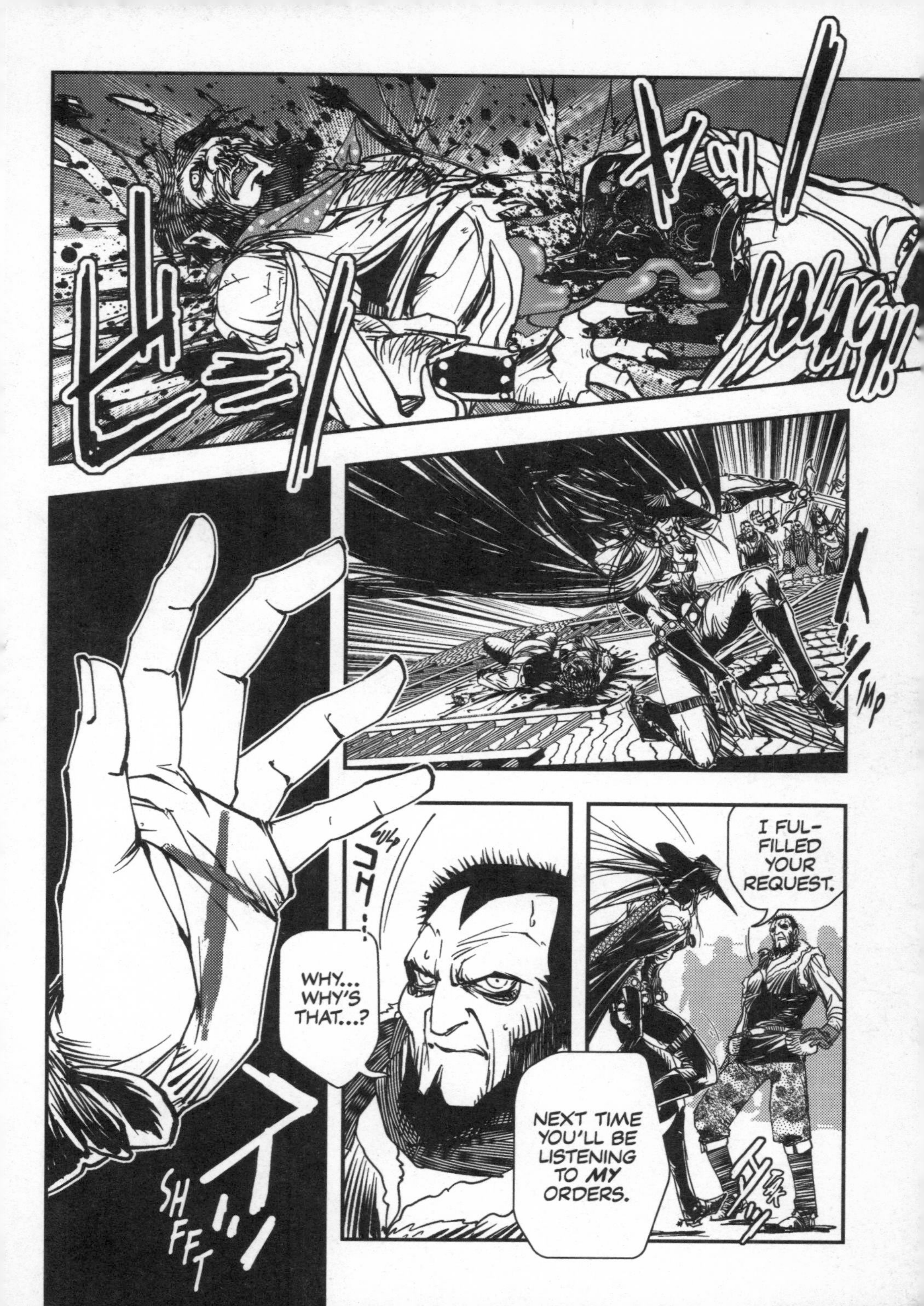
TMP
I FUL-
FILLED
YOUR
REQUEST.
GULP
WHY...
WHY'S
THAT...?
NEXT TIME
YOU'LL BE
LISTENING
TO MY
ORDERS.
SHFFT

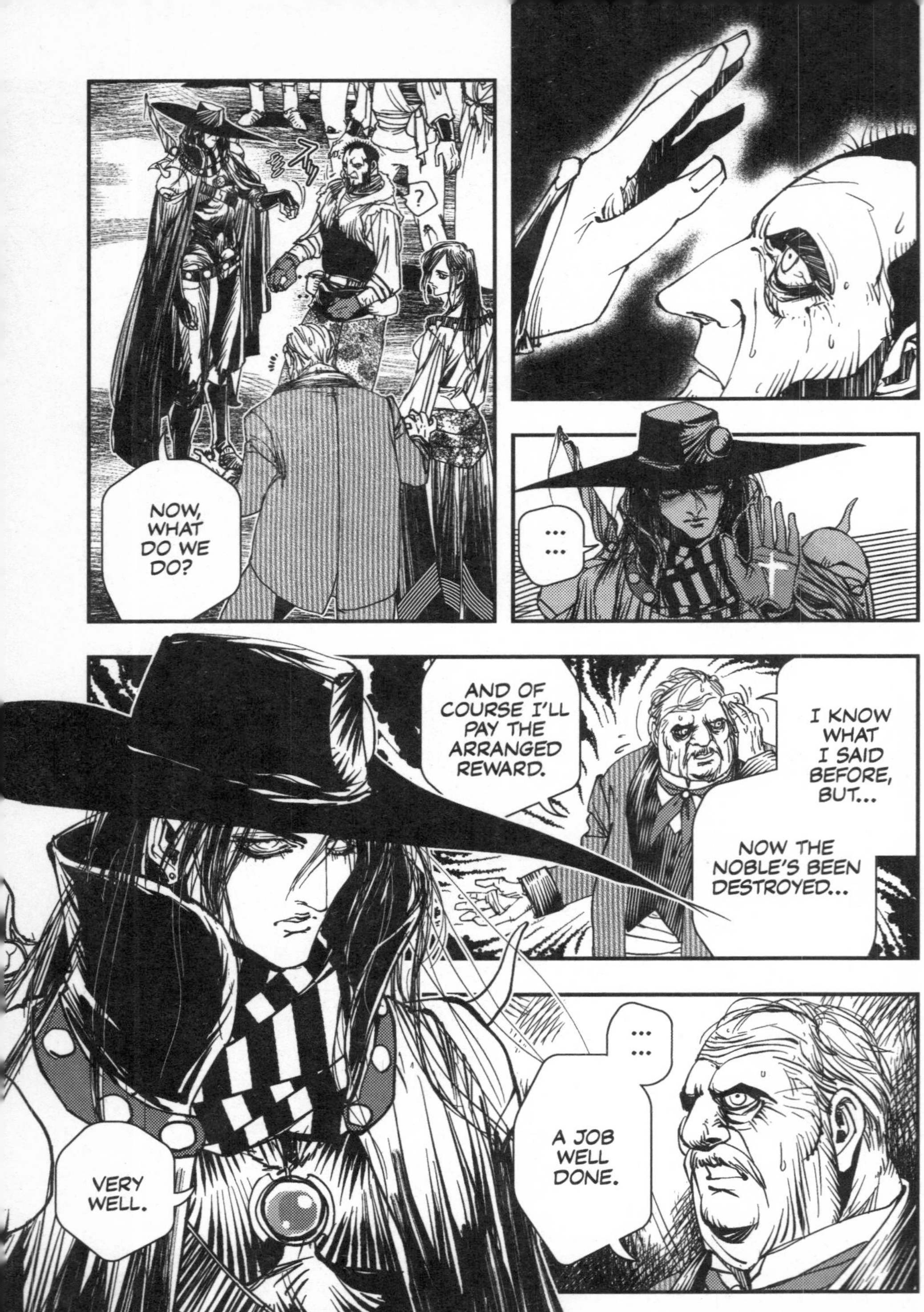
……
……
?
NOW, WHAT DO WE DO?
I KNOW WHAT I SAID BEFORE, BUT...
NOW THE NOBLE'S BEEN DESTROYED...
AND OF COURSE I'LL PAY THE ARRANGED REWARD.
……
……
A JOB WELL DONE.
VERY WELL.

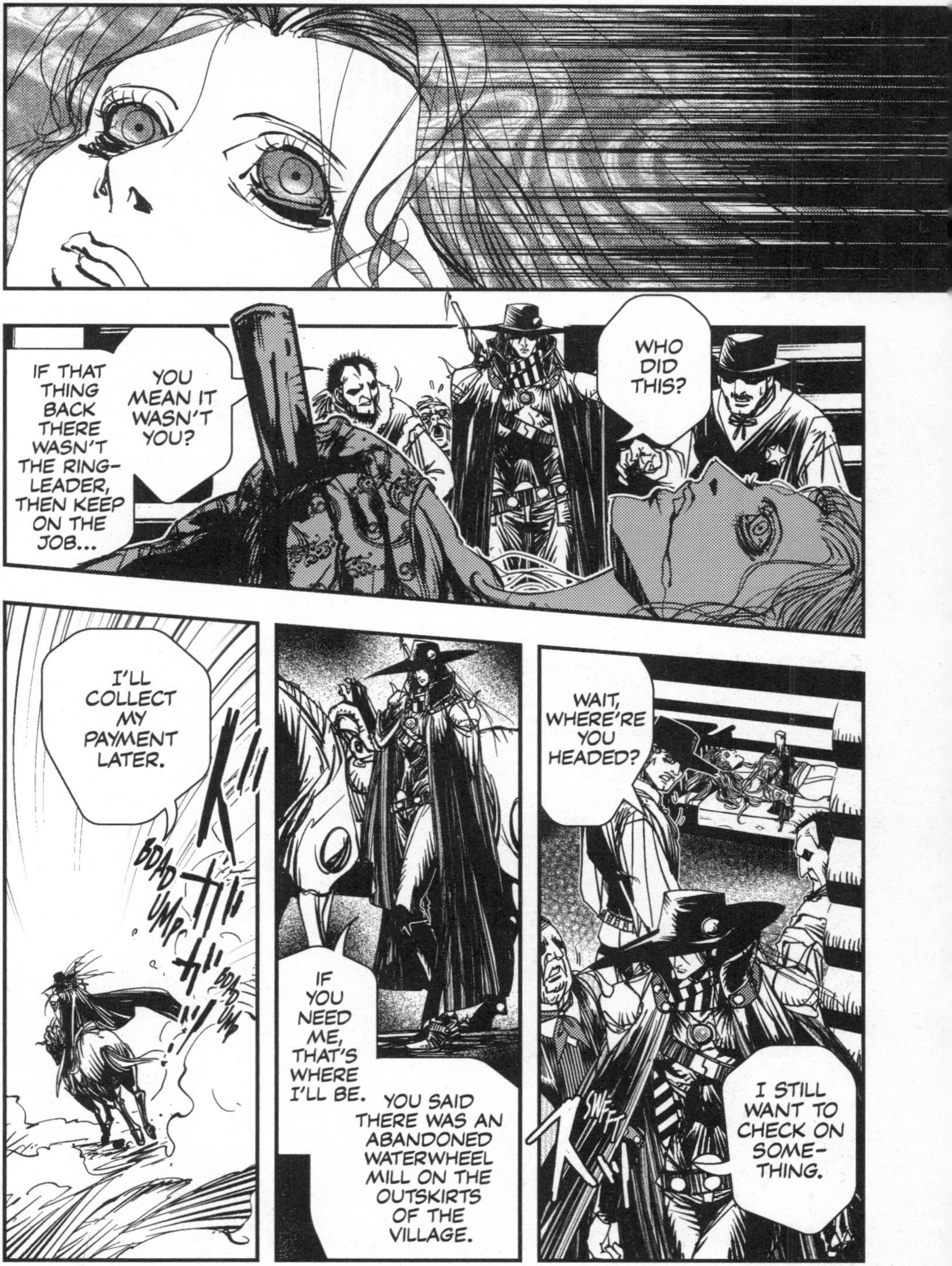
WHO DID THIS?
YOU MEAN IT WASN'T YOU?
IF THAT THING BACK THERE WASN'T THE RING-LEADER, THEN KEEP ON THE JOB...
WAIT, WHERE'RE YOU HEADED?
I STILL WANT TO CHECK ON SOME-THING.
YOU SAID THERE WAS AN ABANDONED WATERWHEEL MILL ON THE OUTSKIRTS OF THE VILLAGE.
IF YOU NEED ME, THAT'S WHERE I'LL BE.
I'LL COLLECT MY PAYMENT LATER.

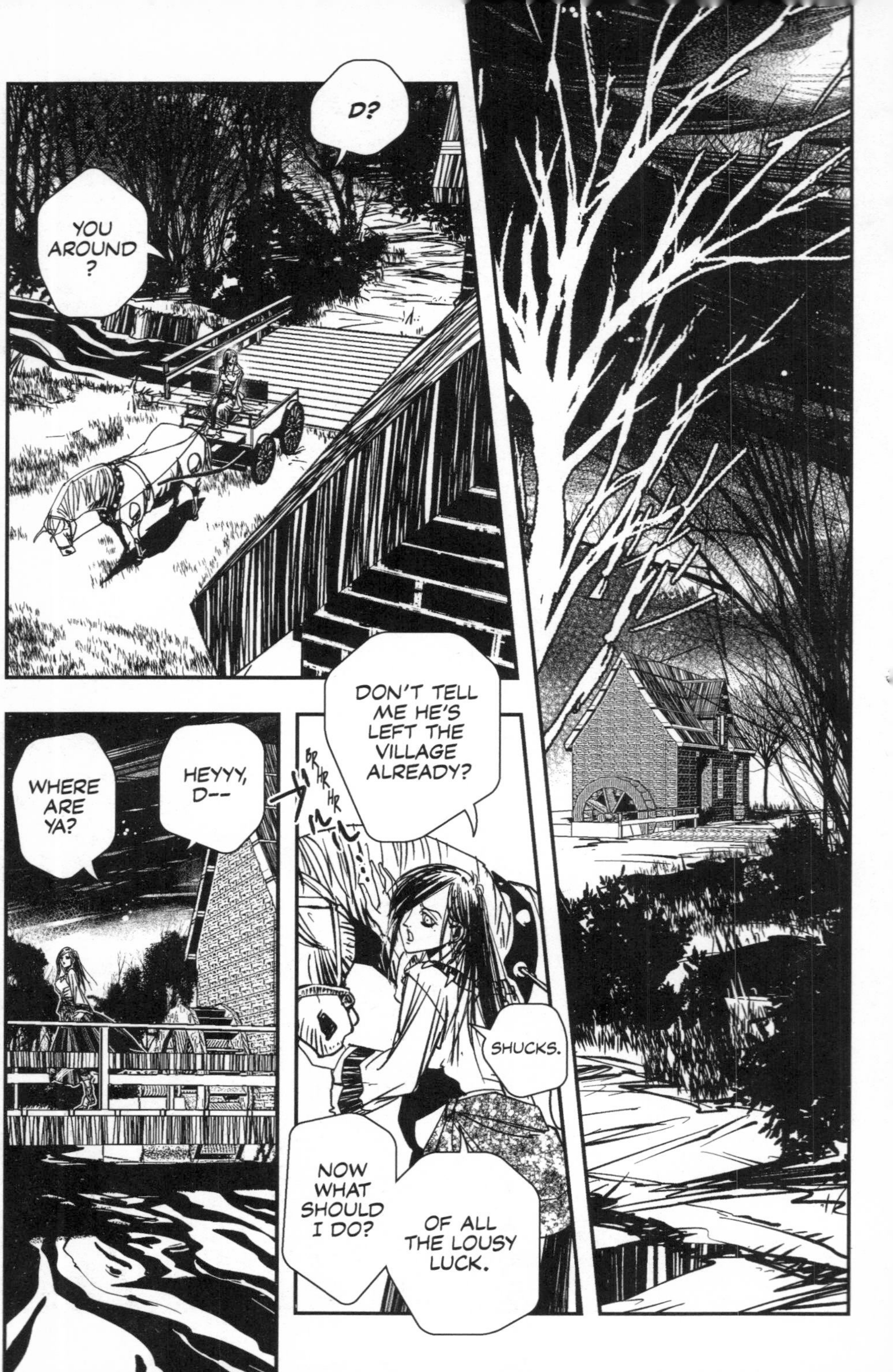
D?
YOU AROUND?
DON'T TELL ME HE'S LEFT THE VILLAGE ALREADY?
BRHRHR
SHUCKS.
OF ALL THE LOUSY LUCK.
NOW WHAT SHOULD I DO?
HEYYY, D--
WHERE ARE YA?

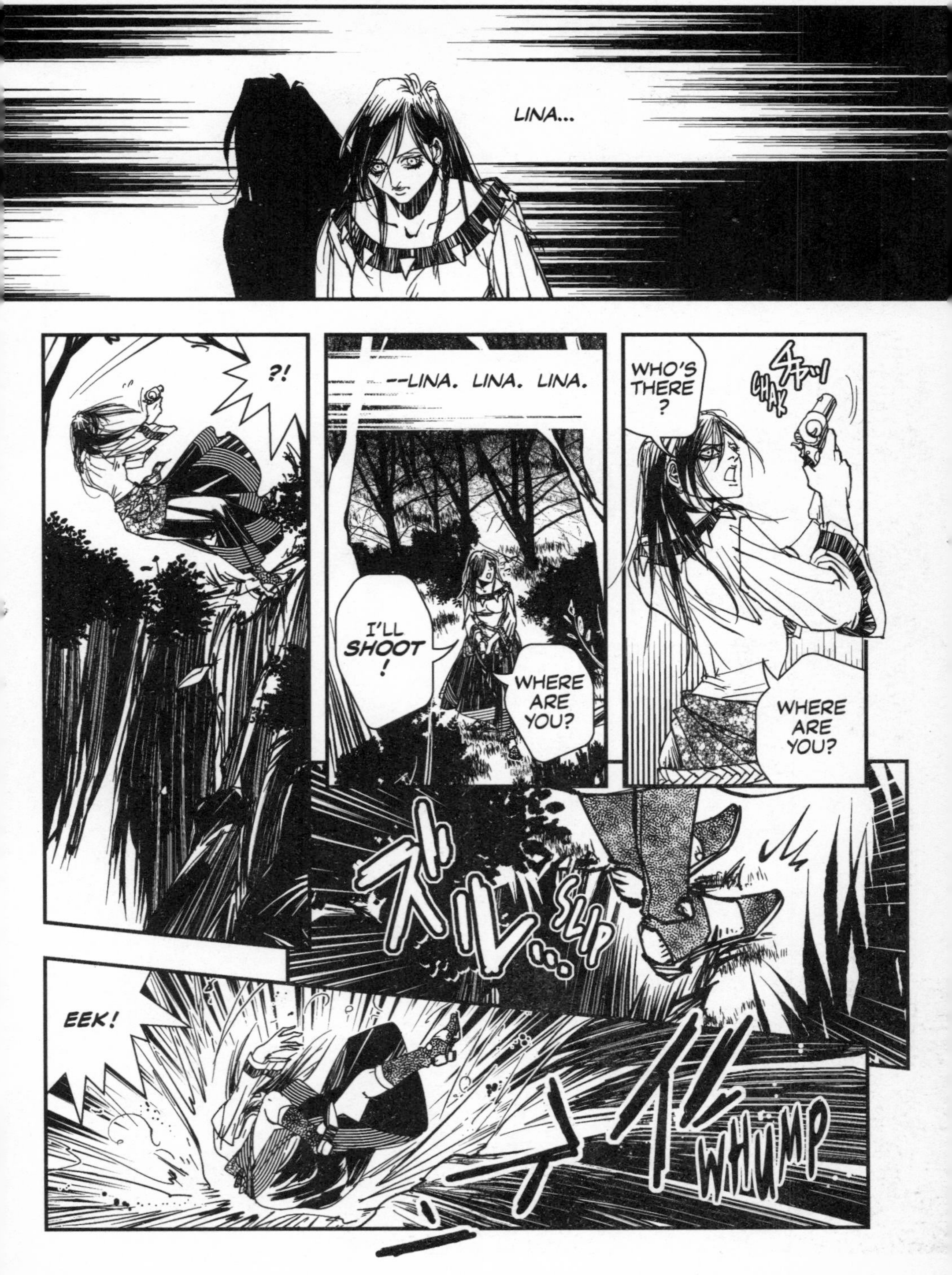
LINA...
WHO'S THERE?
CHAK
WHERE ARE YOU?
--LINA. LINA. LINA.
WHERE ARE YOU?
I'LL SHOOT!
ズル...
SLIP
?!
EEK!
WHUMP

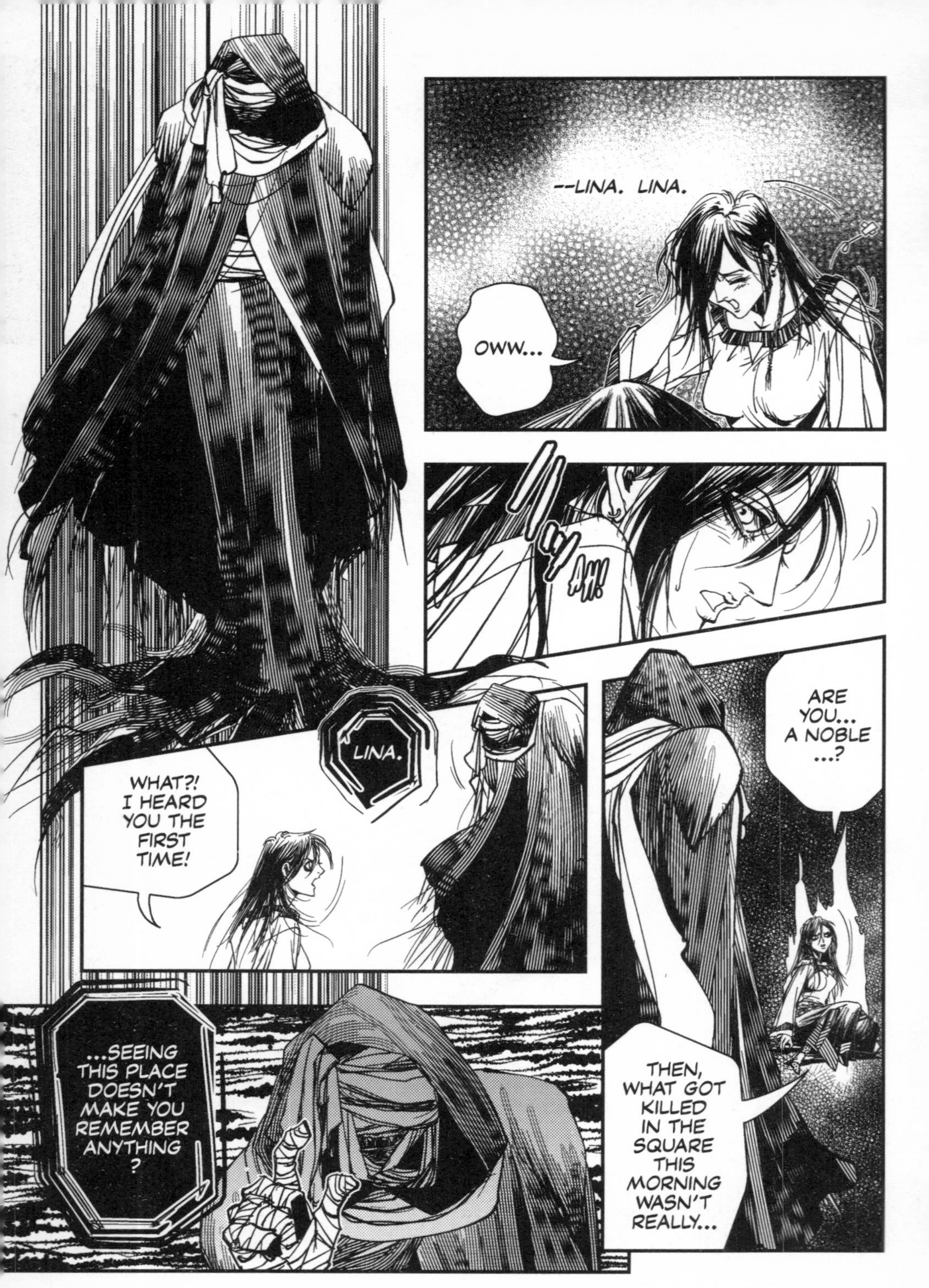

--LINA. LINA.
OWW...
AH!
ARE YOU... A NOBLE ...?
THEN, WHAT GOT KILLED IN THE SQUARE THIS MORNING WASN'T REALLY...
LINA.
WHAT?! I HEARD YOU THE FIRST TIME!
...SEEING THIS PLACE DOESN'T MAKE YOU REMEMBER ANYTHING ?

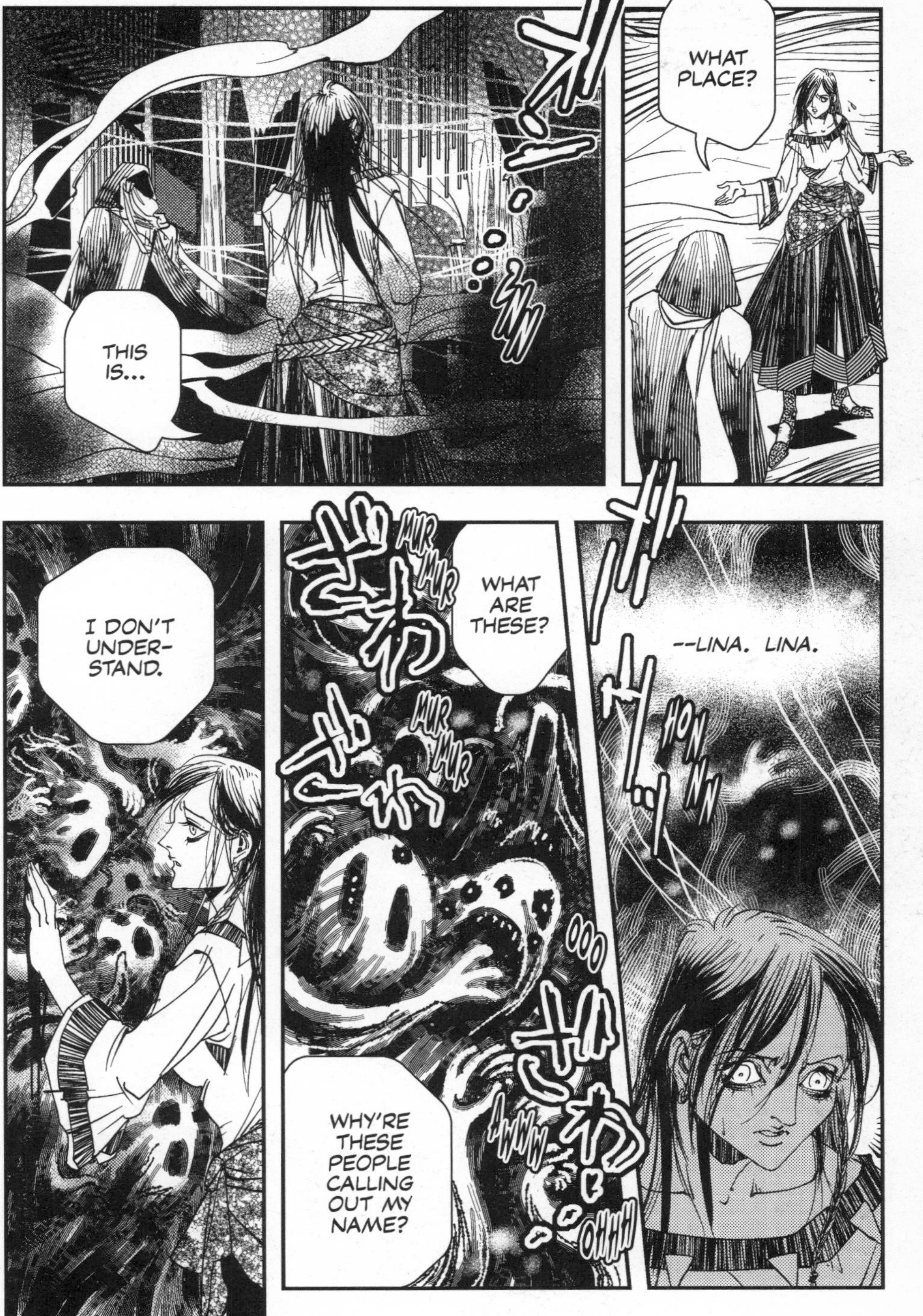
WHAT PLACE?
THIS IS...
ZNN
--LINA. LINA.
HONNN
WHAT ARE THESE?
MUR MUR
MUR MUR
OOO
AWWW
OHHH
WHY'RE THESE PEOPLE CALLING OUT MY NAME?
I DON'T UNDER-STAND.

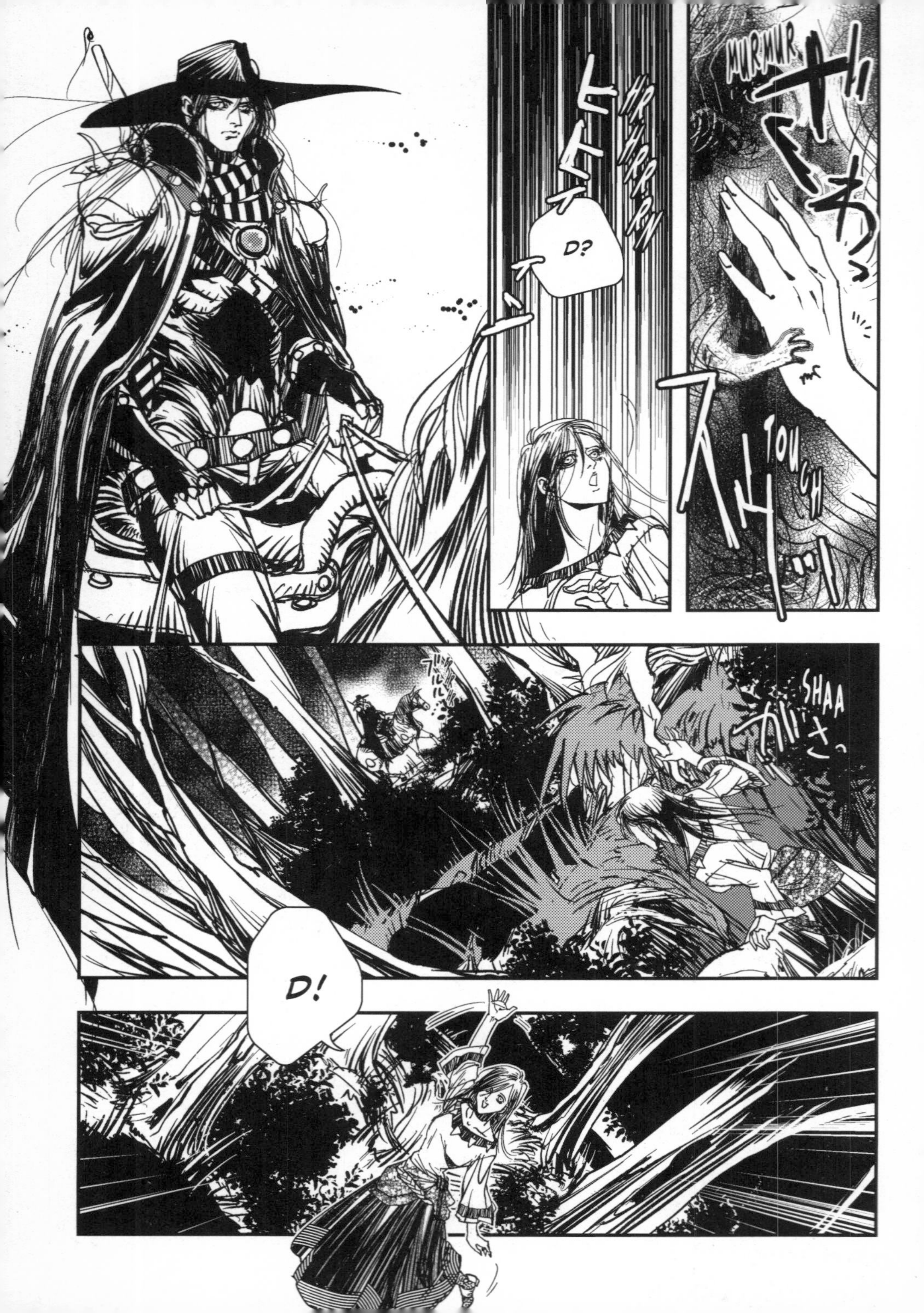
MURMUR
ざわっ
TOUCH
HRHRRRN
D?
SHAA
D!

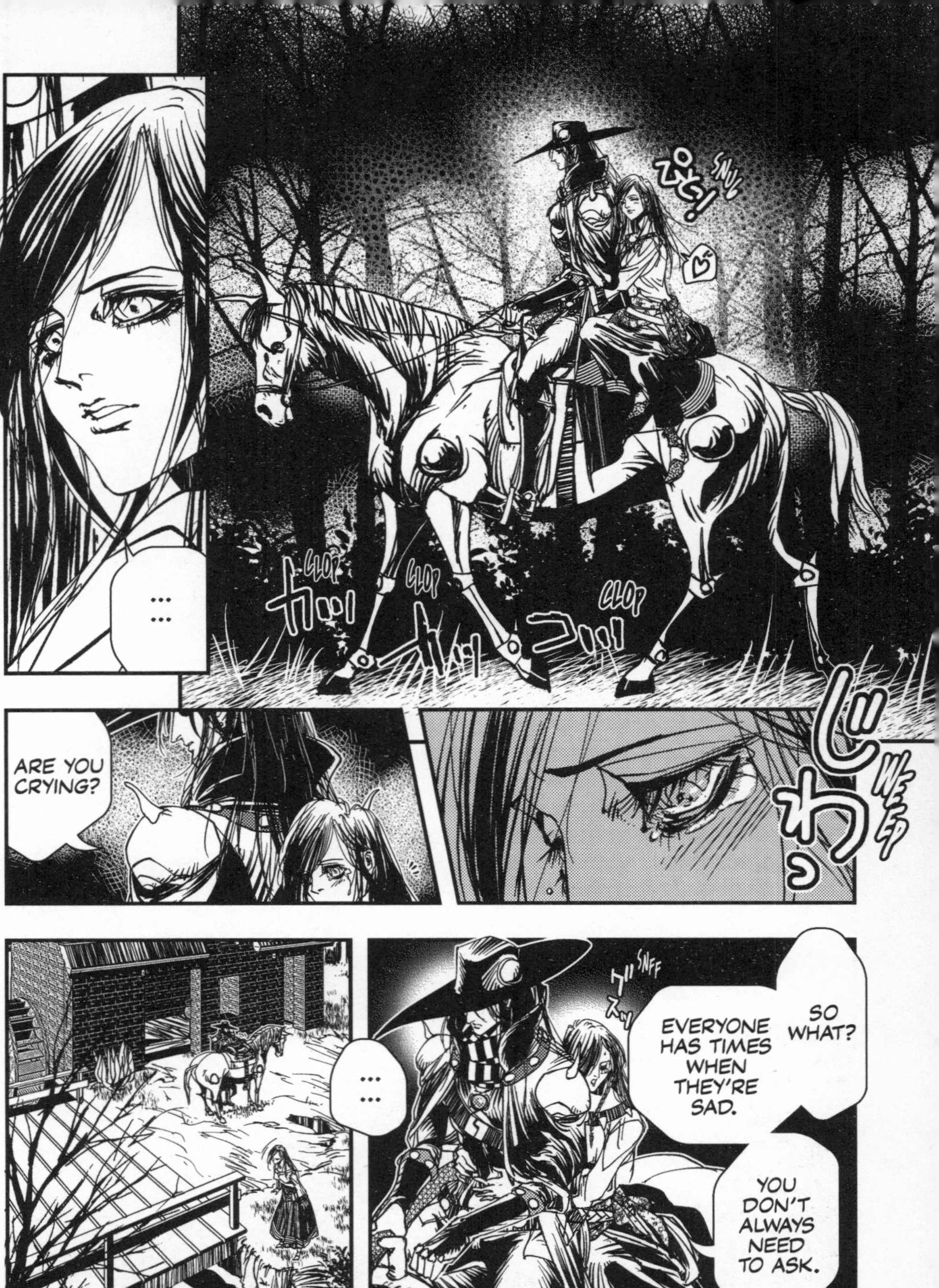
SNUG
ぴとっ!
♡
CLOP
カッ
CLOP
カッ
CLOP
コッ
...
...
WEEP
じわっ
ARE YOU CRYING?
SO WHAT?
EVERYONE HAS TIMES WHEN THEY'RE SAD.
SNFF
YOU DON'T ALWAYS NEED TO ASK.
...
...

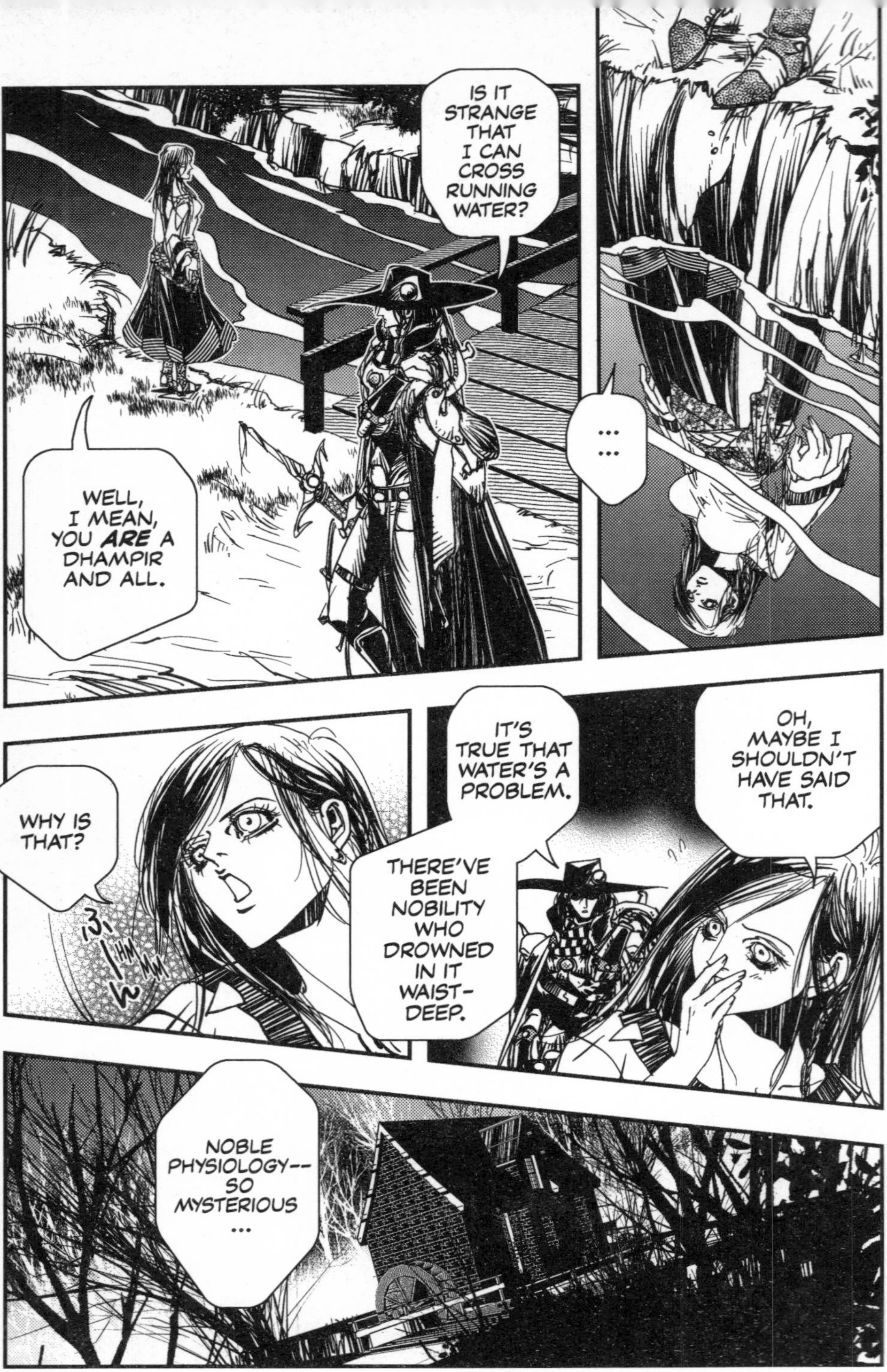
……
IS IT STRANGE THAT I CAN CROSS RUNNING WATER?
WELL, I MEAN, YOU ***ARE*** A DHAMPIR AND ALL.
OH, MAYBE I SHOULDN'T HAVE SAID THAT.
IT'S TRUE THAT WATER'S A PROBLEM.
THERE'VE BEEN NOBILITY WHO DROWNED IN IT WAIST-DEEP.
WHY IS THAT?
HMMM
NOBLE PHYSIOLOGY-- SO MYSTERIOUS …

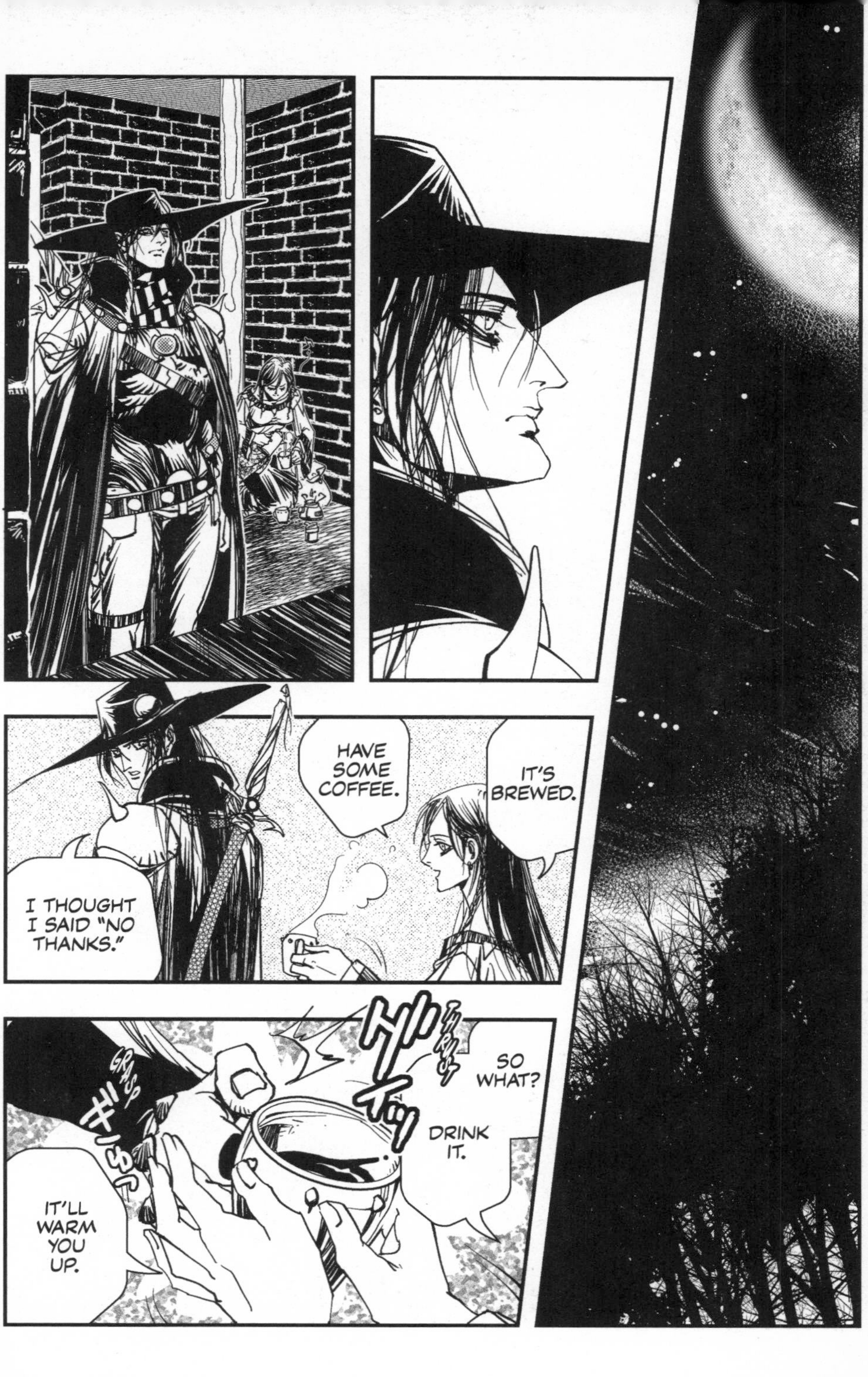
IT'S BREWED.
HAVE SOME COFFEE.
I THOUGHT I SAID "NO THANKS."
THRUST
ズイッ
SO WHAT?
DRINK IT.
GRASP
ギリッ
IT'LL WARM YOU UP.

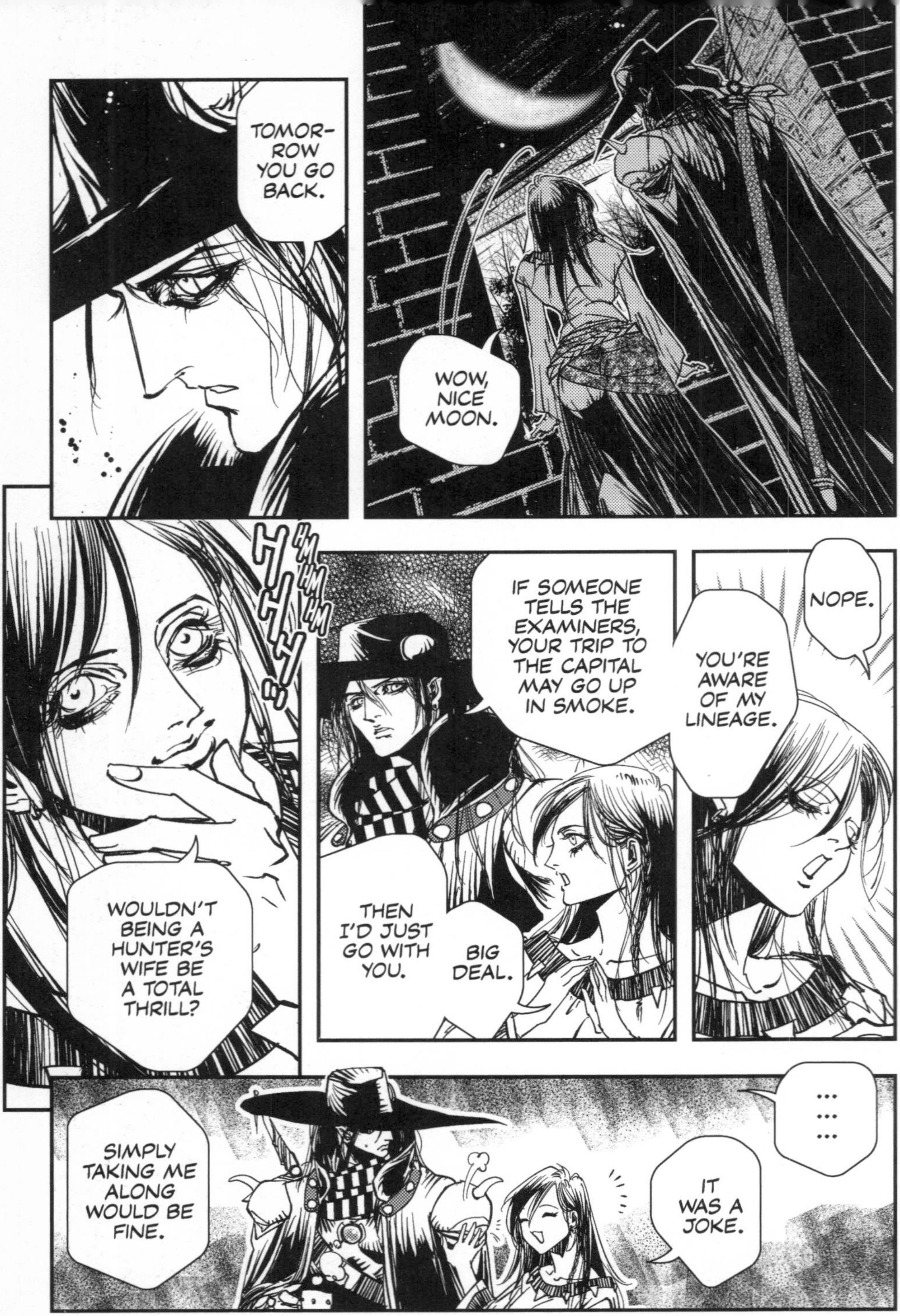
WOW, NICE MOON.
TOMOR-ROW YOU GO BACK.
NOPE.
YOU'RE AWARE OF MY LINEAGE.
IF SOMEONE TELLS THE EXAMINERS, YOUR TRIP TO THE CAPITAL MAY GO UP IN SMOKE.
BIG DEAL.
THEN I'D JUST GO WITH YOU.
WOULDN'T BEING A HUNTER'S WIFE BE A TOTAL THRILL?
...
...
...
IT WAS A JOKE.
SIMPLY TAKING ME ALONG WOULD BE FINE.

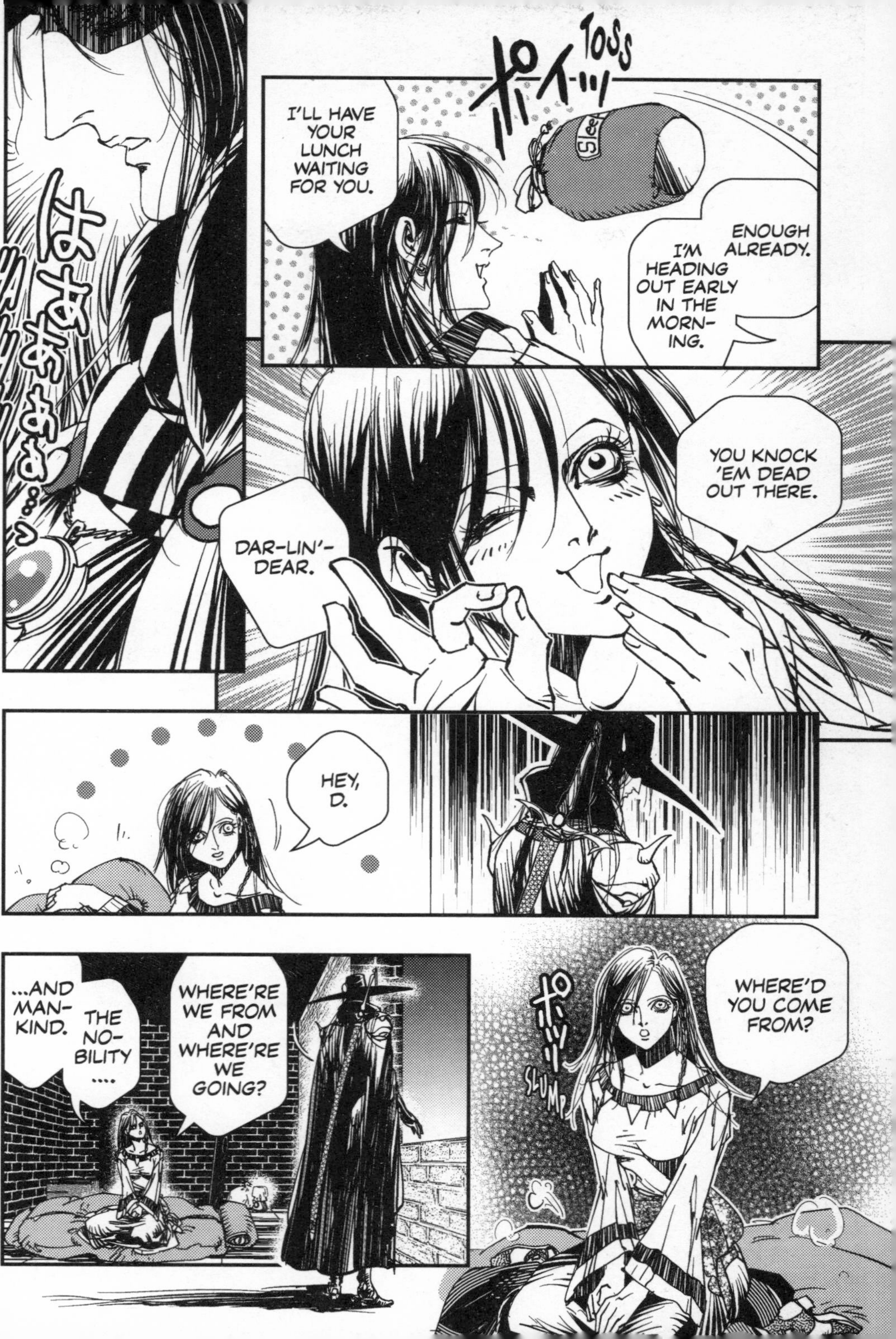
ポイーッ
TOSS
I'LL HAVE YOUR LUNCH WAITING FOR YOU.
ENOUGH ALREADY. I'M HEADING OUT EARLY IN THE MORN-ING.
YOU KNOCK 'EM DEAD OUT THERE.
DAR-LIN'-DEAR.
はあああぁ…
HAHHHH
HEY, D.
ポッ
SLUMP
WHERE'D YOU COME FROM?
WHERE'RE WE FROM AND WHERE'RE WE GOING?
THE NO-BILITY....
...AND MAN-KIND.

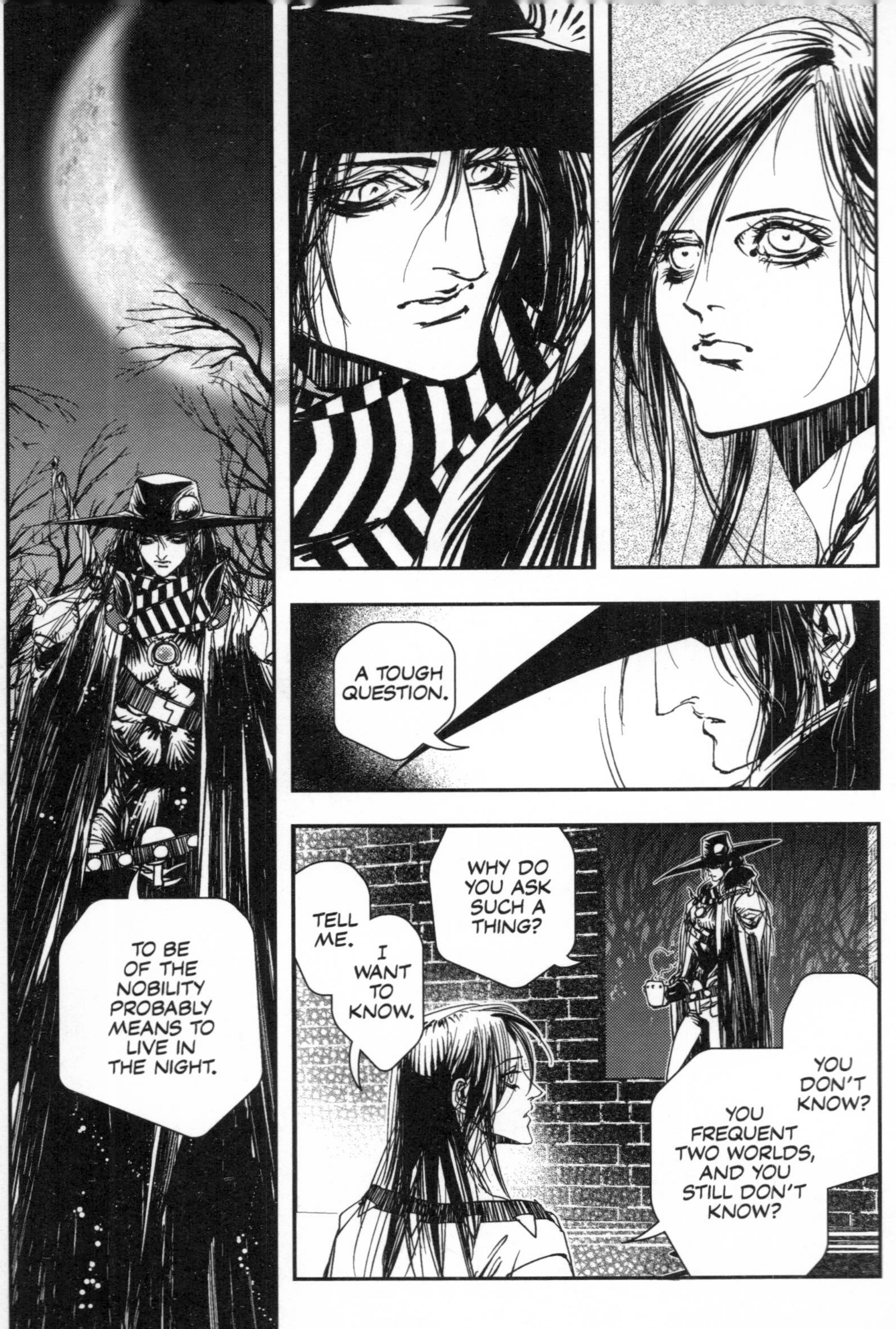
A TOUGH QUESTION.
WHY DO YOU ASK SUCH A THING?
TELL ME.
I WANT TO KNOW.
YOU DON'T KNOW?
YOU FREQUENT TWO WORLDS, AND YOU STILL DON'T KNOW?
TO BE OF THE NOBILITY PROBABLY MEANS TO LIVE IN THE NIGHT.

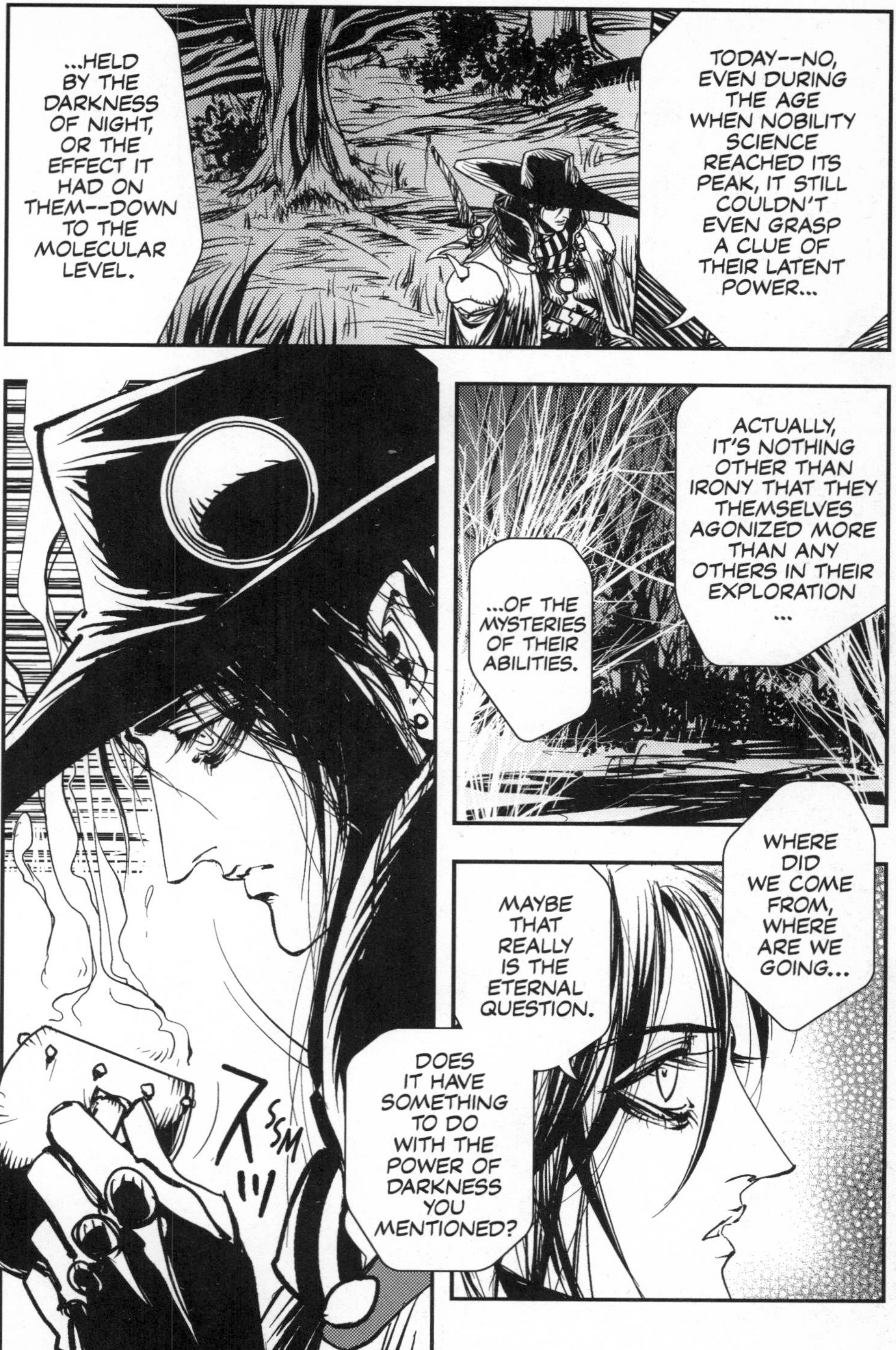
TODAY--NO, EVEN DURING THE AGE WHEN NOBILITY SCIENCE REACHED ITS PEAK, IT STILL COULDN'T EVEN GRASP A CLUE OF THEIR LATENT POWER...
...HELD BY THE DARKNESS OF NIGHT, OR THE EFFECT IT HAD ON THEM--DOWN TO THE MOLECULAR LEVEL.
ACTUALLY, IT'S NOTHING OTHER THAN IRONY THAT THEY THEMSELVES AGONIZED MORE THAN ANY OTHERS IN THEIR EXPLORATION ...
...OF THE MYSTERIES OF THEIR ABILITIES.
WHERE DID WE COME FROM, WHERE ARE WE GOING...
MAYBE THAT REALLY IS THE ETERNAL QUESTION.
DOES IT HAVE SOMETHING TO DO WITH THE POWER OF DARKNESS YOU MENTIONED?
SSSM

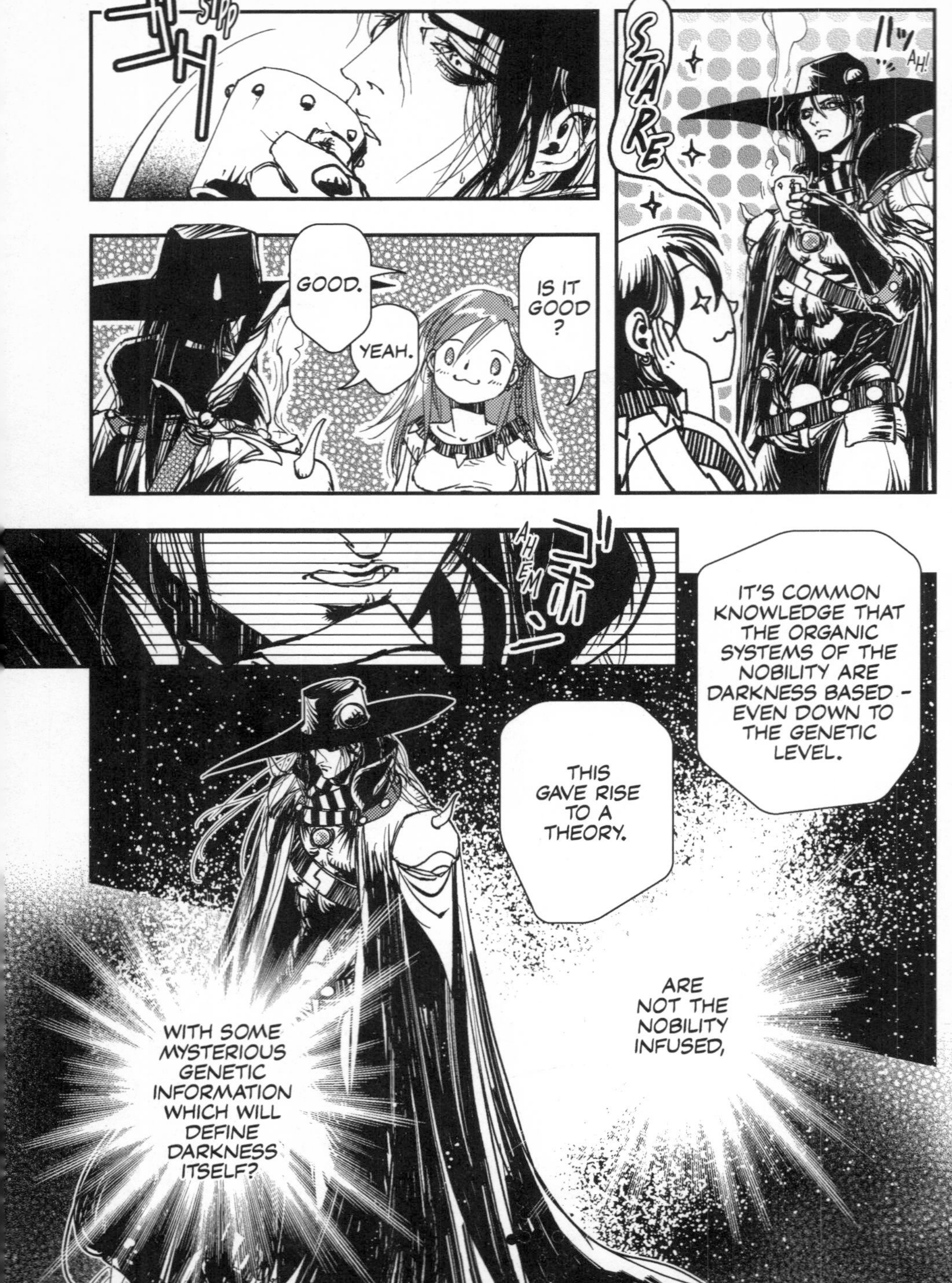
STARE
ハッ
AH!
SIPP
IS IT GOOD?
GOOD.
YEAH.
AHEM
IT'S COMMON KNOWLEDGE THAT THE ORGANIC SYSTEMS OF THE NOBILITY ARE DARKNESS BASED - EVEN DOWN TO THE GENETIC LEVEL.
THIS GAVE RISE TO A THEORY.
ARE NOT THE NOBILITY INFUSED,
WITH SOME MYSTERIOUS GENETIC INFORMATION WHICH WILL DEFINE DARKNESS ITSELF?

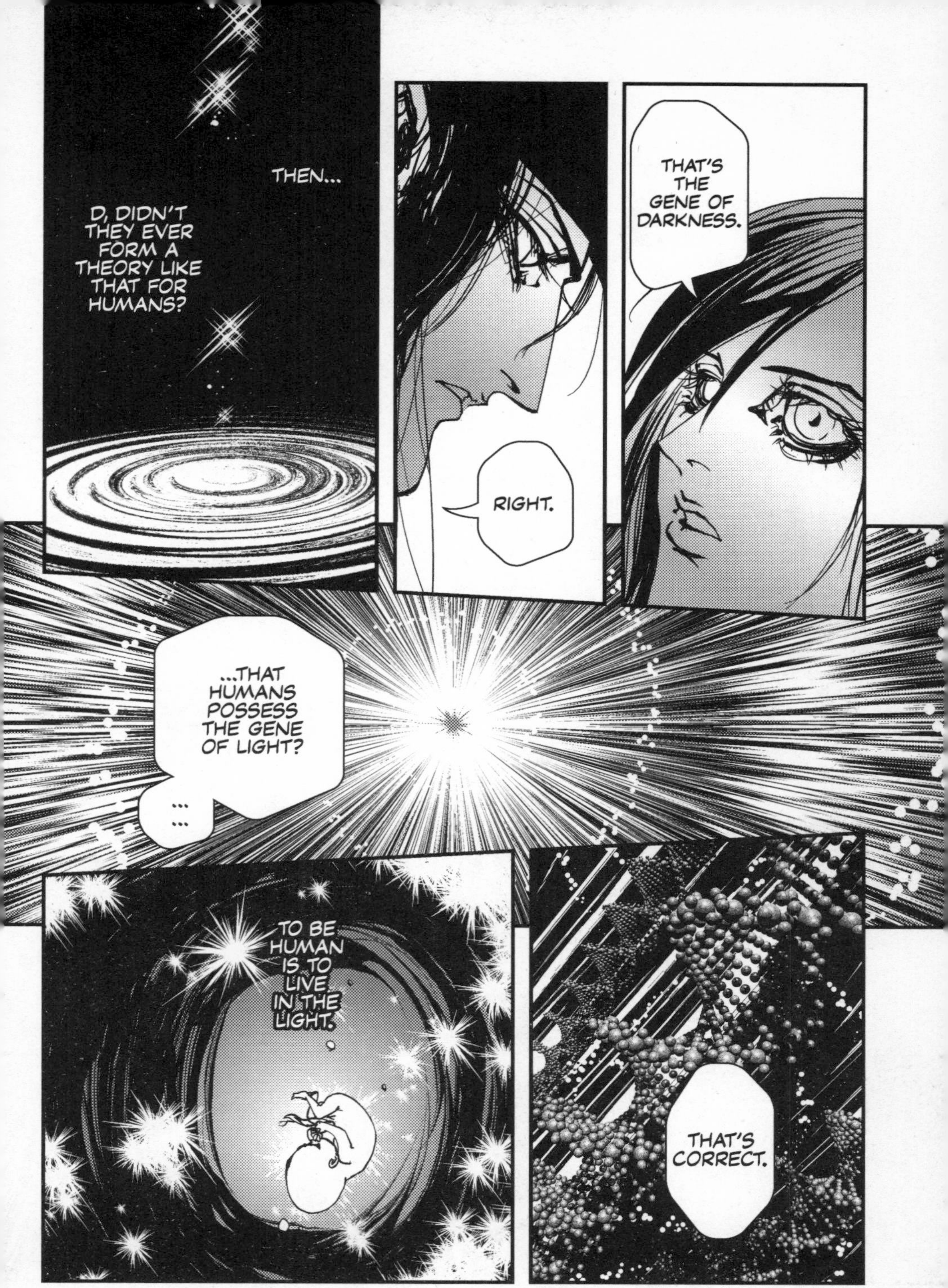
THAT'S THE GENE OF DARKNESS.
RIGHT.
THEN...
D, DIDN'T THEY EVER FORM A THEORY LIKE THAT FOR HUMANS?
...THAT HUMANS POSSESS THE GENE OF LIGHT?
... ...
THAT'S CORRECT.
TO BE HUMAN IS TO LIVE IN THE LIGHT.

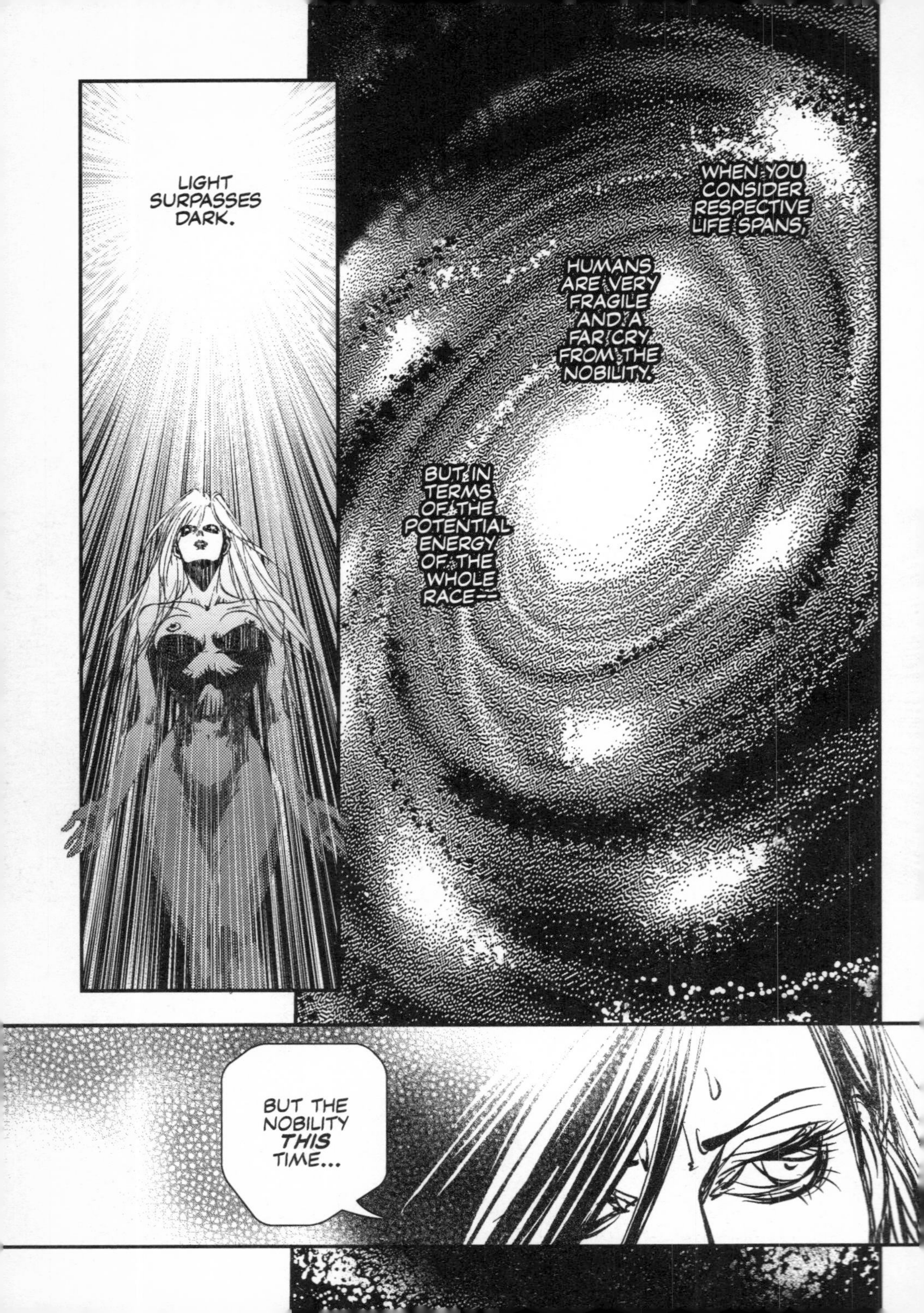
WHEN YOU CONSIDER RESPECTIVE LIFE SPANS,
HUMANS ARE VERY FRAGILE AND A FAR CRY FROM THE NOBILITY.
BUT IN TERMS OF THE POTENTIAL ENERGY OF THE WHOLE RACE--
LIGHT SURPASSES DARK.
BUT THE NOBILITY *THIS* TIME...

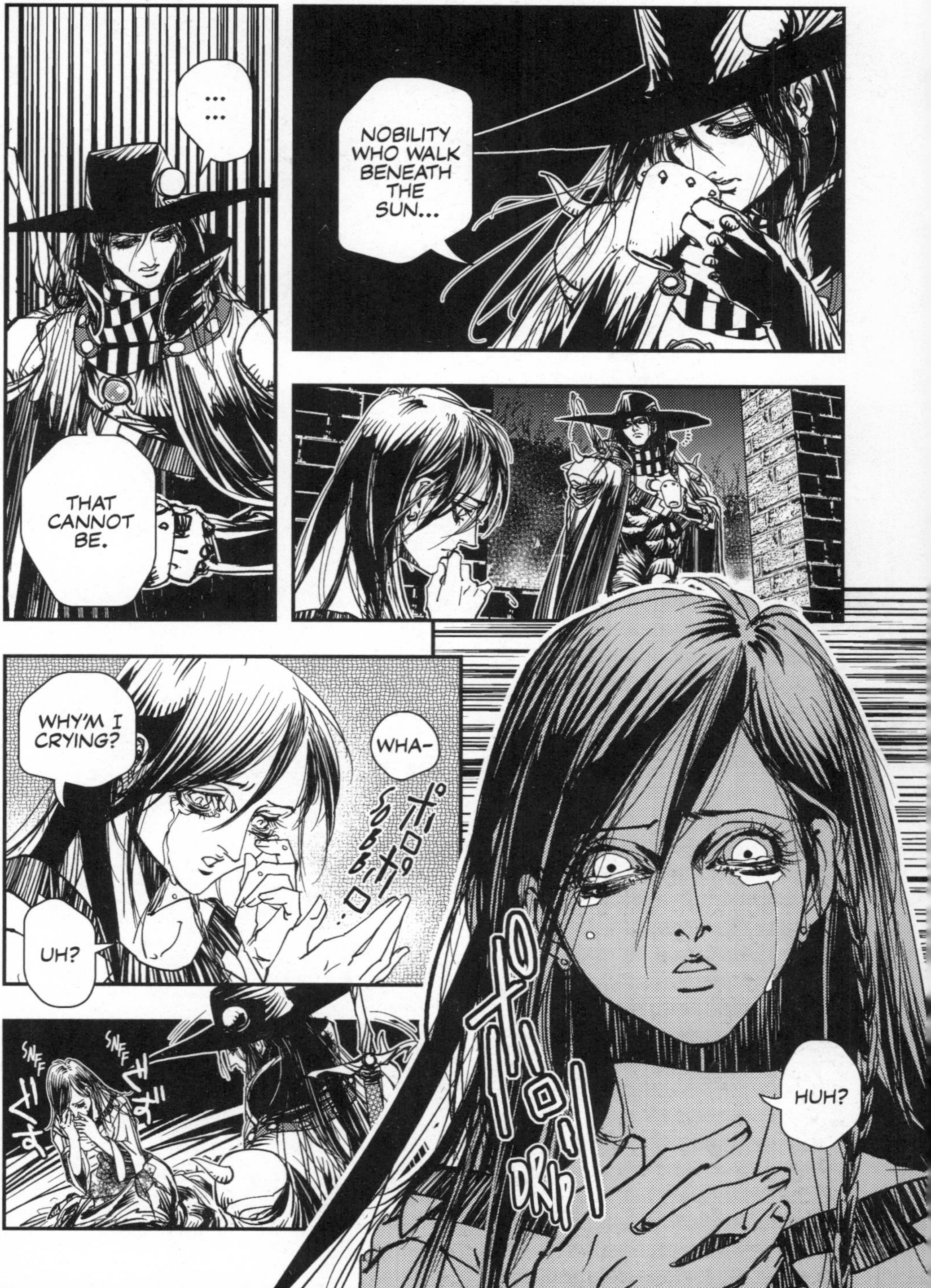
NOBILITY WHO WALK BENEATH THE SUN...
......
THAT CANNOT BE.
HUH?
DRIP
WHY'M I CRYING?
WHA-
UH?
SNFF
SNFF

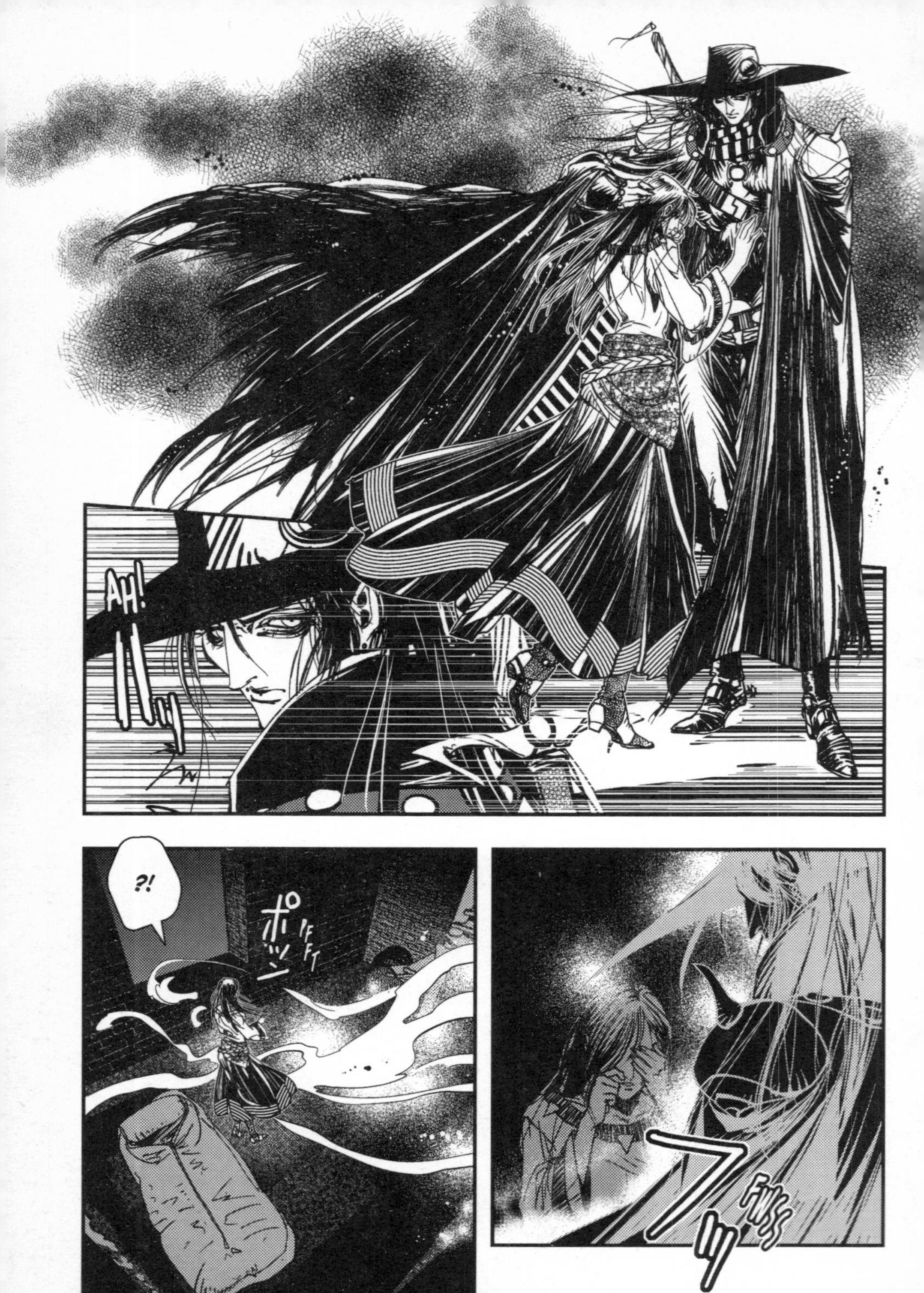
AH!
フ
FWISS
?!
ポツン
PFFT

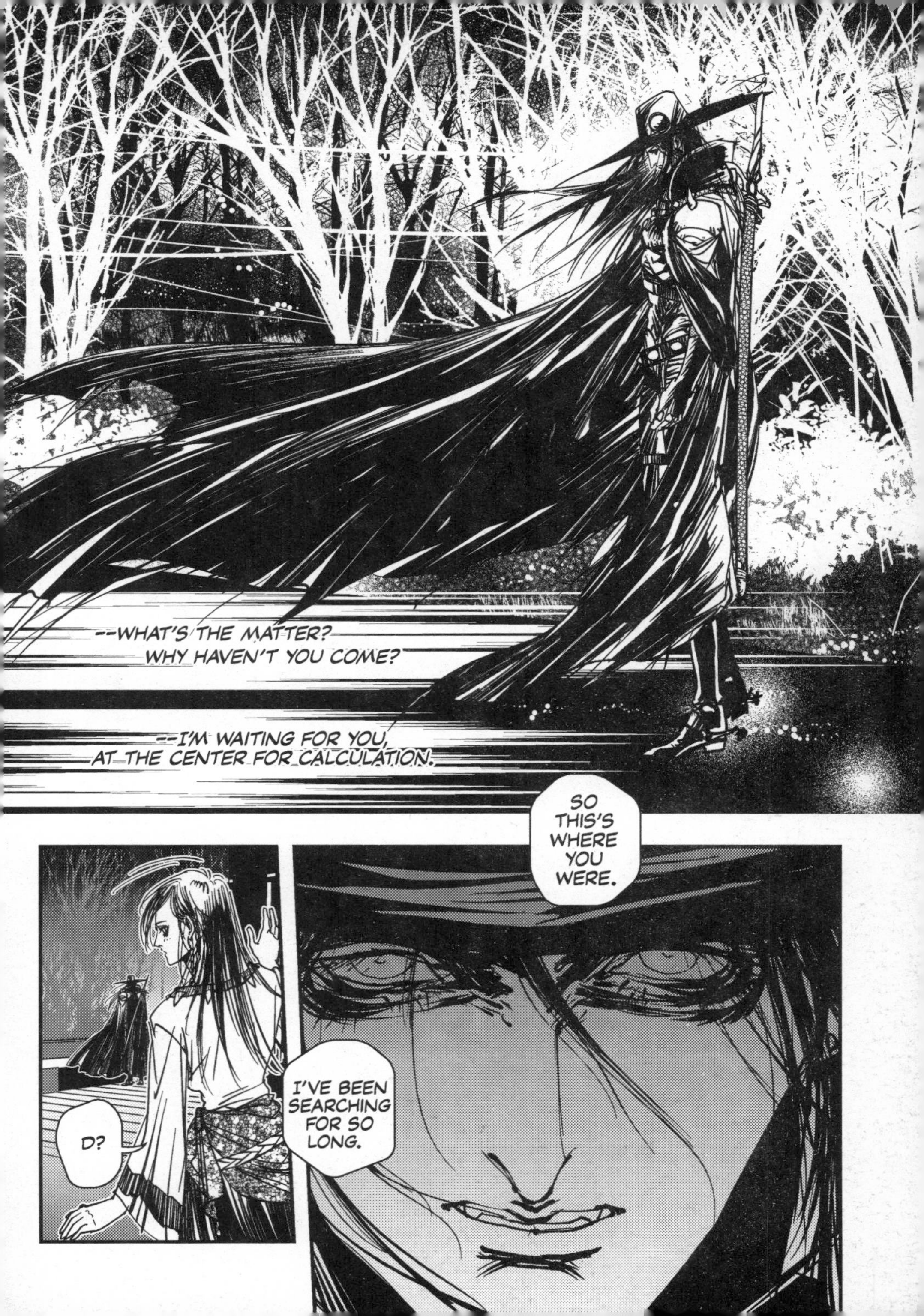
--WHAT'S THE MATTER? WHY HAVEN'T YOU COME?
--I'M WAITING FOR YOU, AT THE CENTER FOR CALCULATION.
SO THIS'S WHERE YOU WERE.
I'VE BEEN SEARCHING FOR SO LONG.
D?

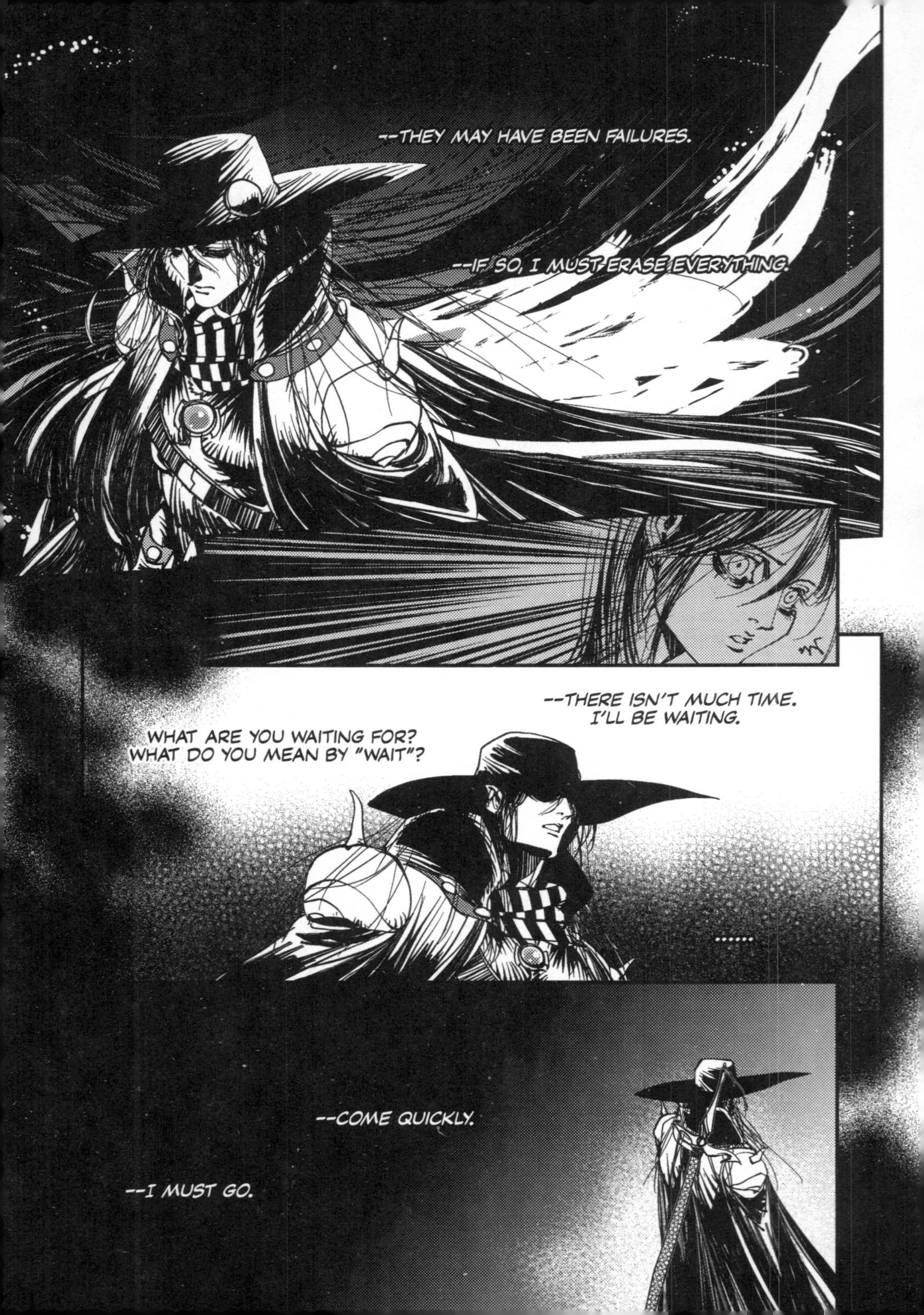
--THEY MAY HAVE BEEN FAILURES.
--IF SO, I MUST ERASE EVERYTHING.
--THERE ISN'T MUCH TIME. I'LL BE WAITING.
WHAT ARE YOU WAITING FOR? WHAT DO YOU MEAN BY "WAIT"?
......
--COME QUICKLY.
--I MUST GO.

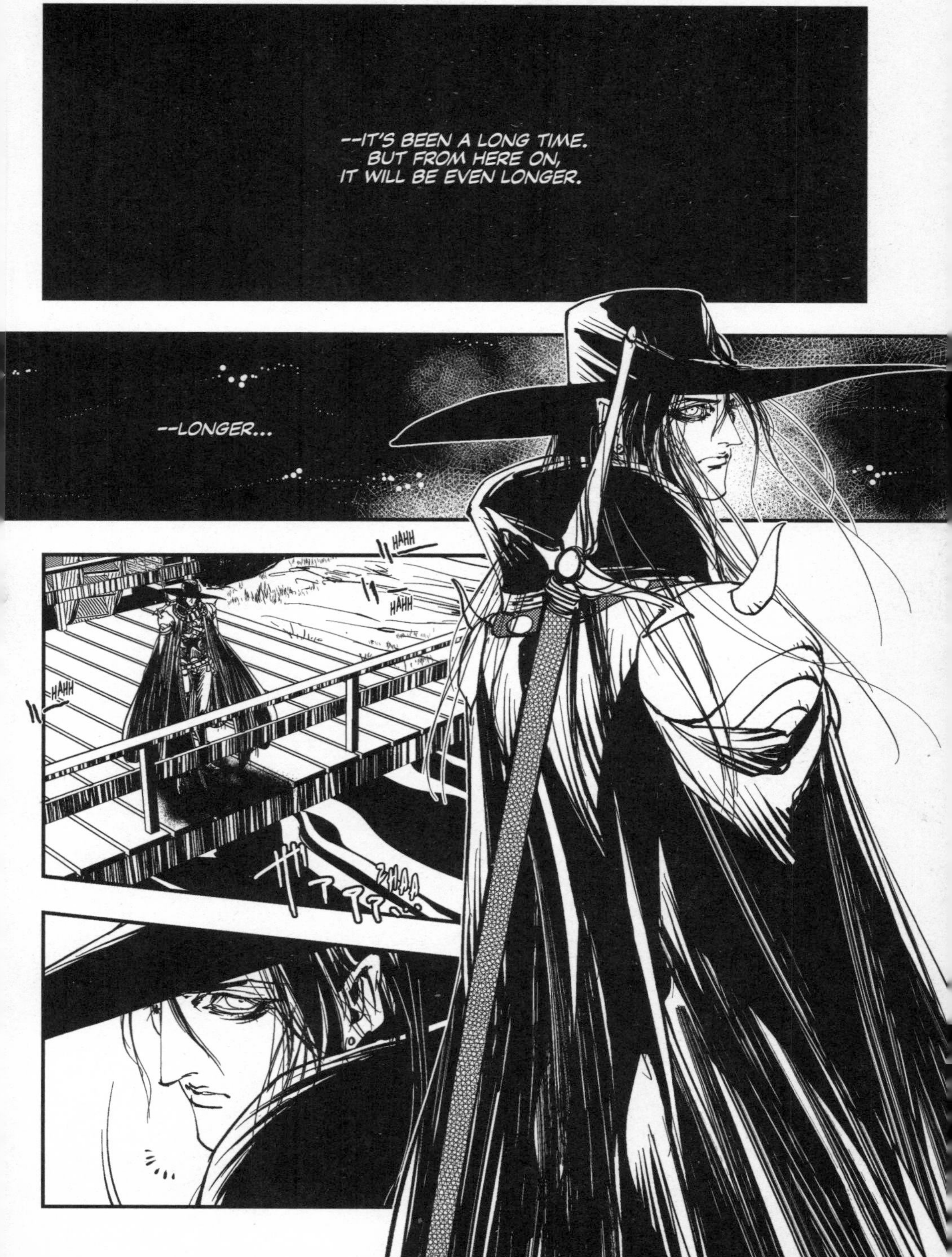
--IT'S BEEN A LONG TIME.
BUT FROM HERE ON,
IT WILL BE EVEN LONGER.
--LONGER...
HAHH
HAHH
HAHH
ZHAA

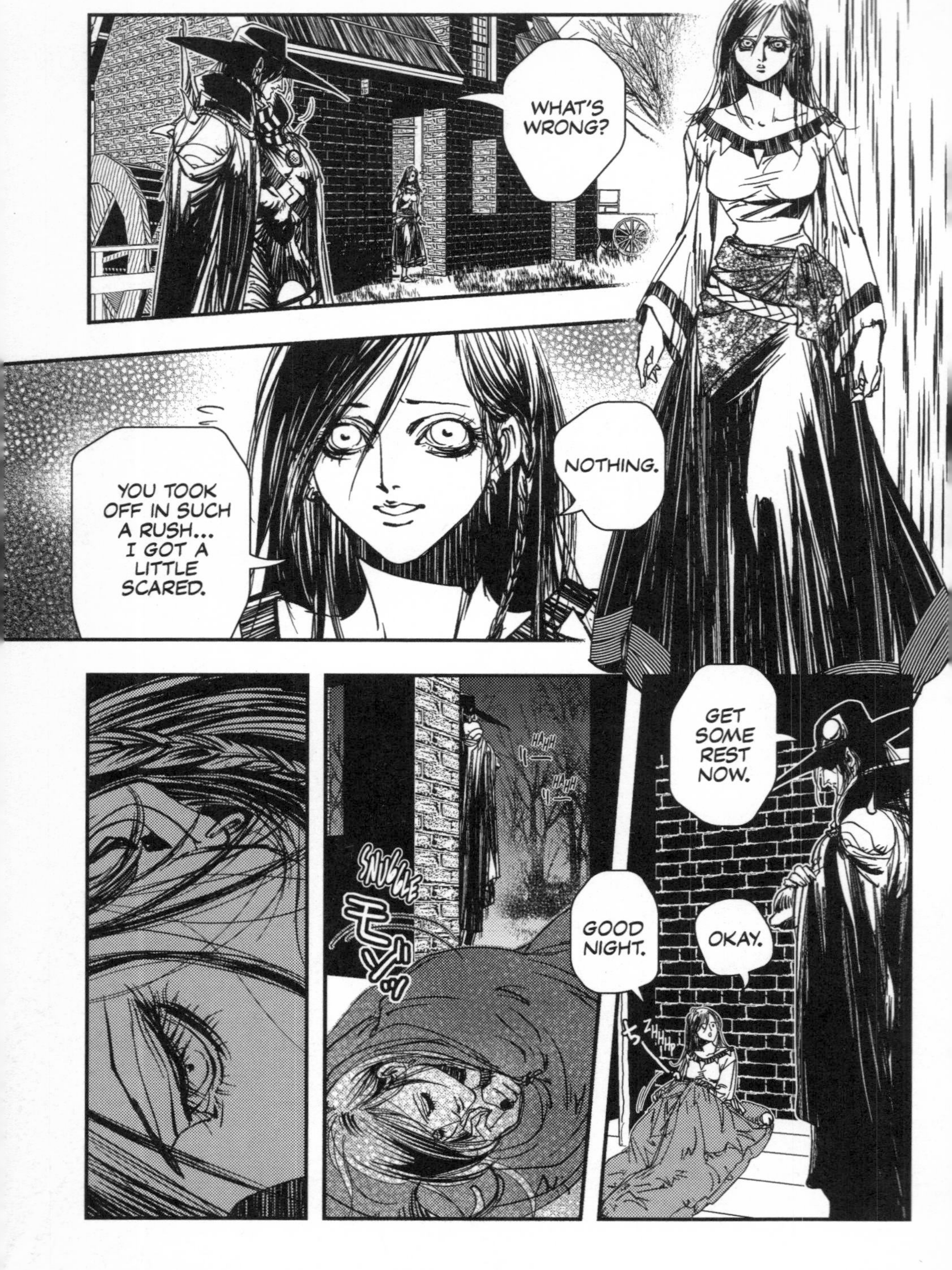
WHAT'S WRONG?
NOTHING.
YOU TOOK OFF IN SUCH A RUSH... I GOT A LITTLE SCARED.
GET SOME REST NOW.
OKAY.
GOOD NIGHT.
ZHHHP
HAHH
HAHH
SNUGGLE

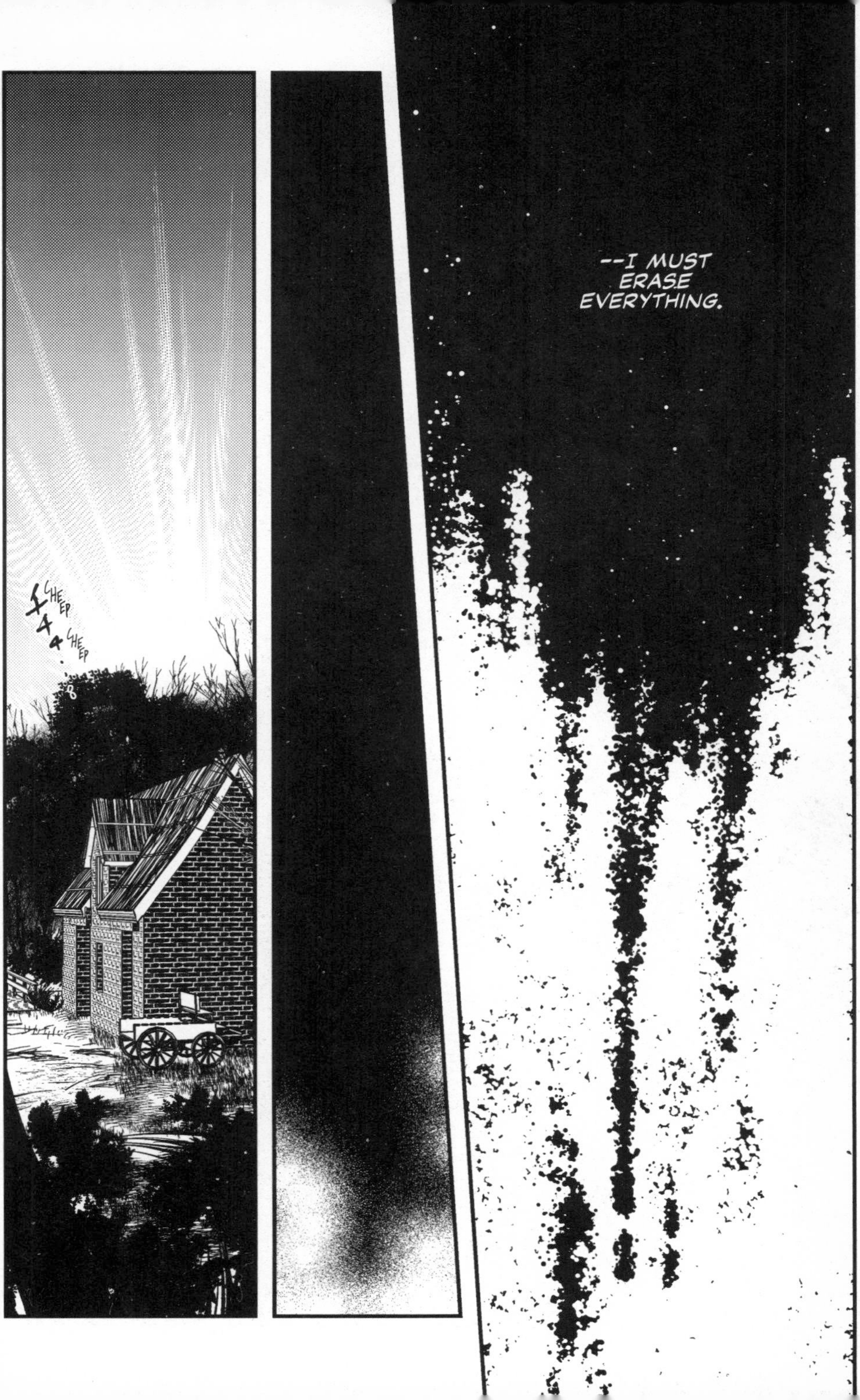
--I MUST
ERASE
EVERYTHING.
CHEEP
CHEEP

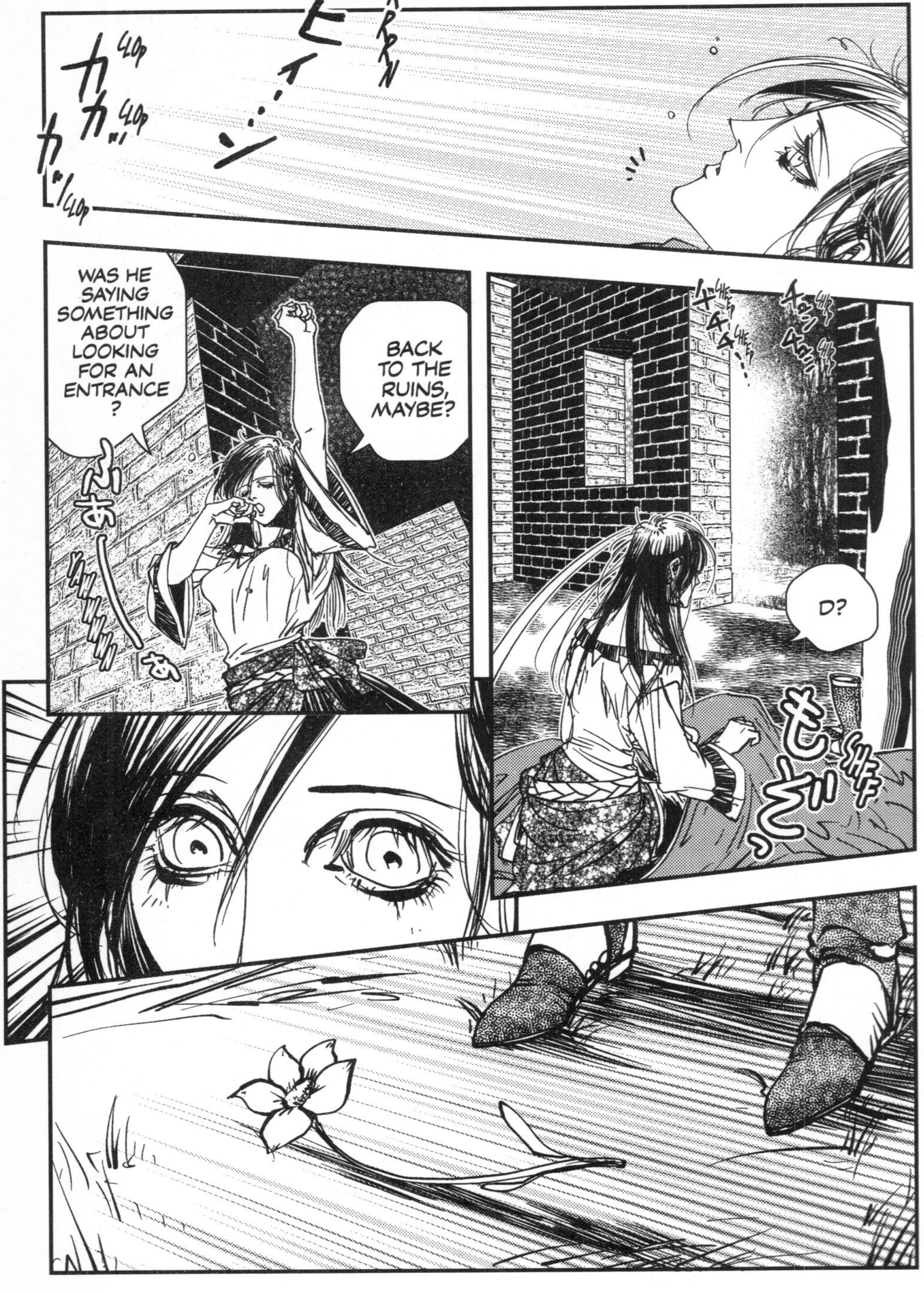
HR HR RRRN
ヒヒィ…ン
CLOP CLOP CLOP
CHEEP CHEEP
D?
もぞ
SHF
BACK TO THE RUINS, MAYBE?
WAS HE SAYING SOMETHING ABOUT LOOKING FOR AN ENTRANCE?
ふあ～

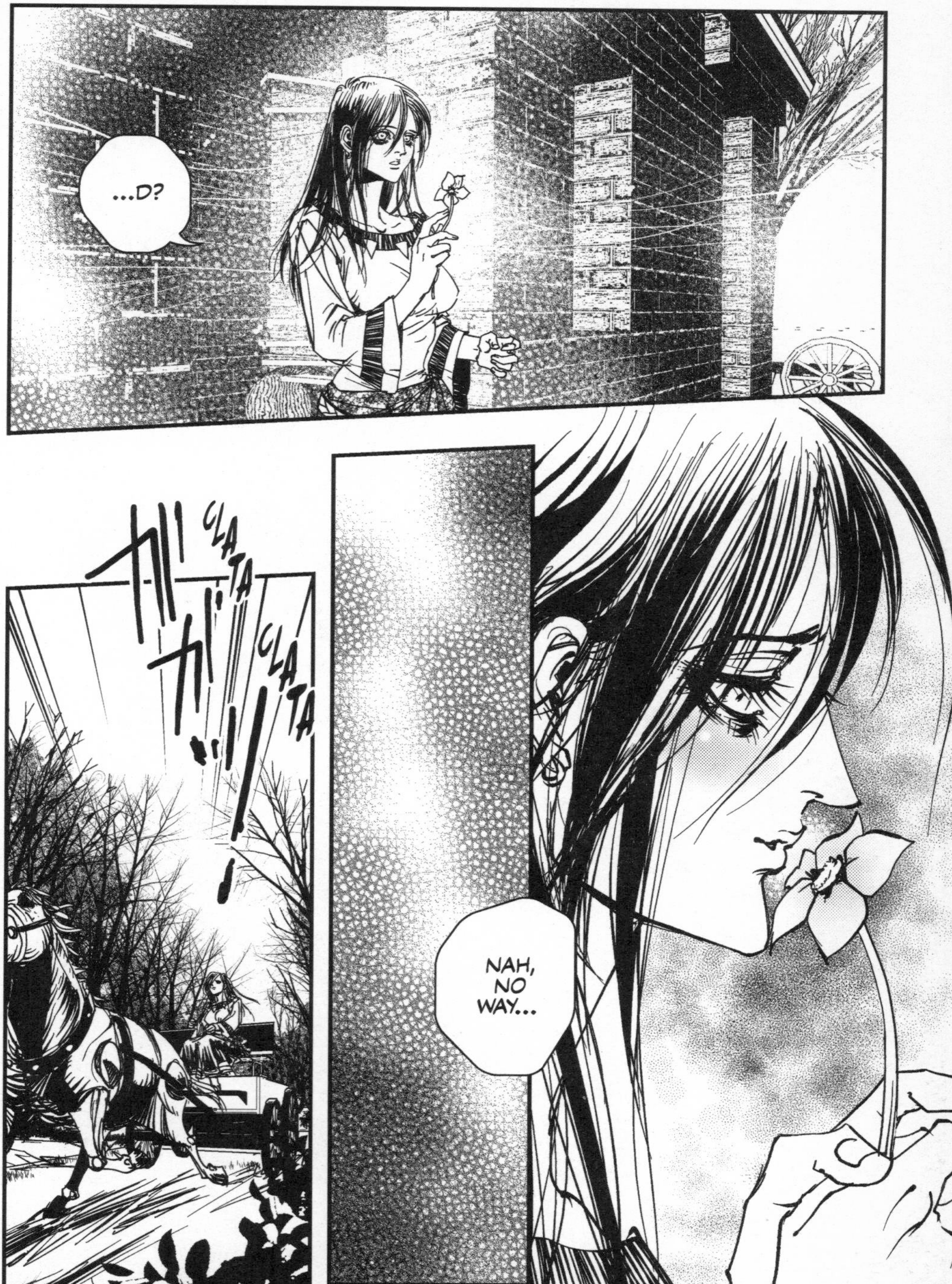
...D?
NAH, NO WAY...
CLATA
CLATA

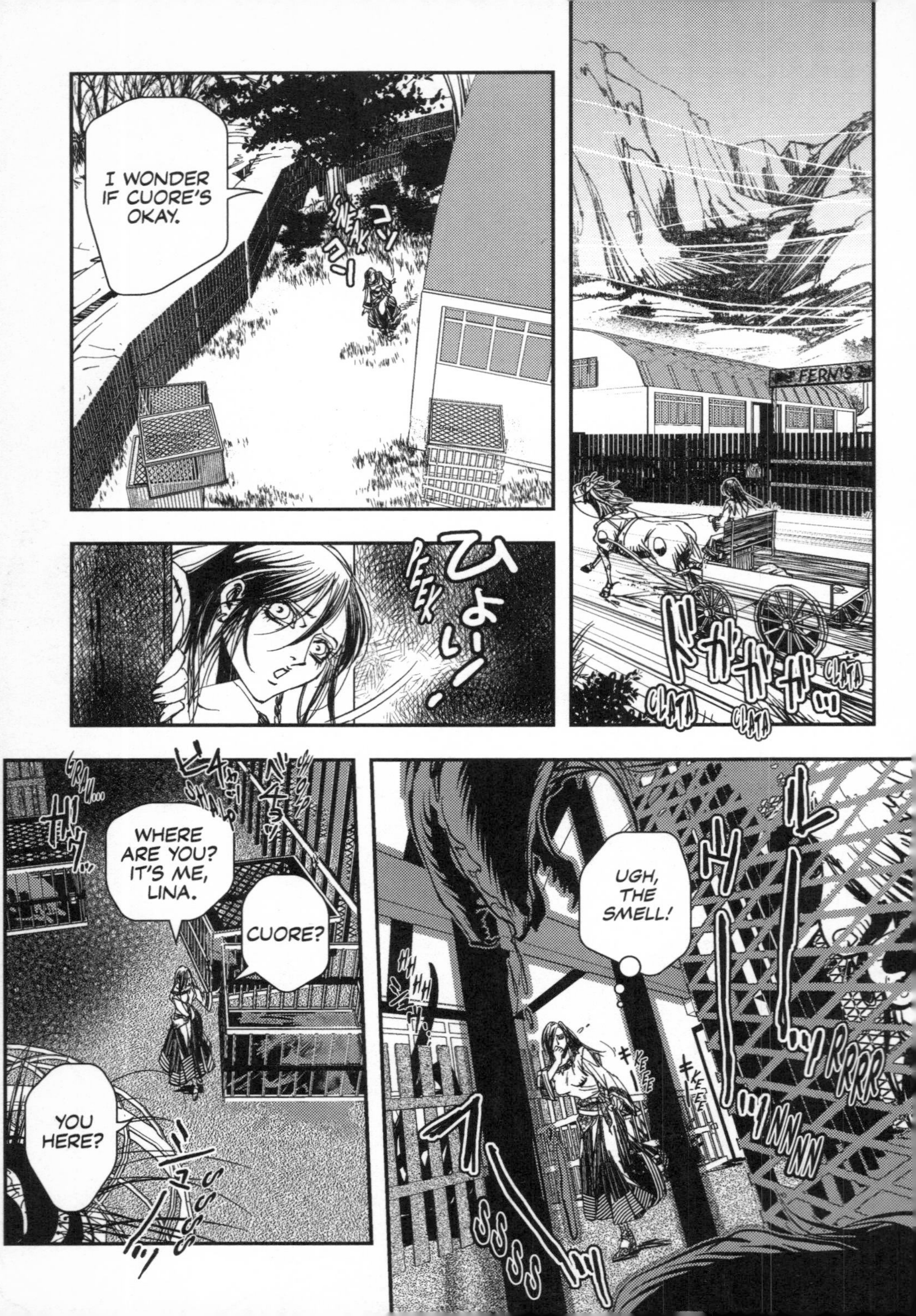
FERN'S
CLATA
CLATA
CLATA
I WONDER IF CUORE'S OKAY.
SNEAK
PEEK
UGH, THE SMELL!
RRRR
NNNN
SSSS
WHERE ARE YOU? IT'S ME, LINA.
CUORE?
YOU HERE?

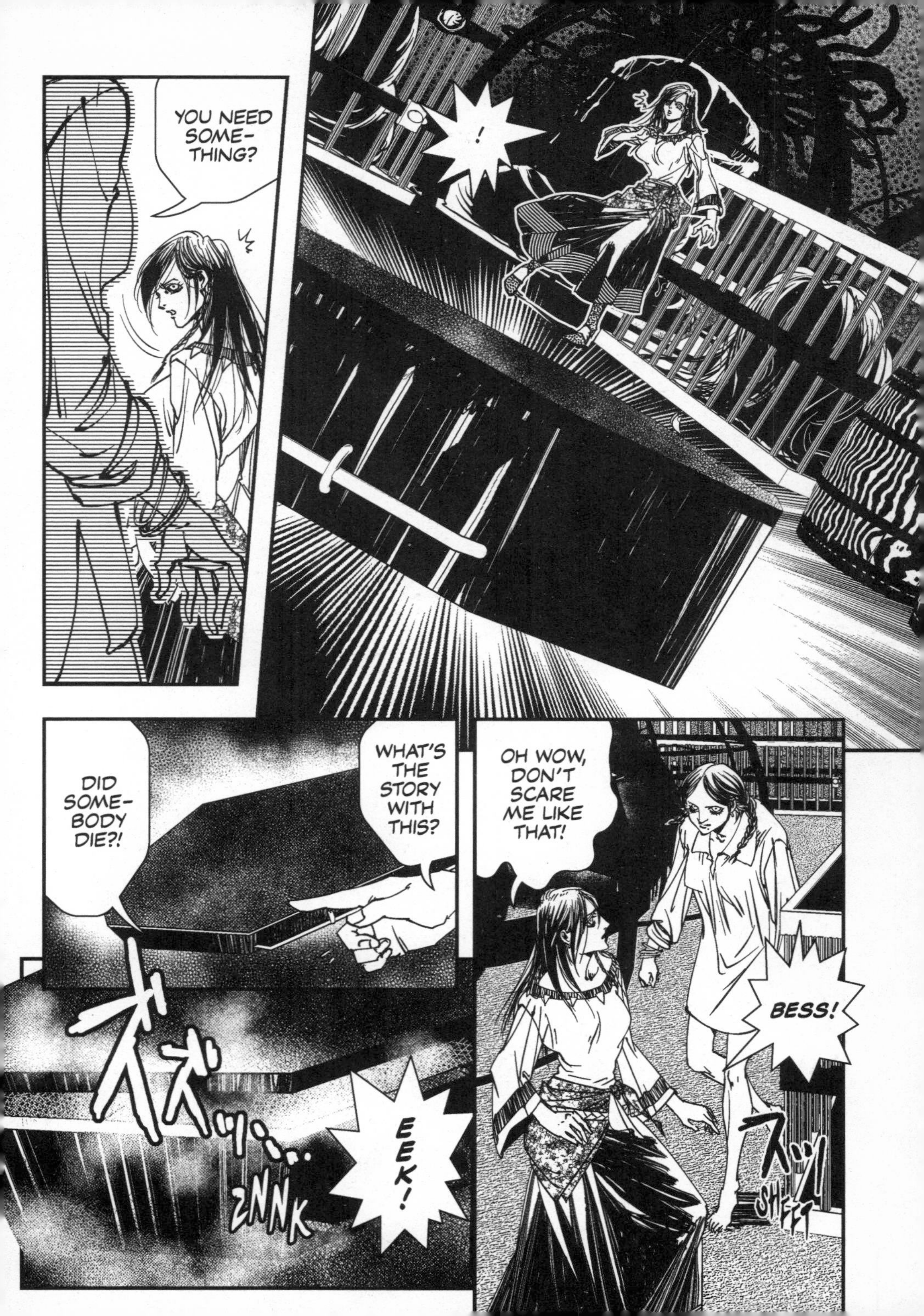
!
YOU NEED SOME-THING?
OH WOW, DON'T SCARE ME LIKE THAT!
BESS!
WHAT'S THE STORY WITH THIS?
DID SOME-BODY DIE?!
EEK!
ZNNK

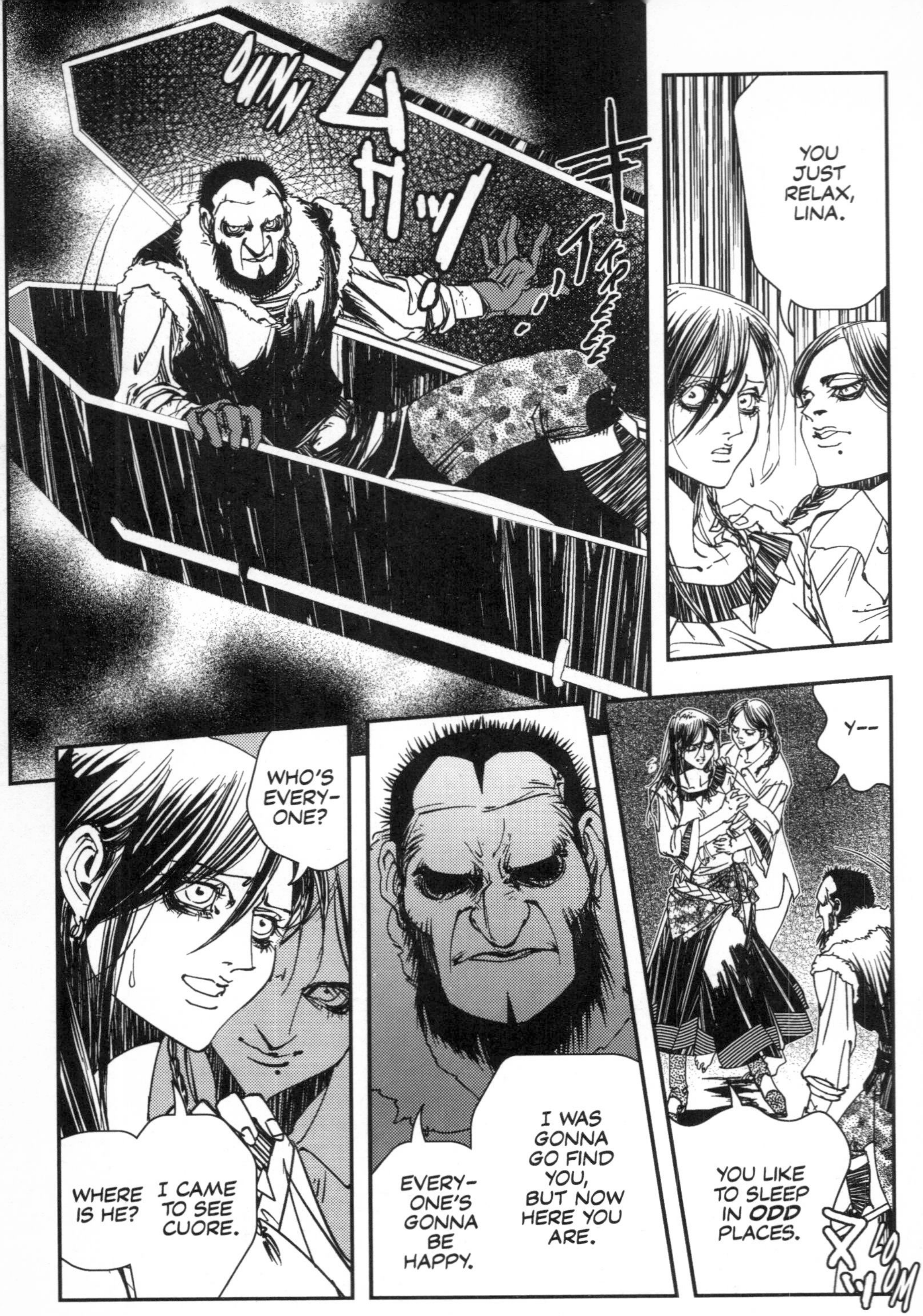
YOU JUST RELAX, LINA.
DUNN
Y--
YOU LIKE TO SLEEP IN ODD PLACES.
I WAS GONNA GO FIND YOU, BUT NOW HERE YOU ARE.
EVERY-ONE'S GONNA BE HAPPY.
WHO'S EVERY-ONE?
I CAME TO SEE CUORE.
WHERE IS HE?

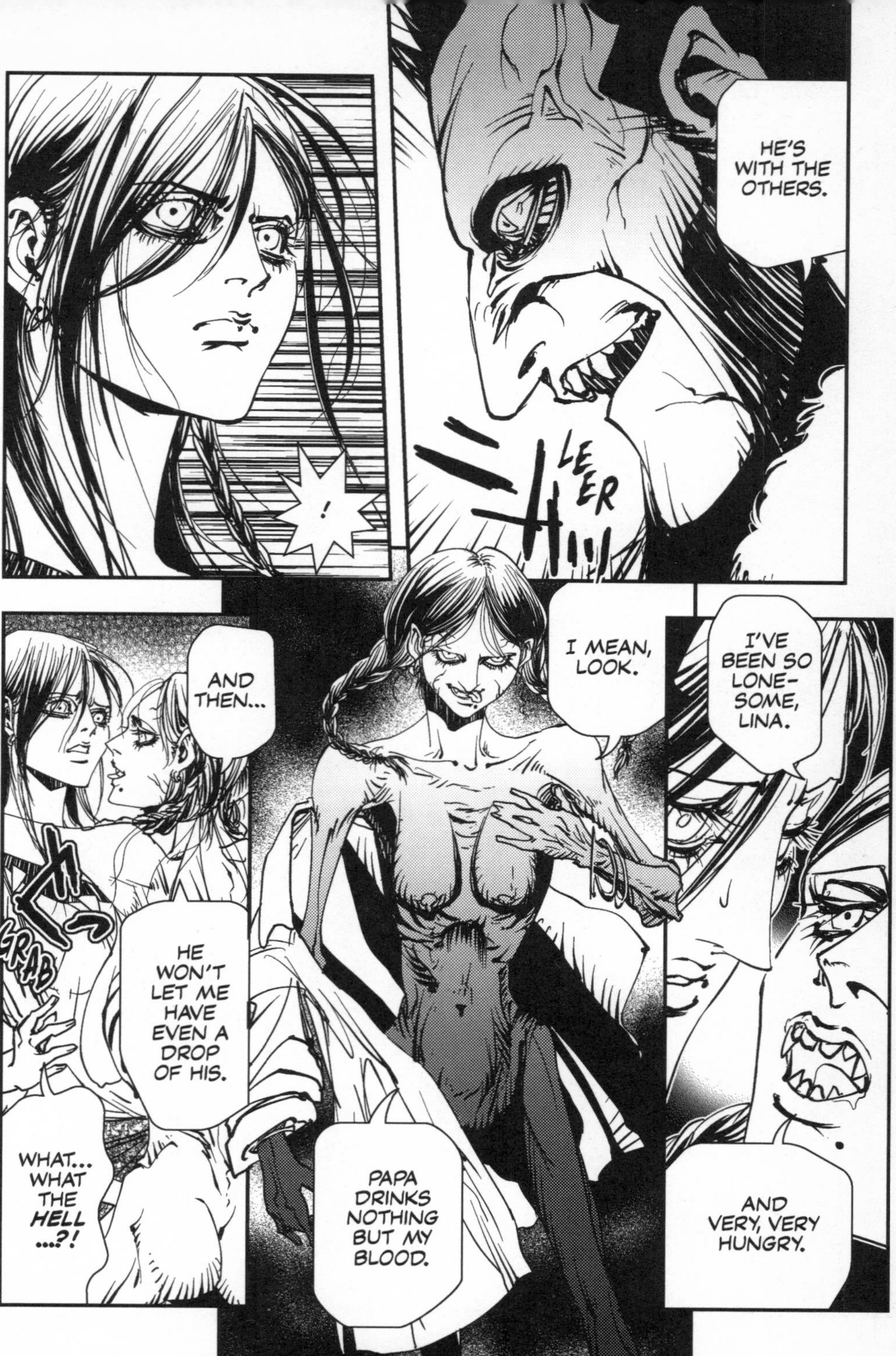
HE'S WITH THE OTHERS.
LEER
!
I'VE BEEN SO LONE-SOME, LINA.
AND VERY, VERY HUNGRY.
I MEAN, LOOK.
PAPA DRINKS NOTHING BUT MY BLOOD.
AND THEN...
GRAB
HE WON'T LET ME HAVE EVEN A DROP OF HIS.
WHAT... WHAT THE HELL ...?!

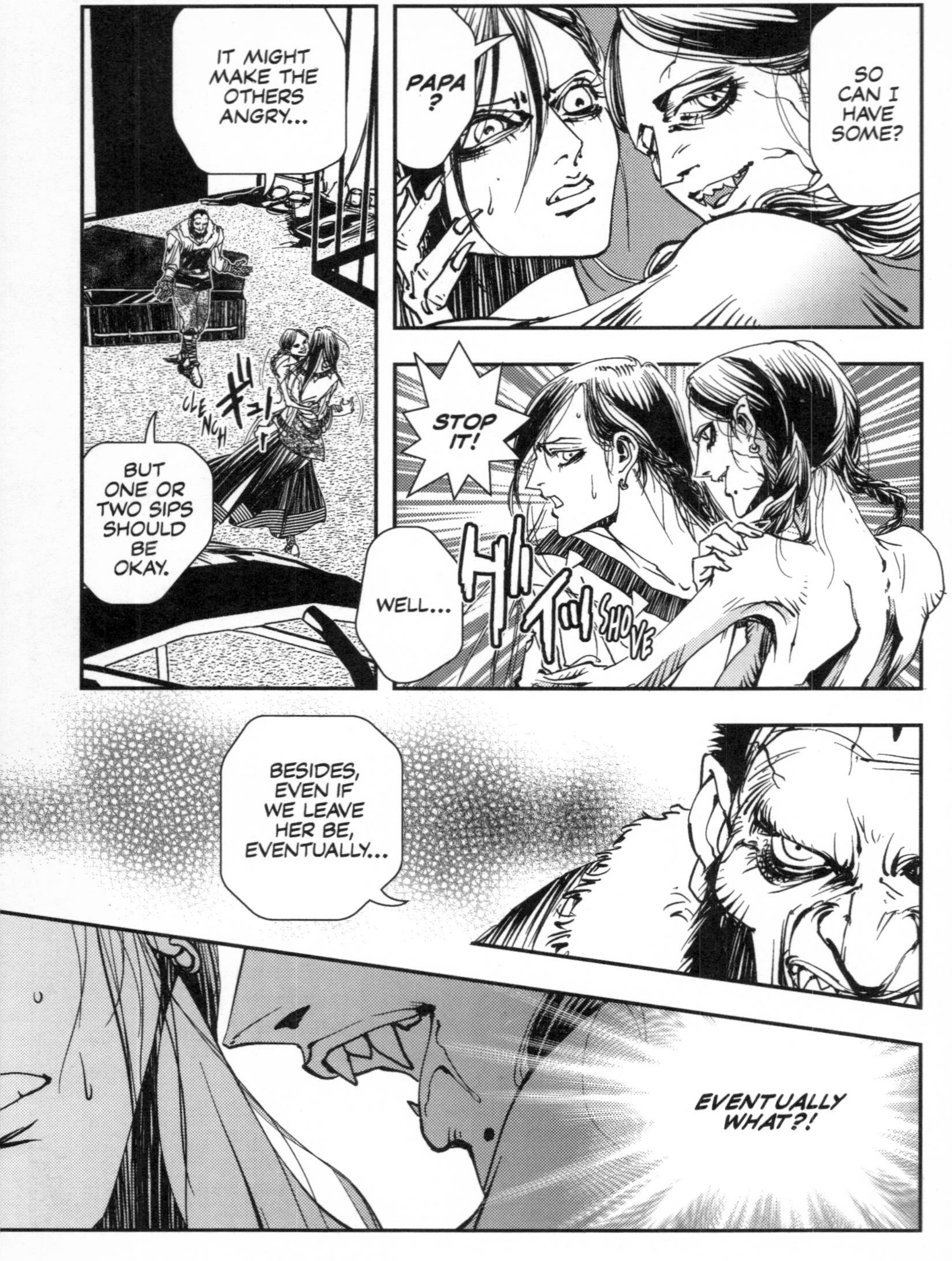
SO CAN I HAVE SOME?
PAPA?
STOP IT!
WELL...
SHOVE
IT MIGHT MAKE THE OTHERS ANGRY...
CLENCH
BUT ONE OR TWO SIPS SHOULD BE OKAY.
BESIDES, EVEN IF WE LEAVE HER BE, EVENTUALLY...
EVENTUALLY WHAT?!

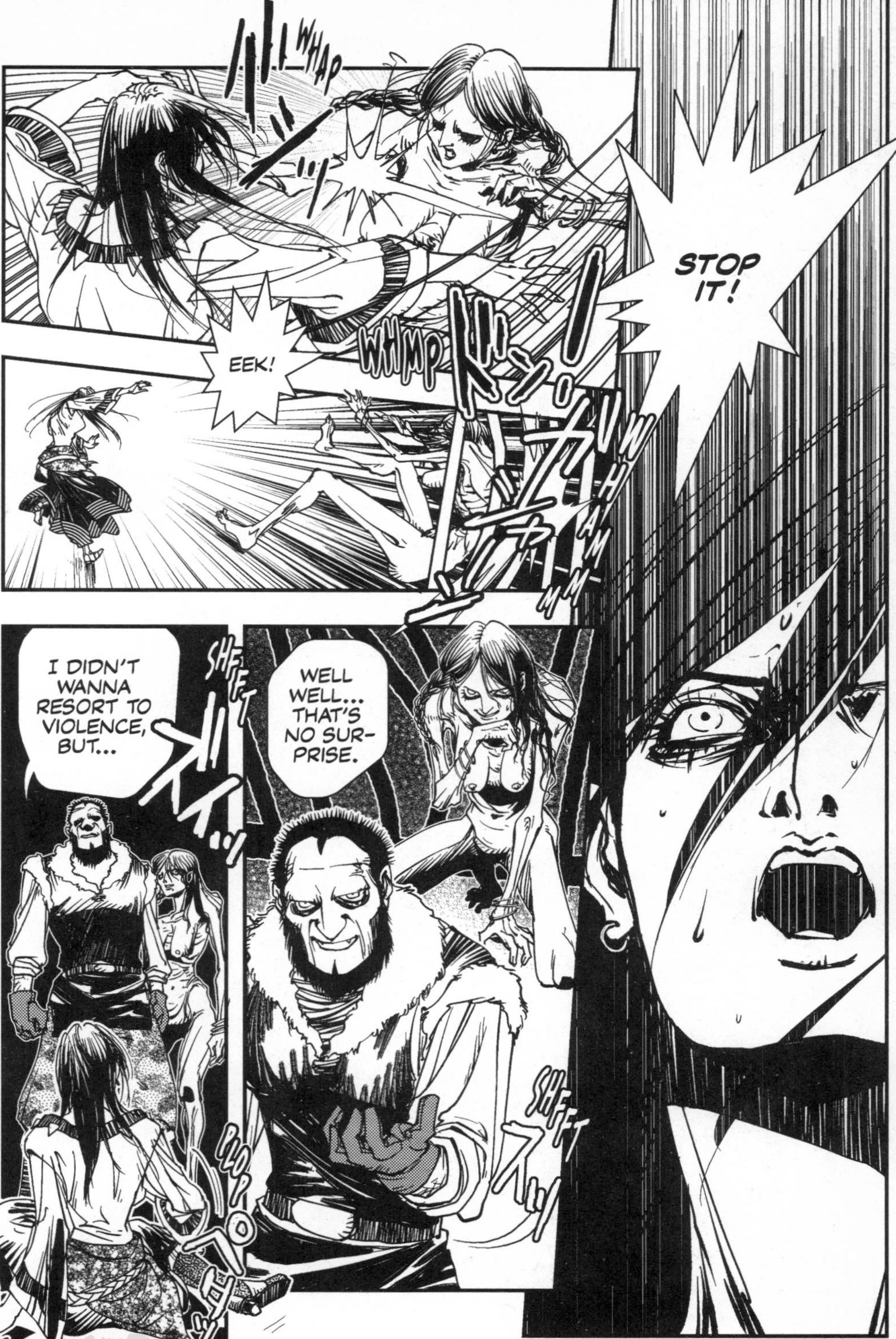
STOP IT!
WHAP
EEK!
WHMP
WHAMM
WELL WELL... THAT'S NO SUR-PRISE.
SHFFT
I DIDN'T WANNA RESORT TO VIOLENCE, BUT...
SHFFT
PLOP

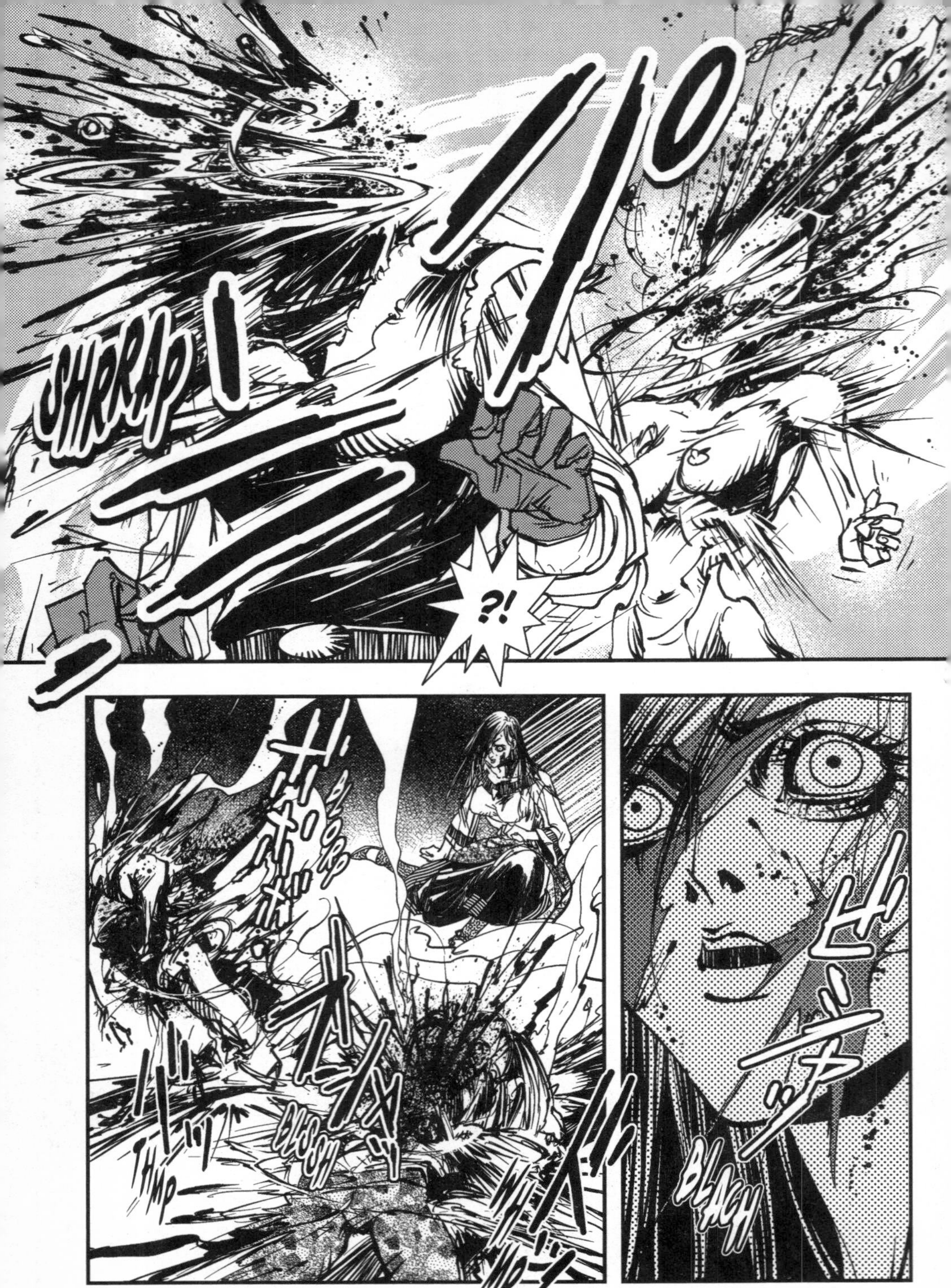
SHKRAP
?!
BLACH
BLOORP
WHUMP
BLOSH
THMP

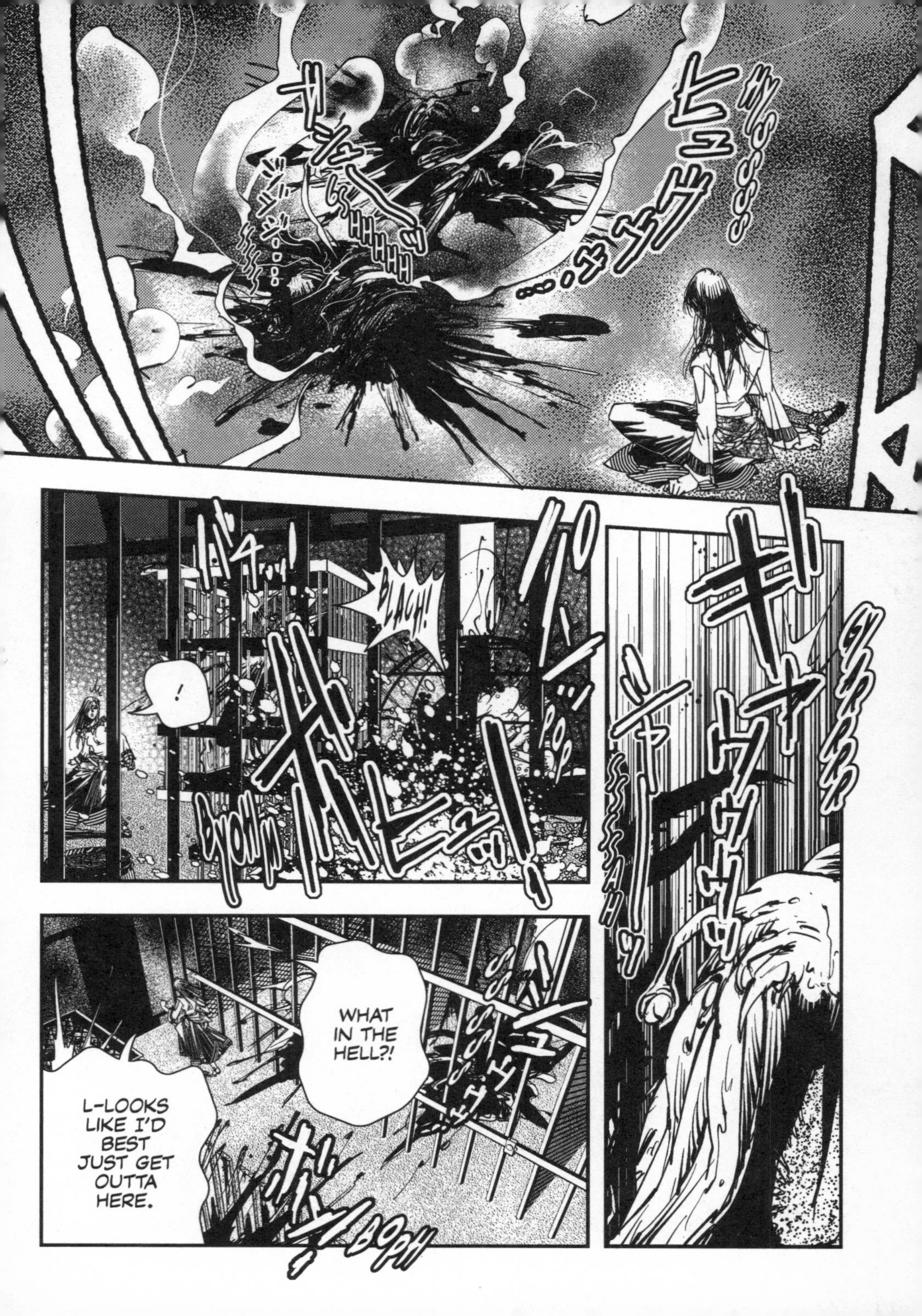
BLACH!
!
WHAT IN THE HELL?!
L-LOOKS LIKE I'D BEST JUST GET OUTTA HERE.

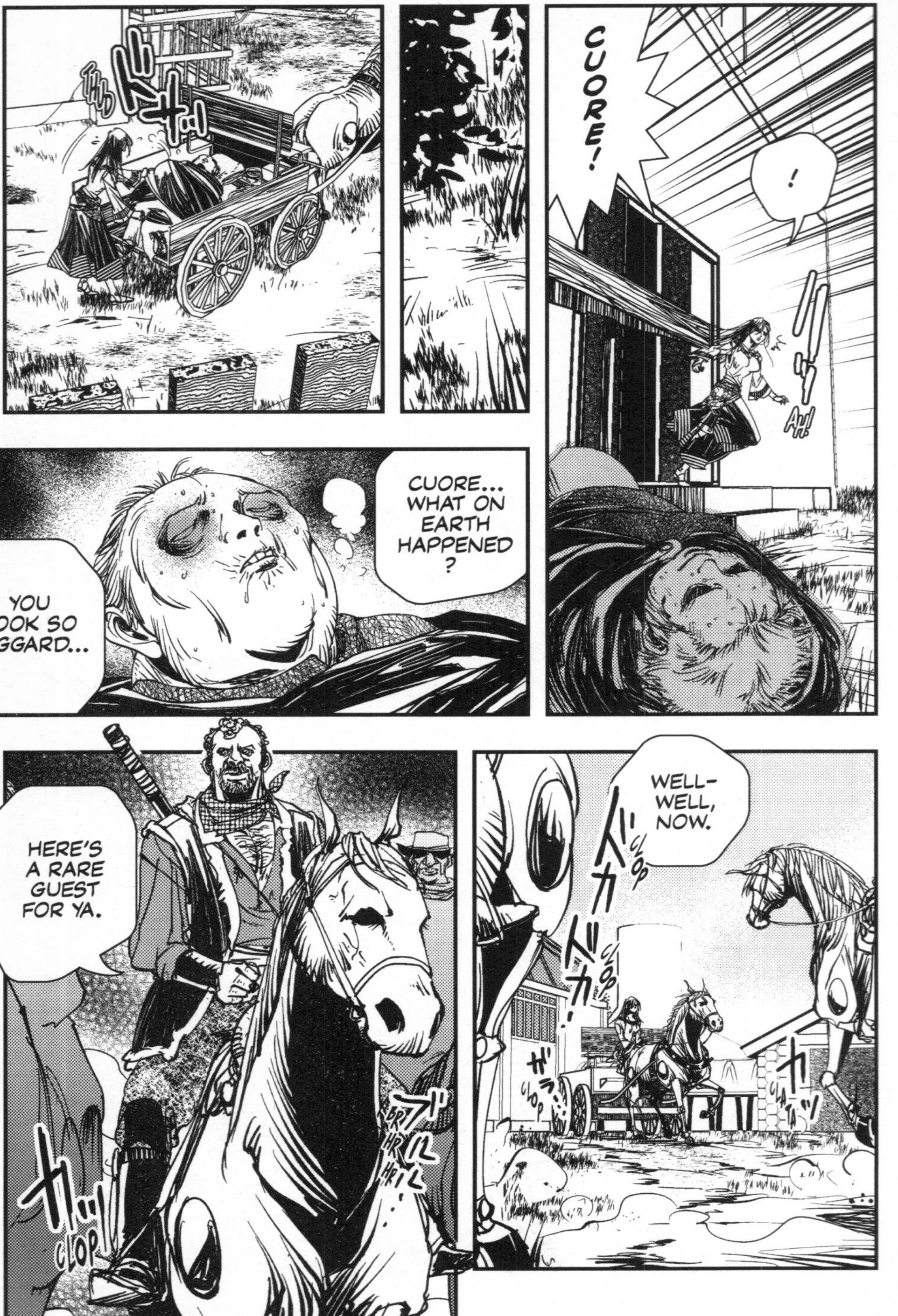

CUORE!
!
AH!
CUORE... WHAT ON EARTH HAPPENED?
YOU LOOK SO HAGGARD...
WELL-WELL, NOW.
CLOP
CLOP
CLOP
HERE'S A RARE GUEST FOR YA.
CLOP

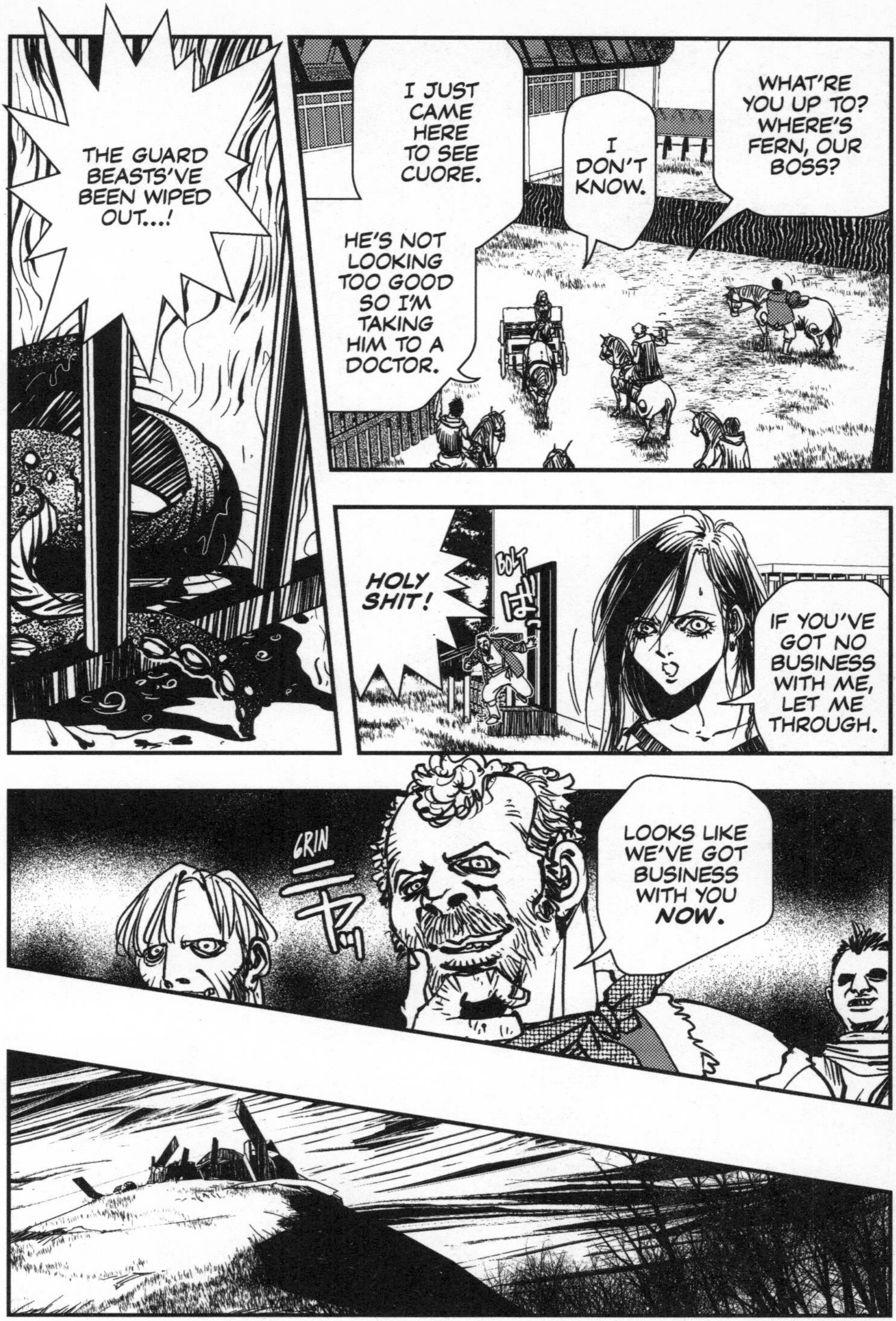
WHAT'RE YOU UP TO? WHERE'S FERN, OUR BOSS?
I DON'T KNOW.
I JUST CAME HERE TO SEE CUORE.
HE'S NOT LOOKING TOO GOOD SO I'M TAKING HIM TO A DOCTOR.
IF YOU'VE GOT NO BUSINESS WITH ME, LET ME THROUGH.
BOLT
ばっ
HOLY SHIT!
THE GUARD BEASTS'VE BEEN WIPED OUT...!
LOOKS LIKE WE'VE GOT BUSINESS WITH YOU NOW.
GRIN
ニヤッ

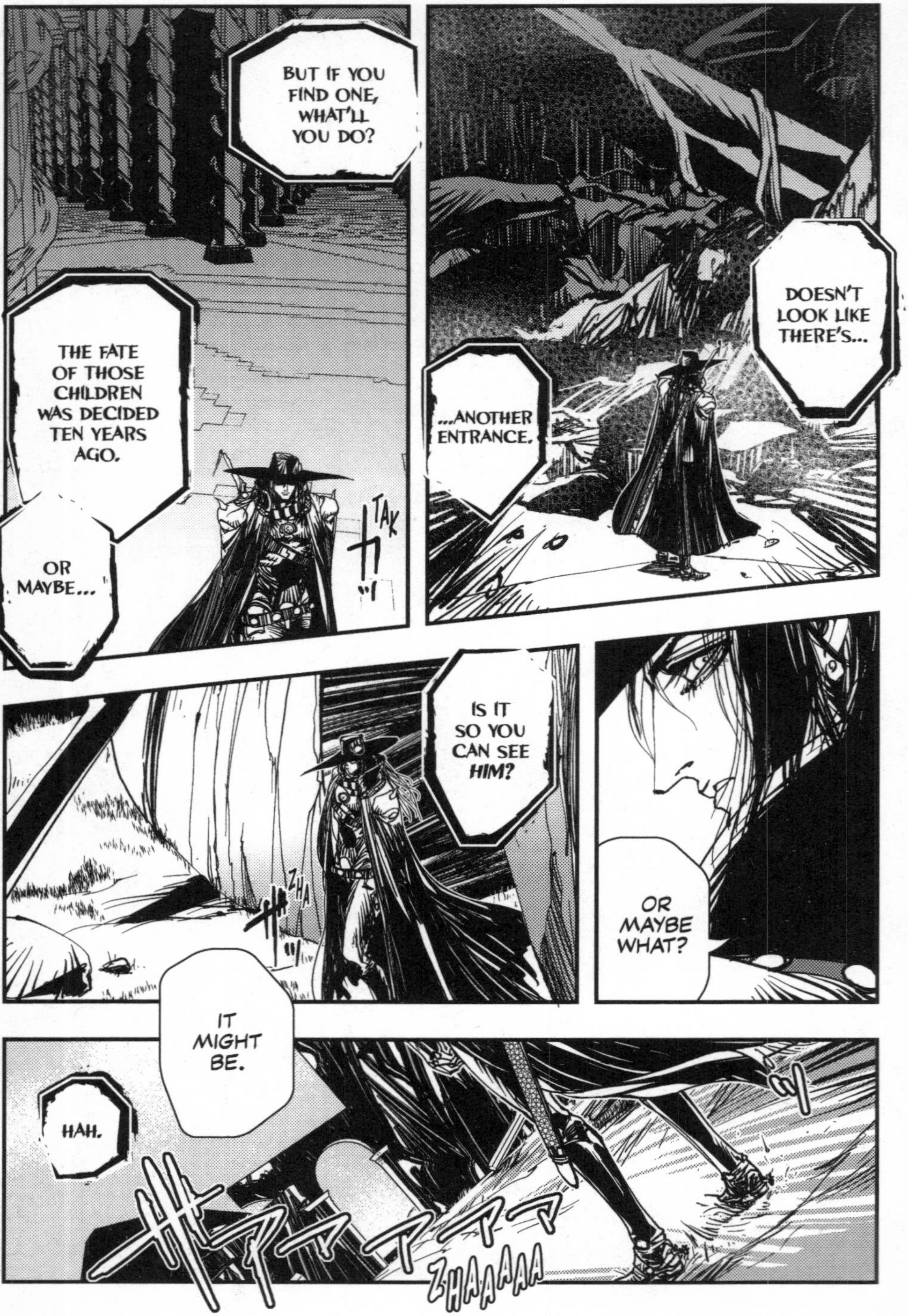
DOESN'T LOOK LIKE THERE'S...
...ANOTHER ENTRANCE.
BUT IF YOU FIND ONE, WHAT'LL YOU DO?
THE FATE OF THOSE CHILDREN WAS DECIDED TEN YEARS AGO.
OR MAYBE...
TAK
OR MAYBE WHAT?
IS IT SO YOU CAN SEE HIM?
ZHA
IT MIGHT BE.
HAH.
ZHAAAAAA

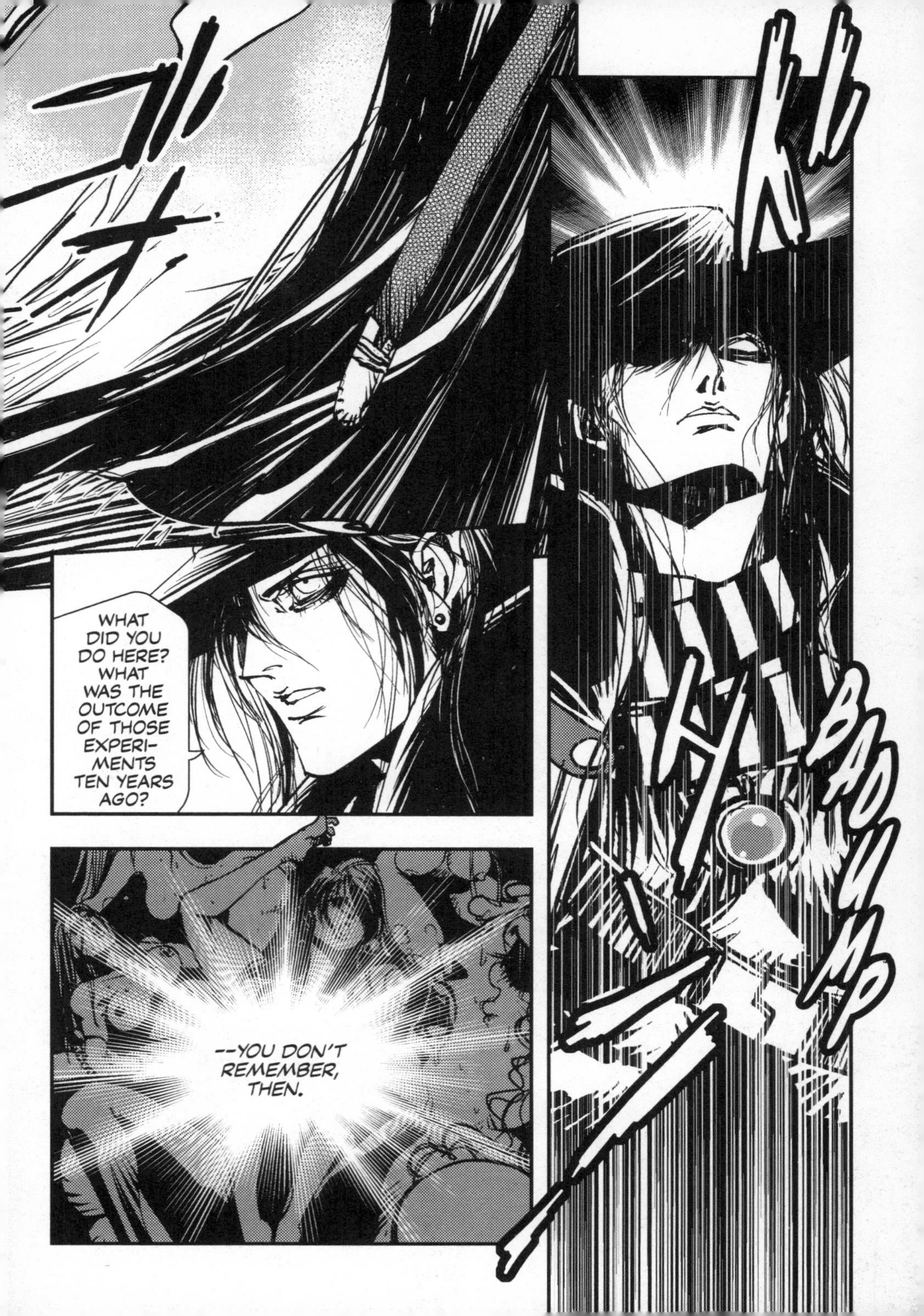
BADUMP
WHAT DID YOU DO HERE? WHAT WAS THE OUTCOME OF THOSE EXPERIMENTS TEN YEARS AGO?
--YOU DON'T REMEMBER, THEN.

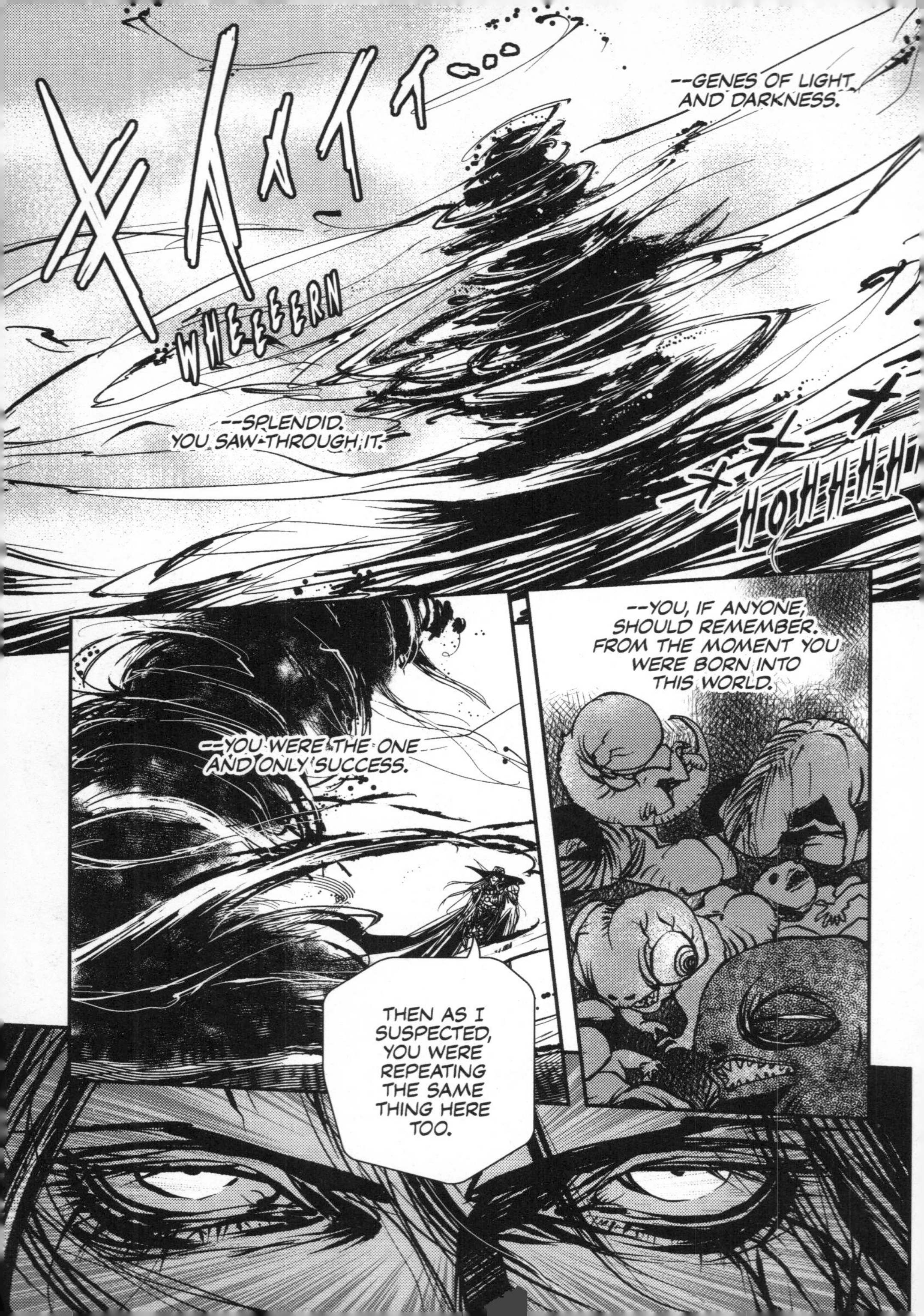
--GENES OF LIGHT AND DARKNESS.
WHEEEERN
--SPLENDID. YOU SAW THROUGH IT.
--YOU, IF ANYONE, SHOULD REMEMBER. FROM THE MOMENT YOU WERE BORN INTO THIS WORLD.
--YOU WERE THE ONE AND ONLY SUCCESS.
THEN AS I SUSPECTED, YOU WERE REPEATING THE SAME THING HERE TOO.

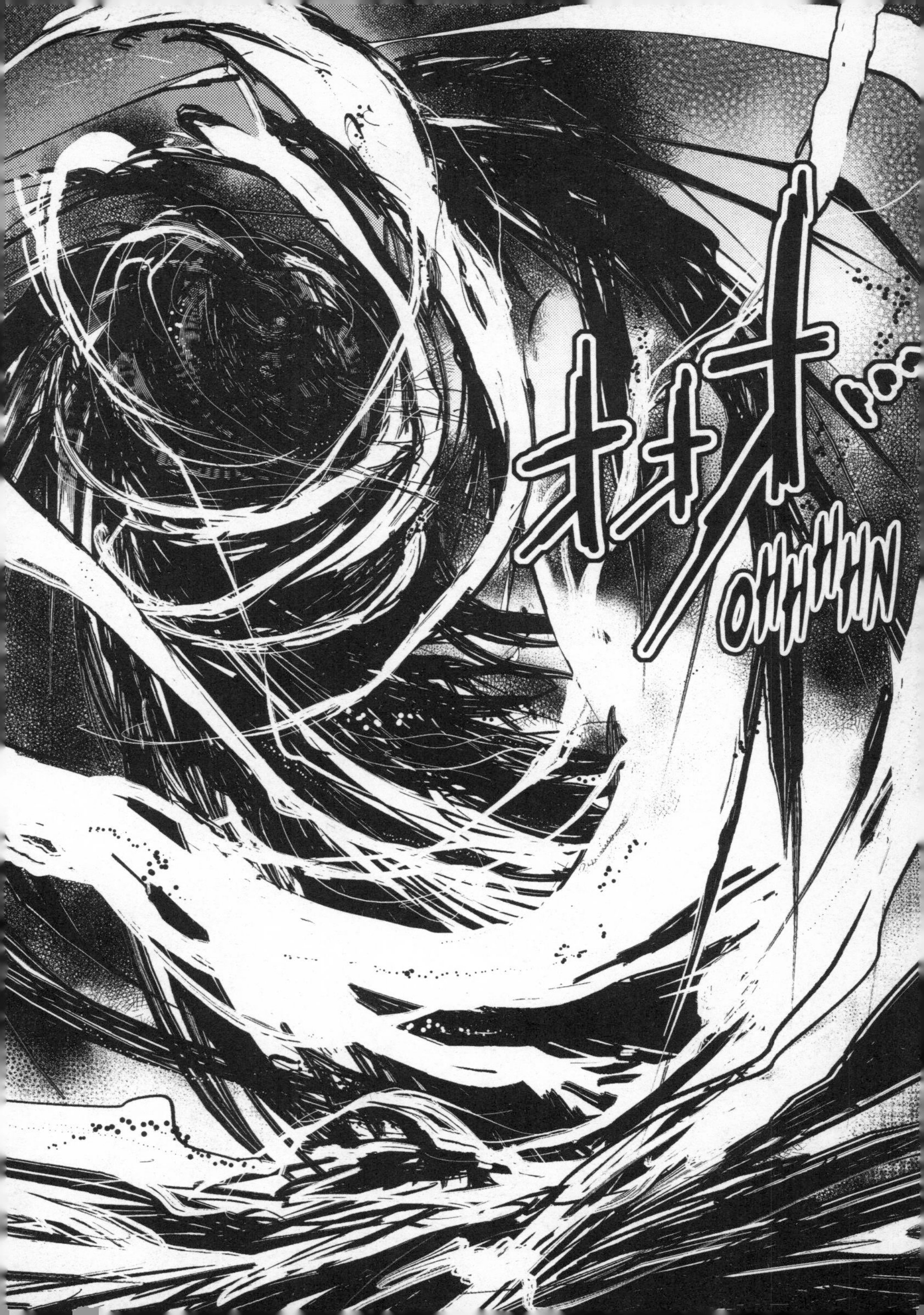
オォオ…
OHHHHN

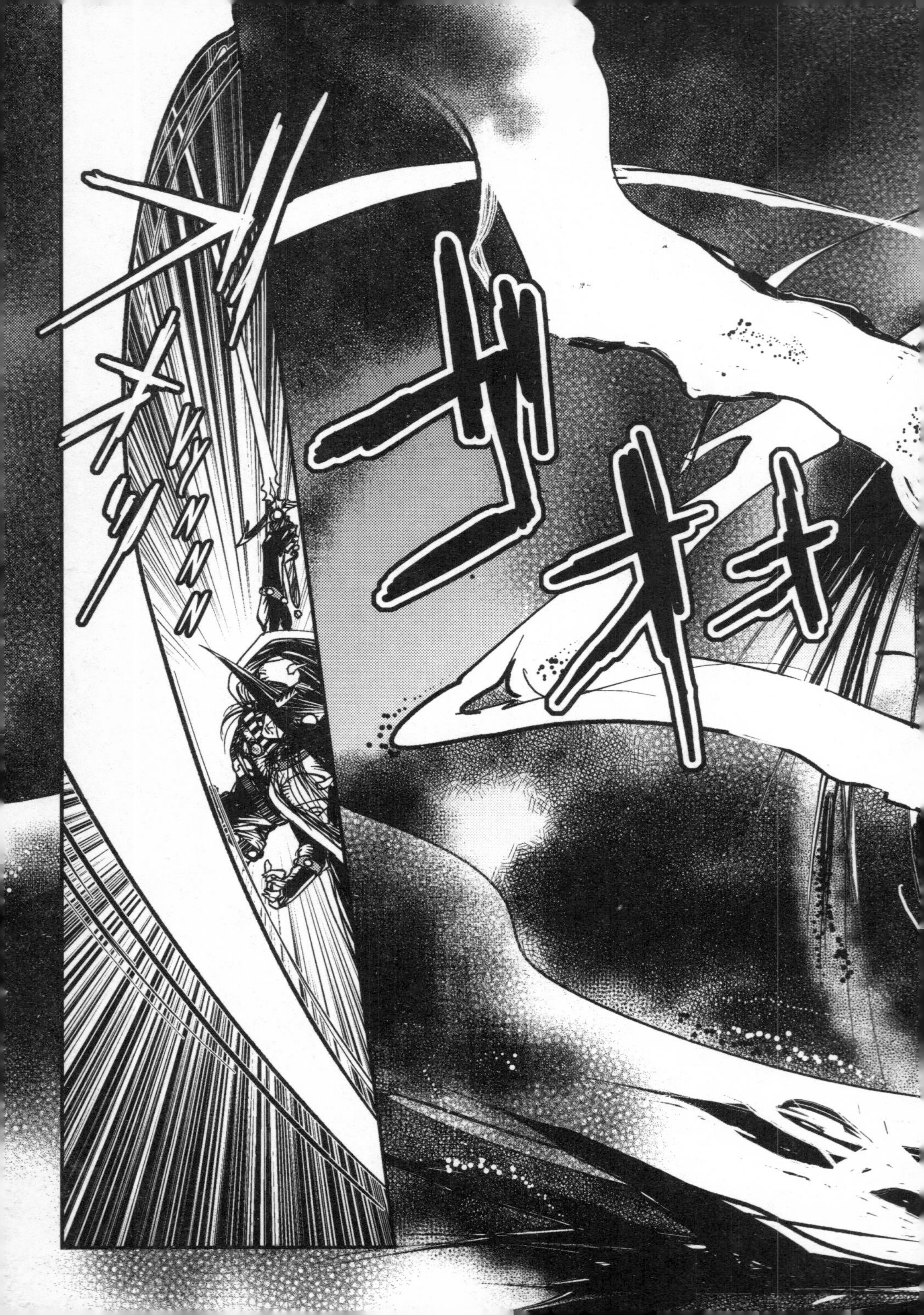
ゴオォ

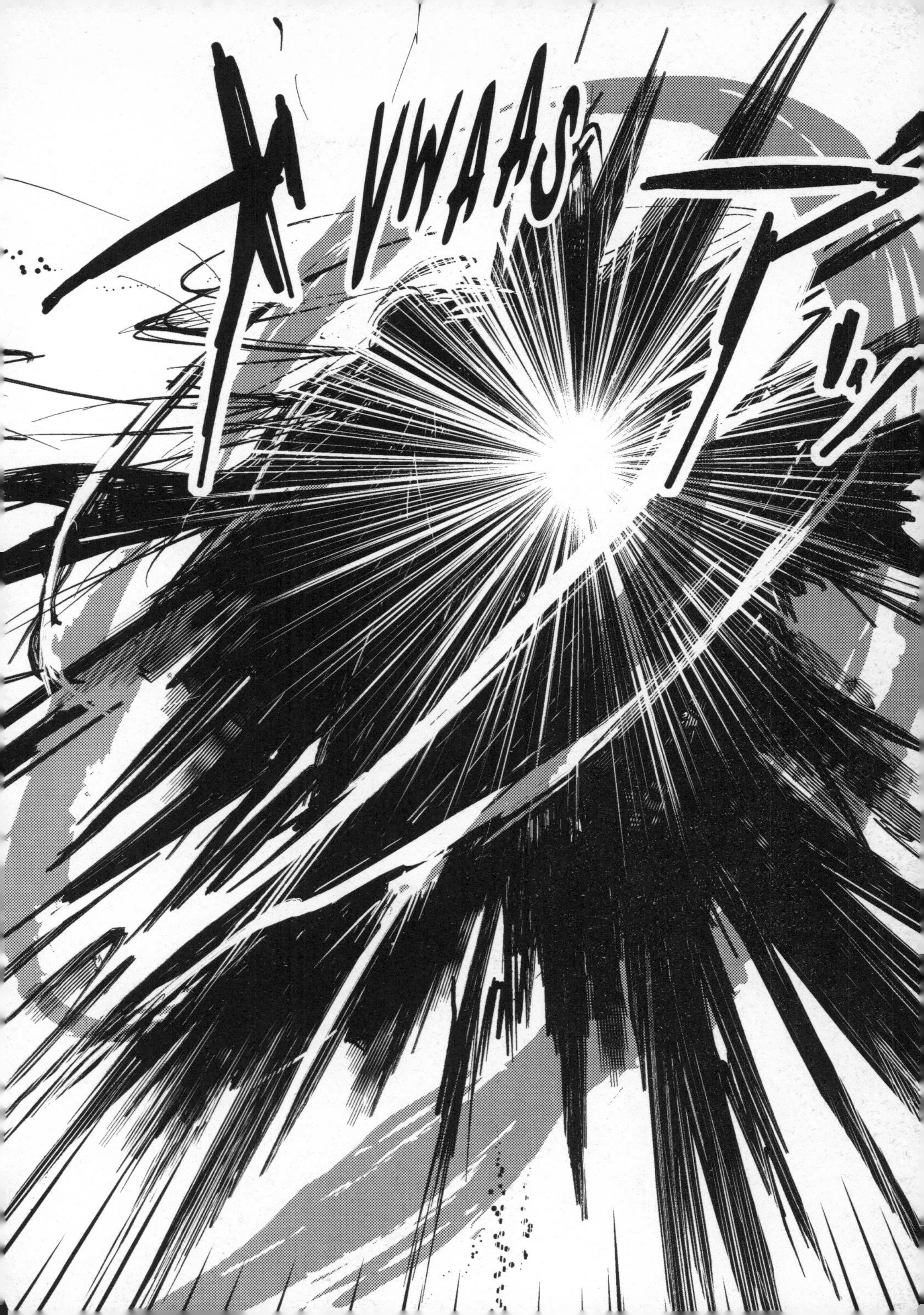
VWAAS

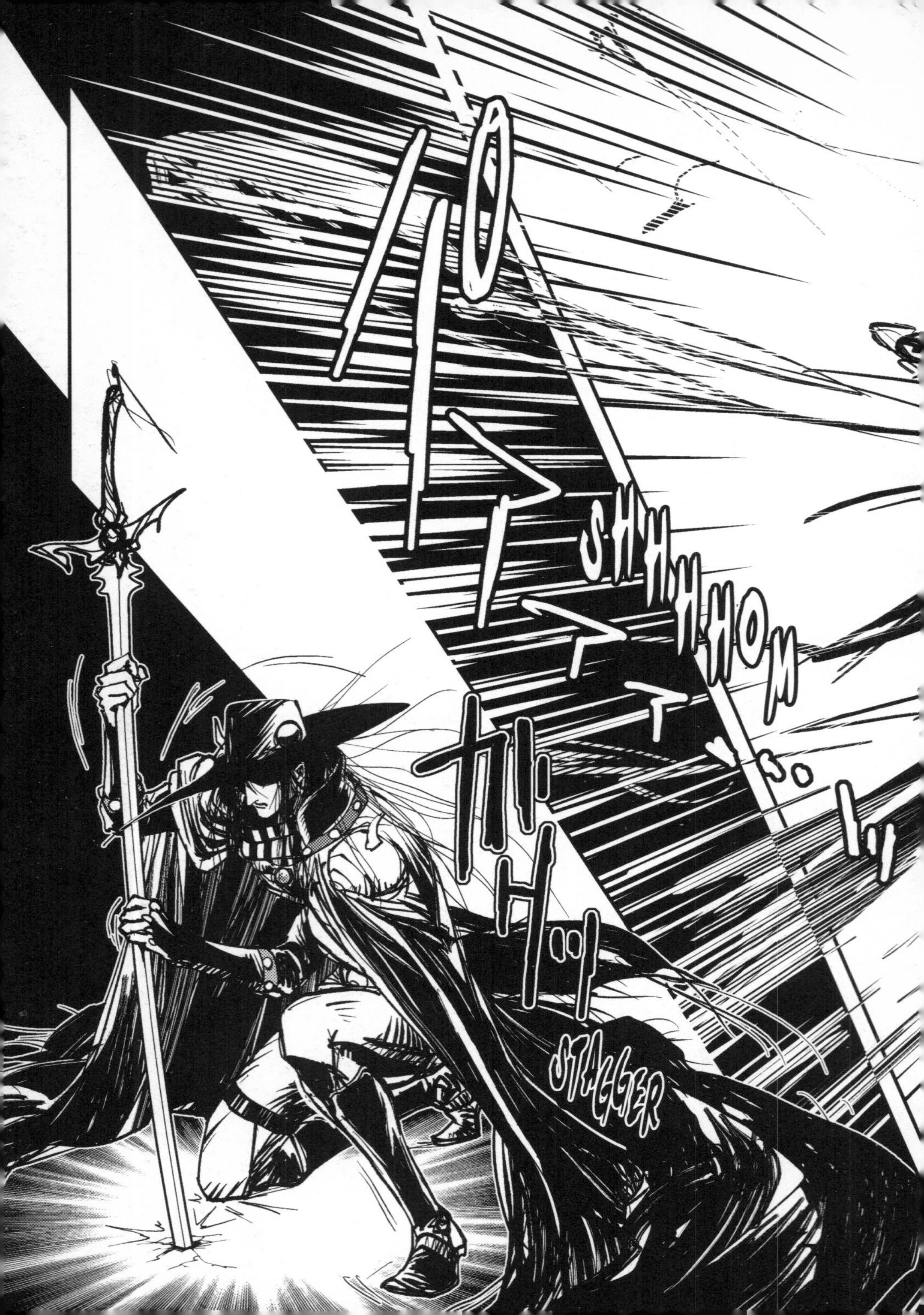
SHHHHHOM
STAGGER

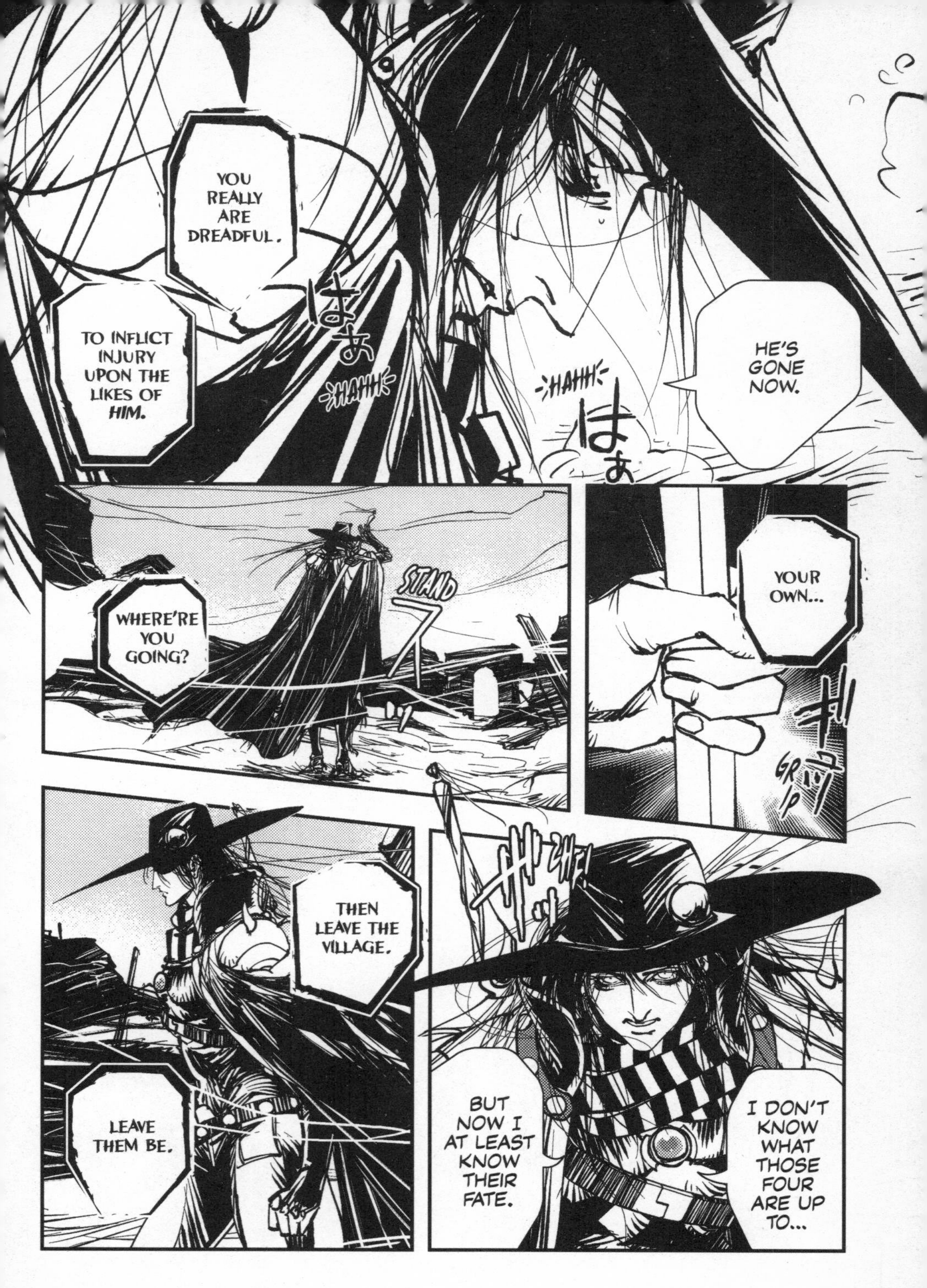
HE'S GONE NOW.
-HAHH-
はぁ
YOU REALLY ARE DREADFUL.
TO INFLICT INJURY UPON THE LIKES OF HIM.
はぁ
-HAHH-
YOUR OWN...
GRIP
STAND
WHERE'RE YOU GOING?
HEH
I DON'T KNOW WHAT THOSE FOUR ARE UP TO...
BUT NOW I AT LEAST KNOW THEIR FATE.
THEN LEAVE THE VILLAGE.
LEAVE THEM BE.

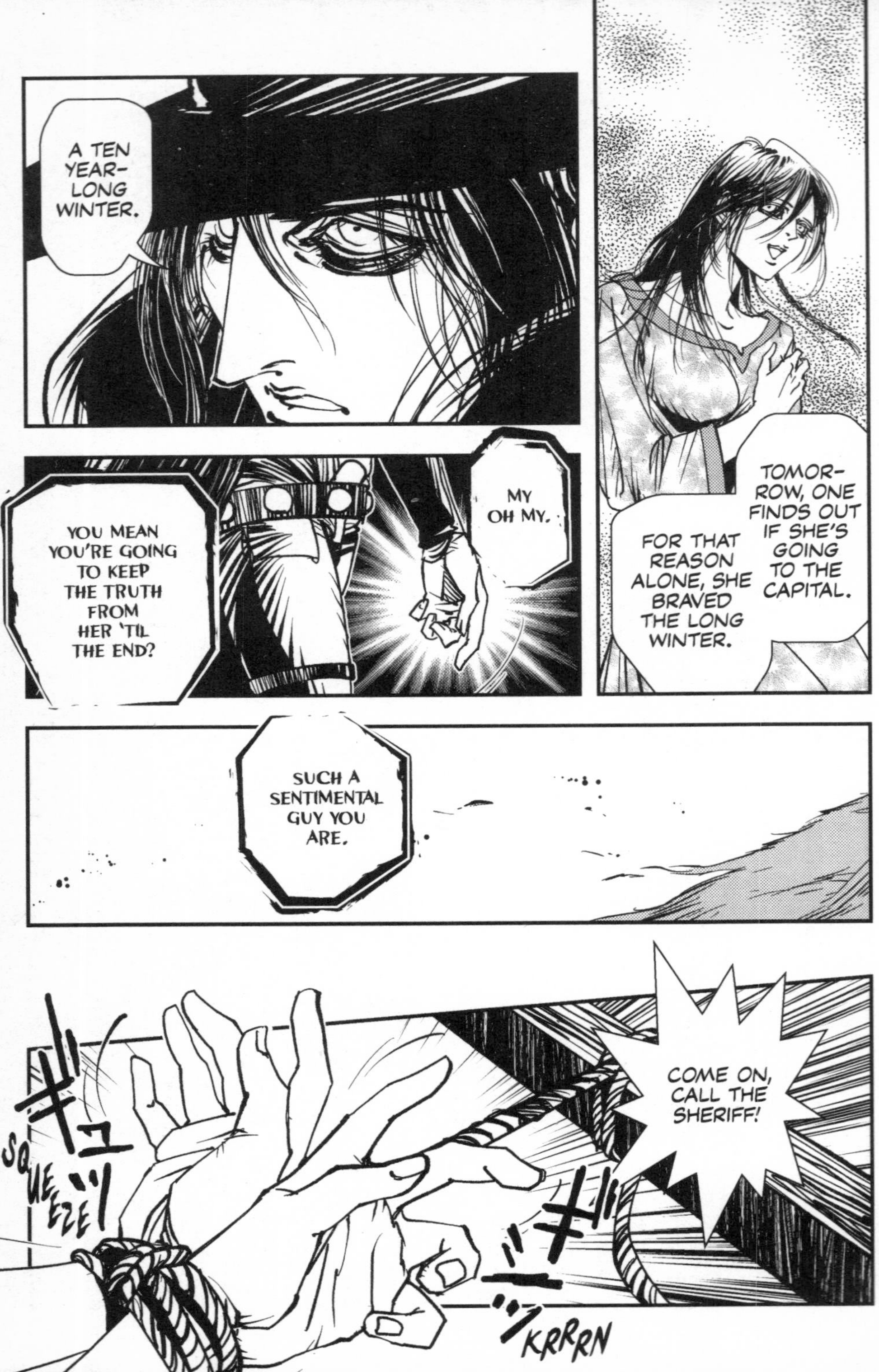
TOMOR-ROW, ONE FINDS OUT IF SHE'S GOING TO THE CAPITAL.
FOR THAT REASON ALONE, SHE BRAVED THE LONG WINTER.
A TEN YEAR-LONG WINTER.
MY OH MY.
YOU MEAN YOU'RE GOING TO KEEP THE TRUTH FROM HER 'TIL THE END?
SUCH A SENTIMENTAL GUY YOU ARE.
COME ON, CALL THE SHERIFF!
SQUEEZE
KRRRN

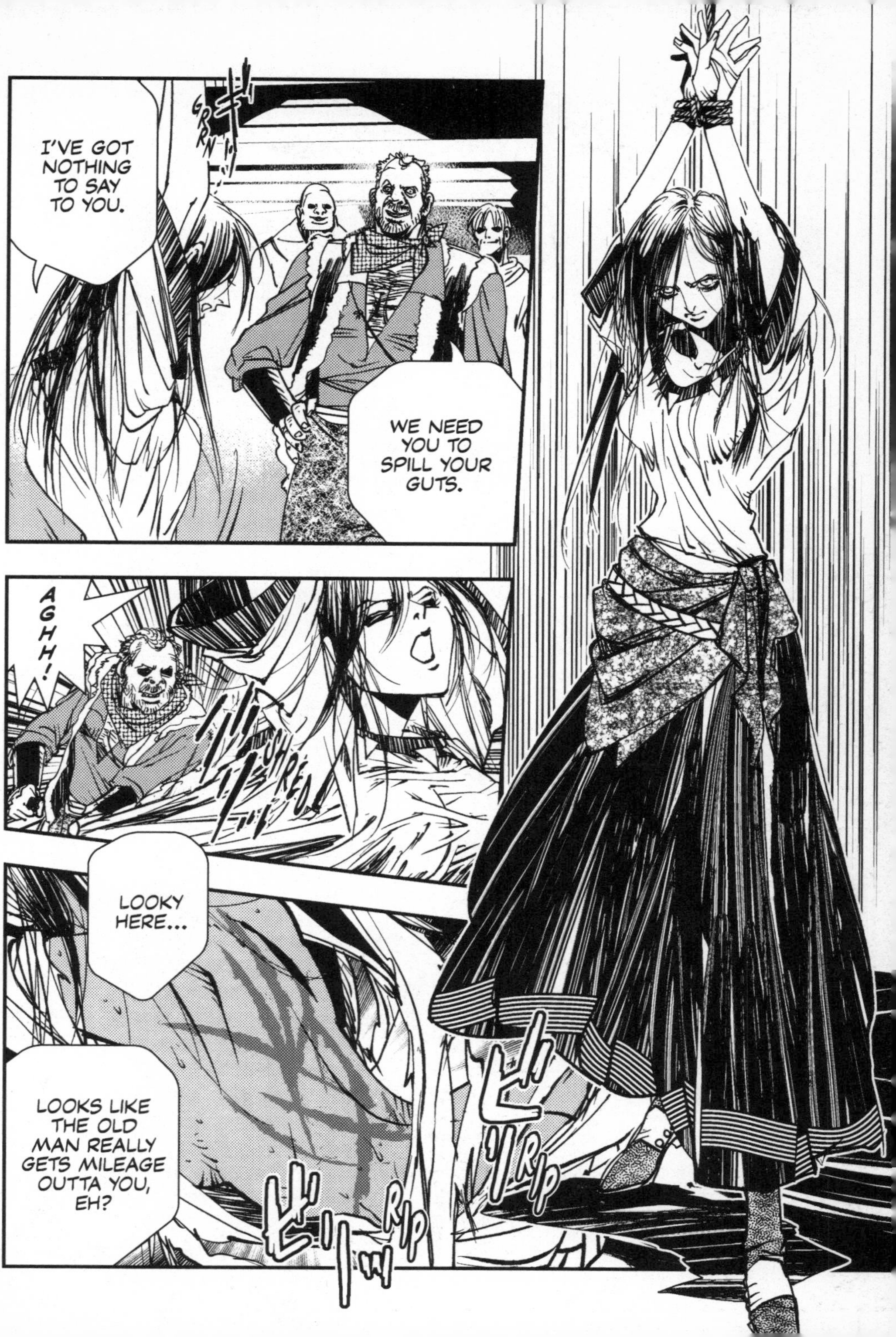
RIP
GRRRN
I'VE GOT NOTHING TO SAY TO YOU.
WE NEED YOU TO SPILL YOUR GUTS.
SHRED
AGHH!
LOOKY HERE...
LOOKS LIKE THE OLD MAN REALLY GETS MILEAGE OUTTA YOU, EH?
RIP

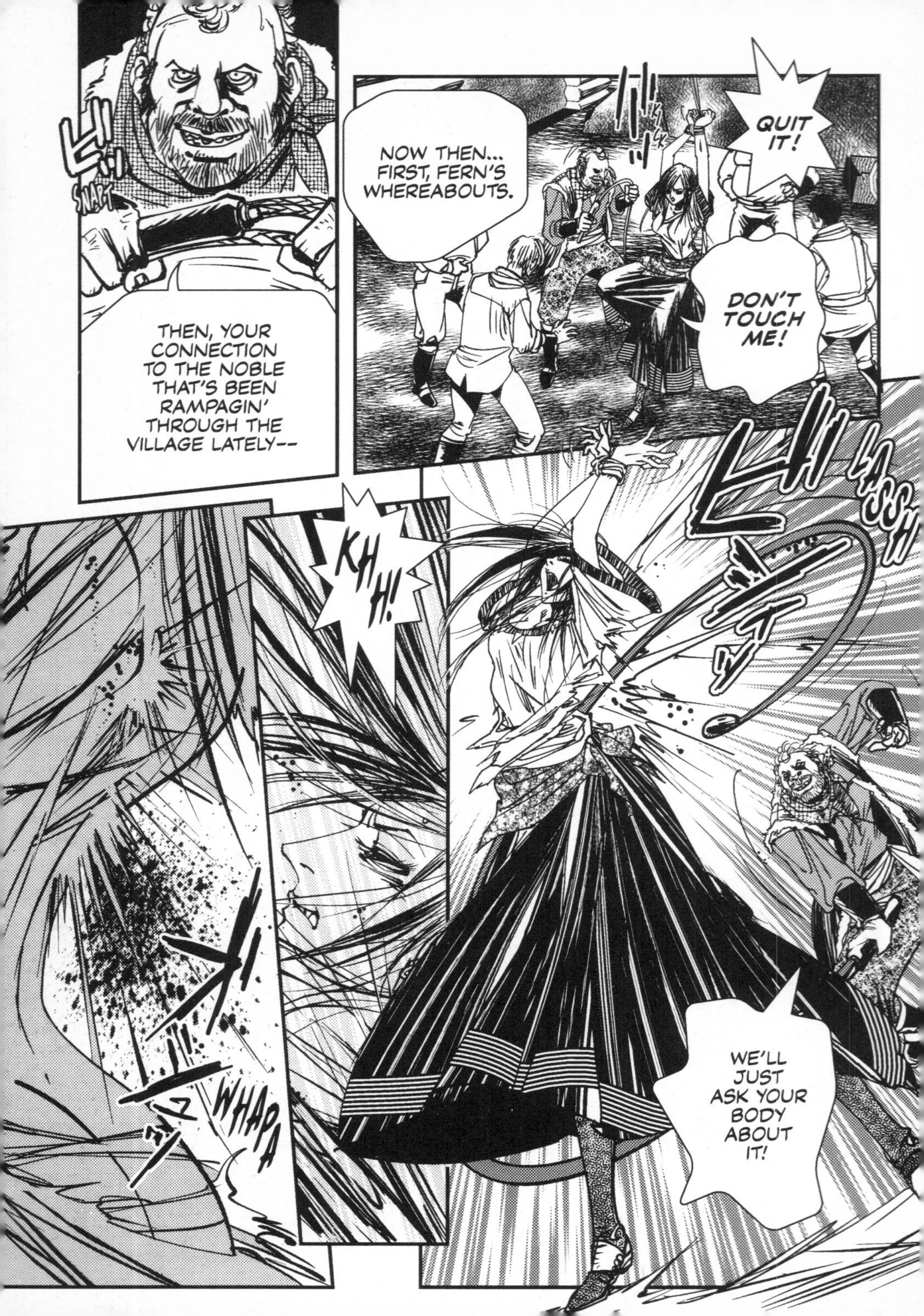
QUIT IT!
NOW THEN... FIRST, FERN'S WHEREABOUTS.
DON'T TOUCH ME!
SNAP
THEN, YOUR CONNECTION TO THE NOBLE THAT'S BEEN RAMPAGIN' THROUGH THE VILLAGE LATELY--
LASSH
WE'LL JUST ASK YOUR BODY ABOUT IT!
KHH!
WHAP

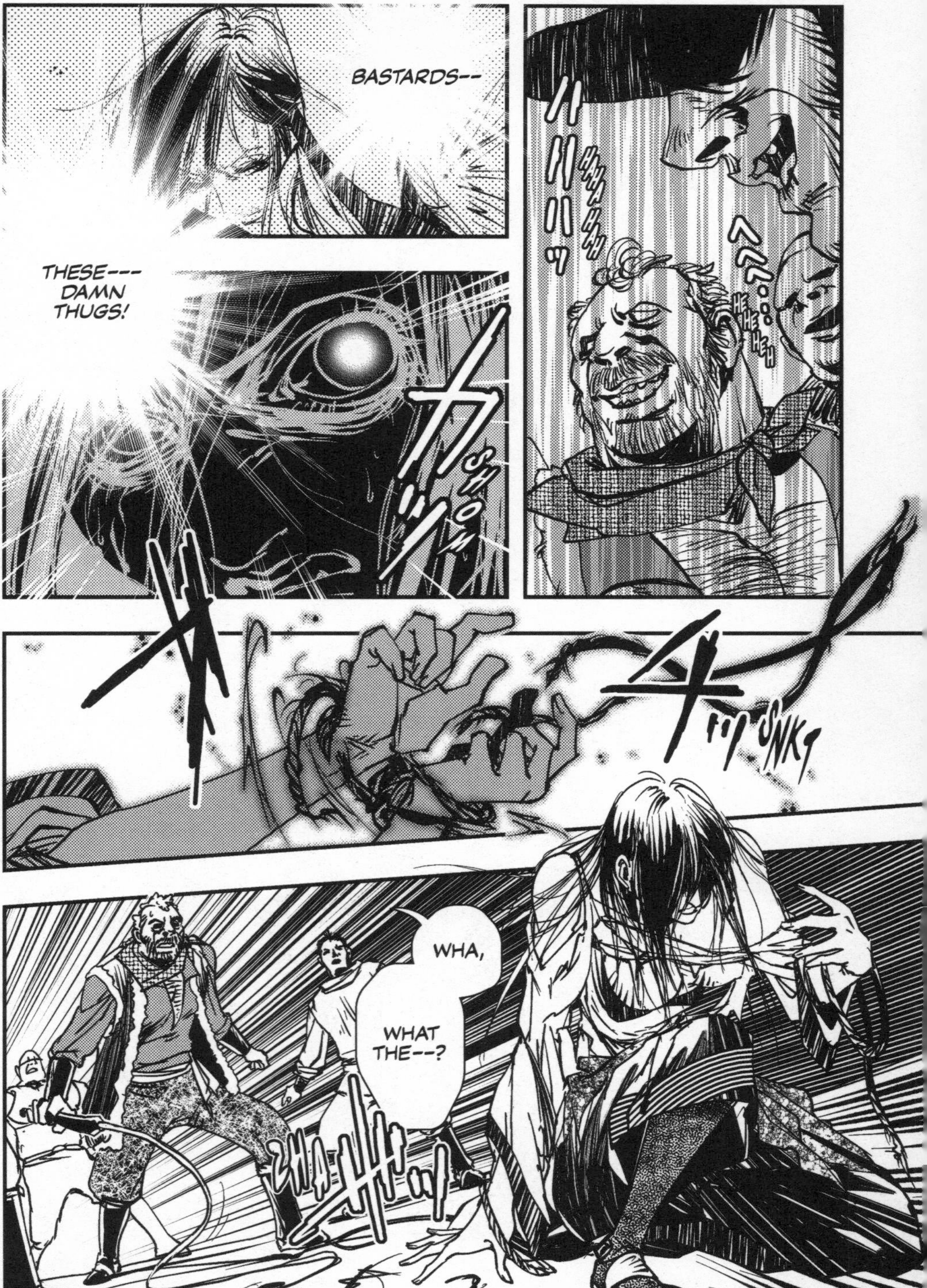
BASTARDS--
THESE--- DAMN THUGS!
SHOOM
SNK
WHA,
WHAT THE--?

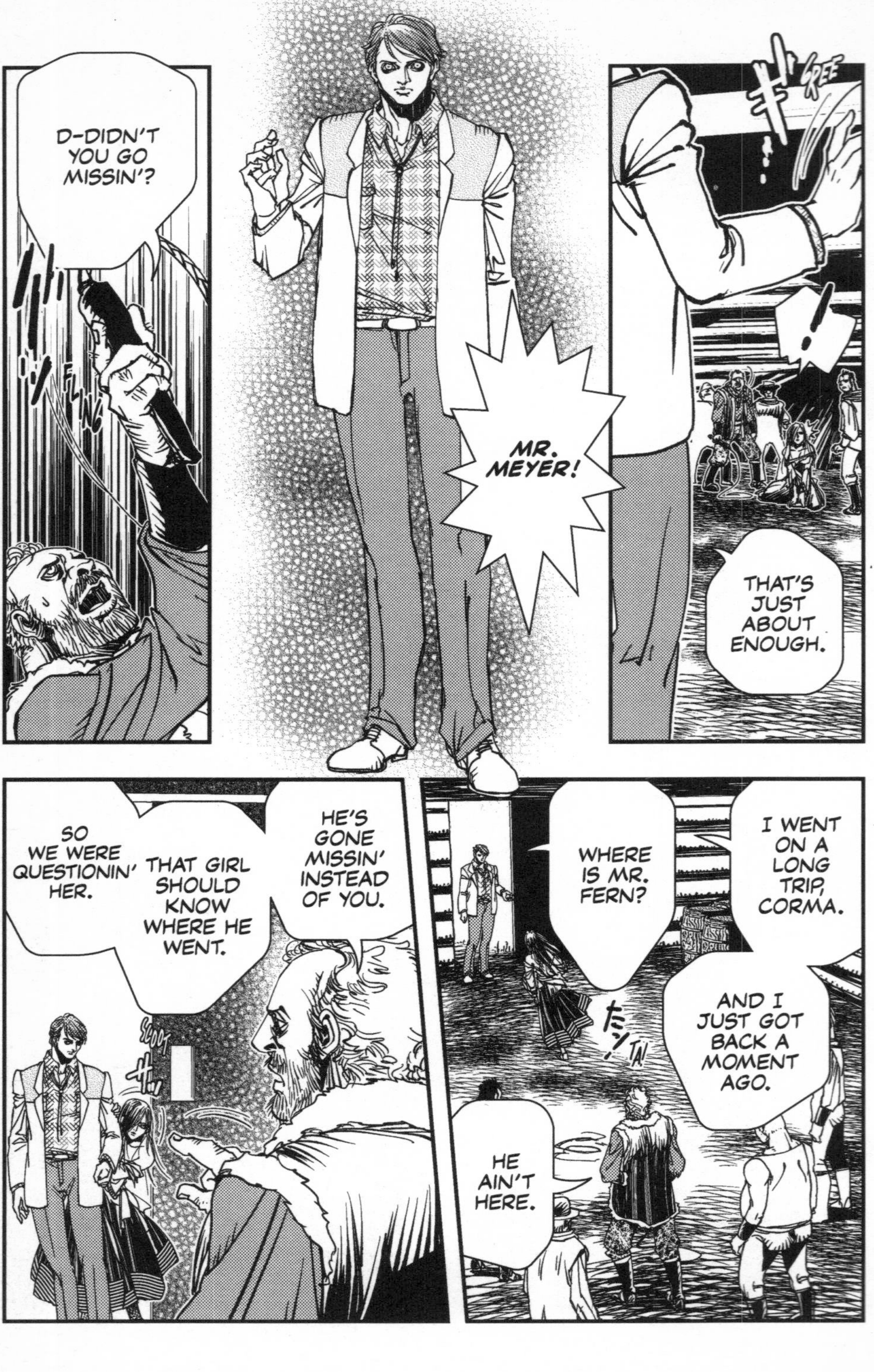
GREE
!
THAT'S JUST ABOUT ENOUGH.
MR. MEYER!
D-DIDN'T YOU GO MISSIN'?
FLING
I WENT ON A LONG TRIP, CORMA.
AND I JUST GOT BACK A MOMENT AGO.
WHERE IS MR. FERN?
TA!
HE AIN'T HERE.
HE'S GONE MISSIN' INSTEAD OF YOU.
THAT GIRL SHOULD KNOW WHERE HE WENT.
SO WE WERE QUESTIONIN' HER.
SCOOT

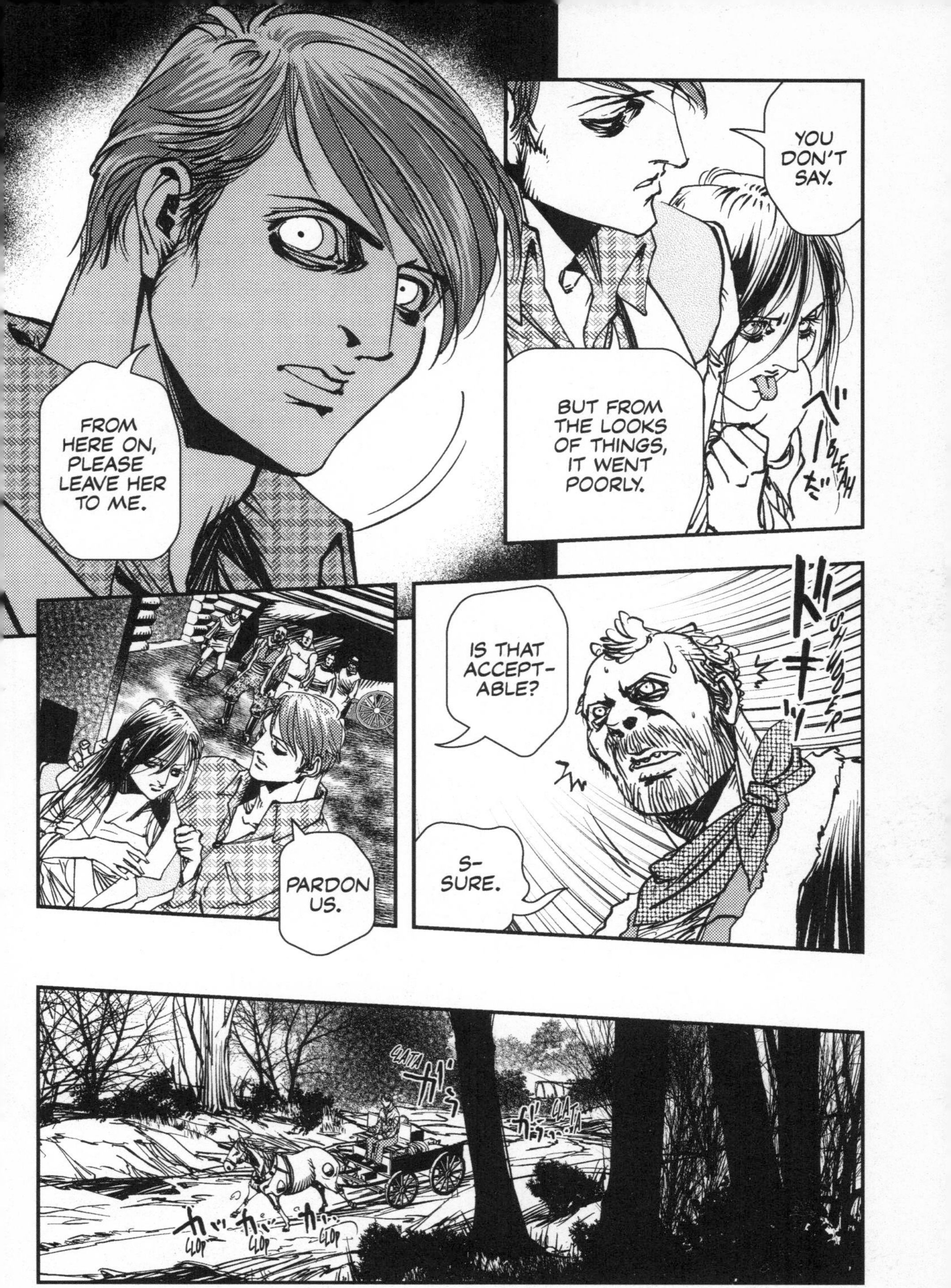
YOU DON'T SAY.
BUT FROM THE LOOKS OF THINGS, IT WENT POORLY.
BLEAH
FROM HERE ON, PLEASE LEAVE HER TO ME.
SHUDDER
IS THAT ACCEPTABLE?
S- SURE.
PARDON US.
CLATTA
CLATTA
CLOP
CLOP
CLOP

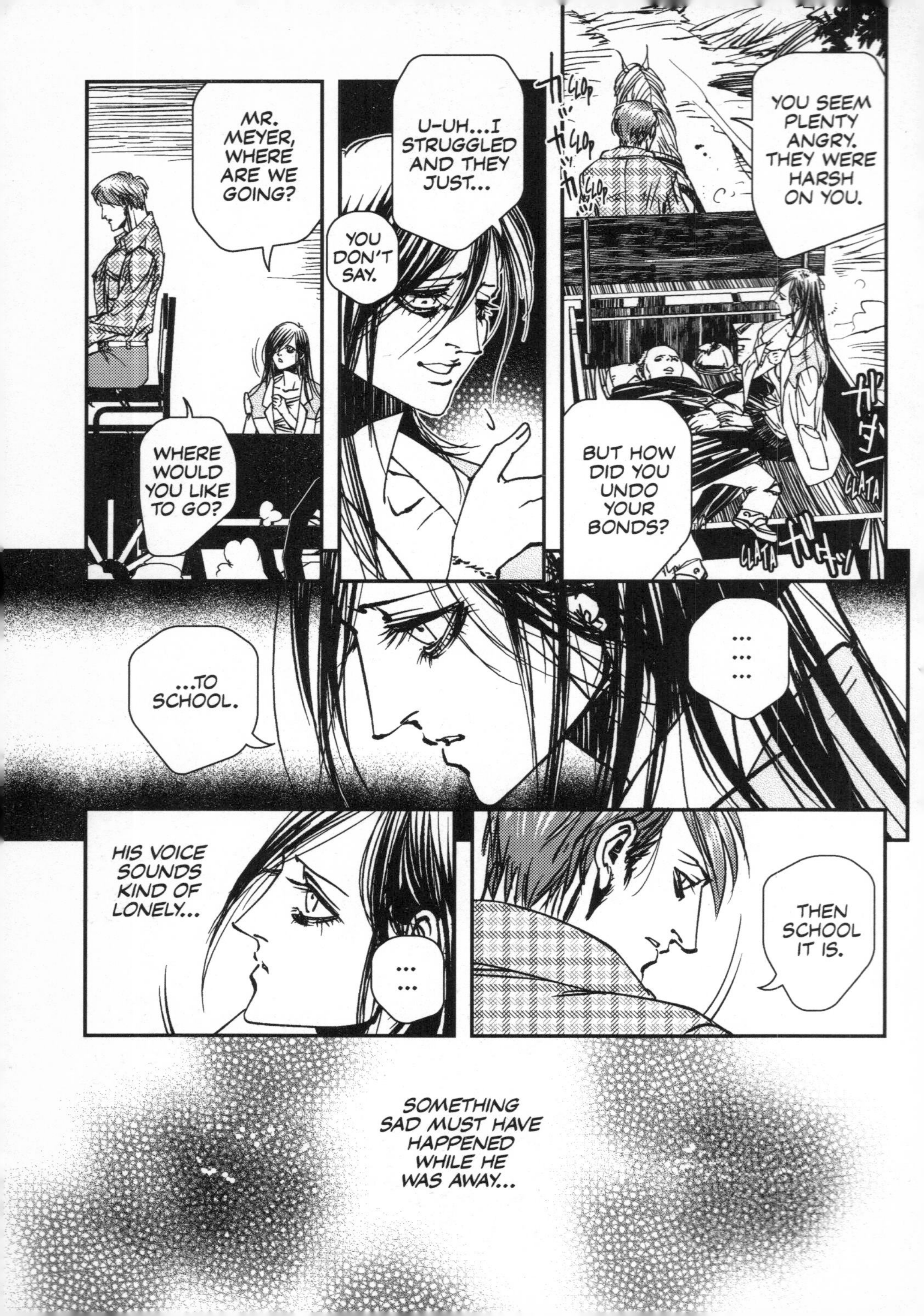
CLOP
CLOP
CLOP
YOU SEEM PLENTY ANGRY. THEY WERE HARSH ON YOU.
BUT HOW DID YOU UNDO YOUR BONDS?
CLATA
CLATA
U-UH...I STRUGGLED AND THEY JUST...
YOU DON'T SAY.
MR. MEYER, WHERE ARE WE GOING?
WHERE WOULD YOU LIKE TO GO?
....
...TO SCHOOL.
THEN SCHOOL IT IS.
HIS VOICE SOUNDS KIND OF LONELY...
......
SOMETHING SAD MUST HAVE HAPPENED WHILE HE WAS AWAY...

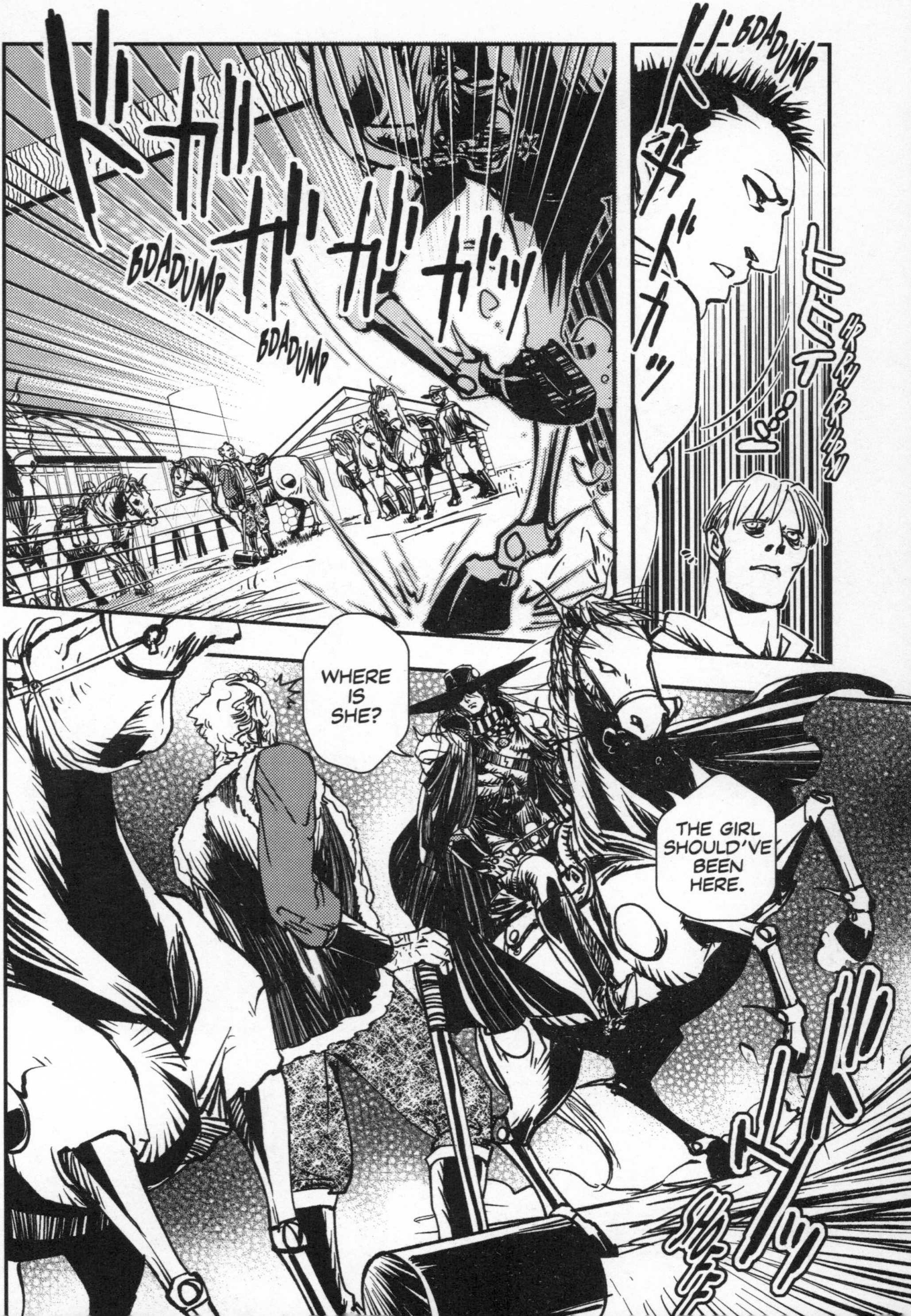
BDADUMP
BDADUMP
BDADUMP
WHERE IS SHE?
THE GIRL SHOULD'VE BEEN HERE.

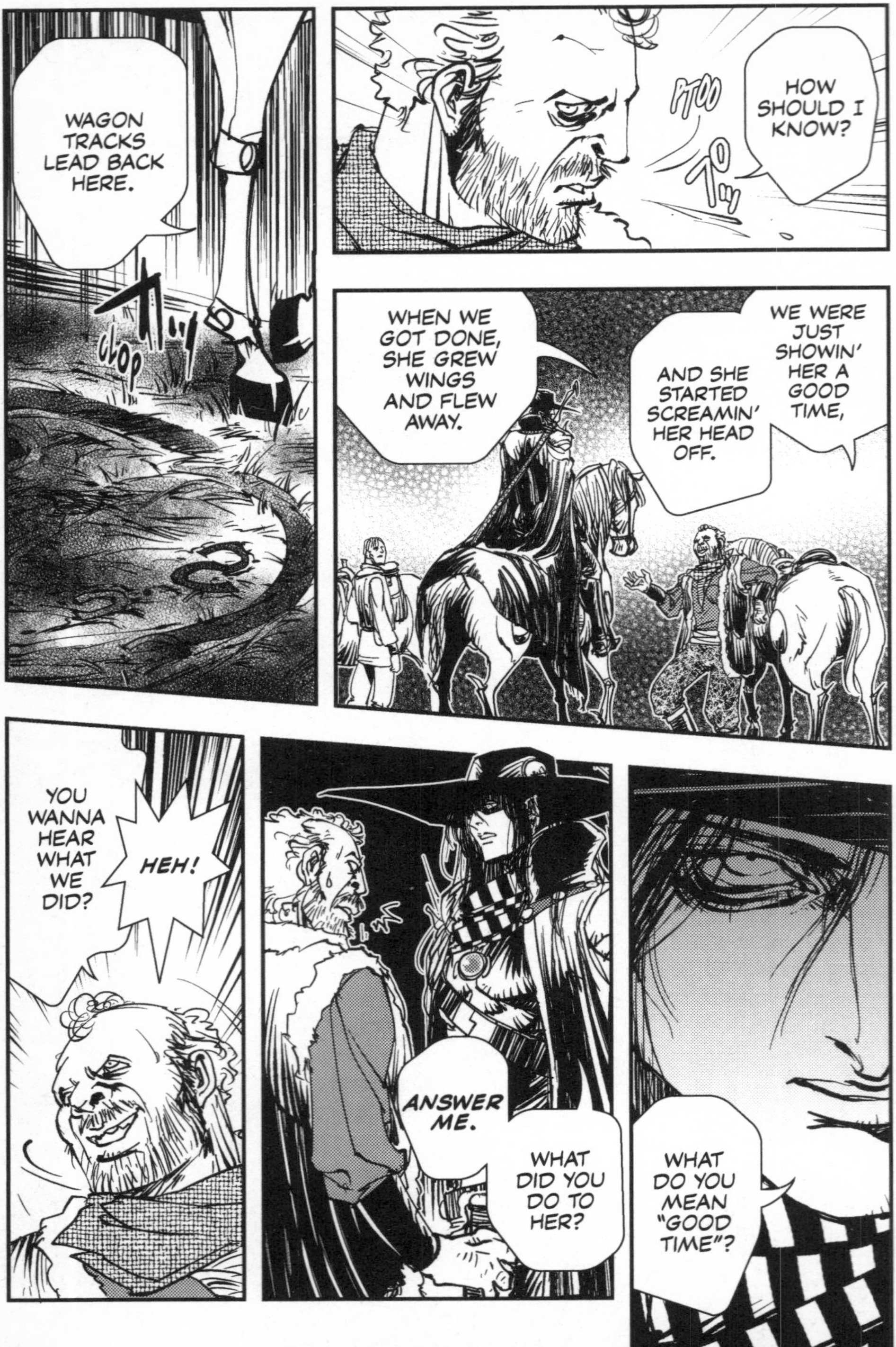
HOW SHOULD I KNOW?
PTOO
WE WERE JUST SHOWIN' HER A GOOD TIME,
AND SHE STARTED SCREAMIN' HER HEAD OFF.
WHEN WE GOT DONE, SHE GREW WINGS AND FLEW AWAY.
WAGON TRACKS LEAD BACK HERE.
CLOP
WHAT DO YOU MEAN "GOOD TIME"?
ANSWER ME.
WHAT DID YOU DO TO HER?
HEH!
YOU WANNA HEAR WHAT WE DID?

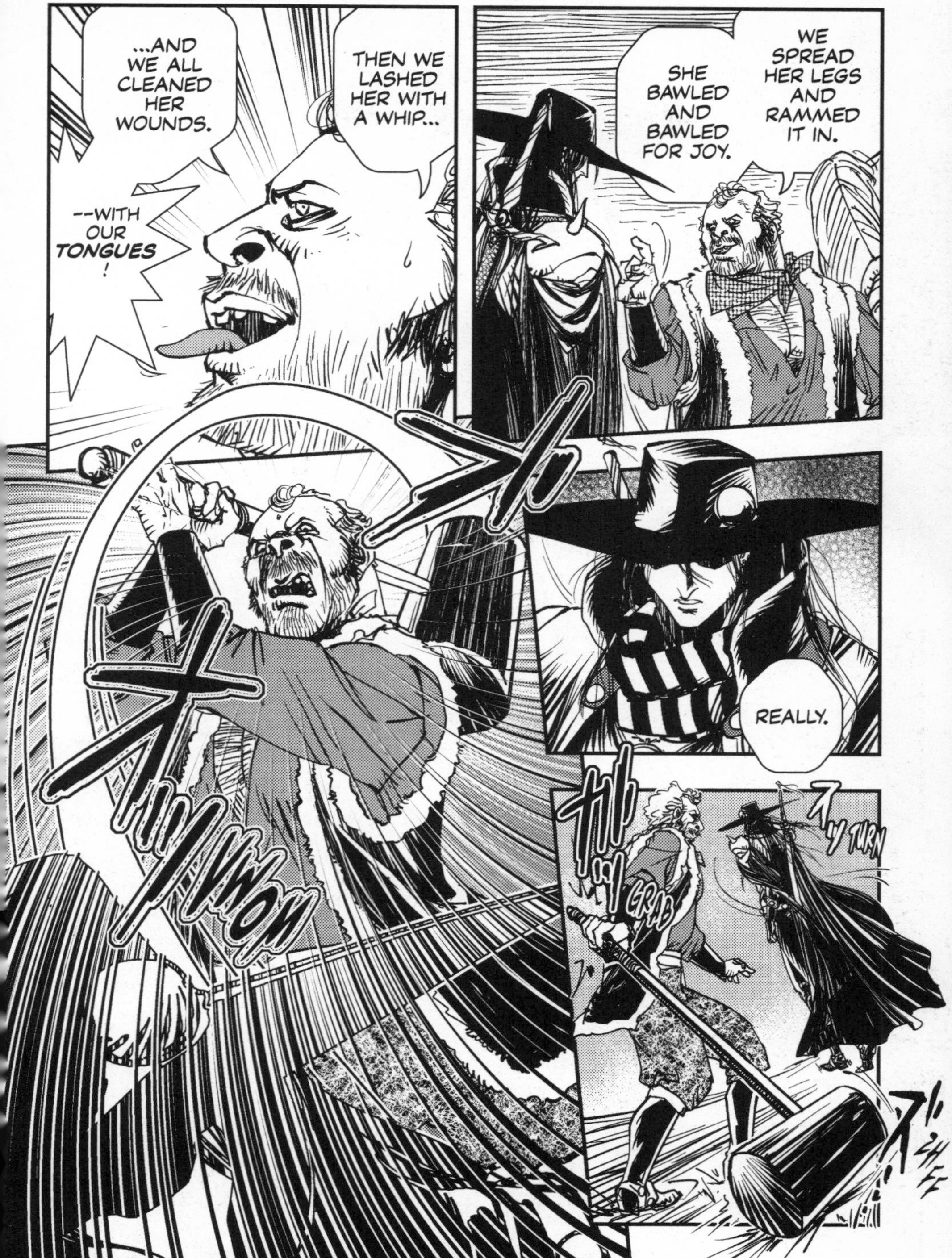
WE SPREAD HER LEGS AND RAMMED IT IN.
SHE BAWLED AND BAWLED FOR JOY.
THEN WE LASHED HER WITH A WHIP...
...AND WE ALL CLEANED HER WOUNDS.
--WITH OUR ***TONGUES***!
REALLY.
TURN
GRAB

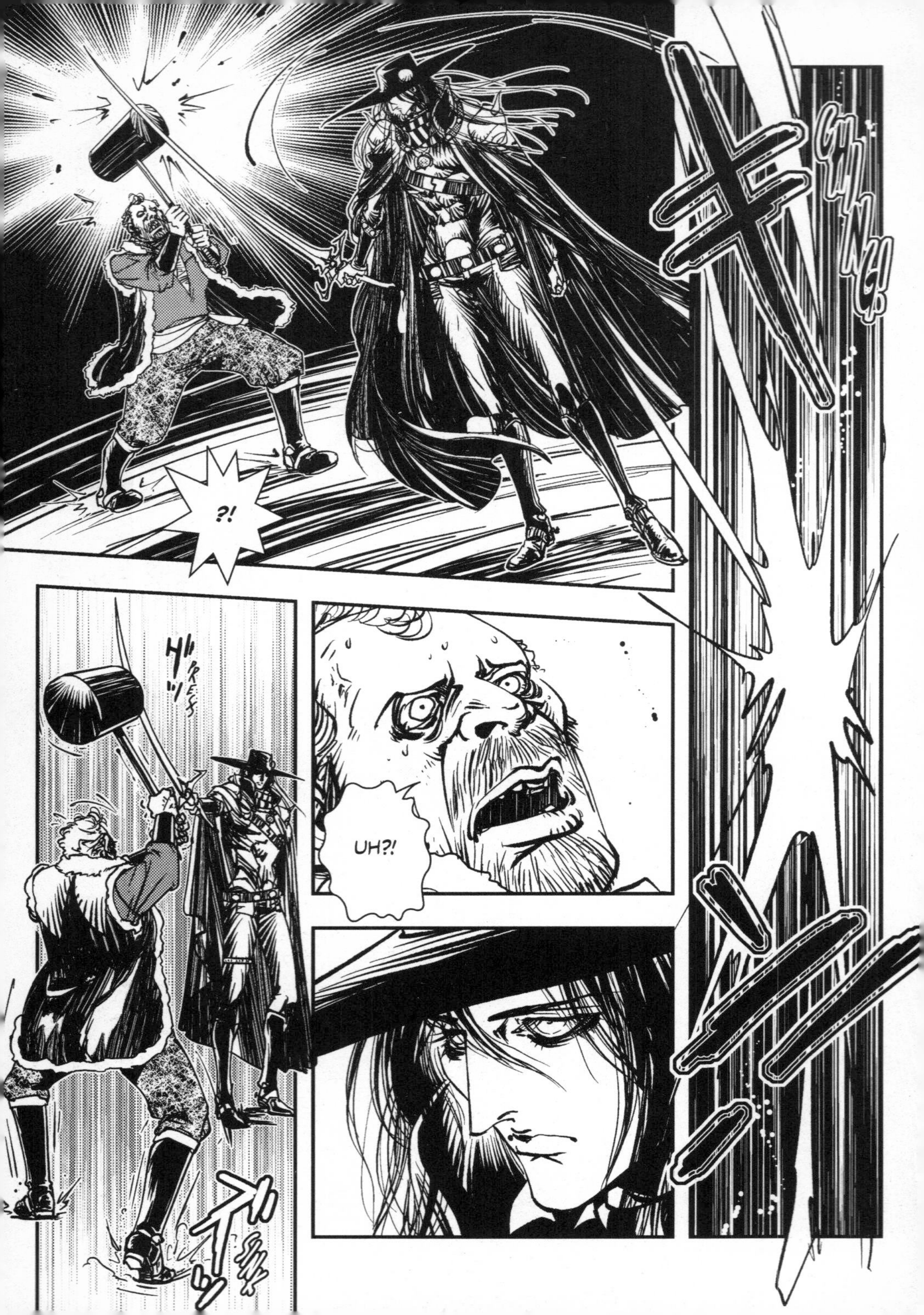
CHIIING!
?!
UH?!
PRESS
SLINK

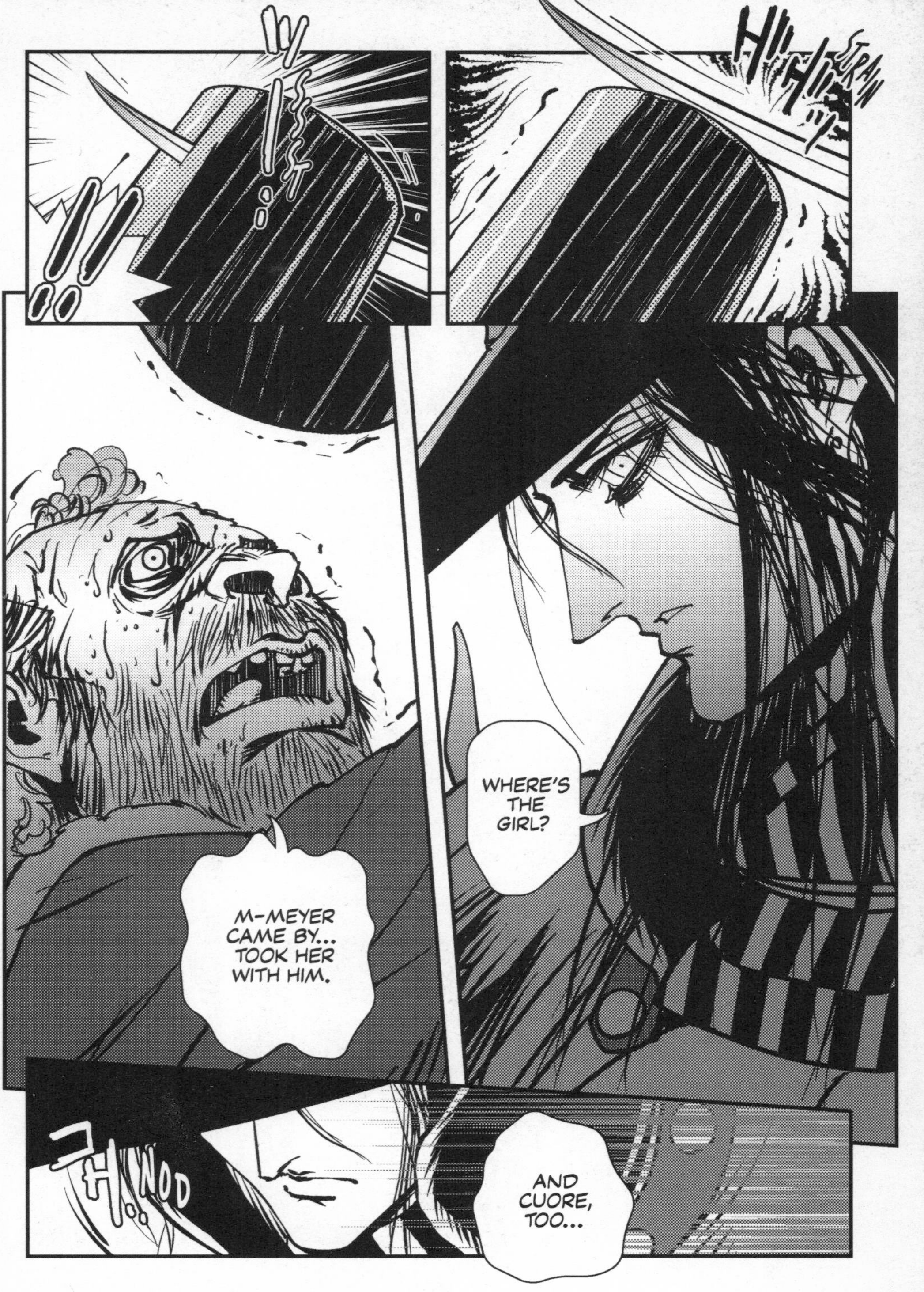
STRAIN
!!
WHERE'S THE GIRL?
M-MEYER CAME BY... TOOK HER WITH HIM.
AND CUORE, TOO...
NOD

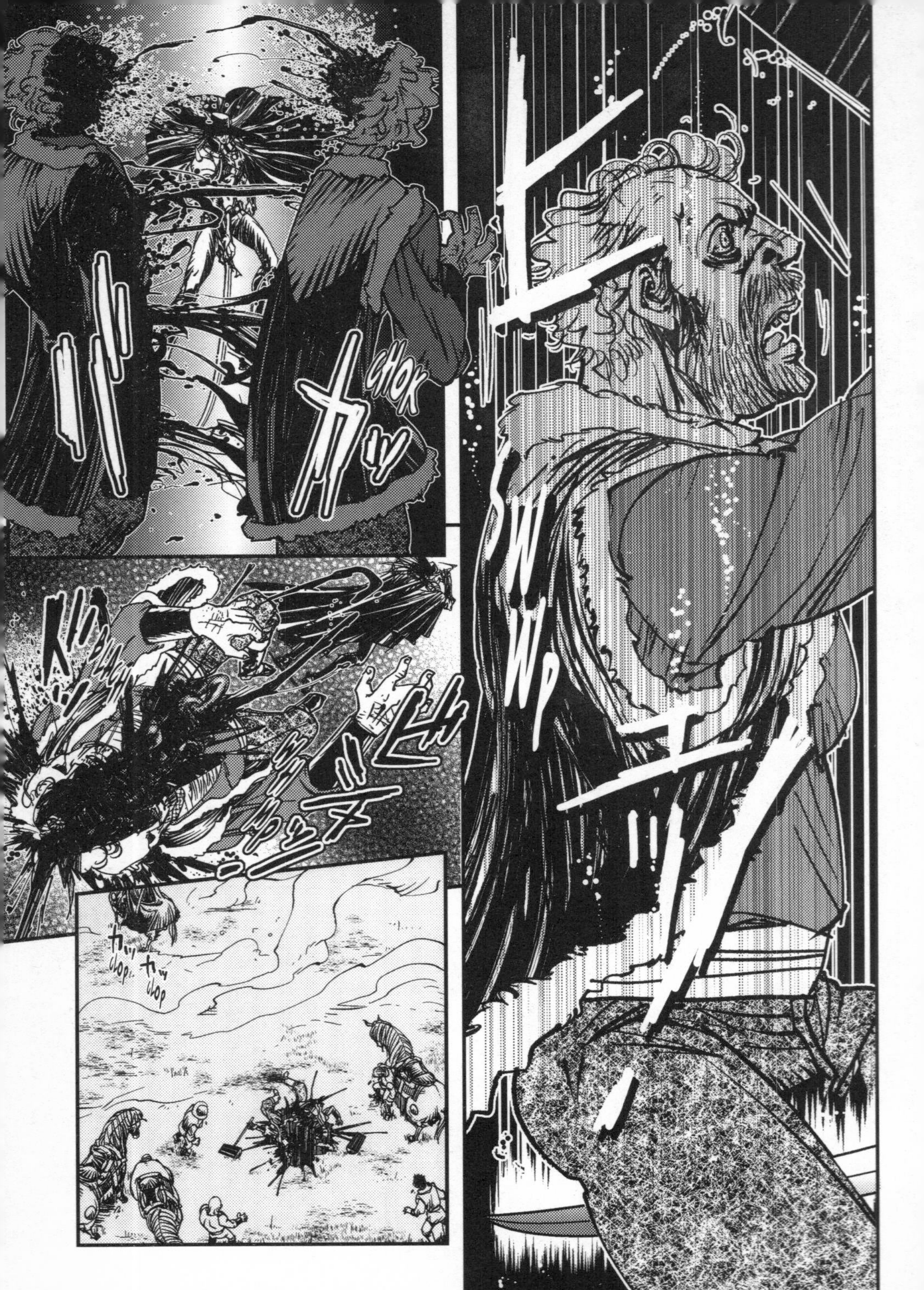
SWWP
CHOK
clop
clop

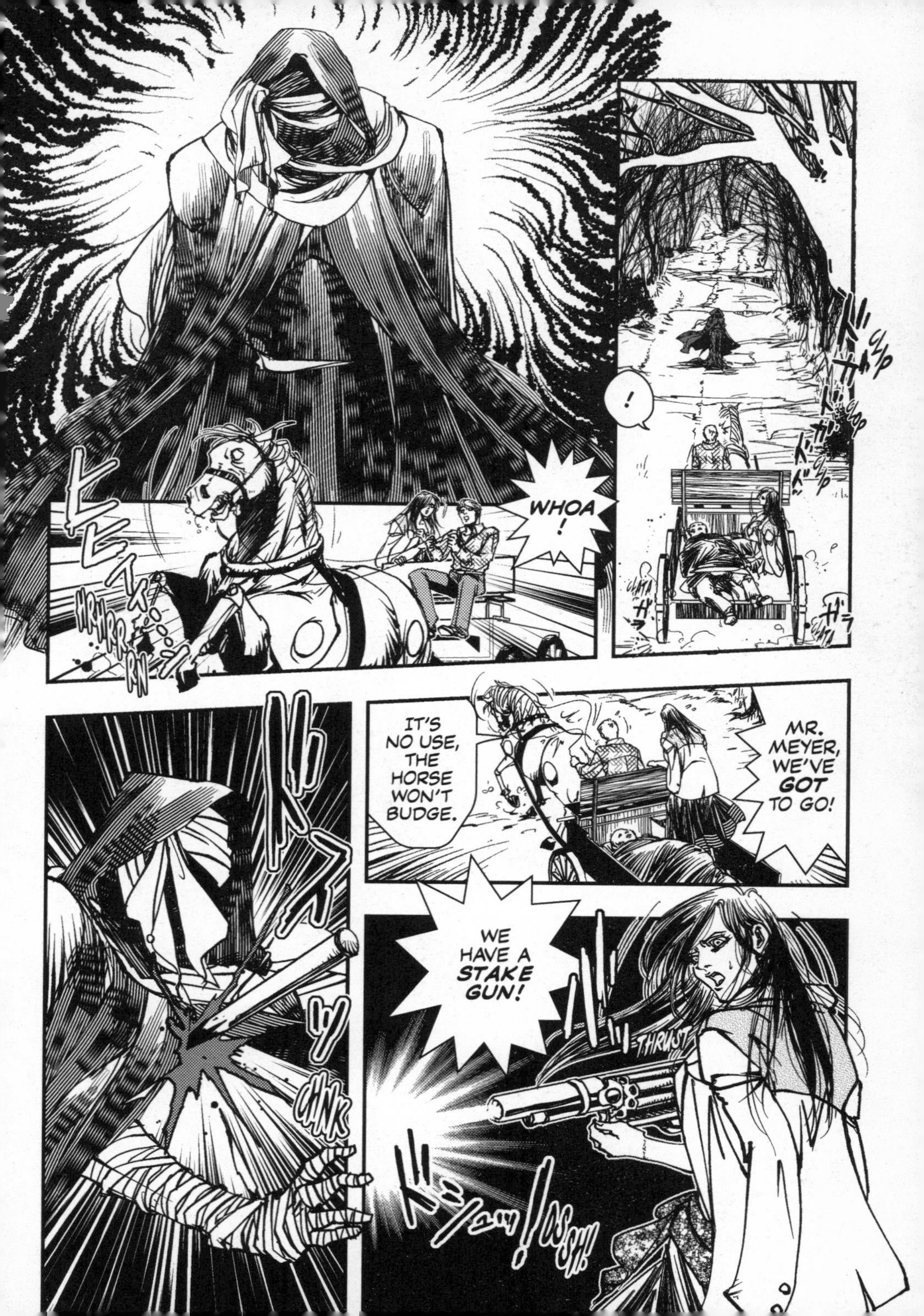
CLIP
CLOP
CLIP
!
CLATA
CLATA
WHOA!
HRHRRRN
MR. MEYER, WE'VE GOT TO GO!
IT'S NO USE, THE HORSE WON'T BUDGE.
WE HAVE A STAKE GUN!
THRUST
CHNK

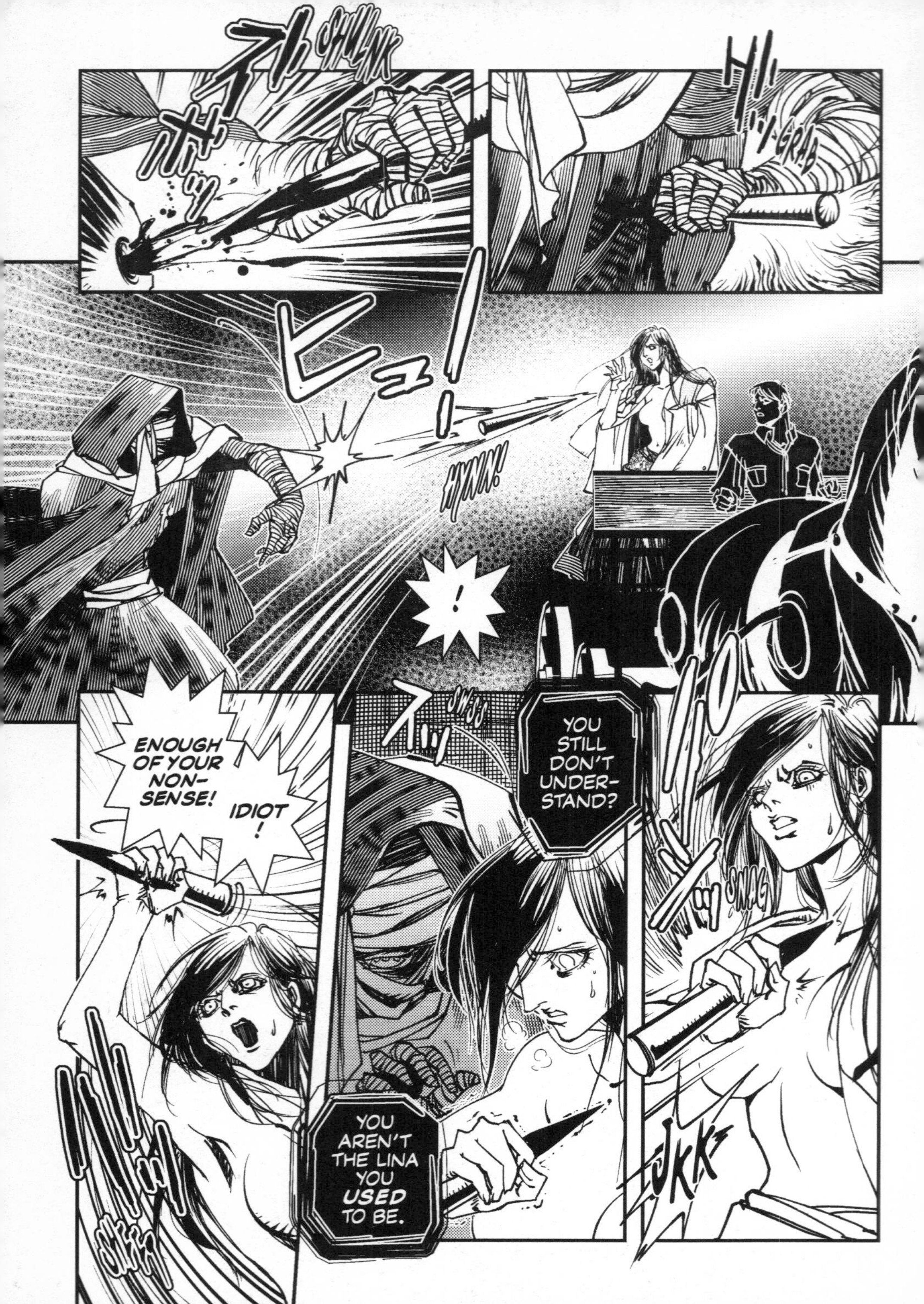
GRAB
SHUNK
HYNN!
!
JKK
SNAG
SWSS
YOU STILL DON'T UNDER-STAND?
YOU AREN'T THE LINA YOU USED TO BE.
ENOUGH OF YOUR NON-SENSE!
IDIOT!

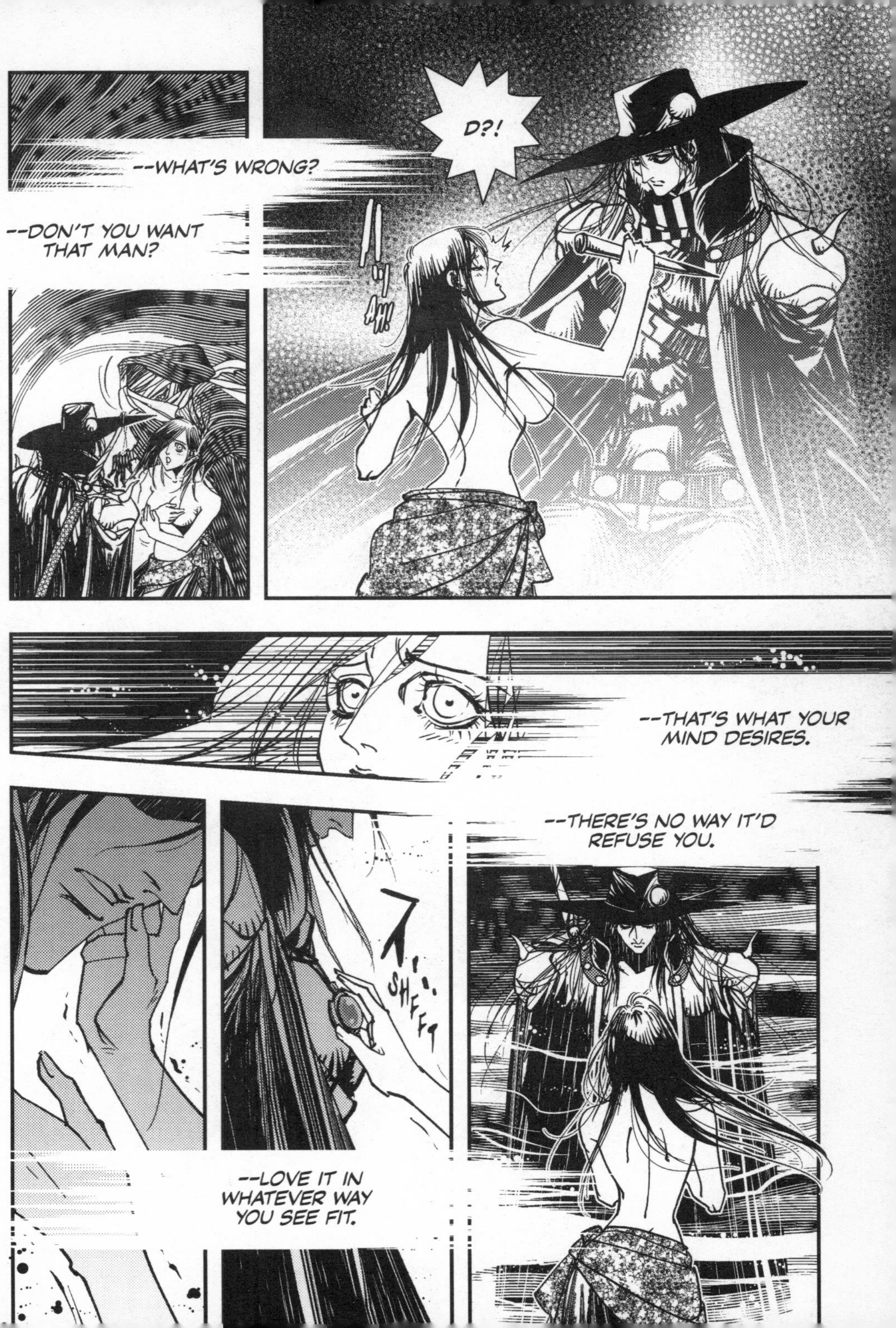
D?!
AH!
--WHAT'S WRONG?
--DON'T YOU WANT THAT MAN?
--THAT'S WHAT YOUR MIND DESIRES.
--THERE'S NO WAY IT'D REFUSE YOU.
--LOVE IT IN WHATEVER WAY YOU SEE FIT.

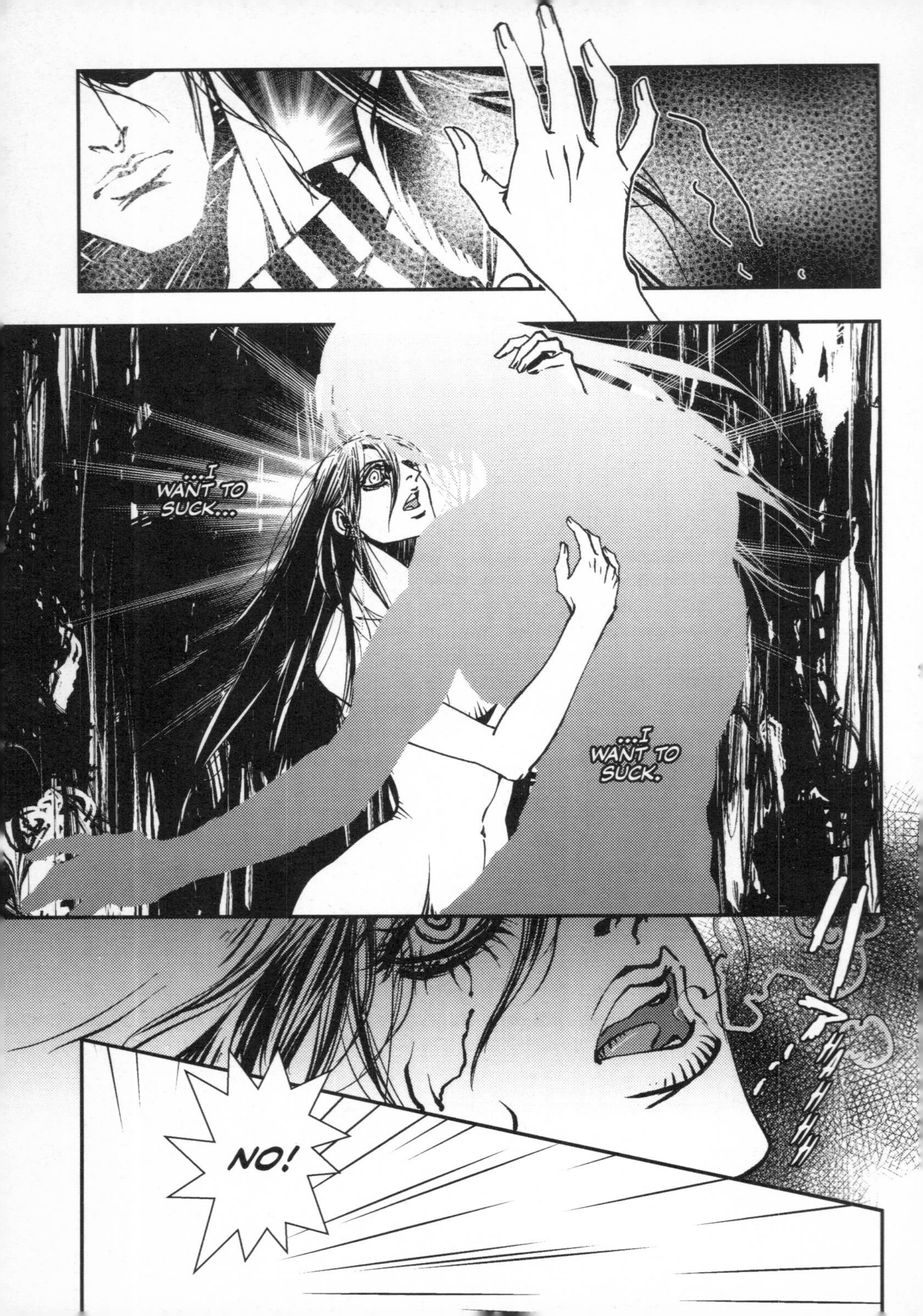
...I WANT TO SUCK.
...I WANT TO SUCK...
NO!

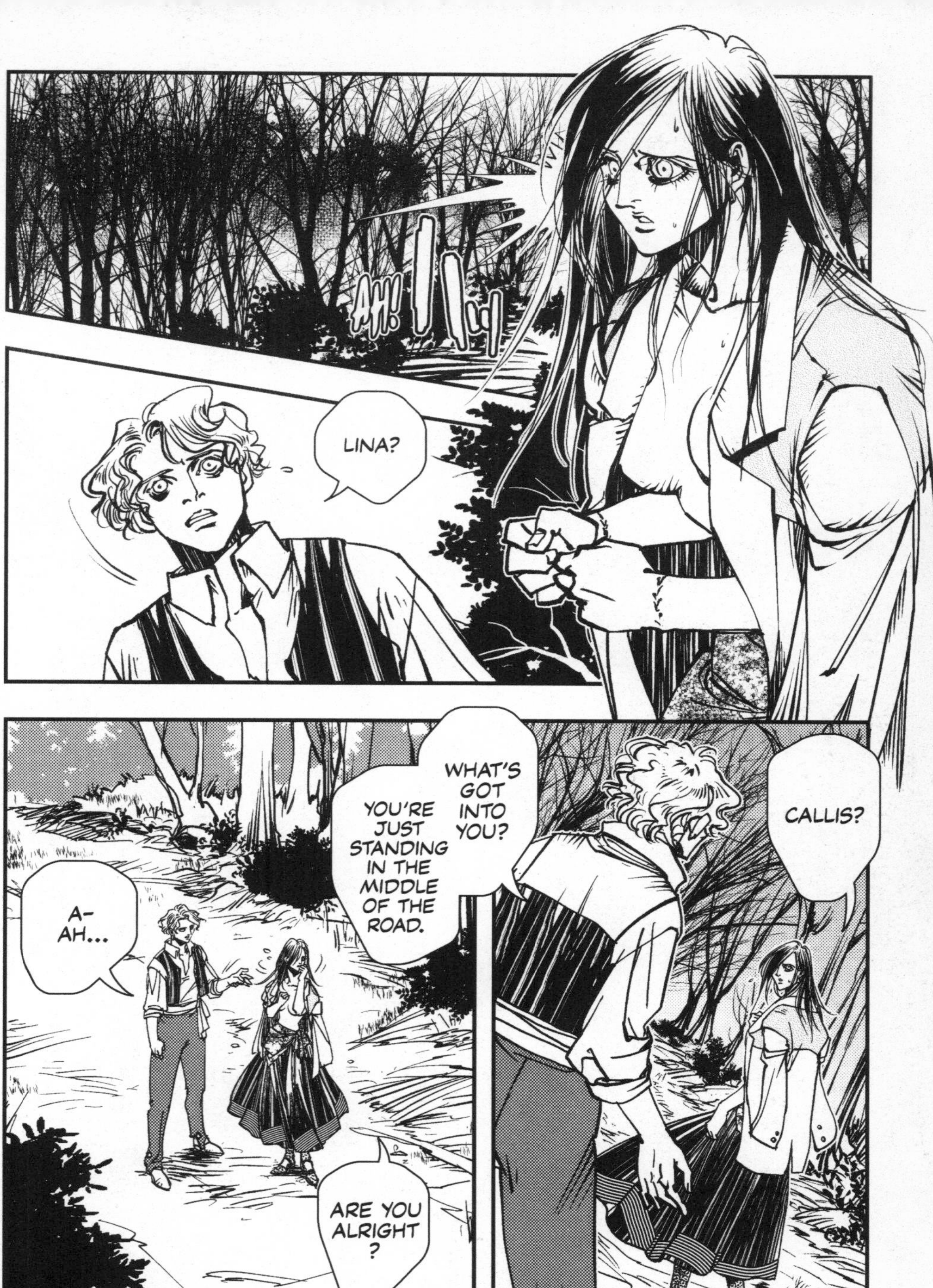
AH!
LINA?
CALLIS?
WHAT'S GOT INTO YOU?
YOU'RE JUST STANDING IN THE MIDDLE OF THE ROAD.
A-AH...
ARE YOU ALRIGHT?

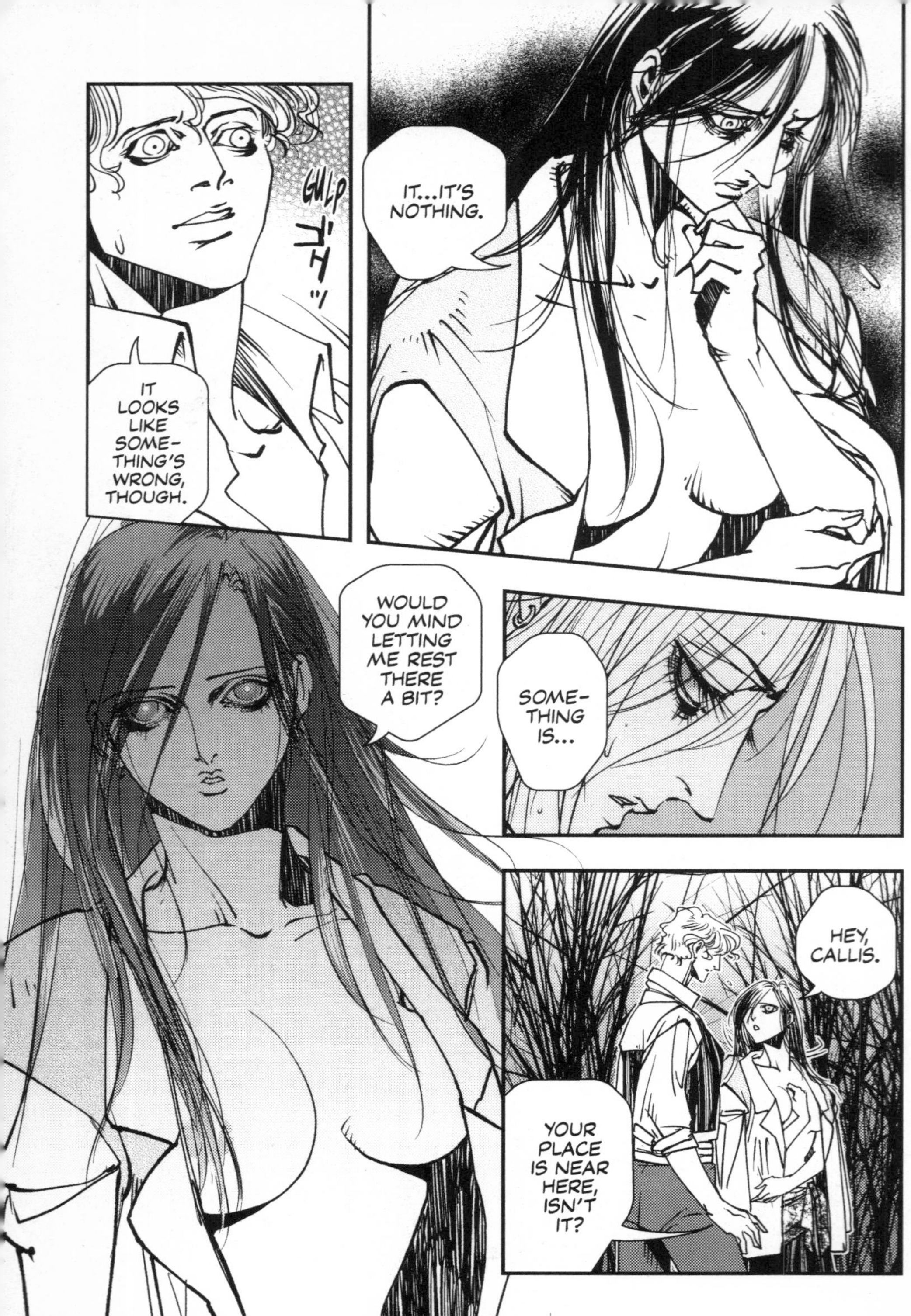
IT...IT'S NOTHING.
GULP
ゴクッ
IT LOOKS LIKE SOME-THING'S WRONG, THOUGH.
SOME-THING IS...
HEY, CALLIS.
YOUR PLACE IS NEAR HERE, ISN'T IT?
WOULD YOU MIND LETTING ME REST THERE A BIT?

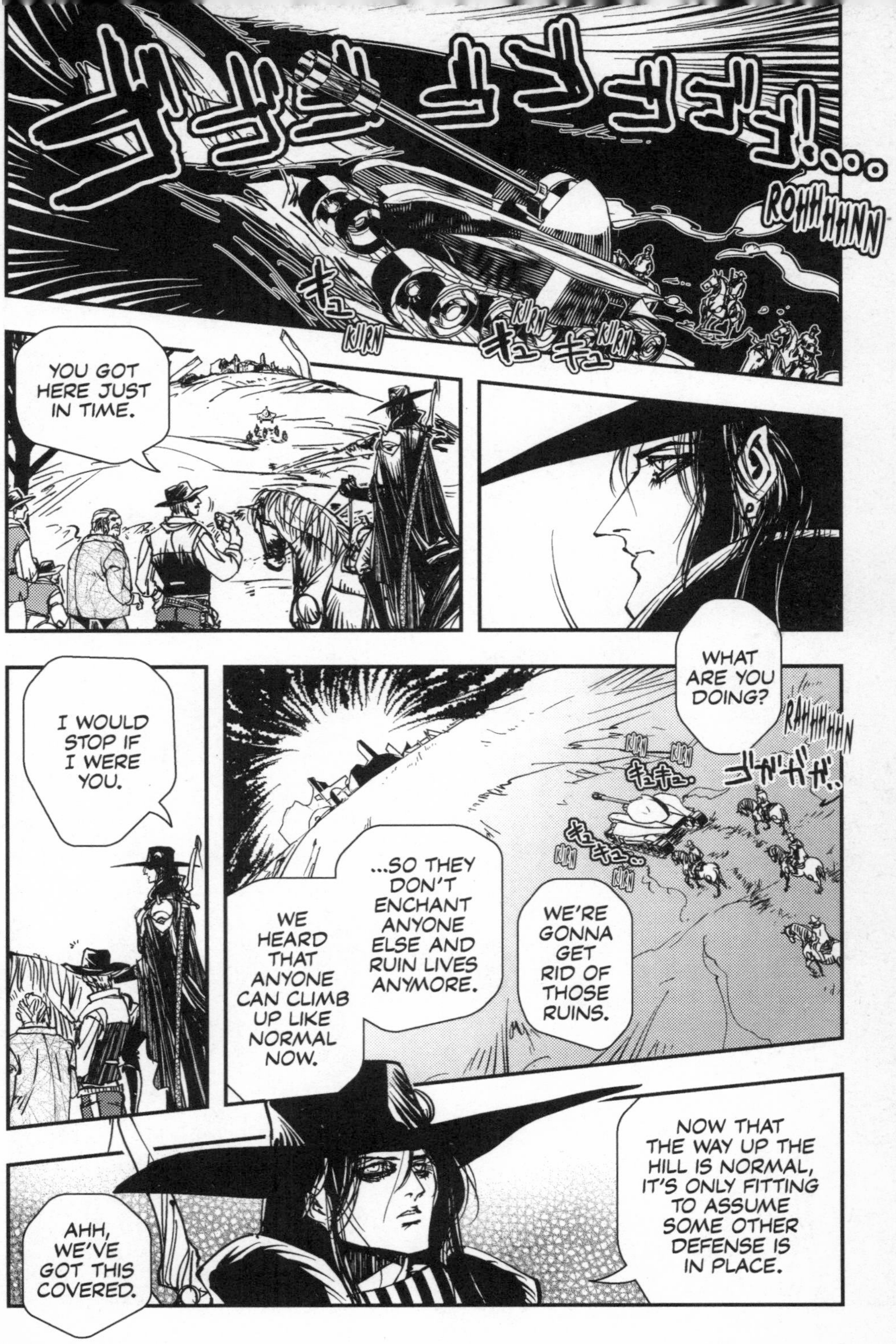
ROHHHHHNN
キュ
KIRN
キュ KIRN
キュ KIRN
YOU GOT HERE JUST IN TIME.
WHAT ARE YOU DOING?
RAHHHHHHN
ゴガガガ..
KIRN KIRN
キュキュ.
キュキュ..
KIRN
KIRN
WE'RE GONNA GET RID OF THOSE RUINS.
...SO THEY DON'T ENCHANT ANYONE ELSE AND RUIN LIVES ANYMORE.
WE HEARD THAT ANYONE CAN CLIMB UP LIKE NORMAL NOW.
I WOULD STOP IF I WERE YOU.
NOW THAT THE WAY UP THE HILL IS NORMAL, IT'S ONLY FITTING TO ASSUME SOME OTHER DEFENSE IS IN PLACE.
AHH, WE'VE GOT THIS COVERED.

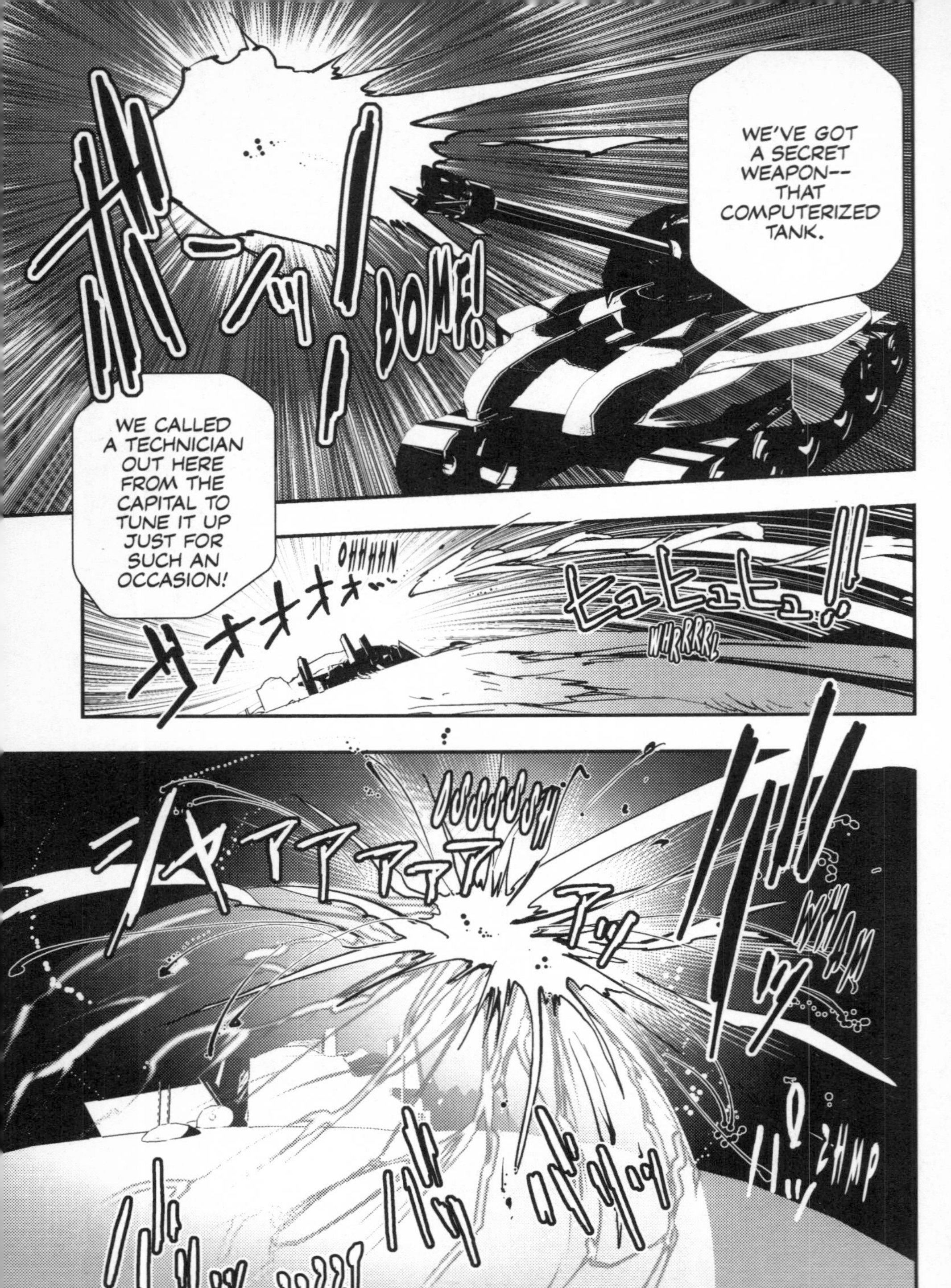
WE'VE GOT A SECRET WEAPON-- THAT COMPUTERIZED TANK.
BOMF!
WE CALLED A TECHNICIAN OUT HERE FROM THE CAPITAL TO TUNE IT UP JUST FOR SUCH AN OCCASION!
ヒュヒュヒュ!!
WHRRRRL
OHHHHHN
ZHMP

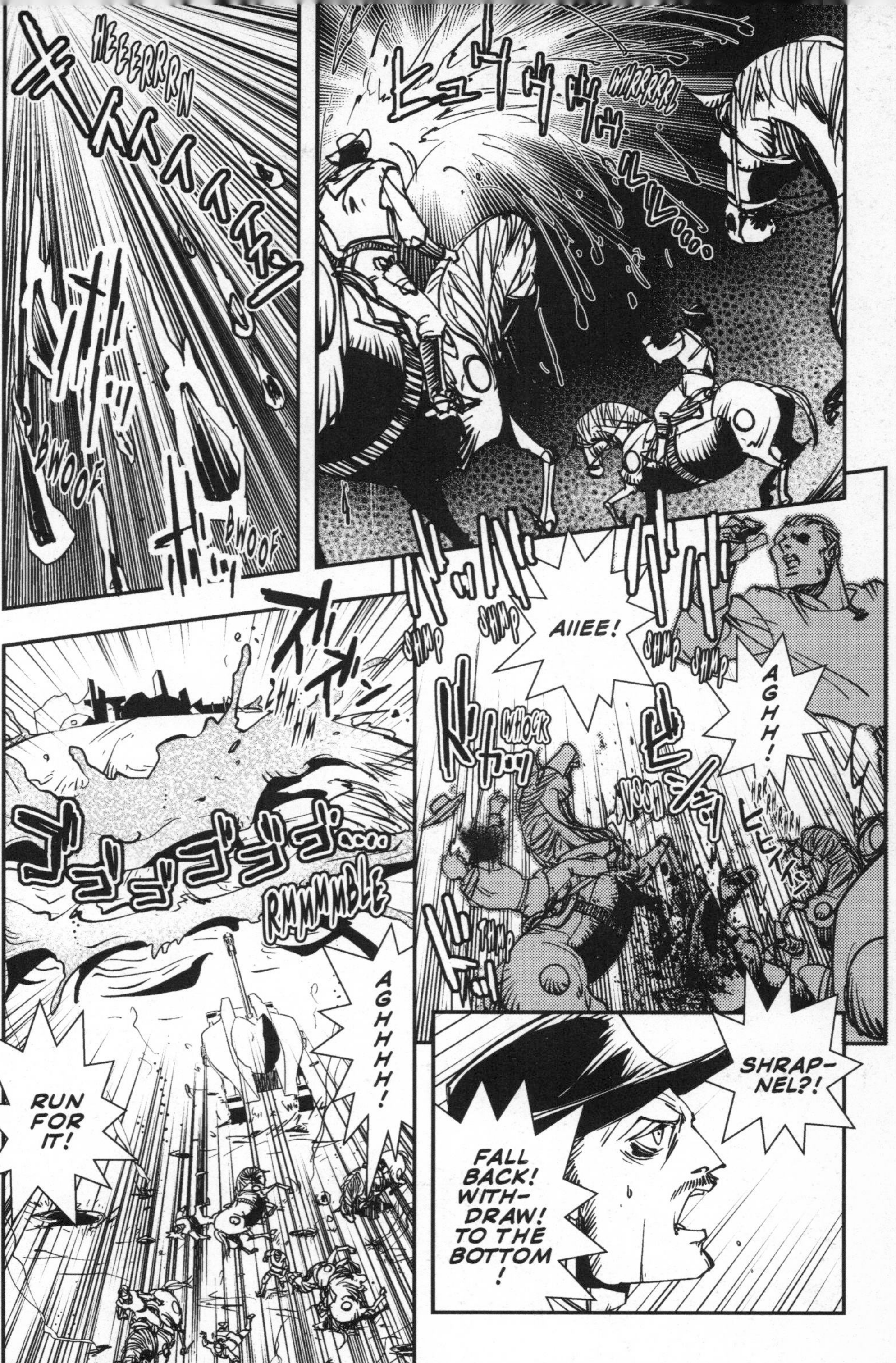

WHRRRRL
HEEERRRN
BWOOF
BWOOF
AIIEE!
AGHH!
WHOCK
SHRAP-NEL?!
FALL BACK! WITH-DRAW! TO THE BOTTOM!
RMMMMBLE
AGHHHH!
RUN FOR IT!

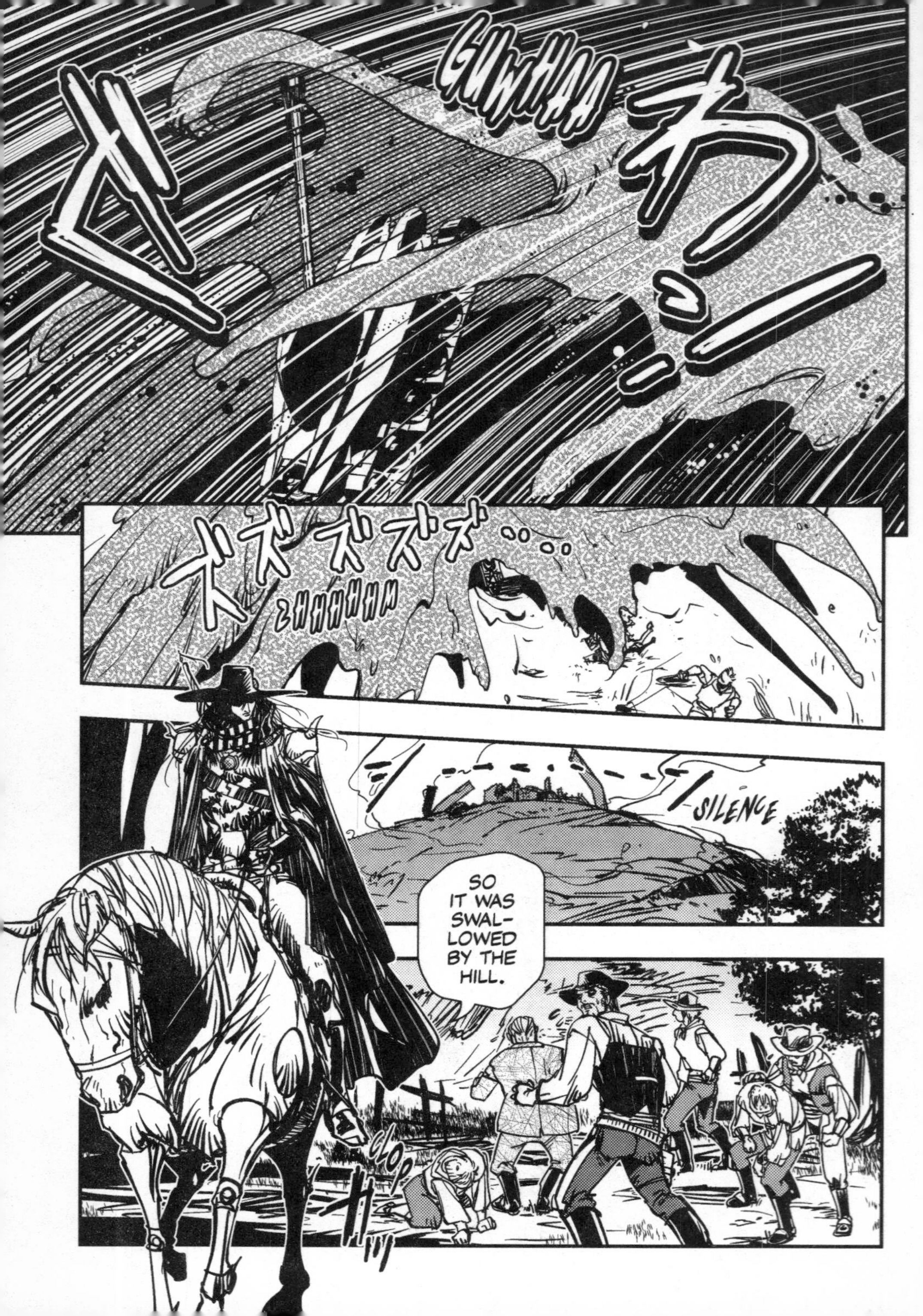
ズわッ!!
ズズズズズ……
ZHHHHHHM
SILENCE
SO IT WAS SWAL-LOWED BY THE HILL.
CLOP

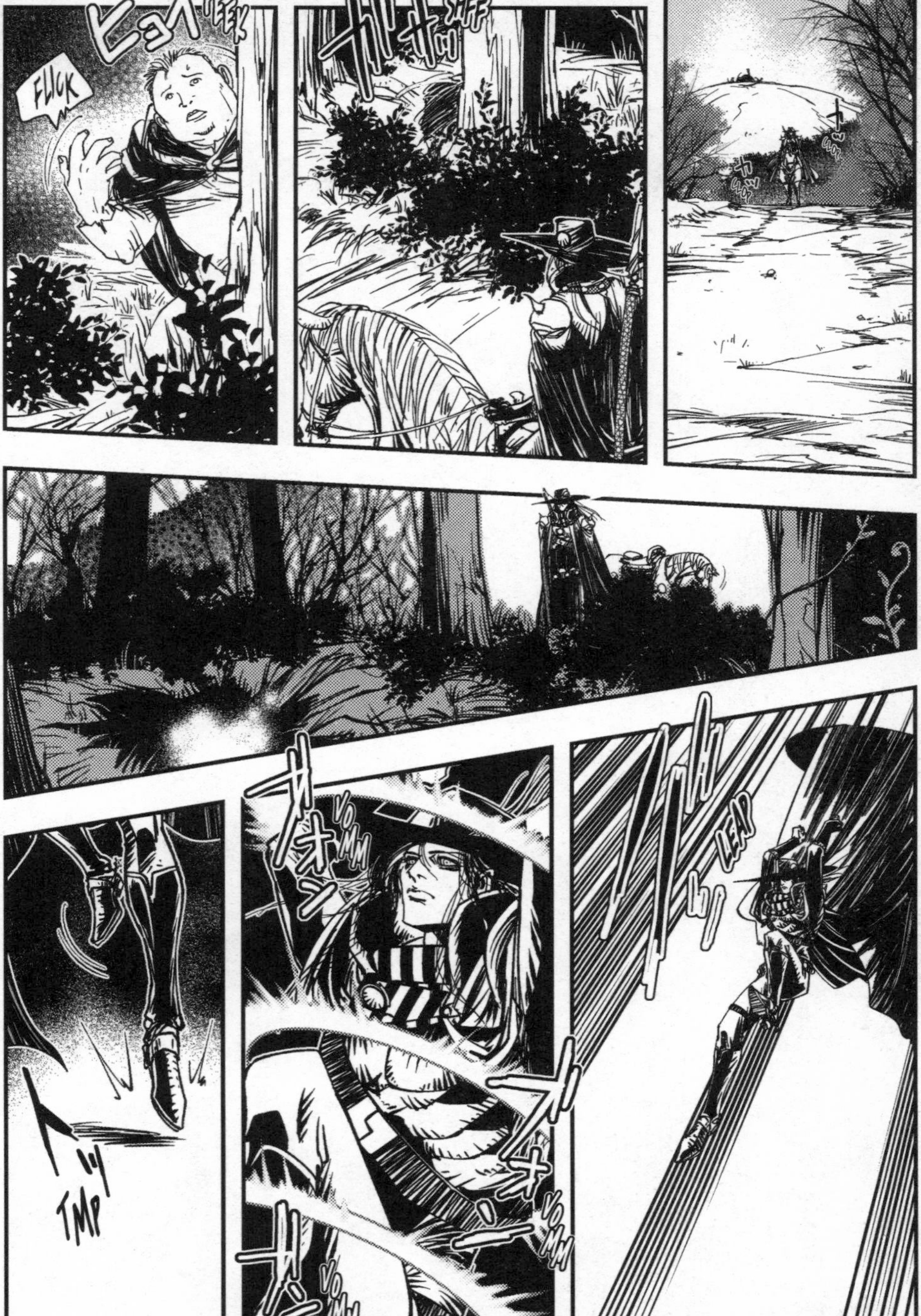
CLOP
CLOP
SHFF
ヒョイ PEEK
FLICK
LEAP
VOMM
VOMM
VOMM
TMP

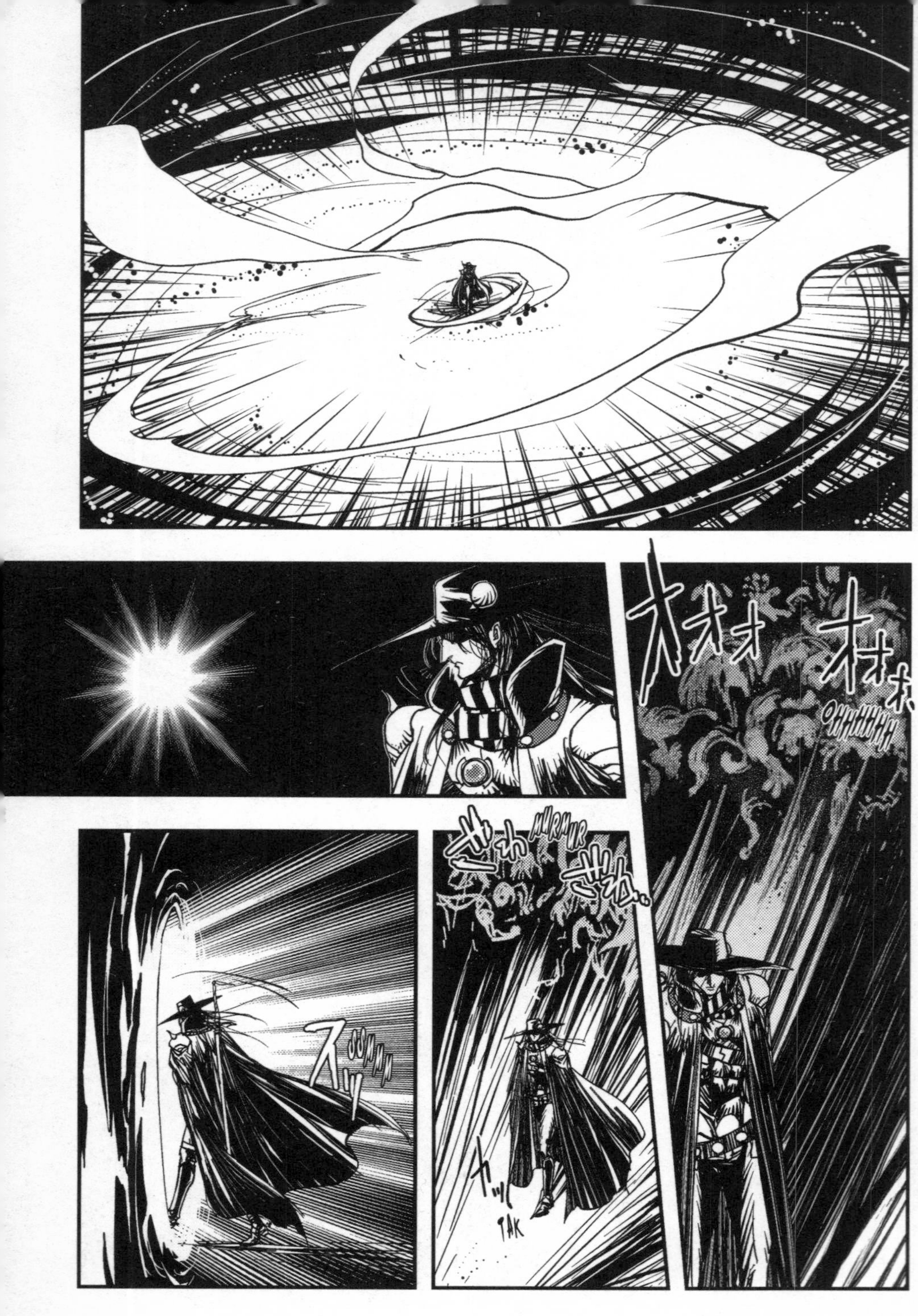
オオオ
オオォ...
OHHHHHH
ざわーざわ...
MURMUR
カツ
TAK
スッ
SSHHHH

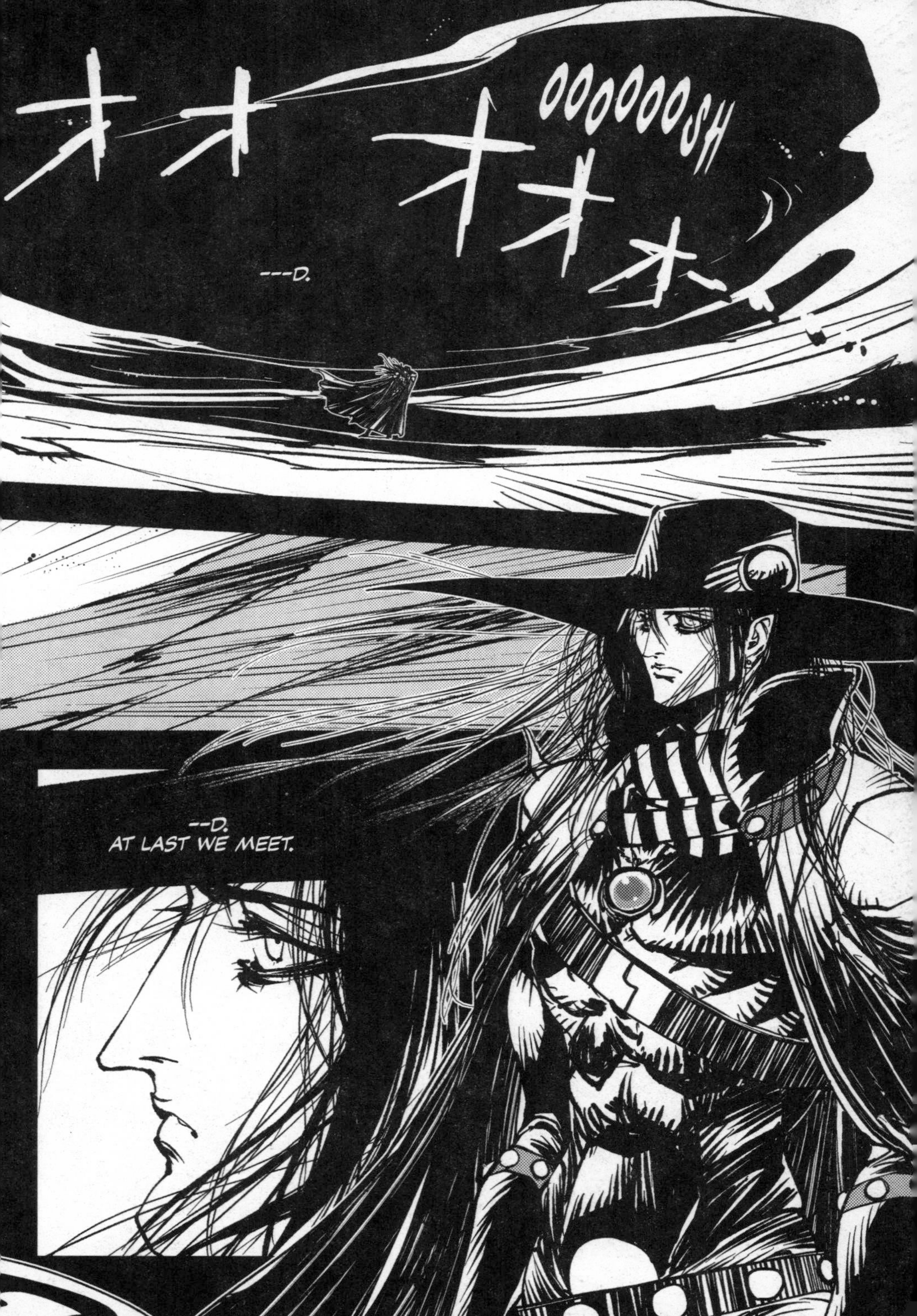

オオオオオオー
OOOOOOOSH
---D.
--D.
AT LAST WE MEET.

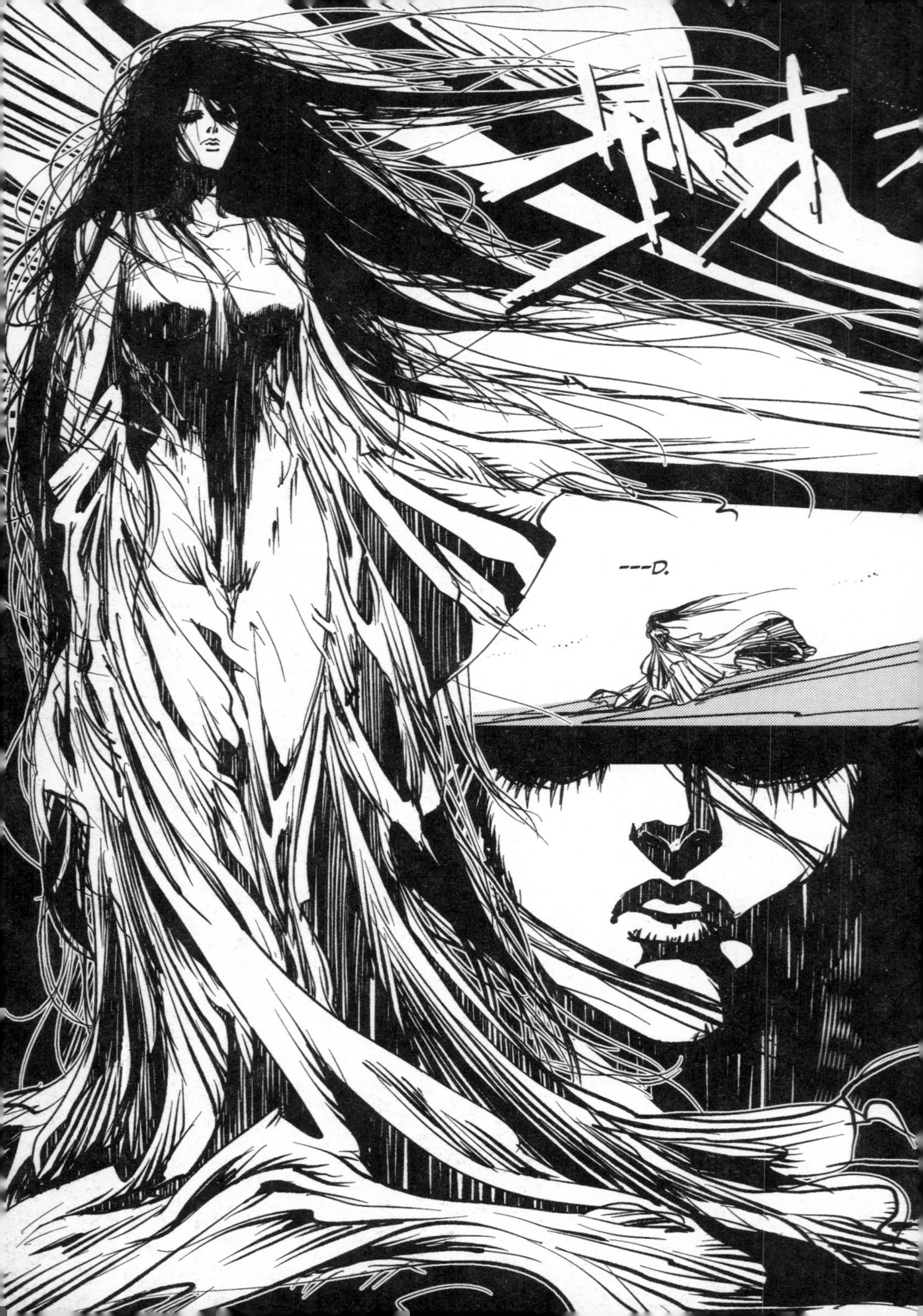
---D.

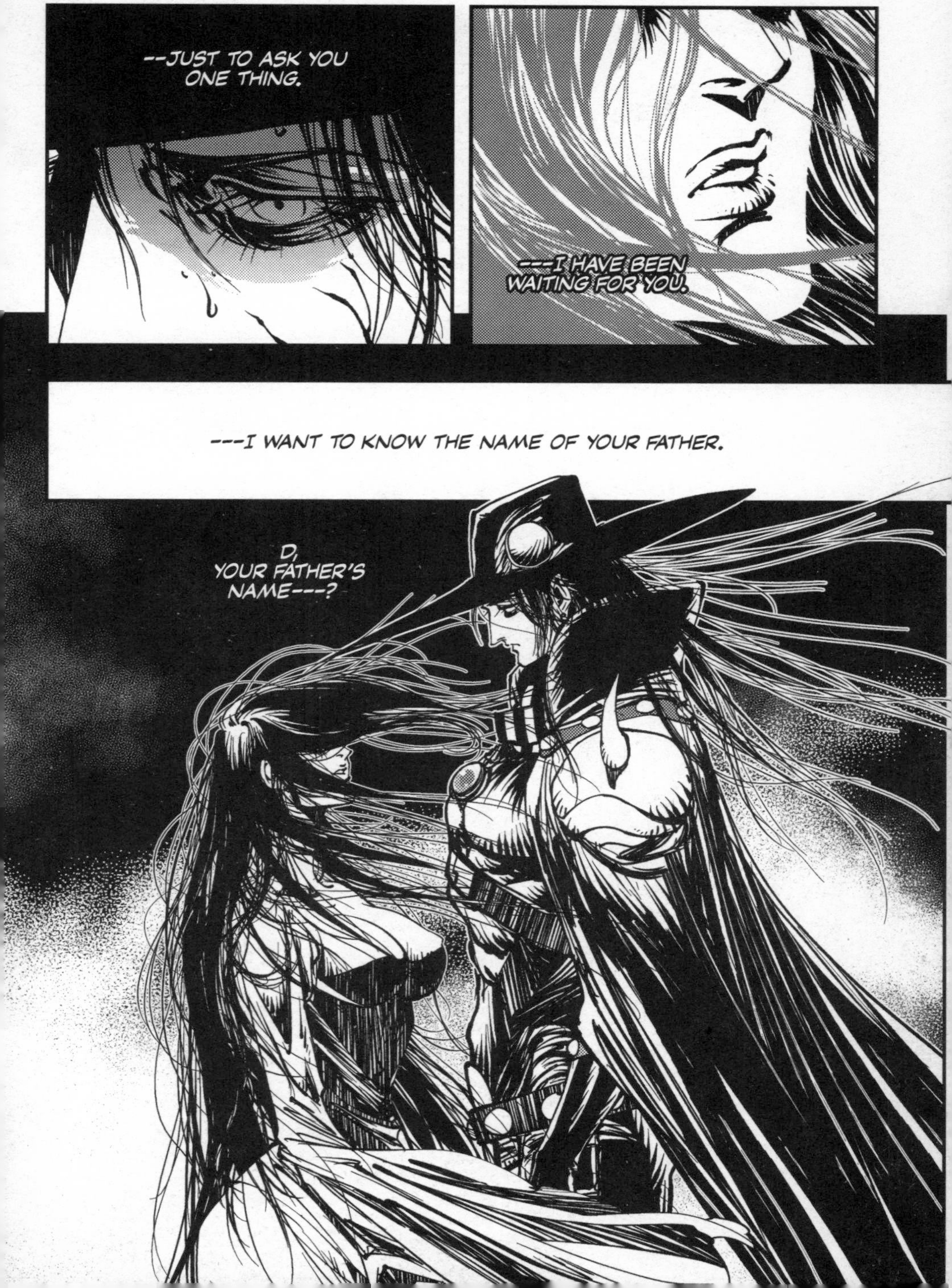
---I HAVE BEEN WAITING FOR YOU.
--JUST TO ASK YOU ONE THING.
---I WANT TO KNOW THE NAME OF YOUR FATHER.
D, YOUR FATHER'S NAME---?

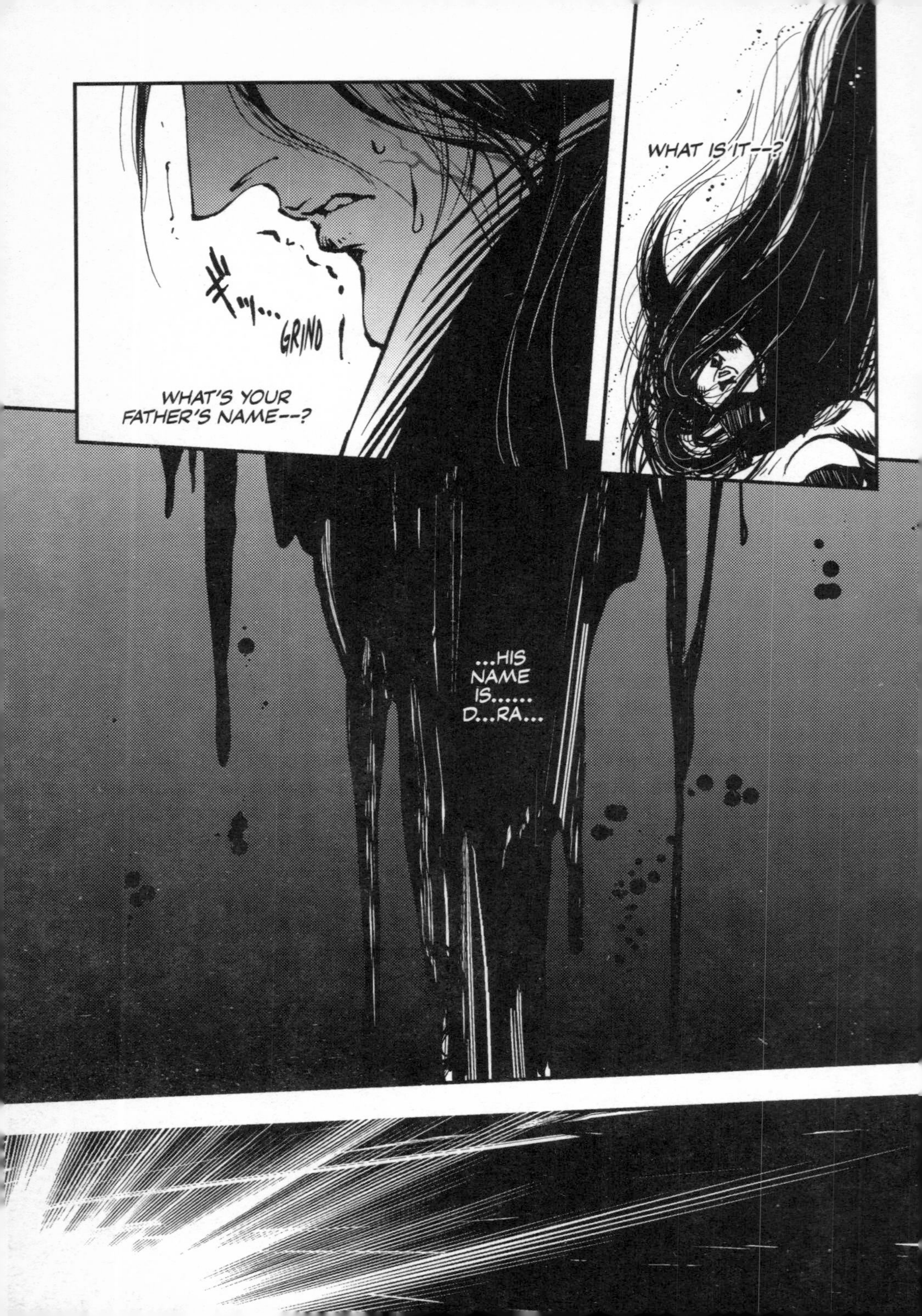
WHAT IS IT--?
GRIND
WHAT'S YOUR FATHER'S NAME--?
...HIS NAME IS...... D...RA...

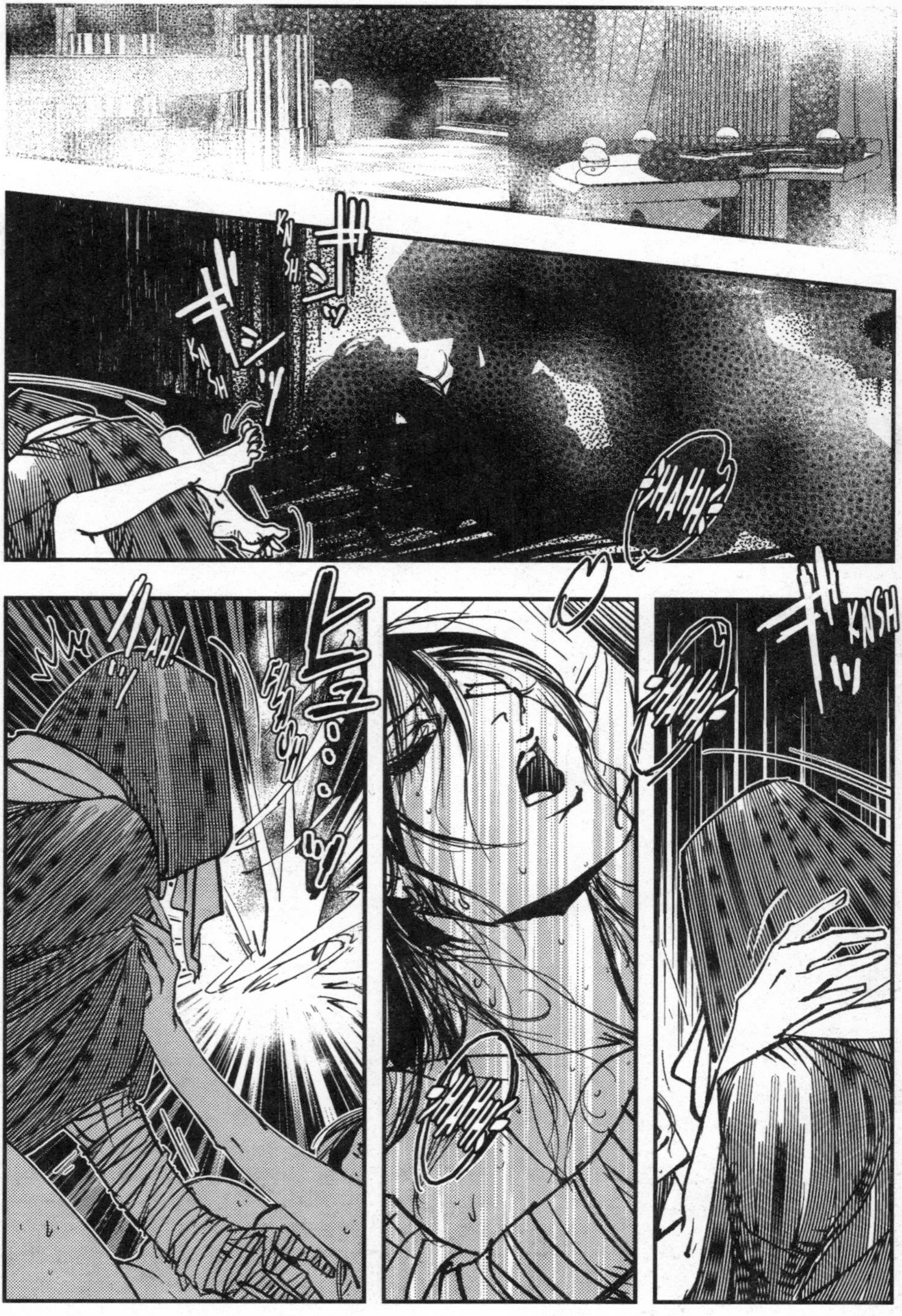

KNSH
KNSH
HAHH
KNSH
HAHH
HAHH
AH!
FLASH

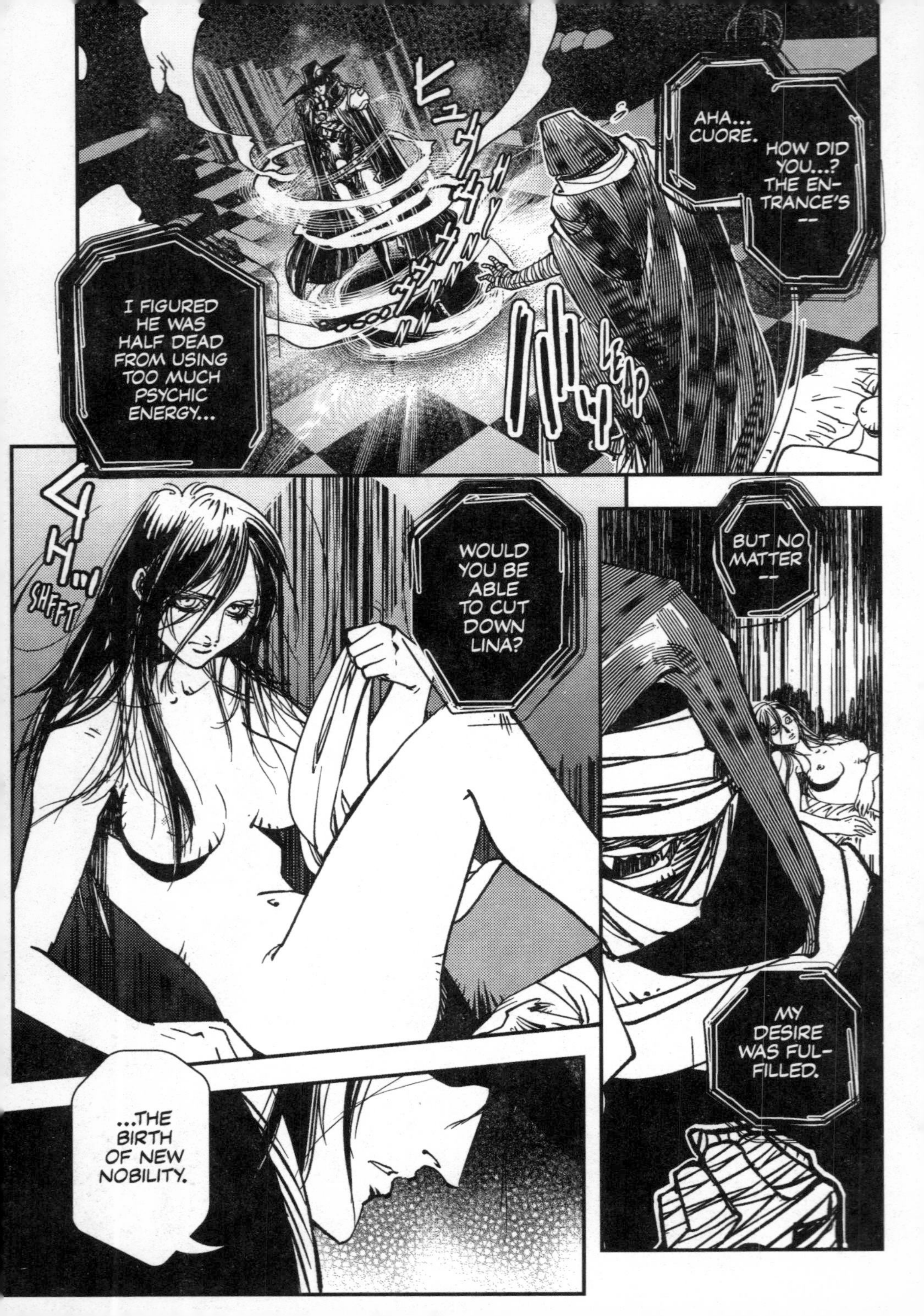
AHA... CUORE.
HOW DID YOU...? THE EN-TRANCE'S --
LEAP
I FIGURED HE WAS HALF DEAD FROM USING TOO MUCH PSYCHIC ENERGY...
BUT NO MATTER --
MY DESIRE WAS FUL-FILLED.
WOULD YOU BE ABLE TO CUT DOWN LINA?
SHFFT
...THE BIRTH OF NEW NOBILITY.

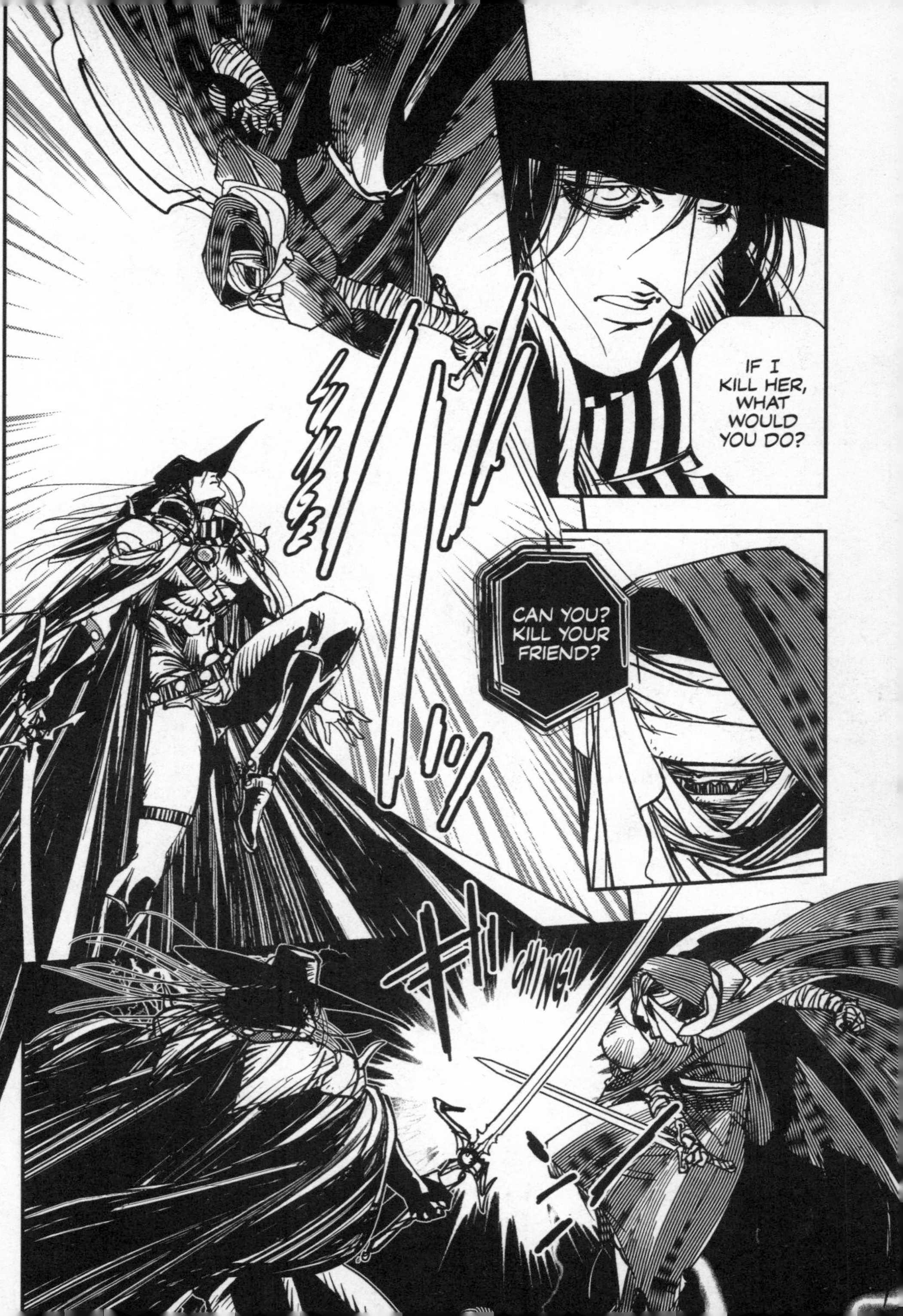
IF I KILL HER, WHAT WOULD YOU DO?
CAN YOU? KILL YOUR FRIEND?
CHING!

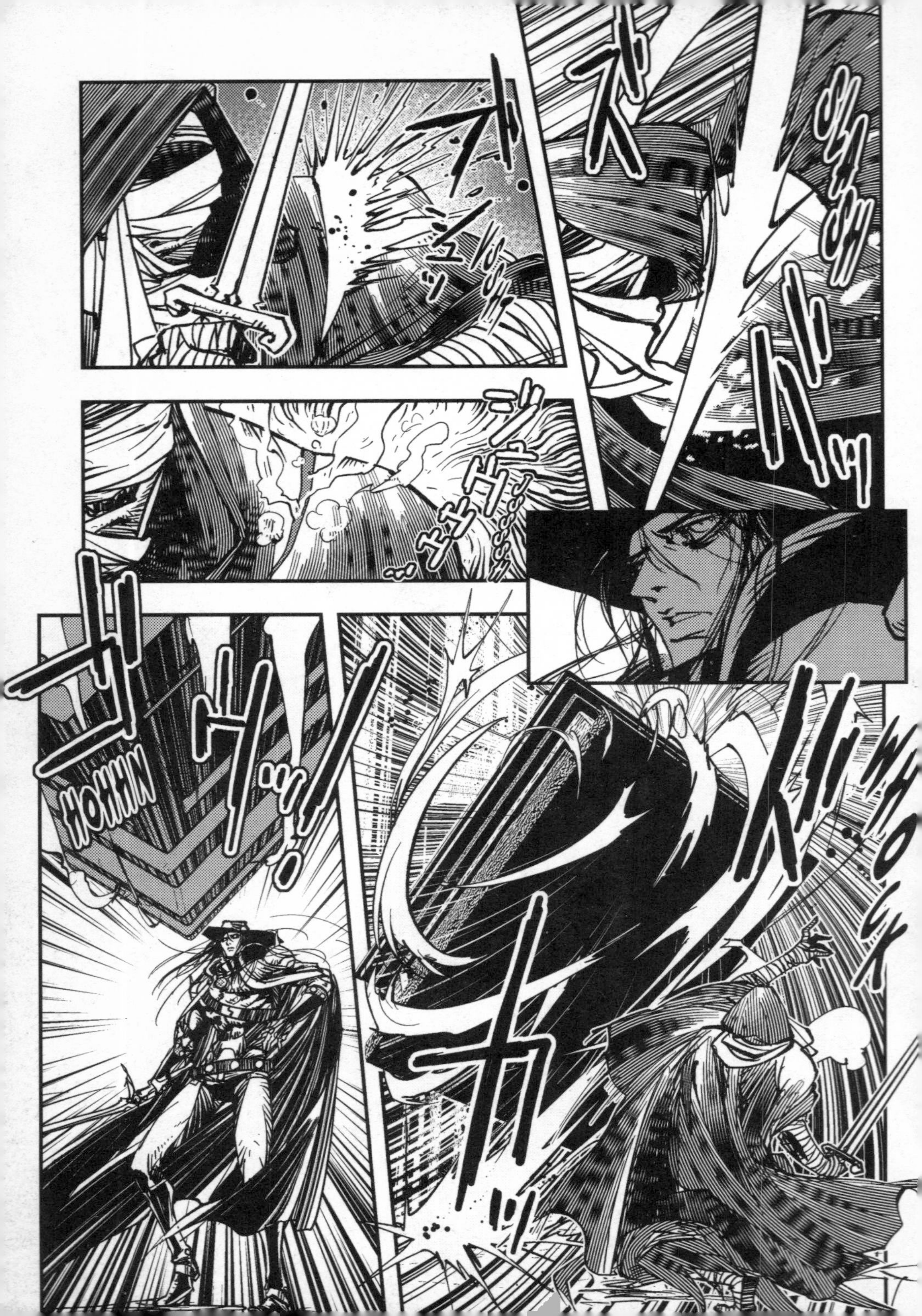

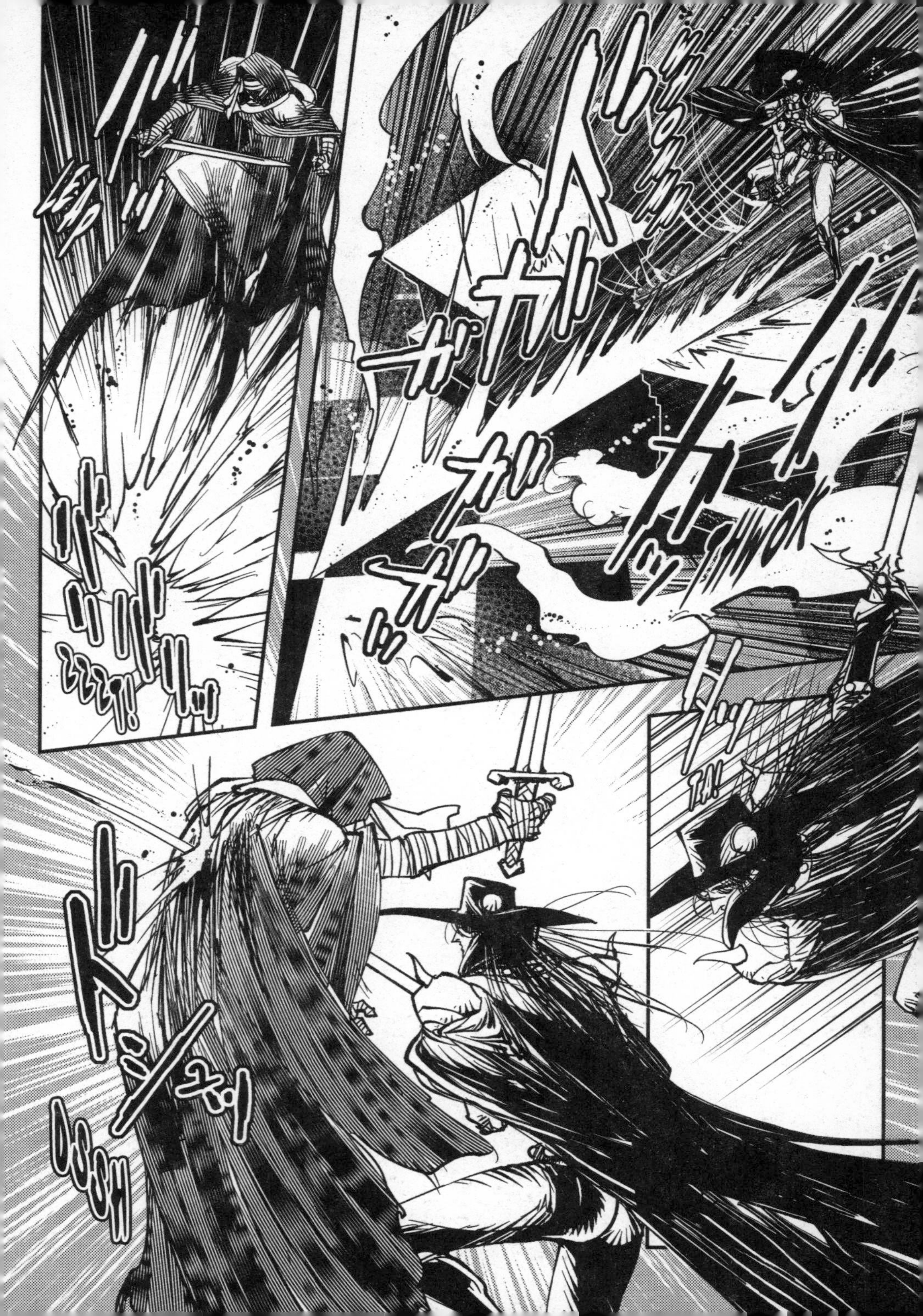
LEAP
ZZZZT!
TA!
DASH

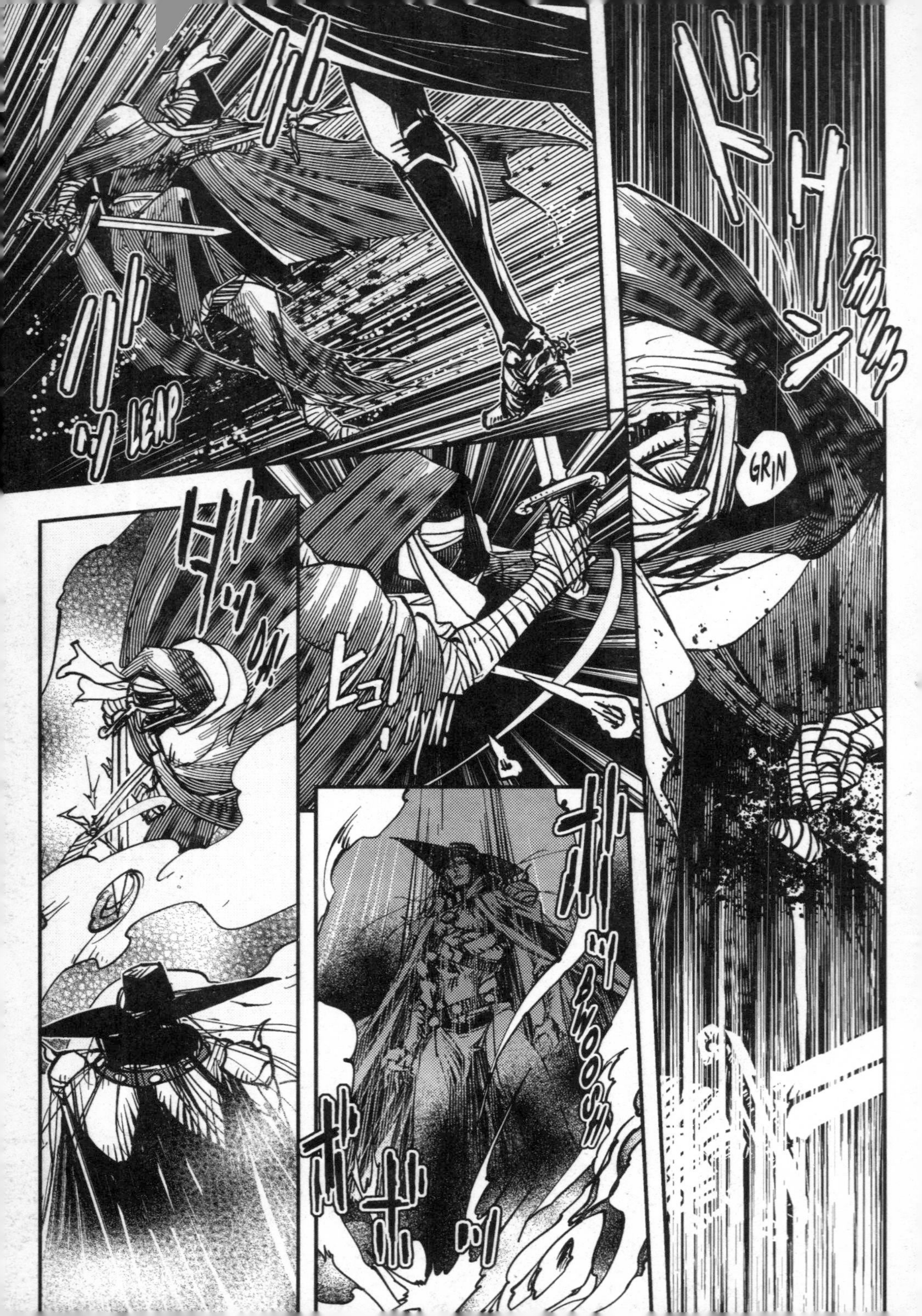
THUMP
GRIN
LEAP
HYN!
WHOOSH

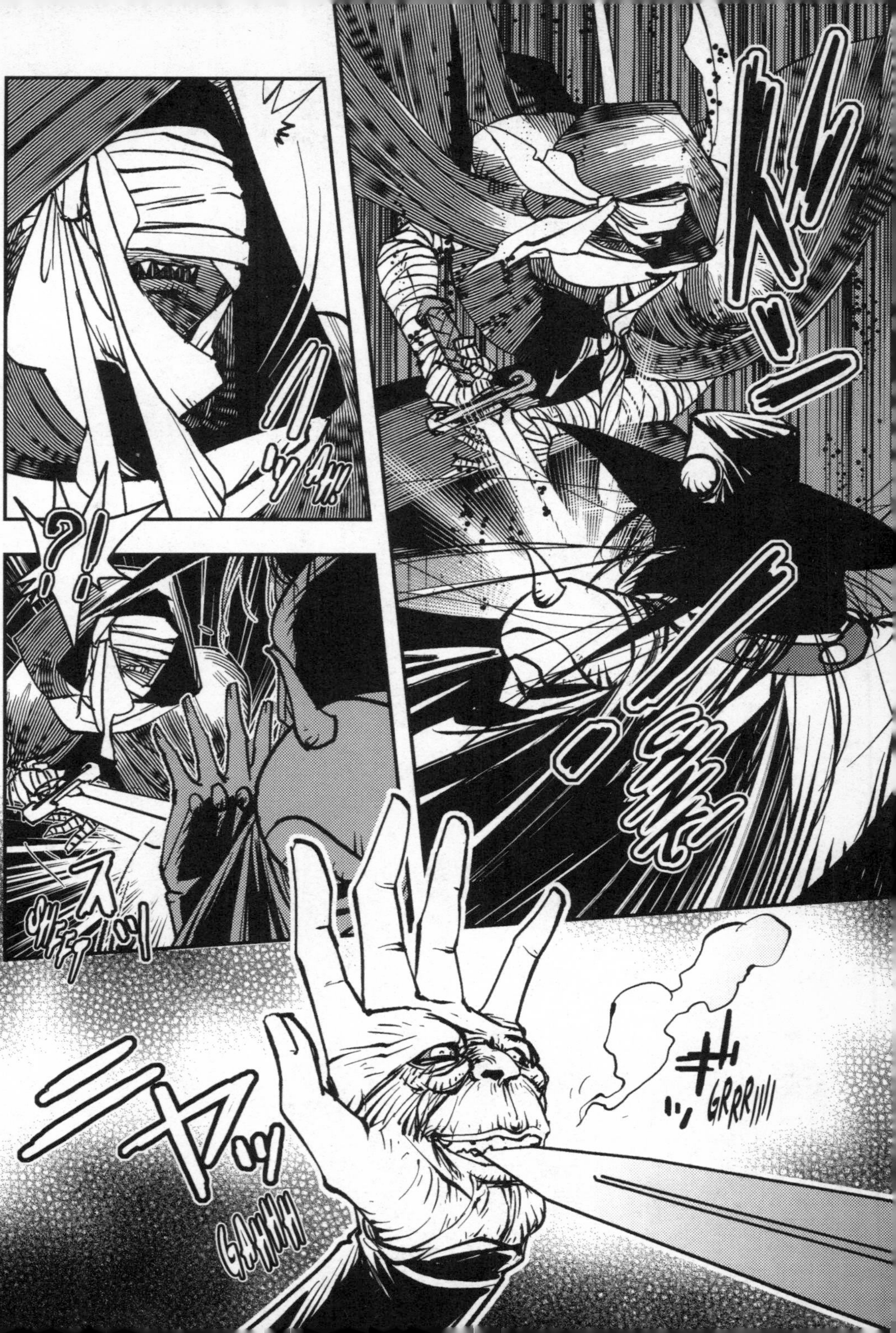
CHUNK
AH!
?!
GRRR
GAHHH

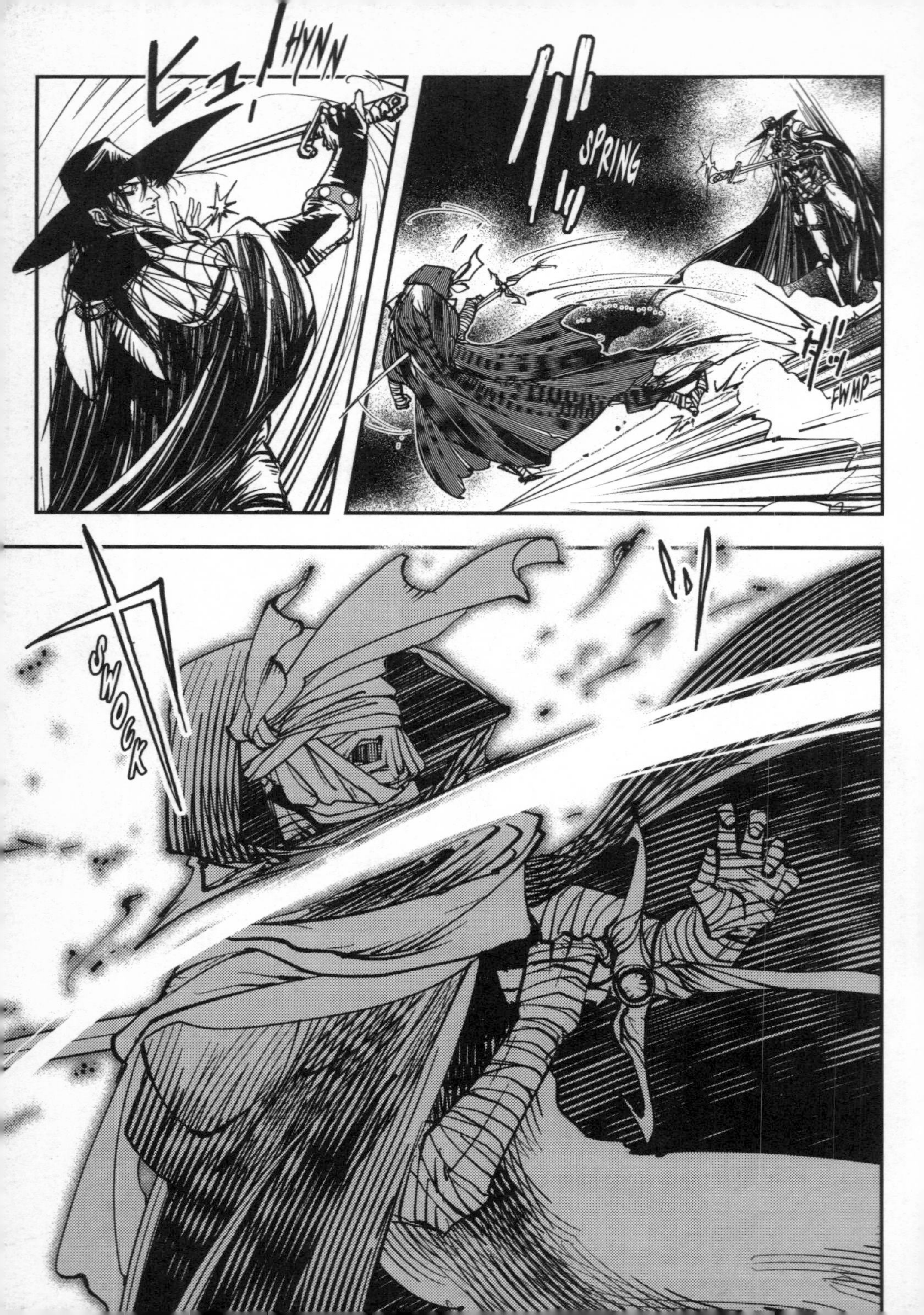
SPRING
FWMP
ヒュ!
HYNN
SWOUK

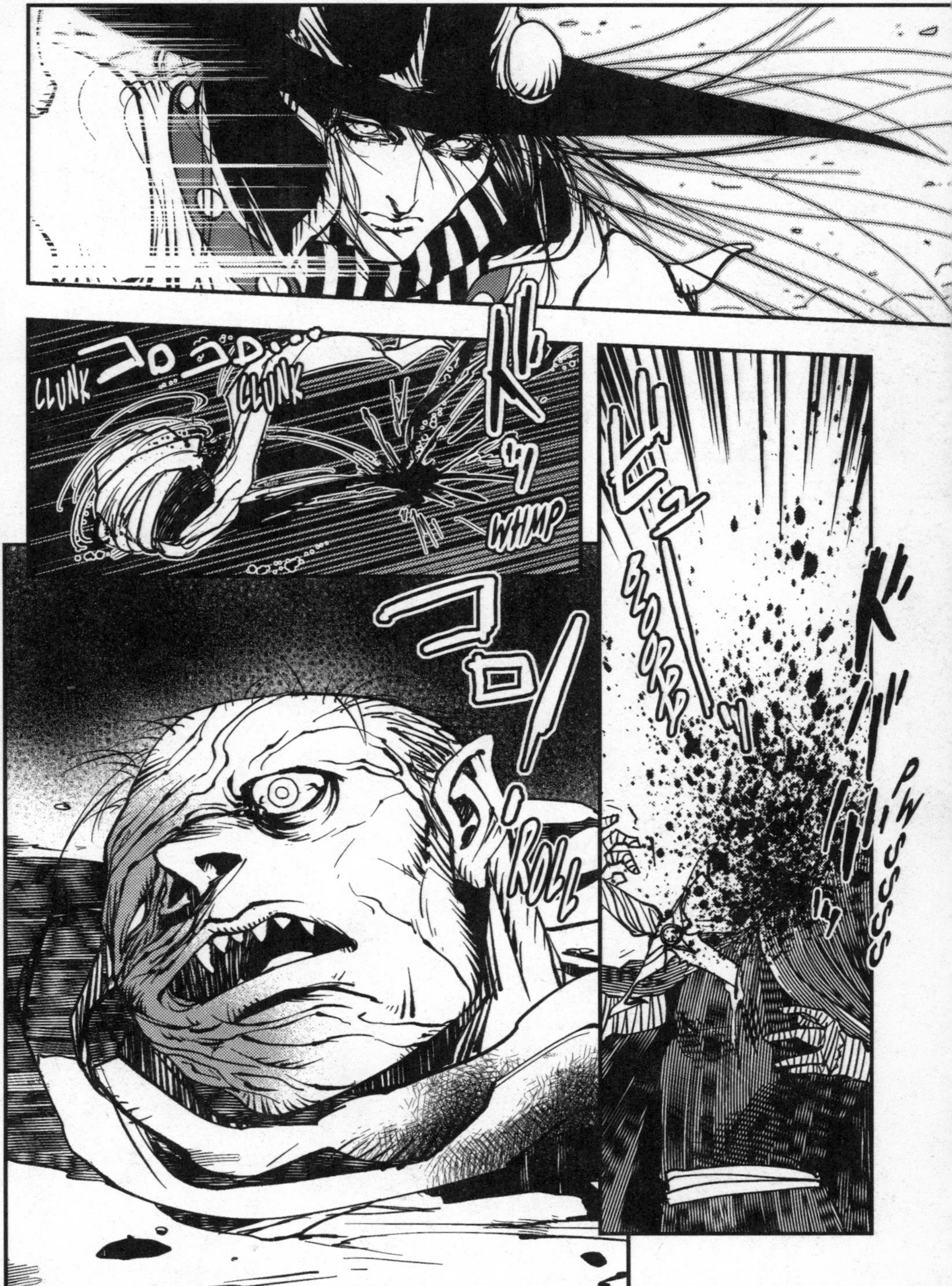
CLUNK
CLUNK
WHMP
ROLL

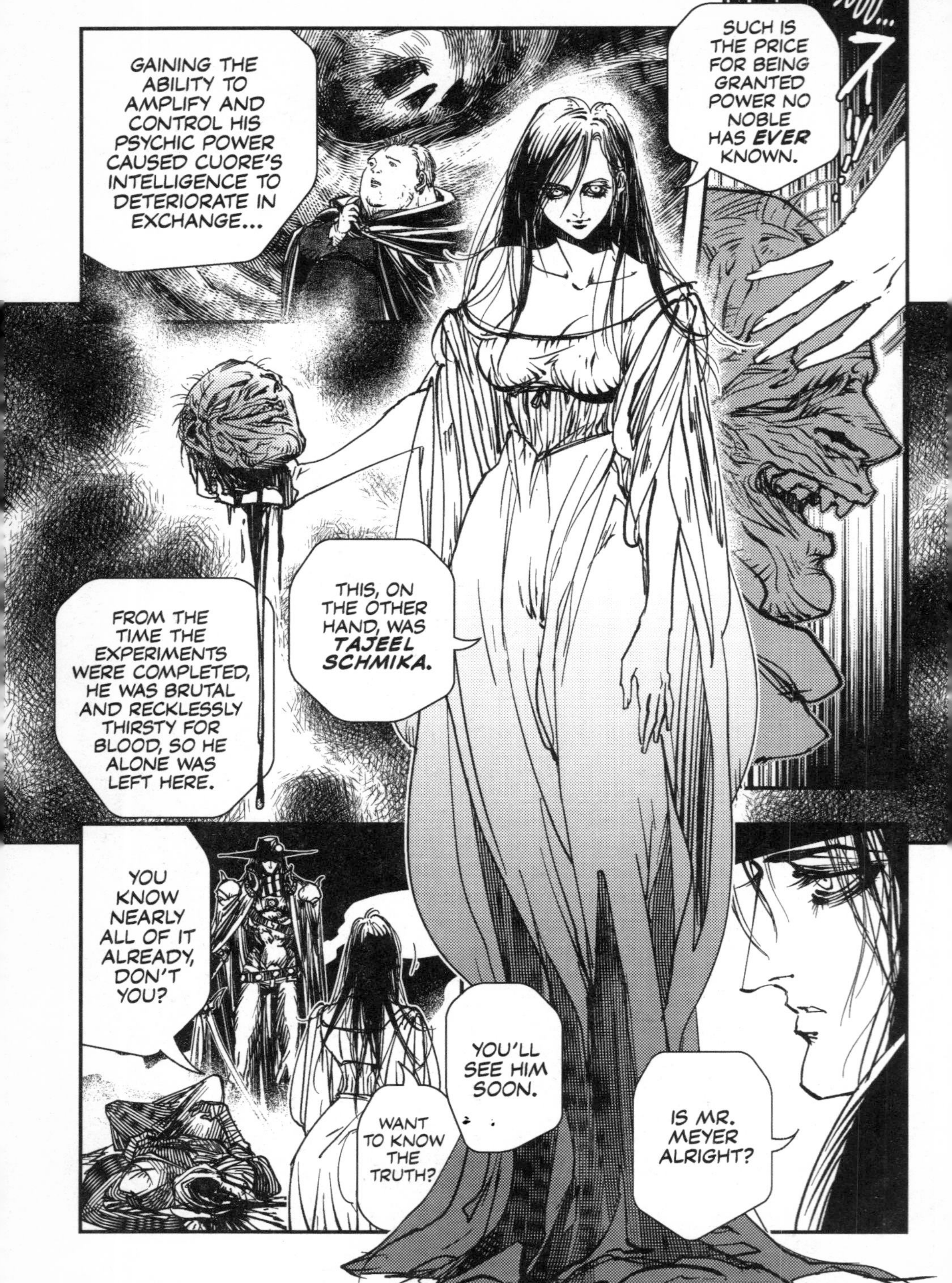
SUUU...
SUCH IS THE PRICE FOR BEING GRANTED POWER NO NOBLE HAS ***EVER*** KNOWN.
GAINING THE ABILITY TO AMPLIFY AND CONTROL HIS PSYCHIC POWER CAUSED CUORE'S INTELLIGENCE TO DETERIORATE IN EXCHANGE...
THIS, ON THE OTHER HAND, WAS ***TAJEEL SCHMIKA.***
FROM THE TIME THE EXPERIMENTS WERE COMPLETED, HE WAS BRUTAL AND RECKLESSLY THIRSTY FOR BLOOD, SO HE ALONE WAS LEFT HERE.
IS MR. MEYER ALRIGHT?
YOU'LL SEE HIM SOON.
WANT TO KNOW THE TRUTH?
YOU KNOW NEARLY ALL OF IT ALREADY, DON'T YOU?

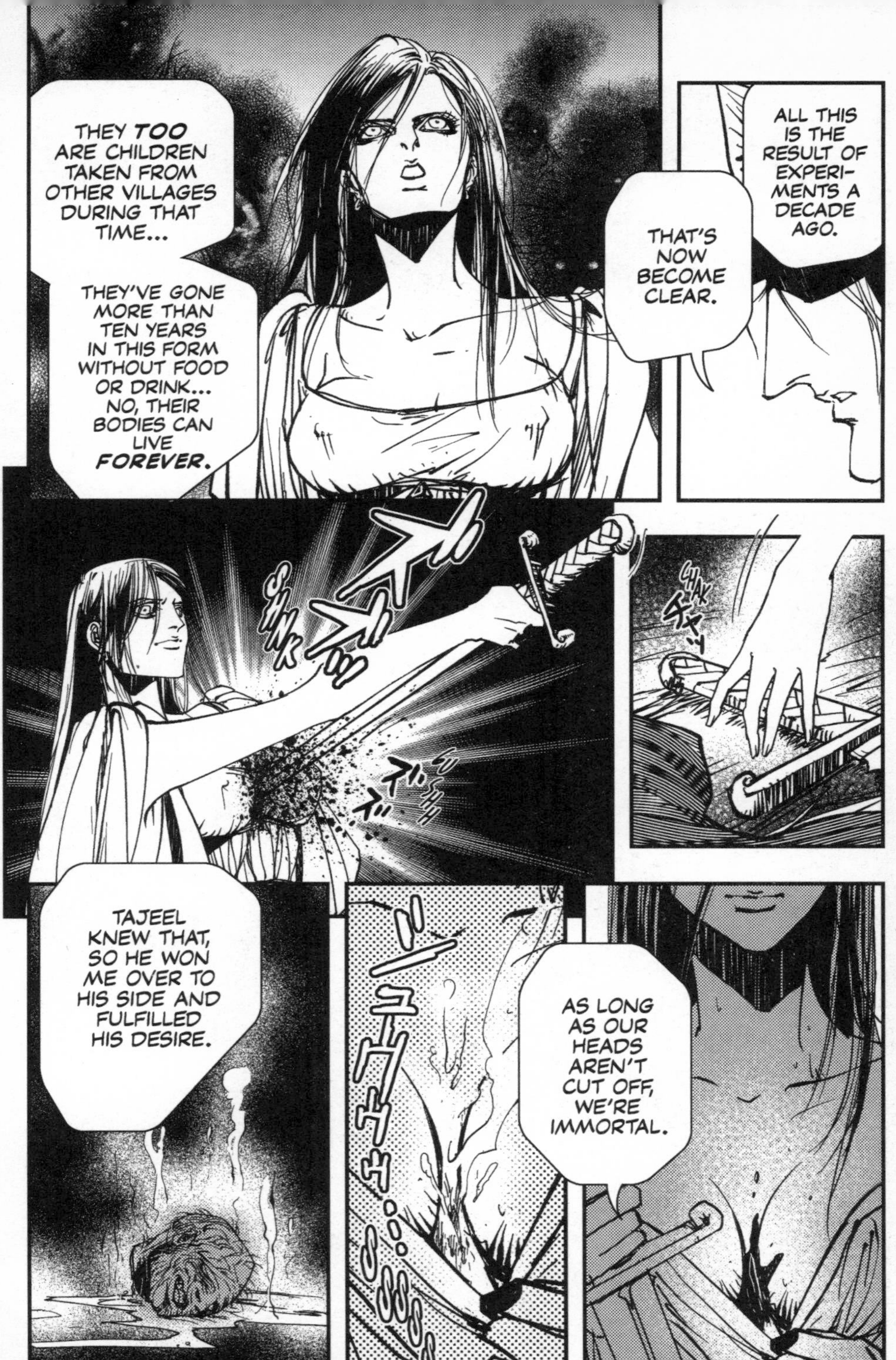
ALL THIS IS THE RESULT OF EXPERIMENTS A DECADE AGO.
THAT'S NOW BECOME CLEAR.
THEY *TOO* ARE CHILDREN TAKEN FROM OTHER VILLAGES DURING THAT TIME...
THEY'VE GONE MORE THAN TEN YEARS IN THIS FORM WITHOUT FOOD OR DRINK... NO, THEIR BODIES CAN LIVE ***FOREVER***.
CHAK
チャッ
SHNK
AS LONG AS OUR HEADS AREN'T CUT OFF, WE'RE IMMORTAL.
SSSS
TAJEEL KNEW THAT, SO HE WON ME OVER TO HIS SIDE AND FULFILLED HIS DESIRE.

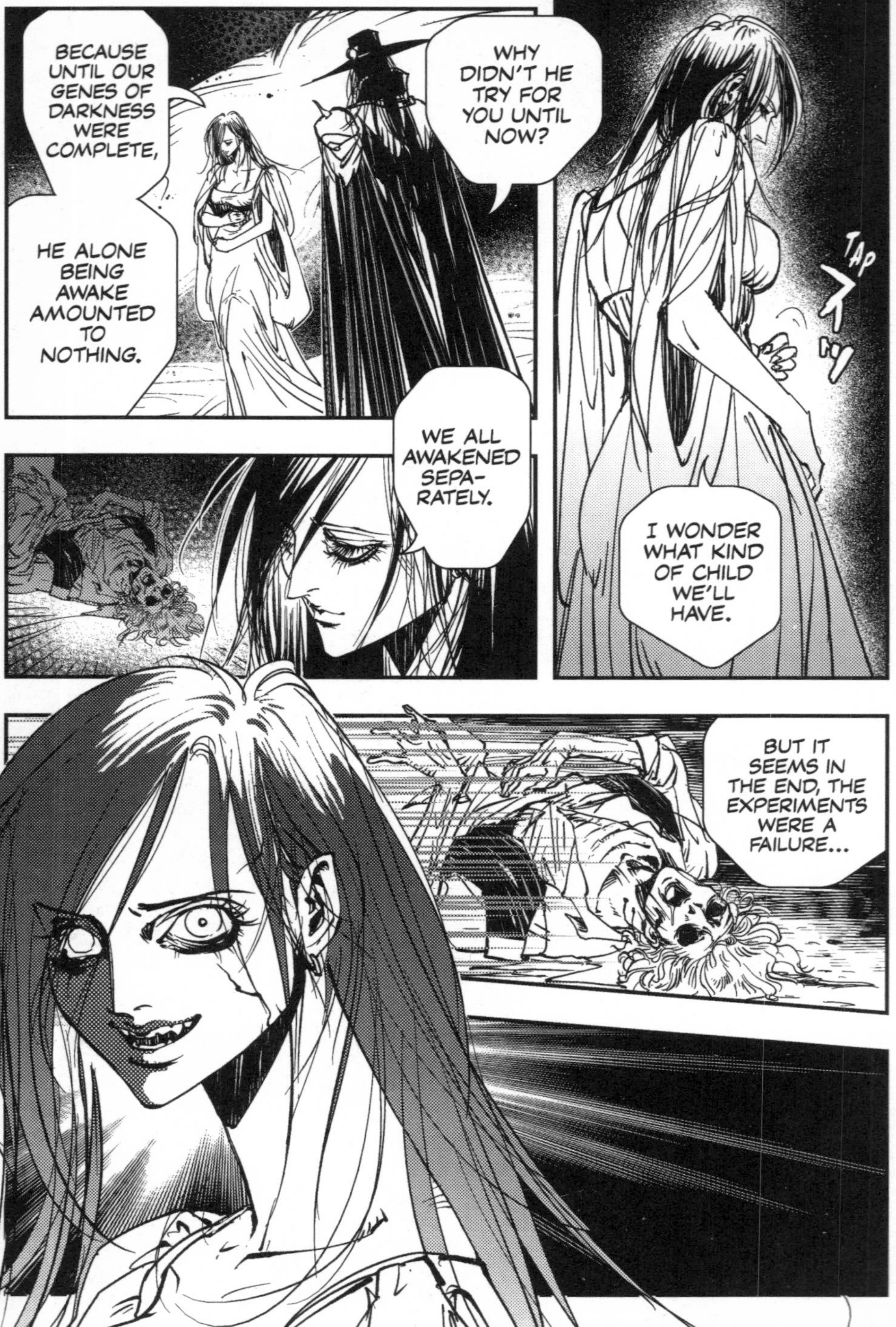
TAP
I WONDER WHAT KIND OF CHILD WE'LL HAVE.
WHY DIDN'T HE TRY FOR YOU UNTIL NOW?
BECAUSE UNTIL OUR GENES OF DARKNESS WERE COMPLETE,
HE ALONE BEING AWAKE AMOUNTED TO NOTHING.
WE ALL AWAKENED SEPA-RATELY.
BUT IT SEEMS IN THE END, THE EXPERIMENTS WERE A FAILURE...

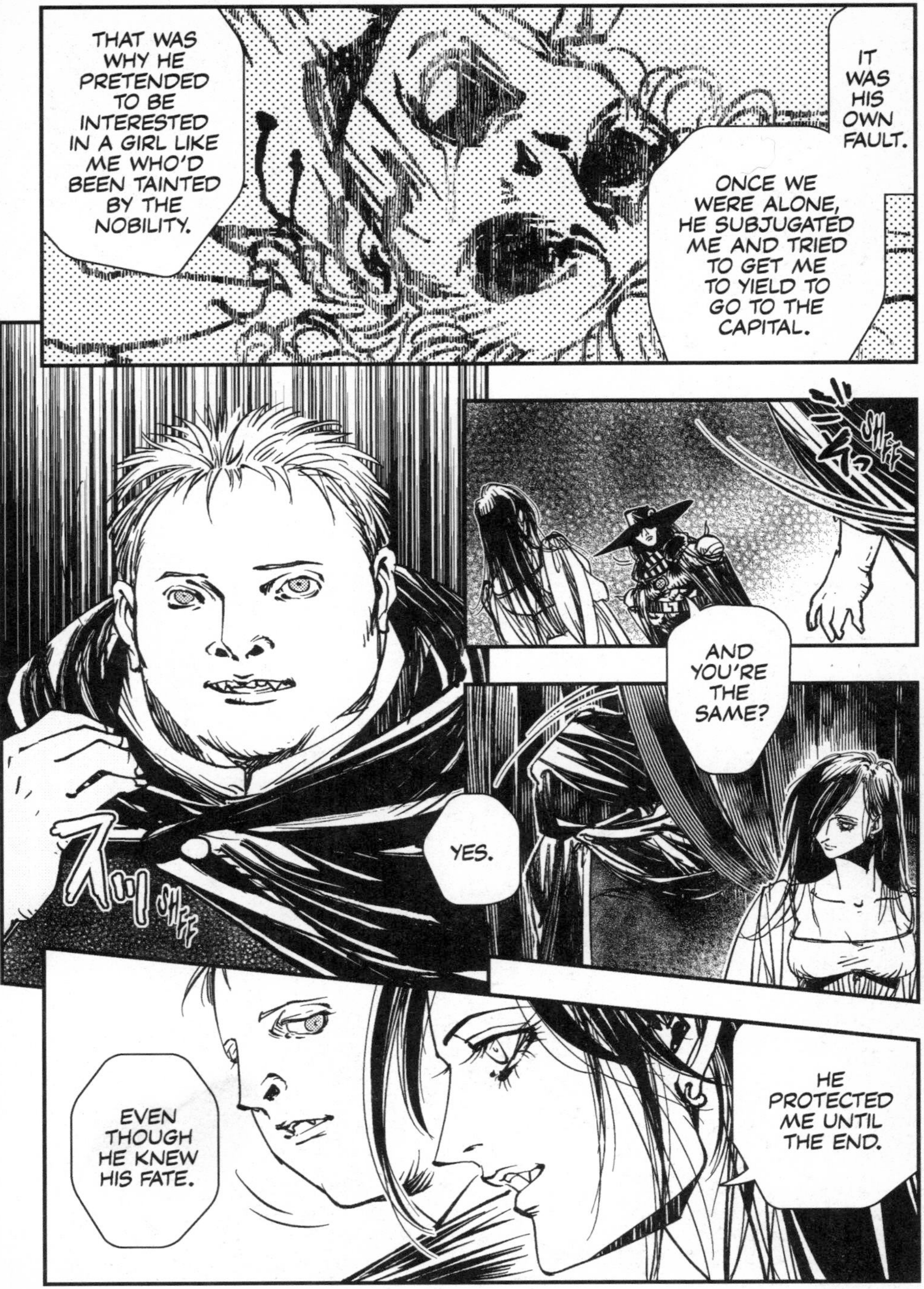
IT WAS HIS OWN FAULT.
ONCE WE WERE ALONE, HE SUBJUGATED ME AND TRIED TO GET ME TO YIELD TO GO TO THE CAPITAL.
THAT WAS WHY HE PRETENDED TO BE INTERESTED IN A GIRL LIKE ME WHO'D BEEN TAINTED BY THE NOBILITY.
SHFF
AND YOU'RE THE SAME?
YES.
SHFF
HE PROTECTED ME UNTIL THE END.
EVEN THOUGH HE KNEW HIS FATE.

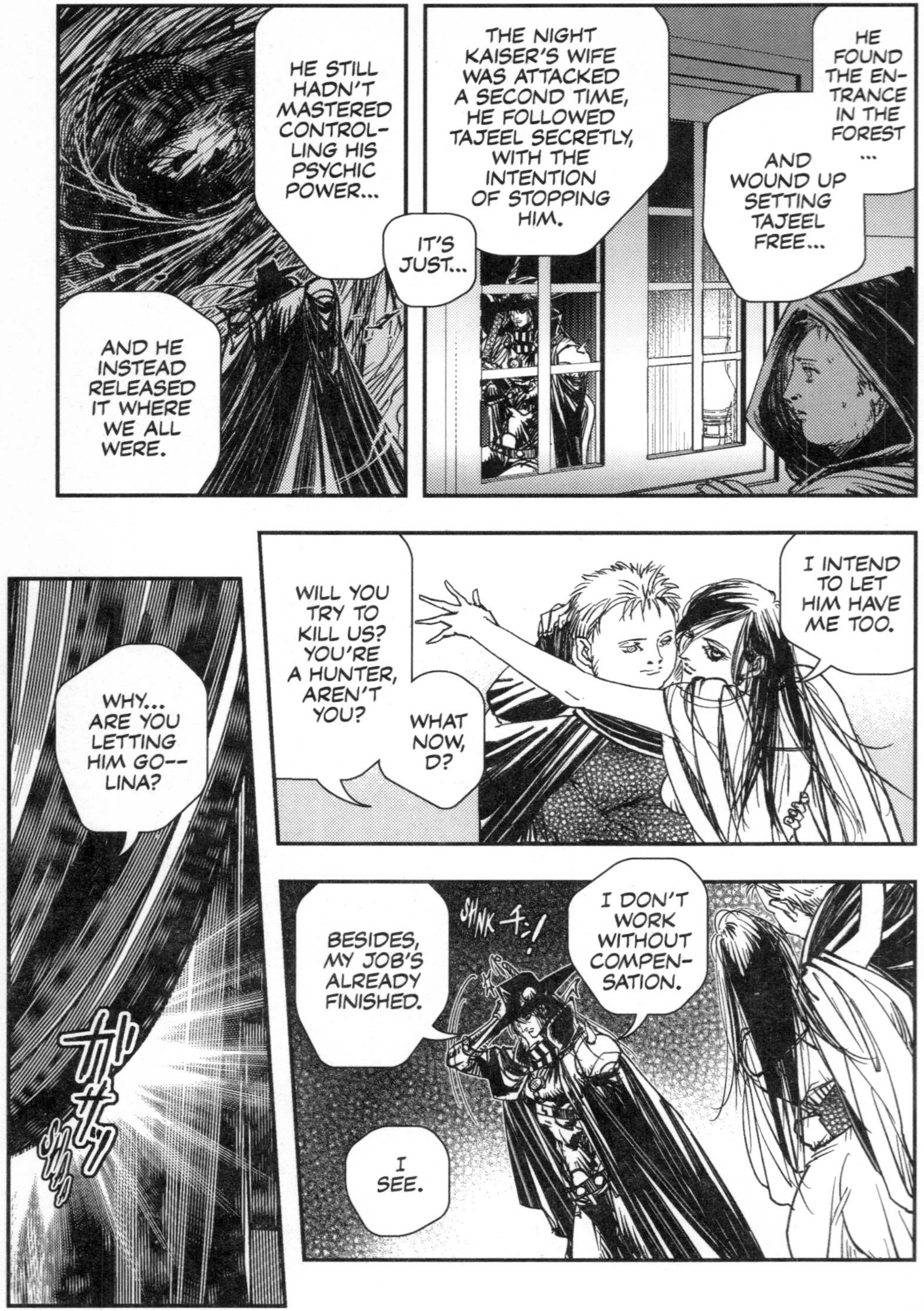
IT'S JUST...
THE NIGHT KAISER'S WIFE WAS ATTACKED A SECOND TIME, HE FOLLOWED TAJEEL SECRETLY, WITH THE INTENTION OF STOPPING HIM.
HE FOUND THE EN- TRANCE IN THE FOREST ...
AND WOUND UP SETTING TAJEEL FREE...
HE STILL HADN'T MASTERED CONTROL- LING HIS PSYCHIC POWER...
AND HE INSTEAD RELEASED IT WHERE WE ALL WERE.
I INTEND TO LET HIM HAVE ME TOO.
WILL YOU TRY TO KILL US? YOU'RE A HUNTER, AREN'T YOU?
WHAT NOW, D?
I DON'T WORK WITHOUT COMPEN- SATION.
SHNK
BESIDES, MY JOB'S ALREADY FINISHED.
I SEE.
WHY... ARE YOU LETTING HIM GO-- LINA?

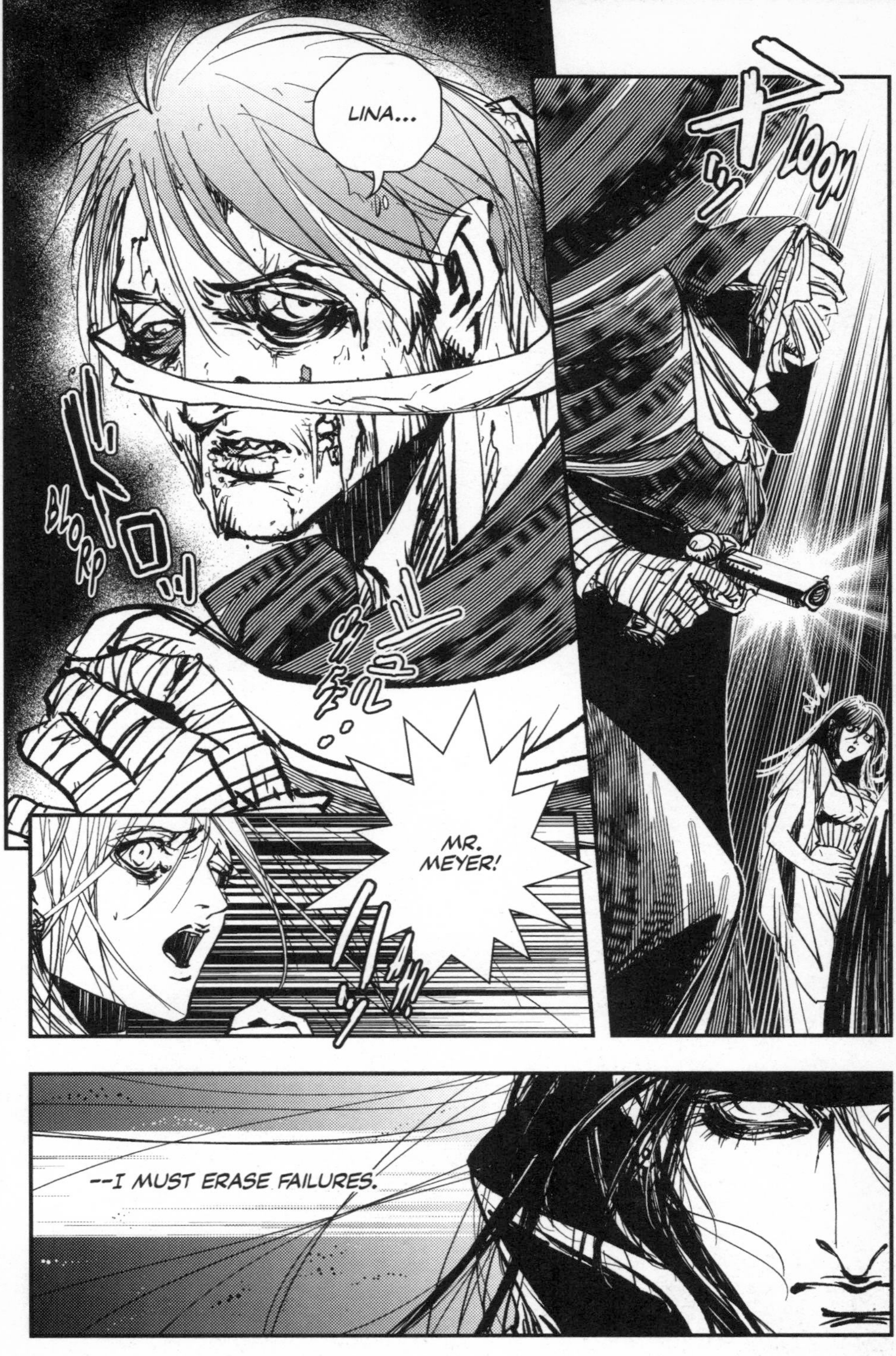
LOOM
LINA...
BLORP
MR. MEYER!
--I MUST ERASE FAILURES.

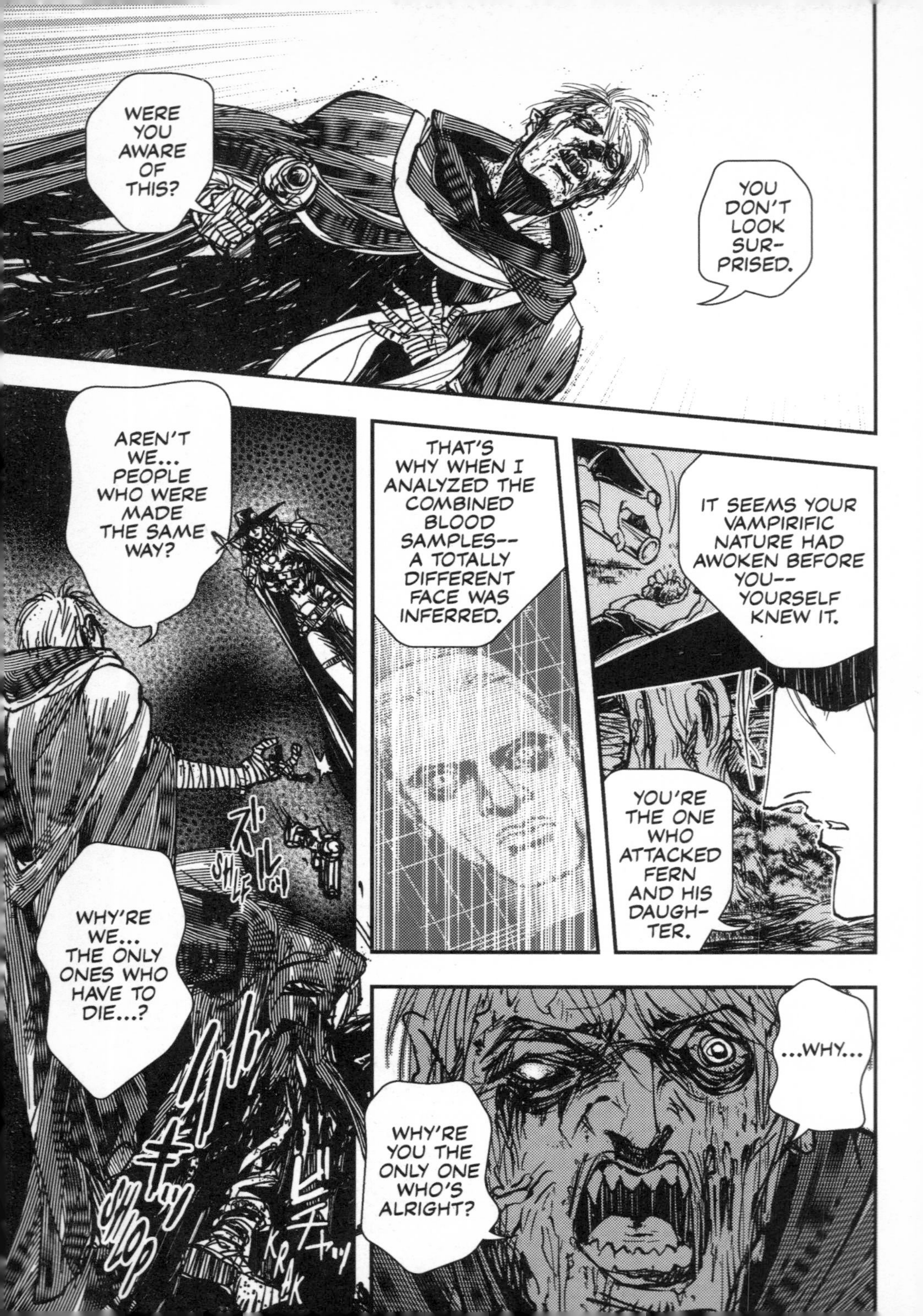
YOU DON'T LOOK SUR-PRISED.
WERE YOU AWARE OF THIS?
IT SEEMS YOUR VAMPIRIFIC NATURE HAD AWOKEN BEFORE YOU-- YOURSELF KNEW IT.
YOU'RE THE ONE WHO ATTACKED FERN AND HIS DAUGH-TER.
THAT'S WHY WHEN I ANALYZED THE COMBINED BLOOD SAMPLES-- A TOTALLY DIFFERENT FACE WAS INFERRED.
...WHY...
WHY'RE YOU THE ONLY ONE WHO'S ALRIGHT?
AREN'T WE... PEOPLE WHO WERE MADE THE SAME WAY?
SHLE
WHY'RE WE... THE ONLY ONES WHO HAVE TO DIE...?
SHLOP
KRAK

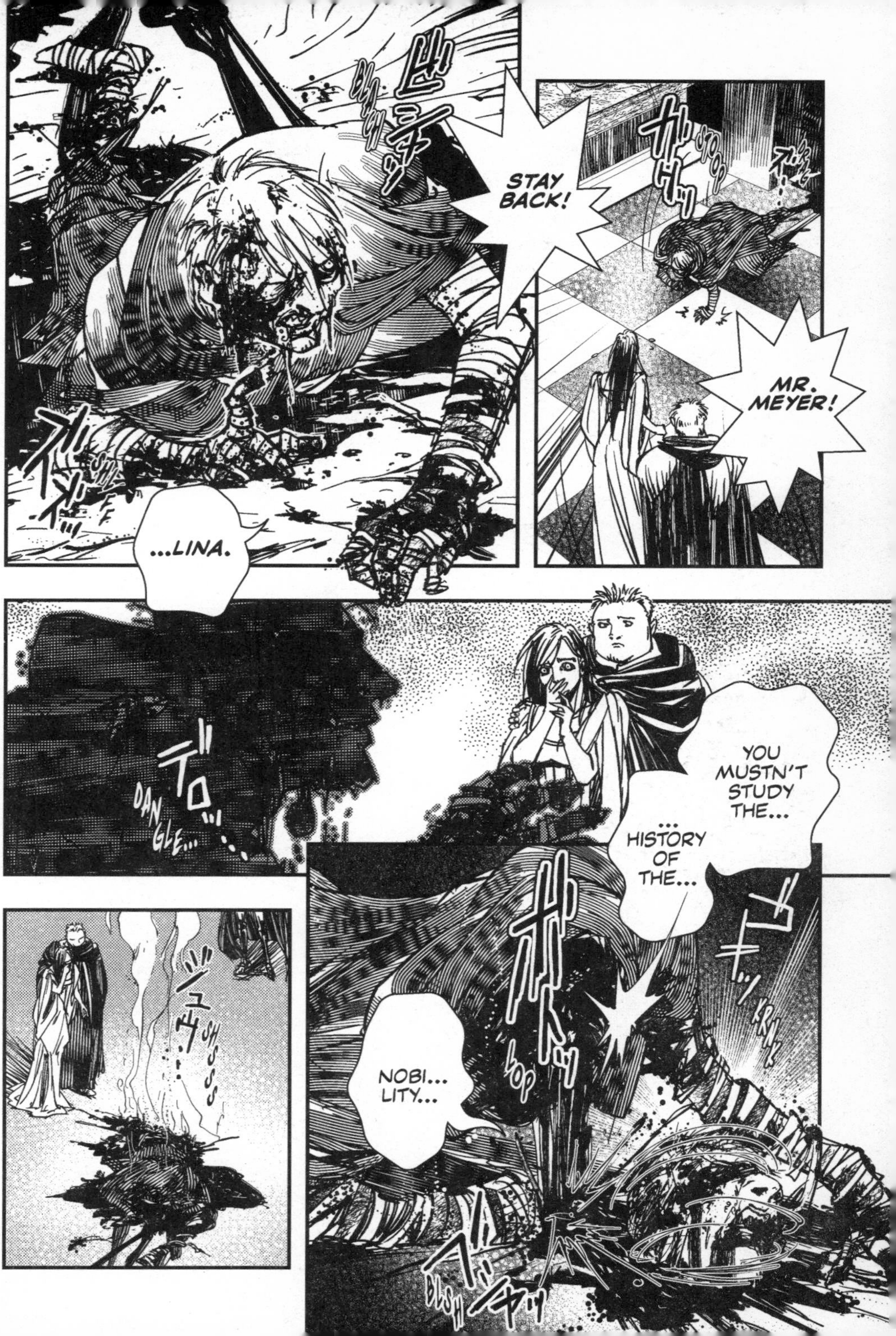
STAY BACK!
MR. MEYER!
...LINA.
YOU MUSTN'T STUDY THE...
DANGLE...
... HISTORY OF THE...
KRNK
BOP
NOBI... LITY...
BLSH
SHSSSS

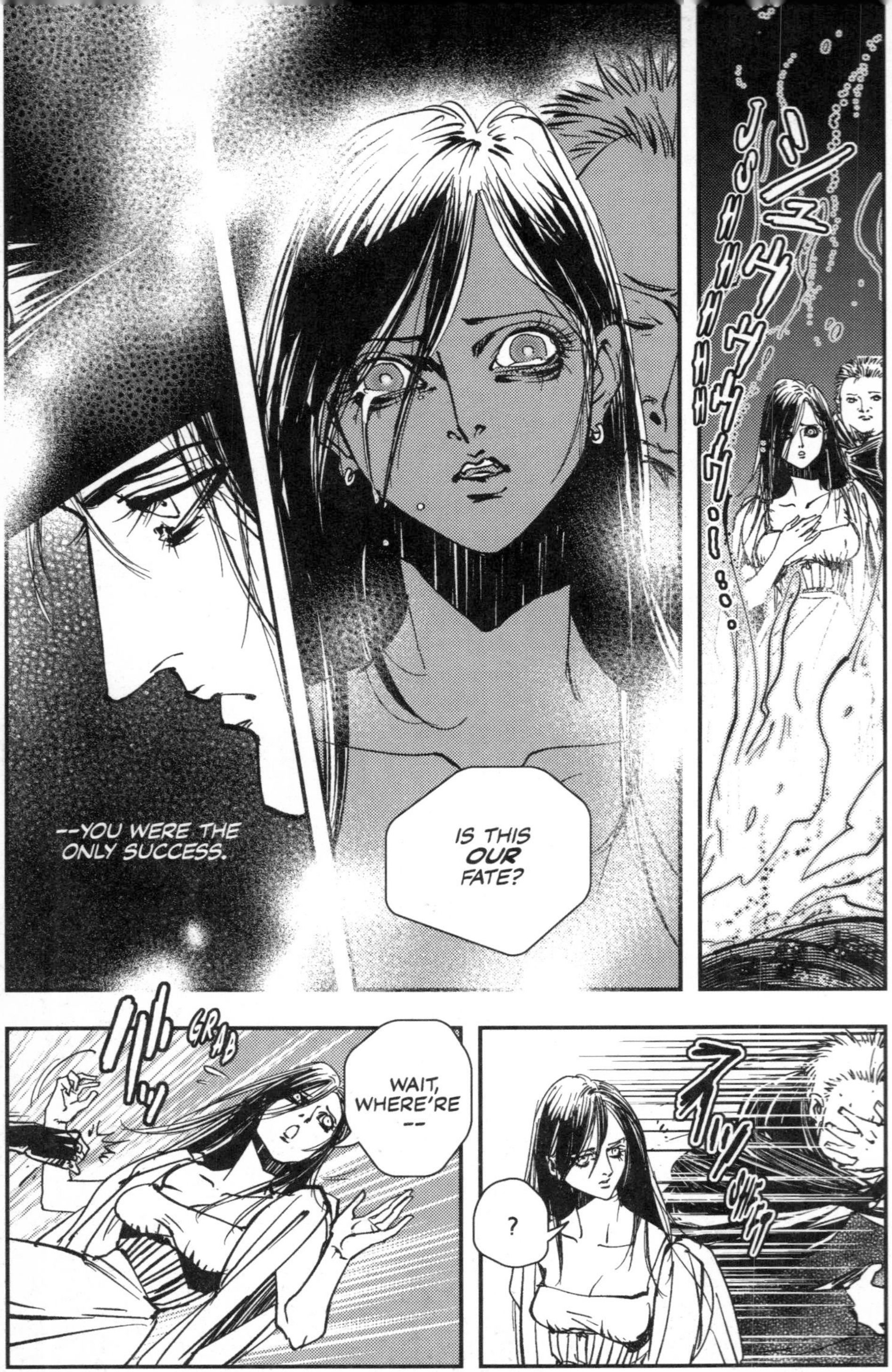
IS THIS **OUR** FATE?
--YOU WERE THE ONLY SUCCESS.
?
GRAB
WAIT, WHERE'RE --

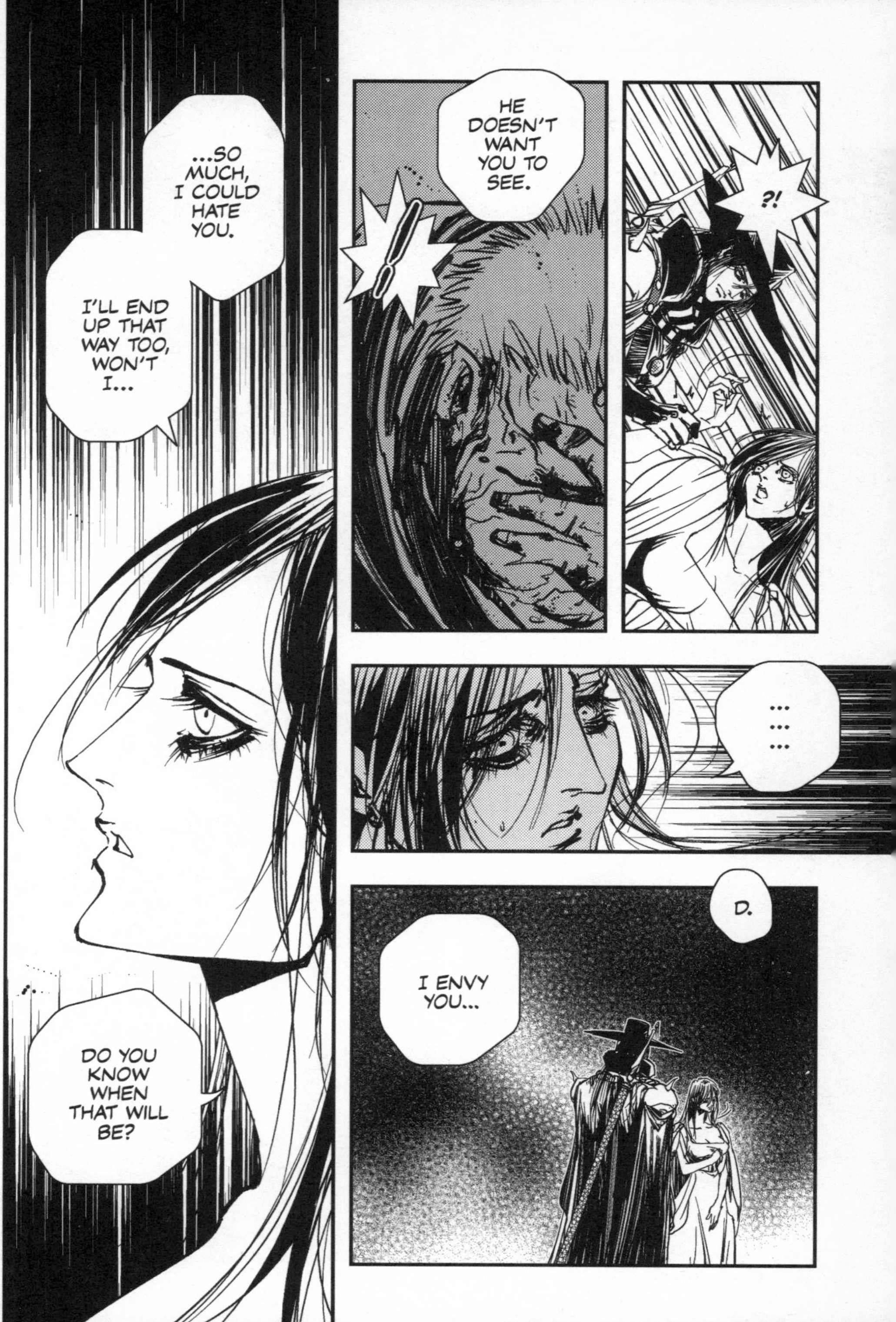
?!
HE DOESN'T WANT YOU TO SEE.
!
... ...
D.
I ENVY YOU...
...SO MUCH, I COULD HATE YOU.
I'LL END UP THAT WAY TOO, WON'T I...
DO YOU KNOW WHEN THAT WILL BE?

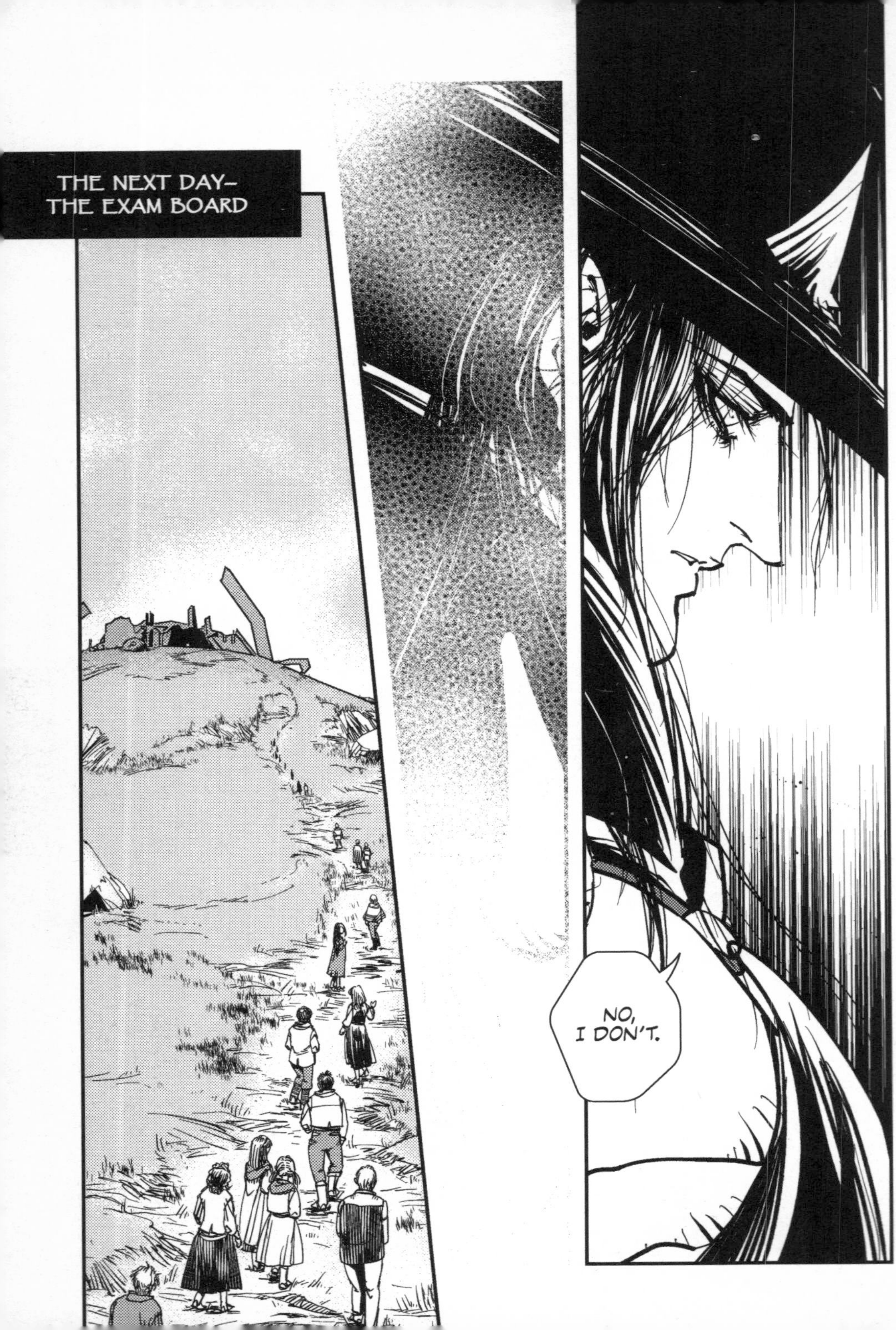
NO, I DON'T.
THE NEXT DAY—
THE EXAM BOARD

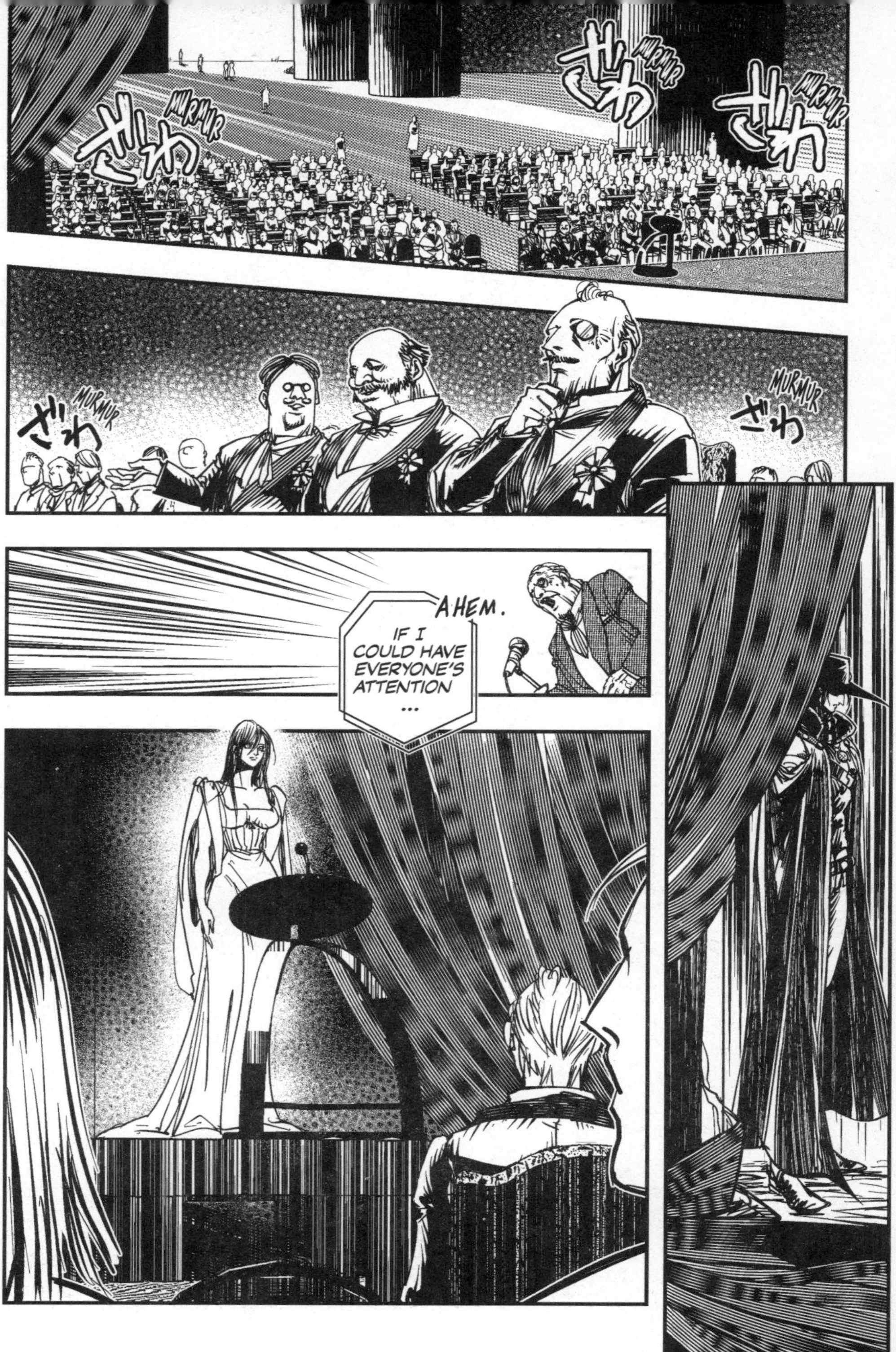
ざわ MURMUR
ざわ MURMUR
ざわ MURMUR
ざわ MURMUR
ざわ MURMUR
AHEM.
IF I COULD HAVE EVERYONE'S ATTENTION ...

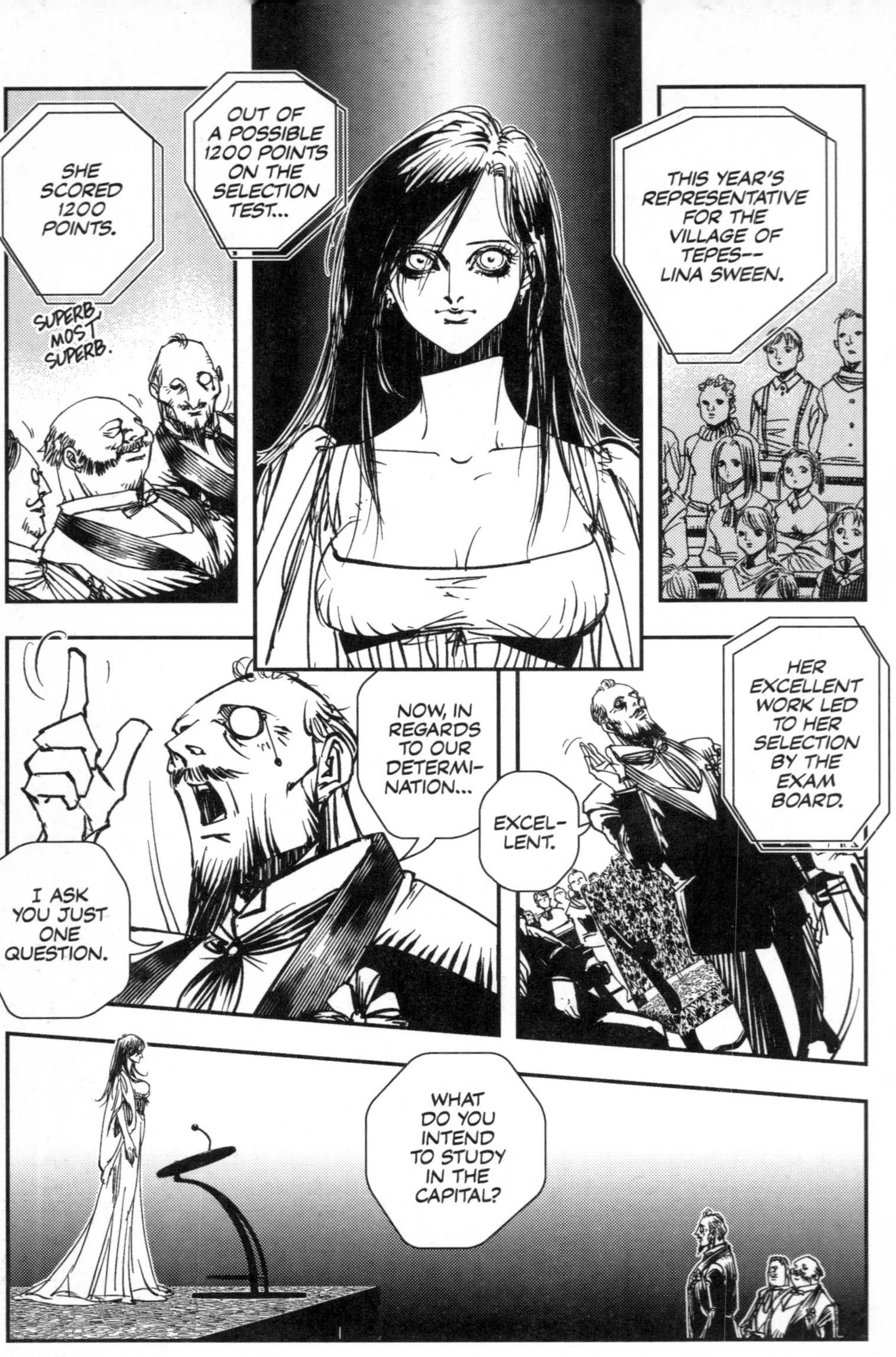
THIS YEAR'S REPRESENTATIVE FOR THE VILLAGE OF TEPES-- LINA SWEEN.
OUT OF A POSSIBLE 1200 POINTS ON THE SELECTION TEST...
SHE SCORED 1200 POINTS.
SUPERB, MOST SUPERB.
HER EXCELLENT WORK LED TO HER SELECTION BY THE EXAM BOARD.
EXCEL-LENT.
NOW, IN REGARDS TO OUR DETERMI-NATION...
I ASK YOU JUST ONE QUESTION.
WHAT DO YOU INTEND TO STUDY IN THE CAPITAL?

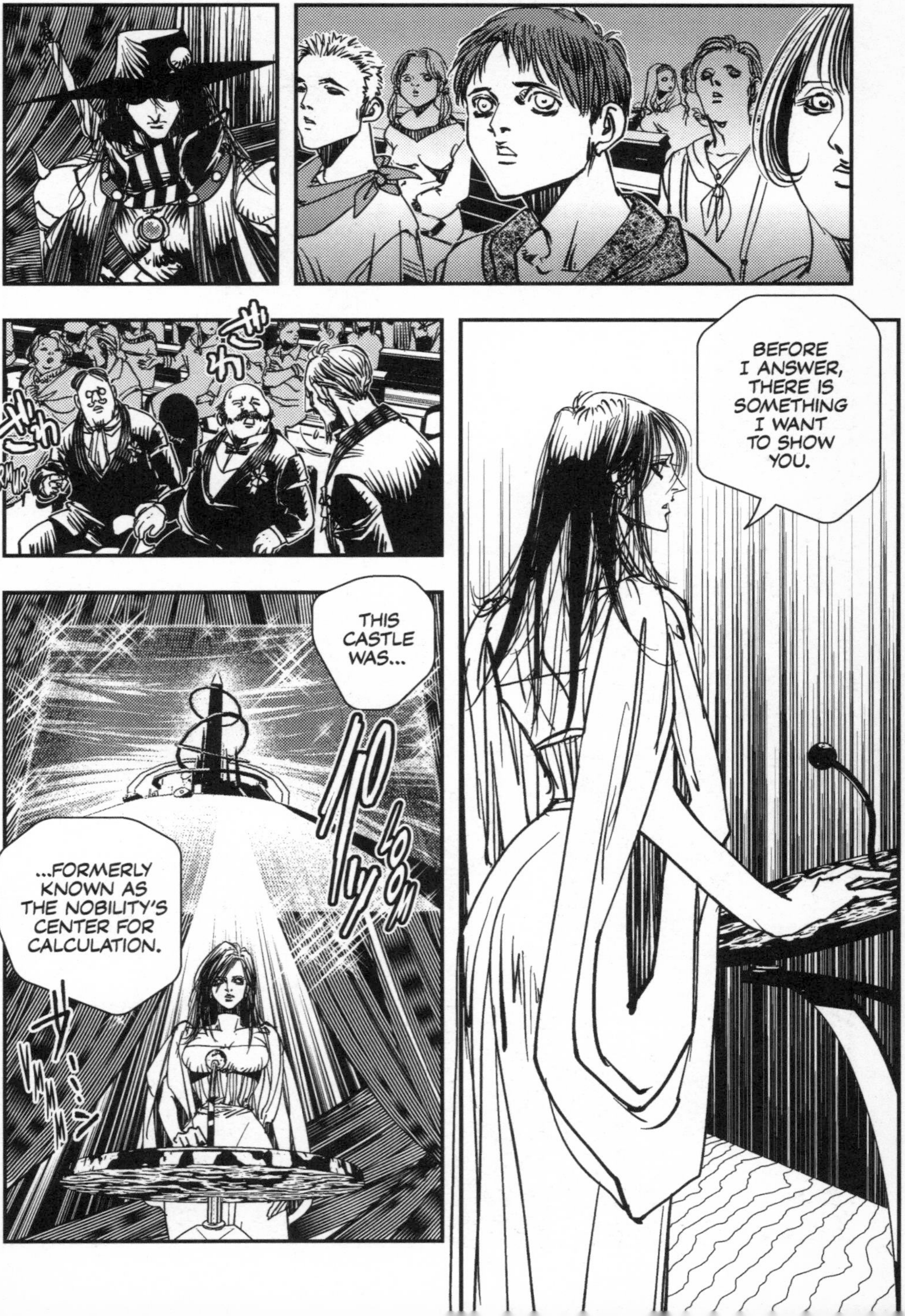
BEFORE I ANSWER, THERE IS SOMETHING I WANT TO SHOW YOU.
ざわ
ざわ
MURMUR
THIS CASTLE WAS...
...FORMERLY KNOWN AS THE NOBILITY'S CENTER FOR CALCULATION.

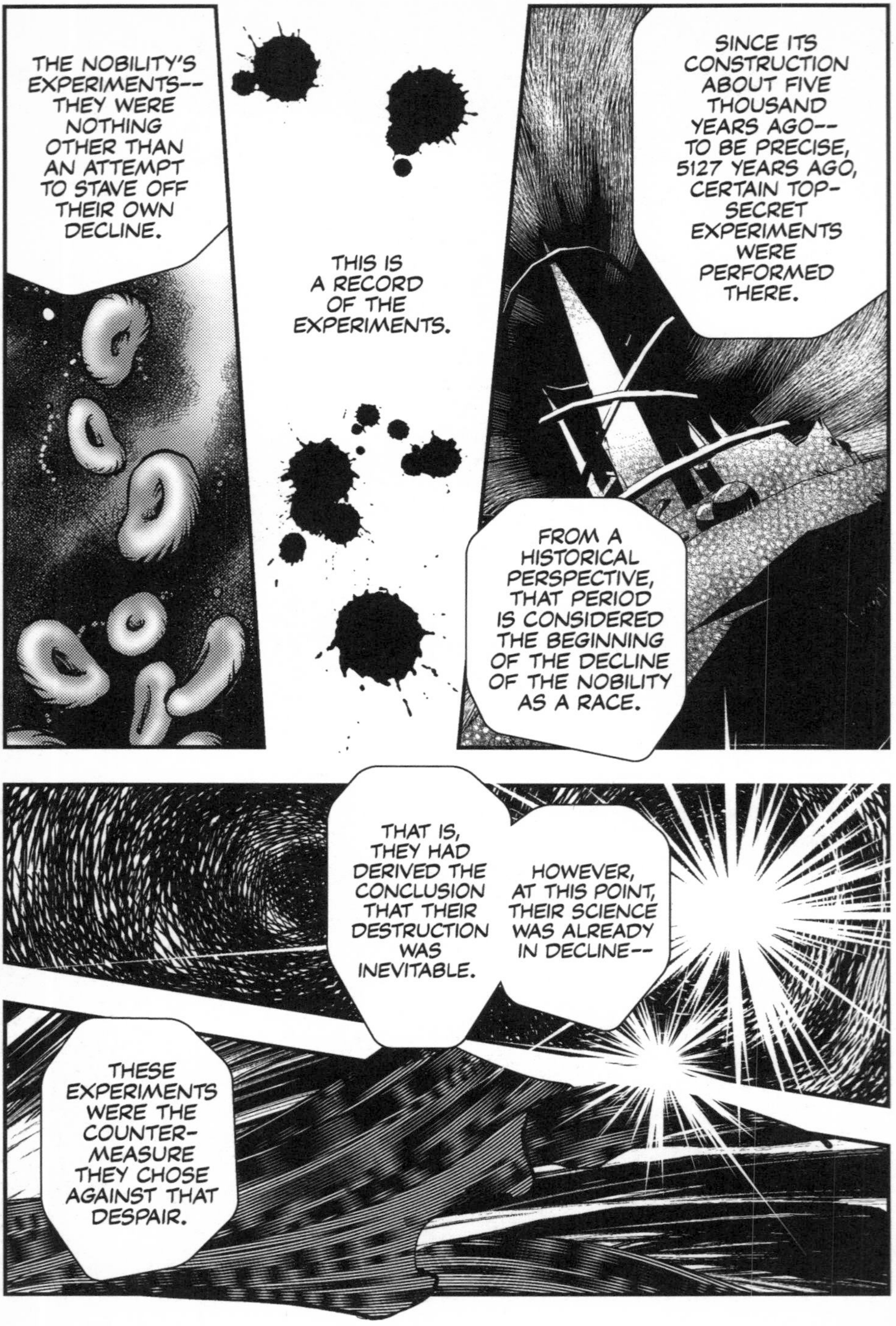
SINCE ITS CONSTRUCTION ABOUT FIVE THOUSAND YEARS AGO-- TO BE PRECISE, 5127 YEARS AGO, CERTAIN TOP-SECRET EXPERIMENTS WERE PERFORMED THERE.
FROM A HISTORICAL PERSPECTIVE, THAT PERIOD IS CONSIDERED THE BEGINNING OF THE DECLINE OF THE NOBILITY AS A RACE.
THIS IS A RECORD OF THE EXPERIMENTS.
THE NOBILITY'S EXPERIMENTS-- THEY WERE NOTHING OTHER THAN AN ATTEMPT TO STAVE OFF THEIR OWN DECLINE.
HOWEVER, AT THIS POINT, THEIR SCIENCE WAS ALREADY IN DECLINE--
THAT IS, THEY HAD DERIVED THE CONCLUSION THAT THEIR DESTRUCTION WAS INEVITABLE.
THESE EXPERIMENTS WERE THE COUNTER-MEASURE THEY CHOSE AGAINST THAT DESPAIR.

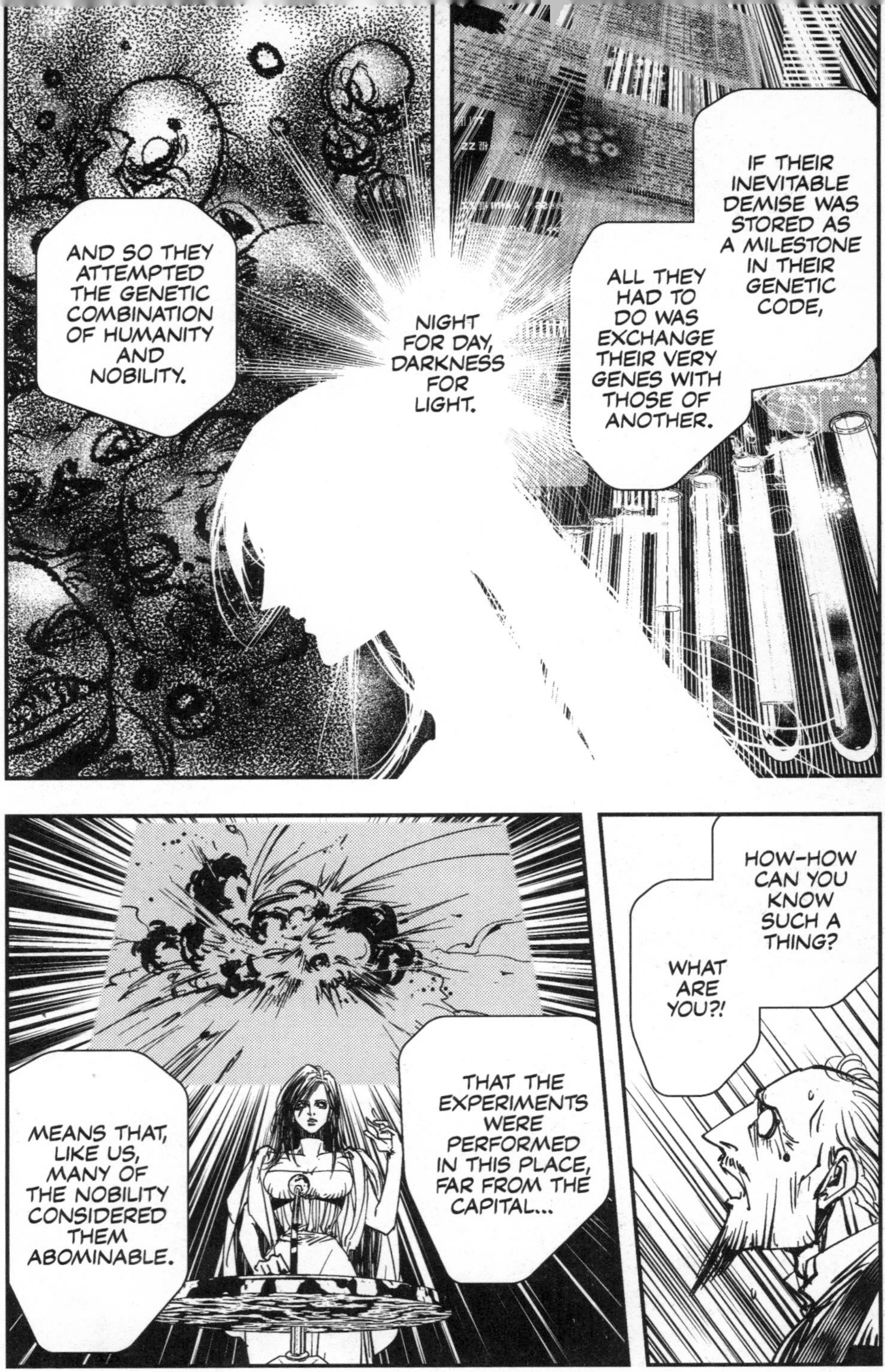
IF THEIR INEVITABLE DEMISE WAS STORED AS A MILESTONE IN THEIR GENETIC CODE,
ALL THEY HAD TO DO WAS EXCHANGE THEIR VERY GENES WITH THOSE OF ANOTHER.
NIGHT FOR DAY, DARKNESS FOR LIGHT.
AND SO THEY ATTEMPTED THE GENETIC COMBINATION OF HUMANITY AND NOBILITY.
HOW-HOW CAN YOU KNOW SUCH A THING?
WHAT ARE YOU?!
THAT THE EXPERIMENTS WERE PERFORMED IN THIS PLACE, FAR FROM THE CAPITAL...
MEANS THAT, LIKE US, MANY OF THE NOBILITY CONSIDERED THEM ABOMINABLE.

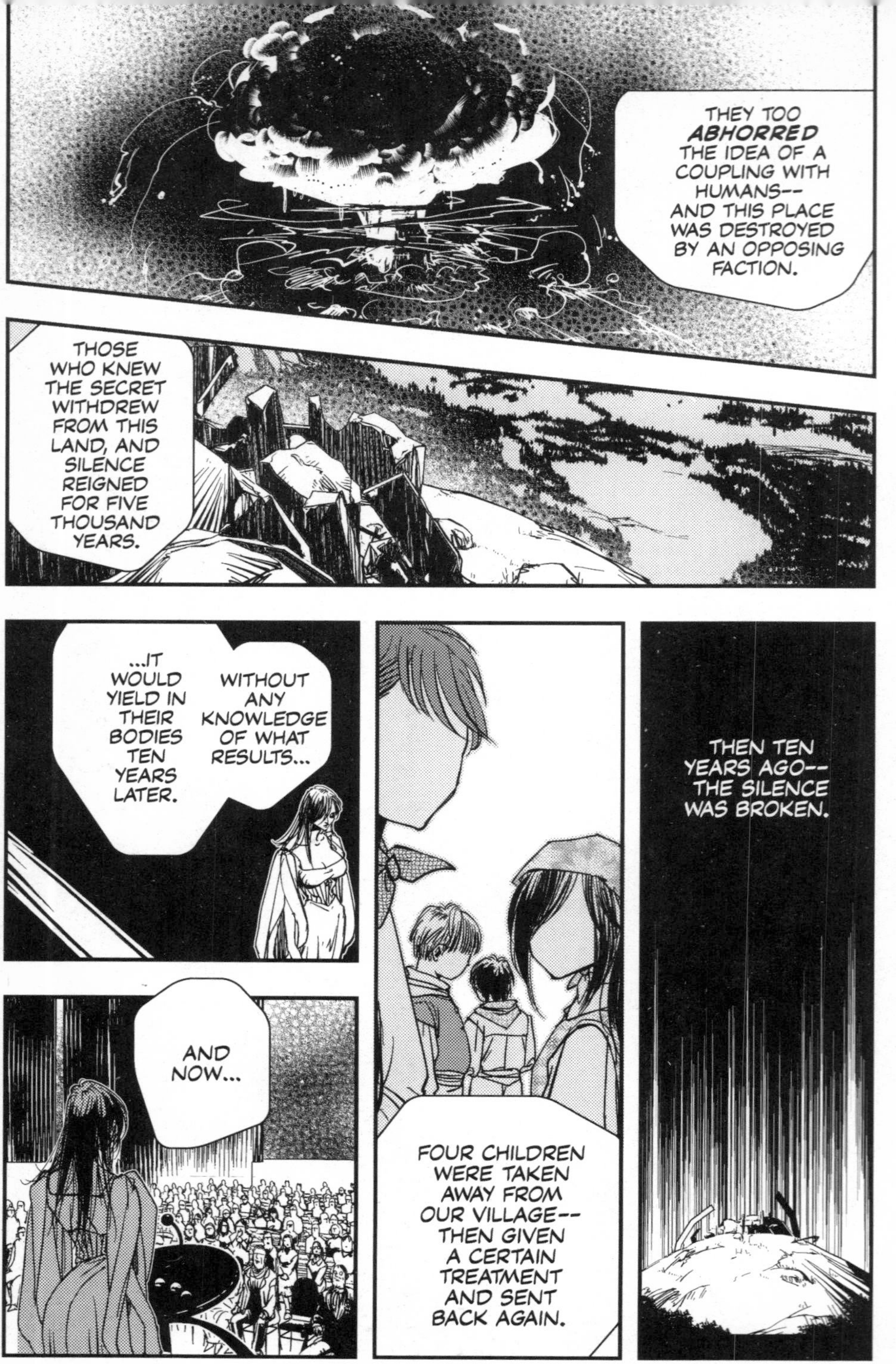
THEY TOO ABHORRED THE IDEA OF A COUPLING WITH HUMANS--AND THIS PLACE WAS DESTROYED BY AN OPPOSING FACTION.
THOSE WHO KNEW THE SECRET WITHDREW FROM THIS LAND, AND SILENCE REIGNED FOR FIVE THOUSAND YEARS.
THEN TEN YEARS AGO--THE SILENCE WAS BROKEN.
FOUR CHILDREN WERE TAKEN AWAY FROM OUR VILLAGE--THEN GIVEN A CERTAIN TREATMENT AND SENT BACK AGAIN.
WITHOUT ANY KNOWLEDGE OF WHAT RESULTS...
...IT WOULD YIELD IN THEIR BODIES TEN YEARS LATER.
AND NOW...

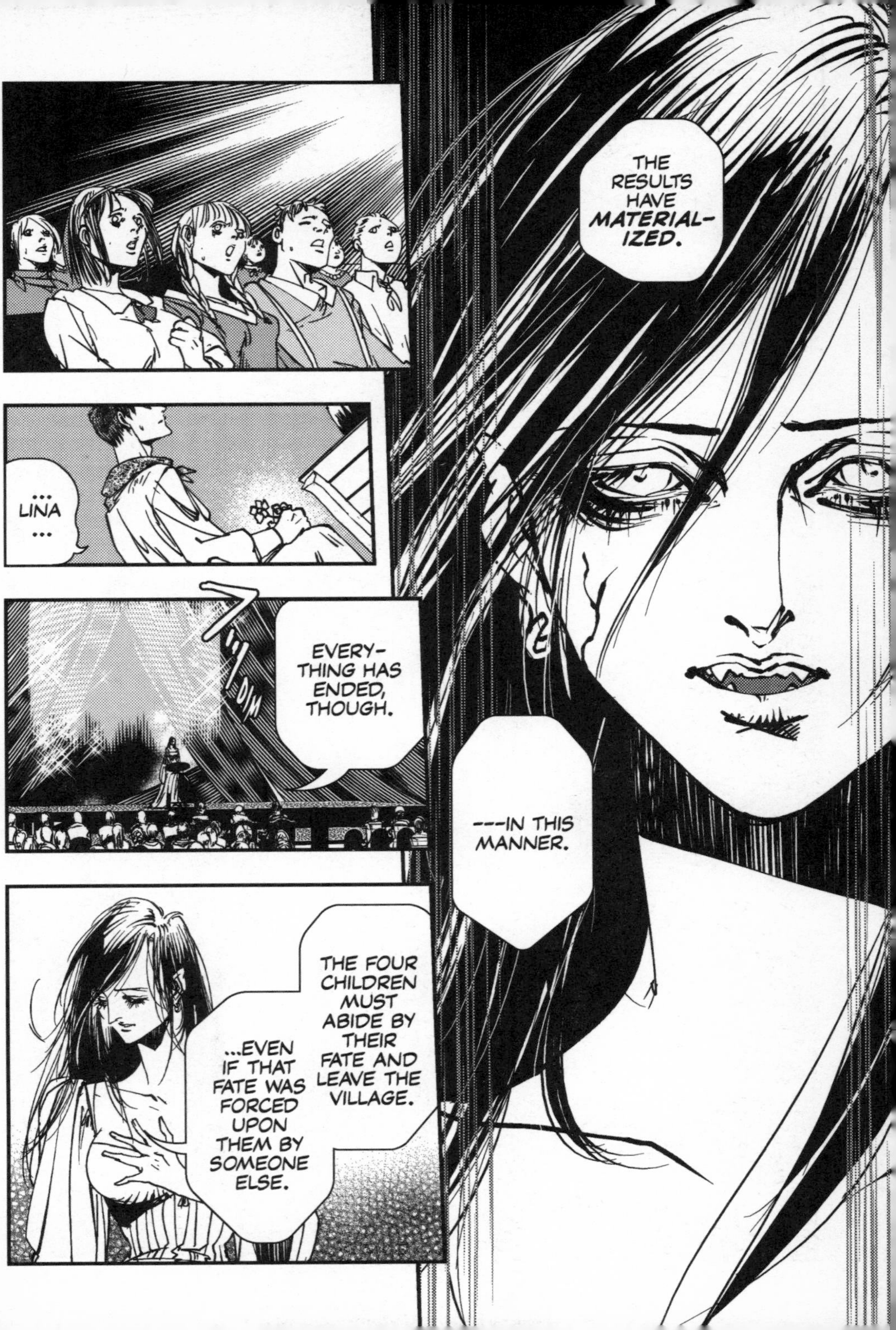
THE RESULTS HAVE MATERIALIZED.
---IN THIS MANNER.
...LINA...
EVERYTHING HAS ENDED, THOUGH.
THE FOUR CHILDREN MUST ABIDE BY THEIR FATE AND LEAVE THE VILLAGE.
...EVEN IF THAT FATE WAS FORCED UPON THEM BY SOMEONE ELSE.

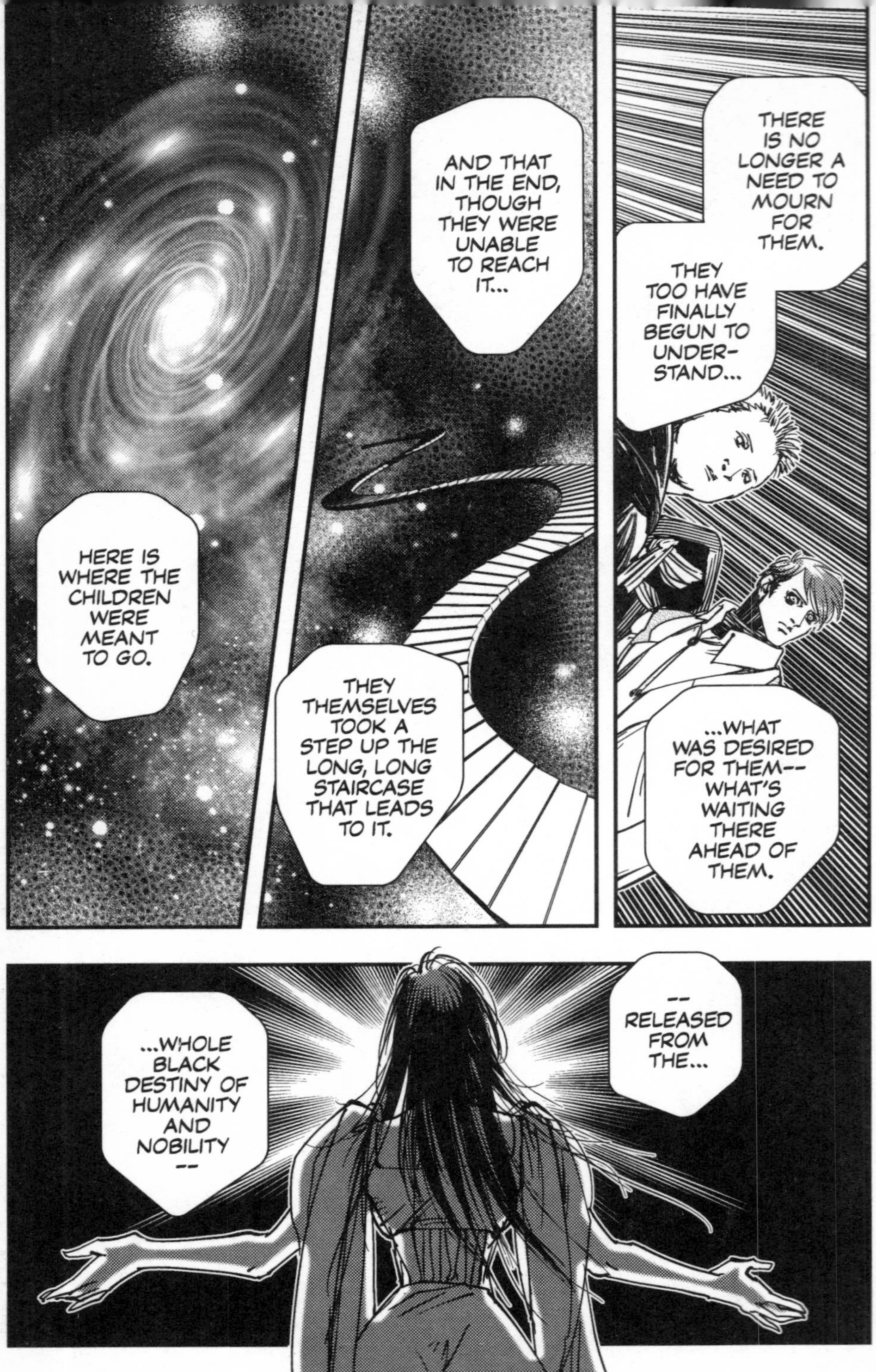
THERE IS NO LONGER A NEED TO MOURN FOR THEM.
THEY TOO HAVE FINALLY BEGUN TO UNDER-STAND...
...WHAT WAS DESIRED FOR THEM-- WHAT'S WAITING THERE AHEAD OF THEM.
AND THAT IN THE END, THOUGH THEY WERE UNABLE TO REACH IT...
THEY THEMSELVES TOOK A STEP UP THE LONG, LONG STAIRCASE THAT LEADS TO IT.
HERE IS WHERE THE CHILDREN WERE MEANT TO GO.
--RELEASED FROM THE...
...WHOLE BLACK DESTINY OF HUMANITY AND NOBILITY--

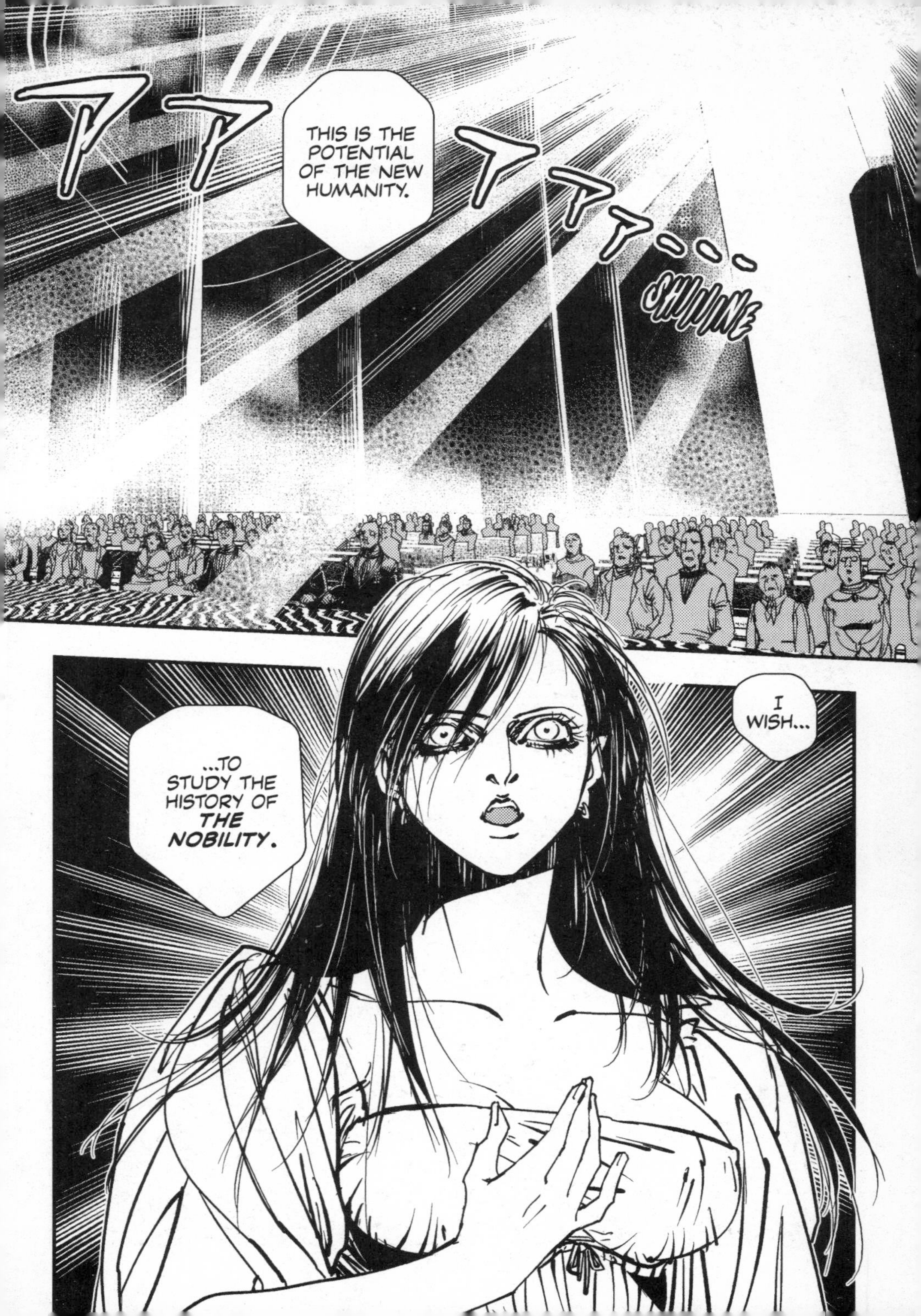
THIS IS THE POTENTIAL OF THE NEW HUMANITY.
アア
アアアー・・・
I WISH...
...TO STUDY THE HISTORY OF ***THE NOBILITY***.

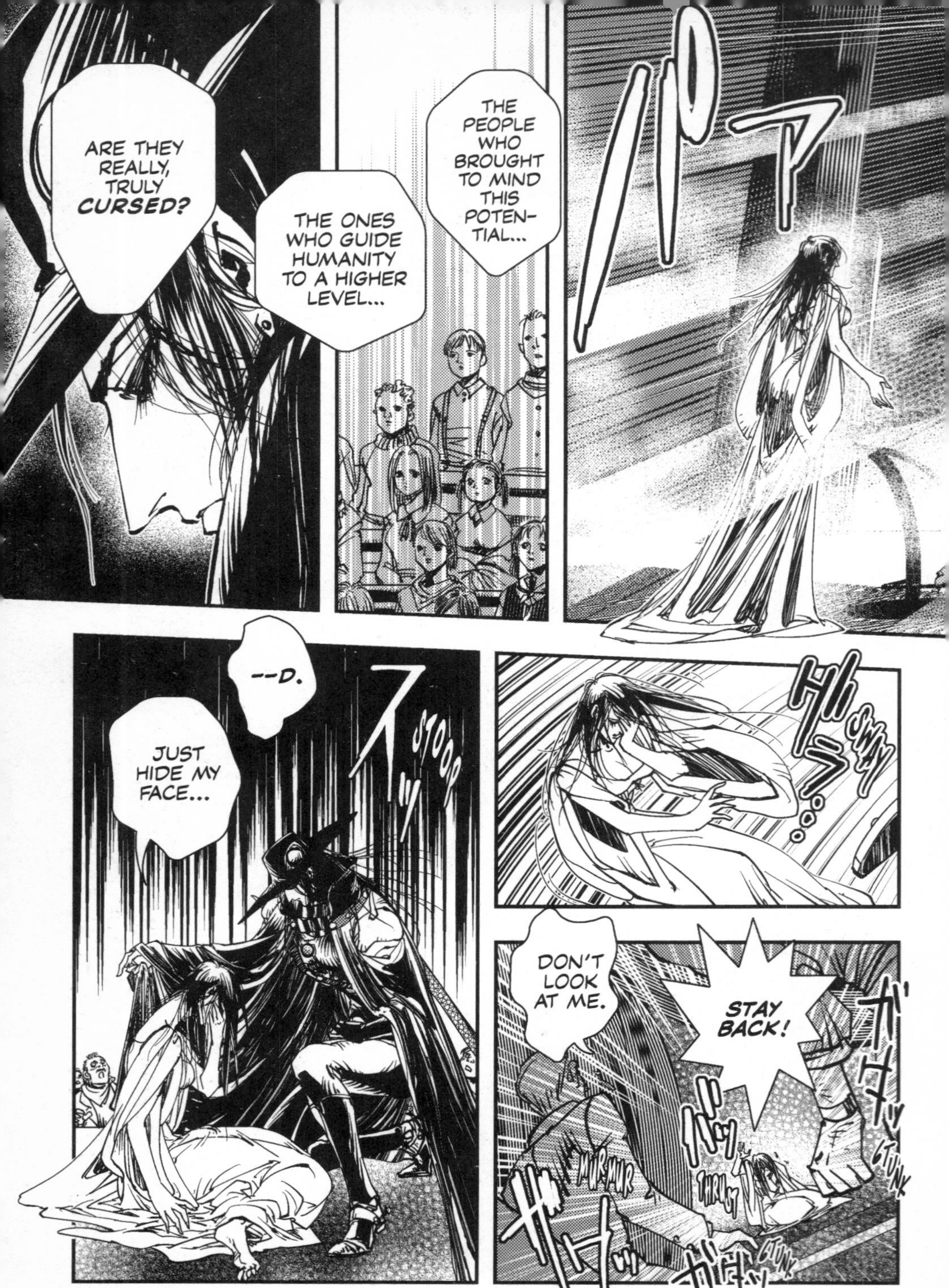
THE PEOPLE WHO BROUGHT TO MIND THIS POTEN-TIAL...
THE ONES WHO GUIDE HUMANITY TO A HIGHER LEVEL...
ARE THEY REALLY, TRULY **CURSED?**
SWAY
STAY BACK!
DON'T LOOK AT ME.
GTUNK
THRUM
MURMUR
GTUNK
--D.
JUST HIDE MY FACE...
STOOP

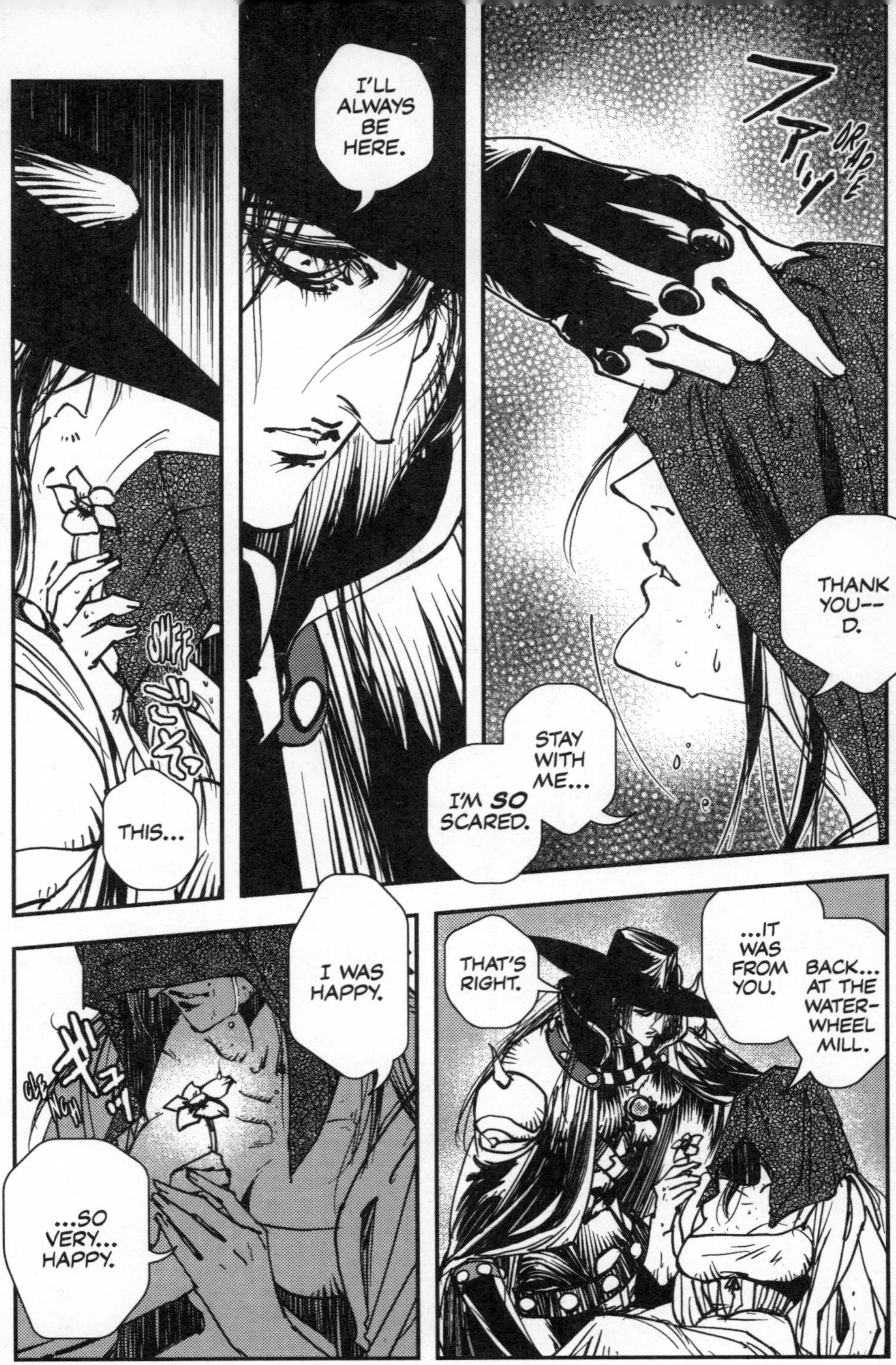
DRAPE
THANK YOU--D.
STAY WITH ME... I'M SO SCARED.
I'LL ALWAYS BE HERE.
SHFF
THIS...
BACK... AT THE WATER-WHEEL MILL.
...IT WAS FROM YOU.
THAT'S RIGHT.
I WAS HAPPY.
CLENCH
...SO VERY... HAPPY.

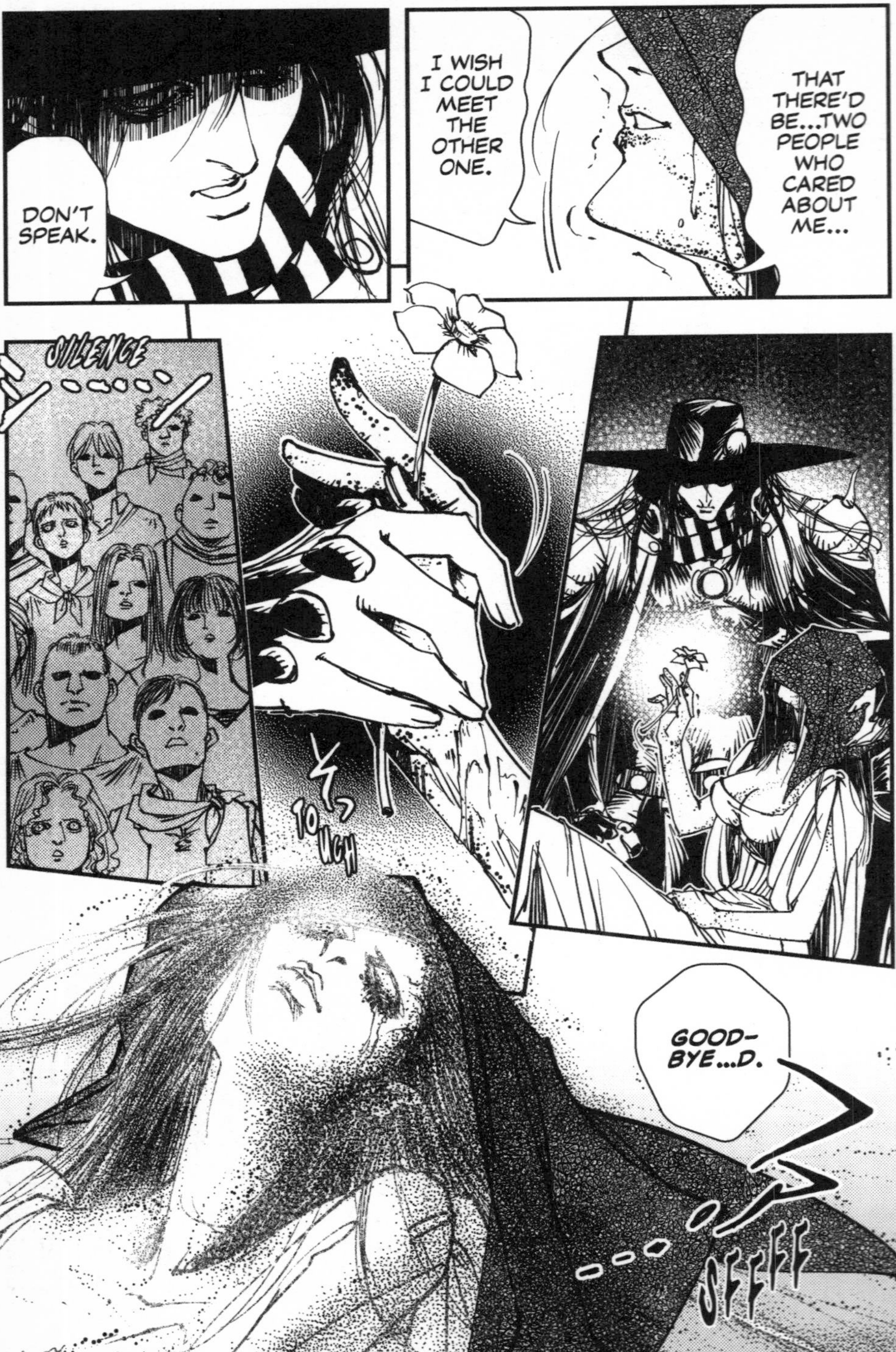

I WISH I COULD MEET THE OTHER ONE.
THAT THERE'D BE...TWO PEOPLE WHO CARED ABOUT ME...
DON'T SPEAK.
TOUGH
SILENCE
......
GOOD-BYE...D.
......
SFFFF

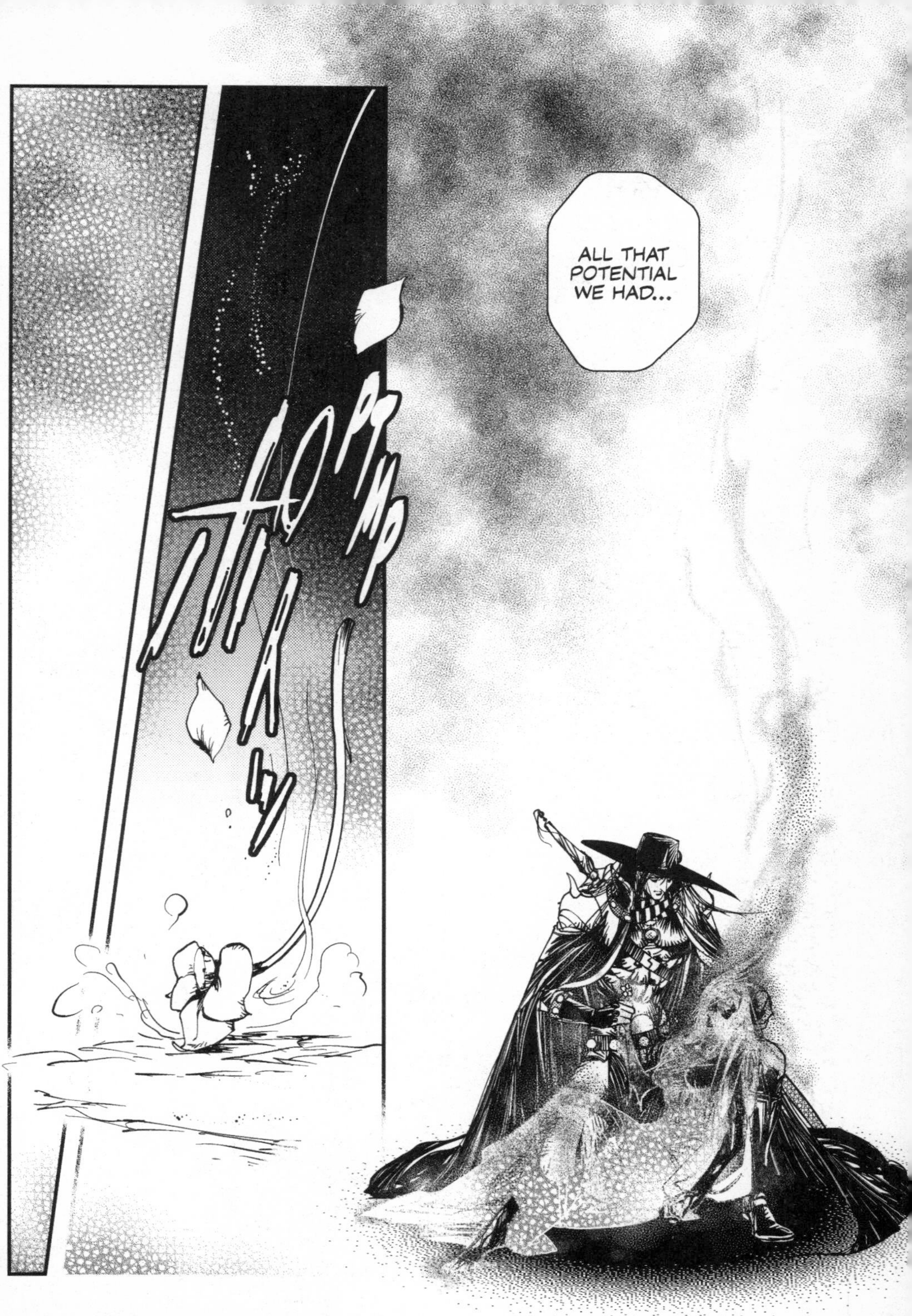
ALL THAT POTENTIAL WE HAD...

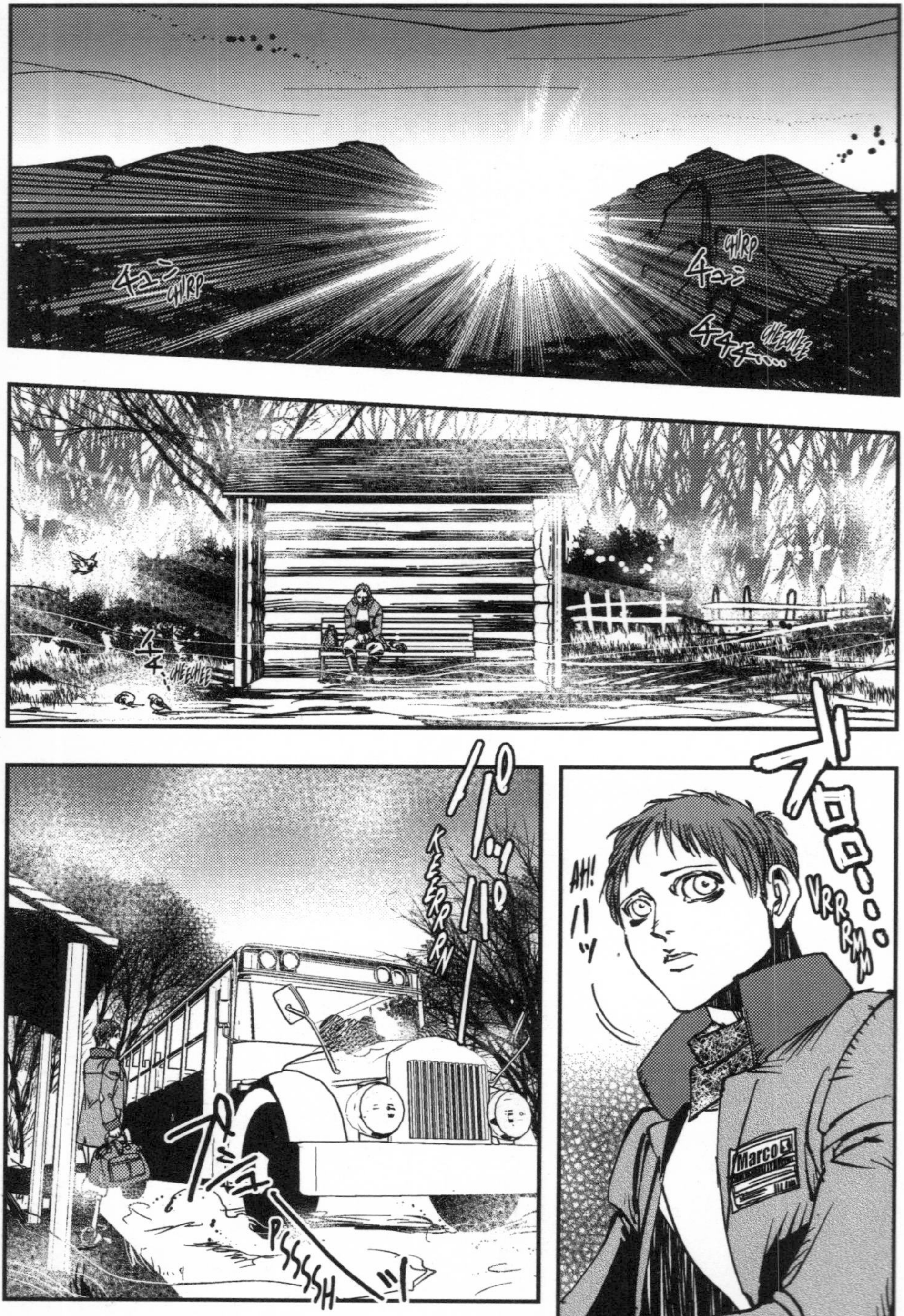
CHIRP
CHEECHEE...
CHIRP
CHEECHEE
VRRRMM
AH!
KEERRRN
PSSSSH

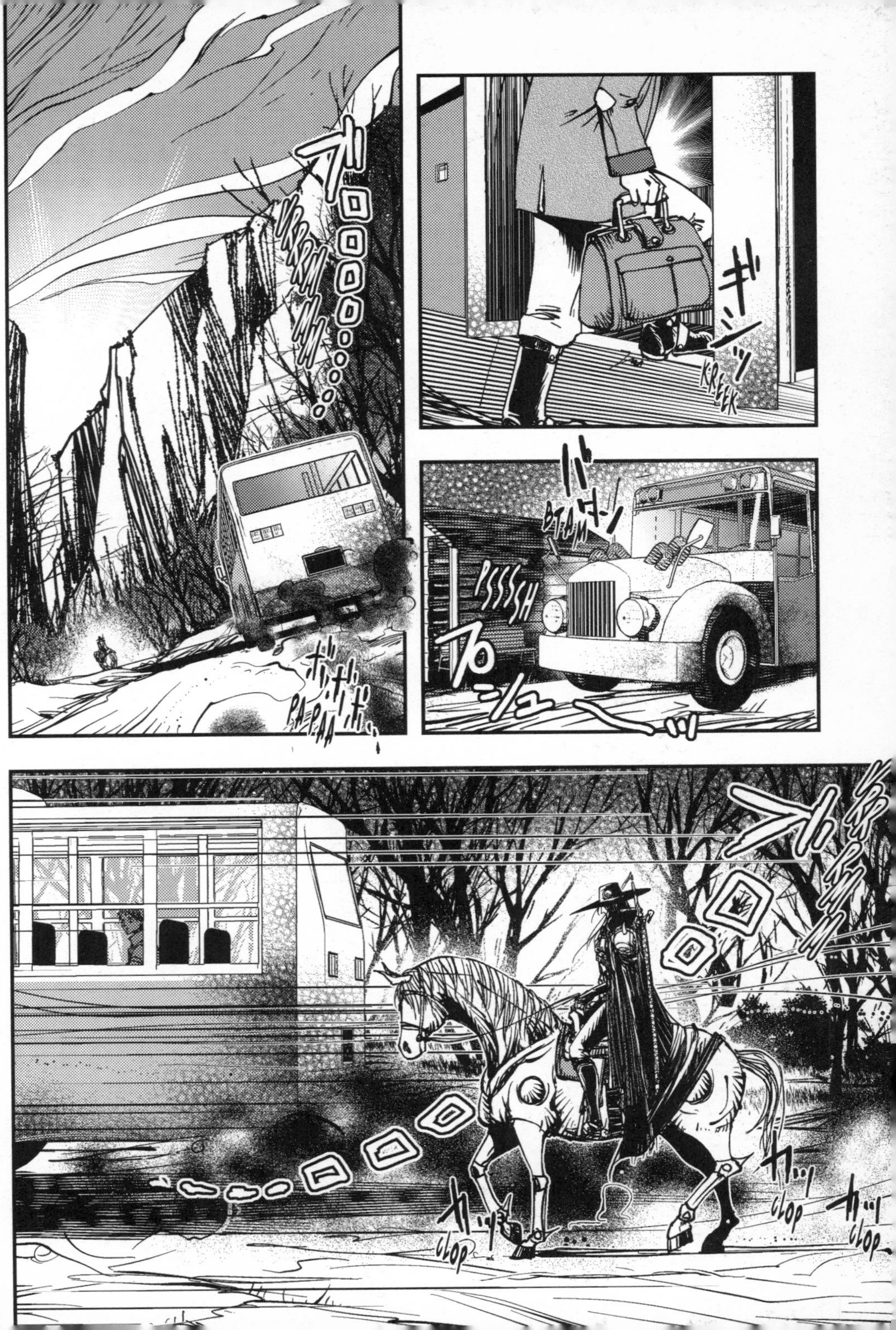
ギシッ
KREEK
バターン
BTAM
PSSSSH
プシューッ
ブロロロロロロ・・・・
VRRRMMMMM...
ガガガガ・・
PAPAA
ブロロロロロロ・・・・
VRRRMMMMM
カッ
CLOP
カッ
CLOP
カッ
CLOP

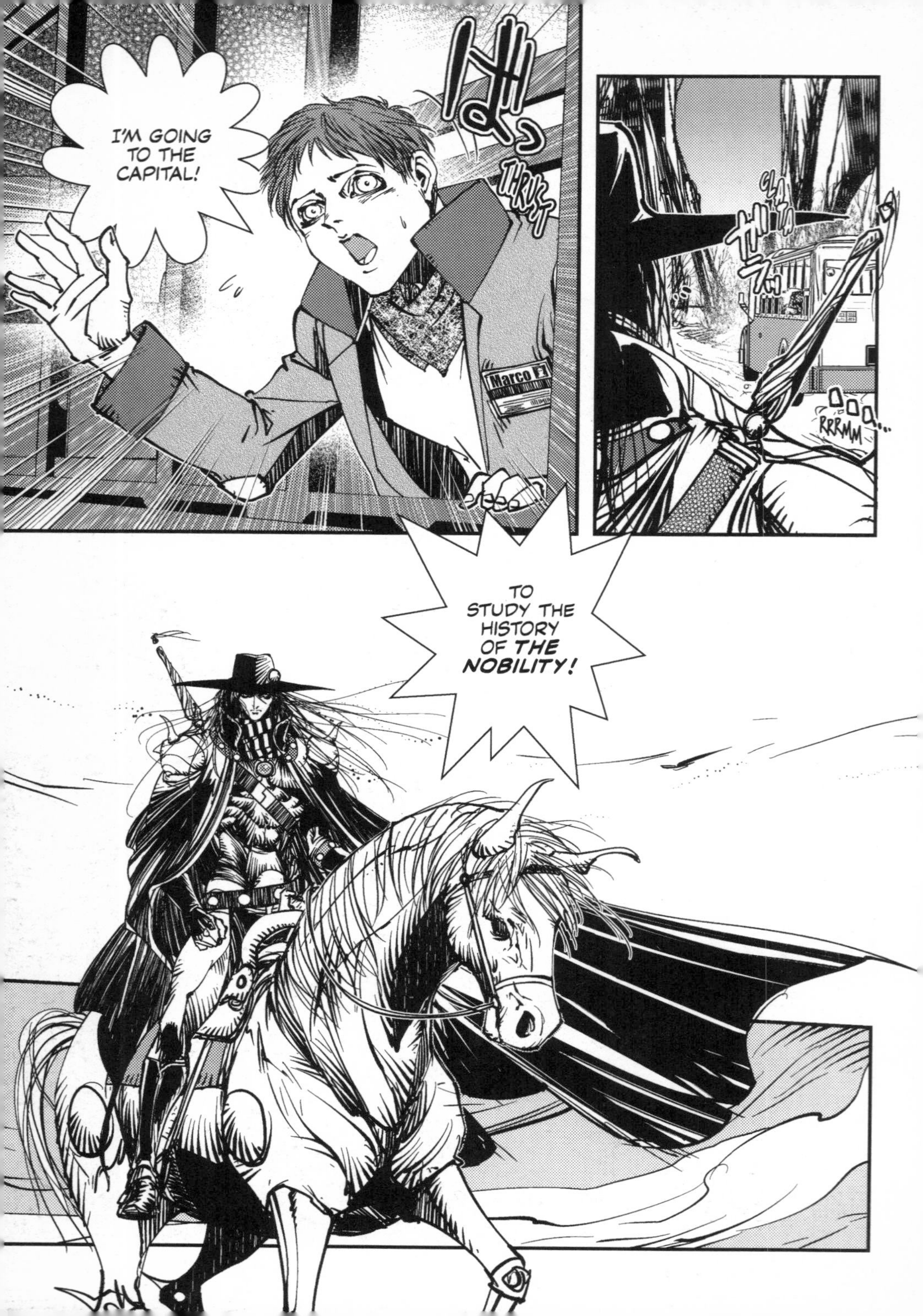
CLATTA
RRRMM...
I'M GOING TO THE CAPITAL!
THRUST
TO STUDY THE HISTORY OF THE NOBILITY!

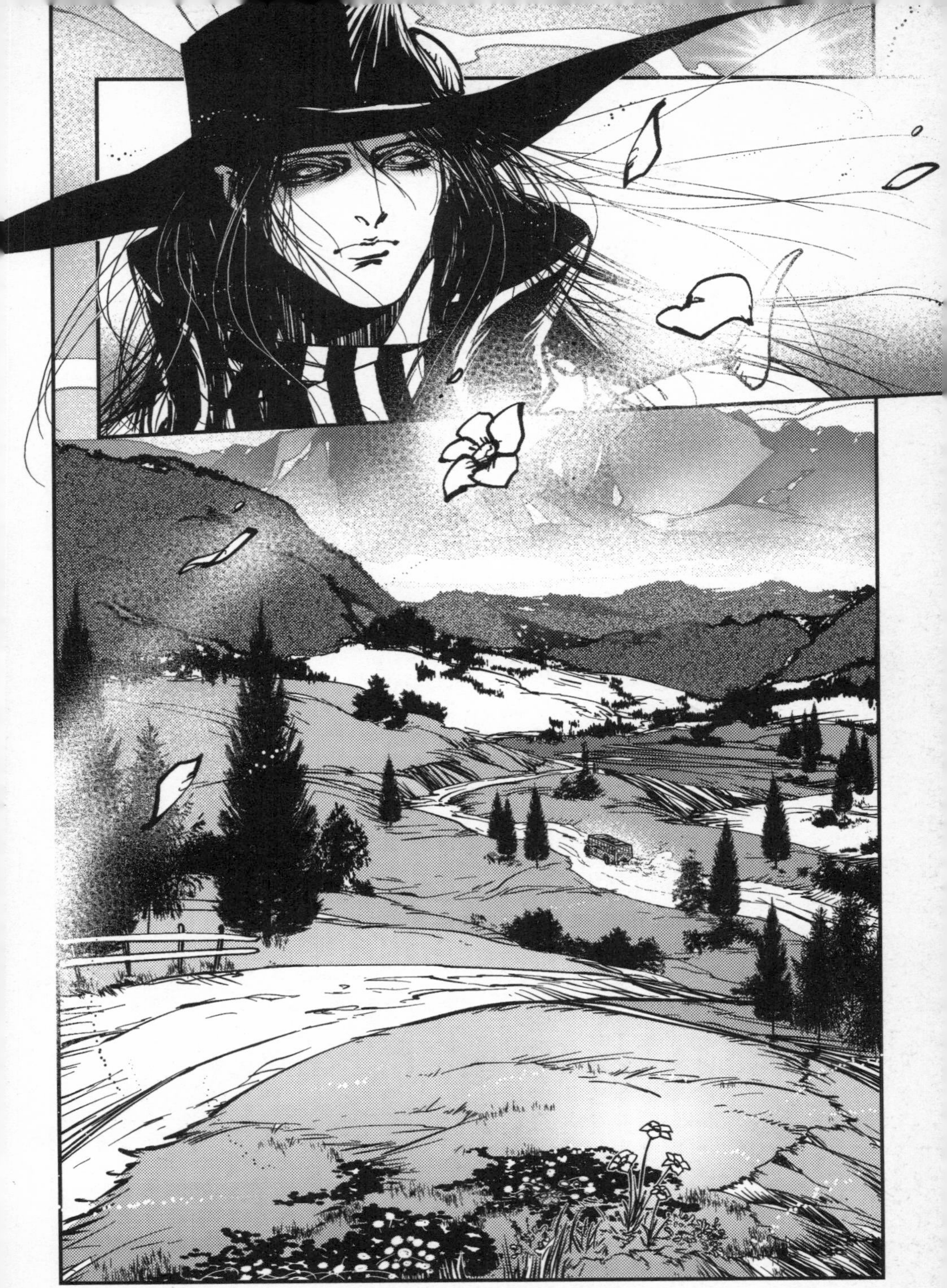

HIDEYUKI KIKUCHI'S VAMPIRE HUNTER D VOL. 2 - END

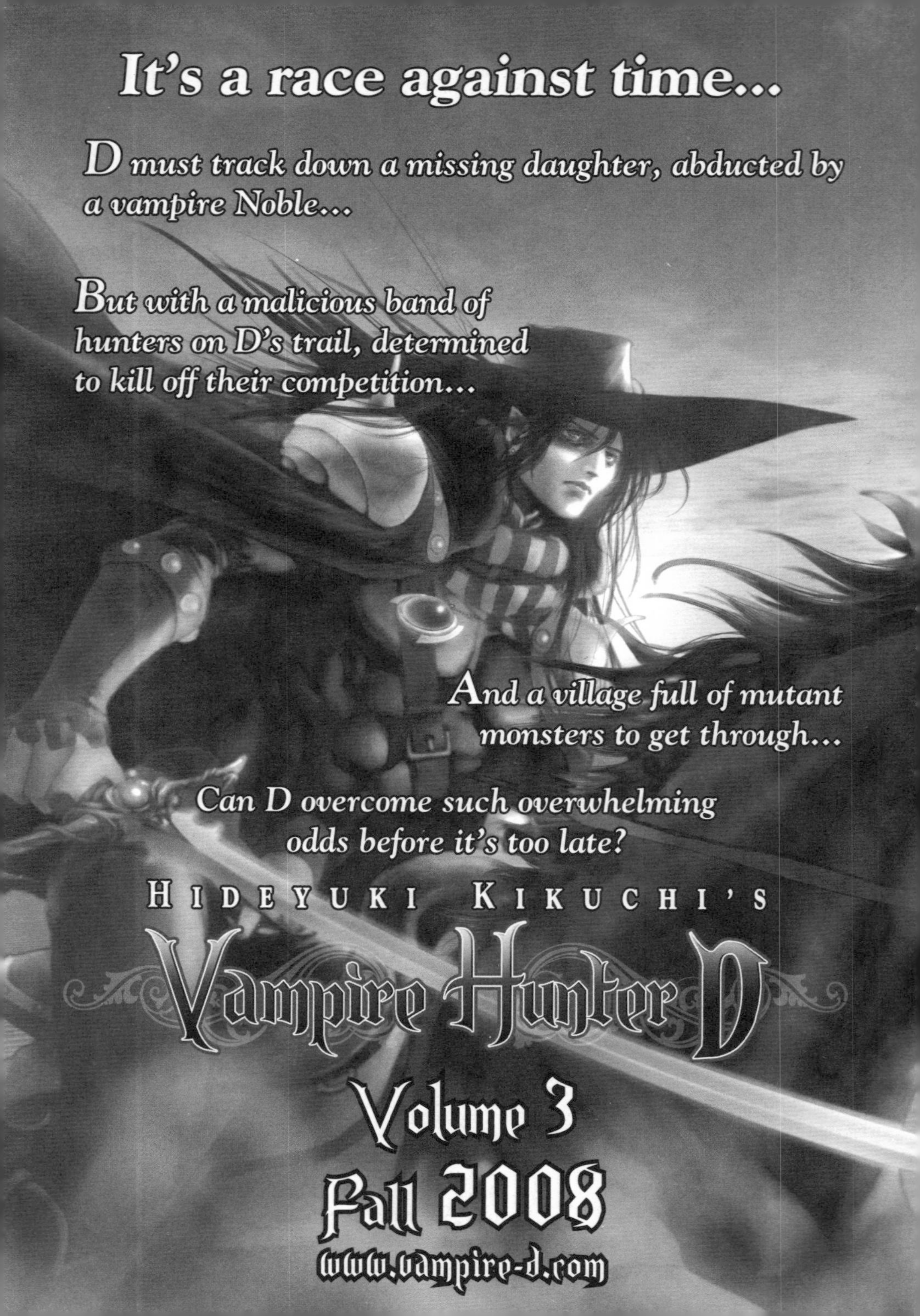
It's a race against time...
D must track down a missing daughter, abducted by a vampire Noble...
But with a malicious band of hunters on D's trail, determined to kill off their competition...
And a village full of mutant monsters to get through...
Can D overcome such overwhelming odds before it's too late?
HIDEYUKI KIKUCHI'S
Vampire Hunter D
Volume 3
Fall 2008
www.vampire-d.com

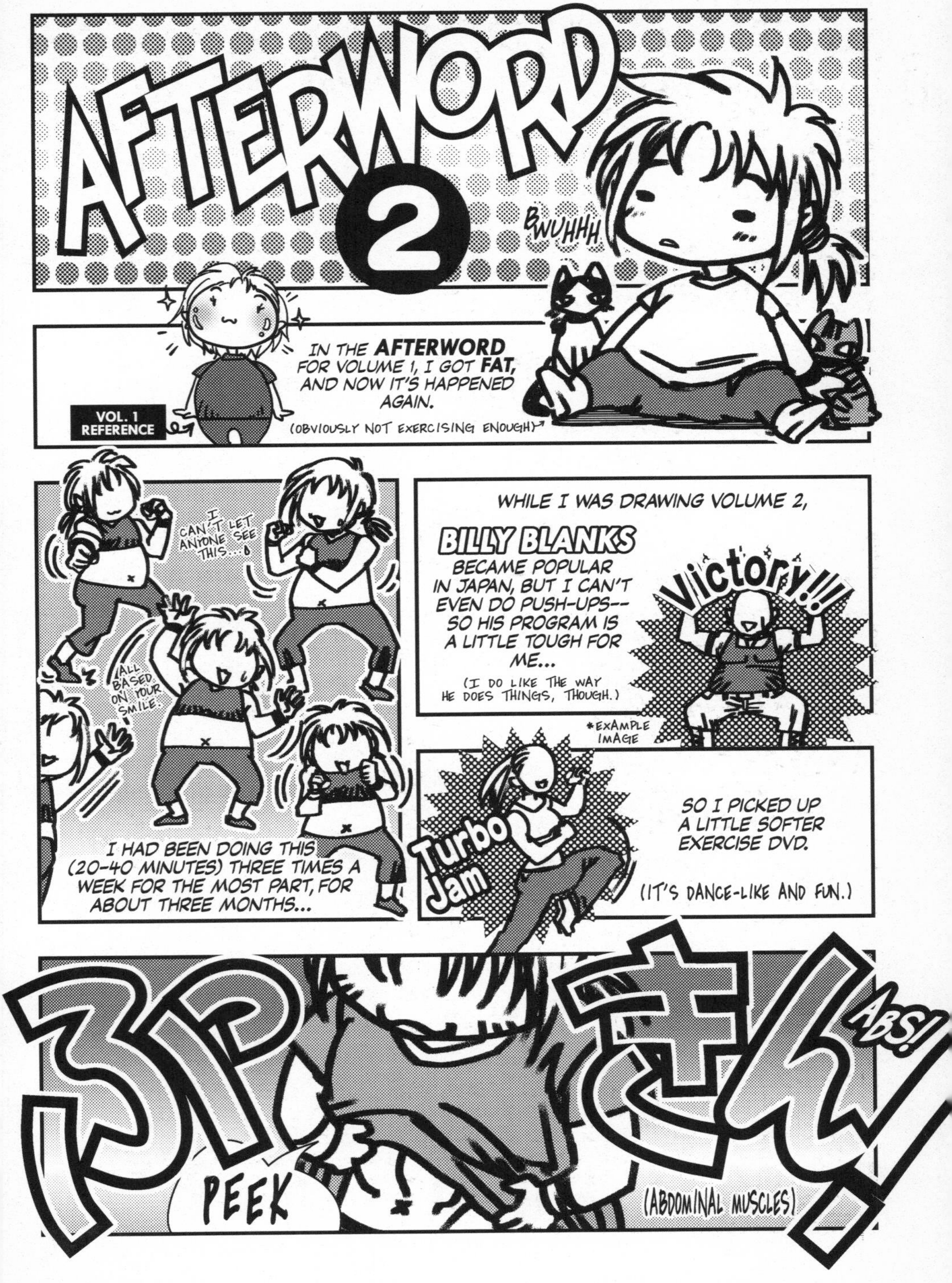

AFTERWORD 2
BWUHHH
IN THE **AFTERWORD** FOR VOLUME 1, I GOT **FAT**, AND NOW IT'S HAPPENED AGAIN.
(OBVIOUSLY NOT EXERCISING ENOUGH)
VOL. 1 REFERENCE
WHILE I WAS DRAWING VOLUME 2,
BILLY BLANKS BECAME POPULAR IN JAPAN, BUT I CAN'T EVEN DO PUSH-UPS--SO HIS PROGRAM IS A LITTLE TOUGH FOR ME...
(I DO LIKE THE WAY HE DOES THINGS, THOUGH.)
Victory!!
*EXAMPLE IMAGE
SO I PICKED UP A LITTLE SOFTER EXERCISE DVD.
(IT'S DANCE-LIKE AND FUN.)
Turbo Jam
I CAN'T LET ANYONE SEE THIS...
ALL BASED ON YOUR SMILE
I HAD BEEN DOING THIS (20-40 MINUTES) THREE TIMES A WEEK FOR THE MOST PART, FOR ABOUT THREE MONTHS...
ABS!
(ABDOMINAL MUSCLES)
PEEK

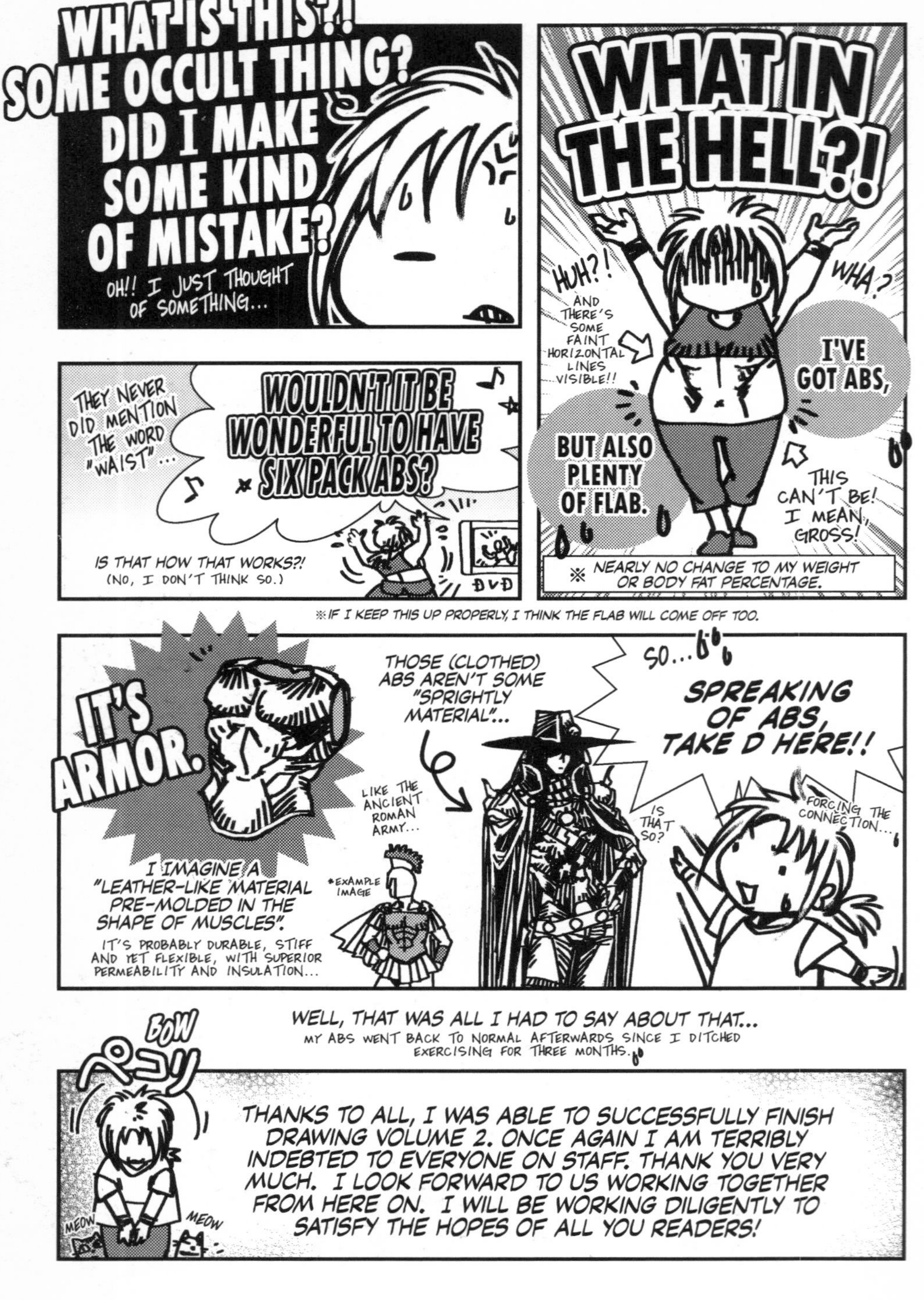
WHAT IN THE HELL?!
WHA?
HUH?!
I'VE GOT ABS,
AND THERE'S SOME FAINT HORIZONTAL LINES VISIBLE!!
BUT ALSO PLENTY OF FLAB.
THIS CAN'T BE! I MEAN, GROSS!
※ NEARLY NO CHANGE TO MY WEIGHT OR BODY FAT PERCENTAGE.
WHAT IS THIS?! SOME OCCULT THING? DID I MAKE SOME KIND OF MISTAKE?
OH!! I JUST THOUGHT OF SOMETHING...
WOULDN'T IT BE WONDERFUL TO HAVE SIX PACK ABS?
THEY NEVER DID MENTION THE WORD "WAIST"...
DVD
IS THAT HOW THAT WORKS?!
(NO, I DON'T THINK SO.)
※IF I KEEP THIS UP PROPERLY, I THINK THE FLAB WILL COME OFF TOO.
SO...
SPREAKING OF ABS, TAKE D HERE!!
FORCING THE CONNECTION...
IS THAT SO?
THOSE (CLOTHED) ABS AREN'T SOME "SPRIGHTLY MATERIAL"...
LIKE THE ANCIENT ROMAN ARMY...
*EXAMPLE IMAGE
IT'S ARMOR.
I IMAGINE A "LEATHER-LIKE MATERIAL PRE-MOLDED IN THE SHAPE OF MUSCLES".
IT'S PROBABLY DURABLE, STIFF AND YET FLEXIBLE, WITH SUPERIOR PERMEABILITY AND INSULATION...
WELL, THAT WAS ALL I HAD TO SAY ABOUT THAT...
MY ABS WENT BACK TO NORMAL AFTERWARDS SINCE I DITCHED EXERCISING FOR THREE MONTHS.
BOW
ペコリ
THANKS TO ALL, I WAS ABLE TO SUCCESSFULLY FINISH DRAWING VOLUME 2. ONCE AGAIN I AM TERRIBLY INDEBTED TO EVERYONE ON STAFF. THANK YOU VERY MUCH. I LOOK FORWARD TO US WORKING TOGETHER FROM HERE ON. I WILL BE WORKING DILIGENTLY TO SATISFY THE HOPES OF ALL YOU READERS!
MEOW
MEOW